THE Directory of Small Press & Magazine Editors & Publishers

LEN FULTON & ELLEN FERBER, EDITORS

15th Edition 1984-85

Dustbooks

The **Directory of Small Magazine/Press Editors and Publishers** is an alphabetical index listing by name all the editors and publishers of small presses and magazines in this directory's main companion volume, the **International Directory of Little Magazines and Small Presses.** This directory should be used when you have the name of an editor or publisher but not the name of his or her associated press or publication.

COVER: JUDITH GROSSMAN, IMPRINT

$13.95/copy $42.00/year subscription
    U.S.A.

ISBN 0-913218-53-7

Copyright 1984 by Len Fulton, Published annually by Dustbooks, P.O. Box 100, Paradise, California 95969, also publishers of SMALL PRESS REVIEW, INTERNATIONAL DIRECTORY OF LITTLE MAGAZINES AND SMALL PRESSES, SMALL PRESS RECORD OF BOOKS IN PRINT and chapbooks of poetry and prose.
Typesetting format and computer programming by Neil McIntyre, P.O. Box 2066, Marysville, CA 95901.

A

Abbott, Steve, Associate Editor (see also Jenkins, Joyce; Silberg, Richard), *POETRY FLASH*, PO Box 4172, Berkeley, CA 94704, 415-548-6871

Abed-Rabbo, Dr. Samir, *JOURNAL FOR ARAB AND ISLAMIC STUDIES*, PO Box 543, Brattleboro, VT 05301, 802-257-5121

5000430

Abed-Rabbo, Dr. Samir, Maple Leaf Press of Jenin, Inc., 58 Elliot Street, Brattleboro, VT 05301, 802-257-0872

Abel, Richard, Senior Editor, Timber Press, PO Box 1631, Beaverton, OR 97075, 503-292-2606

Abercrombie, V.T. (see also Williams, Helen), Brown Rabbit Press, Box 19111, Houston, TX 77024, 713-622-1844/465-1168

Abrahamson, Israel, *INSTEAD OF A MAGAZINE*, Box 433, Willimantic, CT 06226

Acres, Marty, One Percent Publishing Company, 2888 Bluff Street, Suite 143, Boulder, CO 80301, 303-449-8896

Adams, Jan (see also Gordon, Rebecca; Johanna, Betty; Meyerding, Jane), *LESBIAN CONTRADIC-TION-A Journal of Irreverent Feminism*, 584 Castro Street, Suite 263, San Francisco, CA 94114

Adams Suzanne (see also Murphy, Robert A.), Higginson Books, Derby Square, Salem, MA 01970, 617-744-0470

Addleman, Rex (see also Simmons, Jim; Nading, Lee), *VERIDIAN*, PO Box 2324, Bloomington, IN 47402

Adler, Jeremy, *A*, 58, Cedar Road, London NW2 6SP, England

Adler, Jeremy, Alphabox Press, 58 Cedar Road, London NW2, England

Agetstein, Stephen, Editor (see also Sein, Steve), *VIDEO 80 MAGAZINE*, 1250-17th Street, San Francisco, CA 94107, 415-863-8434

Aglietti, Susan L., Editor, Publisher, *VINTAGE '45—A UNIQUELY SUPPORTIVE QUARTERLY JOURNAL FOR WOMEN*, PO Box 266, Orinda, CA 94563, 415-254-7266

Ahern, Colleen, Design (see also Hettich, Michael; Osborne, Karen), Moonsquilt Press, 16401 NE 4th Avenue, North Miami Beach, FL 33162, 305-947-9534

Ahern, Tom, *DIANA'S ALMANAC*, 71 Elmgrove Ave., Providence, RI 02906

Ahern, Tom, Diana's Press, 71 Elmgrove Avenue, Providence, RI 02906, 401-274-5417

Aiello, Kate, Editor, *WINEWOOD JOURNAL*, Box 339, Black Hawk, CO 80422, 303-582-5867

Aiello, Kate, Winewood Publishing, Box 339, Black Hawk, CO 80422, 303-582-5867

Ainlay Jr., Thomas, Coordinator (see also Urushibara, Hideko; Zuckerman, Matthew), Tokyo English Literature Society (TELS), TELS 'Tomeoki', Koishikawa Post Office, Bunkyo-ku, Tokyo 112, Japan, 03-312-0481

Ainsworth, Catherine Harris, The Clyde Press, 373 Lincoln Parkway, Buffalo, NY 14216, 716-875-4713/834-1254

Aisenberg, Nadya (see also Veenendaal, Cornelia; Pedrick, Jean), Rowan Tree Press, 124 Chestnut Street, Boston, MA 02108, 617-523-7627

Alberhasky, P. S., *SANTA FE / POETRY AND THE ARTS*, 3415 Harcourt Driveield, Ames, IA 50010, 505-982-8187

Albert (see also Becker; Huizinga), New Society Publishers, 4722 Baltimore Avenue, Philadelphia, PA 19143, 215-726-6543

Alberti, Robert E., *ASSERT NEWSLETTER*, PO Box 1094, San Luis Obispo, CA 93406, 805-543-5911

Alberti, Robert E., President, Impact Publishers, Inc., PO Box 1094, San Luis Obispo, CA 93406, 805-543-5911

Aldan, Daisy, Folder Editions, 10326 68th Road, #A47, Forest Hills, NY 11375, 212-275-3839

Alenier, Karren L., Secretary (see also Baldwin, Deirdra; Beall, Jim; Sargent, Bob), The Word Works, Inc., PO Box 42164, Washington, DC 20015, (202) 554-3014

Alexander, Charlotte, *OUTERBRIDGE*, English A323, College of Staten Island, 715 Ocean Terrace, Staten Island, NY 10301, 212-390-7654

Alexander, Dr. E. Curtis, ECA Associates, PO Box 15004, Great Bridge Station, Chesapeake, VA 23320, 804-547-5542

Alladyce, Fiona, Publisher (see also Barnett, Anthony), Agneau 2, c/o DS (The Book Shop), 14 Peto Place, London NW1 4DT, England

Allard, Diane (see also Shouldice, Larry), *ELLIPSE*, Univ. de Sherbrooke, Box 10 Faculte des Arts, Sherbrooke, Quebec J1K2R1, Canada, 819-565-4576

Allardt, Linda (see also Kitchen, Judith; Rubin, Stan Sanvel; Bennett, Bruce), State Street Press, PO Box 252, Pittsford, NY 14534, 716-586-0154

Allen, David, Hyst'ry Myst'ry House, Garnerville, NY 10923

Allen, Dean, Allen Enterprises, 2917 Somerset Avenue, Texas City, TX 77590

Allen, Dean, *AMERICAN: Offical Journal of the Constitutional Rights Foundation*, 2917 Somerset Avenue, Texas City, TX 77590

Allen, Donna, Editor (see also Allen, Martha Leslie), *MEDIA REPORT TO WOMEN*, 3306 Ross Place NW, Washington, DC 20008, 202-966-7783

Allen, Donna, Editor, Women's Institute for Freedom of the Press, 3306 Ross Place, N.W., Washington, DC 20008, 202-966-7783

Allen, Jane, Editor (see also Guthrie, Derek), Chicago New Art Association, 230 East Ohio, RM. 207, Chicago, IL 60611, 312-642-6236

Allen, Jane Addams, Founding Editor (see also Guthrie, Derek), *NEW ART EXAMINER*, 230 East Ohio, Chicago, IL 60611, 312-642-6236

Allen, Kelly (see also Godfrey, W.D.; Godfrey, Ellen; Sterling, Sharon; Truscott, Gerry), Press Porcepic Limited, 235-560 Johnson St., Victoria, B.C. V8W 3C6, Canada, 604-381-5502

Allen, Marcus (see also La Russo, Carol), Whatever Publishing, Inc./Rising Sun Records, 61 Camino Alto, Suite 100, PO Box 137, Mill Valley, CA 94941, 415-388-2100

Allen, Martha, *THE CELIBATE WOMAN JOURNAL*, 3306 Ross Place, N.W., Washington, DC 20008, 202-966-7783

Allen, Martha Leslie, *INDEX/DIRECTORY OF WOMEN'S MEDIA*, 3306 Ross Place NW, Washington, DC 20008, 202-966-7783

Allen, Martha Leslie, Associate Editor (see also Allen, Donna), *MEDIA REPORT TO WOMEN*, 3306 Ross Place NW, Washington, DC 20008, 202-966-7783

Allen, Robert (see also Draper, Jan; Luxton, Stephen; Dow, Hugh), *THE MOOSEHEAD REVIEW*, Box 169, Ayer's Cliff, Quebec, Canada, 819-842-2835, 838-4801

Allen, William, Editor (see also Morris, Linda), *THE OHIO JOURNAL*, OSU Dept. of English, 164 W. 17th Avenue, Columbus, OH 43210, 614-422-2242

Allinson, Amy (see also Allinson, Russel), Valley Publishing, PO Box 2223, Lower Burrell, PA 15068

Allinson, Russel (see also Allinson, Amy), *Valley Publishing*, PO Box 2223, Lower Burrell, PA 15068

Allison, Dorothy (see also Bulkin, Elly; Clarke, Cheryl; Otter, Nancy Clarke; Waddy, Adrianne), *CONDITIONS*, PO Box 56, Van Brunt Sta., Brooklyn, NY 11215, 212-788-8654

Allison, Gay, Poetry (see also Lever, Bernice; Hamilton, Helen; Jenoff, Marvyne), *WAVES*, 79 Denham Drive, Thornhill, Ont. L4J 1P2, Canada, 416-889-6703

Allison, R. Bruce, Sol Press, 2025 Dunn Place, Madison, WI 53713, 608-257-4126

Allton, George, Assistant Editor (see also Wilhelm, Roger P.), *THRESHOLD MAGAZINE,* Wilhelm Publishing, Inc., PO Box 922, Columbia, MO 65205, 314-442-6134

Alpin, Gale, Prologue Publications, P.O. Box 640, Menlo Park, CA 94026, 415-322-1663

Alta (see also Jones, Whitney), Shameless Hussy Press, Box 3092, Berkeley, CA 94703

Alurista (see also Xelina), *MAIZE: Notebooks of Xicano Art and Literature,* The Colorado College, Box 10, Colorado Springs, CO 80903, 303-636-3249, 473-2233 ext. 624

Alurista (see also Xelina), Maize Press, The Colorado College, Box 10, Colorado Springs, CO 80903, 303-636-3249; 473-2233, ext. 624

Alyson, Sasha, Alyson Publications, Inc., PO Box 2783, Boston, MA 02208, 617-542-5679

Aman, Reinhold A., Editor & Publisher, *MALEDICTA: The International Journal of Verbal Aggression,* 331 S. Greenfield Ave., Waukesha, WI 53186, 414-542-5853

Aman, Reinhold A., Editor & Publisher, Maledicta Press, 331 S. Greenfield Ave., Waukesha, WI 53186, 414-542-5853

Ambrose, Michael E., *ARGONAUT,* PO Box 7985, Austin, TX 78712

Ames, Patrick, Associate Publisher (see also Anderson, James), Breitenbush Publications, P.O. Box 02137, Portland, OR 97202

Amodeo, Ron (see also Richter, Karl), *ALLEGHENY REVIEW,* Box 32, Allegheny College, Meadville, PA 16335, 814-724-6553; 724-4343

Anastas, Charles (see also Strempek, Stephen; McPhee, Linda), *HARBOR REVIEW,* c/o English Department, UMass/Boston, Boston, MA 02125

Anbian, Robert, Night Horn Books, 495 Ellis Street, Box 1156, San Francisco, CA 94102, 415-431-6198

Anbian, Robert, Editor (see also Spilker, John; King, Dennis; Hellerman, Steve; Kosoua, Anna; Erfurdt, Jamie), *OBOE: A Journal of Literature & Fine Art,* 495 Ellis Street, Box 1156, San Francisco, CA 94102

And, Miekal, *THE ACTS THE SHELFLIFE,* 1341 Williamson, Madison, WI 53703

And, Miekal (see also Was, Elizabeth), *SPEK,* 1341 Williamson, Madison, WI 53703

And, Miekal (see also Was, Elizabeth; Boyer, Chuck), Xerox Sutra Editions, 1341 Williamson #B, Madison, WI 53703

Anders, Irene, Managing Editor (see also Rexner, Romulus), *COSMOPOLITAN CONTACT,* P. O. Box 1566, Fontana, CA 92335

Andersen, Deborah (see also Andersen, Richard), *Shane Press,* 2908 SE Tolman, Portland, OR 97202

Andersen, Len J. (see also Cornish, Sam; Orowan, Florella), *FICTION, LITERATURE & THE ARTS REVIEW,* Arcade, 318 Harvard Street, Brookline, MA 02146, 617-232-2674

Andersen, M., Editor (see also Nuse, B.; Newton, J.; Zavitz, C.; Rooney, F.; Wine, J.; Prentice, A.; Scane, J.; Caplan, Paula; Van Kirk, Sylvia), *RESOURCES FOR FEMINIST RESEARCH/DOCUMEN-TATION SUR LA RECHERCHE FEMINISTE,* Ont Inst for Stud in Educ, Centre for Women's Studies in Education, 252 Bloor Street W., Toronto, Ontario M5S 1V6, Canada, 416-923-6641

Andersen, Richard (see also Andersen, Deborah), *Shane Press,* 2908 SE Tolman, Portland, OR 97202

Anderson, Alex (see also Chaloner, Peter), Heat Press, 129 Cooper Ave, Woodlynne, NJ 08107, 215-662-0586/215-389-6913

Anderson, Christine, Brattle Publications, 4 Brattle Street, Suite 306, Cambridge, MA 02138, 617-661-7467

Anderson, Douglas, Bread & Butter Press, 2582 S Clayton, Denver, CO 80210, 303-753-0912

Anderson, James, Publisher & Executive Editor (see also Ames, Patrick), Breitenbush Publications, P.O. Box 02137, Portland, OR 97202

Anderson, James, Associate Editor (see also Collins, Roy), R.I. Review Inc., PO Box 3028 Wayland Square, Providence, RI 02906, 401-331-1034

Anderson, James, Associate Editor (see also Collins, Roy), *RHODE ISLAND REVIEW*, PO Box 3028 Wayland Square, Providence, RI 02906, 401-331-1034

Anderson, Kathy Elaine, Editor (see also Jones, Keith; Hemphill, Essex C.; Williams, Cynthia L.), *NETHULA JOURNAL OF CONTEMPORARY LITERATURE*, 930 F Street, Suite 610, Washington, DC 20004

Anderson, Kay, Contributing Editor (see also Porter, Andrew; D'Ammassa, Don; DiFate, Vincent; Pohl, Frederik; Silverberg, Robert; Jones, Stephen; Fletcher, Jo; Carmody, Larry), *SCIENCE FICTION CHRONICLE*, PO Box 4175, New York, NY 10163, 212-643-9011

Anderson, Lou Ann, Distribution Manager (see also Coward, Jane), Wimmer Brothers Books, PO Box 18408, Memphis, TN 38181, 901-362-8900

Andre, Michael, *KINGSTON*, 105 Hudston Street #311, New York City, NY 10013

Andreas, Steve, Editor and Owner, Real People Press, Box F, Moab, UT 84532, 801-259-7578

Andrew, Helen (see also Kramer, Aaron; Everitt, Helen; Vondrasek, Bets), *WEST HILLS REVIEW: A WALT WHITMAN JOURNAL*, Walt Whitman Birthplace Assn., 246 Walt Whitman Road, Huntington Station, NY 11746, (516) 427-5240

Andrews, Bruce (see also Bernstein, Charles), *L=A=N=G=U=A=G=E*, 464 Amsterdam Avenue, New York, NY 10024, 212-799-4475

Andrews, Naomi, Editor, Lotus Press, Inc., P.O. Box 21607, Detroit, MI 48221, 313-861-1280

Anees, M. (see also Bilgrami, M.; Gallaghan, Haj Haydar; Mazandarani, Batul H.), Zahra Publications, PO Box 730, Blanco, TX 78606, 512-698-3239

Anger, Lance (see also Wagner, Pete), *MINNE HA! HA!*, PO Box 14009, Minneapolis, MN 55414, 612-378-9156

Anger, Lance, Editor-in-Chief (see also Wagner, Pete), Minne Ha! Ha!, PO Box 14009, Minneapolis, MN 55414

Angyal, Andrew J., Faculty Advisor, *COLONNADES*, Box 5246, Elon College, NC 27244

Anosike, Benji, Executive Editor, Do-It-Yourself Legal Publishers, 150 Fifth Ave., New York, NY 10011, 212-242-2840

Anozie, S.O., *CONCH MAGAZINE*, 102 Normal Avenue, Buffalo, NY 14213, 716-885-3686

Anozie, S.O., General Editor, Conch Magazine Ltd. (Publishers), 102 Normal Avenue, (Symphony Circle), Buffalo, NY 14213, 716-885-3686

Anozie, S.O., *CONCH REVIEW OF BOOKS*, 102 Normal Ave., Buffalo, NY 14213, 716-885-3686

Ansell, Kenneth, *IMPETUS MAGAZINE*, 587 Wandsworth Road, London SW8 3JD, England, 01-720-4460

Anton, Frank, Editor, *N.A.H.B. BUILDER MAGAZINE*, 15th and M Streets N W, Washington, DC 20005, 202-822-0390

Anton, Y Bani (see also Antonitis, Dr. Joseph), Marsh Point Press, 45 Peters Street, Orono, ME 04473, 207-866-2576

Antonitis, Dr. Joseph (see also Anton, Y Bani), *Marsh Point Press*, 45 Peters Street, Orono, ME 04473, 207-866-2576

Antreassian, Jack, Ashod Press, PO Box 1147, Madison Square Station, New York, NY 10159, 212-475-0711

Apglyn, Nic (see also Lang, Tom), *IDO-VIVO*, International Language (IDO) Society of Gt. Britain, 135 Stryd Keppoch, Caerdydd, Wales, 0222-497414

Apglyn, Nic (see also Lang, Tom), International Language (IDO) Society of Great Britain, 135 Stryd Keppoch, Caerdydd, Wales, 0222-497414

Appelhof, Mary, Flower Press, 10332 Shaver Road, Kalamazoo, MI 49002, 616-327-0108

Archard, Cary, *POETRY WALES*, 56, Parcau Avenue, Bridgend, Mid-Glamorgan, Wales

Archard, Cary, Poetry Wales Press, 56, Parcau Avenue, Bridgend, Mid-Glamorgan, Wales

Ardinger, Richard, *THE LIMBERLOST REVIEW*, PO Box 771, Hailey, ID 83333

Argiry, George P., Editor, Beninda Books, P.O. Box 9251, Canton, OH 44711

Argiry, George P., *SUCCESS AND MONEY!*, PO Box 9251, Canton, OH 44711, 492-4025

Armstrong, Alison (see also Bekker, Pieter; Brown, Richard), *JAMES JOYCE BROADSHEET*, James Joyce Centre, University College, Gower Street, London WC1E 6BT, England, 01-986-9456

Armstrong, W.A., Professor (see also Booth, Michael, Professor; Rosenfeld, Dr. Sybil), *THEATRE NOTEBOOK*, 103 Ralph Court, Queensway, London W2 5HU, England

Arnold, Bob, *LONGHOUSE*, Green River R.F.D., Brattleboro, VT 05301

Arnold, Bob, Longhouse, Green River R.F.D., Brattleboro, VT 05301

Arnold, Jeanne (see also Lindquist, Barbara), Mother Courage Press, 1533 Illinois Street, Racine, WI 53405, 414-634-1047

Arnold, Mark, *GOOD*, 292 Turk, San Francisco, CA 94102

Aronson, Arnold (see also Margolis, Tina; Garren, Lois; King, Keith; Wells, Ann; Wolff, Fred M.; Rollins, Brook), *THEATRE DESIGN AND TECHNOLOGY*, 330 W. 42nd Street, New York, NY 10036, 212-563-5551

Aronson, Arnold (see also Davy, Kate), U.S. Institute for Theatre Technology, Inc., 330 W. 42nd Street, New York, NY 10036, 212-563-5551

Arrathoon, Dr. Leigh A. (see also Marecki, Joan), Solaris Press, Inc., PO Box 1009, Rochester, MI 48063, 313-656-0667

Aschwanden, Charles (see also Aschwanden, Richard), Rama Publishing Co., PO Box 889, Canon City, CO 81212, 303-566-0123

Aschwanden, Richard (see also Aschwanden, Charles), *Rama Publishing Co.*, PO Box 889, Canon City, CO 81212, 303-566-0123

Ashley, Robin, V.P. (see also te Neues, Hendrik), te Neues Publishing Company, 15 East 76th Street, New York, NY 10021, 212-288-0265

Ashram, Atmaniketan, Auromere, Inc., 1291 Weber Street, Pomona, CA 91768, 714-629-8255

Aslaksen, Edvard, *IASP NEWSLETTER*, International Association of Scholarly Publishers, PO Box 2959 Toyen, Universitets forlaget, 0608 Oslo 6, Norway

Aster, H. (see also Mayne, S.; Walsh, M.; Potichnyj, P.), Mosaic Press/Valley Editions, PO Box 1032, Oakville, Ontario L6J 5E9, Canada

Atkinson, J. J., First Commonwealth Press, Route 3, PO Box 442, Live Oak, FL 32060, 305-949-7797

Attebury, Jean, Editor (see also Rothwell, Edward), The Garlinghouse Company, 320 S.W. 33rd Street, PO Box 299, Topeka, KS 66601, 913-267-2490

Attley, Marilee, Editor, *NEW ENGLAND RUNNING*, Box 658, Brattleboro, VT 05301, 802-257-0411

Attley, Marilee, Editor, Whetstone Publishing, Box 658, Brattleboro, VT 05301

Attwood, Derek (see also Best, Alan), *NEW GERMAN STUDIES*, Dept Of German, Univ. Hull, Hull HU6 7RX, England, 0482-497649

Atwater, Dorthea (see also Hay, Peter), Sonica Press, PO Box 42720, Los Angeles, CA 90042, 213-222-1026

Aubert, Alvin, *OBSIDIAN: BLACK LITERATURE IN REVIEW*, English Dept., Wayne State Univ., Detroit, MI 48202

Auer, Tom, *THE BLOOMSBURY REVIEW*, PO Box 8928, Denver, CO 80201, 303-455-0593

Auster, Paul, Contributing Editor (see also Quasha, George; Quasha, Susan; Martin, Michele; Coffey, Michael; Stein Charles; Nedds, Trish; Kelly, Robert; Kamin, Franz; McClelland, Bruce), Station Hill Press, Station Hill Road, Barrytown, NY 12507, 914-758-5840

Austin, Alan (see also Zu-Bolton, Ahmos; Wray, Elizabeth; Becker, Anne), *BLACK BOX MAGAZINE*, PO Box 50145, Washington, DC 20004, 202-347-4823

Austin, Alan, Co-Producer (see also Becker, Anne; Wray, Elizabeth), Watershed Tapes, PO Box 50145, Washington, DC 20004

Austin, Alan D. (see also Becker, Anne), Watershed Intermedia, P.O. Box 50145, Washington, DC 20004, 202-347-4823

Avery, Amanda, Associate Editor (see also Ranker, Camille), Mendocino Graphics, PO Box 1580, Mendocino, CA 95460, 707-964-3831

Axelrod, David B. (see also Hand, Joan C.), *WRITERS INK*, 194 Soundview Drive, Rocky Point L.I., NY 11778, 516-744-6160

Axelrod, Jeanette, Editor & Publisher, Adler Publishing Company, PO Box 9342, Rochester, NY 14604, 716-377-5804

Aycock, Shirley, M.O.P. Press, Rt 24, Box 53C, Fort Myers, FL 33908, 813-482-0802

Ayyildiz, Judy (see also Ferguson, Maurice; Bullins, Amanda; Nash, Valery; Sheffler, Natalie; Steinke, Paul; Weinstein, Ann), *ARTEMIS*, PO Box 945, Roanoke, VA 24005, 703-981-9318

Azarnoff, Pat, Editor, *PEDIATRIC MENTAL HEALTH*, PO Box 1880, Santa Monica, CA 90406, 213-459-7710

B

Babbs, Ken (see also Kesey, Ken; my; Leary, Timothy; Marrs, Lee; Loren, Richard), *SPIT IN THE OCEAN*, 85829 Ridgeway Rd, Pleasant Hill, OR 97455, 503-747-5796

Babcock, Kent, Journey Publications, PO Box 423, Woodstock, NY 12498, 914-679-2250

Bach, Pieter, Book Review Editor (see also Shep, R.L.), *THE TEXTILE BOOKLIST*, Box C-20, Lopez Island, WA 98261, 206-468-2021

Backstrand, Brian, Poetry Editor (see also Burnham, R. Peter; Hennessey, Patricia J.), *THE LONG STORY*, 11 Kingston Street, North Andover, MA 01845, 617-686-7638

Bacon, Josephine, Pholiota Press, Inc., PO Box DB, Garden Grove, CA 92642, 714-534-7400; 537-5355

Baehr, Anne-Ruth (see also Hair, Jennie; Jeffery, Mildred; Walker, Lois V.; Yaryura-Tobias, Anibal), Pleasure Dome Press (Long Island Poetry Collective Inc.), Box 773, Huntington, NY 11743, 516-691-2376

Baehr, Anne-Ruth, Editor (see also Hair, Jennie; Jeffrey, Mildred; Walker, Lois V.; Yaryura-Tobias, Anibal; Lucas, Barbara), *XANADU*, Box 773, Huntington, NY 11743, (516) 691-2376

Baer, D. Richard, Editor, Hollywood Film Archive, 8344 Melrose Ave., Hollywood, CA 90069, 213-933-3345

Bagai, Eric (see also Bagai, Judith), Foreworks, Box 9747, North Hollywood, CA 91609, 213-982-0467

Bagai, Judith (see also Bagai, Eric), *Foreworks*, Box 9747, North Hollywood, CA 91609, 213-982-0467

Bailey, Chris (see also Rippington, Geoff; Polley, Simon; Sutherland, Allen; Swinden, Dave), British Science Fiction Assoc. Ltd., 269 Wykeham Road, Reading RG6 1PL, England, 0734-666142

Bailey, Chris (see also Sutherland, Allen; Swinden, Dave), *FOCUS*, 269 Wykeham Road, Reading RG6 1PL, England

Bailey, Marilyn (see also Ulrich, Betty; Hall, John), *THE INKLING JOURNAL*, PO Box 128, Alexandria, MN 56308, 612-762-2020

Bailey, Marilyn (see also Ulrich, Betty; Hall, John), Inkling Publications, Inc., PO Box 128, Alexandria, MN 56308, 612-762-2020

Bailey, Rhonda (see also Smith, Ron; Guppy, Stephen), Oolichan Books, P.O. Box 10, Lantzville, British Columbia V0R2H0, Canada, 604-390-4839

Bailey, Thatcher, Bay Press, 3710 Discovery Road North, Gracie Station, Port Townsend, WA 98368, 206-385-1270

Bain, David, Dream Place Publications, 2938 Magnolia, Berkeley, CA 94705, 415-845-2509

Bainbridge, Dave (see also Deahl, Joseph), The Passive Solar Institute, Box 722, Bascom, OH 44809, 419-937-2226

Baird, A. (see also Gaard, F.; Rath, E.), *ARTPOLICE*, 133 E. 25th Street, Minneapolis, MN 55404, 612-825-3673

Baird, J. Arthur (see also Tapp, Roland W.), The Iona Press, Box C-3181, Wooster, OH 44691, 216-262-2300 ext. 470

Baird, Jo, Managing Editor (see also Howe, Florence), The Feminist Press, Box 334, Old Westbury, NY 11568

Baird, Keith E., Associate Editor (see also Jackson, Esther; Bond, Jean Carey; O'Dell, J. H.; Kaiser, Ernest; Hairston, Loyle), *FREEDOMWAYS - A Quarterly Review of the Freedom Movement*, Freedomways Associates, Inc., 799 Broadway Suite 542, New York, NY 10003

Baizerman, Suzanne, Publisher & Editor (see also Searle, Karen), Arana Press Inc., PO Box 14-23849, St. Paul, MN 55114, 303-449-1170

Baizerman, Suzanne (see also Searle, Karen), Dos Tejedoras Fiber Arts Publications, 3036 N. Snelling, St. Paul, MN 55113

Baizerman, Suzanne, Publisher & Editor (see also Searle, Karen), *THE WEAVER'S JOURNAL*, PO Box 14-238, St. Paul, MN 55114

Baker, Charles L., Assistant Editor (see also Burnhm, Crispin), *ELDRITCH TALES*, 1051 Wellington Road, Lawrence, KS 66044, 913-843-4341

Baker, Charles L., Assistant Editor (see also Burnham, Crispin), Yith Press, 1051 Wellington Road, Lawrence, KS 66044, 913-843-4341

Baker, Frederich Vishnu Dass (see also Baker, Jeannine Paruati), Freestone Publishing Collective, PO Box 398, Monroe, UT 84754, 801-527-3738

Baker, Gail, Hummingbird Press, 2400 Hannett NE, Albuquerque, NM 87106, 505-268-6277

Baker, Jeannine Paruati (see also Baker, Frederich Vishnu Dass), Freestone Publishing Collective, PO Box 398, Monroe, UT 84754, 801-527-3738

Baker, Morrow, Editorial Consultant (see also Mayfield, Carl), *THE MARGARINE MAYPOLE ORANGOUTANG EXPRESS*, 3209 Wellesley, NE 1, Albuquerque, NM 87107

Baker, Rosalie F., *CLASSICAL CALLIOPE*, 20 Grove Street, Peterborough, NH 03458

Baker, Sheila, Akiba Press, PO Box 13086, Oakland, CA 94611, 415-339-1283

Bakos, Barbara (see also Beckett, Tom), Viscerally Press, 1695 Brady Lake Road, Kent, OH 44240

Balakian, Peter (see also Smith, Bruce), *GRAHAM HOUSE REVIEW*, Box 5000, Colgate University, Hamilton, NY 13346

Baldwin, Deirdra, President (see also Alenier, Karren L.; Beall, Jim; Sargent, Bob), The Word Works, Inc., PO Box 42164, Washington, DC 20015, (202) 554-3014

Baldwin, Howard, Managing Editor (see also Pellicano, Cheryl), *LOS GATOS MAGAZINE*, 251 East 7th Street, Long Beach, CA 90813, 408-866-1888

Balkema, Sandra J., *RACKHAM JOURNAL OF THE ARTS AND HUMANITIES*, Rackham Journal of the Arts & Humanities, 4024 Modern Language Bldg. Univ. of Mich., Ann Arbor, MI 48106, 313-764-2537

Ballagas, Manuel F. (see also Madrigal Ecay, Roberto), *TERMINO*, PO Box 8905, Cincinnati, OH 45208, 513-232-1548

Ballentine, Rudolph, M.D., Director (see also Clark, Lawrence), Himalayan Publishers, RD 1, Box 88-A, Honesdale, PA 18431, 717-253-5551

Balogh, Paulette (see also Pride, Anne; McElligot, Pat), *MOTHEROOT JOURNAL*, 214 Dewey Street, Pittsburgh, PA 15218, 412-731-4453

Balogh, Paulette (see also Pride, Anne; McElligott, Pat), Motheroot Publications, 214 Dewey Street, Pittsburgh, PA 15218

Balsamo, Ron (see also Hughes, John E.; Lee, Jean C.; Reed, W.A.; Reed, Vicki; Thompson, Catherine; Dennis, Deborah), *FARMER'S MARKET*, PO Box 1272, Galesburg, IL 61402

Bame, Louise, Vista Publications, 3010 Santa Monica Blvd., Suite 221, Santa Monica, CA 90404, 213-828-3258

Bamford, Christopher (see also Marsh, William Parker), *THE LINDISFARNE LETTER*, R.D. #2, West Stockbridge, MA 01266, 413-232-4377

Bamford, Christopher (see also Marsh, William Parker), The Lindisfarne Press, RD #2, West Stockbridge, MA 01266, 413-232-4377

Banana, Anna, Banana Productions, PO Box 3655, Vancouver, BC V6B 3Y8, Canada, 604-876-8543

Banana, Anna, *BANANA RAG*, PO Box 3655, Vancouver, B.C., V6B 3Y8, Canada, 604-876-8543

Banbury, Lance, Galaxy Press, 71 Recreation Street, Tweed Heads N.S.W., Australia, 075 361997

Bandos, Kate, Promotion Director (see also Everitt, Charles; Kennedy, Linda; Lynch, Kevin), The Globe Pequot Press, Old Chester Road, Chester, CT 06412, 203-526-9571

Bandow, Doug, *INQUIRY MAGAZINE*, Inquirey, 1320 G Street, SE, Washington, DC 20003, 202-547-2770

Bandow, Doug, *Johnson Press*, Inquirey, 1320 G Street, SE, Washington, DC 20003, 202-547-2770

Banner, Bob, *CRITIQUE: A Journal of Conspiracy & Metaphysics*, PO Box 11451, Santa Rosa, CA 95406, 707-528-1060

Banning, Robert (see also Miller, Robert; Jones, Jennifer), Word Power, Inc., PO Box 17034, Seattle, WA 98107, 206-782-1437

Banta, Mary Lu (see also Ross, Charlie), Smithereens Press, Box 1036, Bolinas, CA 94924, 415-868-0149

Banta, Mary Lu (see also Ross, Charlie), *SMITHEREENS SEASONAL SAMPLER*, Box 1036, Bolinas, CA 94924, 415-868-0149

Baptist, Weldon O., Assistant Editor (see also Bogus, Sdiane; De Oca, D.M.; Coleman, Cheryl L.), W. I. M. Publications, Box 367, Department IDSP, College Corner, OH 45003, 513-523-5994

Bard, Michael, Consumer's Advisory Press, PO Box 77107, Greensboro, NC 27407, 919-855-3183

Bareiss, Philip (see also Parsons, James), Gallery West, Inc., Box 1589, Taos, NM 87571, 758-9637

Bargas, Miruim D., Editor, *FOREIGN ARTISTS POETS AND AUTHORS REVIEW (FAPAR)*, 2921 E Madison #7 IDLMSP, Seattle, WA 98112, 206-322-1431

Barker, David (see also Mailman, Leo; Locklin, Gerald; Zepeda, Ray; Snider, Clifton; Salinas, Judy; Kay, John), *MAELSTROM REVIEW*, 8 Farm Hill Road, Cape Elizabeth, ME 04107

Barklam, J. (see also Barklam, John W.B.), *FORESIGHT MAGAZINE*, 29 Beaufort Av., Hodge Hill, Birmingham, England B346AD, England, 021-783-0587

Barklam, John W.B. (see also Barklam, J.), *FORESIGHT MAGAZINE*, 29 Beaufort Av., Hodge Hill, Birmingham, England B346AD, England, 021-783-0587

Barlow, Jackie, *HOUSEWIVES' HANDY HINTS*, PO Box 66, Mount Dora, FL 32757, 904-343-8282

Barlow, Jackie, *SMALL BUSINESSWOMAN'S NEWSLETTER,* PO Box 66, Mount Dora, FL 32757, 904-343-8282

Barnes, Jim, *CHARITON REVIEW,* Northeast Missouri State University, Kirksville, MO 63501, 816-785-4499

Barnes, Jim, Chariton Review Press, Northeast Missouri State University, Kirksville, MO 63501, 816-785-4499 ʹ

Barnes, Sondra Anice, Publisher, Brason-Sargar Publications, PO Box 872, Reseda, CA 91335, 213-851-1229

Barnett, Anthony, Editor (see also Alladyce, Fiona), Agneau 2, c/o DS (The Book Shop), 14 Peto Place, London NW1 4DT, England

Barnett, Anthony, *LAMB,* c/o The Distributor, Nick Kimberley's Book Shop, 14 Peto Place, London NW1, England

Barnett, Anthony, The Literary Supplement, Nothing doing (formally in London), c/o The Distributor, Nick Kimberley's Book Shop, 14 Peto Place, London NW1, England

Barnhart, Clarence L., *THE BARNHART DICTIONARY COMPANION,* PO Box 247, Cold Spring, NY 10516, 265-2822

Barnhart, David K., Lexik House Publishers, PO Box 247, Cold Spring, NY 10516, 265-2822

Baron, Magda, Editor (see also Martin, Leslie), *AMERICAN DANCE GUILD NEWSLETTER,* 570 7 Ave. 20 Floor, New York, NY 10018, 212-944-0557

Baron, Matt (see also Wujciak, Dick; Zuk, Sue), Cornell Design Publishers, PO Box 278, E. Hanover, NJ 07936

Barone, Dennis (see also Ducoff-Barone, Deborah), Tamarisk, 319 S Juniper Street, Philadelphia, PA 19107

Barowitz, Elliott, Executive Editor, *ART & ARTISTS,* 280 Broadway, Suite 412, New York, NY 10007, 212-227-3770

Barrett, Dean, *Hong Kong Publishing Co., Ltd.,* 307 Yu Yuet Lai Building, 43-55 Wyndham Street, Central, Hong Kong, 5-259053

Barringer, Margot, Associate Editor (see also Jackson, Thomas H.), *POESIS: A JOURNAL OF CRITICISM,* Department of English, Bryn Mawr College, Bryn Mawr, PA 19010, 215-645-5306

Barry, James P., Editor, *OHIOANA QUARTERLY,* 1105 Ohio Dept Bldg., 65 S. Front St, Columbus, OH 43215, 614-466-3831

Barry, Jan (see also Ehrhart, W. D.), East River Anthology, 75 Gates Ave, Montclair, NJ 07042, 201-746-5941

Barth, Robert L., Robert L. Barth, 14 Lucas Street, Florence, KY 41042, 606-283-1479

Barthelme, Frederick, Editor (see also Herzinger, Kim A.; Inness-Brown, Elizabeth), *MISSISSIPPI REVIEW,* Box 5144, Southern Station, Hattiesburg, MS 39406, 601-266-4321

Bartlett, Elizabeth, Poetry (see also Michelson, Linda Brown; Hughes, Michael), *CROSSCURRENTS, A QUARTERLY,* 2200 Glastonbury Road, West Lake Village, CA 91361

Bartow, Dennis W., Publisher, Daring Publishing Group, PO Box 526, Canton, OH 44701

Basler, Sabra, *VALLEY SPIRIT,* c/o Sabra Basler, 120 C Street, #2, Davis, CA 95616

Bass, Lorena (see also Lowe, Lorilee), Coriander Press, PO Box 337, Ashland, OR 97520, 503-488-1016

Bassett, Mark T., *Mercury Press,* PO Box 1282, Columbia, MO 65205

Basso, Dave, Falcon Hill Press, Box 1431, Sparks, NV 89431, 702-359-5893

Bates, Owen (see also Michaels, Neal), *BOOK NEWS & BOOK BUSINESS MART,* Box 16254, Fort Worth, TX 76133, 817-293-7030

Bates, Owen (see also Michaels, Neal), Premier Publishers, Inc., Box 16254, Fort Worth, TX 76133, 817-293-7030

Bauer, William, Fiction Editor (see also Conway, Don; Gibbs, Robert; Trethewey, Eric; Hawkes, Robert; Butlin, Ron; Taylor, Michael; Thompson, Kent; Davey, Bill; Boyles, Ann), *THE FIDDLE-HEAD*, The Observatory, Univ. New Brunswick, PO Box 4400, Fredericton, NB E3B 5A3, Canada, 506-454-3591

Bauhan, William L., William L. Bauhan, Publisher, Dublin, NH 03444, 603-563-8020

Bax, Martin, *AMBIT*, 17 Priory Gardens, London, England N6 5QY, England

Bayes, Ron, Founding Editor (see also Roper, John H.; Osmanski, Edna Ann; Diogo, Judith A.), Saint Andrews Press, St Andrews College, Laurinburg, NC 28352, 919-276-3652

Baylis, Janice, Editor, Sun, Man, Moon Inc., PO Box 5084, Huntington Beach, CA 92615, 714-962-8945

Baysans, Greg (see also Willkzie, Philip; Emond, Paul; Young, Tom; Strizek, Norman), *JAMES WHITE REVIEW; a gay men's literary quarterly*, PO Box 3356, Traffic Station, Minneapolis, MN 55403, 612-291-2913; 871-2248

Beahm, George, Heresy Press, 713 Paul Street, Newport News, VA 23605, 804-865-2631

Beall, Jim, Grants Manager (see also Alenier, Karren L.; Baldwin, Deirdra; Sargent, Bob), The Word Works, Inc., PO Box 42164, Washington, DC 20015, (202) 554-3014

Beam, Gordon (see also Cohan, Tony), Acrobat Books Publishers, PO Box 480820, Los Angeles, CA 90048, 213-467-4506

Beam, Joe (see also Bernstein, Carole; Caplan, Leslie; Rorke, Raymond; Simpson, Chris; Sorensen, Sally Jo), *PAINTED BRIDE QUARTERLY*, 230 Vine Street, Philadelphia, PA 19106, 215-925-9914

Bean, Joyce Bean, Fiction (see also Cooper, Peter S.; Fielding, Cynthia), *YAWL (Young Artists & Writers of the Library)*, 3400 West 11th Street, Suite 134, Chicago, IL 60655, 312-233-6002

Bean, Joyce Miller, Fiction Editor (see also Cooper, Peter S.; Steger, Linda; Mitchell, Barbara; Fielding, Cynthia), *MIDWAY REVIEW*, 3400 West 11th Street, Suite 134, Chicago, IL 60655, 312-233-6002

Bean, Joyce Miller, Fiction Editor (see also Cooper, Peter S.; Fielding, Cynthia), Southwest Area Cultural Arts Council, 3400 West 11th Street, Suite 134, Chicago, IL 60655, 312-233-6002

Bearden, Wanda, Art Editor (see also Nemeth, Doris), The Poet, 2314 West Sixth Street, Mishawaka, IN 46544, 219-255-8606

Beatty, Allan, *PHOTRON*, PO Box 1906, Ames, IA 50010

Beaver, Betsey (see also Miriam, Selma; Furie, Noel), Sanguinaria Publishing, 85 Ferris Street, Bridgeport, CT 06605, 203-576-9168

Beck, Jerri (see also George, Anne), Druid Press, 2724 Shades Crest Road, Birmingham, AL 35216, 205-933-7974

Beck, Raymond M., Contrib. Editor (see also Rimm, Virginia M.; Perrin, Arnold; Grierson, Ruth; Briggs, Henry; Boisvert, Donald J.; McIntyre, Joan; Knowles, Ardeana Hamlin; Brown, Ronald G.), *NEW ENGLAND SAMPLER*, RFD #1 Box 2280, Brooks, ME 04921, 207-525-3575

Becker (see also Albert; Huizinga), New Society Publishers, 4722 Baltimore Avenue, Philadelphia, PA 19143, 215-726-6543

Becker, Anne (see also Austin, Alan; Zu-Bolton, Ahmos; Wray, Elizabeth), *BLACK BOX MAGAZINE*, PO Box 50145, Washington, DC 20004, 202-347-4823

Becker, Anne (see also Austin, Alan D.), Watershed Intermedia, P.O. Box 50145, Washington, DC 20004, 202-347-4823

Becker, Anne, Co-Producer (see also Wray, Elizabeth; Austin, Alan), Watershed Tapes, PO Box 50145, Washington, DC 20004

Becker, Roy, Manager, ICS Books, Inc., PO Box 8002, Merrillville, IN 46410, 219-769-0585

Beckett, Tom, *THE DIFFICULTIES*, 1695 Brady Lake Road, Kent, OH 44240

Beckett, Tom (see also Bakos, Barbara), Viscerally Press, 1695 Brady Lake Road, Kent, OH 44240

Beckman, Lanny (see also Maurer, Ralph; Lotgrave, Janet), New Star Books Ltd., 2504 York Avenue, Vancouver, B.C. V6K 1E3, Canada, 604-738-9429

Becknell, John M., *ANOTHER SEASON,* Willowwood Publishing, PO Box 148, Cologne, MN 55322, 612-466-3323

Beebe, Maurice, Editor-in-Chief, *JOURNAL OF MODERN LITERATURE,* Temple Univ., Philadelphia, PA 19122

Beeman, Rockne (see also Muses, Dr. Charles), Sceptre Publishing, 1442A Walnut Street, Suite 61, Berkeley, CA 94709, 415-525-1481

Beesley, Anthony J. (see also Beesley, Barbara), The Twickenham Press, 31 Jane Street, New York, NY 10014, 212-741-2417

Beesley, Barbara (see also Beesley, Anthony J.), *The Twickenham Press,* 31 Jane Street, New York, NY 10014, 212-741-2417

Behm, Richard, Editor (see also Norby, Mary), *SONG,* 808 Illinois, Stevens Pt, WI 54481, 715-344-6836

Behm, Richard, Song Press, 808 Illinois, Stevens Point, WI 54481

Beilke, Irene (see also Beilke, Marlan), Quintessence Publications, 356 Bunker Hill Mine Road, Amador City, CA 95601, 209-267-5470

Beilke, Marlan (see also Beilke, Irene), *Quintessence Publications,* 356 Bunker Hill Mine Road, Amador City, CA 95601, 209-267-5470

Beisel, David, Editor, *THE JOURNAL of PSYCHOHISTORY,* 2315 Broadway, NY, NY 10024, 212-873-5900

Beisel, David, Editor, Psychohistory Press, 2315 Broadway, New York City, NY 10024, 212-873-5900

Bekker, Pieter (see also Armstrong, Alison; Brown, Richard), *JAMES JOYCE BROADSHEET,* James Joyce Centre, University College, Gower Street, London WC1E 6BT, England, 01-986-9456

Belfiglio, Genevieve, Editor (see also Tarlen, Carol), *REAL FICTION,* 298-9th Avenue, San Francisco, CA 94118

Bell, Rebecca S. (see also Severin, C. Sherman), CSS Publications, PO Box 23, Iowa Falls, IA 50126, 515-648-2716; 243-6407

Bellis, Lewis, Business Manager (see also Robinson, Chris), *RECON,* P.O. Box 14602, Philadelphia, PA 19134

Bellis, Lewis, Business Manager (see also Robinson, Chris), Recon Publications, PO Box 14602, Philadelphia, PA 19134

Bench, Carson E. (see also Carpenter, Maryann), *SHARING,* Box 1470, 290 S 1st Ave., Ste. 300, Yuma, AZ 85364, 602-782-4646

Bender, Eleanor M. (see also Dillingham, Thomas), *OPEN PLACES,* Box 2085, Stephens College, Columbia, MO 65215, 314-442-2211

Benedict, Elinor, Editor-in-Chief (see also Hackenbruch, Carol), *PASSAGES NORTH,* William Bonifas Fine Arts Center, Escanaba, MI 49829, 906-786-3833

Benedict, Roy G. (see also Lind, Alan R.; Hansen, Zenon R.), Transport History Press, PO Box 201, Park Forest, IL 60466, 312-799-1785

Benesh, Carolyn L.E., Assoc. Editor (see also Liu, Robert K.; Kennedy, Sylvia), *ORNAMENT, A Quarterly of Jewelry and Personal Adornment,* PO Box 35029, Los Angeles, CA 90035, 213-652-9914

Benington, George, Editor, Coyote Love Press, 27 Deering Street, Portland, ME 04101, 207-774-8451

Bennani, Ben, Ishtar Press, Inc., English & Foreign Language, Georgia Southwestern College, Americus, GA 31709, 912-928-1350

Bennani, Ben, *PAINTBRUSH: A Journal of Poetry, Translations & Letters,* Dept. of English & Foreign Languages, Georgia Southwestern College, Americus, GA 31709, 912-928-1350

Bennett, Bruce (see also Kitchen, Judith; Rubin, Stan Sanvel; Allardt, Linda), State Street Press, PO Box 252, Pittsford, NY 14534, 716-586-0154

Bennett, Carolyn, Gull Books, 657 East 26th Street, #4S, Brooklyn, NY 11210, 212-434-0094

Bennett, Dr. Clifford A., Nationwide Press, Inc., 2860 S Circle Drive, South Bldg., Suite 108, Colorado Springs, CO 80906, 303-576-6777

Bennett, John, Vagabond Press, 1610 N. Water Street, Ellensburg, WA 98926, 509-925-5634

Bennett, John M., *LOST AND FOUND TIMES*, 137 Leland Ave, Columbus, OH 43214

Bennett, John M., Luna Bisonte Prods, 137 Leland Ave, Columbus, OH 43214, 614-846-4126

Bennett, John M., Guest Editor (see also Curry, J.W.; Laba, Mark), *1Cent*, 729a Queen Street East, Toronto, Ontario M4M 1H1, Canada

Benseler, David P., Editor, *THE MODERN LANGUAGE JOURNAL*, 314 Cunz Hall, Ohio State University, Columbus, OH 43210, 614-422-6985

Bensky, Larry, *MEDIAFILE*, Media Alliance Fort Mason, San Francisco, CA 94123, 415-441-2557

Benstock, Sharon S., *TULSA STUDIES IN WOMEN'S LITERATURE*, 600 S. College, Tulsa, OK 74104, 918-592-6000-2503

Bentheim, Steve, *THE INTERIOR VOICE*, PO Box 117, Kelowna, B.C. V1Y 7N3, Canada, 763-8199

Bercholz, Samuel, Editor-in-Chief (see also Emily Hilburn), Great Eastern Book Company, PO Box 271, Boulder, CO 80306, 303-449-6113

Berg, Neal (see also Szabo, Marilyn; Udinotti, Angese), *CHIMERA*, 4215 N. Marshall Way, Scottsdale, AZ 85251, 602-275-7924

Berg, Stephen (see also Vogelsang, Arthur; Bonanno, David), *AMERICAN POETRY REVIEW*, 1616 Walnut St., Room 405, Philadelphia, PA 19103, 215-732-6770

Bergdoll, Erwin R., The Pray Curser Press, c/oErwin R. Bergdoll, Elm Bank, Dutton, VA 23050, 804-693-2823

Berge, Carol, *CENTER*, c/o General Delivery, Ranches of Taos, NM 87557

Berge, Carol, Center Press, c/o General Delivery, Ranches of Taos, NM 87557

Berger, John, Consulting Editor (see also Lesser, Wendy; Bowles, Paul; Hass, Robert; Vidal, Gore; Wasserman, Steve), *THE THREEPENNY REVIEW*, PO Box 9131, Berkeley, CA 94709, 415-849-4545

Berger, Stu, Paragon Publishing, PO Box 53, Santa Rosa, CA 95402, 707-527-8185

Bergstrom, Janet (see also Lyon, Elisabeth; Penley, Constance), *CAMERA OBSCURA: A Journal of Feminism and Film Theory*, PO Box 25899, Los Angeles, CA 90025

Berkzhill, Emma Joe, *NONVIOLENT ANARCHIST NEWSLETTER*, Box 1385, Austin, TX 78767

Bernard, Sidney (see also Smith, Harry; Tolnay, Tom), *PULPSMITH*, 5 Beekman Street, New York, NY 10038

Berne, Stanley (see also Goodson, Arthur; Zekowski, Arlene; Zaage, Herman), Berne, PO Box 5645, Coronado Station, Santa Fe, NM 87502, 505-356-4082

Bernstein, Carole (see also Beam, Joe; Caplan, Leslie; Rorke, Raymond; Simpson, Chris; Sorensen, Sally Jo), *PAINTED BRIDE QUARTERLY*, 230 Vine Street, Philadelphia, PA 19106, 215-925-9914

Bernstein, Charles (see also Andrews, Bruce), *L=A=N=G=U=A=G=E*, 464 Amsterdam Avenue, New York, NY 10024, 212-799-4475

Bernstein, Joel (see also Burk, Dale A), Stoneydale Press Publishing Company, 295 Kootenai Creek Road, Stevensville, MT 59870, 406-777-5269

Berry, Frank, *BOTTOMFISH MAGAZINE*, 21250 Stevens Creek Blvd., Cupertino, CA 95014, 408-996-4550, 996-4547

Berry-Horton, Glenna (see also Luschei, Glenna), *CAFE SOLO*, 7975 San Marcos, Atascadero, CA 93422, 805-466-0947

Bertholf, Robert, *CREDENCES: A Journal of Twentieth Century Poetry and Poetics,* 420 Capen Hall, New York State University, c/o Poetry Collection, Buffalo, NY 14260, 716-673-2917

Bertolet, Bebe, Designer & Art Production Consultant (see also Gravelle, Barbara; Lumpkin, Kirk), *ZYGA MAGAZINE ASSEMBLAGE,* PO Box 7452, Oakland, CA 94601, 415-261-6837

Bertolet, Bebe, Designer & Art Production Consultant (see also Gravelle, Barbara; Lumpkin, Kirk), Zyga Multimedia Research, PO Box 7452, Oakland, CA 94601, 415-261-6837

Besa, David, Wine Country Publishers, 706 Mariano Drive, Sonoma, CA 95476, 707-938-0485

Best, Alan (see also Attwood, Derek), *NEW GERMAN STUDIES,* Dept Of German, Univ. Hull, Hull HU6 7RX, England, 0482-497649

Betz, Daniel R., Editor (see also Gold, Alexander), Ansuda Publications, Box 158, Harris, IA 51345

Betz, Daniel R. (see also Gold, Alexander), *THE PUB,* Box 158, Harris, IA 51345

Bevington, Stan (see also Young, David; Davey, Frank; James, Clifford; Nichol, bp; Ondaatje, Michael; McCartney, Linda; Sheard, Sarah; Reid, Dennis), Coach House Press, 95 Rivercrest Road, Toronto, Ontario M6S 4H7, Canada, 416-767-6317

Bevis, Mary Morgan, Editor (see also Brown, Carol L.), *COTTAGE CHEESE,* 8620 Portland, Bloomington, MN 55420

Bey, Galen, *SIERRA VIEW,* Sierra View Publishing, 22450 deKalb Drive, Woodland Hills, CA 91364, 818-347-7998

Bhavan, Rabindra (see also Malik, Keshav), *INDIAN Literature,* 35 Feroze Shah Road, New Delhi 110001, India, 388667

Bhikshuni Heng Ch'ih, Editor-in-Chief (see also Bhikshuni Heng Ch'ing; Bhikshuni Heng Tao; Upasaka Chou Li-ren), *VAJRA BODHI SEA,* 1731 15th St, Gold Mountain Monastery, San Francisco, CA 94103, 861-9672

Bhikshuni Heng Ch'ing, Editor (see also Bhikshuni Heng Ch'ih; Bhikshuni Heng Tao; Upasaka Chou Li-ren), *VAJRA BODHI SEA,* 1731 15th St, Gold Mountain Monastery, San Francisco, CA 94103, 861-9672

Bhikshuni Heng Tao, Editor (see also Bhikshuni Heng Ch'ih; Bhikshuni Heng Ch'ing; Upasaka Chou Li-ren), *VAJRA BODHI SEA,* 1731 15th St, Gold Mountain Monastery, San Francisco, CA 94103, 861-9672

Bianco, David, Director (see also Myers Jr., George), The Lunchroom Press, PO Box 36027, Grosse Pointe Farms, MI 48236

Bieberle, Gordon F., Editor, Publisher (see also Ullman, Rosanne; Davis, Allison; Shinn, Sharon), *PUBLISHING TRADE,* 1495 Oakwood, Des Plaines, IL 60016, 312-298-8291

BigEagle, Duane (see also Bradd, William), Ten Mile River Press, 2155 Eastman Lane, Petaluma, CA 94952, 707-964-5579

Bigelow, Charles, Associate Editor (see also Kirshenbaum, Sandra; Taylor, W. Thomas), *FINE PRINT: A Review for the Arts of the Book,* P O Box 3394, San Francisco, CA 94119, 415-776-1530

Biggs, Margaret Key, *PURPLE PEGASUS,* Purple Pegasus Poetry Club, 800 Niles Rd Port St Joe Jr-Sr High, Port St. Joe, FL 32456, 904-229-8251

Biggs, Margaret Key, Editor (see also Biggs, Wayne S.), Red Key Press, PO Box 551, Port St Joe, FL 32456, 904-227-1305

Biggs, S., Visual Arts (see also Dutkiewicz, Adam; Brakmanis, M.; Hastwell, G.; Franklin, C.), *WORDS AND VISIONS/WAV MAGAZINE,* 499 The Parade, Magill, Australia, 08-3329529

Biggs, Wayne S., Art Editor (see also Biggs, Margaret Key), Red Key Press, PO Box 551, Port St Joe, FL 32456, 904-227-1305

Bilgrami, M. (see also Anees, M.; Gallaghan, Haj Haydar; Mazandarani, Batul H.), Zahra Publications, PO Box 730, Blanco, TX 78606, 512-698-3239

BILLINGS, ROBERT, *NEWSLETTER (LEAGUE OF CANADIAN POETS),* 24 Ryerson Avenue, Toronto, Ontario M5T 2P3, Canada, 416-363-5047

13

Billings, Robert, Editor (see also Jacobs, Maria), *POETRY TORONTO,* 217 Northwood Drive, Willowdale, Ontario M2M 2K5, Canada

Birner, Linda D., *MOM...GUESS WHAT! MAGAZINE & TYPESETTING,* 1400 S Street, Suite 100B, Sacramento, CA 95814, 916-441-6397

Birtch, Sara, Co-Publisher (see also Green, Samuel), Jawbone Press, Waldron Island, WA 98297

Bish, Curt, *SUNSHINE & HEALTH, THE NUDIST MAGAZINE,* The Sunshine & Health Publishing Co., PO box 4281, Pittsburgh, PA 15203

Bissinger, Tom, *COMMON GROUND,* PO Box 83, St. Peters, PA 19470, 215-469-0191

Bjorklund, Paul R., *KEEPSAKE MAGAZINE FOR BRIDES,* 3009 North 67th Place, Scottsdale, AZ 85251, 602-252-9257

Black, Harold, Review Editor (see also Strahan, Bradley R.; Sullivan, Shirley G.; Gill, Ursula), *VISIONS,* 4705 South 8th Road, Arlington, VA 22204, 703-521-0142

Black, Joel, Associate Editor (see also Lehman, David; Green, Stefanie; Hartley, Glen T.), Nobodaddy Press, 159 Ludlowville Road, Lansing, NY 14882

Black, Joel (see also Lehman, David; Green, Stefanie; Hartley, Glen T.), *POETRY IN MOTION,* 159 Ludlowville Road, Lansing, NY 14882

Blackburn, Alex, *WRITERS FORUM,* University of Colorado at Colorado Springs, Colorado Springs, CO 80907, 303-593-3155 or 303-599-4023

Blackburn, Michael (see also Silkin, Jon; Tracy, Lorna; Morgan, Richard), *STAND,* 179 Wingrove Road, Newcastle-on-Tyne NE49DA, England

Blackford, Staige D., Editor, *THE VIRGINIA QUARTERLY REVIEW,* One West Range, Charlottesville, VA 22903, 804-924-3124

Blaikie, John (see also Brockway, R.; Brockway, Katie; West, Linda; Blanar, Mike; Hanly, Ken; Gentleman, Dorothy Corbett), Pierian Press, 5, Brandon University, Brandon, Manitoba, Canada, 727-2577

Blaikie, John (see also Brockway, R.; Brockway, Katie; West, Linda; Blanar, Mike; Hanly, Ken; Gentleman, Dorothy Corbett), *PIERIAN SPRING,* 5, Brandon University, Brandon, Manitoba, Canada, 727-2577

Blake, Jeri, DoubLeo Publications, 227 East 11th St, New York, NY 10003, 212-473-2739

Blake, Mona (see also Ianniello, Tom; Ianniello, Pat), *THE CHORD,* Musician's Contact Service, PO Box 40708, Rochester, NY 14604, 716-244-3188

Blanar, Mike (see also Brockway, R.; Brockway, Katie; West, Linda; Hanly, Ken; Blaikie, John; Gentleman, Dorothy Corbett), Pierian Press, 5, Brandon University, Brandon, Manitoba, Canada, 727-2577

Blanar, Mike (see also Brockway, R.; Brockway, Katie; West, Linda; Hanly, Ken; Blaikie, John; Gentleman, Dorothy Corbett), *PIERIAN SPRING,* 5, Brandon University, Brandon, Manitoba, Canada, 727-2577

Blank, Joani, Down There Press, PO Box 2086, Burlingame, CA 94010, 415-342-9867

Blasing, M.K., Director (see also Blasing, Randy; Honig, Edwin), Copper Beech Press, Box 1852 Brown Univ., Providence, RI 02912, 401-863-2393

Blasing, Randy, Editor (see also Blasing, M.K.; Honig, Edwin), *Copper Beech Press,* Box 1852 Brown Univ., Providence, RI 02912, 401-863-2393

Blench, J.W., *THE DURHAM UNIVERSITY JOURNAL,* Department of English Studies, Elvet Riverside, New Elvet, Durham, England

Bliss, Kevin, *NORTHERN NEW ENGLAND REVIEW,* 825 Franklin Pierce College, Rindge, NH 03461, 603-899-5111

Blostein, Fay (see also Byers, Barbara), Ontario Library Association, 73 Richmond Street, W., Suite 402, Toronto, Ontario M5H 1Z4, Canada, 416-363-3389

Blostein, Fay, *REVIEWING LIBRARIAN*, 73 Richmond Street W., Suite 402, Toronto, Ontario M5H 1Z4, Canada, 416-363-3389

Blue, Helen M., Editor, *THE CIRCLE*, 105 S Huntington Avenue, Blue, Helen M.*Editor, Jamaica Plain, MA 02130, 617-232-0343

Bluestein, Dan T., Business Manager (see also Schechter, Ruth Lisa; Thomas, Dan B.; Crisci, Pat J.; Merrill, Susan; Stettan, Leonard), *CROTON REVIEW*, P.O. Box 277, Croton on Hudson, NY 10520, 914-271-3144

Bluestein, Eleanor (see also Freilicher, Melvyn), *CRAWL OUT YOUR WINDOW*, 4641 Park Blvd, San Diego, CA 92116, 619-299-4859

Blum, John, Asst. Editor (see also Plath, James; Emery, Mary Ann; Williams, Elizabeth), *CLOCKWATCH REVIEW*, 737 Penbrook Way, Hartland, WI 53029, 414-367-8315

Blum, Peter, Math Counseling Institute Press, 4518 Corliss Avenue, N, Seattle, WA 98103, 206-632-8639

Blythe, Joanne S., Editor, *TRANET*, Box 567, Rangeley, ME 04970, 207-864-2252

Blythe, Randall, Managing Editor (see also Pickelsimer, Lisa), *NEW BEGINNINGS MAGAZINE*, Route #2, Box 27-D, Pisgah Forest, NC 28768, 704-883-3973

Blythe, Will, Editor (see also Carroll, Ron; Morrison, John), *THE BLACK WARRIOR REVIEW*, P.O. Box 2936, University, AL 35486, 205-348-4518

Boatright, Philip, *STEPPENWOLF*, PO Box 43576, Tucson, AZ 85733

Boatwright, James, Editor (see also Howard, Richard), *SHENANDOAH*, PO Box 722, Lexington, VA 24450, 703-463-9111 ext 283

Boccio, Paul, The First East Coast Theatre and Publishing Company, Inc., PO Box A244, Village Station, NY 10014, 212-947-1253

Bodek, Norman, Editor, Publisher, *PRODUCTIVITY*, PO Box 16722, Stamford, CT 06905, 203-322-8388

Boggs, Redd, Fiction (see also Sapiro, Leland; Smith, Sheryl; Emerson, Mary), *RIVERSIDE QUARTERLY*, Box 863-388, Wildcat Station, Plano, TX 75086, 214-234-6795

Bogstad, Janice, *NEW MOON*, SF 3, PO Box 2056, Madison, WI 53701, 608-251-3854

Bogus, Sdiane (see also De Oca, D.M.; Baptist, Weldon O.; Coleman, Cheryl L.), W. I. M. Publications, Box 367, Department IDSP, College Corner, OH 45003, 513-523-5994

Boisvert, Donald J., Contributing Editor (see also Rimm, Virginia M.; Perrin, Arnold; Grierson, Ruth; Briggs, Henry; McIntyre, Joan; Knowles, Ardeana Hamlin; Brown, Ronald G.; Beck, Raymond M.), *NEW ENGLAND SAMPLER*, RFD #1 Box 2280, Brooks, ME 04921, 207-525-3575

Bokhara, Elias (see also Georgakas, Dan; Janda, Judy), Smyrna Press, Box 1803 GPO, Brooklyn, NY 11202

Bolane, Jamie E., Childbirth Graphics Ltd., PO Box 17025, Irondequoit, Rochester, NY 14617, 716-266-6769 (message phone)

Bollinger, Taree, *JOURNAL OF FORMS MANAGEMENT*, 1818 SE Division Street, Portland, OR 97202, 503-232-0232

Bolotin, Norm, Editor & Publisher (see also Laing, Christine), Creative Options, Box 601, Edmonds, WA 98020, 206-789-5808

Bolton, Stanwood, Poetry (see also Reynolds, Louise T.; Jackel, Harry; Reynolds, Louise E.; Madrigal, Sylvia), *THE NEW RENAISSANCE, An International Magazine of Ideas & Opinions, Emphasizing Literature & The Arts*, 9 Heath Road, Arlington, MA 02174

Bomberger, Irvin (see also Flower, Ruth), *DRAFT ACTION*, #534 Washington Bldg, 1435 G St. NW, Washington, DC 20005, 202-393-4870

Bonanno, David (see also Vogelsang, Arthur; Berg, Stephen), *AMERICAN POETRY REVIEW*, 1616 Walnut St., Room 405, Philadelphia, PA 19103, 215-732-6770

15

Bond, Jean Carey, Editor (see also Jackson, Esther; O'Dell, J. H.; Kaiser, Ernest; Baird, Keith E.; Hairston, Loyle), *FREEDOMWAYS - A Quarterly Review of the Freedom Movement*, Freedomways Associates, Inc., 799 Broadway Suite 542, New York, NY 10003

Bondell, Martin (see also Galant, Juliette), Fotofolio, Inc., 96 Spring Street, New York, NY 10012, 212-226-0923

Bondy, Melissa (see also Edelson, Morris; Fellner, Mike; McGilligan, Pat; Edelson, Olga), Quixote Press, 1812 Marshall, Houston, TX 77098

Bonetti, Kay, Director, American Audio Prose Library (non-print), 915 East Broadway, Columbia, MO 65201, 314-874-5676

Bonewits, P.E.I., Contributing Editor (see also Clifton, Charles; Clifton, Mary), *IRON MOUNTAIN: A JOURNAL OF MAGICAL RELIGION*, PO Box 6423, Colorado Springs, CO 80934, 303-685-5849

Bookbinder, Sarah, Publisher, Programmed Press, 2301 Baylis Avenue, Elmont, NY 11003, 516-775-0933

Booth, Michael, Professor (see also Armstrong, W.A., Professor; Rosenfeld, Dr. Sybil), *THEATRE NOTEBOOK*, 103 Ralph Court, Queensway, London W2 5HU, England

Borgatti, Robert (see also Sicoli, Dan; Farallo, Livio), *SLIPSTREAM*, Slipstream Publications, Box 2071, New Market Station, Niagara Falls, NY 14301, 716-282-2616

B'orlaug, Ruby, Executive Vice President (see also Thorsgood, Antoinette), Ide House, Inc., 4631 Harvey Drive, Mesquite, TX 75149, 214-681-2552

Borman, Kevin (see also Tipton, David), Rivelin Press, 24 Aireville Road, Bradford, England, 0274-498135

Borneman, Bill (see also Piper, Paul), *WORLD WAR IV*, 1733 South 5th W., Missoula, MT 59801, 442-0656

Borowski, Steven J., Big "B" Publications, 1818 Woodbine Street, Ridgewood, NY 11385, 212-381-7872

Borrelli, Peter, Editor (see also von Rosenberg, Helena), *THE AMICUS JOURNAL*, 122 E 42nd Street, New York, NY 10168, 949-0049

Boss, Laura, *LIPS*, PO Box 1345, Montclair, NJ 07042

Bossong, Ken (see also Holzman, David; Pilarski, Jan), Citizen's Energy Project, 1110 6th Street, NW, Washington, DC 20001

Bossong, Ken, *SOFT SOLAR NOTES*, 1110 6th Street, NW, Washington, DC 20001

Botnick, Ken, Co-Editor (see also Miller, Steve), The Red Ozier Press, PO Box 101, Old Chelsea Station, New York, NY 10113, 212-620-3154

Boucher, Tania K., Aeolian Palace Press, Box 8, Pocopson, PA 19366, 215-793-1139

Boudreau, Diane (see also Boudreau, Jean), Winter Trees Productions Ltd., Box 20072, Jackson, WY 83001, 307-733-3152

Boudreau, Jean (see also Boudreau, Diane), *Winter Trees Productions Ltd.*, Box 20072, Jackson, WY 83001, 307-733-3152

Bounds, Art, *THE PEGASUS REVIEW*, PO Box 134, Flanders, NJ 07836, 201-927-0749

Bourasaw, Noel V., Publisher, Editor, *NORTHWEST WINE ALMANAC*, First Noel Publishing Co., PO Box 85595, Seattle, WA 98145, 206-522-3050

Bourne, Daniel, Editor (see also Kavacik, Karen), *ARTFUL DODGE*, PO Box 1473, Bloomington, IN 47402, 812-332-0310

Bowden, Michael (see also Wojahn, David), San Pedro Press, 212 Clawson Street, Bisbee, AZ 85603

Bowden, Michael (see also Wojahn, David), *WHETSTONE*, 212 Clawson Street, Bisbee, AZ 85603

Bowles, Paul, Consulting Editor (see also Lesser, Wendy; Berger, John; Hass, Robert; Vidal, Gore; Wasserman, Steve), *THE THREEPENNY REVIEW*, PO Box 9131, Berkeley, CA 94709, 415-849-4545

Boyars, Marion, Marion Boyars, Inc., PO Box 223, Canal Street Station, New York, NY 10013

Boyd, Blair, Editor (see also Loyd, Bonnie), *LANDSCAPE*, PO Box 7107, Berkeley, CA 94707, 415-549-3233

Boyer, Chuck (see also And, Miekal; Was, Elizabeth), Xerox Sutra Editions, 1341 Williamson #B, Madison, WI 53703

Boyer, D. (see also Trusky, T.; Burmaster, O.), Ahsahta, Boise State University, Department of English, Boise, ID 83725, 208-385-1190 or 1999

Boyer, Susan, Editor (see also Ljungkull, Christine), *THE TOWNSHIPS SUN*, Box 28, Lennoxville, Quebec, Canada

Boyles, Ann, Fiction Editor (see also Conway, Don; Gibbs, Robert; Trethewey, Eric; Hawkes, Robert; Butlin, Ron; Taylor, Michael; Thompson, Kent; Davey, Bill; Bauer, William), *THE FIDDLEHEAD*, The Observatory, Univ. New Brunswick, PO Box 4400, Fredericton, NB E3B 5A3, Canada, 506-454-3591

Brabec, Barbara, Editor & Publisher, *NATIONAL HOME BUSINESS REPORT*, PO Box 10423, Springfield, MO 65808

Bradd, William (see also BigEagle, Duane), Ten Mile River Press, 2155 Eastman Lane, Petaluma, CA 94952, 707-964-5579

Bradford, James, *COPULA*, W1114 Indiana Street, Spokane, WA 99205, 325-2985

Bradford, Jean I., Copley Books, 7776 Ivanhoe Avenue, P O Box 957, La Jolla, CA 92038, 619-454-1842, 619-454-0411

Bradley, Beth (see also Thompson, Sandra S.; Teague, Toney), *ANGELSTONE*, 316 Woodland Drive, Birmingham, AL 35209, 205-870-7281

Bradley, Beth (see also Thompson, Sandra S.; Teague, Toney), Angelstone Press, 316 Woodland Drive, Birmingham, AL 35209, 205-870-7281

Bradley, Jacqueline, Editor, publisher (see also Kelly, Patrick), Blue Horse Publications, PO Box 6061, Augusta, GA 30906, (404) 798-5628

Bradley, Jacqueline T., Editor, publisher (see also Kelly, Patrick; Weissmann, G. Warren; Brunswick, S.J.; Mallory, Eugenia P.), *BLUE HORSE*, P.O. Box 6061, Augusta, GA 30906, 404-798-5628

Bradley, Jerry (see also Rothfork, John), Saurian Press, Box A, New Mexico Tech., Socorro, NM 87801, 505-835-5445

Bradley, Matt, Bradley Publishing, PO Box 7383, Little Rock, AR 72217, 501-224-0692

Bradt, George (see also Walters, James L.), Bradt Enterprises, 93 Harvey Street, Cambridge, MA 02140

Brady, Steven R., Editor (see also Mitchell, Char), *CACHE REVIEW*, 4805 E. 29th Street, Tucson, AZ 85711, 602-748-0600

Brady, William, Editorial Director, *HARVEST BOOK SERIES*, PO Box 2466, Los Angeles, CA 90078

Brady, William, Editorial Director, Harvest Publishers, PO Box 2466, Los Angeles, CA 90078

Bragg, Patricia, Ph.D. (see also Bragg, Paul C., Ph.D.), Health Science, Box 7, Santa Barbara, CA 93117, 805-968-1028

Bragg, Paul C., Ph.D. (see also Bragg, Patricia, Ph.D.), *Health Science*, Box 7, Santa Barbara, CA 93117, 805-968-1028

Brakkee, E., American Medical Publishing Association, PO Box 1900, Santa Barbara, CA 93102, 805-682-7475

Brakmanis, M., Poetry (see also Dutkiewicz, Adam; Hastwell, G.; Biggs, S.; Franklin, C.), *WORDS AND VISIONS/WAV MAGAZINE*, 499 The Parade, Magill, Australia, 08-3329529

Bramann, Jorn K., *NIGHTSUN*, Department of Philosophy, Frostburg State College, Frostburg, MD 21532, 301-689-4249

Brand, Stewart, *COEVOLUTION QUARTERLY,* Box 428, Sausalito, CA 94966, 415-332-1716

Brandenburg, William, GRF, Ltd., PO Box 715, Roosevelt, UT 84066, 801-353-4586

Brandi, John, Tooth of Time Books, 634 E Garcia, Santa Fe, NM 87501

Brashers, Charles, Associated Creative Writers, 9231 Molly Woods Ave, La Mesa, CA 92041, 619-460-4107

Brashers, Charles (see also Kuhlken, Ken), Helix House, 9231 Molly Woods Avenue, La Mesa, CA 92041, 619-460-4107

Bratman, David (see also Leverant, Robert), Images Press, PO Box 756, Sebastopol, CA 95472, 707-823-4351

Bratton, Joe, Pau Hana Press, 1750 Kalakaua Ave., Suite 3-577, Honolulu, HI 96826, 808-735-5650

Breakey, Jeff, Sprouting Publications, Box 62, Ashland, OR 97520, 503-482-5627

Breakey, Jeff, *THE SPROUTLETTER,* Box 62, Ashland, OR 97520, 503-482-5627

Breger, Brian (see also Lewis, Harry; Wachtel, Chuck), *# MAGAZINE,* 339 W. 4th Street #2R, New York, NY 10014

Breit, Luke (see also Grizzell, Patrick), *POET NEWS,* 2791 24th St. #8, Sacramento, CA 95818, 916-739-1885

Breitman, Wallace E., *FEDERAL NOTES,* PO Box 986, Saratoga, CA 95070, 408-356-4557

Brennan, Barbara, Designer (see also Laughter, Fred), Moonlight Publications, PO Drawer 2850, La Jolla, CA 92038

Brewer, Daryln, Editor, *CODA: Poets & Writers Newsletter,* 201 West 54th St., New York, NY 10019, 212-757-1766

Brewer, Daryln, Editor (see also Merrill, Lisa), Poets & Writers, Inc., 201 West 54th Street, New York, NY 10019, 212-757-1766

Brewer, Merry, Editor (see also Lind, Lars), Poet Papers, P.O. Box 528, Topanga, CA 90290

Brewer, Merry, Editor, *THE RECORD SUN,* PO Box 528, Topanga, CA 90290

Bridwell, Tom, Salt-Works Press, RFD 1 Box 141, Grenada, MS 38901, 617-385-3948

Briggs, Henry, Contributing Editor (see also Rimm, Virginia M.; Perrin, Arnold; Grierson, Ruth; Boisvert, Donald J.; McIntyre, Joan; Knowles, Ardeana Hamlin; Brown, Ronald G.; Beck, Raymond M.), *NEW ENGLAND SAMPLER,* RFD #1 Box 2280, Brooks, ME 04921, 207-525-3575

Brill, Kastle, Co-Editor (see also Johnson, Bonnie; Willoughby, Robin; Zuckerman, Ryki), *EARTH'S DAUGHTERS,* Box 41, c/o Bonnie Johnson, Central Park Stn., NY 14215, 716-837-7778

Brilliant, Marilyn A., Acquisitions Editor (see also Knier, Timothy; Schultz, Cathy; Sitz, Carlton), Pine Mountain Press, Inc., Box 19746, West Allis, WI 53219, 414-778-1120

Brittain, Larry, *JUNCTION MAG.,* Brooklyn College, Bedford Ave. & Avenue H., English Dept, Brooklyn, NY 11210

Britton, Jack, *HOBBY BOOKWATCH (MILITARY, GUN & HOBBY BOOK REVIEW),* PO Box 52033, Tulsa, OK 74152, 918-743-6048

Brockway, Katie (see also Brockway, R.; West, Linda; Blanar, Mike; Hanly, Ken; Blaikie, John; Gentleman, Dorothy Corbett), Pierian Press, 5, Brandon University, Brandon, Manitoba, Canada, 727-2577

Brockway, Katie (see also Brockway, R.; West, Linda; Blanar, Mike; Hanly, Ken; Blaikie, John; Gentleman, Dorothy Corbett), *PIERIAN SPRING,* 5, Brandon University, Brandon, Manitoba, Canada, 727-2577

Brockway, Laurie Sue, Publishing Director (see also Weingarten, Henry), ASI Publishers, Inc., 63 West 38th Street, New York, NY 10018, 212-679-0645

Brockway, R. (see also Brockway, Katie; West, Linda; Blanar, Mike; Hanly, Ken; Blaikie, John; Gentleman, Dorothy Corbett), Pierian Press, 5, Brandon University, Brandon, Manitoba, Canada, 727-2577

Brockway, R. (see also Brockway, Katie; West, Linda; Blanar, Mike; Hanly, Ken; Blaikie, John; Gentleman, Dorothy Corbett), *PIERIAN SPRING*, 5, Brandon University, Brandon, Manitoba, Canada, 727-2577

Bromell, Nicholas, Editor (see also Parson, Ann), Boston Critic, Inc., 991 Massachusetts Avenue, No. 4, Cambridge, MA 02138

Bromell, Nicholas, Editor (see also Parson, Ann), *BOSTON REVIEW*, 991 Massachusetts Avenue, No.4, Cambridge, MA 02138, 617-492-5478

Brook, Walter, World Press Watch Press, PO Box 4177, Lantana, FL 33465, 305-585-7797

Brooks, Marshall, Editor (see also Greene, Stephanie), Arts End Books, Box 162, Newton, MA 02168, 617-965-2478

Brooks, Marshall, Editor (see also Greene, Stephanie), *NOSTOC*, Box 162, Newton, MA 02168

Brooks, Randy (see also Brooks, Shirley), High/Coo Press, Route 1, Battleground, IN 47920, 317-567-2596

Brooks, Shirley (see also Brooks, Randy), *High/Coo Press*, Route 1, Battleground, IN 47920, 317-567-2596

Brooks, Walter, *WORLD PRESS WATCH*, PO Box 4177, Lantana, FL 33465, 585-7797

Broome, Dean, Plantagenet House, Inc., PO Box 271, Blackshear, GA 31516, 912-449-6601

Brown, Barbara, Editor, Naturegraph Publishers, Inc., P. O. Box 1075, Happy Camp, CA 96039, 916-493-5353

Brown, Beth (see also Brown, Otis), Overtone Press, 4421 Chestnut Street, Philadelphia, PA 19104, 215-386-4279

Brown, Beth (see also Brown, Otis), *OVERTONE SERIES*, 4421 Chestnut Street, Philadelphia, PA 19104, 215-386-4279

Brown, Bruce (see also Brown, Joan), *POOR MAN'S PRESS*, Box 1291, Station B, Ottawa, Ontario K1P 5R3, Canada

Brown, Carol L., Associate Editor (see also Bevis, Mary Morgan), *COTTAGE CHEESE*, 8620 Portland, Bloomington, MN 55420

Brown, Charles N., Editor & Publisher (see also Miller, Faren; Holmen, Rachel), *LOCUS: The Newspaper of the Science Fiction Field*, Box 13305, Oakland, CA 94661, 415-339-9196

Brown, David (see also Letsinger, Sue; Halsted, Deb), Left Bank Books, 92 Pike Street, Seattle, WA 98101

Brown, Douglas A., Phoenix Publishing Co., PO Box 10, Custer, WA 98240, 206-467-8219

Brown, Eben A., E. Arthur Brown Company, 3404 Pawnee Drive, Alexandria, MN 56308, 612-762-8847

Brown, Harold M., *CONSTELLATIONS*, PO Box 4378, Santa Rosa, CA 95402, 707-526-6020

Brown, Harvey (see also Warner, Elizabeth), Frontier Press, P O Box 5023, Santa Rosa, CA 95402, 707-544-5174

Brown, Jae, Editor-in-Chief (see also Moore, Mary Jane), *A LETTER AMONG FRIENDS*, PO Box 1198, Groton, CT 06340, 203-536-3494

Brown, Joan (see also Brown, Bruce), *POOR MAN'S PRESS*, Box 1291, Station B, Ottawa, Ontario K1P 5R3, Canada

Brown, Karenne, Editor, *PHOEBE*, G.M.U. 4400 University Dr., Fairfax, VA 22030, 703-323-3730

Brown, Lee (see also Duberstein, Larry), Darkhorse Bookmakers, Jones Hill Road, Ashby, MA 01431

Brown, Marc, Editor (see also Sanders, Ken; Firmage, Richard), Dream Garden Press, 1199 Iola Avenue, Salt Lake City, UT 84104, 801-355-2154

Brown, Melvin E., Assistant Editor (see also Weaver, Michael S.), *BLIND ALLEYS*, PO Box 13224, Baltimore, MD 21203, 301-235-3857

Brown, Melvin E. (see also Weaver, Michael S.), Seventh Son Press, PO Box 13224, Baltimore, MD 21203, 301-235-3857

Brown, Otis (see also Brown, Beth), Overtone Press, 4421 Chestnut Street, Philadelphia, PA 19104, 215-386-4279

Brown, Otis (see also Brown, Beth), *OVERTONE SERIES*, 4421 Chestnut Street, Philadelphia, PA 19104, 215-386-4279

Brown, Richard (see also Armstrong, Alison; Bekker, Pieter), *JAMES JOYCE BROADSHEET*, James Joyce Centre, University College, Gower Street, London WC1E 6BT, England, 01-986-9456

Brown, Ronald G., Contrib. Editor (see also Rimm, Virginia M.; Perrin, Arnold; Grierson, Ruth; Briggs, Henry; Boisvert, Donald J.; McIntyre, Joan; Knowles, Ardeana Hamlin; Beck, Raymond M.), *NEW ENGLAND SAMPLER*, RFD #1 Box 2280, Brooks, ME 04921, 207-525-3575

Brown, Steven Ford, Editor, Thunder City Press, PO Box 600574, Houston, TX 77260

Brown, Steven Ford, Editor, *THUNDER MOUNTAIN REVIEW*, PO Box 600574, Houston, TX 77260

Brown, Stuart, Administrative Assistant (see also Knipe, Tony), Ceolfrith Press, Sunderland, Tyne & Wear SR27DF, England, 0783-41214

Brown, Toni, Managing Editor (see also Kippel, Leslie D.), *RELIX*, PO Box 94, Brooklyn, NY 11229, 212-645-0818

Brown, Wilfred, *THE ARCHER*, PO Box 41, Camas Valley, OR 97416, 503-445-2327

Bruccoli, Matthew J., Bruccoli Clark Collector's Editions, 1700 Lone Pine Road, Bloomfield Hills, MI 48013, 313-642-8897

Bruce, Bud, Good Earth Press, 546 S. Villa, Villa Park, IL 60181

Bruchac, Carol (see also Bruchac, Joseph), *THE GREENFIELD REVIEW*, R.D. 1, P.O. Box 80, Greenfield Center, NY 12833, 518-584-1728

Bruchac, Carol W., Editor (see also Bruchac, Joseph, III), *THE PRISON WRITING REVIEW*, R.D. 1, Box 80, C/O The Greenfield Review, Greenfield Center, NY 12833

Bruchac, Carol Worthen, Editor (see also Bruchac, Joseph, III), The Greenfield Review Press, P.O. Box 80, Greenfield Center, NY 12833

Bruchac, Joseph (see also Bruchac, Carol), *THE GREENFIELD REVIEW*, R.D. 1, P.O. Box 80, Greenfield Center, NY 12833, 518-584-1728

Bruchac, Joseph, III, Editor (see also Bruchac, Carol Worthen), The Greenfield Review Press, P.O. Box 80, Greenfield Center, NY 12833

Bruchac, Joseph, III, Editor (see also Bruchac, Carol W.), *THE PRISON WRITING REVIEW*, R.D. 1, Box 80, C/O The Greenfield Review, Greenfield Center, NY 12833

Brummels, J.V. (see also Sanders, Mark), Sandhills Press, 219 S 19th Street, Ord, NE 68862

Brummet, John, Co-Editor (see also Curran, Keelin), *SCAPE*, 1506 4th Avenue, Apt #11, Oakland, CA 94606, 415-763-2012

Bruner, Mark, Jump River Press, Inc., 810 Oak Street, Medina, OH 44256

Bruner, Mark, *JUMP RIVER REVIEW*, 810 Oak Street, Medina, OH 44256

Brunswick, S.J., Fiction Editor (see also Bradley, Jacqueline T.; Kelly, Patrick; Weissmann, G. Warren; Mallory, Eugenia P.), *BLUE HORSE*, P.O. Box 6061, Augusta, GA 30906, 404-798-5628

Bryan, Carol, *CREATIVE PERSON*, 1000 Byus Drive, Charleston, WV 25311, 304-345-2378

Bryan, Carol, *THE LIBRARY IMAGINATION PAPER!*, 1000 Byus Drive, Charleston, WV 25311, 304-345-2378

Bryant, Dorothy, Ata Books, 1928 Stuart Street, Berkeley, CA 94703, 415-841-9613

Buccellati, Giorgio, Undena Publications, PO Box 97, Malibu, CA 90265, 213-366-1744

Buchman, Chris (see also Schneider, Rex), Blue Mouse Studio, Box 312, Union, MI 49130

Buchmann, Hank (see also Clifton, Linda J.), *CRAB CREEK REVIEW*, 806 N 42nd, Seattle, WA 98103, 206-543-6548

Buchsbaum, Ralph, Editor, The Boxwood Press, 183 Ocean View Blvd, Pacific Grove, CA 93950, 408-375-9110

Buchwald, Emilie, Editor (see also Scholes, Randall W.), *MILKWEED CHRONICLE*, Box 24303, Minneapolis, MN 55424, 612-332-3192

Buck, E.A., Goldfinch Press, Box 304, Iowa City, IA 52244

Buck, Harry (see also Nisley, Rebecca), *ANIMA*, 1053 Wilson Avenue, Chambersburg, PA 17201, 717-263-8303

Buck, Harry M, Executive Editor, Anima Publications, c/o Concocheague Associates, Inc., 1053 Wilson Avenue, Chambersburg, PA 17201, 717-263-8303

Buck, Paul, *CURTAINS*, 4 Bower Street, Maidstone, Kent ME16 8SD, England, 0622-63681

Buck, Paul, Pressed Curtains, 4 Bower Street, Maidstone, Kent ME16 8SD, England, 0622-63681

Buck, Paul (see also Vas Dias, Robert; Patterson, Ian), Spectacular Diseases, 83(b) London Road, Peterborough, Cambs, England

Buckland, Raymond (see also Buckland, Tara), Taray Publications, Route 2, Box 206, Scottsville, VA 24590, 804-286-3198

Buckland, Tara (see also Buckland, Raymond), *Taray Publications*, Route 2, Box 206, Scottsville, VA 24590, 804-286-3198

Budd, Louis J., Managing Editor (see also Cady, Edwin H.), *AMERICAN LITERATURE*, 210 West Duke Building, Duke University, Durham, NC 27708, 919-684-3948

Buehler, Laurie, *RHINO*, 3915 Foster Street, Evanston, IL 60203, 312-433-3536

Buford, Bill, *GRANTA*, 44a, Hobson Street, Cambridge CB1 1NL, England, (0223) 315290

Buford, Bill, Granta Publications Ltd, 44a, Hobson Street, Cambridge CB1 1NL, England, (0223) 315290

Bugbee, Helen, Traumwald Press, 3550 Lake Shore Drive, Suite 10, Chicago, IL 60657, 312-525-5303

Buh, Lisa (see also Sowell, Carol), Barrington Press, 5933 Armaga Springs Road, Suite A, Palos Verdes, CA 90274, 213-544-2597

Bukowski, Charles, Contributing Editor (see also Golden, Michael; Elias, Viki; Harrison, Jim; Mungo, Raymond; Placidus, Max; Codrescu, Andrei; Horotwitz, Mikhail; Ligi; Kramer, Glenn; Mitchell, Donna; Riedel, Robert), *SMOKE SIGNALS*, 1516 Beverly Road, Brooklyn, NY 11226

Bulkin, Elly (see also Allison, Dorothy; Clarke, Cheryl; Otter, Nancy Clarke; Waddy, Adrianne), *CONDITIONS*, PO Box 56, Van Brunt Sta., Brooklyn, NY 11215, 212-788-8654

Bull, David C., Bull Publishing Co., P O Box 208, Palo Alto, CA 94302, 415-322-2855

Bullen, Donald (see also Sennett, John), *MAGIC CHANGES*, 553 W Oakdale #317, Chicago, IL 60657, 312-327-5606

Bullins, Amanda (see also Ayyildiz, Judy; Ferguson, Maurice; Nash, Valery; Sheffler, Natalie; Steinke, Paul; Weinstein, Ann), *ARTEMIS*, PO Box 945, Roanoke, VA 24005, 703-981-9318

Bullock, Ben, Gourmet Guides, 1767 Stockton Street, San Francisco, CA 94133, 415-391-5903

Bullock, Robert, Inglewood Discoveries, Box 1653, Rockefeller Center Station, New York, NY 10185

Bumppo, Natty (see also Hebhoe, Hank T.), Borf Books, Box 413, Brownsville, KY 42210, 502-597-2187

Burch, Charlton, Designer and Editor (see also Martin, Andrea), *LIGHTWORKS MAGAZINE*, PO Box 1202, Birmingham, MI 48012, 313-642-7207

Burger, Henry G., The Wordtree, 7306 Brittany W-8, Merriam, KS 66203, 913-236-7733

Burgess, Mary, Editor (see also Reginald, Robert), The Borgo Press, Box 2845, San Bernardino, CA 92406, (714) 884-5813

Burghard, Sr. Shirley, R.N., A.A.S., B.A., O.S.L., *CONSTRUCTIVE ACTION NEWSLETTER*, Act/ Action, B 1104 Ross Towers 710 Lodi St., Syracuse, NY 13203, 315-471-4644

Burgin, Robert, Editor-in-Chief, *NORTH CAROLINA LIBRARIES*, Route 2, Box 28A, Wake Forest, NC 27587, 919-556-2940

Burk, Dale A (see also Bernstein, Joel), Stoneydale Press Publishing Company, 295 Kootenai Creek Road, Stevensville, MT 59870, 406-777-5269

Burke, E. J., Mouvement Publications, 109 East State Street, Ithaca, NY 14850, 607-272-2157

Burkhardt, Minnie, Pussycat Press, 11 rue du Vidollet, 1202 Geneva, Switzerland, (022) 34 97 90

Burmaster, O. (see also Trusky, T.; Boyer, D.), Ahsahta, Boise State University, Department of English, Boise, ID 83725, 208-385-1190 or 1999

Burnham, Crispin, Editor-in-Chief, Publisher (see also Baker, Charles L.), Yith Press, 1051 Wellington Road, Lawrence, KS 66044, 913-843-4341

Burnham, Linda Frye, Editor (see also Durland, Steven), Astro Artz, 240 So Broadway, 5th Floor, Los Angeles, CA 90012, 213-687-7362

Burnham, Linda Frye, Editor (see also Durland, Steven), *HIGH PERFORMANCE*, 240 S. Broadway, 5th Floor, Los Angeles, CA 90012, 213-687-7362

Burnham, Michael (see also Burnham, Ruth), Our Gang Publications, 630 Woodlawn Avenue, Canon City, CO 81212, 303-275-6227

Burnham, R. Peter, Fiction Editor (see also Hennessey, Patricia J.; Backstrand, Brian), *THE LONG STORY*, 11 Kingston Street, North Andover, MA 01845, 617-686-7638

Burnham, Ruth (see also Burnham, Michael), Our Gang Publications, 630 Woodlawn Avenue, Canon City, CO 81212, 303-275-6227

Burnhm, Crispin, Editor-in-Chief, Publisher (see also Baker, Charles L.), *ELDRITCH TALES*, 1051 Wellington Road, Lawrence, KS 66044, 913-843-4341

Burns, Grant (see also Hill, Casey), *NEW PAGES: News & Reviews of the Progressive Booktrade*, 4426 South Belsay Road, Grand Blanc, MI 48439

Burns, Richard, Editor (see also Krelove, Lillian), *COME-ALL-YE*, P.O. Box 494, Hatboro, PA 19040, 215-675-6762

Burns, Richard (see also Cumbie, Richard), *NANTUCKET REVIEW*, P.O. Box 1234, Nantucket, MA 02554

Burns, Richard K. (see also Krelove, Lillian), Legacy Books (formerly Folklore Associates), PO Box 494, Hatboro, PA 19040, 215-675-6762

Burns, Roland (see also Cooke, Roger; Kindred, Wendy), *THE BLACK FLY REVIEW*, University of Maine at Fort Kent, Fort Kent, ME 04743, 207-834-3162

Burns, William, Editor (see also Empereur, Jake, S.J.; Mudd, C.P.), *MODERN LITURGY*, Box 444, Saratoga, CA 95071, 408-252-4195

Burns, William, Editor, Advertising Manager, Resource Publications, Inc., 160 East Virginia Street #290, San Jose, CA 95112

Burnstein, Saul, Editorial Director (see also Goldman, Susan), New Bedford Press, 5800 W Century Blvd., Suite 91502, Los Angeles, CA 90009, 837-2961

Burrows, Arthur A. (see also Clark, Raymond C.; Moran, Patrick R.), ProLingua Associates, 15 Elm Street, Brattleboro, VT 05301, 802-257-7779

Burton, Brenda (see also Green, Lewis), New Horizons Publishers, 737 Tenth Avenue East, Seattle, WA 98102, 206-323-1102

Burton, Mary A. (see also Goldsmith, P.A.), Golden Sails Press, 6263 Cahaba Valley Road, Birmingham, AL 35243, 205-991-5548

Burton, Mary A. (see also Goldsmith, P.A.), *SHADOW VOYAGES*, 6263 Cahaba Valley Road, Birmingham, AL 35243, 205-991-5548

Burwell, Helen P., Burwell Enterprises, 5106 F.M. 1960 West Suite 349, Houston, TX 77069

Bush, Erwin H., Burning Bush Publications, 103 Middleton Place, Jeffersonville, PA 19403, 215-255-5162

Bush, Erwin H. (see also Rogers, Katherin A.), *PHILOSOHICAL SPECULATIONS in Science Fiction & Fantasy,* 103 Middleton Place, Jeffersonville, PA 19403, 215-275-5396

Bush, G. F., Publisher (see also Nash, Helen), *LETTERS MAGAZINE*, MAINE WRITERS WORKSHOP, RFD 1, Box 905, Stonington, ME 04681

Bush, G. F., Publisher (see also Nash, Helen), Mainespring Press, MAINE WRITERS WORKSHOP, Box 905, R. F. D., Stonington, ME 04681

Butkus, Greg (see also Worden, Mark; Lybrand, Lisa), *POETRY TODAY*, Box 20822, Portland, OR 97220, 213-334-4732

Butler, Edith, *WOMEN WISE*, 38 South Main Street, Concord, NH 03301, 603-225-2739

Butlin, Ron, Poetry Editor (see also Conway, Don; Gibbs, Robert; Trethewey, Eric; Hawkes, Robert; Taylor, Michael; Thompson, Kent; Davey, Bill; Boyles, Ann; Bauer, William), *THE FIDDLEHEAD*, The Observatory, Univ. New Brunswick, PO Box 4400, Fredericton, NB E3B 5A3, Canada, 506-454-3591

Buttaci, Sal St. John (see also Gerstle, Susan Linda), New Worlds Unlimited, PO Box 556, Saddle Brook, NJ 07662

Button, John (see also Gaston, Robin; Lines, Marianna), The Findhorn Press, The Park, Forres, Morayshire 1V360TZ, Scotland, 030-93-2582

Buxton, Karen, Production (see also McFarland, Ron; Snyder, Margaret; Foriyes, Tina), *SNAP-DRAGON*, English Department, University of Idaho, Moscow, ID 83843, 208-885-6156

Byers, Barbara (see also Blostein, Fay), Ontario Library Association, 73 Richmond Street, W., Suite 402, Toronto, Ontario M5H 1Z4, Canada, 416-363-3389

Bynum, W.F. (see also Nutton, V.), *MEDICAL HISTORY*, 183 Euston Road, London NW1 2BP, England

Byron, Ken, *'2D' (DRAMA AND DANCE)*, Knighton Fields Drama Centre, Herrick Road, Leicester LE2 6DJ, England, 0533-700850-701525

C

C., G.C. (see also Matthews, David; Oliveros, Chuck), Dead Angel Press, 1206 Lyndale Drive SE, Atlanta, GA 30316, 404-624-1524

C., G.C. (see also Oliveros, Chuck; Matthews, David), *DEAD ANGEL*, 1206 Lyndale Drive SE, Atlanta, GA 30316

Cabello-Argandona, Roberto, Editor-in-chief (see also Pisano, Vivian M.; Claire Splan), *LECTOR*, PO Box 4273, Berkeley, CA 94704, 415-893-8702

Caccia, Fulvio (see also D'Alfonso, Antonio; Tassinar, Lamberto; Ramirez, Bruno), *VICE VERSA*, P.O. Box 633, Sta N.D.G., Montreal, Quebec H4A 3R1, Canada

Caday, Jan (see also Donnelly, Margarita; Malone, Ruth; Wendt, Ingrid; Wilner, Eleanor; Thompson, Joyce; Mclean, Cheryl; Gordon, Rebecca; Domitrovich, Lisa; Jenkins, Meredith), *CALYX: A Journal of Art and Literature by Women,* PO Box B, Corvallis, OR 97339, 503-753-9384

Cadet, Melissa, Trans Tech Management Press, PO Box 23032, Sacramento, CA 95823, 916-421-9382

Cady, Edwin H., Editor (see also Budd, Louis J.), *AMERICAN LITERATURE*, 210 West Duke Building, Duke University, Durham, NC 27708, 919-684-3948

Cairncross, George, British Editor (see also Elsberg, John), *BOGG MAGAZINE,* 422 N Cleveland Street, Arlington, VA 22201

Cairncross, George (see also Elsberg, John), Bogg Publications, 422 N Cleveland Street, Arlington, VA 22201

Calder, Dr. Angus (see also Niven, Dr. Alastair), *THE JOURNAL OF COMMONWEALTH LITERATURE,* Africa Centre, 38 King Street, London, England, 01-836-1973

Caldwell, E.T. (see also Prohlo, Irwin M.), Heavy Evidence Productions, 1315½ 7th Street, Menomonie, WI 54751

Caldwell, E.T. (see also Prohlo, Irwin M.), *HEAVY EVIDENCE,* 1315½ 7th Street, Milwaukee, WI 54751

Calhoun, Harry, *PIG IN A POKE,* PO Box 19426, Pittsburgh, PA 15273, 412-621-1835

Calhoun, Richard, Editor (see also Johnson, Carol; Hill, Robert), *SOUTH CAROLINA REVIEW,* English Dept, Clemson Univ, Clemson, SC 29631, 803-656-3229

Calkins, Jean, J&C Transcripts, PO Box 41-2749, Garland, TX 75041

Calkins, Jean, *JEAN'S JOURNAL,* Box 15, Kanona, NY 14856

Callaghan, Barry, *EXILE,* Box 546, Downsview, Ontario, Canada, 416-967-9391; 667-3892

Callaghan, Barry, Exile Editions Ltd, 69 Sullivan Street, Toronto, Ontario M5T 1C2, Canada, 416-667-3892 or 977-7937

Callenbach, Ernest, *FILM QUARTERLY,* University of California Press, Berkeley, CA 94720, 415-642-6333

Caloren, F. (see also Roussopoulos, D.; Kowaluk, L.; Young, B.), *OUR GENERATION,* 3981 boul St Laurent, Montreal, Quebec H2W 1Y5, Canada

Calvert Jr., Robert, Garrett Park Press, Garrett Park, MD 20896, 301-946-2553

Cameron, Kenneth P., President (see also Philips, Graham), Alchemy Books, 681 Market, Suite 755, San Francisco, CA 94105, 415-777-9509

Camp, Bill (see also Lewis, Dale), Sunbeam Books, 23630 Old Owen Road, Monroe, WA 98272, 206-794-5919

Campagna, Richard, Campagna Press, 314 West 53rd, New York, NY 10101, 212-621-9955

Campbell, Gregory, The Bare Feet and Happy People Press, Box 84, Jemez Springs, NM 87025, 505-829-3854

Campbell, Gregory, *'YES, YOU CAN KISS MY BARE FEET...' OUR CHILDREN ARE ALWAYS SAYING,* Box 84, Jemez Springs, NM 87025, 505-829-3854

Campbell, John (see also Pink, Holly), *CROWDANCING,* Route 1, Box 189A, Winters, CA 95694, 916-795-4323

Campbell, John T., Editor & Publisher (see also Cole, Eddie-Lou; Joy, Julie), *WORLD OF POETRY,* 2431 Stockton Blvd., Sacramento, CA 95817, 916-731-8463

Campbell, Kalynn (see also King, Rey), Cosmic Circus Productions, 414 So 41st Street, Richmond, CA 94804, 415-529-0716

Campbell, Kalynn, *SPASTIC CULTURE MAGAZINE,* 414 So. 41st Street, Richmond, CA 94804, 415-529-0716

Campbell, Kimo, Editor (see also Vorhies, Aleen), Pueo Press, PO Box 2066, San Rafael, CA 94912, 415-456-6480

Campbell, P. Michael, Editor, *BERKELEY POETRY REVIEW,* 102 Sproul Hall, University of California, Berkeley, CA 94720

Campbell, Randy, Bovincular Atavists Co., 629 State Street #211, Santa Barbara, CA 93101, 966-3536

Campbell, Randy, Editor-in-Chief, *NIGHT LIGHT MAGAZINE,* 629 State Street #211, Santa Barbara, CA 93101, 966-3536

Canan, Craig T., *SOUTHERN PROGRESSIVE PERIODICALS UPDATE DIRECTORY*, PO Box 120574, Nashville, TN 37212

Cane, Crescenzio (see also Scammacca, Nat), *COOP. ANTIGRUPPO SICILIANO*, Villa Schammacha-nat, Via Argenteria Km 4, Trapani, Sicily, Italy, 0923-38681

Cannon, Melissa (see also Savage, Alice), *CAT'S EYE*, 1005 Clearview Drive, Nashville, TN 37205

Cannon, Steve (see also Reed, Ishmael), I. Reed Books, 1446 Sixth Street #D, Berkeley, CA 94710, 415-527-1586

Cantor, Aviva, Acting Executive Editor (see also Yaffe, Richard), *ISRAEL HORIZONS*, 150 Fifth Avenue, Room 1002, New York, NY 10011, 212-255-8760

Cantor, Aviva, Editor (see also Schneider, Susan W.; Freedman, Reena Sigman), *LILITH*, 250 W 57th, Suite 1328, New York, NY 10019, (212) 757-0818

Caplan, Leslie (see also Beam, Joe; Bernstein, Carole; Rorke, Raymond; Simpson, Chris; Sorensen, Sally Jo), *PAINTED BRIDE QUARTERLY*, 230 Vine Street, Philadelphia, PA 19106, 215-925-9914

Caplan, Paula, Editor (see also Nuse, B.; Newton, J.; Zavitz, C.; Rooney, F.; Andersen, M.; Wine, J.; Prentice, A.; Scane, J.; Van Kirk, Sylvia), *RESOURCES FOR FEMINIST RESEARCH/DOCUMENTA-TION SUR LA RECHERCHE FEMINISTE*, Ont Inst for Stud in Educ, Centre for Women's Studies in Education, 252 Bloor Street W., Toronto, Ontario M5S 1V6, Canada, 416-923-6641

Cappello, Rosemary Petracca, *PHILADELPHIA POETS*, 330 Bainbridge Street, Apt. 13, Philadelphia, PA 19147, 215-238-0463

Caquelin, Anthony, Book Review Editor (see also Woodhams, Stephen; Gabbard, D.C.; Gabbard, Dwight C.; Overson, Beth E.; Salmon-Heynemen, Jana; Goodwin, Tema; Shames, Terry; Rajfur, Ted), *FICTION MONTHLY*, Malvolio Press, 545 Haight Street, Suite 67, San Francisco, CA 94117, 415-621-1646

Carey, Margaret Standish, Co-Owner, Co-Editor (see also Hainline, Patricia Hoy), Calapooia Publications, 27006 Gap Road, Brownsville, OR 97327

Carey, M.R., *LANCASTER INDEPENDENT PRESS*, PO Box 275, Lancaster, PA 17604, 717-393-7811

Cargin, Peter, *FILM*, 81 Dean St., London W1V6AA, England, 01-437-4355

Carlisle, Kathleen (see also Carlisle, Tomas), Angst World Library, 1160 Forest Creek Road, Selma, OR 97538

Carlisle, Tomas (see also Carlisle, Kathleen), *Angst World Library*, 1160 Forest Creek Road, Selma, OR 97538

Carlson, Suzanne (see also Emblen, D.L.), Clamshell Press, 160 California Avenue, Santa Rosa, CA 95405

Carlton, Charles (see also Simms, Norman), *MIORITA*, Dept of F.L.L.L., Univ of Rochester, Dewey Hall 482, Rochester, NY 14627

Carmody, Larry, Contributing Editor (see also Porter, Andrew; D'Ammassa, Don; Anderson, Kay; DiFate, Vincent; Pohl, Frederik; Silverberg, Robert; Jones, Stephen; Fletcher, Jo), *SCIENCE FICTION CHRONICLE*, PO Box 4175, New York, NY 10163, 212-643-9011

Carney, Matthew (see also Leimroth, Carol), Caislan Press, Box 28371, San Jose, CA 95159, 408-723-8514

Carothers, Joel (see also Grace, Marian), Blazon Books, 1934 West Belle Plaine, Chicago, IL 60613, 312-975-0317

Carpenter, Blyth, Vice President (see also Carpenter, Russell), Natural World Press, 607 Chiltern Road, Hillsborough, CA 94010, 415-344-4154

Carpenter, Maryann (see also Bench, Carson E.), *SHARING*, Box 1470, 290 S 1st Ave., Ste. 300, Yuma, AZ 85364, 602-782-4646

Carpenter, Russell (see also Carpenter, Blyth), Natural World Press, 607 Chiltern Road, Hillsborough, CA 94010, 415-344-4154

Carr, Dan (see also Ferrarie, Julia), Four Zoas Night House Ltd., 30 Main St, PO Box 111, Ashuelot, NH 03441

Carrell, Ann, Associate Editor (see also Clift, G.W.; Roper, J.V.; Mosher, Robin; Salah-Din, Hakim), *LITERARY MAGAZINE REVIEW*, English Department, Kansas State University, Manhattan, KS 66506, 913-532-6719

Carrington, Stephen M., Poetry Editor (see also O'Callaghan, Robert J.), Pine Tree Publishing, PO Box 93, Phippsburg, ME 04562, 207-389-2428

Carroll, Jane, Poetry Editor (see also Gilborn, Alice), *BLUELINE*, Blue Mountain Lake, NY 12812, 518-352-7365

Carroll, Nina, *ALLIN*, 27 Harpes Road, Oxford, England

Carroll, Ron, Fiction Editor (see also Blythe, Will; Morrison, John), *THE BLACK WARRIOR REVIEW*, P.O. Box 2936, University, AL 35486, 205-348-4518

Carter, Dyson, *NORTHERN NEIGHBORS*, PO Box 1210, Gravenhurst, Ont. P0C 1G0, Canada

Carter, Kaye Edwards (see also Holley, Barbara; Vilips, Kathryn L.), *EARTHWISE LITERARY CALENDAR*, PO Box 680-536, Miami, FL 33168

Carthew, Sally (see also Kay, Phillip), The Firebird Press, PO Box 10, Kingswood, N.S.W. 2750, Australia, 047 360344

Carthew, Sally (see also Kay, Phillip), *THE NEPEAN REVIEW*, PO Box 10, Kingswood, N.S.W. 2750, Australia, 047 360344

Cartier, John (see also Hegedus, Debbie), *DELAWARE ALTERNATIVE PRESS*, PO Box 4592, Newark, DE 19711

Carver, Raymond, Contributing Editor (see also Murphy, George; Gallagher, Tess; Galvin, Brendan; Matthews, William; McBride, Mekeel; Mueller, Lisel), *TENDRIL*, Box 512, Green Harbor, MA 02041, 617-834-4137

Casale, Anne Schettino, Editor-in-Chief, *WOMEN'S RIGHTS LAW REPORTER*, 15 Washington Street, Newark, NJ 07104

Casey, Deb, Fiction Editor (see also Witte, John; Scates, Maxine), *NORTHWEST REVIEW*, 369 P.L.C., University of Oregon, Eugene, OR 97403, 503-686-3957

Casey, W. Wilson, Managing Editor (see also Johnson, W. Max), CaseCo Publications, 1138 Edisto Drive, Spartanburg, SC 29302, 803-585-3298

Cassell, Dana K., Cassell Communications Inc., 3600 NW 34th Street, PO Box 9844, Ft. Lauderdale, FL 33310, 305-485-0795

Cassell, Dana K., *FREELANCE WRITER'S REPORT*, 3600 NW 34th Street, PO Box 9844, Ft. Lauderdale, FL 33310, 305-878-2328

Cassidy, John, Klutz Enterprises, PO Box 2992, Stanford, CA 94305, 415-857-0888

Cassidy, Maureen, *BRITISH COLUMBIA HISTORICAL NEWS*, PO Box 35326, Station E, Vancouver, B.C. V6M 4G5, Canada

Castro, Jan Garden, Big River Association, 7420 Cornell Ave, St. Louis, MO 63130

Castro, Jan Garden, *RIVER STYX*, 7420 Cornell Avenue, St. Louis, MO 63130, 314-725-0602

Caswell, Donald, Anhinga Press, Department of English, Florida State University, Tallahassee, FL 32306, 904-644-1248

Cates, William R., W R C Publishing, 2915 Fenimore Road, Silver Spring, MD 20902, 301-949-6787

Catley, Lucille M., Sal Magundi Enterprises, PO Box 25625, S.W. Canyon Lane, Portland, OR 97225, 503-297-6658

Caton, Margaret, Associate Editor (see also Lee, Anthony A.), Kalimat Press, 10889 Wilshire Blvd #700, Los Angeles, CA 90024, 213-208-8059

Cavanaugh, Micheal A., *CIVIL WAR BOOK EXCHANGE*, Box 15432, Philadelphia, PA 19149, 609-786-1865

26

Cave, George P., *ONE WORLD*, Trans-Species Unlimited, PO Box 1351, State College, PA 16804, 814-238-0793

Ceconi, Isabel, Associate Editor (see also Juergensen, Hans; Juergensen, Ilse; Collins, Pat), *GRYPHON*, Dept. of Humanities-LE3 370, The University of South Florida, Tampa, FL 33620

Certa, Rolando (see also Scammacca, Nat), *IMPEGNO 80*, Villa Schammachanat, Via Argentaria Km 4, Trapani, Sicily, Italy

Certa, Rolando (see also Scammacca, Nat), Sicilian Antigruppo/Cross-Cultural Communications, Villa Schammchanat, via Argenteria Km 4, Trapani, Sicily, Italy, 0923-38681

Chache, Miss Kalamu (see also Juba, Robert Davis "Dr. Juba"; Lewis, Al), *JOYFUL NOISE INTERNATIONAL*, 109 Minna St., Suite 153, San Francisco, CA 94105, 415-931-1009

Chaffee, Eric, Foursquare Press, 648 Ransom Road, Lancaster, NY 14086, 716-681-2586

Chaloner, Peter (see also Anderson, Alex), Heat Press, 129 Cooper Ave, Woodlynne, NJ 08107, 215-662-0586/215-389-6913

Chambers, Bradford, Council on Interracial Books For Children, 1841 Broadway, New York, NY 10023, 212-757-5339

Chambers, Bradford, *INTERRACIAL BOOKS FOR CHILDREN BULLETIN*, 1841 Broadway, New York, NY 10023, 212-757-5339

Chambers, Catherine, Seraphim Press, 7439 La Palma Avenue Ste 263, Buena Park, CA 90620, 714-527-4475

Chantikian, Kosrof, *KOSMOS*, 381 Arlington Street, San Francisco, CA 94131

Chantikian, Kosrof, KOSMOS, 381 Arlington Street, San Francisco, CA 94131

Chapman, Mary Lewis, *LITERARY SKETCHES*, Box 711, Williamsburg, VA 23187, 804-229-2901

Char, Carlene, Comber Press, 735 Ekekela Place, Honolulu, HI 96817, 808-595-7337

Char, Carlene, Editor & Publisher, *COMPUTER BOOK REVIEW*, 735 Ekekela Place, Honolulu, HI 96817, 808-595-7337

Charleworth, Edward A., Ph.D. (see also Nathan, Ronald G., Ph.D), Biobehavioral Publishers and Distributors, Inc., 10603 Grant, Suite #204, PO Box 1102, Houston, TX 77251, 713-890-8575

Charne, James I., Executive Vice President, Legal Management Services, Inc., 329 Prospect Street, Ridgewood, NJ 07450, 201-447-4327

Chase, Bernard L., Managing Editor, Linwood Publishers, PO Box 70152, North Charleston, SC 29415, 803-873-2719

Checole, Kassahun, Africa Research & Publications Project, P.O.Box 1892, Trenton, NJ 08607, 609-392-7370

Checole, Kassahun, Africa World Press, PO Box 1892, Trenton, NJ 08607, 609-392-7370

Cherin, Robin (see also Rohmer, Harriet), Children's Book Press/Imprenta de Libros Infantiles, 1461 9th Ave., San Francisco, CA 94122, 415-664-8500

Chernoff, Maxine (see also Hoover, Paul), *OINK!*, 1446 W Jarvis #3-D, Chicago, IL 60626

Chesson, Lela (see also Morgan, Melanie), Falls of the Tar Publications, PO Box 4194, Rocky Mount, NC 27801

Chichinskas, Pamela, Managing Director (see also Clarkson, Sherri), Eden Press, 4626 St. Catherine Street West, Montreal, Quebec H3Z 1S3, Canada, (514) 931-3910

Chichinskas, Pamela, Managing Director (see also Clarkson, Sherri), *INTERNATIONAL JOURNAL OF WOMEN'S STUDIES*, 4626 St. Catherine Street West, Montreal, Quebec H3Z 1S3, Canada, (514) 931-3910

Chickering, A. Lawrence, Executive Editor (see also Lammi, Walter J.; Glynn, Patrick), Institute for Contemporary Studies, 785 Market Street, Suite 750, San Francisco, CA 94103, 415-543-6213

Chickering, A. Lawrence, Editor (see also Lammi, Walter J.; Glynn, Patrick), *JOURNAL OF CONTEMPORARY STUDIES*, 785 Market Street, Suite 750, San Francisco, CA 94103, 415-543-6213

Chilcote, Ronald H., Managing Editor, *LATIN AMERICAN PERSPECTIVES*, PO Box 5703, Riverside, CA 92517, 714-787-5508

Chin, R. (see also Tajima, Renee; Lee, C.N.; Chow, P.; Chu, B.; Francia, L.; Wu, S.; Lew, Walter; Hahn, Tomie; Kwan, S.), *BRIDGE: ASIAN AMERICAN PERSPECTIVES*, Asian Cine-Vision, Inc., 32 E Broadway, New York, NY 10002, 212-925-8685

Ching, C.T.K., Total Concepts, PO Box 90607, Honolulu, HI 96835, 808-595-4410

Chitwood, Dr. Terry, Polestar Publications, 620 S Minnesota Avenue, Sioux Falls, SD 57104, 605-338-2888

Chitwood, Garrett, Editor, The Pushkin Press, 1930 Columbia Road, NW, Washington, DC 20009, 202-265-1871

Choate, Albert G., Syzygy, Box 428, Rush, NY 14543, 716-226-2127

Choate, Lon, Consulting Editor (see also Galasso, Al; Schubert, Cynthia), American Bookdealers Exchange, PO Box 2525, La Mesa, CA 92041, 619-462-3297

Choate, Lon, Consulting Editor (see also Galasso, Al; Schubert, Cynthia), *BOOK DEALERS WORLD*, PO Box 2525, La Mesa, CA 92041, 619-462-3297

Chock, Eric (see also Lum, Darrell), *BAMBOO RIDGE, THE HAWAII WRITERS' QUARTERLY*, 990 Hahaione Street, Honolulu, HI 96825, 808-395-7098

Chock, Eric (see also Lum, Darrell), Bamboo Ridge Press, 990 Hahaione Street, Honolulu, HI 96825, 808-395-7098

Chouliaras, Y. (see also Kitroeff, A.; Pappas, P.; Roubatis, Y.), *JOURNAL OF THE HELLENIC DIASPORA*, 337 West 36th Street, New York, NY 10018, 212-279-9586

Chow, P. (see also Tajima, Renee; Lee, C.N.; Chin, R.; Chu, B.; Francia, L.; Wu, S.; Lew, Walter; Hahn, Tomie; Kwan, S.), *BRIDGE: ASIAN AMERICAN PERSPECTIVES*, Asian Cine-Vision, Inc., 32 E Broadway, New York, NY 10002, 212-925-8685

Choyke, Arthur (see also Ford-Choyke, Phyllis), *GALLERY SERIES/POETS*, 401 W. Ontario St., c/o Artcrest Products, Chicago, IL 60610

Choyke, Arthur (see also Ford-Choyke, Phyllis), Harper Square Press, c/o Artcrest Products Co., Inc., 401 W Ontario Street, Chicago, IL 60610, 312-751-1650

Chrisman, Robert, Editor, *THE BLACK SCHOLAR: Journal of Black Studies and Research*, PO Box 7106, San Francisco, CA 94120, 415-541-0311

Christ, Ronald, Managing Editor (see also Dollens, Dennis), *SITES-ARCHITECTURAL MAGAZINE*, Lumen, Inc., 446 West 20th Street, New York, NY 10011, 212-924-0642

Christensen, Erleen, Editor (see also Warner, Sharon Oard), *COTTONWOOD (formerly COTTONWOOD REVIEW)*, Box J, Kansas Union, Univ. of Kansas, Lawrence, KS 66045

Christensen, Paul, Cedarshouse Press, 406 W. 28th St., Bryan, TX 77801, 713-822-5615

Christensen, Thomas, Assistant Editor, North Point Press, PO Box 6275, Berkeley, CA 94706

Christian, Paula, Associate Editor (see also Craig, David; McCoy, Barbara; White, Gail), *PIEDMONT LITERARY REVIEW*, P.O.Box 3656, Danville, VA 24541, 804-793-0956

Christina, Dye, Managing Editor (see also Parker, Jim), D.I.N. Publications, PO Box 5115, Phoenix, AZ 85010, 602-257-0797

Christina, Martha, Director, Ampersand Press, Creative Writing Program, Roger Williams College, Bristol, RI 02809

Christina, Martha, Editor, *CALLIOPE*, Creative Writing Program, Roger Williams College, Bristol, RI 02809

Chu, B. (see also Tajima, Renee; Lee, C.N.; Chow, P.; Chin, R.; Francia, L.; Wu, S.; Lew, Walter; Hahn, Tomie; Kwan, S.), *BRIDGE: ASIAN AMERICAN PERSPECTIVES*, Asian Cine-Vision, Inc., 32 E Broadway, New York, NY 10002, 212-925-8685

Church, Philip D., Editor (see also Crump, Galbraith M.; Daniel, Robert W.; Klein, William F.), *THE KENYON REVIEW*, Kenyon College, Gambier, OH 43022, 614-427-3339

Cin, Clifford Cannon, Cin Publications, PO Box 11277, San Francisco, CA 94101

Citino, David, *CORNFIELD REVIEW,* The Ohio State University Marion Campus, 1465 Mt. Vernon Avenue, Marion, OH 43302, 614-389-2361

Claire, F.B. (see also Richie, E. Daniel; Wasserman, Rosanne; Rovner, Arkady), The Groundwater Press, 40 Clinton Street #1A, New York, NY 10002, 212-228-5750

Claire Splan, Assistant Editor (see also Pisano, Vivian M.; Cabello-Argandona, Roberto), *LECTOR,* PO Box 4273, Berkeley, CA 94704, 415-893-8702

Clancy, John (see also James, Susan), *INSIGHT NORTHWEST,* 9123-25th NE, Seattle, WA 98115, 206-523-2101

Clare, Robert (see also Ford, Eric), *EUROSHAVIAN,* 125 Markyate Rd, Dagenham, Essex RM8 2LB, England

Clare, Robert (see also Ford, Eric; King, Royston; Cooper-Brown, Howard), High Orchard Press, 125 Markyate Road, Dagenham, Essex, England RM8 2LB, England

Clarges, Robert, Managing Editor (see also Hutchison-Cleaves, Geoffrey), Papyrus Publishers, PO Box 466, Yonkers, NY 10704, 914-664-0840

Clark, Duane (see also Schain, Stephen; Volz, Bill; Lang, Lillian), *VERNAL,* 522 E. Third Avenue, Durango, CO 81301, 303-259-0221

Clark, Lawrence, Editor (see also Ballentine, Rudolph, M.D.), Himalayan Publishers, RD 1, Box 88-A, Honesdale, PA 18431, 717-253-5551

Clark, Mary, *A JOURNAL OF INNOCENCE,* 646 9th Avenue, 423 West 46th Street, New York, NY 10036, 212-246-7277

Clark, Mary, The Public Press, 646 9th Avenue, New York, NY 10036

Clark, Michael, *THE WIDENER REVIEW,* Humanities Division, Widener Univ., Chester, PA 19013, 215-499-4266

Clark, Patricia, Sales + Subscriptions Manager (see also Higham, Robin; Socolofsky, Homer), *JOURNAL OF THE WEST,* 1531 Yuma, Manhattan, KS 66502, 913-532-6733; 539-3668

Clark, Patricia P., General Manager (see also Higham, Robin), Sunflower University Press, 1531 Yuma, Manhattan, KS 66502, 913-532-6733

Clark, Raymond C. (see also Burrows, Arthur A.; Moran, Patrick R.), ProLingua Associates, 15 Elm Street, Brattleboro, VT 05301, 802-257-7779

Clark, Robert A., Arthur H. Clark Co., PO Box 230, Glendale, CA 91209, 213-245-9119

Clark, Stephen (see also McWaters, Barry), Evolutionary Press, Santa Barbara Office, PO Box 40391, Santa Barbara, CA 93103, 415-221-9222

Clark, Susan (see also Conrad, Margaret; Smyth, Donna), *ATLANTIS: A Women's Studies Journal/ Journal D'Etudes Sur La Femme,* Mount Saint Vincent University, Halifax Nova Scotia B3M 2J6, Canada

Clark, Susan, Editor-in-Chief (see also McLeod, Kathy; Marple, Vivian), *THE RADDLE MOON,* Creative Writing Department, Univ. of Victoria, Box 1700, B.C., Victoria, B.C. V8W 2Y2, Canada, 604-721-7306

Clark, Trevor, Cove Press, PO Box 325, Severna Park, MD 21146, 301-757-0134

Clarke, Cheryl (see also Allison, Dorothy; Bulkin, Elly; Otter, Nancy Clarke; Waddy, Adrianne), *CONDITIONS,* PO Box 56, Van Brunt Sta., Brooklyn, NY 11215, 212-788-8654

Clarke, Gillian (see also Hill, Greg), *THE ANGLO-WELSH REVIEW,* 1 Cyncoed Ave., Cyncoed, Cardiff, Wales, United Kingdom, 0222-755100

Clarke, Mary (see also Clarke, Nicholas), The Bold Strummer Ltd, 1 Webb Road, Westport, CT 06880, 203-226-8230

Clarke, Nicholas (see also Clarke, Mary), *The Bold Strummer Ltd,* 1 Webb Road, Westport, CT 06880, 203-226-8230

Clarke, Robert, Between The Lines, 427 Bloor St. W., Toronto, Ontario M5S 1X7, Canada, 416-964-6560

Clarkson, Sherri, Editor (see also Chichinskas, Pamela), Eden Press, 4626 St. Catherine Street West, Montreal, Quebec H3Z 1S3, Canada, (514) 931-3910

Clarkson, Sherri, Editor (see also Chichinskas, Pamela), *INTERNATIONAL JOURNAL OF WOMEN'S STUDIES*, 4626 St. Catherine Street West, Montreal, Quebec H3Z 1S3, Canada, (514) 931-3910

Claudel, Calvin A., Assistant Editor for Translations (see also Grue, Lee Meitzen), *THE NEW LAUREL REVIEW*, 828 Lesseps Street, New Orleans, LA 70117, 504-947-6001

Clayton, Alec, Co-Editor (see also Clayton, Gabi), *MISSISSIPPI ARTS & LETTERS*, PO Box 3510, Hatiesburg, MS 39403

Clayton, Alec (see also Clayton, Gabi), *PERSONS*, PO Box 3510, Hattiesburg, MS 39403, 601-545-7624

Clayton, Alec, Co-Editor (see also Clayton, Gabi), *Persons Publishing*, PO Box 3510, Hattiesburg, MS 39403

Clayton, Gabi, Co-Editor (see also Clayton, Alec), *MISSISSIPPI ARTS & LETTERS*, PO Box 3510, Hatiesburg, MS 39403

Clayton, Gabi (see also Clayton, Alec), *PERSONS*, PO Box 3510, Hattiesburg, MS 39403, 601-545-7624

Clayton, Gabi, Co-Editor (see also Clayton, Alec), *Persons Publishing*, PO Box 3510, Hattiesburg, MS 39403

Cleary, Michael (see also Saricyan-Jamieson, Ligia; Schwartz, Magi), *THE SOUTH FLORIDA POETRY REVIEW*, PO Box 7072, Hollywood, FL 33081, 305-474-5285

Clements, Robert W. (see also Tetreault, Wilfred F.), American Business Consultants, Inc., 1540 Nuthatch Lane, Sunnyvale, CA 94087, 408-732-8931/738-3011

Clendaniel, Nancy (see also Cotolo, F.M.; Tabor, B. Lyle; Savion, Thom; Stevroid, Lionel), *FAT TUESDAY*, 853 N Citrus, Los Angeles, CA 90038

Clever, Glenn (see also Tierney, Frank), Borealis Press Limited, 9 Ashburn Drive, Nepean Ontario, Canada, 613-224-6837

Clever, W. Glenn (see also Tierney, Frank M.), *JOURNAL OF CANADIAN POETRY*, 9 Ashburn Drive, Nepean Ontario, Canada, (613) 224-6837

Clift, G.W. (see also Carrell, Ann; Roper, J.V.; Mosher, Robin; Salah-Din, Hakim), *LITERARY MAGAZINE REVIEW*, English Department, Kansas State University, Manhattan, KS 66506, 913-532-6719

Clifton, Charles, Co-Editor (see also Clifton, Mary; Bonewits, P.E.I.), *IRON MOUNTAIN: A JOURNAL OF MAGICAL RELIGION*, PO Box 6423, Colorado Springs, CO 80934, 303-685-5849

Clifton, Linda J. (see also Buchmann, Hank), *CRAB CREEK REVIEW*, 806 N 42nd, Seattle, WA 98103, 206-543-6548

Clifton, Mary, Co-Editor (see also Clifton, Charles; Bonewits, P.E.I.), *IRON MOUNTAIN: A JOURNAL OF MAGICAL RELIGION* , PO Box 6423, Colorado Springs, CO 80934, 303-685-5849

Clifton, Merritt, Editor-in-Chief (see also Clifton, Robin Michelle), *SAMISDAT*, Box 129, Richford, VT 05476, 514-263-4439

Clifton, Merritt, Contributing Editor ('Help') (see also Fulton, Len; Ferber, Ellen; Urioste, Pat; Jerome, Judson), *THE SMALL PRESS REVIEW*, P.O. Box 100, Paradise, CA 95969, 916-877-6110

Clifton, Robin Michelle, Reviews Editor (see also Clifton, Merritt), *SAMISDAT*, Box 129, Richford, VT 05476, 514-263-4439

Clifton, Whiten, Poetry Canada Poesie Review Inc., PO Box 1280, Station A, Toronto, Ontario, Canada, 416-927-8001

Clinton, D., Editor, *SALTHOUSE*, Salthouse, PO Box 11537, Milwaukee, WI 53211, 414-332-4582

Cloke, Richard (see also Smith, Lori C.; Rodecker, Shirley J.), Cerulean Press (Subsidiary of Kent Publiations), 18301 Halsted St., Northridge, CA 91325

Cloke, Richard, General Manager (see also Smith, Lori C.; Rodecker, Shirley J.), Kent Publications, Inc., 18301 Halsted Street, Northridge, CA 91325, 213-349-2080

Cloke, Richard, Editor-in-Chief (see also Rodecker, Shirley J.; Smith, Lori C.), *SAN FERNANDO POETRY JOURNAL*, 18301 Halstead Street, Northridge, CA 91325

Coakley, William Leo (see also Prising, Robin), Helikon Press, 120 West 71st Street, New York City, NY 10023

Cobbing, Bob (see also Rowan, John), Writers Forum, 262 Randolph Ave., London W9, England, 01-624-8565

Cochrane, Shirley, Vice President (see also Sargent, Robert; Wyman, Hastings), Washington Writers Publishing House, PO Box 50068, Washington, DC 20004, 202-546-1020

Codrescu, Andrei (see also Markert, Lawrence), *EXQUISITE CORPSE*, PO Box 20889, Baltimore, MD 21209, 301-578-0146

Codrescu, Andrei, Contributing Editor (see also Golden, Michael; Elias, Viki; Harrison, Jim; Mungo, Raymond; Bukowski, Charles; Placidus, Max; Horotwitz, Mikhail; Ligi; Kramer, Glenn; Mitchell, Donna; Riedel, Robert), *SMOKE SIGNALS*, 1516 Beverly Road, Brooklyn, NY 11226

Cody, James, Editor, Place of Herons Press, PO Box 1952, Austin, TX 78767, 512-467-9413

Cody, James, Editor, *WOOD IBIS*, PO Box 1952, Austin, TX 78767, 512-467-9413

Coffey, Michael, Associate Editor (see also Quasha, George; Quasha, Susan; Martin, Michele), Open Book Publications, A Division of Station Hill Press, Station Hill Road, Barrytown, NY 12507

Coffey, Michael, Associate Editor (see also Quasha, George; Quasha, Susan; Martin, Michele; Stein Charles; Nedds, Trish; Kelly, Robert; Auster, Paul; Kamin, Franz; McClelland, Bruce), Station Hill Press, Station Hill Road, Barrytown, NY 12507, 914-758-5840

Coghill, Sheila (see also Koontz, Tom; Lowe, Kyrla; Tammaro, Thom), *BARNWOOD*, RR 2, Box 11C, Daleville, IN 47334

Coghill, Sheila (see also Koontz, Tom; Tammaro, Thom), The Barnwood Press, RR 2, Box 11C, Daleville, IN 47334, 317-378-0921

Cohan, Tony (see also Beam, Gordon), Acrobat Books Publishers, PO Box 480820, Los Angeles, CA 90048, 213-467-4506

Cohen, Jocelyn Helaine (see also Poore, Nancy Victoria), Helaine Victoria Press,Inc., 4080 Dynasty Lane, Martinsville, IN 46151, 317-537-2868

Cohen, M. (see also Huang, J.; Thoenen, B.; Jacobson, J.; McKale, A.), *THE DROOD REVIEW OF MYSTERY*, Box 8872, Boston, MA 02114

Cohen, Sande, Co-Editor (see also Reimers, Ronald), *THE PALIMPSEST REVIEW*, PO Box 1280, Santa Monica, CA 90406

Coldewey, John C., *MODERN LANGUAGE QUARTERLY*, 4045 Brooklyn Ave. N.E., Seattle, WA 98105, 206-543-2992

Cole, Eddie-Lou, Poetry Editor (see also Campbell, John T.; Joy, Julie), *WORLD OF POETRY*, 2431 Stockton Blvd., Sacramento, CA 95817, 916-731-8463

Cole, Tom (see also Magary, Alan), Lexikos, 1012 14th Street, San Francisco, CA 94114, 415-861-4916

Coleman, Cheryl L., Associate Editor (see also Bogus, Sdiane; De Oca, D.M.; Baptist, Weldon O.), W. I. M. Publications, Box 367, Department IDSP, College Corner, OH 45003, 513-523-5994

Coleman, Ellen, Earl M Coleman Enterprises, Inc, PO Box T, Crugers, NY 10521, 914-271-5124/5125

Collins, Chris (see also Wenig, M. Judith; Freundlich, Paul; Hirsch, Audrey), *COMMUNITIES*, Box 426, Louisa, VA 23093, 703-894-5126

Collins, Chris (see also Wenig, M. Judith; Freundlich, Paul; Hirsch, Audrey), *Communities Publishing Cooperative*, Box 426, Louisa, VA 23093, 703-894-5126

Collins, Don, *CLEVELAND CHESS BULLETIN*, 10902 Brainard Drive, Parma, OH 44130, 888-3755

Collins, Joyce, Publications Officer, Primary Communications Research Centre, University of Leicester, Leicester, United Kingdom, 0533 556223

Collins, Pat, Fiction Editor (see also Juergensen, Hans; Ceconi, Isabel; Juergensen, Ilse), *GRYPHON*, Dept. of Humanities-LE3 370, The University of South Florida, Tampa, FL 33620

Collins, Robert A., *FANTASY NEWSLETTER*, College of Humanities, Florida Atlantic University, Boca Raton, FL 33431, 305-393-3839

Collins, Roy, Editor (see also Anderson, James), R.I. Review Inc., PO Box 3028 Wayland Square, Providence, RI 02906, 401-331-1034

Collins, Roy, Editor (see also Anderson, James), *RHODE ISLAND REVIEW*, PO Box 3028 Wayland Square, Providence, RI 02906, 401-331-1034

Colon, Laurent E., Dynamic Information Publishing, 8311 Greeley Boulevard, Springfield, VA 22152, 202-676-3869, 703-569-5507

Colquitt, Betsy Feagan (see also Opperman, Harry), *DESCANT*, English Department, TCU, Fort Worth, TX 76129

Colquitt, Betsy Feagan (see also Opperman, Harry), Texas Christian University Press, English Department, TCU, Fort Worth, TX 76129

Combs, Bruce, *TAURUS*, Box 28, Gladstone, OR 97027

Comen, Diane, Administrator (see also Lawson, Todd S.J.; Marsic, John; Samolis, William; Comen, Diane; Graham, Joan; Rader, Steve), Peace & Pieces Press, Box 99394, San Francisco, CA 94109, 415-771-3431

Comen, Diane, Contributing Editor (see also Comen, Diane; Lawson, Todd S.J.; Marsic, John; Samolis, William; Graham, Joan; Rader, Steve), *Peace & Pieces Press*, Box 99394, San Francisco, CA 94109, 415-771-3431

Comen, Dr. Diane, Associate Editor (see also Lawson, Dr. Todd; Marsic, John; Rader, Steve; Monte, Oscar; Nishi, Mio; Ginsberg, Allen; Samolis, Dr. Sam; Graham, Joan; Ferlinghetti, Lawrence; Ramirez, Julio; Haynes, Dr. Robert; Snyder, Gary; Morris, Dr. Richard), *ALPS MONTHLY*, PO Box 99394, San Francisco, CA 94109, 415-771-3431

Coney, Denise (see also Southward, Keith; Hryciuk, Marshall), *INKSTONE*, PO Box 67, Station H, Toronto, Ontario M4C 5H7, Canada, 656-0356

Coney, Denise (see also Southward, Keith; Hryciak, Marshall), Inkstone Press, PO Box 67, Station H, Toronto, Ontario M4C 5H7, Canada

Congobardi, David, President, *THE HARVARD ADVOCATE*, 21 South St., Cambridge, MA 02138, 617-495-7820

Conlon, Ann, Sheriar Press, 1414 Madison Street, Myrtle Beach, SC 29577, 803-272-5333

Conlon, Faith (see also Wilson, Barbara; da Silva, Rachel), The Seal Press, Box 13, Seattle, WA 98111, 624-5262

Connell, Donna, Can Do Books, 2119 Lone Oak Avenue, Napa, CA 94558, 707-224-0197

Connelly, Dolores (see also Straayer, Arny Christine; Johnson, Christine L.; Soule, S. Janet), Metis Press, Inc., PO Box 25187, Chicago, IL 60625

Conner, Don R., *PROOF ROCK*, Proof Rock Press, PO Box 607, Halifax, VA 24558

Conoley, Gillian (see also Rayher, Ed; McGuill, Mike; Stansberry, Domenic; Ruhl, Steven), *TIGHTROPE*, 72 Colonial Village, Amherst, MA 01002

Conrad, Margaret, Co-Editor (see also Clark, Susan; Smyth, Donna), *ATLANTIS: A Women's Studies Journal/Journal D'Etudes Sur La Femme*, Mount Saint Vincent University, Halifax Nova Scotia B3M 2J6, Canada

Conway, Connie (see also Tuel, Ted), *MISSOURI VALLEY SOCIALIST*, PO Box 31321, Omaha, NE 68131, 402-553-2314

Conway, Don, Managing Editor (see also Gibbs, Robert; Trethewey, Eric; Hawkes, Robert; Butlin, Ron; Taylor, Michael; Thompson, Kent; Davey, Bill; Boyles, Ann; Bauer, William), *THE FIDDLE-HEAD*, The Observatory, Univ. New Brunswick, PO Box 4400, Fredericton, NB E3B 5A3, Canada, 506-454-3591

Cook, Deborah (see also Cook, Ralph; Polkinhorn, Harry; Polkinhorn, Christa), Atticus Press, PO Box 34044, San Diego, CA 92103, 619-299-3088

Cook, Diane G.H., Managing Editor (see also Payne, Robert; Smith, William Jay; MacShane, Frank), *TRANSLATION*, 307A Mathematics, Columbia University, New York, NY 10027, 212-280-2305

Cook, Diane G.H., Managing Editor (see also MacShane, Frank; Payne, Robert; Smith, William Jay; Galvin, Dallas), Translation, 307A Mathematics, Columbia University, New York, NY 10027, 280-2305

Cook, Ralph (see also Polkinhorn, Harry; Cook, Deborah; Polkinhorn, Christa), Atticus Press, PO Box 34044, San Diego, CA 92103, 619-299-3088

Cook, Ralph (see also Polkinhorn, Harry), *ATTICUS REVIEW*, PO Box 34044, San Diego, CA 92103, 619-299-3088

Cook, R.L., The Lomond Press, 4 Whitecraigs, Kinnesswood, Kinross KY13 7JN, Scotland, 059 284 301

Cook, Stanley, *POETRY NOTTINGHAM*, 600 Barnsley Road, Sheffield, S5 6VA, South Yorkshire, England

Cook, Stanley, Editor, Poetry Nottingham Society Publications, 600 Bainsley Road, Sheffield S5 6VA, South Yourkshire, England

Cooke, Roger (see also Burns, Roland; Kindred, Wendy), *THE BLACK FLY REVIEW*, University of Maine at Fort Kent, Fort Kent, ME 04743, 207-834-3162

Cookson, William (see also Dale, Peter), *AGENDA*, 5 Cranbourne Court, Albert Bridge Road, London, England SW11 4PE, England, 01-228-0700

Cookson, William, Agenda Editions, 5 Cranbourne Court, Albert Bridge Rd, London, England SW114PE, England, 01-228-0700

Cooley, Peter, Advisor (see also Strauss, Susan), *THE TULANE LITERARY MAGAZINE*, University Center, New Orleans, LA 70118

Cooney, Ellen, Duir Press, 919 Sutter #9, San Francisco, CA 94109

Cooney, Rian (see also Mirchandani, Ravi), *THE CAMBRIDGE POETRY MAGAZINE*, 602 King's College, Cambridge CB2 1ST, England

Cooper, Michael (see also Shelton, Donald), GloryPatri Publishers, 2891 Richmond Road Suite 202, Lexington, KY 40509, 606-269-3391

Cooper, Peter S., Editor (see also Bean, Joyce Miller; Steger, Linda; Mitchell, Barbara; Fielding, Cynthia), *MIDWAY REVIEW*, 3400 West 11th Street, Suite 134, Chicago, IL 60655, 312-233-6002

Cooper, Peter S., Managing Editor (see also Bean, Joyce Miller; Fielding, Cynthia), Southwest Area Cultural Arts Council, 3400 West 11th Street, Suite 134, Chicago, IL 60655, 312-233-6002

Cooper, Peter S., Editor (see also Bean, Joyce Bean; Fielding, Cynthia), *YAWL (Young Artists & Writers of the Library)*, 3400 West 11th Street, Suite 134, Chicago, IL 60655, 312-233-6002

Cooper, W. Norman (see also Schorre, Val), Truth Center, A Universal Fellowship, 6940 Oporto Drive, Los Angeles, CA 90068, 213-876-6295

Cooper, Wyn, *QUARTERLY WEST*, 317 Olpin Union, U. of Utah, Salt Lake City, UT 84112, 801-581-3938

Cooper-Brown, Howard (see also Ford, Eric), *THE BULWER LYTTON CHRONICLE*, High Orchard, 125 Markyate Rd, Dagenham, Essex RM8 2LB, England

Cooper-Brown, Howard (see also Ford, Eric; King, Royston; Clare, Robert), High Orchard Press, 125 Markyate Road, Dagenham, Essex, England RM8 2LB, England

Cope, David (see also Cope, Susan), *BIG SCREAM*, 2782 Dixie S.W., Grandville, MI 49418, 616-531-1442

Cope, David (see also Cope, Susan), Nada, 2782 Dixie S.W., Grandville, MI 49418, 616-531-1442

Cope, Susan (see also Cope, David), *BIG SCREAM*, 2782 Dixie S.W., Grandville, MI 49418, 616-531-1442

Cope, Susan (see also Cope, David), Nada, 2782 Dixie S.W., Grandville, MI 49418, 616-531-1442

Copeland, Colone M. (see also Copeland, Robert W.), Jordan Valley Heritage House, Inc., 43592 Hwy 226, Stayton, OR 97383, 503-859-3144

Copeland, Robert W. (see also Copeland, Colone M.), *Jordan Valley Heritage House, Inc.*, 43592 Hwy 226, Stayton, OR 97383, 503-859-3144

Coppola, Carlo (see also Dulai, Surjit), *JOURNAL OF SOUTH ASIAN LITERATURE*, Area Studies Program, Oakland University, Rochester, MI 48063, (313) 377-2076

Corbett, Bayliss, *CENSORED*, PO Box 1526, Bonita Springs, FL 33923, (813) 294-5555

Core, George, Editor (see also Cornelius, Mary Lucia S.), *SEWANEE REVIEW*, Univ. of the South, Sewanee, TN 37375, 615-598-5931

Corey, Orlin, Editor (see also Gowdy, Anne R.), Anchorage Press, Inc., Box 8067, New Orleans, LA 70182, 504-283-8868

Corey, Stephen, Assistant Editor (see also Lindberg, Stanley W.), *THE GEORGIA REVIEW*, Univ. of Georgia, Athens, GA 30602, 404-542-3481

Corkum, Collin J., Ph.D. (see also Girard-Corkum, Jerria, Ph.D.), BrainStorm Books, PO Box 1407, Tustin, CA 92681, 714-731-4802

Corman, Cid, *ORIGIN*, Paideuma 305 EM Building, UMO, Utano, ME 04469, 207-581-3814

Cornelius, Mary Lucia S., Managing Editor (see also Core, George), *SEWANEE REVIEW*, Univ. of the South, Sewanee, TN 37375, 615-598-5931

Cornish, Sam (see also Andersen, Len J.; Orowan, Florella), *FICTION, LITERATURE & THE ARTS REVIEW*, Arcade, 318 Harvard Street, Brookline, MA 02146, 617-232-2674

Cornwall, Claudia, Nerve Press, 5875 Elm Street, Vancouver, B.C. V6N 1A6, Canada, 604-266-7905

Cortez, Joseph J., Hari Kari Products, Publishing Division, PO Box 610053, Houston, TX 77208, 713-827-1651

Costello, Catherine (see also O'Brien, Aline; Rasmussen, Chrys), Continuing Saga Press, PO Box 194, San Anselmo, CA 94960, 415-454-4411

Costello, Debbie (see also Kellman, Lisa), Black Oyster Press, PO Box 8550, Chicago, IL 60680, 312-743-5744

Costello, James A., *EN PASSANT/POETRY*, 4612 Sylvanus Drive, Wilmington, DE 19803

Costello, James A., En Passant Poetry Press, 4612 Sylvanus Drive, Wilmington, DE 19803

Cotolo, F.M. (see also Tabor, B. Lyle; Savion, Thom; Stevroid, Lionel; Clendaniel, Nancy), *FAT TUESDAY*, 853 N Citrus, Los Angeles, CA 90038

Cottier, Chockie (see also Ortiz, Roxanne Dunbar), *INDIGENOUS WORLD/EL MUNDO INDIGE-NA*, 275 Grand View Avenue #103, San Francisco, CA 94114, 415-647-1966

Coughlin, Michael E., Michael E. Coughlin, Publisher, 1985 Selby Avenue, St Paul, MN 55104, 612-646-8917

Coughlin, Michael E., *THE DANDELION*, 1985 Selby Ave, St Paul, MN 55104, 612-646-8917

Coulter, Art, *CHANGE*, 1825 North Lake Shore Dr, Chapel Hill, NC 27514, 919-942-2994

Cousins, Linda, Publisher & Editor, *THE UNIVERSAL BLACK WRITER*, PO Box 5, Radio City Station, New York, NY 10101, 212-622-5996

Covina, Gina, Barn Owl Books, 1101 Keeler Avenue, Berkeley, CA 94708, 415-549-2149

Cowan, Alice, Publisher, Megalon Publications, 7337 Peony Court, Citrus Heights, CA 95610, 805-968-2329

Cowan, James C., *THE D.H. LAWRENCE REVIEW*, Box 2474, University of Arkansas, Fayetteville, AR 72701

Coward, Jane, Editor (see also Anderson, Lou Ann), Wimmer Brothers Books, PO Box 18408, Memphis, TN 38181, 901-362-8900

Cowen, John, Publisher (see also Villa, Jose Garcia), *BRAVO*, 1081 Trafalgar Street, Teaneck, NJ 07666, 201-836-5922

Cox, Bill, Quantal Publishing B, PO Box 1598, Goleta, CA 93116, 805-964-7293

Cox, James A., *THE MIDWEST BOOKWATCH*, 278 Orchard Drive, Oregon, WI 53575, 608-835-7937

Cozens, Andrew, Avalon Editions, 66 Millfield Road, York, Y02 INQ, England

Cozens, Andrew, *DOUBLE HARNESS*, 66 Millfield Road, York, Y02 INQ, England

Crabb, Michael, Editor, *DANCE IN CANADA*, 38 Charles Street East, Toronto ON M4Y 1T1, Canada

Crabb, Riley Hansard, Borderland Sciences Research Foundation, P.O. Box 549, Vista, CA 92083, 724-2043

Crabb, Riley Hansard, *JOURNAL OF BORDERLAND RESEARCH*, P.O. Box 549, Vista, CA 92083, 724-2043

Craig, David, Editor (see also Christian, Paula; McCoy, Barbara; White, Gail), *PIEDMONT LITERARY REVIEW*, P.O.Box 3656, Danville, VA 24541, 804-793-0956

Craig, Gary, *COMMUNITY DEVELOPMENT JOURNAL*, Brookside, Seaton Burn, Newcastle upon Tyne NL136EY, England, 0632-363023

Craig, James (see also Craig, Marguerite), ProActive Press, PO Box 296, Berkeley, CA 94701, 415-549-0839

Craig, Marguerite (see also Craig, James), *ProActive Press*, PO Box 296, Berkeley, CA 94701, 415-549-0839

Craig, Timothy, The Murray Hill Press, (Timothy Craig), 108 MacGregor Avenue, Roslyn Heights, NY 11577, 516-883-1612

Crary, Elizabeth, Parenting Press, 7750 31st Avenue, NE, Seattle, WA 98115, 206-525-4660

Craven, Jerry, *SEPARATE DOORS*, 911 W T Station, Canyon, TX 79016

Cravey, Robin, Tilted Planet Press, PO Box 8646, Austin, TX 78712, 512-447-7619

Crawford, Gary William (see also Eng, Steve), Gothic Press, 4998 Perkins Road, Baton Rouge, LA 70808, 504-766-2906

Crawford, John, Editor and Publisher, West End Press, PO Box 7232, Minneapolis, MN 55407

Crawford, Marc, *TIME CAPSULE*, General PO Box 1185, New York, NY 10116, 212-219-0542

Crawford, Marc, Editor-in-Chief (see also Hejna, Matthew), Time Capsule, Inc., GPO Box 1185, New York, NY 10116, 212-219-0542

Crisci, Pat J., Associate Editor (see also Schechter, Ruth Lisa; Thomas, Dan B.; Bluestein, Dan T.; Merrill, Susan; Stettan, Leonard), *CROTON REVIEW*, P.O. Box 277, Croton on Hudson, NY 10520, 914-271-3144

Critchley, Cecily, Assistant Editor (see also Ferrier, Carole; Levy, Bronwen), *HECATE*, P.O. Box 99, St. Lucia, Queensland 4067, Australia

Crombie, Daniel, Jr., Editor (see also Wilson, Del), Crossroads Communications, PO Box 7, Carpentersville, IL 60110

Crosby, Candace, Bitterroot Educational Resources for Women, 315 South 4th E., Missoula, MT 59801, 406-728-3041

Crow, Mary, Translations (see also Tremblay, Bill; Ude, Wayne), *COLORADO STATE REVIEW*, 322 Eddy, English Department, Colorado State University, Fort Collins, CO 80523, 303-491-6428

Crowdus, Gary (see also Georgakas, Dan; Rubenstein, Lenny), *CINEASTE MAGAZINE*, 200 Park Avenue South, Room 1320, New York, NY 10003

Crowell, Shirley, Editorial Assistant (see also Gegenheimer, Albert F.), *ARIZONA QUARTERLY*, Univ. Of Arizona, Tucson, AZ 85721, Main Library B541 602-621-6396

Crowley, J., Assistant Editor (see also Kennedy, Alan), *THE DALHOUSIE REVIEW*, Dalhousie Univ. Helen L. Gorman, Bus. Mgr., Sir James Dunn Bldg. Suite 314, Halifax, Nova Scotia B3H 3J5, Canada

Crown, Kathleen, Editor, *RED CEDAR REVIEW*, 325 Morrill Hall, Dept. of English, Mich. State Univ., E. Lansing, MI 48824, 517-355-9656

Crudup, Sonya, Editorial Assistant (see also White, Patricia), Bond Publishing Company, 226 Massachusetts Avenue NE, Suite 21, Washington, DC 20002, 202-547-3140

Cruickshank, Douglas, Senior Editor (see also Luneau, Lynn; McGowan, Cese), Mho & Mho Works, Box 33135, San Diego, CA 92103, 619-488-4991

Crump, Galbraith M., Editor (see also Church, Philip D.; Daniel, Robert W.; Klein, William F.), *THE KENYON REVIEW*, Kenyon College, Gambier, OH 43022, 614-427-3339

Cuddihy, Michael, *IRONWOOD*, P.O.Box 40907, Tucson, AZ 85717

Cuddihy, Michael, Ironwood Press, PO Box 40907, Tucson, AZ 85717

Cuelho, Art, *BLACK JACK & VALLEY GRAPEVINE*, Box 249, Big Timber, MT 59011

Cuelho, Art, Seven Buffaloes Press, Box 249, Big Timber, MT 59011

Culligan, Bridget, Managing Editor (see also McNamara, Bob), L'Epervier Press, 762 Hayes #15, Seattle, WA 98109

Cully, Kendig Brubaker, *THE REVIEW OF BOOKS AND RELIGION*, Duke University Divinity School, Durham, NC 27706

Culp, Marguerite (see also McGivern, Gary), *CLEARWATER NAVIGATOR*, 112 Market Street, Poughkeepsie, NY 12601, 914-454-7673

Cumbie, Richard (see also Burns, Richard), *NANTUCKET REVIEW*, P.O. Box 1234, Nantucket, MA 02554

Cumming, W. (see also Keyishian, M.; Zander, W.; Decavalles, A.), *JOURNAL OF NEW JERSEY POETS*, Fairleigh Dickinson Univ., English Dept., 285 Madison Avenue, Madison, NJ 07940, 01-377-4700

Cummings, Albert (see also O'Shaunnessay, William), Golden West Historical Publications, PO Box 1906, Ventura, CA 93002

Cummings, Kathleen J., Publisher (see also Dominguez, Leonard J.; Hunt, Larry), *NIT&WIT, Chicago's Arts Magazine*, PO Box 14685, Chicago, IL 60614, 312-248-1183

Cummins, Rich, Managing Editor (see also Nelson, Tony), *SONORA REVIEW*, Dept of English, University of Arizona, Tucson, AZ 85721, (602) 626-1387

Cummins, Walter, Editor-in-Chief (see also Green, Martin; Keyishian, Harry), *THE LITERARY REVIEW*, Fairleigh Dickinson University, 285 Madison Avenue, Madison, NJ 07940, 201 377-4050

Cunliffe, Dave, BB Books, 1 Spring Bank, Salesbury, Blackburn, Lancs BB1 9EU, England, 0254 49128

Cunliffe, Dave, *GLOBAL TAPESTRY JOURNAL*, 1 Spring Bank, Salesbury, Blackburn, Lancs BB1 9EU, England, 0254 49128

Curl, John, Homeward Press, PO Box 2307, Berkeley, CA 94702, (412) 526-3254

Curran, Keelin, Co-Editor (see also Brummet, John), *SCAPE*, 1506 4th Avenue, Apt #11, Oakland, CA 94606, 415-763-2012

Currier, Donald, *THE LAS VEGAS INSIDER*, Good 'n' Lucky, PO Box 370, Henderson, NV 89015, 702-564-3895

Curry, J.W., Curvd H&Z, 729A Queen Street East, Toronto, Ontario M4M 1H1, Canada, 416-463-5867

Curry, J.W. (see also Laba, Mark; Lefler, Peggy), *INDUSTRIAL SABOTAGE*, 729A Queen Street East, Toronto, Ontario M4M 1H1, Canada, 416-463-5867

Curry, J.W. (see also Bennett, John M.; Laba, Mark), *1Cent*, 729a Queen Street East, Toronto, Ontario M4M 1H1, Canada

Curry, J.W. (see also Laba, Mark), Spider Plots in Rat-Holes, 729A Queen Street East, Toronto, Ontario M4M 1H1, Canada, 416-463-5867

Curry, J.W., Utopic Furnace Press, 729A Queen Street East, Toronto, Ontario M4M 1H1, Canada, 416-463-5867

Curtin, Nancy (see also Tarakan, Sheldon L.), *E. A. R. for Children*, 40 Holly Lane, Roslyn Heights, NY 11577, 516-621-2445

Curtis, Cecil, Placebo Press, 4311 Bayou Blvd #T-199, Pensacola, FL 32503, 904-477-3995

Cushman, Kathleen, Harvard Common Press, 535 Albany Street, Boston, MA 02118, 617-423-5803

Cussen, June, Pineapple Press, Inc., PO Box 314, Englewood, FL 33533, 813-475-2238

Cutts, Wiliam J., Balmy Press, Box 972, Minneapolis, MN 55440, 612-333-8076

Cutts, William J., *THE FOOTLOOSE LIBRARIAN*, Box 972, Minneapolis, MN 55440, 612-333-8076

Cutty, Robert B., Associate Editor (see also Paladino, Thomas; Stanson, Diane), *THE THIRD WIND*, PO Box 8277, Boston, MA 02114

Cyphers, Lucille, *MUSCADINE*, 1111 Lincoln Place, Boulder, CO 80302, 303-443-9748

Cyrus, Stanley A. (see also Smart, Ian I.), *AFRO-HISPANIC REVIEW*, 3306 Ross Place, NW, Washington, DC 20008, 202-966-7783

Czompo, Andor (see also Czompo, Ann I.), AC Publications, PO Box 238, Homer, NY 13077, 607-749-4040

Czompo, Ann I. (see also Czompo, Andor), *AC Publications*, PO Box 238, Homer, NY 13077, 607-749-4040

D

da Silva, Rachel (see also Wilson, Barbara; Conlon, Faith), The Seal Press, Box 13, Seattle, WA 98111, 624-5262

Dahl, Bard (see also Schoenberg, Al), *PANGLOSS PAPERS*, Box 18917, Los Angeles, CA 90018, 213-663-1950

Dahl, Bard (see also Schoenberg, Al), Pangloss Press, Box 18917, Los Angeles, CA 90018, 213-663-1950

Dahlberg, Rlene H., Pequod Press, 344 Third Ave, Apt 3A, New York, NY 10010, 212-686-4789

Daigon, Ruth, *POETS ON:*, Box 255, Chaplin, CT 06235, 203-455-9671

Dailey, Joel (see also Mangan, Patricia), Acre Press, 1804 E Main Street, Endicott, NY 13760

Daitzman, Reid J., World University Press, 1425 Bedford Street #1A, Stamford, CT 06905, 203-359-1779

Dale, Peter (see also Cookson, William), *AGENDA*, 5 Cranbourne Court, Albert Bridge Road, London, England SW11 4PE, England, 01-228-0700

Daley, Debora (see also Daley, John), *INK*, 111 Elmwood Avenue, Buffalo, NY 14201, 716-885-6400

Daley, Debora (see also Daley, John), Just Buffalo Press, 111 Elmwood Avenue, Buffalo, NY 14201, 716-885-6400

Daley, John (see also Daley, Debora), *INK*, 111 Elmwood Avenue, Buffalo, NY 14201, 716-885-6400

Daley, John (see also Daley, Debora), Just Buffalo Press, 111 Elmwood Avenue, Buffalo, NY 14201, 716-885-6400

D'Alfonso, Antonio, Guernica Editions, PO Box 633, Station N.D.G., Montreal, Quebec H4A 3R1, Canada, 514-254-2917/481-5569

D'Alfonso, Antonio (see also Tassinar, Lamberto; Caccia, Fulvio; Ramirez, Bruno), *VICE VERSA*, P.O. Box 633, Sta N.D.G., Montreal, Quebec H4A 3R1, Canada

Dallman, Elaine, Editor-in-Chief, *WOMAN POET*, PO Box 60550, Reno, NV 89506, 702-972-1671

Dallman, Elaine, Editor-in-Chief, Women-in-Literature, Inc., PO Box 60550, Reno, NV 89506, 702-972-1671

Dalton, Bill, Founder, Moon Publications, PO Box 1696, Chico, CA 95927, (916) 345-5473

Dalton, Bill, Tree By The River Publishing, 4375 Highland Place, Riverside, CA 92506, 714-682-8942

Dame, Enid (see also Lev, Donald), *HOME PLANET NEWS*, P.O. Box 415 Stuyvesant Station, New York, NY 10009, 212-769-2854

Dame, Enid (see also Lev, Donald), Home Planet Publications, PO Box 415 Stuyvesant Station, New York, NY 10009, 212-769-2854

D'Ammassa, Don, Book Critic (see also Porter, Andrew; Anderson, Kay; DiFate, Vincent; Pohl, Frederik; Silverberg, Robert; Jones, Stephen; Fletcher, Jo; Carmody, Larry), *SCIENCE FICTION CHRONICLE*, PO Box 4175, New York, NY 10163, 212-643-9011

Damon, John Edward, Poetry Assistant (see also Freeman, Stephanie Anne; Rouig, Lynn), *JEOPARDY*, Western Washington University, Humanities 350, WWU, Bellingham, WA 98225

Danbury, Richard S., III (see also Olmsted, Robert; Olmsted, Elaine), Dan River Press, PO Box 88, Thomaston, ME 04861

Daniel, Bruce, Book Reviews (see also Schick, James B.; Heffernan, Michael), *THE MIDWEST QUARTERLY*, Pittsburg State University, Pittsburg, KS 66762, 316-231-7000

Daniel, Eddee (see also Kapitan, Lynn), *THIRD COAST ARCHIVES*, PO Box 11204, Shorewood, WI 53211, 414-964-0173

Daniel, Robert W., Editor (see also Church, Philip D.; Crump, Galbraith M.; Klein, William F.), *THE KENYON REVIEW*, Kenyon College, Gambier, OH 43022, 614-427-3339

Daniels, Guy (see also Hedley, Leslie Woolf), Exile Press, PO Box 1768, Novato, CA 94948, 883-2132

Daniels, Kate (see also Jones, Richard), *POETRY EAST*, Star Rt. 1 Box 50, Earlysville, VA 22936, 804-973-5299

Daniels, P. (see also Gordon, M.; Ehrenfeld, H.), *THE FOUR ZOAS JOURNAL OF POETRY & LETTERS*, 30 Main St, PO Box 111, Ashuelot, NH 03441

D'arcy, Anne J., *TELEWOMAN*, PO Box 2306, Pleasant Hill, CA 94523

Dardess, George, Associate Editor (see also Walsh, Joy), Moody Street Irregulars, Inc., PO Box 157, Clarence Center, NY 14032, (716) 741-3393

Dardess, George, Associate Editor (see also Walsh, Joy), *MOODY STREET IRREGULARS: A Jack Kerouac Magazine*, PO Box 157, Clarence Center, NY 14032, 716-741-3393

Darling, Denise L., Director Publications and Marketing (see also Tennyson, Doris M.), Hanley-Wood, Inc., 15th and M Streets N W, Washington, DC 20005, 202-822-0394

Darling, Harold, Editor-in-Chief, Green Tiger Press, 1061 India, San Diego, CA 92101, 619-238-1001

Darling, Ritchie, Green Knight Press, PO Box 111, Amherst, MA 01002, 413-253-9780

Darling, Ritchie, Northern New England Review Press, PO Box 111, Amherst, MA 01002, 413-253-9780

Darling, Ritchie, Rat & Mole Press, PO Box 111, Amherst, MA 01002, 413-253-9780

Darlington, Andrew, Eight Miles High Home Entertainment, 44 Spa Croft Road, Teall Street, Ossett, W. Yorks WF5 0HE, England

Darlington, Andrew, *LUDD'S MILL*, 44 Spa Croft Road, Teall Street, Ossett, West Yorkshire WF50HE, England, Wakefield 275814

Darlington, Sandy (see also Reynolds, Julie), Arrowhead Press, 3005 Fulton, Berkeley, CA 94705, 415-540-7010

Darroch, Lynn (see also Weinstein, Joel), Mud Press, 1336 S.E. Marion Street, Portland, OR 97202

Darwin, Victoria, Darwin Publications, 850 N. Hollywood Way, Burbank, CA 91505, 818-848-0944

DasGupta, Ellen, Editor, *POPULAR WOODWORKER*, 1300 Galaxy Way, Concord, CA 94520, 415-671-6852

Davenport, Eileen, Associate Editor (see also Fleming, Harold), *BLACK WILLOW POETRY*, 401 Independence Drive 'Sunrise', Towamencin Township, Harleysville, PA 19438, 215-362-5546

Davenport, Eileen, Associate Editor (see also Fleming, Harold), Black Willow Press, 401 Independence Drive 'Sunrise', Towamencin Township, Harleysville, PA 19438, 215-362-5546

Davey, Bill, Fiction Editor (see also Conway, Don; Gibbs, Robert; Trethewey, Eric; Hawkes, Robert; Butlin, Ron; Taylor, Michael; Thompson, Kent; Boyles, Ann; Bauer, William), *THE FIDDLEHEAD*, The Observatory, Univ. New Brunswick, PO Box 4400, Fredericton, NB E3B 5A3, Canada, 506-454-3591

Davey, Frank (see also Bevington, Stan; Young, David; James, Clifford; Nichol, bp; Ondaatje, Michael; McCartney, Linda; Sheard, Sarah; Reid, Dennis), Coach House Press, 95 Rivercrest Road, Toronto, Ontario M6S 4H7, Canada, 416-767-6317

David, Joe, Books for All Times, Inc., PO Box 2, Alexandria, VA 22313, 703-548-0457

Davids, Betsy (see also Petrillo, Jim), Rebis Press, P.O. Box 2233, Berkeley, CA 94702, 415-527-3845

Davidson, Michael, Archive for New Poetry, University of California, San Diego, C-075, La Jolla, CA 92093, 714-452-6766

Davidson, Michael, *DOCUMENTS FOR NEW POETRY*, University of California, San Diego C-075, c/o Archive for New Poetry, La Jolla, CA 92093, 714-452-6766

Davie, Donald (see also Kilroy, James; Touster, Eva), *CUMBERLAND POETRY REVIEW*, Poetics, Inc., PO Box 120128 Acklen Station, Nashville, TN 37212, 615-373-8948

Davies, Glynn, Aya Press, PO Box 303, Station A, Toronto, Ontario M5W 1C2, Canada, 416-782-9984

Davies, Hilary, Editor (see also Fleming, Ray), *ARGO incorporating DELTA*, Old Fire Station, 40 George St., Oxford, England

Davies, Robert A. (see also Gogol, John M.), *MR. COGITO*, PO Box 627, Pacific University, Forest Grove, OR 97116, 503-357-6151 ext 250

Davies, Robert A. (see also Gogol, John M.), Mr. Cogito Press, U C Box 627, Pacific University, Forest Grove, OR 97116

Davis, Allison, Special Projects Editor (see also Bieberle, Gordon F.; Ullman, Rosanne; Shinn, Sharon), *PUBLISHING TRADE*, 1495 Oakwood, Des Plaines, IL 60016, 312-298-8291

Davis, Annette (see also Walatka, Pam Portugal; Stephens, Helen; Main, Jody; Jamello, Nancy Portugal), Wild Horses Publishing Company, 12310 Concepcion Road, Los Altos Hills, CA 94022, 415-941-3396

Davis, Jon (see also Hackett, Suzanne), *CUTBANK*, English Dept., U. of Montana, Missoula, MT 59812

Davis, Jon (see also Hackett, Suzanne), SmokeRoot, Dept of English/Univ of Mont, Missoula, MT 59812

Davis, Mark (see also Gleeson, Andrew), *ON DIT*, PO Box 498, Adelaide 5001, Australia, 223-2685

Davis, Susan, Managing Editor, *POET LORE*, 4000 Albemarle Street, N.W., Washington, DC 20016, 202-362-6445

Davis, Ty, Managing Editor (see also Papineau, Lou), *THE NEWPAPER*, Box 2393, Providence, RI 02906, 401-273-NEWP

Davy, Kate (see also Aronson, Arnold), U.S. Institute for Theatre Technology, Inc., 330 W. 42nd Street, New York, NY 10036, 212-563-5551

Dawes, Kathleen A., New Capernaum Works, 4615 NE Emerson Street, Portland, OR 97218, (503) 281-1307; 284-1339

Day, Robert A., ISI Press, 3501 Market Street, Philadelphia, PA 19104, 215-386-0100

De Angelis, Jacqueline (see also Rodriguez, Aleida), Books of a Feather, PO Box 3095, Terminal Annex, Los Angeles, CA 90051

De Angelis, Jacqueline (see also Rodriguez, Aleida), *RARA AVIS*, P.O. Box 3095, Terminal Annex, Los Angeles, CA 90051

de Faymonville, Denise (see also Lawrence, E.S.; Sheroan, Dorsey F.), Wheat Forders, Box 6317, Washington, DC 20015, 202-362-1588

De Foe, Mark, Editor (see also Keating, Martha; Gamble, Mort; McAleavey, David; Pierce, Constance), *THE LAUREL REVIEW*, West Virginia Wesleyan College, Buckhannon, WV 26201, 304-473-8006

de Jim, Strange, Ash-Kar Press, PO Box 14547, San Francisco, CA 94114

de la Fuente, Patricia, Assoc. Ed. (see also Schmidt, Dorey), *RIVERSEDGE*, PO Box 3185, Edinburg, TX 78539, 512-381-3429

de la Fuente, Patricia, Assoc. Ed (see also Schmidt, Dorey), Riversedge Press, PO Box 3185, Edinburg, TX 78539

de la Torre Bueno, Anka (see also Kopelman, Sikander; Kopelman, Sajjada), Sufi Order Publications/Omega Press, PO Box 574, Lebanon Spring, NY 12114, 518-794-8181

De Loach, Allen, *BEAU FLEUVE SERIES*, PO Box 110, Central Park Station, Buffalo, NY 14215

De Mente, Boye (see also Stewart, Fern), Phoenix Books/Publishers, P.O.Box 32008, Phoenix, AZ 85064, 602-952-0163

De Oca, D.M., Marketing & Research (see also Bogus, Sdiane; Baptist, Weldon O.; Coleman, Cheryl L.), W. I. M. Publications, Box 367, Department IDSP, College Corner, OH 45003, 513-523-5994

de Palchi, Alfredo, Associate Editor (see also Raiziss, Sonia; Swann, Brian; Foerster, Richard), *CHELSEA*, Box 5880, Grand Central Station, New York, NY 10163

de Vinck, Jose M., Owner, Alleluia Press, Box 103, Allendale, NJ 07401, 201-327-3513

Deacon, Gene, President (see also Deacon, Nell), Gold Crest Publishing, 5644 Londonderry Road, Drawer 21, Charlotte, NC 28210, 704-552-6255

Deacon, Nell, Secretary-Treasurer (see also Deacon, Gene), *Gold Crest Publishing*, 5644 Londonderry Road, Drawer 21, Charlotte, NC 28210, 704-552-6255

Deahl, Joseph (see also Bainbridge, Dave), The Passive Solar Institute, Box 722, Bascom, OH 44809, 419-937-2226

Deahl, Joseph (see also Evans, Mike), *WIND POWER DIGEST*, Box 700, Bascom, OH 44809, 419-937-2299

Deahl, Joseph (see also Evans, Mike), Wind Power Publishing, Box 700, Bascom, OH 44809, 419-937-2299

Deal, Shirley Herd, S. Deal & Assoc., 1629 Guizot St., San Diego, CA 92107

Dean, Barbara, Island Press - A Division of Round Valley Agrarian Institute, Star Route 1, Box 38, Covelo, CA 95428, 707-983-6432

Dean, Tim, Editor, *THIRD WAY*, 37 Elm Road, New Malden, Surrey KT3 3HB, England, 01-942-9761

Deanovich, Connie (see also Mesmer, Sharon; Pintonelli, Debbie), *B-CITY*, B-City Press, 1555 W. Pratt Boulevard, Chicago, IL 60626, 312-743-4806

DeBrincat, Matthew, Bible-Speak Enterprises, 1940 Mount Vernon Court #4, Mountain View, CA 94040, 415-965-9020

Decavalles, A. (see also Keyishian, M.; Zander, W.; Cumming, W.), *JOURNAL OF NEW JERSEY POETS*, Fairleigh Dickinson Univ., English Dept., 285 Madison Avenue, Madison, NJ 07940, 01-377-4700

Decker, Virginia A., Managing Editor, Community Collaborators, PO Box 5429, Charlottesville, VA 22905, 804-977-1126

Dee, Anne Patterson, *CRAFTSWOMAN*, 1153 Oxford Road, Deerfield, IL 60015, 312-945-1769

Dee, Anne Patterson, Daedalus Publications, Inc., 1153 Oxford Road, Deerfield, IL 60015, 312-945-1769

DeFremery, P.W., Tamal Vista Publications, 222 Madrone Ave, Larkspur, CA 94939, 924-7289

Degenhart, Karen, *LAPIS*, 18420 Klimm Avenue, Homewood, IL 60430, 312-957-5856

Degenhart, Karen, Lapis Educational Association, Inc., 18420 Klimm Avenue, Homewood, IL 60430, 312-957-5856

Degnore, R.P. (see also Rose, I.), I.R.D. Productions - Alien Prods, Box 366, Canal Street Station, New York, NY 10013, 212-420-9043

DeGrazia, Emilio, General Editor (see also Wadden, Paul; Williams, Susan; Lund, Orval J.; Leukovins, Deborah), *GREAT RIVER REVIEW*, 211 W 7th, Winona, MN 55987

Deitz, Paula, Co-editor (see also Morgan, Frederick), *THE HUDSON REVIEW*, 684 Park Avenue, New York, NY 10021, 212-650-0020

deJaeger, H.K., *INFORMATION RESOURCES ANNUAL/IRA*, Bibliotheque Royale/CNDST, 4 boulevard de l'Empereur, B-1000 Brussels, Belgium

Dejanikus, Tacie (see also Leonard, Vickie; Douglas, Carol Anne; Lootens, Tricia; Henry, Alice; Fugh-Berman, Adrianne; Moira, Fran; Kulp, Denise; Sorrel, Lorraine), *OFF OUR BACKS*, 1841 Columbia Road NW Rm 212, Room 212, Washington, DC 20009, 202-234-8072

Delacoste, Frederique (see also Newman, Felice), Cleis Press, PO Box 8933, Pittsburgh, PA 15221

Dell, Barbara (see also Naatz, Robert), Precipice Press, 106 Pinion Lane, Manitou Springs, CO 80829

Dellenbaugh, Anne G., Co-Editor (see also Weil, Lise), *TRIVIA, A JOURNAL OF IDEAS*, Box 606, North Amherst, MA 01059, 413-367-2254

Dellutri, Mary (see also Goldman, Richard; Lennon, Nancy), *RAMBUNCTIOUS REVIEW*, Rambunctious Press, Inc., 1221 West Pratt, Chicago, IL 60626

DeLoach, Allen, *INTREPID*, PO Box 110, Central Park Station, Buffalo, NY 14215

DeLoach, Allen, Intrepid Press, PO Box 110, Central Park Station, Buffalo, NY 14215

DeLoach, Allen, *23 CLUB SERIES*, PO Box 110, Central Park Station, Buffalo, NY 14215

Delson, Donn (see also Posner, Neil), Bradson Press, 120 Longfellow Street, Thousand Oaks, CA 91360, 805-496-8212

DeLuca, Geraldine (see also Natov, Roni), *THE LION AND THE UNICORN: A Critical Journal of Children's Literature*, Dept of English, Brooklyn College, Brooklyn, NY 11210, 780-5195

deMause, Lloyd, Creative Roots, Inc., PO Box 401, Planetarium Station, New York, NY 10024, 212-799-2294

Demeter, John P., *RADICAL AMERICA*, 38 Union Square, Somerville, MA 02143, 617-628-6585

Demeter, Lise (see also Weeds, Betty), Hungarica Publishing House, Fraser Valley Region, PO Box 86788, North Vancouver, B.C. V7L 4L3, Canada, 604-986-3539

Dempsey, Hugh A., *ALBERTA HISTORY*, 95 Holmwood Ave NW, Calgary Alberta T2K 2G7, Canada, 403-289-8149

Dempsey, Hugh A., Historical Society of Alberta, 95 Holmwood Ave. NW, Calgary, Alberta T2K 2G7, Canada

Denham, Robert, Editor and Publisher, Iron Mountain Press, Box D, Emory, VA 24327, 703-944-5363

Denison, John, President, The Boston Mills Press, 98 Main Street, Erin, Ontario N0B 1T0, Canada, 519-833-2407

Dennis, Deborah (see also Balsamo, Ron; Hughes, John E.; Lee, Jean C.; Reed, W.A.; Reed, Vicki; Thompson, Catherine), *FARMER'S MARKET*, PO Box 1272, Galesburg, IL 61402

Dennis, John, National Stereoscopic Association, Box 14801, Columbus, OH 43214, 614-263-4296

Dennis, John, *STEREO WORLD*, Box 14801, Columbus, OH 43214, 614-263-4296

Deno, Cynthia, University of California Press, Berkeley, CA 94720, 415-642-6333

Dent, Peter, Interim Press, 3 Thornton Close, Budleigh Salterton, Devon EX9 6PJ, England, 5231

DeRay, Norton, Director (see also Sura, Thurman), Seed Center, PO Box 658, Garberville, CA 95440, 707-986-7575

Derman, Sylvia, Managing Editor, *GESAR- Buddhist Perspectives*, 2425 Hillside Ave., Berkeley, CA 94704, 415-548-5407

Dern, Marie C., Jungle Garden Press, 47 Oak Rd, Fairfax, CA 94930

DeSalvo, Jules (see also Vorda, Allan; Sullivan, Jamie), *THE FABULIST REVIEW*, PO Box 770851, Houston, TX 77215, 713-978-6191

DeSalvo, Jules, *RIVERFRONT*, Metropolitan Technical Community College, PO Box 3777, Omaha, NE 68103, 402-449-8322

Detjen, Gustav, Jr., Philatelic Directory Publishing Co, 154 Laguna Court, St. Augustine Shores, FL 32086, 904-797-3513

Detjen, Gustav, Jr., *THE PHILATELIC JOURNALIST*, 154 Laguna Court, St. Augustine, FL 32086

Deutsch, Diana, *MUSIC PERCEPTION*, Department of Psychology, C-009, University of California, San Diego, La Jolla, CA 92093

Devons, Vernon (see also Nyerges, Christopher), Survival News Service, Box 42152, Los Angeles, CA 90042, 213-255-9502

Deyans, Vernon (see also Nyerges, Christopher), *BURWOOD JOURNAL*, Box 42152, Los Angeles, CA 90042, 213-255-9502

Di Piero, Mary Jane, Alexandrian Press, 1070 Arastradero Road, PO Box 1000, Palo Alto, CA 94303, 415-494-8450 ext. 282

Diana Witt (see also Frompovich, Catherine J.; Koppenhaver, April M.), C J Frompovich Publications, RD 1, Chestnut Road, Coopersburg, PA 18036, 215-346-8461

Dibz, A. (see also Kaplan, Tobey), Ground Under Press, 2913 Shattuck Avenue, Berkeley, CA 94705

Dickson, Anne, Pressworks, Inc., PO Box 190441, Dallas, TX 75219, 214-749-1044

Dietz, Chris (see also Gregory, Michael; Thornton, Elizabeth), The Bisbee Press Collective, Drawer HA, Bisbee, AZ 85617

DiFate, Vincent, Contributing Editor (see also Porter, Andrew; D'Ammassa, Don; Anderson, Kay; Pohl, Frederik; Silverberg, Robert; Jones, Stephen; Fletcher, Jo; Carmody, Larry), *SCIENCE FICTION CHRONICLE*, PO Box 4175, New York, NY 10163, 212-643-9011

Diffey, Dr. T.J., *BRITISH JOURNAL OF AESTHETICS*, Oxford Journals, Journal Subscription Department, Walton Street, Oxford, 0X2 6DP, England

DiFranco, Anthony (see also Steinke, Russell; O'Brien, William), *LONG POND REVIEW*, English Dept, Suffolk Community College, Selden Long Island, NY 11784

Dillingham, Thomas, Bk. Review Ed. (see also Bender, Eleanor M.), *OPEN PLACES*, Box 2085, Stephens College, Columbia, MO 65215, 314-442-2211

Dilsaver, Paul, *BLUE LIGHT REVIEW*, PO Box 31, Helena, MT 59624

Dimeo, Steven, Ph.D., Editor-in-Chief, *NEW OREGON REVIEW*, 537 N.E. Lincoln St., Hillsboro, OR 97124, 503-640-1375

Dimitrios, Bro. (see also Wade, David), *FROZEN WAFFLES*, Writers-Action, PO Box 1941, Bloomington, IN 47402, 812-334-0381

Dimitrios, Bro. (see also Wade, David), Frozen Waffles Press & Tapes, Writers-Action, Inc., PO Box 1941, Bloomington, IN 47402, 812-334-0381

Dimitrios, Brother (see also Wade, David), Pitjon Press/BackPack Media, Writers-Action, Inc., PO Box 1941, Bloomington, IN 47402, 812-334-0381

Diogo, Judith A., Editorial Assistant, Executive Secretary (see also Bayes, Ron; Roper, John H.; Osmanski, Edna Ann), Saint Andrews Press, St Andrews College, Laurinburg, NC 28352, 919-276-3652

DiPresso, Stephen J. (see also McGlynn, Brian), *RAPSCALLION'S DREAM*, PO Box 183, Bronx, NY 10470, (212) 549-2374

Dixon, Marlene, Editor, *CONTEMPORARY MARXISM*, 2703 Folsom Street, San Francisco, CA 94110, 415-550-1703

Dixon, Peter (see also Wesolowski, Paul G.; Gorman, Neal E.), *THE FREEDONIA GAZETTE*, Darien B-28 at Village II, New Hope, PA 18938, 215-862-9734

Dochniak, Jim, Editor, *SEZ: A Multi-Racial Journal of Poetry & People's Culture*, PO Box 8803, Minneapolis, MN 55408, 612-822-3488

Dochniak, Jim, Editor, Shadow Press, U.S.A., PO Box 8803, Minneapolis, MN 55408, 612-822-3488

Dodd, Wayne, *THE OHIO REVIEW*, Ellis Hall, Ohio University, Athens, OH 45701, 614-594-5889

Doering, Steven, *RANDOM WEIRDNESS*, 6092 N. Newburg Avenue, Chicago, IL 60631

Dolan, Jill, Managing Editor (see also Kirby, Michael), *THE DRAMA REVIEW*, MIT Press For New York University, 300 South Bldg. 51 W. 4th Street, New York, NY 10003, 212-598-2597

Dolan, John M., Co-Editor (see also Glick, Wendell), *THOREAU QUARTERLY*, 355 Ford Hall, Univ of Minnesota, 224 Church Street SE, Minneapolis, MN 55455, 612-373-3612

Dollens, Dennis, Editor (see also Christ, Ronald), *SITES-ARCHITECTURAL MAGAZINE*, Lumen, Inc., 446 West 20th Street, New York, NY 10011, 212-924-0642

Dominguez, Leonard J., Editor-in-chief (see also Cummings, Kathleen J.; Hunt, Larry), *NIT&WIT, Chicago's Arts Magazine*, PO Box 14685, Chicago, IL 60614, 312-248-1183

Domitrovich, Lisa (see also Donnelly, Margarita; Malone, Ruth; Wendt, Ingrid; Wilner, Eleanor; Thompson, Joyce; Caday, Jan; Mclean, Cheryl; Gordon, Rebecca; Jenkins, Meredith), *CALYX: A Journal of Art and Literature by Women*, PO Box B, Corvallis, OR 97339, 503-753-9384

Donaldson, Janet M., Glenhurst Publications, Inc., Central Community Center, 6300 Walker Street, St. Louis Park, MN 55416, 612-925-3632

Donato, Vince (see also Poole, Gary), *THE LAUGH FACTORY*, Fell Great Publishing Co., 1370 Windsor Road, Teaneck, NJ 07666, 201-833-0068

Donley, Carol (see also Fratus, David), *HIRAM POETRY REVIEW*, Box 162, Hiram, OH 44234, 216-569-3211

Donnelly, Margarita, Managing Editor (see also Malone, Ruth; Wendt, Ingrid; Wilner, Eleanor; Thompson, Joyce; Caday, Jan; Mclean, Cheryl; Gordon, Rebecca; Domitrovich, Lisa; Jenkins, Meredith), *CALYX: A Journal of Art and Literature by Women*, PO Box B, Corvallis, OR 97339, 503-753-9384

Donovan, Diana, Manager, Celo Press, Route #5, Burnsville, NC 28714, 702-675-4925

Doran, Susan, Editor (see also Murray, Steven T.), Fjord Press, PO Box 615, Corte Madera, CA 94925, 415-924-9566/549-1910

Dore, Ian, Osprey Books, PO Box 965, Huntington, NY 11743, 516-549-0143

Doremus, Paul N. (see also Spangler, David M.), *LORIAN JOURNAL*, PO Box 147, Middleton, WI 53562, 608-833-0455

Doremus, Paul N. (see also Spangler, David M.), Lorian Press, PO Box 147, Middleton, WI 53562, 608-833-0455

Doria, Charles, Publisher, Editor (see also Succop, Greg), *ASSEMBLING*, Box 1967, Brooklyn, NY 11202

Doria, Charles (see also Succop, Greg), Assembling Press, PO Box 1967, Brooklyn, NY 11202

Dorman, Sean, The Raffeen Press, 4 Union Place, Fowey, Cornwall PL23 1BY, England

Dorman, Sean, *WRITING*, 4 Union Place, Fowey, Cornwall PL23 1BY, England

Dorosh, Ellen M., Antietam Press, P.O. Box 62, Boonsboro, MD 21713, (301) 432-8079

Dorset, Gerald, New England Press, 45 Tudor City #1903, New York, NY 10017

Dorsett, Robert (see also Ko, Loretta), *THE ATAVIST*, Box 5643, Berkeley, CA 94705

Dorsett, Thomas (see also Nirmala, Kammana), *KAVITHA*, 4408 Wickford Road, Baltimore, MD 21210, 301-467-4316

Doss, Donna, *THE INDIAN VOICE*, 102-423 West Broadway, Vancouver, British Columbia V5Y1R4, Canada, 604-112-876-0944

Dossin, Jennifer, Art & Submissions (see also Galef, Jack), Elizabeth Street Press, 240 Elizabeth Street, New York, NY 10012

Doty, Ruth (see also Urban, Tom; Valentine, Jody), *BLUE BUILDINGS*, 1215 25th Street #F, Des Moines, IA 50311, 515-277-2709

Doughty, Dale W., Scarborough Publishing Incorp., PO Box 384, Scarborough, ME 04074, 207-883-5194

Douglas, Carol Anne (see also Leonard, Vickie; Lootens, Tricia; Henry, Alice; Fugh-Berman, Adrianne; Moira, Fran; Dejanikus, Tacie; Kulp, Denise; Sorrel, Lorraine), *OFF OUR BACKS*, 1841 Columbia Road NW Rm 212, Room 212, Washington, DC 20009, 202-234-8072

Douglas, Prentice (see also Malaschak, Dolores), *LINCOLN LOG (POETRY JOURNAL)*, Route 2, Box 126-C, Raymond, IL 62560

Douthit, Peter (see also MacNaughton, Anne; McCallum, Tracy), Minor Heron Press, PO Box 2615, Taos, NM 87571, 505-758-0081

Dow, Hugh (see also Allen, Robert; Draper, Jan; Luxton, Stephen), *THE MOOSEHEAD REVIEW*, Box 169, Ayer's Cliff, Quebec, Canada, 819-842-2835, 838-4801

Dowbenko, Uri, Sirius Publications, 270 S. La Cienega Blvd, Suite 301, Beverly Hills, CA 90211

Doyle, Judy (see also Taylor, Alexander), Curbstone Press, 321 Jackson Street, Willimantic, CT 06226, 423-9190

Doyle, R.F., Poor Richards Press, 17854 Lyons Street, Forest Lake, MN 55025

Dragland, Stan (see also McKay, Jean), *BRICK: A Journal Of Reviews*, Box 219, Ilderton, Ontario N0M 2AO, Canada, (519) 666-0283

Dragland, Stan (see also McKay, Don), Brick Books, Box 219, Ilderton, Ontario N0M 2AO, Canada, 519-666-0283

Drake, Albert, *HAPPINESS HOLDING TANK*, 1790 Grand River, Okemos, MI 48864

Drake, Albert, Stone Press, 1790 Grand River, Okemos, MI 48864

Draper, Jan (see also Allen, Robert; Luxton, Stephen; Dow, Hugh), *THE MOOSEHEAD REVIEW*, Box 169, Ayer's Cliff, Quebec, Canada, 819-842-2835, 838-4801

Dreher, Denise, Madhatter Press, 3101 12th Avenue, S. #5, Minneapolis, MN 55407, 612-722-8951

Drucker, Joseph, Editor (see also Grimes, John), *ALLY*, 234 High Street #6, Santa Cruz, CA 95060, 408-423-4946

du Passage, Mary (see also Malinowitz, Michael; Horowitz, Evelyn), *THE BAD HENRY REVIEW*, Box 45, Van Brunt Station, Brooklyn, NY 11215

du Passage, Mary (see also Malinowitz, Michael; Horowitz, Evelyn), 44 Press, Inc., Box 45, Van Brant Station, Brooklyn, NY 11215

Duane, Kit (see also Rosenwasser, Rena; Lisanevich, Xenia; Loeb, Emily; Kitrilakis, Thalia), Kelsey St. Press, PO Box 9235, Berkeley, CA 94709, AM: 415-845-2260; PM: 415-548-3826

Duberstein, Larry (see also Brown, Lee), Darkhorse Bookmakers, Jones Hill Road, Ashby, MA 01431

Dubois, Rochelle, *VALHALLA*, 59 Sandra Circle A-3, Westfield, NJ 07090, 232-7224

DuBois, Rochelle H., Editor (see also Erdmann, Diane C.), Merging Media, 59 Sandra Circle A-3, Westfield, NJ 07090, 232-7224

Ducoff-Barone, Deborah (see also Barone, Dennis), Tamarisk, 319 S Juniper Street, Philadelphia, PA 19107

Duddy, Linda W., Associate Editor (see also Duddy, Neil T.), *UPDATE-A Quarterly Journal on New Religious Movements*, The Dialog Center, Klvermarksvej 4, 8200 Aarhus N, Denmark, 06- 10 50 01

Duddy, Neil T., Editor (see also Duddy, Linda W.), *UPDATE-A Quarterly Journal on New Religious Movements*, The Dialog Center, Klvermarksvej 4, 8200 Aarhus N, Denmark, 06- 10 50 01

Dudewicz, Edward J., *AMERICAN JOURNAL OF MATHEMATICAL AND MANAGEMENT SCIENCES*, 20 Cross Road, Syracuse, NY 13224

Dudewicz, Edward J., American Sciences Press, Inc., 20 Cross Road, Syracuse, NY 13224

Dudley, B.G., Chess Enterprises, Inc., 107 Crosstree Road, Coraopolis, PA 15108

Duer, David (see also Merians, Valerie), Dog Hair Press, PO Box 372, West Branch, IA 52358, 319-643-7324

Duer, David, *LUNA TACK*, PO Box 372, West Branch, IA 52358, 319-338-2980

Dufour, A., *BIBLIOTHEQUE D'HUMANISME ET RENAISSANCE*, Librairie Droz S.A., 11r.Massot, 1211 Geneve 12, Switzerland

Dufour, A., Librairie Droz S.A., Librairie Droz S.A., 11r.Massot, 1211 Geneve 12, Switzerland

Duggan, Joseph J., *ROMANCE PHILOLOGY*, University of California Press, Berkeley, CA 94720

Duke, Donald, Golden West Books, PO Box 80250, San Marino, CA 91108, 213-283-3446

Dukes, Norman, Associate Editor (see also Dunn, Sharon; Melnyczuk, Askold), *THE AGNI REVIEW*, PO Box 229, Cambridge, MA 02238, 617-491-1079

Dulai, Surjit (see also Coppola, Carlo), *JOURNAL OF SOUTH ASIAN LITERATURE*, Area Studies Program, Oakland University, Rochester, MI 48063, (313) 377-2076

Dunn, David (see also Michael, Ann E.), LiMbo bar&grill Books, 7446 Overhill Road, Melrose Park, PA 19126

Dunn, Sharon, Editor (see also Dukes, Norman; Melnyczuk, Askold), *THE AGNI REVIEW*, PO Box 229, Cambridge, MA 02238, 617-491-1079

Dunn, Tom, *THE PIPE SMOKER'S EPHEMERIS*, 20-37 120th Street, College Point, NY 11356

Dunning, Barbara Renkens, Editor, Cape Cod Writers Inc, Box 333, Cummaquid, MA 02637

Dunning, Barbara Renkens, Editor (see also Lunn, Jean), *SANDSCRIPT*, Box 333, Cummaquid, MA 02637, 617-362-6078

DuPriest, Mabel (see also DuPriest, Travis), Southport Press, Dept. of English, Carthage College, Kenosha, WI 53141, 414-551-8500 (252)

DuPriest, Travis (see also DuPriest, Mabel), *Southport Press*, Dept. of English, Carthage College, Kenosha, WI 53141, 414-551-8500 (252)

45

Duran, Erin, Editor, Art Director (see also Smith, Chuck), Word for Today, PO Box 8000, Costa Mesa, CA 92628, 714-979-0706

Durland, Steven, Managing Editor (see also Burnham, Linda Frye), Astro Artz, 240 So Broadway, 5th Floor, Los Angeles, CA 90012, 213-687-7362

Durland, Steven, Managing Editor (see also Burnham, Linda Frye), *HIGH PERFORMANCE*, 240 S. Broadway, 5th Floor, Los Angeles, CA 90012, 213-687-7362

Durst, Gary Michael, Center for the Art of Living, Box 788, Evanston, IL 60204, 312-864-8664

Durst, James, Publisher (see also Torczyner, Leslie), *SONGSMITH JOURNAL*, PO Box 608036, Chicago, IL 60626, 312-274-0054

Dutch, Peter, Publisher (see also Moot, Andrew), *PACIFIC BRIDGE*, PO Box 6328, San Francisco, CA 94101, 415-863-3622

Dutcher, Roger, *URANUS*, 1537 Washburn, Beloit, WI 53511, 608-362-4493

Dutkiewicz, Adam, Coordinator, Span, Fiction, Music (see also Brakmanis, M.; Hastwell, G.; Biggs, S.; Franklin, C.), *WORDS AND VISIONS/WAV MAGAZINE*, 499 The Parade, Magill, Australia, 08-3329529

Dutton, Sandra, *RIVER CITY REVIEW*, PO Box 34275, Louisville, KY 40232, 502-459-8040

Dworkin, Marc Steven, *SHIRIM*, Hillel Ext. 900 Hilgard Avenue, Los Angeles, CA 90024

Dwyer, John N., North Star Press, PO Box 451, St. Cloud, MN 56301, 612-253-1636

Dynes, Wayne, Gai Saber Monographs, c/o Gau, Box 480, Lenox Hill Station, New York, NY 10021, 212-864-0361

E

Eades, Dan, Editor (see also Eades, Joan; Ohlsen, Linda), *BLOODROOT*, PO Box 891, Grand Forks, ND 58206, 701-775-6079

Eades, Dan, Editor (see also Eades, Joan; Ohlsen, Linda), Bloodroot, Inc., PO Box 891, Grand Forks, ND 58206, 70l-775-6079

Eades, Joan, Editor (see also Ohlsen, Linda; Eades, Dan), *BLOODROOT*, PO Box 891, Grand Forks, ND 58206, 701-775-6079

Eades, Joan, Editor (see also Eades, Dan; Ohlsen, Linda), Bloodroot, Inc., PO Box 891, Grand Forks, ND 58206, 70l-775-6079

Eads, Valerie, *FIGHTING WOMAN NEWS*, PO Box 1459, Grand Central Station, New York, NY 10163, 212-228-0900

Eads, Valerie, Fighting Woman News Press, PO Box 1459, Grand Central Station, New York, NY 10163

Eagan, Peggy (see also Names, Larry D.), Larantor Press, Box 253, 211 Main Street, Neshkoro, WI 54960, 414-293-4377

Eagleson, John, Editor (see also Scharper, Philip J.; Higgins, Elizabeth), Orbis Books, Attention: Robert N. Quigley, Maryknoll, NY 10545, 914-941-7590

Earl, Rob, *VING*, 3 Pleasant Villas, 189 Kent Street, Mereworth, Maidstone, Kent ME18 5QN, England, (0622) 812804

Early, Robert, *MID-AMERICAN REVIEW*, Dept of English, Bowling Green State University, Bowling Green, OH 43403, 419-372-2725

Early, Sarah, *SPUR*, WDM, Bedford Chambers, Covent Garden, London WC2E 8HA, England

Eason, Deborah, *CREATIVE LOAFING*, 1011 West Peachtree, Atlanta, GA 30308, 404-873-5623

Eason, Roger R., Managing Editor (see also Tickle, Phyllis; Spicer, David), St. Luke's Press, Suite 401, 1407 Union Avenue, Memphis, TN 38104, 901-357-5441

Eaton, Jonathan, Editor, International Marine Publishing Co., 21 Elm Street, Camden, ME 04843, 207-236-4342

Eaves, Morris (see also Paley, Morton D.), *BLAKE, AN ILLUSTRATED QUARTERLY*, Dept. of English, Univ. of New Mexico, Albuquerque, NM 87131, 505-277-3103

Ebel, Charles W., *AFRICA NEWS*, P.O. Box 3851, Durham, NC 27702, 919-286-0747

Eberth, Theresa, *OUT-LOOK*, 1315 E. Columbia #1, Colorado Springs, CO 80909

Edelson, Elihu, Editor, *BOTH SIDES NOW*, Rt 6, Box 28, Tyler, TX 75704, 214-592-4263

Edelson, Morris (see also Bondy, Melissa; Fellner, Mike; McGilligan, Pat; Edelson, Olga), Quixote Press, 1812 Marshall, Houston, TX 77098

Edelson, Olga (see also Edelson, Morris; Bondy, Melissa; Fellner, Mike; McGilligan, Pat), *Quixote Press*, 1812 Marshall, Houston, TX 77098

Edwards, David D., Editor & Publisher, Occasional Productions, 593 Vasona Avenue, Los Gatos, CA 95030

Edwards, Ellen, Co-Editor (see also Ray, MaryEllen), Rising Publishing, PO Box 72478, Los Angeles, CA 90002, 213-746-7483

Edwards, Ken, Editor, *REALITY STUDIOS*, Flat H, 85 Balfour Street, London SE17, United Kingdom, 01-708-0652

Edwards, Ken, Reality Studios Press, 75 Balfour Street, London SE17, United Kingdom, 01-708-0652

Edwards, Kimberly A., Publisher, *WRITING UPDATE*, 4812 Folsom Boulevard, Sacramento, CA 95819

Edwards, Michael (see also Green, J.C.R.), Aquila Publishing, PO Box 1, Portree, Isle of Skye, Scotland

Edwards, Michael (see also Green, J.C.R.), *PROSPICE*, PO Box 1, Isle of Skye, Portree, IV51 9BT, England

Edwards, Ronald, Little River Press, 10 Lowell Avenue, Westfield, MA 01085, 413-568-5598

Edwards, Thomas R., Exec. Ed. (see also Poirier, Richard; Hyman, Suzanne K.), *RARITAN: A Quarterly Review*, 165 College Avenue, New Brunswick, NJ 08903, 201-932-7852

Edwords, Frederick, *CREATION/EVOLUTION JOURNAL*, PO Box 146 Amherst Branch, Buffalo, NY 14226, 716-839-5083

Efron, Arthur, *PAUNCH*, 123 Woodward Ave, Buffalo, NY 14214, 716-836-7332

Efros, Susan (see also Levinson, Joan), Waterfall Press, 2122 Junction Avenue, El Cerrito, CA 94530, 415-232-5539

Eggleston, John, *STUDIES IN DESIGN EDUCATION CRAFT AND TECHNOLOGY*, Keele University, Department of Education, Keele, Staffordshire ST5 5BG, England, 0782-621111

Eglash, Albert, San Luis Quest Press, Box 998, San Luis Obispo, CA 93406, 805-543-8500

Ehrenfeld, H. (see also Gordon, M.; Daniels, P.), *THE FOUR ZOAS JOURNAL OF POETRY & LETTERS*, 30 Main St, PO Box 111, Ashuelot, NH 03441

Ehrenreich, Barbara, Co-Editor (see also Harrington, Michael; Phillips, Maxine), *DEMOCRATIC LEFT*, 853 Broadway, Suite 801, New York, NY 10003, 212-260-3270

Ehrhart, W. D. (see also Barry, Jan), East River Anthology, 75 Gates Ave, Montclair, NJ 07042, 201-746-5941

Ehrlich, Howard J., *SOCIAL ANARCHISM*, 2743 Maryland Avenue, Baltimore, MD 21218, 301-243-6987

Eilenberg, Jeff (see also Moss, Mark; Gorka, John), *SING OUT! The Folk Song Magazine*, PO Box 1071, Easton, PA 18042, 215-253-8105

Eilertson, D.F., Opus Associates, Inc., 106-B Lake Side Drive, Smyrna, TN 37167, 919-223-5796

Eisner, Will, Editor, *WILL EISNER'S QUARTERLY*

Elbert, N.E. (see also Mottet, Arthur L., Jr.; Fox, C.L.), Pacific Scientific Press, Inc., 3506 Pennsylvania, Longview, WA 98632, 206-425-8592

Elder, Gary, Editor (see also Elder, Jeane), Holmgangers Press, 95 Carson Court Shelter Cove, Shelter Cove, Whitethorn, CA 95489, 707-986-7700

Elder, Jeane, Editor (see also Elder, Gary), *Holmgangers Press*, 95 Carson Court Shelter Cove, Shelter Cove, Whitethorn, CA 95489, 707-986-7700

Elder, John, Poetry Editor (see also Steinzor, Seth; Johnson, Ronna; Mabe, Eirard), *DARK HORSE*, Box 9, Somerville, MA 02143

Elder, Karl, Editor (see also Worman, A. Lee), *SEEMS*, c/o Lakeland College, Box 359, Sheboygan, WI 53082

Eldrege, Joss (see also Marilyn, Sandra), *TRADESWOMEN MAGAZINE*, Tradeswomen Inc., PO Box 40664, San Francisco, CA 94140, 415-989-1566

Elevitch, M. D., First Person, Box 604, Palisades, NY 10964

Eley, Glen D., GDE Publications, PO Box 304, Lima, OH 45802, 419-227-8101

Eley, Glen D., *SOFTBALL ILLUSTRATED*, PO Box 304, Lima, OH 45802, 419-227-8101

Elias, Stephen, Senior Editor (see also Warner, Ralph), Nolo Press, 950 Parker Street, Berkeley, CA 94710, 415-549-1976

Elias, Viki, Executive Editor (see also Golden, Michael; Harrison, Jim; Mungo, Raymond; Bukowski, Charles; Placidus, Max; Codrescu, Andrei; Horotwitz, Mikhail; Ligi; Kramer, Glenn; Mitchell, Donna; Riedel, Robert), *SMOKE SIGNALS*, 1516 Beverly Road, Brooklyn, NY 11226

Elitzik, Paul, Director, Lake View Press, PO Box 25421, Chicago, IL 60625, 312-935-2694

Elkhadem, Saad, *THE INTERNATIONAL FICTION REVIEW*, Dept. of German & Russian, UNB, Fredericton, N.B., Canada

Ellenbogen, Glenn C., *JOURNAL OF POLYMORPHOUS PERVERSITY*, 20 Waterside Plaza, Suite 24-H, New York, NY 10010, 212-689-5473

Ellingham, Patrick M., *THE CATHARTIC*, PO Box 1391, Ft Lauderdale, FL 33302, 305-764-4574

Elliot, Sharon, Fresh Press, 774 Allen Court, Palo Alto, CA 94303, 415-493-3596

Elliott, Andrew (see also Huehes, John), *NORTH*, 10 Stranmillis Park, Belfast BT9 5AU, Northern Ireland, 0232-662271

Elliott, William, Poetry Editor (see also Rossi, Betty; Sliney, Jean), *LOONFEATHER: Minnesota North Country Art*, Bemidji Community Arts Center, 426 Bemidji Avenue, Bemidji, MN 56601, 218-751-7570

Ellis, Don, Publisher, Creative Arts Book Company, 833 Bancroft Way, Berkeley, CA 94710, 415-848-4777

Ellis, Ron, *WINDFALL*, Dept of English, University of Wisconsin, Whitewater, WI 53190, 414-472-1036

Ellison, Heidi, Managing Editor (see also Schaefer, Jay), *FICTION NETWORK MAGAZINE*, PO Box 5651, San Francisco, CA 94101, 415-552-3223

Ellison, Tom, Live Oak Publications, Box 2193, Boulder, CO 80306, 303-530-1087

Elman, Barbara (see also Schiffman, Glenn), *WORD PROCESSING NEWS*, 211 East Olive #210, Burbank, CA 91502, 818-845-7809

Elsberg, John, USA Editor (see also Cairncross, George), *BOGG MAGAZINE*, 422 N Cleveland Street, Arlington, VA 22201

Elsberg, John (see also Cairncross, George), Bogg Publications, 422 N Cleveland Street, Arlington, VA 22201

Emblen, D.L. (see also Carlson, Suzanne), Clamshell Press, 160 California Avenue, Santa Rosa, CA 95405

Embry, Charles R., *SULPHUR RIVER*, PO Box 3044, East Texas Station, Commerce, TX 75428, 214-886-7450

Emerson, Ann (see also Harrod, Elizabeth; Plante, Tom), Owlseye Publications, 23650 Stratton Court, Hayward, CA 94541, 415-537-6858

Emerson, Ann (see also Harrod, Elizabeth; Plante, Tom), *POETALK QUARTERLY*, 23650 Stratton Court, Hayward, CA 94541, 415-537-6858

Emerson, Mary, Art (see also Sapiro, Leland; Boggs, Redd; Smith, Sheryl), *RIVERSIDE QUARTER-LY*, Box 863-388, Wildcat Station, Plano, TX 75086, 214-234-6795

Emery, Mary Ann, Asst. Editor (see also Plath, James; Blum, John; Williams, Elizabeth), *CLOCKWATCH REVIEW*, 737 Penbrook Way, Hartland, WI 53029, 414-367-8315

Emily Hilburn, Managing Editor (see also Bercholz, Samuel), Great Eastern Book Company, PO Box 271, Boulder, CO 80306, 303-449-6113

Emmett, Katherine C., Editor-in-Chief, *THE COW CREEK REVIEW*, Pittsburg State University, Pittsburg, KS 66762, 316-231-7000-306

Emond, Paul (see also Willkzie, Philip; Young, Tom; Baysans, Greg; Strizek, Norman), *JAMES WHITE REVIEW; a gay men's literary quarterly*, PO Box 3356, Traffic Station, Minneapolis, MN 55403, 612-291-2913; 871-2248

Empereur, Jake, S.J., Editor-in-Chief (see also Burns, William; Mudd, C.P.), *MODERN LITURGY*, Box 444, Saratoga, CA 95071, 408-252-4195

Empfield (see also Kilgore; Holsapple), *CONTRABAND MAGAZINE*, PO Box 4073, Station A, Portland, ME 04101

Empfield (see also Kilgore; Holsapple), Contraband Press, PO Box 4073, Sta A, Portland, ME 04101

Emry, Douglas K., Publisher, *WRITERS WEST*, PO Box 16097, San Diego, CA 92116

Emuss, John (see also George, Margaret; Pain, Margaret; James, Susan), Guildford Poets Press, 9 White Rose Lane, Woking, Surrey, GU22 73A, England

Emuss, John (see also George, Margaret; Pain, Margaret; James, Susan), *WEYFARERS*, 9 Whiterose Lane, Woking, Surrey, England

Endemann, Carl T., Alta Napa Press, 1969 Mora Avenue07, Calistoga, CA 94515, 707-942-4444

Eng, Steve, Associate Editor (see also Moran, John C.; Herron, Don), The F. Marion Crawford Memorial Society, Saracinesca House, 3610 Meadowbrook Avenue, Nashville, TN 37205

Eng, Steve, Literary Editor (see also Yeatman, Ted P.), Depot Press, PO Box 60072, Nashville, TN 37206, 226-1890

Eng, Steve (see also Crawford, Gary William), Gothic Press, 4998 Perkins Road, Baton Rouge, LA 70808, 504-766-2906

Eng, Steve, Associate Editor (see also Moran, John C.; Herron, Don), *THE ROMANTIST*, Saracinesca House, 3610 Meadowbrook Avenue, Nashville, TN 37205, 615-228-5939

Engebretsen, Alan C., *POETIC JUSTICE*, 8220 Rayford Drive, Los Angeles, CA 90045, 213-649-1491

Engh (see also Eriksen; Madsen; Seglen; Ostenstad), Futurum Forlag, Hjelmsgt. 3, 0355 Oslo 3, Norway, (02) 69 12 84

Engh (see also Eriksen; Madsen; Selgen; Ostenstad), *GATEAVISA*, Hjelmsgt 3, 0355 Oslo 3, Norway, (02) 69 12 84

Engstrom, Barbie, Publisher, Kurios Press, Box 946, Bryn Mawr, PA 19010, 215-527-4635

Enright, John, Tinkers Dam Press, 1703 East Michigan Avenue, Jackson, MI 49202

49

Ensler, Eve (see also Martin, Stephen-Paul; Royal, Richard; Millis, Christopher; Kiefer, Paul; Sullivan, Mary Jane; Sanders, Catherine Marie), *CENTRAL PARK*, P.O. Box 1446, New York, NY 10023

Entrekin, Charles, Managing Editor, *BERKELEY POETS COOPERATIVE*, PO Box 459, Berkeley, CA 94701, 415-528-2252

Entrekin, Charles, Managing Editor, Berkeley Poets Workshop and Press, PO Box 459, Berkeley, CA 94701, 415-528-2252

Eppinga, Jane, *TOPSY TURVY-PATAS ARRIBAS*, 7060 Calle del Sol, Tucson, AZ 85710, 602-747-9352

Epstein, Joseph, *THE AMERICAN SCHOLAR*, 1811 Q Street NW, Washington, DC 20009, 202-265-3808

Epstein, Joseph, The William Byrd Press, 1811 Q Street NW, Washington, DC 20009, 202-265-3808

Erdmann, Diane C., Publisher (see also DuBois, Rochelle H.), Merging Media, 59 Sandra Circle A-3, Westfield, NJ 07090, 232-7224

Erfurdt, Jamie, Associate Editor (see also Anbian, Robert; Spilker, John; King, Dennis; Hellerman, Steve; Kosoua, Anna), *OBOE: A Journal of Literature & Fine Art*, 495 Ellis Street, Box 1156, San Francisco, CA 94102

Erickson, Dave, Fiction Editor (see also Prophet, Colleen; Shaw, Darla K.), *COE REVIEW:Annual Anthology of Experimental Literature*, 1220 First Avenue N.E., Coe College, Cedar Rapids, IA 52402, 319-399-8660

Eriksen (see also Engh; Madsen; Seglen; Ostenstad), Futurum Forlag, Hjelmsgt. 3, 0355 Oslo 3, Norway, (02) 69 12 84

Eriksen (see also Engh; Madsen; Selgen; Ostenstad), *GATEAVISA*, Hjelmsgt 3, 0355 Oslo 3, Norway, (02) 69 12 84

Erikson, Kai T., Editor (see also Laurans, Penelope; Wipprecht, Wendy), *THE YALE REVIEW*, 1902A Yale Station, New Haven, CT 06520

Ernst, John, Valley Lights Publications, PO Box 1537, Ojai, CA 93023, 805-646-9888

Ernst, Kathy S., Press Me Close, PO Box 250, Farmingdale, NJ 07727, 201-938-4297

Ernst, K.S., *PLACE STAMP HERE*, PO Box 250, Farmingdale, NJ 07727, 201-938-4297

Eshelman, Wm. R., Pres & Editor (see also Lee, Barbara), Scarecrow Press, P O Box 656, Metuchen, NJ 08840, 201-548-8600

Eshleman, Clayton, *SULFUR*, 852 S. Bedford Street, Los Angeles, CA 90035

Essary, Loris (see also Loeffler, Mark), *INTERSTATE*, PO Box 7068, U.T. Sta., Austin, TX 78713

Essary, Loris (see also Loeffler, Mark), Noumenon Press, PO Box 7068, University Station, Austin, TX 78713

Essary, Loris (see also Kostelanetz, Richard; Scobie, Stephen; Frank, Sheldon; Zelevansky, Paul; Higgins, Dick; Young, Karl), *PRECISELY*, PO Box 73, Canal Street, New York, NY 10013

Estrin, Jerry, *VANISHING CAB*, 827 Pacific Street, Box 101, San Francisco, CA 94133

et al (student editors vary), *COLD-DRILL*, 1910 University Drive, Boise, ID 83725, 208-385-1999

Evans, D. Ellis (see also Smith, J. Beverley; Livens, R. G.), *BULLETIN OF THE BOARD OF CELTIC STUDIES*, Univ. of Wales Press, 6 Gwennyth Street, Cathays, Cardiff CF2 4YD, Wales

Evans, Larry (see also Evans, Leslie), *MILL HUNK HERALD*, 916 Middle Street, Pittsburgh, PA 15212, 412-321-4767

Evans, Leslie (see also Evans, Larry), *MILL HUNK HERALD*, 916 Middle Street, Pittsburgh, PA 15212, 412-321-4767

Evans, Mark, Editor, Synergy Publishers, PO Box 18268, Denver, CO 80218

Evans, Mike (see also Deahl, Joseph), *WIND POWER DIGEST*, Box 700, Bascom, OH 44809, 419-937-2299

Evans, Mike (see also Deahl, Joseph), Wind Power Publishing, Box 700, Bascom, OH 44809, 419-937-2299

Evans, Robert L., Publisher (see also Gragert, Steven K.), Evans Publications Inc., 133 S. Main, PO Box 520, Perkins, OK 74059, 405-547-2144

Evans, Rose, Sea Fog Press, 447 20th Avenue, San Francisco, CA 94121, 415-221-8527

Everett, Graham, Secretary-Treasurer (see also Planz, Allen; Miller, Marge), Backstreet Editions, Inc., c/o Box 555, Port Jefferson, NY 11777

Everett, Graham, *STREET MAGAZINE*, Box 555, Port Jefferson, NY 11777

Everett, Graham, Street Press, Box 555, Port Jefferson, NY 11777

Everhart, Bob, Editor, *TRADITION*, 106 Navajo, Council Bluffs, IA 51501, 712-366-1136

Everitt, Charles, President (see also Kennedy, Linda; Lynch, Kevin; Bandos, Kate), The Globe Pequot Press, Old Chester Road, Chester, CT 06412, 203-526-9571

Everitt, Helen (see also Kramer, Aaron; Vondrasek, Bets; Andrew, Helen), *WEST HILLS REVIEW: A WALT WHITMAN JOURNAL*, Walt Whitman Birthplace Assn., 246 Walt Whitman Road, Huntington Station, NY 11746, (516) 427-5240

Everly, Kathleen, Ph.D., Ed-U Press, Inc., Box 583, Fayetteville, NY 13066

Exander, Max (see also Reed, Paul Richard), *Folsom House*, PO Box 14793, San Francisco, CA 94114

F

Fabian, R. Gerry, Raw Dog Press, 129 Worthington Ave, Doylestown, PA 18901, 215-345-7692

Fair, Anthony, Consulting Editor, *AMERICAN BOOK COLLECTOR*, 274 Madison Avenue, New York, NY 10016, 212-685-2250

Fair, Anthony ABC, Consulting Editor (see also Fricks, E.E. CCP), The Moretus Press, Inc., 274 Madison Avenue, New York, NY 10016, 212-685-2250

Faiss, Janet Wullner, Publisher & Editor, The Green Hut Press, 1015 East Jardin Street, Appleton, WI 54911, 414-734-9728

Falkenberg, Philippe R., Greencrest Press Inc., Box 7745, Winston-Salem, NC 27109, 919-722-6463

Fallon, Tom, *CHARTENG WORKSHOP*, 226 Linden Street, Rumford, ME 04276, 364-7237

Fallon, Tom, Small-Small Press, 226 Linden Street, Rumford, ME 04276, 364-7237

Fankuchen, Steve, *SHMATE*, Box 4228, Berkeley, CA 94704

Fankuchen, Steve, Shmate Press, Box 4228, Berkeley, CA 94704

Fanning, Robbie (see also Green, Marilyn), Fibar Designs, P.O.Box 2634, Menlo Park, CA 94026, 415-323-2549

Fanning, Robbie (see also Green, Marilyn), *OPEN CHAIN*, PO Box 2634, Menlo Park, CA 94025

Farallo, Livio (see also Sicoli, Dan; Borgatti, Robert), *SLIPSTREAM*, Slipstream Publications, Box 2071, New Market Station, Niagara Falls, NY 14301, 716-282-2616

Farley, Gay, News Editor (see also Ryan, William; Gellen, Karen), *GUARDIAN*, 33 W 17th St, New York, NY 10011, 212-691-0404

Farley, Gay, News Editor (see also Ryan, William; Gellen, Karen), Institute for Independent Social Journalism, Inc., 33 W 17th St, New York, NY 10011, 212-691-0404

Farmer, Joyce, Nanny Goat Productions, Box 845, Laguna Beach, CA 92652, (714) 494-7930

Farren, Pat, *PEACEWORK*, 2161 Massachusetts Avenue, Cambridge, MA 02140, 617-661-6130

Farris, John C., Quail Productions, Box 312, Roseland, NJ 07068, 201-992-5865

Faust, Dikko (see also Smith, Esther K.), Purgatory Pie Press, 238 Mott 4B, New York, NY 10072, 212-925-3462

Fawcett, Richard H., *August Derleth Society Newsletter*, 61 Teecomwas Drive, Uncasville, CT 06382, (203) 848-0636

Feinberg, Karen, Fiction Editor (see also Gonzalez, Lupe A.; Vitucci, Donna D.), La Reina Press, PO Box 8182, Cincinnati, OH 45208

Feingold, S. Norman, Consulting Editor, Bellman Publishing Co., PO Box 164, Arlington, MA 02174

Feingold, S. Norman, Consulting Editor, *SCHOLARSHIPS, FELLOWSHIPS & LOANS NEWS SERVICE & COUNSELORS INFORMATION SERVICES*, PO Box 164, Arlington, MA 02174, 617-648-7243

Feinstein, Karen Wolk, *URBAN & SOCIAL CHANGE REVIEW*, Boston College, McGuinn Hall, Chestnut Hill, MA 02167

Felder, Fred E., Editor, Cragmont Publications, 1308 East 38th Street, Oakland, CA 94602, 415-546-0646

Fellner, Mike (see also Edelson, Morris; Bondy, Melissa; McGilligan, Pat; Edelson, Olga), Quixote Press, 1812 Marshall, Houston, TX 77098

Ferber, Ellen (see also Fulton, Len), Dustbooks, Box 100, Paradise, CA 95969, 916-877-6110

Ferber, Ellen, Executive Editor (see also Fulton, Len; Urioste, Pat; Clifton, Merritt; Jerome, Judson), *THE SMALL PRESS REVIEW*, P.O. Box 100, Paradise, CA 95969, 916-877-6110

Ferguson, David, Editor In Chief (see also Marunas, P. Raymond; Garber, Thomas; Padol, Brian; Gateff, Amy H.; Smith, Charlotte; Goldman, Bill), *BOX 749*, Box 749, Old Chelsea Station, New York, NY 10011, 212-98-0519

Ferguson, David, Editor-in-Chief, The Printable Arts Society, Inc., Box 749, Old Chelsea Station, New York, NY 10011, (212) 989-0519

Ferguson, David, *RE:PRINT (AN OCCASIONAL MAGAZINE)*, c/o BOX 749, Box 749 Old Chelsea Station, New York, NY 10011

Ferguson, Gordon, Associate Editor (see also Glass Jr., Jesse), *CREAM CITY REVIEW*, PO Box 413, English Dept, Curtin Hall, Univ of Wisconsin, Milwaukee, WI 53201

Ferguson, Marilyn, Editor-Publisher (see also Zweig, Connie), *BRAIN/MIND BULLETIN*, P O Box 42211, Los Angeles, CA 90042, 213-223-2500

Ferguson, Marilyn, Editor-Publisher (see also Zweig, Connie), Interface Press, PO Box 42211, Los Angeles, CA 90042, 213-223-2500

Ferguson, Marilyn, Editor-Publisher (see also Zweig, Connie), *LEADING EDGE*, PO Box 42211, Los Angeles, CA 90042, 213-223-2500

Ferguson, Maurice (see also Ayyildiz, Judy; Bullins, Amanda; Nash, Valery; Sheffler, Natalie; Steinke, Paul; Weinstein, Ann), *ARTEMIS*, PO Box 945, Roanoke, VA 24005, 703-981-9318

Ferguson, Nancy (see also Ferguson, William), Metacom Press, 31 Beaver Street, Worcester, MA 01603, 617-757-1683

Ferguson, Tom, M.D., *MEDICAL SELF-CARE*, Boxx 718, Inverness, CA 94937, 415-663-8462

Ferguson, William (see also Ferguson, Nancy), Metacom Press, 31 Beaver Street, Worcester, MA 01603, 617-757-1683

Fericano, Katherine (see also Fericano, Paul F.; Langton, Roger W.), Poor Souls Press/ Scaramouche Books, PO Box 236, Millbrae, CA 94030

Fericano, Paul F. (see also Langton, Roger W.; Fericano, Katherine), *Poor Souls Press/Scaramouche Books*, PO Box 236, Millbrae, CA 94030

Ferlinghetti, Lawrence, Poetry Critic (see also Lawson, Dr. Todd; Comen, Dr. Diane; Marsic, John; Rader, Steve; Monte, Oscar; Nishi, Mio; Ginsberg, Allen; Samolis, Dr. Sam; Graham, Joan; Ramirez, Julio; Haynes, Dr. Robert; Snyder, Gary; Morris, Dr. Richard), *ALPS MONTHLY*, PO Box 99394, San Francisco, CA 94109, 415-771-3431

Ferlinghetti, Lawrence (see also Peters, Nancy J.; Sharrard, Robert), City Lights Books, 261 Columbus Ave., San Francisco, CA 94133, 415-362-8193

Ferlinghetti, Lawrence (see also Peters, Nancy J.; Sharrard, Robert), *CITY LIGHTS JOURNAL*, 261 Columbus Avenue, San Francisco, CA 94133, 415-362-8193

Feroe, Paul, Ally Press, PO Box 30340, St. Paul, MN 55175, 612-227-1567

Ferrarie, Julia (see also Carr, Dan), Four Zoas Night House Ltd., 30 Main St, PO Box 111, Ashuelot, NH 03441

Ferrier, C., Hecate Press, PO Box 99, St. Lucia, QLD 4067, Australia

Ferrier, Carole, Editor (see also Levy, Bronwen; Critchley, Cecily), *HECATE*, P.O. Box 99, St. Lucia, Queensland 4067, Australia

Fessler, Diane M., Primer Publishers, 5738 North Central, Phoenix, AZ 85012, 602-266-1043

Feuerstein, Georg, Editor-in-Chief (see also Rohe, Fred), The Dawn Horse Press, PO Box 3270, Clearlake, CA 95422, 707-994-8281

Feuerstein, Georg, Senior Editor (see also Rohe, Fred), *THE LAUGHING MAN: On the Principles and Secrets of Religion, Spirituality and Human Culture*, PO Box 3270, Clearlake, CA 95422, 707-928-5469

Field, Filip (see also Witt, Roselyn), *AGAPE*, 6940 Oporto Drive, Los Angeles, CA 90068, 213-876-6295

Fielding, Cynthia, Production (see also Cooper, Peter S.; Bean, Joyce Miller; Steger, Linda; Mitchell, Barbara), *MIDWAY REVIEW*, 3400 West 11th Street, Suite 134, Chicago, IL 60655, 312-233-6002

Fielding, Cynthia, Production (see also Cooper, Peter S.; Bean, Joyce Miller), Southwest Area Cultural Arts Council, 3400 West 11th Street, Suite 134, Chicago, IL 60655, 312-233-6002

Fielding, Cynthia, Production (see also Cooper, Peter S.; Bean, Joyce Bean), *YAWL (Young Artists & Writers of the Library)*, 3400 West 11th Street, Suite 134, Chicago, IL 60655, 312-233-6002

Fielding, P. M., *PIP COLLEGE 'HELPS' NEWSLETTER*, Box 50347, Tulsa, OK 74150, 918-584-5906

Fielding, P.M., Partners In Publishing, Box 50347, Tulsa, OK 74150, 918-584-5906

Fife, Darlene (see also Head, Robert), *STUDIES*, 104 South Jefferson Street, Lewisburg, WV 24901

Fillingham, Patricia, Warthog Press, 29 South Valley Road, West Orange, NJ 07052, 201-731-9269

Filyer, Lorraine, Managing Editor, *THIS MAGAZINE*, 70 The Esplanade, Third Floor, Toronto, Ontario M5E 1R2, Canada, 364-2431

Finch, Peter (see also Stephens, Meic), Oriel, 53 Charles St., Cardiff, Wales CF14ED, Great Britain, 0222-395548

Finch, Peter, Second Aeon Publications, 19 Southminster Road, PENYLAN, Cardiff, Wales CF2 5AT, Great Britain, 0222-493093

Finch, Vivienne (see also Pryor, William), *TANGENT*, 58 Blakes Lane, New Malden, Surrey, England KT3 6NX, England

Finch, Vivienne (see also Pryor, William), Tangent Books, 58 Blakes Lane, New Malden, Surrey, England KT3 6NX, England, 01-942-0979

Findlater, Richard, *THE AUTHOR*, 84 Drayton Gardens, London, England SW10 9SD, England

Findlater, Richard, Society Of Authors, 84, Drayton Gardens, London, England SW10 9SD, United Kingdom, 01-373-6642

Fine, Elsa Honig, *WOMAN'S ART JOURNAL*, 7008 Sherwood Drive, Knoxville, TN 37919, 615-584-7467

Finegan, T.J., Chairman (see also Godfrey, Samuel T.), *THE GOOFUS OFFICE GAZETTE*, The Goofus Office, #4 Rockland Avenue, Nanuet, NY 10954, 914-623-6154

Fingland, Randy, Prose Editor (see also Moser, N.), Illuminations Press, 2110 9th Street, Apt B, Berkeley, CA 94710, 415-849-2102

Fingland, Randy, Wingbow Press, 12929 Fifth Street, Berkeley, CA 94710, 415-549-3030

Fink, Bob, *CROSSCURRENTS*, 516 Ave K South, Saskatoon, Saskatchewan, Canada

Fink, Bob, Greenwich-Meridian, 516 Ave K So, Saskatoon Sask, Canada

Finkelstein, Kathryn (see also Finkelstein, Norman), House of Keys Press, PO Box 8940, Cincinnati, OH 45208, 513-351-3050

Finkelstein, Norman (see also Finkelstein, Kathryn), *House of Keys Press*, PO Box 8940, Cincinnati, OH 45208, 513-351-3050

Finlay, Alison (see also Snyder, Arnold), *BLACKJACK FORUM*, 2000 Center St. #1067, Berkeley, CA 94704, 415-540-5209

Finlay, Alison (see also Snyder, Arnold), R.G.E., 2000 Center St. #1067, Berkeley, CA 94704

Finley, Sara (see also Thorne, J.; McAllister, Paul W.), Three Tree Press, PO Box 10044, Lansing, MI 48901

Finnegan, James J. (see also Summers, Anthony J.; Ravens, Debi), Cornerstone Press, PO Box 28048, St. Louis, MO 63119, 314-752-3703

Finnegan, James J., Assistant Editor (see also Summers, Anthony J.; Ravens, Debi), *IMAGE MAGAZINE*, P.O. Box 28048, St. Louis, MO 63119, 314-752-3703

Firmage, Richard, Editor & Designer (see also Sanders, Ken; Brown, Marc), Dream Garden Press, 1199 Iola Avenue, Salt Lake City, UT 84104, 801-355-2154

Fischer-Galati, Stephen, *EAST EUROPEAN QUARTERLY*, Box 29 Regent Hall, University of Colorado, Boulder, CO 80309, 303-492-6157

Fish, Mara (see also Raphael, Dan), Skydog Press, 6735 S E 78th, Portland, OR 97206

Fisher, Barbara, Co-Editor (see also Spiegel, Richard), Ten Penny Players, Inc., 799 Greenwich Street, New York, NY 10014, 212-929-3169

Fisher, Barbara, Co-Editor (see also Spiegel, Richard), *WATERWAYS: Poetry in the Main Stream*, 799 Greenwich St., New York, NY 10014

Fisher, Eunice M., Managing Editor (see also McKinney, Ruth), *THE ROCKFORD REVIEW*, PO Box 858, Rockford, IL 61105, 815-962-1353

Fisher, Jocelyn, Editor (see also Garrett, Alexandra), Beyond Baroque Foundation Publications, PO Box 806, 681 Venice Blvd., Venice, CA 90291, 213-822-3006

Fisher, Jocelyn, Editor (see also Garrett, Alexandra), *MAGAZINE*, PO Box 806, Venice, CA 90291, 213-822-3006

Fisher, Thomas Michael, *STAR-WEB PAPER*, General Delivery, La Mesilla, NM 88046, 505-523-7923

Fishman, Charles, Award Editor (see also Gordon, Coco), Water Mark Press, 175 E Shore Road, Huntington Bay, NY 11743, 516-549-1150

Fitting, Frances (see also Thomson, T.L.), San Diego Publishing Company, PO Box 9222, San Diego, CA 92109, 619-698-5105

FitzGerald, Gregory, Fiction (see also Judge, Frank), *EXIT*, 50 Inglewood Dr, Rochester, NY 14619

FitzPatrick, Kevin, Editor, *LAKE STREET REVIEW*, Box 7188, Powderhorn Station, Minneapolis, MN 55407

Fitzsimmons, Thomas (see also Hargreaves Fitzsimmons, Karen), Katydid Books, c/o English Dept, Oakland University, Rochester, MI 48063

Fleeman, J.D. (see also Stanley, E.G.; Hewitt, D.), *NOTES & QUERIES: for Readers & Writers, Collectors & Librarians*, Oxford Journals, Walton Street, Oxford 0X2 6DP, England

54

Fleming, Harold, Editor,Publisher (see also Davenport, Eileen), *BLACK WILLOW POETRY*, 401 Independence Drive 'Sunrise', Towamencin Township, Harleysville, PA 19438, 215-362-5546

Fleming, Harold, Editor,Publisher (see also Davenport, Eileen), Black Willow Press, 401 Independence Drive 'Sunrise', Towamencin Township, Harleysville, PA 19438, 215-362-5546

Fleming, Lee, Art Editor, Film Reviews (see also Swift, Mary; Lang, Doug; Rosenzweig, Phyllis; Wittenberg, Clarissa), *WASHINGTON REVIEW*, P O Box 50132, Washington, DC 20004, 202-638-0515

Fleming, Ray, American Literary Editor (see also Davies, Hilary), *ARGO incorporating DELTA*, Old Fire Station, 40 George St., Oxford, England

Fletcher, Barbara (see also Fletcher, Donald), Rainbow Publications, 1493 South Columbian Way, Suite 1, Seattle, WA 98144, 206-767-4653

Fletcher, Donald (see also Fletcher, Barbara), *Rainbow Publications*, 1493 South Columbian Way, Suite 1, Seattle, WA 98144, 206-767-4653

Fletcher, Jo, Contributing Editor (see also Porter, Andrew; D'Ammassa, Don; Anderson, Kay; DiFate, Vincent; Pohl, Frederik; Silverberg, Robert; Jones, Stephen; Carmody, Larry), *SCIENCE FICTION CHRONICLE*, PO Box 4175, New York, NY 10163, 212-643-9011

Fletcher, Marjorie, President, Alice James Books, 138 Mount Auburn Street, Cambridge, MA 02138, 617-354-1408

Florence, Jerry, Co-Editor (see also Shankel-Lecrenski, Miklyn), *HARDSCRABBLE*, Blue Sheep Press, 10th & Ingersoll, Coos Bay, OR 97420, 267-3104 ext. 244

Flower, Ruth (see also Bomberger, Irvin), *DRAFT ACTION*, #534 Washington Bldg, 1435 G St. NW, Washington, DC 20005, 202-393-4870

Flynn, Richard, Editor (see also Walthall, Hugh; Pappas, Evangeline; Weber, Lilian; Weber, Ron), S.O.S. Books, 1821 Kalorama Road NW, Washington, DC 20009, 703-524-4460

Foerster, Richard, Associate Editor (see also Raiziss, Sonia; de Palchi, Alfredo; Swann, Brian), *CHELSEA*, Box 5880, Grand Central Station, New York, NY 10163

Foery, Raymond, *THE DOWNTOWN REVIEW*, 21 Vandam Street, New York, NY 10013, 212-662-0899

Fogarty, Robert, Editor (see also St. John, David; Holyoke, Tom; Miller, Nolan), *THE ANTIOCH REVIEW*, PO Box 148, Yellow Springs, OH 45387, 513-767-7386

Foldvary, Fred (see also Fulmer, Sandra), The Gutenberg Press, PO Box 26345, San Francisco, CA 94126, 415-548-3776

Foldvary, Fred E., *THE LIBERTARIAN DIGEST*, 1920 Cedar Street, Berkeley, CA 94709, 415-548-3776

Folsom, Ed, Co-Editor (see also White, William; Perlman, Jim), *WALT WHITMAN QUARTERLY REVIEW*, 308 EPB The University of Iowa, Iowa City, IA 52240, 319-353-3698; 353-5650

Folsom, Eric (see also Harrison, Jeanne; Saunders, Leslie), *NEXT EXIT*, Box 143, Tamworth, Ontario K0K 3G0, Canada, 613-379-2339

Foner, Martin F., Professional Press Corporation, PO Box 505, Lake Jem, FL 32745, 904-383-1200

Foote, A. Edward, Thornwood Book Publishers, PO Box 1442, Florence, AL 35630, 205-766-6782

Foran, Rita (see also Halldorson, Lynette), Timeless Books, P.O. Box 60, Porthill, ID 83853, 604-227-9224

Ford, E., Executive (see also Roy, Terina Lee), Edwardian Studies Association, 125 Markyate Road, Dagenham Essex RM8 2LB, England

Ford, E., *SHAW NEWSLETTER*, High Orchard, 125 Markyate Road, Dagenham, Essex RM8 2LB, England

Ford, E., Shaw Society, High Orchard, 125 Markyate Road, Dagenham, Essex RM8 2LB, England

Ford, Eric (see also Cooper-Brown, Howard), *THE BULWER LYTTON CHRONICLE*, High Orchard, 125 Markyate Rd, Dagenham, Essex RM8 2LB, England

Ford, Eric, *EDWARDIAN STUDIES,* High Orchard, 125 Markyate Road, Dagenham, Essex RM8 2LB, England

Ford, Eric (see also Clare, Robert), *EUROSHAVIAN,* 125 Markyate Rd, Dagenham, Essex RM8 2LB, England

Ford, Eric, Exec. (see also King, Royston; Cooper-Brown, Howard; Clare, Robert), High Orchard Press, 125 Markyate Road, Dagenham, Essex, England RM8 2LB, England

Ford, Eric, Exec. Editor (see also King, Royston), *WELLSIANA, The World Of H.G. Wells,* High Orchard, 125 Markyate Rd, Dagenham, Essex RM8 2LB, England

Ford-Choyke, Phyllis (see also Choyke, Arthur), *GALLERY SERIES/POETS,* 401 W. Ontario St., c/o Artcrest Products, Chicago, IL 60610

Ford-Choyke, Phyllis (see also Choyke, Arthur), Harper Square Press, c/o Artcrest Products Co., Inc., 401 W Ontario Street, Chicago, IL 60610, 312-751-1650

Fordham, Monroe, Ed. (see also Watkins, Melvin; Williams, Lillian S.), *AFRO-AMERICANS in NEW YORK LIFE & HISTORY,* PO Box 1663, Buffalo, NY 14216

Foreman, Paul (see also Robertson, Foster), Thorp Springs Press, 803 Red River, Austin, TX 78701

Foreman, R. H., Foreman Press, PO Box 7430, Glendale, CA 91205

Foriyes, Tina, Editor (see also McFarland, Ron; Snyder, Margaret; Buxton, Karen), *SNAPDRAGON,* English Department, University of Idaho, Moscow, ID 83843, 208-885-6156

Forrie, Allan (see also Sorestad, Glen; Sorestad, Sonia; O'Rourke, Paddy), Thistledown Press Ltd., 668 East Place, Saskatoon, Saskatchewan S7J2Z5, Canada, 374-1730

Fortune, Nigel (see also Olleson, Edward), *MUSIC AND LETTERS,* Oxford Journals, Walton Street, Oxford 0X2 6DP, England

Foster, Craig, Golf Sports Publishing, PO Box 3687, Lacey, WA 98503, 206-491-8067

Foster, John, Editor (see also Squires, Dana Leigh), Lost Music Network, PO Box 2391, Olympia, WA 98507, 206-352-9735

Foster, John (see also Squires, Dana Leigh), *OP: Independent Music,* PO Box 2391, Olympia, WA 98507, 206-866-7955, 352-9735

Foster, Mary E., Marilee Publications, PO Box 2351, Bonita Springs, FL 33923, 813-992-1800

Fowler, Gus (see also White, Shirley), Amistad Brands, Inc., 22 Division Ave., N.E., Washington, DC 20019, 301-593-7276

Fowler, William M., Managing Editor (see also Rhoads, Linda Smith), *THE NEW ENGLAND QUARTERLY,* 243 Meserve Hall, Northeastern University, Boston, MA 02115, 617-437-2734

Fowler, William M., Jr., Managing Editor (see also Rhoads, Linda Smith), The New England Quarterly, Inc., 243 Meserve Hall, Northeastern University, Boston, MA 02115, 617-437-2734

Fox, Bob, Publisher & Editor (see also Fox, Susan), Carpenter Press, Route 4, Pomeroy, OH 45769, 614-992-7520

Fox, C.L. (see also Mottet, Arthur L., Jr.; Elbert, N.E.), Pacific Scientific Press, Inc., 3506 Pennsylvania, Longview, WA 98632, 206-425-8592

Fox, Dr. Michael, Quarterly Committee of Queen's University, Queen's University, Kingston, Ontario K7L 3N6, Canada

Fox, Dr. Michael, *QUEEN'S QUARTERLY: A Canadian Review,* Queen's University, Kingston, Ontario K7L3N6, Canada, 613-547-6968

Fox, Howard N. (see also Messerli, Douglas), Sun & Moon Press, 4330 Hartwick Road, #418, College Park, MD 20740, 301-864-6921

Fox, Hugh, *Ghost Dance: THE INTERNATIONAL QUARTERLY OF EXPERIMENTAL POETRY,* 526 Forest, E. Lansing, MI 48823

Fox, Hugh, Ghost Dance Press, 526 Forest, E. Lansing, MI 48823

56

Fox, Hugh, Contributing Editor (see also Kruchkow, Diane; Johnson, Curt; Savitt, Lynne; Melnicove, Mark), *STONY HILLS: News & Review of the Small Press*, Weeks Mills, New Sharon, ME 04955, 207-778-3436

Fox, Jane, Director (see also Stroblas, Laurie), *CAROUSEL*, 4800 Sangamore Road, Bethesdn, MD 20816, 301-229-0930

Fox, Skip, Kore, 126 Glynnwood Avenue, Lafayette, LA 70506

Fox, Susan (see also Fox, Bob), Carpenter Press, Route 4, Pomeroy, OH 45769, 614-992-7520

Fox, William L. (see also McAllister, Bruce), West Coast Poetry Review Press, 1335 Dartmouth Dr, Reno, NV 89509, 702-322-4467

Frakes, Carol (see also Frink, Sharon; Singer, Patricia), Seaworthy Press, 4200 Wisconsin Avenue NW, Suite 106-143, Washington, DC 20016, 1983

Francia, L. (see also Tajima, Renee; Lee, C.N.; Chow, P.; Chin, R.; Chu, B.; Wu, S.; Lew, Walter; Hahn, Tomie; Kwan, S.), *BRIDGE: ASIAN AMERICAN PERSPECTIVES*, Asian Cine-Vision, Inc., 32 E Broadway, New York, NY 10002, 212-925-8685

Frank, Sheldon (see also Kostelanetz, Richard; Scobie, Stephen; Zelevansky, Paul; Higgins, Dick; Essary, Loris; Young, Karl), *PRECISELY*, PO Box 73, Canal Street, New York, NY 10013

Franklin, C., Design & Layout (see also Dutkiewicz, Adam; Brakmanis, M.; Hastwell, G.; Biggs, S.), *WORDS AND VISIONS/WAV MAGAZINE*, 499 The Parade, Magill, Australia, 08-3329529

Franklin, Robert, President, McFarland & Company, Inc., Publishers, Box 611, Jefferson, NC 28640, 919-246-4460

Franzen, Cole (see also Wellman, Don; Turner, Irene), *O.ARS*, Box 179, Cambridge, MA 02238, 617-641-1027

Fraterdeus, Peter, Epic, 1024 Judson Avenue, Lakeside Studio, Evanston, IL 60202, 312-475-8517

Fraticelli, Marco, *THE ALCHEMIST*, PO Box 123, LaSalle, Quebec H8R 3T7, Canada

Fratus, David (see also Donley, Carol), *HIRAM POETRY REVIEW*, Box 162, Hiram, OH 44234, 216-569-3211

Fratz, D. Douglas, *THRUST: Science Fiction in Review*, 8217 Langport Terrace, Gaithersburg, MD 20877, 301-948-2514

Frauenglas, Robert A., SOMRIE Press, Ryder Street Station, Box 328, Brooklyn, NY 11234, 212-763-0134

Frazer, Tony (see also Vas Dias, Robert; Robinson, Ian), *NINTH DECADE*, 52 Cascade Avenue, London N10, United Kingdom, 01-444-8591

Frazer, Tony, Shearsman Books, 47 Dayton Close, Plymouth, Devon PL6 5DX, England, 0752-779682

Frazier, Louie (see also Sussman, Art), Garcia River Press, PO Box 527, Pt. Arena, CA 95468, 707-882-9956

Frazier, Robert (see also Van Troyer, Gene), Science Fiction Poetry Assoc., 8350 Poole Avenue, Sun Valley, CA 91352, 818-768-4970

Frederick, Filis, *THE AWAKENER MAGAZINE*, 938 18th Street, Hermosa Beach, CA 90254, 213-379-2656

Frederick, Filis, The Awakener Press, 938 18th Street, Hermosa Beach, CA 90254, 213-379-2656

Freed, Teresa, *THE FOODLETTER*, 3430-D Coon Road, Gregory, MI 48137, 313-498-2633

Freedman, Reena Sigman, News Editor (see also Schneider, Susan W.; Cantor, Aviva), *LILITH*, 250 W 57th, Suite 1328, New York, NY 10019, (212) 757-0818

Freedom, Jefferson, *SEXUAL FREEDOM*, PO Box 0105, College Grove Station, San Diego, CA 92115

Freeman, Elizabeth, Crones' Own Press, 310 Driver Street, Durham, NC 27703, 919-596-7708

Freeman, Jim, Cosmotic Concerns, PO Box 3574, Granada Hills, CA 91344, 213-462-8865

Freeman, Lenore (see also Rubin, Lorna), Triad Publishing Co. Inc., 1110 NN 8th Avenue Suite C, Gainesville, FL 32601, 904-373-5308

Freeman, Stephanie Anne, Editor (see also Damon, John Edward; Rouig, Lynn), *JEOPARDY*, Western Washington University, Humanities 350, WWU, Bellingham, WA 98225

Freeman, Victoria (see also Reid, Gayla; Wachtel, Eleanor; Schendlinger, Mary; Wexler, Jeannie), *ROOM OF ONE'S OWN*, PO Box 46160, Station G, Vancouver, British Columbia V6R 4G5, Canada, 604-733-3889

Freethy, Ron, *BRITISH NATURALISTS' ASSOCIATION (PUBLISHERS)*, Thorneyholme Hall, Roughlee, Near Burnley, Lancs BB129LH, England, 66568

Freethy, Ron, *COUNTRY-SIDE*, Thorneyholme Hall, Roughlee, Near Burnley, Lancs BB129LH, England, 66568

Freilicher, Melvyn (see also Bluestein, Eleanor), *CRAWL OUT YOUR WINDOW*, 4641 Park Blvd, San Diego, CA 92116, 619-299-4859

Freundlich, Paul (see also Wenig, M. Judith; Collins, Chris; Hirsch, Audrey), *COMMUNITIES*, Box 426, Louisa, VA 23093, 703-894-5126

Freundlich, Paul (see also Wenig, M. Judith; Collins, Chris; Hirsch, Audrey), *Communities Publishing Cooperative*, Box 426, Louisa, VA 23093, 703-894-5126

Fricks, E.E., Editor, *COLLECTORS CLUB PHILATELIST*, 274 Madison Avenue, New York, NY 10016, 212-685-2250

Fricks, E.E. CCP, Editor (see also Fair, Anthony ABC), The Moretus Press, Inc., 274 Madison Avenue, New York, NY 10016, 212-685-2250

Friebert, Stuart (see also Young, David), *FIELD*, Rice Hall, Oberlin College, Oberlin, OH 44074

Fried, Emanuel, Labor Arts Books, 1064 Amherst St., Buffalo, NY 14216, 716-873-4131

Fried, Philip, Founder and Editor, *THE MANHATTAN REVIEW*, c/o Philip Fried, 304 Third Avenue, 4A, New York, NY 10010

Fried, Philip, Founder and Editor, Manhattan Review Press, c/o Philip Fried, 304 Third Avenue, 4A, New York, NY 10010

Friedland, Helen, Editor, *POETRY/LA*, Peggor Press, PO Box 84271, Los Angeles, CA 90073, 213-472-6171

Friedlander, Albert H., *EUROPEAN JUDAISM*, Kent House,, Rutland Gardens,, London SW7 1BX, England, 01-584-2754

Friedman, John S., Co-Editor (see also Gottesman, Irving), *SHANTIH*, Box 125, Bay Ridge St., Brooklyn, NY 11220

Friedman, Richard (see also Kostakis, Peter; Pearlstein, Darlene), The Yellow Press, 2394 Blue Island Ave, Chicago, IL 60608

Friedman, Robert S., The Donning Company / Publishers, 5659 Virginia Beach Blvd., Norfolk, VA 23502, 804-499-0589

Friedmann, Peggy, Project Director (see also Wilson, Sharon), *KALLIOPE, A Journal of Women's Art*, 3939 Roosevelt Blvd, Florida Junior College at Jacksonville, Jacksonville, FL 32205, 904-387-8211 or 904-387-8272

Frink, Sharon (see also Singer, Patricia; Frakes, Carol), Seaworthy Press, 4200 Wisconsin Avenue NW, Suite 106-143, Washington, DC 20016, 1983

Frisch, Annette (see also Raynes, Livia), Odin Press, PO Box 536, New York, NY 10021, 212-744-2538

Frisch, Peter, Publisher (see also McQueen, Robert I.), *THE ADVOCATE*, 1730 S. Amphlett, Suite 225, San Mateo, CA 94402, 415-573-7100

Frompovich, Catherine J. (see also Koppenhaver, April M.; Diana Witt), C J Frompovich Publications, RD 1, Chestnut Road, Coopersburg, PA 18036, 215-346-8461

Frost, Cheryl, Co-ordinating Editor (see also Perkins, E.), English Language Literature Association, English Department, James Cook University of North Quebec, Townsville 4811, Australia

Frost, Cheryl, Co-ordinating Editor (see also Perkins, E.), *LINQ,* English Dept., James Cook University of North Queensland, Townsville 4811, Australia

Frost, David Duane, Summer Stream Press, PO Box 6056, Santa Barbara, CA 93160, 805-682-4626

Frost, John, Chief Editor, *AMERICAN POETRY ANTHOLOGY,* Dept. DB-1984, Box 2279, Santa Cruz, CA 95063, 408-429-1122

Frost, John, American Poetry Association, Dept. DB-1984, Box 2279, Santa Cruz, CA 95063, 408-429-1122

Fuchs, Laurie, *LADYSLIPPER CATALOG + RESOURCE GUIDE OF RECORDS & TAPES BY WOMEN,* PO Box 3124, Durham, NC 27705, 919-683-1570

Fuchs, Laurie, Ladyslipper, Inc., PO Box 3124, Durham, NC 27705, 919-683-1570

Fudge, Gloria, Editor and Publisher (see also Hosler, Laddie), *THE WISHING WELL,* Box 117, Novato, CA 94948

Fugh-Berman, Adrianne (see also Leonard, Vickie; Douglas, Carol Anne; Lootens, Tricia; Henry, Alice; Moira, Fran; Dejanikus, Tacie; Kulp, Denise; Sorrel, Lorraine), *OFF OUR BACKS,* 1841 Columbia Road NW Rm 212, Room 212, Washington, DC 20009, 202-234-8072

Fuller, George, Jazz Press, 345-A Coral Street, Santa Cruz, CA 95060, 409-423-6275

Fulmer, Sandra (see also Foldvary, Fred), The Gutenberg Press, PO Box 26345, San Francisco, CA 94126, 415-548-3776

Fulton, Len (see also Ferber, Ellen), Dustbooks, Box 100, Paradise, CA 95969, 916-877-6110

Fulton, Len, Editor-Publisher (see also Ferber, Ellen; Urioste, Pat; Clifton, Merritt; Jerome, Judson), *THE SMALL PRESS REVIEW,* P.O. Box 100, Paradise, CA 95969, 916-877-6110

Furie, Noel (see also Miriam, Selma; Beaver, Betsey), Sanguinaria Publishing, 85 Ferris Street, Bridgeport, CT 06605, 203-576-9168

Furnival, John (see also Houedard, Dom Silvester), Openings Press, Rooksmoor House, Woodchester, Glos, England

Fusek, Serena, Associate Editor (see also Hinnebusch, Patricia Doherty), *ORPHIC LUTE,* PO Box 2815, Newport News, VA 23602

Fyri, Ragnar, *ZELOT,* Solliveien 37, 1370 Asker, Norway

G

Gaard, F. (see also Baird, A.; Rath, E.), *ARTPOLICE,* 133 E. 25th Street, Minneapolis, MN 55404, 612-825-3673

Gabbard, Dana, Editor, *THE DUCKBURG TIMES,* 400 Valleyview, Selah, WA 98942, 509-697-4634

Gabbard, D.C., Publisher (see also Woodhams, Stephen; Gabbard, Dwight C.; Overson, Beth E.; Caquelin, Anthony; Salmon-Heynemen, Jana; Goodwin, Tema; Shames, Terry; Rajfur, Ted), *FICTION MONTHLY,* Malvolio Press, 545 Haight Street, Suite 67, San Francisco, CA 94117, 415-621-1646

Gabbard, Dwight C., Bookstore Guide Editor (see also Woodhams, Stephen; Gabbard, D.C.; Overson, Beth E.; Caquelin, Anthony; Salmon-Heynemen, Jana; Goodwin, Tema; Shames, Terry; Rajfur, Ted), *FICTION MONTHLY,* Malvolio Press, 545 Haight Street, Suite 67, San Francisco, CA 94117, 415-621-1646

Gabriele, Mary (see also Michael, Ann; Small, Robert; Steptoe, Lamont B.), *HEAT,* 1220 S. 12th Street, 3rd Floor, Philadelphia, PA 19147, 215-271-6569 or 382-6644

Gach, Michael Reed, *ACUPRESSURE WORKSHOP,* 1533 Shattuck Avenue, Berkeley, CA 94709

Gadney, Alan, Editor, Festival Publications, P.O. Box 10180, Glendale, CA 91209, 213-222-8626

Gaffney, Rachel, Editor (see also Wilber, Ken), *ReVISION JOURNAL*, PO Box 316, Cambridge, MA 02238, 617-354-5827

Gaida, David J., Editor, *PLAINS CHESS*, 3003 South 119th Street West, Wichita, KS 67215

Galant, Juliette (see also Bondell, Martin), Fotofolio, Inc., 96 Spring Street, New York, NY 10012, 212-226-0923

Galasso, Al, Editorial Director (see also Schubert, Cynthia; Choate, Lon), American Bookdealers Exchange, PO Box 2525, La Mesa, CA 92041, 619-462-3297

Galasso, Al, Editorial Director (see also Schubert, Cynthia; Choate, Lon), *BOOK DEALERS WORLD*, PO Box 2525, La Mesa, CA 92041, 619-462-3297

Gale, Vi, Editor, Publisher, Prescott Street Press, PO Box 40312, Portland, OR 97240

Galef, Jack (see also Dossin, Jennifer), Elizabeth Street Press, 240 Elizabeth Street, New York, NY 10012

Gallaghan, Haj Haydar (see also Anees, M.; Bilgrami, M.; Mazandarani, Batul H.), Zahra Publications, PO Box 730, Blanco, TX 78606, 512-698-3239

Gallaghan, Haj Hayder (see also Mazandarani, Aliya B.H.), *NURADEEN*, PO Box 730, Blanco, TX 78606, 512-698-3239

Gallagher, Tess, Contributing Editor (see also Murphy, George; Carver, Raymond; Galvin, Brendan; Matthews, William; McBride, Mekeel; Mueller, Lisel), *TENDRIL*, Box 512, Green Harbor, MA 02041, 617-834-4137

Gallaher, Cynthia, *BEFORE THE RAPTURE: POETRY OF SPIRITUAL LIBERATION*, Before The Rapture Press, PO Box A3604, Chicago, IL 60690

Galt, John, Associate Editor (see also Pinsonneault, Claude; Paine, T.), *COMMON SENSE*, PO Box 650051, Miami, FL 33165, 305-937-6080

Galvin, Brendan (see also Garrett, George), *POULTRY*, Box 727, Truro, MA 02666

Galvin, Brendan, Contributing Editor (see also Murphy, George; Carver, Raymond; Gallagher, Tess; Matthews, William; McBride, Mekeel; Mueller, Lisel), *TENDRIL*, Box 512, Green Harbor, MA 02041, 617-834-4137

Galvin, Dallas (see also Cook, Diane G.H.; MacShane, Frank; Payne, Robert; Smith, William Jay), Translation, 307A Mathematics, Columbia University, New York, NY 10027, 280-2305

Galvin, Zanne T., Production Editor (see also Taylor, Duane), *ILLINOIS WRITERS REVIEW*, PO Box 562, Macomb, IL 61455, 217-357-2225

Gamble, Mort, Fiction Editor (see also De Foe, Mark; Keating, Martha; McAleavey, David; Pierce, Constance), *THE LAUREL REVIEW*, West Virginia Wesleyan College, Buckhannon, WV 26201, 304-473-8006

Gamboa, Manazar, *CHISMEARTE MAGAZINE*, 849 S. Broadway, #674, Los Angeles, CA 90014, 213-622-1411

Ganci, Joseph A., Co-Author,Editor Officer; Secretary & Treasurer (see also Ganci, Michael T.; Monti, David A.), Avanti Assocciates, Publishers Inc., 9 Marrietta Lane, Mercerville, NJ 08619

Ganci, Michael T., Co-Author,Editor & Officer; President (see also Monti, David A.; Ganci, Joseph A.), *Avanti Associates, Publishers Inc.*, 9 Marrietta Lane, Mercerville, NJ 08619

Gander, Forrest, Editor (see also Wright, C. D.), Lost Roads Publishers, PO Box 5848, Weybosset Hill Station, Providence, RI 02903, 401-941-4188

Ganick, Peter, *ABACUS*, 181 Edgemont Avenue, Elmwood, CT 06110

Ganick, Peter, Potes & Poets Press, 181 Edgemont Avenue, Elmwood, CT 06110, 203-233-2023

Garber, Thomas, Music Editor (see also Ferguson, David; Marunas, P. Raymond; Padol, Brian; Gateff, Amy H.; Smith, Charlotte; Goldman, Bill), *BOX 749*, Box 749, Old Chelsea Station, New York, NY 10011, 212-98-0519

Garcia, Martha, *WESTART,* PO Box 1396, Auburn, CA 95603, 916-885-0969

Gardiner, Linda, *THE WOMEN'S REVIEW OF BOOKS,* Wellesley College, Center For Research On Women, Wellesley, MA 02181, 617-431-1453

Gardner, Geoffrey, *THE ARK,* 106 Woodstock Street, Somerville, MA 02144

Gardner, James Louis, *JAPAN AND AMERICA: A JOURNAL OF CULTURAL STUDIES,* Pacific Insititute of Cultural Studies, PO Box 774, Pleasant Grove, UT 84062, 801-785-4353

Gardner, John, Founder (see also Rosenberg, L.M.; Higgins, Joanna), *MSS (Manuscripts),* SUNY, Binghamton, NY 13901, 607-798-2000

Garland, Margaret, Editor & Treasurer, *MIDWEST CHAPARRAL,* 1309 2nd Avenue SW, Waverly, IA 50677

Garlington, Jack, Editor (see also Shapard, Robert; Roberts, Nancy), *WESTERN HUMANITIES REVIEW,* University of Utah, Salt Lake City, UT 84112, 801-581-7438

Garren, Lois, Associate Editor (see also Aronson, Arnold; Margolis, Tina; King, Keith; Wells, Ann; Wolff, Fred M.; Rollins, Brook), *THEATRE DESIGN AND TECHNOLOGY,* 330 W. 42nd Street, New York, NY 10036, 212-563-5551

Garrett, Alexandra, Managing Editor, Fiction & Poetry (see also Fisher, Jocelyn), Beyond Baroque Foundation Publications, PO Box 806, 681 Venice Blvd., Venice, CA 90291, 213-822-3006

Garrett, Alexandra, Managing Editor, Fiction & Poetry (see also Fisher, Jocelyn), *MAGAZINE,* PO Box 806, Venice, CA 90291, 213-822-3006

Garrett, George (see also Galvin, Brendan), *POULTRY,* Box 727, Truro, MA 02666

Garrison, Thomas S., *CURRENT WORLD LEADERS,* 2074 Alameda Padre Serra, Santa Barbara, CA 93103, 805-965-5010

Garrison, Thomas S. (see also Williams, Susan; Krakowiak, Mary), International Academy at Santa Barbara, 2074 Alameda Padre Serra, Santa Barbara, CA 93103, 805-965-5010

Gartner, Audrey, Managing Editor (see also Riessman, Frank), *SOCIAL POLICY,* Room 1212, 33 W 42nd St, New York, NY 10036, 212-840-7619

Garvin, Harry R., *BUCKNELL REVIEW,* Bucknell University, Lewisburg, PA 17837, 717-524-3674

Garvy, Helen, Shire Press, PO Box 1728, Santa Cruz, CA 95061, 408-425-0842

Gaspari, Walter, Director, *FETICHE JOURNAL,* Via C. Battisti 43-24060, Chiuduno (BG), Italy

Gaston, Robin (see also Button, John; Lines, Marianna), The Findhorn Press, The Park, Forres, Morayshire 1V360TZ, Scotland, 030-93-2582

Gaston, Robyn (see also Inglis, Mary; Platts, David Earl), *ONE EARTH,* Findhorn Foundation, The Park, Forres, Morayshire 1V36 0TZ, Scotland, 030-93-2582

Gateff, Amy H. (see also Ferguson, David; Marunas, P. Raymond; Garber, Thomas; Padol, Brian; Smith, Charlotte; Goldman, Bill), *BOX 749,* Box 749, Old Chelsea Station, New York, NY 10011, 212-98-0519

Gates, J. M., *CIRCLE,* PO Box 176, Portland, OR 97207

Gates, J. M., Editor, Circle Forum, PO Box 176, Portland, OR 97207

Gay, Reginald, *BOSS,* Box 370, Madison Square Station, New York, NY 10159

Gay, Reginald, Boss Books, Box 370, Madison Square Station, New York, NY 10159

Gaylor, Annie Laurie, *THE FEMINIST CONNECTION,* PO Box 429, Madison, WI 53701, 608-256-1400, 238-3338

Gegenheimer, Albert F. (see also Crowell, Shirley), *ARIZONA QUARTERLY,* Univ. Of Arizona, Tucson, AZ 85721, Main Library B541 602-621-6396

Geiger, K. (see also Sargent, L.; Herman, E.; Walsh, S.), South End Press, 302 Columbus Avenue, Boston, MA 02116, 617-266-0629

Geiger, Loren D., *BOOMBAH HERALD,* 15 Park Boulevard, Lancaster, NY 14086

Geiselman, Lucy Ann, *MOBIUS: A Journal for Continuing Education Professionals in Health Sciences &* *Health Policy,* University of California Press, 2120 Berkeley Way, Berkeley, CA 94720, 415-642-7485

Geist, Anthony (see also Janney, Frank; Pope, Randolph), Ediciones del Norte, Box A130, Hanover, NH 03755, 603-795-2433

Gellen, Karen, Foreign Editor (see also Ryan, William; Farley, Gay), *GUARDIAN,* 33 W 17th St, New York, NY 10011, 212-691-0404

Gellen, Karen, Foreign Editor (see also Ryan, William; Farley, Gay), Institute for Independent Social Journalism, Inc., 33 W 17th St, New York, NY 10011, 212-691-0404

Gelpi, Barbara Charlesworth, Editor, *SIGNS: JOURNAL OF WOMEN IN CULTURE AND SOCIETY,* Center for Research on Women, Serra House, Stanford University, Stanford, CA 94305, 415-497-0970

Geltrich, Brigitta, Senior Editor, Creative With Words Publications (CWW), PO Box 223226, Carmel, CA 93922, 408-625-3542

Genis, Alexandro M., Manager, Summit University Press, Box A, Malibu, CA 90265, 213-991-4751

Gennrich, Suzanne J., Fiction (see also Rumsey, Anne M.), *THE MADISON REVIEW,* Dept of English, H.C. White Hall, 600 N. Park Street, Madison, WI 53706, 263-3303

Gentleman, Dorothy Corbett (see also Brockway, R.; Brockway, Katie; West, Linda; Blanar, Mike; Hanly, Ken; Blaikie, John), Pierian Press, 5, Brandon University, Brandon, Manitoba, Canada, 727-2577

Gentleman, Dorothy Corbett (see also Brockway, R.; Brockway, Katie; West, Linda; Blanar, Mike; Hanly, Ken; Blaikie, John), *PIERIAN SPRING,* 5, Brandon University, Brandon, Manitoba, Canada, 727-2577

Georgakas, Dan (see also Crowdus, Gary; Rubenstein, Lenny), *CINEASTE MAGAZINE,* 200 Park Avenue South, Room 1320, New York, NY 10003

Georgakas, Dan (see also Bokhara, Elias; Janda, Judy), Smyrna Press, Box 1803 GPO, Brooklyn, NY 11202

George, Anne (see also Beck, Jerri), Druid Press, 2724 Shades Crest Road, Birmingham, AL 35216, 205-933-7974

George, Barbara, Editor, Velo-News Corporation, Box 1257, Brattleboro, VT 05301, 802-254-2305

George, C. William, Ed.-Publ., *AGAINST THE WALL,* PO Box 444, Westfield, NJ 07091, 201-233-4082

George, C. William, Editor, Publisher, Porcupine Productions, PO Box 444, Westfield, NJ 07091, 201-233-4082

George, Kathi, Editor, *FRONTIERS: A Journal of Women Studies,* c/o Women Studies, University of Colorado, Boulder, CO 80309, 303-492-5065

George, Margaret (see also Emuss, John; Pain, Margaret; James, Susan), Guildford Poets Press, 9 White Rose Lane, Woking, Surrey, GU22 73A, England

George, Margaret (see also Emuss, John; Pain, Margaret; James, Susan), *WEYFARERS,* 9 Whiterose Lane, Woking, Surrey, England

George Peffer, Poetry (see also Villani, Jim; Sayre, Rose; Murcko, Terry), Pig Iron Press, P.O. Box 237, Youngstown, OH 44501

Georges, T.M., Syntax Publications, 4419 Driftwood Place, Boulder, CO 80301, 303-530-2692

Gershator, David (see also Gershator, Phillis), Downtown Poets Co-op, G.P.O. Box 1720, Brooklyn, NY 11202

Gershator, Phillis (see also Gershator, David), *Downtown Poets Co-op,* G.P.O. Box 1720, Brooklyn, NY 11202

Gerstein, Marvin, Director, Red Herring Press, c/o Channing-Murray Foundation, 1209 W. Oregon, Urbana, IL 61801, 217-367-8770

Gerstle, Susan Linda (see also Buttaci, Sal St. John), New Worlds Unlimited, PO Box 556, Saddle Brook, NJ 07662

Gibbons, Reginald, Editor (see also LaRusso, Joseph; Penlongo, Bob; Hahn, Susan), *TRIQUAR-TERLY*, 1735 Benson Avenue, Northwestern Univ., Evanston, IL 60201, 312-492-3490

Gibbs, Michael, Kontexts Publications, Overtoom 444, 1054 JW Amsterdam, The Netherlands, 020-836665

Gibbs, Robert, Poetry Editor (see also Conway, Don; Trethewey, Eric; Hawkes, Robert; Butlin, Ron; Taylor, Michael; Thompson, Kent; Davey, Bill; Boyles, Ann; Bauer, William), *THE FIDDLEHEAD*, The Observatory, Univ. New Brunswick, PO Box 4400, Fredericton, NB E3B 5A3, Canada, 506-454-3591

Gibson, Becky Gould, Poetry Editor (see also Shar, Bob), *THE CRESCENT REVIEW*, PO Box 15065, Winston-Salem, NC 27103, 919-768-5943

Gibson, Brenda, Markets Editor (see also Osborne, Anne; Martindale, Sheila; Hancock, Geoff; Thom, Heather; Lennard, Susan), *CANADIAN AUTHOR & BOOKMAN*, 25 Ryerson Aveune, 131 Bloor Street W, Toronto, Ontario M5t 2P3, Canada, 416-364-4203

Gidley, Mick, *AMERICAN ARTS PAMPHLET SERIES*, Queens Bldg., Univ. of Exeter, Exeter EX4 4QH, England

Gilbert, Elliot, Editor (see also Swanson, Robert; Schell, Nixa), *THE CALIFORNIA QUARTERLY*, 100 Sproul Hall, Univ of Calif, Davis, CA 95616

Gilbert, Herman C., Executive Vice President (see also Johnson, Bennett J.), Path Press, Inc., 53 West Jackson Blvd Suite 1040, Chicago, IL 60604, 312-663-0167

Gilborn, Alice, Editor (see also Carroll, Jane), *BLUELINE*, Blue Mountain Lake, NY 12812, 518-352-7365

Giles, Mary E., Editor (see also Hohlwein, Kathryn), *STUDIA MYSTICA*, Calif. State Univ., 6000 J Street, Sacramento, CA 95819

Gill, Elaine (see also Gill, John), The Crossing Press, 17 W Main Street Box 640, Trumansburg, NY 14886, 607-387-6217

Gill, Joan E., President, Grapetree Productions, Inc., Box 10CN, 600 Grapetree Drive, Key Biscayne, FL 33149, 361-2060

Gill, John (see also Gill, Elaine), The Crossing Press, 17 W Main Street Box 640, Trumansburg, NY 14886, 607-387-6217

Gill, Stephen, Editor-in-Chief, Vesta Publications Limited, PO Box 1641, Cornwall, Ont. K6H 5V6, Canada, 613-932-2135

Gill, Stephen, Editor, *WRITER'S LIFELINE*, PO Box 1641, Cornwall, Ont. K6H 5V6, Canada

Gill, Ursula, Art Editor (see also Strahan, Bradley R.; Sullivan, Shirley G.; Black, Harold), *VISIONS*, 4705 South 8th Road, Arlington, VA 22204, 703-521-0142

Gillan, Maria, Editor, *FOOTWORK MAGAZINE*, Passaic County Community College, College Boulevard, Paterson, NJ 07509, 201-279-5000ext. 219

Gillett, J.T. (see also Gross, Alfred), Homunculus Press, Box 27, Deadwood, OR 97430, 503-964-3554

Gillies, Marilyn J., Publisher, Earth-Song Press, 202 Hartnell Place, Sacramento, CA 95825, 916-927-6863

Gilliland, Hap, Council For Indian Education, PO Box 31215, Billings, MT 59107, 252-1800

Gilman, Robert, *IN CONTEXT: A Quarterly of Humane Sustainable Culture*, PO Box 215, Sequim, WA 98382, 206-683-4411

Ginsberg, Allen, Assistant Editor-at-Large (see also Lawson, Dr. Todd; Comen, Dr. Diane; Marsic, John; Rader, Steve; Monte, Oscar; Nishi, Mio; Samolis, Dr. Sam; Graham, Joan; Ferlinghetti, Lawrence; Ramirez, Julio; Haynes, Dr. Robert; Snyder, Gary; Morris, Dr. Richard), *ALPS MONTHLY*, PO Box 99394, San Francisco, CA 94109, 415-771-3431

Giorno, John, *DIAL-A-POEM POETS LP'S*, 222 Bowery, New York, NY 10012, 212-925-6372

Giorno, John, Giorno Poetry Systems Records, 222 Bowery, New York City, NY 10012

Giovannini, Carolyn (see also McGovern, Jack), The Rubicon Press, 5638 Riverdsle Road S, Salem, OR 97302

Girard-Corkum, Jerria, Ph.D. (see also Corkum, Collin J., Ph.D.), BrainStorm Books, PO Box 1407, Tustin, CA 92681, 714-731-4802

Giscombe, C.S., Editor, *EPOCH*, 245 Goldwin Smith Hall, Cornell Univ., Ithaca, NY 14853, 607-256-3385

Glancy, Diane, Myrtle Wood, 1610 S. Quaker, Tulsa, OK 74120, 918-299-9535

Glass Jr., Jesse, Editor (see also Ferguson, Gordon), *CREAM CITY REVIEW*, PO Box 413, English Dept, Curtin Hall, Univ of Wisconsin, Milwaukee, WI 53201

Glazer, Irvin R. (see also Headley, Robert), *MARQUEE*, 624 Wynne Road, Springfield, PA 19064, 215-543-8378

Glazier, Loss (see also Riley, Jan), *ORO MADRE*, 4429 Gibraltar Drive, Fremont, CA 94536, 415-797-9096

Glazier, Loss (see also Riley, Jan), Ruddy Duck Press, 4429 Gibraltar Drive, Fremont, CA 94536, 415-797-9096

Glean, Katherine B. (see also Manthe, George L.), Cube Publications Inc, 1 Buena Vista Road, Port Jefferson, NY 11777, 516-331-4990

Gleeson, Andrew (see also Davis, Mark), *ON DIT*, PO Box 498, Adelaide 5001, Australia, 223-2685

Glenn, Peggy, Aames-Allen Publishing Co., 924 Main Street, Huntington Beach, CA 92648, 714-536-4926

Glick, Wendell, Co-Editor (see also Dolan, John M.), *THOREAU QUARTERLY*, 355 Ford Hall, Univ of Minnesota, 224 Church Street SE, Minneapolis, MN 55455, 612-373-3612

Glover, Jon (see also Silkin, Jon; Wainwright, Jeffrey), Northern House, 179 Wingrove Road, Newcastle upon Tyne NE49DA, England

Glynn, Patrick, Editor (see also Chickering, A. Lawrence; Lammi, Walter J.), Institute for Contemporary Studies, 785 Market Street, Suite 750, San Francisco, CA 94103, 415-543-6213

Glynn, Patrick, Editor (see also Chickering, A. Lawrence; Lammi, Walter J.), *JOURNAL OF CONTEMPORARY STUDIES*, 785 Market Street, Suite 750, San Francisco, CA 94103, 415-543-6213

Glynn, Thomas, Co-Director (see also Leyner, Mark; White, Curtis), Fiction Collective, Inc., Brooklyn College, Dept. of English, Brooklyn, NY 11210, 212-780-5547

Gocek, Matilda A., Library Research Associates, RD #5, Box 41, Dunderberg Road, Monroe, NY 10950, 914-783-1144

Godbert, G. H., *ONLY POETRY*, 121 Gloucester Place, London W1, England

Godbert, Geoffrey, Only Poetry Publications, 121 Gloucester Place, London W1, England

Godbert, Geoffrey (see also Ramsay, Jay; Paskin, Sylvia), *THE THIRD EYE*, 3 South Villas, Camden Square, London NW1, England

Godfrey, Ellen (see also Godfrey, W.D.; Sterling, Sharon; Truscott, Gerry; Allen, Kelly), Press Porcepic Limited, 235-560 Johnson St., Victoria, B.C. V8W 3C6, Canada, 604-381-5502

Godfrey, Samuel T., Chief-of-Stuff (see also Finegan, T.J.), *THE GOOFUS OFFICE GAZETTE*, The Goofus Office, #4 Rockland Avenue, Nanuet, NY 10954, 914-623-6154

Godfrey, W.D. (see also Godfrey, Ellen; Sterling, Sharon; Truscott, Gerry; Allen, Kelly), Press Porcepic Limited, 235-560 Johnson St., Victoria, B.C. V8W 3C6, Canada, 604-381-5502

Goebel, Robert, Associate Editor (see also Rogers, Steven B.), Rainfeather Press, 3201 Taylor Street, Mt. Rainier, MD 20712

Goebel, Robert, Assisant Editor (see also Rogers, Steven B.), *ROADRUNNER-BIO: A Broadside Series*, 3201 Taylor Street, Mt. Rainier, MD 20712

Gogal, John M, *AMERICAN INDIAN BASKETRY*, PO Box 66124, Portland, OR 97266, 503-771-8540

Gogol, John M., Institute for the Study of Traditional American Indian Arts Press, PO Box 66124, Portland, OR 97266, 503-771-8540

Gogol, John M. (see also Davies, Robert A.), *MR. COGITO*, PO Box 627, Pacific University, Forest Grove, OR 97116, 503-357-6151 ext 250

Gogol, John M. (see also Davies, Robert A.), Mr. Cogito Press, U C Box 627, Pacific University, Forest Grove, OR 97116

Goines, David Lance, Saint Heironymous Press, Inc., PO Box 9431, Berkeley, CA 94709, 415-549-1405

Gold, Alexander, Assistant Editor (see also Betz, Daniel R.), Ansuda Publications, Box 158, Harris, IA 51345

Gold, Alexander, Assistant Editor (see also Betz, Daniel R.), *THE PUB*, Box 158, Harris, IA 51345

Gold, Doris B., Editor, Publisher, Biblio Press, PO Box 22, Fresh Meadows, NY 11365, 212-361-3141

Gold, Herman, Co-Editor (see also Holley, Barbara), *EARTHWISE: A Journal of Poetry*, PO Box 680-536, Miami, FL 33168

Gold, Herman, Co-Editor (see also Holley, Barbara), Earthwise Publications, PO Box 680-536, Miami, FL 33168, 305-688-8558

Gold, Herman, Co-Editor (see also Holley, Barbara), *TEMPEST: Avant-Garde Poetry*, PO Box 680-536, Miami, FL 33168, 305-688-8558

Goldberg, Jay (see also Mcelhearn, Kirk), *BOGUS REVIEW*, 120 West 97th Street #10A, New York, NY 10025, 222-1731

Goldberg, Jay (see also Mcelhearn, Kirk), Bogusbooks, 120 West 97th Street #10A, New York, NY 10025

Goldberg, S. L., Editor (see also Tomlinson, T. B.), *THE CRITICAL REVIEW*, History of Ideas Unit, Australian National University, G.P.O. Box 4, Canberra, A.C.T. 2601, Australia

Golden, Michael, Editor, Black Market Press, 1516 Beverly Road, Brooklyn, NY 11226, 212-856-3643

Golden, Michael, Editor (see also Elias, Viki; Harrison, Jim; Mungo, Raymond; Bukowski, Charles; Placidus, Max; Codrescu, Andrei; Horotwitz, Mikhail; Ligi; Kramer, Glenn; Mitchell, Donna; Riedel, Robert), *SMOKE SIGNALS*, 1516 Beverly Road, Brooklyn, NY 11226

Golden, Sandy, Editor, Quince Mill Books, 21 Quince Mill Court, Gaithersburg, MD 20878, 301-840-0081

Goldfarb, Reuven, Editor (see also Goldfarb, Yehudit; Grafstein, Sarah Leah), *AGADA*, 2020 Essex Street, Berkeley, CA 94703, 415-848-0965

Goldfarb, Yehudit, Associate Editor (see also Goldfarb, Reuven; Grafstein, Sarah Leah), *AGADA*, 2020 Essex Street, Berkeley, CA 94703, 415-848-0965

Goldman, Bill (see also Ferguson, David; Marunas, P. Raymond; Garber, Thomas; Padol, Brian; Gateff, Amy H.; Smith, Charlotte), *BOX 749*, Box 749, Old Chelsea Station, New York, NY 10011, 212-98-0519

Goldman, Liela, *SAUL BELLOW JOURNAL*, 6533 Post Oak Drive, West Bloomfield, MI 48033

Goldman, Richard (see also Dellutri, Mary; Lennon, Nancy), *RAMBUNCTIOUS REVIEW*, Rambunctious Press, Inc., 1221 West Pratt, Chicago, IL 60626

Goldman, Susan, Assoc. Editor (see also Burnstein, Saul), New Bedford Press, 5800 W Century Blvd., Suite 91502, Los Angeles, CA 90009, 837-2961

Goldsmith, P.A. (see also Burton, Mary A.), Golden Sails Press, 6263 Cahaba Valley Road, Birmingham, AL 35243, 205-991-5548

Goldsmith, P.A. (see also Burton, Mary A.), *SHADOW VOYAGES*, 6263 Cahaba Valley Road, Birmingham, AL 35243, 205-991-5548

Goldstein, Laurence, *MICHIGAN QUARTERLY REVIEW*, 3032 Rackham Bldg., University of Michigan, Ann Arbor, MI 48109, 313-764-9265

Golz, Jon L., Spirit Press, PO Box 69, Altamonte Springs, FL 32715, 305-339-9324

Gomez-Quinones, Juan (see also McKenna, Teresa; Macias, Reynaldo; Romero, Annelisa), *AZTLAN: International Journal of Chicano Studies Research*, University of California-Los Angeles, 405 Hilgard Avenue, Los Angeles, CA 90025, 213-825-2642

Gomez-Quinones, Juan (see also McKenna, Teresa; Macias, Reynaldo F.; Romero, Annelisa), Chicano Studies Research Center Publications, University of California-Los Angeles, 405 Hilgard Avenue, Los Angeles, CA 90024, 213-825-2642

Gompertz, Mark, The Overlook Press, Route 212, PO Box 427, Woodstock, NY 12498, 914-679-6838

Gompertz, Rolf, The Wordoctor Publications, PO Box 9761, North Hollywood, CA 91609, 818-980-3576/818-763-2224

Gonzales, Christopher A., Editor, *CONCEPTIONS SOUTHWEST*, University of New Mexico, Box 20 UNM Post Office, Albuquerque, NM 87131, 505-277-5656

Gonzalez, Lupe A., Publisher, Editor (see also Feinberg, Karen; Vitucci, Donna D.), La Reina Press, PO Box 8182, Cincinnati, OH 45208

Goode, J. Norman, *MICRO MOONLIGHTER NEWSLETTER*, 4121 Buckthorn Ct., Lewisville, TX 75028, 615-539-1115

Goodell, Larry, Duende Press, Box 571, Placitas, NM 87043, 505-867-5877/262-1619

Goodknight, Glen H. (see also Speth, Lee), *MYTHLORE*, PO Box 4671, Whittier, CA 90607

Goodman, Arifa, Guest Editor (see also Graham, Munir), *THE MESSAGE*, Route 15 Box 270, Tucson, AZ 85715, 505-988-4411

Goodman, Michael (see also Super, Gary Lee), Nexus Press, 608 Ralph McGill Boulevard N.E., Atlanta, GA 30312, (404) 577-3579

Goodson, Arthur, Ed. Director (see also Zekowski, Arlene; Berne, Stanley; Zaage, Herman), Berne, PO Box 5645, Coronado Station, Santa Fe, NM 87502, 505-356-4082

Goodwin, Tema, Copy Editor (see also Woodhams, Stephen; Gabbard, D.C.; Gabbard, Dwight C.; Overson, Beth E.; Caquelin, Anthony; Salmon-Heynemen, Jana; Shames, Terry; Rajfur, Ted), *FICTION MONTHLY*, Malvolio Press, 545 Haight Street, Suite 67, San Francisco, CA 94117, 415-621-1646

Goossens, Elisabeth (see also Miner, Tom), *PINCHPENNY*, 4851 Q Street, Sacramento, CA 95819, 916-451-3042

Gordon, Bonnie (see also Kaplan, Edward), *SAPIENS*, PO Box 209, Millburn, NJ 07041

Gordon, Bonnie (see also Kaplan, Edward), Sapiens Press, 3704 Hyde Park Avenue, Cincinnati, OH 45209

Gordon, Coco (see also Fishman, Charles), Water Mark Press, 175 E Shore Road, Huntington Bay, NY 11743, 516-549-1150

Gordon, M. (see also Daniels, P.; Ehrenfeld, H.), *THE FOUR ZOAS JOURNAL OF POETRY & LETTERS*, 30 Main St, PO Box 111, Ashuelot, NH 03441

Gordon, Paul, Assistant Editor (see also Poole, Robert, Jr.; Marti, Eric), *FRONTLINES*, Box 40105, Santa Barbara, CA 93103, 805-963-5993

Gordon, Rebecca (see also Donnelly, Margarita; Malone, Ruth; Wendt, Ingrid; Wilner, Eleanor; Thompson, Joyce; Caday, Jan; Mclean, Cheryl; Domitrovich, Lisa; Jenkins, Meredith), *CALYX: A Journal of Art and Literature by Women*, PO Box B, Corvallis, OR 97339, 503-753-9384

Gordon, Rebecca (see also Adams, Jan; Johanna, Betty; Meyerding, Jane), *LESBIAN CONTRADIC-TION-A Journal of Irreverent Feminism*, 584 Castro Street, Suite 263, San Francisco, CA 94114

Gore, Tom, Open Space Gallery Photographic Series, PO Box 5207 Station B, Victoria, B.C., V8R 6N4, Canada, 604-383-8833

Gore, Tom, Photography at Open Space, P O Box 5207 Stn B, Victoria BC V8R 6N4, Canada, 604-383-8833

Gorham, Daniel J., *AXIOS,* 800 South Euclid Avenue, Fullerton, CA 92634

Gorham, Daniel J. (see also Magnin, Joseph T.), Axios Newletter, Inc., 800 South Euclid Avenue, Fullerton, CA 92634

Gorham, Daniel J., *GORHAM,* 800 South Euclid Street, Fullerton, CA 92632, 714-526-2131

Gorham, Daniel J., *THE VORTEX (A Historical and Wargamers Jornal),* 800 South Euclid Street, Fullerton, CA 92632, 714-526-2131

Gorka, John (see also Moss, Mark; Eilenberg, Jeff), *SING OUT! The Folk Song Magazine,* PO Box 1071, Easton, PA 18042, 215-253-8105

Gorman, Neal E. (see also Wesolowski, Paul G.; Dixon, Peter), *THE FREEDONIA GAZETTE,* Darien B-28 at Village II, New Hope, PA 18938, 215-862-9734

Gormezan, Keith S., Editor, *LE BEACON REVIEW,* c/o Keith S. Gormezano, 2921 E Madison #7, Seattle, WA 98112, 206-322-1431

Gormezano, Keith, Publisher, Editor-in-Chief, Le Beacon Presse, 2921 E Madison #7 IDLMSP, Seattle, WA 98112

Gormezano, Keith, *GORMEZANO'S BOOK REVIEW FOR LIBRARIES AND BOOKSTORES,* 2921 E Madison #7 IDUMSP, Seattle, WA 98112

Gormezano, Shabatai D., Editor, *M'GODOLIM: THE JEWISH LITERARY MAGAZINE,* 2921 E Madison #7, Seattle, WA 98112, 206-322-1431

Gorton, Gregg (see also Reimers, Ronald), *PRAXIS: A Journal of Cultural Criticism,* PO Box 1280, Santa Monica, CA 90406

Gosciak, J.G. (see also Kenny, Maurice), *CONTACT/11: A Bimonthly Poetry Review Magazine,* PO Box 451, Bowling Green Station, New York, NY 10004, 212-425-5979 or 212-522-3227

Gosciak, J.G. (see also Kenny, Maurice), Contact II: Publications, PO Box 451, Bowling Green Station, New York, NY 10004, 212-522-3227

Gosney, Michael (see also Lapolla, Paul; Tobias, Michael), Avant Books, 3719 Sixth Avenue, San Diego, CA 92103, 619-295-0473

Gottesman, Irving, Co-Editor (see also Friedman, John S.), *SHANTIH,* Box 125, Bay Ridge St., Brooklyn, NY 11220

Gottstein, Ruth, Volcano Press, Inc, 330 Ellis Street, San Francisco, CA 94102, 415-664-5600

Gould, Bruce, Bruce Gould Publications, PO Box 16, Seattle, WA 98111, 284-6144

Gould, Eric, Editor (see also Richardson Jr, Robert D.), *DENVER QUARTERLY,* University of Denver, Denver, CO 80208, 303-753-2869

Gould, Roberta C., *LIGHT: A Poetry Review,* PO Box 380, High Falls, NY 12440

Gove, Jim, Editor (see also Mitchell, Charles; Leddy, Chris), *MINOTAUR,* P.O. Box 4094, Burlingame, CA 94010

Govig, Valerie, Publisher & Editor, Aeolus Press, Inc., 7106 Campfield Road, Baltimore, MD 21207, 301-484-6287

Govig, Valerie, Publisher & Editor, *KITE LINES,* 7106 Campfield Road, Baltimore, MD 21207, 301-484-6287

Gowdy, Anne R., Editorial Assistant (see also Corey, Orlin), Anchorage Press, Inc., Box 8067, New Orleans, LA 70182, 504-283-8868

Gowland, E., National Behavior Systems, 11601 Balboa Blvd., Granada Hills, CA 91344, 213-363-7160

Grace, Marian (see also Carothers, Joel), Blazon Books, 1934 West Belle Plaine, Chicago, IL 60613, 312-975-0317

Grady, Wayne, Managing Editor (see also Smith, Michael), *BOOKS IN CANADA: A National Review Of Books*, 366 Adelaide St East, Toronto, Ontario M5A 3X9, Canada, 416-363-5426

Graf, Jess, Mountain Cat Press, 14 Washington #1, Denver, CO 80203

Graf, Jess, *MOUNTAIN CAT REVIEW*, 14 Washington #1, Denver, CO 80203

Grafstein, Sarah Leah, Art Director (see also Goldfarb, Reuven; Goldfarb, Yehudit), *AGADA*, 2020 Essex Street, Berkeley, CA 94703, 415-848-0965

Gragert, Steven K., Managing Editor (see also Evans, Robert L.), Evans Publications Inc., 133 S. Main, PO Box 520, Perkins, OK 74059, 405-547-2144

Graham, Chael (see also Prochak, Michael), & (Ampersand) Press, Michael S. Prochak, 141 Barrack Street, Colchester, Essex, United Kingdom

Graham, Chael, Co-Editor (see also Prochak, Michael S.), *STARDANCER*, 141 Barracks Street, Colchester, Essex, England

Graham, Joan, Television Associate (see also Lawson, Dr. Todd; Comen, Dr. Diane; Marsic, John; Rader, Steve; Monte, Oscar; Nishi, Mio; Ginsberg, Allen; Samolis, Dr. Sam; Ferlinghetti, Lawrence; Ramirez, Julio; Haynes, Dr. Robert; Snyder, Gary; Morris, Dr. Richard), *ALPS MONTHLY*, PO Box 99394, San Francisco, CA 94109, 415-771-3431

Graham, Joan, Contributing Editor (see also Comen, Diane; Lawson, Todd S.J.; Marsic, John; Samolis, William; Comen, Diane; Rader, Steve), Peace & Pieces Press, Box 99394, San Francisco, CA 94109, 415-771-3431

Graham, Munir, Editor (see also Goodman, Arifa), *THE MESSAGE*, Route 15 Box 270, Tucson, AZ 85715, 505-988-4411

Grande, Frank D., President (see also Paolucci, Anne; Paolucci, Henry), Griffon House Publications, PO Box 81, Whitestone, NY 11357

Gransden, Dr. Antonia, *NOTTINGHAM MEDIEVAL STUDIES*, The University, Nottingham NG7 2RD, England

Grant, C.D. (see also Johnston, Gary), Blind Beggar Press, Box 437, Bronx, NY 10467

Graubard, Stephen R., Editor, *DAEDALUS, Journal of the American Academy of Arts and Sciences,* American Academy of Arts and Sciences, 136 Irving Street, Cambridge, MA 02138, 617-491-2600

Gravelle, Barbara, Literary Editor (see also Lumpkin, Kirk; Bertolet, Bebe), *ZYGA MAGAZINE ASSEMBLAGE*, PO Box 7452, Oakland, CA 94601, 415-261-6837

Gravelle, Barbara, Literary Editor (see also Lumpkin, Kirk; Bertolet, Bebe), Zyga Multimedia Research, PO Box 7452, Oakland, CA 94601, 415-261-6837

Gravelle, Carolyn, *aag-aag!*, Box G, Kendrick, ID 83537, 208-289-5731

Gray, Don (see also Kahn, Dr. Sy M.), Sydon, Inc., c/o Drama Dept, University of the Pacific, Stockton, CA 95211

Graziano, Frank, Editor (see also Graziano, Laura H.), Logbridge - Rhodes, Inc., PO Box 3254, Durango, CO 81301, 303-259-3271

Graziano, Laura H., Managing Editor (see also Graziano, Frank), *Logbridge - Rhodes, Inc.*, PO Box 3254, Durango, CO 81301, 303-259-3271

Green, David, Clover Press, Box 3236, Regina, Saskatchewan S4P 3H1, Canada

Green, David, *GREEN'S MAGAZINE*, Box 3236, Regina, Saskatchewan S4P 3H1, Canada

Green, Dr. J.C.R., The Moorlands Press/Anne Johnston, 11 Novi Lane, Leek, Staffs ST13 6NS, England

Green, Frances, *GAYELLOW PAGES*, Box 292 Village Station, New York, NY 10014, 212-929-7720

Green, James, Director, Johnston Green & Co. (Publishers) Ltd., PO Box 1, Portree, Isle of Skye, Scotland

Green, J.C.R. (see also Edwards, Michael), Aquila Publishing, PO Box 1, Portree, Isle of Skye, Scotland

Green, J.C.R., Managing Editor (see also Neill, William), Club Leabhar, PO Box 1, Portree, Isle of Skye, Scotland

Green, J.C.R., Editor, *INTERNATIONAL REVIEW*, PO Box 1, Portree, Isle of Skye, Scotland

Green, J.C.R., Editor, *PRINTERS PIE*, PO Box 1, Portree, Isle of Skye, Scotland

Green, J.C.R. (see also Edwards, Michael), *PROSPICE*, PO Box 1, Isle of Skye, Portree, IV51 9BT, England

Green, Lewis (see also Burton, Brenda), New Horizons Publishers, 737 Tenth Avenue East, Seattle, WA 98102, 206-323-1102

Green, Marilyn (see also Fanning, Robbie), Fibar Designs, P.O.Box 2634, Menlo Park, CA 94026, 415-323-2549

Green, Marilyn (see also Fanning, Robbie), *OPEN CHAIN*, PO Box 2634, Menlo Park, CA 94025

Green, Martin, Co-Editor (see also Cummins, Walter; Keyishian, Harry), *THE LITERARY REVIEW*, Fairleigh Dickinson University, 285 Madison Avenue, Madison, NJ 07940, 201 377-4050

Green, Paul, *LOOT*, 83(b) London Road, Peterborough, Cambs, England

Green, Paul, *SPECTACULAR DISEASES*, 83(b) London Road, Peterborough, Cambs, England

Green, Perry John, Assistant Editor (see also Walker, William D.; Griggs, Lonnie R.), *JOINT ENDEAVOR*, PO Box 32, Huntsville, TX 77340

Green, Samuel, Co-Publisher (see also Birtch, Sara), Jawbone Press, Waldron Island, WA 98297

Green, Stefanie, Art Director (see also Lehman, David; Black, Joel; Hartley, Glen T.), Nobodaddy Press, 159 Ludlowville Road, Lansing, NY 14882

Green, Stefanie (see also Lehman, David; Black, Joel; Hartley, Glen T.), *POETRY IN MOTION*, 159 Ludlowville Road, Lansing, NY 14882

Green, Theo (see also O'Rourke, Seamus), Inkblot Press, 439-49th Street #11, Oakland, CA 94609, 415-652-7127

Green, Theo (see also O'Roarke, Seamus), *INKBLOT*, 439-49th Street #11, Oakland, CA 94609, 415-652-7127

Greenberg, Harry (see also Zirlin, Larry; Ziegler, Alan), Release Press, 411 Clinton Street, Apt 8, Brooklyn, NY 11231

Greenberg, Sidney, Bridgeberg Books, 245 N. Ridgewood Place #1C, Los Angeles, CA 90004, 213-469-9972

Greene, Jacqueline, Pascal Publishers, 21 Sunnyside Avenue, Wellesley, MA 02181, 617-235-4278

Greene, Stephanie, Managing Editor (see also Brooks, Marshall), Arts End Books, Box 162, Newton, MA 02168, 617-965-2478

Greene, Stephanie, Managing Editor (see also Brooks, Marshall), *NOSTOC*, Box 162, Newton, MA 02168

Greenfield, Deborah, Managing Editor, The George Whittell Memorial Press, 3722 South Avenue, Youngstown, OH 44502

Greenwald, Roger (see also Lush, Richard M.), Anjou, PO Box 322 Station P, Toronto Ontario, Canada, 416-368-9739

Greenwald, Roger, Editor (see also Lush, Richard M), *WRIT* , Two Sussex Avenue, Toronto, Canada, 416-978-4871

Greenwood, Judy (see also Greenwood, Larry), Willowood Press, PO Box 22321, Lexington, KY 40522, 606-272-5693

Greenwood, Larry (see also Greenwood, Judy), *Willowood Press*, PO Box 22321, Lexington, KY 40522, 606-272-5693

Greenwood, William, Green Horse Press, 471 Carr Avenue, Aromas, CA 95004, 408-726-1705

Greer, Jane, *PLAINS POETRY JOURNAL (PPJ)*, Box 2337, Bismarck, ND 58502

Greer, Jane, Stronghold Press, Box 2337, Bismarck, ND 58502

Gregory, Libby, *COLUMBUS FREE PRESS*, Box 3162, Columbus, OH 43210, 299-2497

Gregory, Michael (see also Dietz, Chris; Thornton, Elizabeth), The Bisbee Press Collective, Drawer HA, Bisbee, AZ 85617

Gregory, Michael, The Mother Duck Press, Rt. 1, Box 25A, McNeal, AZ 85617

Greig, J., Rose Publications, PO Box 35033, Tucson, AZ 85740, 602-297-3606

Greisman, David, *ABBEY*, 5360 Fallriver Row Court, Columbia, MD 21044

Grey, Robert W., Editor, *SOUTHERN POETRY REVIEW*, Department of English, Univ of North Carolina, Charlotte, Charlotte, NC 28223, 704-597-4225

Gribble, Dorothy Rose, Director of Productions, *PLANTAGENET PRODUCTIONS, Libraries of Spoken Word Recordings and of Stagescripts*, Westridge, Highclere, Nr. Newbury, Royal Berkshire RG15 9PJ, England

Grier, Barbara, The Naiad Press, Inc., PO Box 10543, Tallahassee, FL 32333, 904-539-9322

Grierson, Ruth, Assistant Editor (see also Rimm, Virginia M.; Perrin, Arnold; Briggs, Henry; Boisvert, Donald J.; McIntyre, Joan; Knowles, Ardeana Hamlin; Brown, Ronald G.; Beck, Raymond M.), *NEW ENGLAND SAMPLER*, RFD #1 Box 2280, Brooks, ME 04921, 207-525-3575

Griffin, Joan S. (see also Horwitz, Adele D.), Presidio Press, 31 Pamaron Way, Novato, CA 94947, 415-883-1373

Griffin, Larry D., Assoc. Editor (see also Parman, Frank), *TERRITORY OF OKLAHOMA: Literature & the Arts*, PO Box 5036, Norman, OK 73070, 405-521-0046

Griffith, E.V., *POETRY NOW*, 3118 K Street, Eureka, CA 95501

Griffith, Roger, Editor (see also Storey, M. John), Garden Way Publishing Company, Schoolhouse Road, Pownal, VT 05261, 802-823-5108

Griffiths, Bill, Pirate Press, 107 Valley Drive, Kingsbury, London NW9 9NT, England

Griffiths, Bill, Pyrofiche, 107 Valley Drive, London NW9 9NT, England

Griffiths, Ralph A. (see also Morgan, Kenneth O.), *WELSH HISTORY REVIEW*, 6 Gwenyth Street, Cathays, Cardiff CF2 4YD, Wales, Cardiff 31919

Griggs, Lonnie R., Associate Editor (see also Walker, William D.; Green, Perry John), *JOINT ENDEAVOR*, PO Box 32, Huntsville, TX 77340

Grimes, John, Consultant (see also Drucker, Joseph), *ALLY*, 234 High Street #6, Santa Cruz, CA 95060, 408-423-4946

Grinberg, Gordon (see also Ritter, Jeff), *BROADSIDE*, Broadside Ltd., PO Box 1464, New York, NY 10023

Griswold, Deidre, World View Publishers, 46 West 21 Street, New York, NY 10010

Gritta, Patricia E. (see also Maltz, Patricia M.), Peregrine Associates, PO Box 22292, Ft. Lauderdale, FL 33316, 987-2423

Grizzell, Patrick (see also Breit, Luke), *POET NEWS*, 2791 24th St. #8, Sacramento, CA 95818, 916-739-1885

Gross, Alfred (see also Gillett, J.T.), Homunculus Press, Box 27, Deadwood, OR 97430, 503-964-3554

Gross, Edmand J., Publisher & President, Halls of Ivy Press, 4545 Industrial St. #5R, Simi Valley, CA 93063, 805-527-0525

Gross, Michael D., Woodstock Publications, 6220 Owens Mouth Avenue #226, Woodland Hills, CA 91367, 213-999-3196

Grossberg, Michael (see also Mueller, Milton), *FREE PRESS NETWORK*, PO Box 1743, Apple Valley, CA 92307, 619-242-4899, 415-834-6880

Grossinger, Richard (see also Hough, Lindy), *IO (named after moon of Jupiter)*, 2320 Blake St., Berkeley, CA 94704, 415-540-7934

Grossinger, Richard (see also Hough, Lindy), North Atlantic Books, 2320 Blake St., Berkeley, CA 94704, 415-540-7934

Grossman, Ron, *BROKEN STREETS*, 57 Morningside Drive, East, Bristol, CT 06010

Grossman, Sharon, Editor, *DEAR CONTRIBUTOR*, Inter-Verba Agency for Authors, 227 East 11th Street, New York, NY 10003, 212-473-2739

Grue, Lee Meitzen, Editor (see also Claudel, Calvin A.), *THE NEW LAUREL REVIEW*, 828 Lesseps Street, New Orleans, LA 70117, 504-947-6001

Gruffudd, Robat (see also Ioan, Elwyn), *LOL*, Lolfa, Y, Talybont, Dyfed, Wales SY24 5ER, United Kingdom, 0970 86 304

Gubernat, Susan (see also Hogan, Ed; Johnson, Ronna; Sagan, Miriam; Zeitlin, Leora), Zephyr Press, 13 Robinson Street, Somerville, MA 02145

Guerra, Jorge, *OVO MAGAZINE*, 307, rue Ste-Catherine, ouest Local 300, Montreal, Quebec H2X 2A3, Canada, 514-849-6253

Gullickson, James R. (see also Procario, Saverio), Sleepy Hollow Press, 150 White Plains Road, Tarrytown, NY 10591, 914-631-8200

Gullikson, Sandy (see also McNamara, Kevin), *CLEARWATER JOURNAL*, 1115 V Avenue, La Grande, OR 97850, 503-963-8212

Gullikson, Sandy, Clearwater Press, 1115 V Avenue, La Grande, OR 97850, 503-963-8212

Gulling, Dennis, *CRAWLSPACE*, Crawlspace Press, 908 W 5th Street, Belvidere, IL 61008, 815-547-4567

Gunderson, Joanna, Red Dust, PO Box 630, Gracie Station, New York, NY 10028, 212-348-4388

Gunn, Barbara, Senior Editor, *UNKNOWNS*, 1900 Century Blvd. N E, Suite One, Atlanta, GA 30345, 404-636-3145

Guppy, Stephen (see also Smith, Ron; Bailey, Rhonda), Oolichan Books, P.O. Box 10, Lantzville, British Columbia V0R2H0, Canada, 604-390-4839

Guss, David (see also Koran, Dennis), Panjandrum Books, 11321 Iowa Ave., Ste.1, Los Angeles, CA 90025, 213-477-8771

Guss, David, Assoc. Ed. (see also Koran, Dennis), *PANJANDRUM POETRY JOURNAL*, 11321 Iowa Ave. Ste.1, Los Angeles, CA 90025, 213-477-8771

Guthrie, Derek, Associate Editor (see also Allen, Jane), Chicago New Art Association, 230 East Ohio, RM. 207, Chicago, IL 60611, 312-642-6236

Guthrie, Derek, Publisher (see also Allen, Jane Addams), *NEW ART EXAMINER*, 230 East Ohio, Chicago, IL 60611, 312-642-6236

Gwynne, James B., Editor, *STEPPINGSTONES: a literary anthology toward Liberation*, Box 1856, Harlem, NY 10027, 212-474-5063

Gwynne, James B., Editor, Steppingstones Press, Box 1856, Harlem, NY 10027, 212-474-5063

Gyongy, Adrienne, Associate Editor (see also McFale, Patricia), *SCANDINAVIAN REVIEW*, 127 East 73rd Street, New York, NY 10021, 212-879-9779

Hackenbruch, Carol, Managing Editor (see also Benedict, Elinor), *PASSAGES NORTH*, William Bonifas Fine Arts Center, Escanaba, MI 49829, 906-786-3833

Hacker, Marilyn, Editor, *13th MOON*, PO Box 309, Catherdral Station, New York, NY 10025, 212-678-1074

Hackett, Neil J., Editor-in-Chief (see also Wray, Jeanne Adams), *CIMARRON REVIEW*, Oklahoma State University Press, Oklahoma State University, Stillwater, OK 74074, (405) 624-6573

Hackett, Suzanne (see also Davis, Jon), *CUTBANK*, English Dept., U. of Montana, Missoula, MT 59812

Hackett, Suzanne (see also Davis, Jon), SmokeRoot, Dept of English/Univ of Mont, Missoula, MT 59812

Hahn, Susan, Manuscripts Editor (see also Gibbons, Reginald; LaRusso, Joseph; Penlongo, Bob), *TRIQUARTERLY*, 1735 Benson Avenue, Northwestern Univ., Evanston, IL 60201, 312-492-3490

Hahn, Tomie (see also Tajima, Renee; Lee, C.N.; Chow, P.; Chin, R.; Chu, B.; Francia, L.; Wu, S.; Lew, Walter; Kwan, S.), *BRIDGE: ASIAN AMERICAN PERSPECTIVES*, Asian Cine-Vision, Inc., 32 E Broadway, New York, NY 10002, 212-925-8685

Haiek, Joseph, *THE NEWS CIRCLE MAGAZINE*, PO Box 3384, Glendale, CA 91201, 213-240-1918

Haiek, Joseph R., *ARAB AMERICAN ALMANAC*, PO Box 3384, Glendale, CA 91201, 213-240-1918

Haiek, Joseph R., The News Circle Publishing Co., PO Box 3384, Glendale, CA 91201, 213-240-1918

Haining, James, *LUCKY HEART BOOKS*, 1804 East 38 1/2, Austin, TX 78722

Haining, James, *SALT LICK*, 1804 East 38 1/2, Austin, TX 78722

Haining, James, Salt Lick Press, 1804 East 38 1/2, Austin, TX 78722

Hainline, Patricia Hoy, Co-Owner, Co-Editor (see also Carey, Margaret Standish), Calapooia Publications, 27006 Gap Road, Brownsville, OR 97327

Hair, Jennie, Contributing Editor (see also Kain, Sue; Walker, Lois V.; Steinle, Rita Juul; Penha, James), *NEWSLETTER*, PO Box 773, Huntington, NY 11743

Hair, Jennie (see also Baehr, Anne-Ruth; Jeffery, Mildred; Walker, Lois V.; Yaryura-Tobias, Anibal), Pleasure Dome Press (Long Island Poetry Collective Inc.), Box 773, Huntington, NY 11743, 516-691-2376

Hair, Jennie, Editor (see also Baehr, Anne-Ruth; Jeffrey, Mildred; Walker, Lois V.; Yaryura-Tobias, Anibal; Lucas, Barbara), *XANADU*, Box 773, Huntington, NY 11743, (516) 691-2376

Hairston, Loyle, Associate Editor (see also Jackson, Esther; Bond, Jean Carey; O'Dell, J. H.; Kaiser, Ernest; Baird, Keith E.), *FREEDOMWAYS - A Quarterly Review of the Freedom Movement*, Freedomways Associates, Inc., 799 Broadway Suite 542, New York, NY 10003

Haley, Patrick, East Eagle Press, PO Box 812, Huron, SD 57350, 605-352-5875

Hall, B.C, Fiction (see also Lake, Paul), *NEBO: A LITERARY JOURNAL*, Department of English, Arkansas Tech University, Russellville, AR 72801, 501-968-0256

Hall, Bob, Managing Editor, *SOUTHERN EXPOSURE*, PO Box 531, Durham, NC 27702, 919-688-8167

Hall, Candace C., *YET ANOTHER SMALL MAGAZINE*, PO Box 14353, Hartford, CT 06114

Hall, Candace Catlin, Andrew Mountain Press, PO Box 14353, Hartford, CT 06114

Hall, Christopher, *THE COUNTRYMAN*, Sheep Street, Burford, Oxford OX8 4LH, England, Burford 2258

Hall, C.J., *G.W. REVIEW*, Marvin Center Box 20, George Washington University, Washington, DC 20052

Hall, David B., Assistant Editor, *TODAY*, 37 Elm Road, New Malden, Surrey KT3 3HB, England, 01-942-9761

Hall, John (see also Bailey, Marilyn; Ulrich, Betty), *THE INKLING JOURNAL*, PO Box 128, Alexandria, MN 56308, 612-762-2020

Hall, John (see also Bailey, Marilyn; Ulrich, Betty), Inkling Publications, Inc., PO Box 128, Alexandria, MN 56308, 612-762-2020

Hall, Timothy, Director (see also White, Richard), White Tower Inc. Press, PO Box 42216, Los Angeles, CA 90042, 213-254-1326

Halldorson, Lynette (see also Foran, Rita), Timeless Books, P.O. Box 60, Porthill, ID 83853, 604-227-9224

Halpern, Daniel (see also Ratner, Megan), *ANTAEUS*, 18 West 30th Street, New York, NY 10001, 212-685-8240

Halpern, Daniel (see also Ratner, Megan), The Ecco Press, 18 West 30th Street, New York City, NY 10001, 212-685-8240

Halsted, Deb (see also Brown, David; Letsinger, Sue), Left Bank Books, 92 Pike Street, Seattle, WA 98101

Hamby, Barbara (see also Woodman, Allen), *APALACHEE QUARTERLY*, DDB Press, PO Box 20106, Tallahassee, FL 32316

Hamel, Guy F. Claude, Editor & Publisher, *C.S.P. WORLD NEWS*, P.O. Box 2608, Station D. Ottawa K1P5W7, Canada, 613-741-8675

Hamel, Guy F Claude, Editor, Publisher, Edition Stencil, PO Box 2608, Station D, Ottawa, Ontario K1P 5W7, Canada, 741-8675

Hamill, Sam (see also Swenson, Tree), Copper Canyon Press/Copperhead, P.O. Box 271, Port Townsend, WA 98368

Hamilton, Bruce T., Executive Editor of Publications, Oregon Historical Society, 1230 S.W. Park Avenue, Portland, OR 97205, 503-222-1741

Hamilton, Helen, Art (see also Lever, Bernice; Allison, Gay; Jenoff, Marvyne), *WAVES*, 79 Denham Drive, Thornhill, Ont. L4J 1P2, Canada, 416-889-6703

Hamilton, Michael (see also Ward, Dan S.), *The Publishing Ward, Inc.*, PO Box 9077, Fort Collins, CO 80525, 303-226-5107

Hamilton, Virginia V., Overbrook House, PO Box 7688, Mountain Brook, AL 35253, 205-879-8222

Hammer, Louis (see also Jaeger, Sharon Ann), Sachem Press, PO Box 9, Old Chatham, NY 12136, 518-794-8077

Hammer, Roger A., The Place In The Woods, 3900 Glenwood Avenue, Golden Valley, MN 55422, 612-374-2120

Hammes, Ken (see also Lewis, Monte; Rattan, Cleatus), *CROSS TIMBERS REVIEW*, Cisco Junior College, Cisco, TX 76437, 817-442-2567

Hammond-Tooke, W.D., Professor, *AFRICAN STUDIES*, 1 Jan Smuts Avenue, 2001 Johannesburg, Republic of South Africa

Hampsten, Elizabeth, Editor, *PLAINSWOMAN*, PO Box 8027, Grand Forks, ND 58202, 701-781-4234

Hancock, Geoff, Fiction Editor (see also Osborne, Anne; Martindale, Sheila; Thom, Heather; Gibson, Brenda; Lennard, Susan), *CANADIAN AUTHOR & BOOKMAN*, 25 Ryerson Aveune, 131 Bloor Street W, Toronto, Ontario M5t 2P3, Canada, 416-364-4203

Hancock, Geoffrey, *CANADIAN FICTION MAGAZINE*, PO Box 946, Station F, Toronto, Ontario M4Y 2N9, Canada

Hand, Joan C. (see also Axelrod, David B.), *WRITERS INK*, 194 Soundview Drive, Rocky Point L.I., NY 11778, 516-744-6160

Hanly, Ken (see also Brockway, R.; Brockway, Katie; West, Linda; Blanar, Mike; Blaikie, John; Gentleman, Dorothy Corbett), Pierian Press, 5, Brandon University, Brandon, Manitoba, Canada, 727-2577

Hanly, Ken (see also Brockway, R.; Brockway, Katie; West, Linda; Blanar, Mike; Blaikie, John; Gentleman, Dorothy Corbett), *PIERIAN SPRING*, 5, Brandon University, Brandon, Manitoba, Canada, 727-2577

Hannan, Jack (see also Louder, Fred; Sarah, Robyn), *FOUR BY FOUR: A SELECTION OF POETS*, 4647, rue Hutchison, Montreal, Quebec H2V 4A2, Canada, 514-274-1902

Hansen, Gunnar, LoonBooks, PO Box 901, Northeast Harbor, ME 04662, 207-276-3693

Hansen, Zenon R. (see also Lind, Alan R.; Benedict, Roy G.), Transport History Press, PO Box 201, Park Forest, IL 60466, 312-799-1785

Hanson, Sharon D., Managing Editor, *MIDWEST ARTS & LITERATURE*, PO Box 1623, Jefferson City, MO 65102

Hanson, Sharon D., Managing Editor, Sheba Review, Inc., Po Box 1623, Jefferson City, MO 65102

Harding, May, Co-Editor (see also Young, Virginia Brady; Ulisse, Peter), *CONNECTICUT RIVER REVIEW: A Journal of Poetry* , 184 Centerbrook Road, Hamden, CT 06518, 203-281-0235

Hargreaves Fitzsimmons, Karen (see also Fitzsimmons, Thomas), Katydid Books, c/o English Dept, Oakland University, Rochester, MI 48063

Hargreaves, G. D., *THE BIBLIOTHECK*, National Library of Scotland, George IV Bridge, Edinburgh EH 1 1EW, Scotland, 031-226-4531

Harkey, Joseph, Editor (see also Hite, Rick; Magnuson, Gordon; Orr, Anderson), *INLET*, Virginia Wesleyan College, Norfolk, VA 23455

Harkness, Donald R., President & Editor-in-Chief, American Studies Press, Inc., 13511 Palmwood Lane, Tampa, FL 33624, 813-961-7200; 813-974-2857

Harllee, John T., *SOUTHERN LIBERTARIAN MESSENGER*, Rt. 10 Box 52 A, Florence, SC 29501

Harman, Ms. Padi, *CALLIOPES CORNER*, SRA Box 1712 C, Anchorage, AK 99507

Harman, Willis (see also O'Regan, Brendan; McNeill, Barbara; Hurley, Tom), *INSTITUTE OF NOETIC SCIENCES NEWSLETTER*, Inst. Noetic Sciences, 475 Gate Five Road, Suite 300, Sausalito, CA 94965, 415-331-5650

Harms, Valerie, Magic Circle Press, 10 Hyde Ridge Rd, Weston, CT 06883

Harnack, William J., Assistant Editor (see also Morain, Lloyd L.), *THE HUMANIST*, 7 Harwood Drive, Amherst, NY 14226, 716-839-5080

Harper, William, The Cotton Lane Press, 18-8th Street, Augusta, GA 30901, 404-722-0232

Harr, Carl F., Associate (see also Harr, Lorraine Ellis; Yagi, Kametaro; Sato, Kazuo), *DRAGONFLY: A Quarterly Of Haiku*, 4102 N.E. 130th Pl., Portland, OR 97230

Harr, Lorraine Ellis (see also Harr, Carl F.; Yagi, Kametaro; Sato, Kazuo), *DRAGONFLY: A Quarterly Of Haiku*, 4102 N.E. 130th Pl., Portland, OR 97230

Harrington, Michael, Co-Editor (see also Ehrenreich, Barbara; Phillips, Maxine), *DEMOCRATIC LEFT*, 853 Broadway, Suite 801, New York, NY 10003, 212-260-3270

Harris, L. John, Aris Books, 77 Menlo Place, Berkeley, CA 94707, 843-0330

Harris, Tina (see also Lanoux, Claude), Fablewaves Press, PO Box 7874, Van Nuys, CA 91409, 213-322-0236

Harrison, Jeanne (see also Folsom, Eric; Saunders, Leslie), *NEXT EXIT*, Box 143, Tamworth, Ontario K0K 3G0, Canada, 613-379-2339

Harrison, Jim, Contributing Editor (see also Golden, Michael; Elias, Viki; Mungo, Raymond; Bukowski, Charles; Placidus, Max; Codrescu, Andrei; Horotwitz, Mikhail; Ligi; Kramer, Glenn; Mitchell, Donna; Riedel, Robert), *SMOKE SIGNALS*, 1516 Beverly Road, Brooklyn, NY 11226

Harrison, Randall, The Communication Press, PO Box 22541, San Francisco, CA 94122, 415-383-1914

Harrison, W. J. (see also Shannon, Mike), *SPITBALL*, 1721 Scott Street, Covington, KY 41011, 606-261-3024

Harrod, Elizabeth (see also Plante, Tom; Emerson, Ann), Owlseye Publications, 23650 Stratton Court, Hayward, CA 94541, 415-537-6858

Harrod, Elizabeth (see also Plante, Tom; Emerson, Ann), *POETALK QUARTERLY*, 23650 Stratton Court, Hayward, CA 94541, 415-537-6858

Hart, Clive, *A WAKE NEWSLITTER, Studies Of James Joyce's Finnegans Wake,* Department of Literature, University of Essex, Wivenhoe Park, Colchester, Essex CO4 3SQ, England

Hart, Clive, A Wake Newslitter Press, Dept. of Literature, Univ. of Essex, Wivenhoe Park, Colchester, Essex CO4 3SQ, England

Hart, Jim (see also Wheeler, Tony), Lonely Planet Publications, P.O. Box 88, South Yarra, Victoria 3141, Australia, 03 429-5100

Harter, Penny (see also Higginson, William J.), From Here Press, Box 219, Fanwood, NJ 07023

Harter, Penny (see also Higginson, William J.), *XTRAS*, Box 219, Fanwood, NJ 07023, (201) 322-5928

Hartford, Professor G.F., *ENGLISH STUDIES IN AFRICA-A Journal of the Humanities,* Witwatersrand University Press, 1 Jan Smuts Ave., 2001 Johannesburg, Republic of South Africa, 011-716-2029

Hartford, Professor G.F., Witwatersrand University Press, 1 Jan Smuts Avenue, 2001 Johannesburg, Republic of South Africa, 011-716-2029

Hartley, Glen T., Associate Editor (see also Lehman, David; Green, Stefanie; Black, Joel), Nobodaddy Press, 159 Ludlowville Road, Lansing, NY 14882

Hartley, Glen T. (see also Lehman, David; Green, Stefanie; Black, Joel), *POETRY IN MOTION,* 159 Ludlowville Road, Lansing, NY 14882

Harvey, Alex, *HOLLOW SPRING REVIEW OF POETRY*, RD 1, Bancroft Road, Chester, MA 01011

Harvey, Alexander, Hollow Spring Press, RD 1, Bancroft Rd, Chester, MA 01011

Harvey, Gordon, Editor, *SEQUOIA, STANFORD LITERARY MAGAZINE*, Storke Publications Bldg., Stanford, CA 94305

Haslam, Gerry, Old Adobe Press, Box 115, Penngrove, CA 94951

Hass, Robert, Consulting Editor (see also Lesser, Wendy; Bowles, Paul; Berger, John; Vidal, Gore; Wasserman, Steve), *THE THREEPENNY REVIEW*, PO Box 9131, Berkeley, CA 94709, 415-849-4545

Hasselstrom, Linda M., Lame Johnny Press, Star Route 3 Box 9A, Hermosa, SD 57744, 605-255-4466

Hastwell, G., Photography (see also Dutkiewicz, Adam; Brakmanis, M.; Biggs, S.; Franklin, C.), *WORDS AND VISIONS/WAV MAGAZINE*, 499 The Parade, Magill, Australia, 08-3329529

Hatfield, Lee Bates, *THE AMERICAN LITERARY REVIEW*, 45 Thurston Road, Newton, MA 02164, 617-527-8556

Hathaway, Baxter (see also Henkel, Christopher; Latta, John), Ithaca House, 108 North Plain Street, Ithaca, NY 14850, 607-272-1233

Hathaway, Michael, *THE KINDRED SPIRIT*, Groovy Gray Cat Publications, Route 2, Box 111, Saint John, KS 67576, 316-549-3933

Hatlen, Burton (see also Terrell, C.F.), National Poetry Foundation, 305 EM Building, University of Maine, Orono, ME 04469, 207-581-3814

Hatlen, Burton (see also Terrell, C.F.), *PAIDEUMA*, 305 EM Building, University of Maine, Orono, ME 04469, 207-581-3814

Hatlen, Burton (see also Terrell, C.F.), *SAGETRIEB*, 305 EM Building, University of Maine, Orono, ME 04469, 207-581-3814

Haus, Henn, Editor (see also Rodriquez, E.), *LOCAL DRIZZLE*, farmOut, P.O.Box 388, Carnation, WA 98014, (206) 333-4980

Hausen, Rena, Editor (see also Navaretta, Cynthia), *WOMEN ARTISTS NEWS*, Box 3304, Grand Central, New York City, NY 10163, 212-666-6990

Hauser, Glenn, *REVIEW OF INTERNATIONAL BROADCASTING*, Box 6287, Knoxville, TN 37914, 615-522-4497

Hauser, Susan, *RASPBERRY PRESS (magazine)*, Route 1, Box 81, Puposky, MN 56667, 218-243-2402

Hawkes, John E. (see also Spiro, Penelope), *FEDORA*, PO Box 577, Siletz, OR 97380, 503-444-2757

Hawkes, Robert, Poetry Editor (see also Conway, Don; Gibbs, Robert; Trethewey, Eric; Butlin, Ron; Taylor, Michael; Thompson, Kent; Davey, Bill; Boyles, Ann; Bauer, William), *THE FIDDLEHEAD*, The Observatory, Univ. New Brunswick, PO Box 4400, Fredericton, NB E3B 5A3, Canada, 506-454-3591

Hawkins Jr., Laurence F., Editor, Trout Creek Press, PO Box 125, Parkdale, OR 97041, 503-352-6494

Hawkins, Laurence F., Jr., Editor, *DOG RIVER REVIEW*, PO Box 125, Parkdale, OR 97041, 503-352-6494

Hawley, Edward A., Exec. Editor (see also Shepherd, George W., Jr.; LeMelle, Tilden J.), *AFRICA TODAY*, c/o G.S.I.S, Univ of Denver, Denver, CO 80208

Hawley, Robert, Oyez, PO Box 5134, Berkeley, CA 94705

Hay, Peter (see also Atwater, Dorthea), Sonica Press, PO Box 42720, Los Angeles, CA 90042, 213-222-1026

Haycock, Carol-Ann (see also Haycock, Ken), Dyad Services, PO Box 46258, Station G, Vancouver VGR 466, Canada

Haycock, Carol-Ann (see also Haycock, Ken), *EMERGENCY LIBRARIAN*, PO Box 46258, Station G, Vancouver VGR 466, Canada

Haycock, Ken (see also Haycock, Carol-Ann), Dyad Services, PO Box 46258, Station G, Vancouver VGR 466, Canada

Haycock, Ken (see also Haycock, Carol-Ann), *EMERGENCY LIBRARIAN*, PO Box 46258, Station G, Vancouver VGR 466, Canada

Hayes, Ann M. (see also Peterson, Perry L.), *WOODROSE*, PO Box 2537, Madison, WI 53701

Hayes, Ann M. (see also Peterson, Perry L.), Woodrose Editions, PO Box 2537, Madison, WI 53701, 608-256-6155

Hayes, Marshall, Editor (see also Wood, Marilyn), *BOOK FORUM*, Hudson River Press, 38 East 76 Street, New York, NY 10021, 212-861-8328

Haynes, Dr. Robert, Critic-at-Large (see also Lawson, Dr. Todd; Comen, Dr. Diane; Marsic, John; Rader, Steve; Monte, Oscar; Nishi, Mio; Ginsberg, Allen; Samolis, Dr. Sam; Graham, Joan; Ferlinghetti, Lawrence; Ramirez, Julio; Snyder, Gary; Morris, Dr. Richard), *ALPS MONTHLY*, PO Box 99394, San Francisco, CA 94109, 415-771-3431

Haynes, Jim (see also Moore, Jack Henry), *'THE CASSETTE GAZETTE'*, Atelier A2, 83 rue de la Tombe-Issoire, Paris 75014, France, 327-1767

Haynes, Jim, Handshake Editions, Atelier A2, 83 rue de la Tombe-Issoire, Paris 75014, France, 327-1767

Hays, J.V., J.V. Hays, Inc., 110 S Woodland Blvd #130, DeLand, FL 32720, 904-738-1210

Head, Gwen, Dragon Gate, Inc., 914 East Miller, Seattle, WA 98102

Head, Robert (see also Fife, Darlene), *STUDIES*, 104 South Jefferson Street, Lewisburg, WV 24901

Headley, Robert (see also Glazer, Irvin R.), *MARQUEE*, 624 Wynne Road, Springfield, PA 19064, 215-543-8378

Heaphy, Jim, *SPACE FOR ALL PEOPLE*, 1724 Sacramento Street, Suite 105, San Francisco, CA 94109, 415-673-1079

Hebert, Thomas W., *VIETNAM WAR NEWSLETTER,* Box 122, Collinsville, CT 06022, 203-582-9784

Hebhoe, Hank T. (see also Bumppo, Natty), Borf Books, Box 413, Brownsville, KY 42210, 502-597-2187

Hecht, Harvey, *THE CAPE ROCK,* English Dept, Southeast Missouri State, Cape Girardeau, MO 63701, 314-651-2151

Hedley, Leslie Woolf (see also Daniels, Guy), Exile Press, PO Box 1768, Novato, CA 94948, 883-2132

Heffernan, Michael, Poetry (see also Schick, James B.; Daniel, Bruce), *THE MIDWEST QUARTERLY,* Pittsburg State University, Pittsburg, KS 66762, 316-231-7000

Hegedus, Debbie (see also Cartier, John), *DELAWARE ALTERNATIVE PRESS,* PO Box 4592, Newark, DE 19711

Hegener, Helen (see also Hegener, Mark), *HOME EDUCATION MAGAZINE,* PO Box 218, Tonasket, WA 98855, 509-486-2449

Hegener, Karen C., Editor-in-Chief, Peterson's Guides, 166 Bunn Drive, PO Box 2123, Princeton, NJ 08540, 609-924-5338

Hegener, Mark (see also Hegener, Helen), *HOME EDUCATION MAGAZINE,* PO Box 218, Tonasket, WA 98855, 509-486-2449

Heilbron, J.L., *HISTORICAL STUDIES IN THE PHYSICAL SCIENCES,* University of California Press, Berkeley, CA 94720, 415-642-7485

Heineman, Barbara, Managing Editor (see also Howe, Florence), *WOMEN'S STUDIES QUARTERLY,* Box 334, Old Westbury, NY 11568, 516-997-7660

Heiner Jr., Carson, Editor, Publication Director, *KALEIDOSCOPE INTERNATIONAL LITERARY/ART MAGAZINE,* UCPSH, 326 Locust, Akron, OH 44302, 216-762-9755 ext. 475

Hejinian, Lyn (see also Watten, Barrett), *POETICS JOURNAL,* 2639 Russell Street, Berkeley, CA 94705, 415-535-1952

Hejinian, Lyn, *TUUMBA,* 2639 Russell Street, Berkeley, CA 94705

Hejinian, Lyn, Tuumba Press, 2639 Russell St, Berkeley, CA 94705

Hejna, Matthew, Editor, *INSIDE/OUT,* GPO Box 1185, New York, NY 10116, 212-219-0542

Hejna, Matthew, Editor (see also Crawford, Marc), Time Capsule, Inc., GPO Box 1185, New York, NY 10116, 212-219-0542

Helbing, Terry, JH Press, PO Box 294, Village Station, New York, NY 10014, 255-4713

Heldrich, Eleanor, Prospect Hill, 216 Wendover Road, Baltimore, MD 21218, 301-235-1026

Hellen, Shelley (see also Lloyd, D H), Applezaba Press, PO Box 4134, Long Beach, CA 90804, 213-591-0015

Hellerman, Steve, Associate Editor (see also Anbian, Robert; Spilker, John; King, Dennis; Kosoua, Anna; Erfurdt, Jamie), *OBOE: A Journal of Literature & Fine Art,* 495 Ellis Street, Box 1156, San Francisco, CA 94102

Helm, Mike, Rainy Day Press, PO Box 3035, Eugene, OR 97403, 503-484-4626

Helminski, Edmund, Threshold Books, Dusty Ridge Road, RD 3 Box 1350, Putney, VT 05346, 802-387-4586 or 245-8300

Hemenway, Phillip, Poetry Editor (see also Jackson, Larry S.), *PHANTASM,* 1116D Wendy Way, Chico, CA 95926, 916-342-6582

Heminger, Steve (see also Schroer, Steve), *CHICAGO REVIEW,* University of Chicago, Faculty Exchange, Box C, Chicago, IL 60637, 312-753-3571

Hemphill, Essex C., Publisher (see also Anderson, Kathy Elaine; Jones, Keith; Williams, Cynthia L.), *NETHULA JOURNAL OF CONTEMPORARY LITERATURE,* 930 F Street, Suite 610, Washington, DC 20004

Henderson, Arn (see also Parman, Frank), Point Riders Press, PO Box 2731, Norman, OK 73070

Henderson, Bill, Pushcart Press, PO Box 380, Wainscott, NY 11975, 516-324-9300

Henderson, Jock (see also McBee, Denis; van Valkenburg, Rick), *BEATNIKS FROM SPACE*, Box 8043, Ann Arbor, MI 48107, 313-668-6867

Henderson, Jock (see also McBee, Denis; van Valkenburg, Rick), The Neither/Nor Press, Box 8043, Ann Arbor, MI 48107, 313-668-6867

Henderson, Mildred K., *HOB-NOB*, 715 Dorsea Road, Lancaster, PA 17601

Hendry, Joy M., *CHAPMAN*, 35 East Claremont Street, Edinburgh, EH7 4HT, Scotland

Hendry, Joy M., Lothlorien, 35 East Claremont Street, Edinburg EH7 4HT, Scotland, 031-556-5363

Henisch, B.A. (see also Henisch, H.K.), The Carnation Press, PO Box 101, State College, PA 16801, 814-238-3577

Henisch, H.K. (see also Henisch, B.A.), *The Carnation Press*, PO Box 101, State College, PA 16801, 814-238-3577

Henkel, Chris (see also Latta, John), *CHIAROSCURO*, 108 North Plain Street, Ithaca, NY 14850, 607-272-1233

Henkel, Chris (see also Latta, John), Clearly Obscure Press, 108 North Plain Street, Ithaca, NY 14850

Henkel, Christopher (see also Hathaway, Baxter; Latta, John), Ithaca House, 108 North Plain Street, Ithaca, NY 14850, 607-272-1233

Hennessey, Patricia J., Fiction Editor (see also Burnham, R. Peter; Backstrand, Brian), *THE LONG STORY*, 11 Kingston Street, North Andover, MA 01845, 617-686-7638

Henris, Marilyn, Associate Editor (see also Lunde, David), The Basilisk Press, P.O. Box 71, Fredonia, NY 14063, 716-934-4199

Henry, Alice (see also Leonard, Vickie; Douglas, Carol Anne; Lootens, Tricia; Fugh-Berman, Adrianne; Moira, Fran; Dejanikus, Tacie; Kulp, Denise; Sorrel, Lorraine), *OFF OUR BACKS*, 1841 Columbia Road NW Rm 212, Room 212, Washington, DC 20009, 202-234-8072

Henry, DeWitt (see also O'Malley, Peter; Lee, Susannah; Peseroff, Joyce), *PLOUGHSHARES*, Box 529, Cambridge, MA 02139

Henry, Jeannette, Indian Historian Press, 1451 Masonic Avenue, San Francisco, CA 94117

Henschel, Lee, Guthrie Publishing Company, 230 W. Eagle Lake Drive, Maple Grove, MN 55369, 218-224-2118

Hepfer, Will, Co-Editor (see also Mark, Linda; Mueller, Carolyn), *SERIALS REVIEW*, PO Box 1808, Ann Arbor, MI 48106, 313-434-5530

Hepworth, James, Managing Editor (see also Wrigley, Robert), Confluence Press, Inc., Spalding Hall, Lewis-Clark State College, Lewiston, ID 83501

Hepworth, James, Managing Editor (see also Wrigley, Robert), *THE SLACKWATER REVIEW*, Spalding Hall, Lewis-Clark Campus, Lewiston, ID 83501, 208-746-2341

Herdeck, Donald, Editor and Publisher (see also Ware, Norman), Three Continents Press, Inc., 1346 Connecticut Ave NW, Suite 224, Washington, DC 20036, 202-457-0288

Heriard, Jack B., *WHISPERING WIND MAGAZINE*, 8009 Wales Street, New Orleans, LA 70126, 504-241-5866

Herman, E. (see also Sargent, L.; Walsh, S.; Geiger, K.), South End Press, 302 Columbus Avenue, Boston, MA 02116, 617-266-0629

Hernandez Jr., Ernie, Frontline Publications, PO Box 1104, El Toro, CA 92630

Herrin, Dawn, *CORNERSTONE*, 4707 N. Malden, Chicago, IL 60640, 312-561-2450

Herron, Don, Associate Editor (see also Moran, John C.; Eng, Steve), The F. Marion Crawford Memorial Society, Saracinesca House, 3610 Meadowbrook Avenue, Nashville, TN 37205

Herron, Don, Associate Editor (see also Moran, John C.; Eng, Steve), *THE ROMANTIST*, Saracinesca House, 3610 Meadowbrook Avenue, Nashville, TN 37205, 615-228-5939

Hershey, Jon (see also Starnes, Jo Anne), *THE OLD RED KIMONO*, Humanities, Floyd College, PO Box 1864, Rome, GA 30161, 404-295-6312

Hershon, Robert (see also Lourie, Dick; Pawlak, Mark; Schreiber, Ron; Levertov, Denise; Jarrett, Emmett), *HANGING LOOSE*, 231 Wyckoff St, Brooklyn, NY 11217

Hertz, Robert S., *CONSPIRACIES UNLIMITED*, PO Box 3085, St Paul, MN 55165

Herzinger, Kim A., Associate Editor (see also Barthelme, Frederick; Inness-Brown, Elizabeth), *MISSISSIPPI REVIEW*, Box 5144, Southern Station, Hattiesburg, MS 39406, 601-266-4321

Heseltine, Nigel (see also Pope, Chris), *RENEWABLE ENERGY NEWS*, Box 4869, Station E, Ottawa, Ontario K1S 5J1, Canada, 613-238-5591

Hesford, Dr. B., *MUSICAL OPINION*, 3/11, Spring Road, Bournemouth, Dorset, England, 23397/23177

Hess, John (see also Kleinhans, Chuck; Lesage, Julia), *JUMP CUT, A Review of Contemporary Cinema*, P.O. Box 865, Berkeley, CA 94701, 415-658-4482

Hester, Susan, Frog in the Well, 430 Oakdale Road, East Palo Alto, CA 94303, 415-323-1237

Hettich, Michael (see also Osborne, Karen; Ahern, Colleen), Moonsquilt Press, 16401 NE 4th Avenue, North Miami Beach, FL 33162, 305-947-9534

Hewett, James (see also Shannon, Foster H.), Green Leaf Press, PO Box 6880, Alhambra, CA 91802, 818-281-6809

Hewitt, D. (see also Stanley, E.G.; Fleeman, J.D.), *NOTES & QUERIES: for Readers & Writers, Collectors & Librarians*, Oxford Journals, Walton Street, Oxford 0X2 6DP, England

Hickman, Irene (see also Hickman, Jack), Hickman Systems - Books, 4 Woodland Lane, Kirksville, MO 63501, 816-665-1836

Hickman, Jack (see also Hickman, Irene), *Hickman Systems - Books*, 4 Woodland Lane, Kirksville, MO 63501, 816-665-1836

Hickok, Gloria Vando, Editor, *HELICON NINE: The Journal of Women's Arts and Letters*, PO Box 22412, Kansas City, MO 64113, 913-381-6383

Hicks, John, *THE MASSACHUSETTS REVIEW*, Memorial Hall, Univ. of Mass, Amherst, MA 01003, 413-545-2689

Higdon, David Leon, *CONRADIANA*, Dept. of English, Box 4530, Texas Tech University, Lubbock, TX 79409

Higgins, Dick (see also Kostelanetz, Richard; Scobie, Stephen; Frank, Sheldon; Zelevansky, Paul; Essary, Loris; Young, Karl), *PRECISELY*, PO Box 73, Canal Street, New York, NY 10013

Higgins, Dick, Printed Editions, PO Box 27, Station Hill Road, Barrytown, NY 12507, 914-758-6488

Higgins, Elizabeth, Editor (see also Scharper, Philip J.; Eagleson, John), Orbis Books, Attention: Robert N. Quigley, Maryknoll, NY 10545, 914-941-7590

Higgins, Joanna, Co-Editor (see also Rosenberg, L.M.; Gardner, John), *MSS (Manuscripts)*, SUNY, Binghamton, NY 13901, 607-798-2000

Higginson, William J. (see also Harter, Penny), From Here Press, Box 219, Fanwood, NJ 07023

Higginson, William J. (see also Harter, Penny), *XTRAS*, Box 219, Fanwood, NJ 07023, (201) 322-5928

Higham, Robin, Editor & President (see also Socolofsky, Homer; Clark, Patricia), *JOURNAL OF THE WEST*, 1531 Yuma, Manhattan, KS 66502, 913-532-6733; 539-3668

Higham, Robin, President (see also Clark, Patricia P.), Sunflower University Press, 1531 Yuma, Manhattan, KS 66502, 913-532-6733

Hilberry, Jane, Editor (see also McGraw, Erin), *INDIANA REVIEW*, 316 North Jordan Avenue, Indiana University, Bloomington, IN 47405, 812-335-3439

Hill, Brian Merrikin, *PENNINE PLATFORM*, 4 Ingmanthorpe Hall Farm, Wetherby, West Yorks LS22 5EQ, England, 0927-64674

Hill, Casey (see also Burns, Grant), *NEW PAGES: News & Reviews of the Progressive Booktrade*, 4426 South Belsay Road, Grand Blanc, MI 48439

Hill, Chris, Editor (see also Schimmel, Bruce), *PHILADELPHIA CITY PAPER*, 6381 Germantown Avenue, Philadelphia, PA 19144, 215-848-3885

Hill, Greg (see also Clarke, Gillian), *THE ANGLO-WELSH REVIEW*, 1 Cyncoed Ave., Cyncoed, Cardiff, Wales, United Kingdom, 0222-755100

Hill, Lawrence, Lawrence Hill & Company, Publishers, Inc., 520 Riverside Ave., Westport, CT 06880, 203-226-9392

Hill, Robert, Editor (see also Johnson, Carol; Calhoun, Richard), *SOUTH CAROLINA REVIEW*, English Dept, Clemson Univ, Clemson, SC 29631, 803-656-3229

Hillman, Aaron W., Editor, *THE CONFLUENT EDUCATION JOURNAL*, 833 Via Granada, Santa Barbara, CA 93103, 805-569-1754

Hillman, Aaron W., Editor, *THE SANTA BARBARA BOOK REVIEW*, 833 Via Granada, Santa Barbara, CA 93103, 805-569-1754

Hillman, James, *SPRING: An Annual of Archetypal Psychology and Jungian Thought*, PO Box 222069, Dallas, TX 75222, 214-698-0933, 0934

Hillman, James, Spring Publications Inc, PO Box 222069, Dallas, TX 75222, 214-698-0933, 0934

Hillman, Paul, Owner, Editor, Hillman Publishing Co., Inc., 2342 Distinctive Drive8, Colorado Springs, CO 80918, 503-682-2505

Hilton, David, Contributing (see also Swanberg, Ingrid; Woessner, Warren), *ABRAXAS*, 2518 Gregory St., Madison, WI 53711, 608-238-0175

Hinnebusch, Patricia Doherty (see also Fusek, Serena), *ORPHIC LUTE*, PO Box 2815, Newport News, VA 23602

Hirsch, Audrey (see also Wenig, M. Judith; Freundlich, Paul; Collins, Chris), *COMMUNITIES*, Box 426, Louisa, VA 23093, 703-894-5126

Hirsch, Audrey (see also Wenig, M. Judith; Freundlich, Paul; Collins, Chris), *Communities Publishing Cooperative*, Box 426, Louisa, VA 23093, 703-894-5126

Hite, Rick, Associate Editor (see also Harkey, Joseph; Magnuson, Gordon; Orr, Anderson), *INLET*, Virginia Wesleyan College, Norfolk, VA 23455

Hobson, Louis, Sunnyvale Marketing, 2627-19th Street, Rockford, IL 61109, 815-397-6299

Hodgkiss, Peter, Galloping Dog Press, 45 Salisbury Gardens, Newcastle upon Tyne, London, England NE2 1HP, England

Hodson, Stanley, Associate Editor (see also Skinner, Knute), *THE BELLINGHAM REVIEW*, 412 N State Street, Bellingham, WA 98225, 206-734-9781

Hodson, Stanley, Associate Editor (see also Skinner, Knute), Signpost Press Inc., 412 N State Street, Bellingham, WA 98225

Hoey, Allen (see also Hoey, Cynthia), Tamarack Editions, 128 Benedict Avenue, Syracuse, NY 13210, 315-478-6495

Hoey, Cynthia (see also Hoey, Allen), *Tamarack Editions*, 128 Benedict Avenue, Syracuse, NY 13210, 315-478-6495

Hoffberg, Judith A., *ARTISTS' PUBLICATIONS IN PRINT*, PO Box 3692, Glendale, CA 91201, 213-797-0514

Hoffberg, Judith A., *UMBRELLA*, PO Box 3692, Glendale, CA 91201, 213-797-0514

Hoffberg, Judith A., Umbrella Associates, PO Box 3692, Glendale, CA 91201, 213-797-0514

Hoffman, D. S. (see also Lloyd, Robert), Durak, RD 1 Box 20C, Rock Stream, NY 14878

Hoffman, Marjorie Mendenhall, *THE BLUEGRASS LITERARY REVIEW,* Midway College, Midway, KY 40347

Hoffmaster, Susan, Managing Editor, Graphic Image Publications, PO Box 1740, La Jolla, CA 92038, 619-457-0344

Hofstrand, Richard K., Editor, Bench Mark Publications, PO Box 755, Charleston, IL 61920, 217-345-7581

Hogan, Ed, Non-Fiction (see also Gubernat, Susan; Johnson, Ronna; Sagan, Miriam; Zeitlin, Leora), Zephyr Press, 13 Robinson Street, Somerville, MA 02145

Hogan, Judy, The Carolina Wren Press, 300 Barclay Road, Chapel Hill, NC 27514, 919-967-8666

Hogan, Mary Suzanne, *BIOLOGY DIGEST,* 143 Old Marlton Pike, Medford, NJ 08055, 609-654-6500

Hogan, Thomas H., Plexus Publishing, Inc., 143 Old Marlton Pike, Medford, NJ 08055, 609-654-6500

Hohlwein, Kathryn, Art & Poetry Editor (see also Giles, Mary E.), *STUDIA MYSTICA,* Calif. State Univ., 6000 J Street, Sacramento, CA 95819

Hol, Jim (see also Munday, Georgette), *THE AGENT,* New Agency, 46 Denbigh Street, London SW1, England

Holdridge, Barbara, Stemmer House Publishers, Inc., 2627 Caves Road, Owings Mills, MD 21117

Holland, Peter (see also Yurechko, John; Lance, Jeanne), *GALLERY WORKS,* 1465 Hammersley Avenue, Bronx, NY 10469, 212-379-1519

Hollenbeck, Joan, Peppertree Publishing, Box 1712, Newport Beach, CA 92663, 714-642-3669

Holley, Barbara, Co-Editor (see also Gold, Herman), *EARTHWISE: A Journal of Poetry,* PO Box 680-536, Miami, FL 33168

Holley, Barbara (see also Vilips, Kathryn L.; Carter, Kaye Edwards), *EARTHWISE LITERARY CALENDAR,* PO Box 680-536, Miami, FL 33168

Holley, Barbara, Chief Editor (see also Newhouse, Sally), *EARTHWISE NEWSLETTER,* PO Box 680-536, Miami, FL 33168, 305-688-8558

Holley, Barbara, Editor, Publisher (see also Gold, Herman), Earthwise Publications, PO Box 680-536, Miami, FL 33168, 305-688-8558

Holley, Barbara, Editor (see also Gold, Herman), *TEMPEST: Avant-Garde Poetry,* PO Box 680-536, Miami, FL 33168, 305-688-8558

Holmen, Rachel, Managing Editor (see also Brown, Charles N.; Miller, Faren), *LOCUS: The Newspaper of the Science Fiction Field,* Box 13305, Oakland, CA 94661, 415-339-9196

Holsapple (see also Kilgore; Empfield), *CONTRABAND MAGAZINE,* PO Box 4073, Station A, Portland, ME 04101

Holsapple (see also Kilgore; Empfield), Contraband Press, PO Box 4073, Sta A, Portland, ME 04101

Holte, Susan, Editor (see also Ramey, Frederick), Arden Press, 1127 Pennsylvania, Denver, CO 80203, 303-837-8913

Holyoke, Tom, Bk. Rev. Ed. (see also Fogarty, Robert; St. John, David; Miller, Nolan), *THE ANTIOCH REVIEW,* PO Box 148, Yellow Springs, OH 45387, 513-767-7386

Holzman, David (see also Bossong, Ken; Pilarski, Jan), Citizen's Energy Project, 1110 6th Street, NW, Washington, DC 20001

Honig, Edwin, Editor (see also Blasing, M.K.; Blasing, Randy), Copper Beech Press, Box 1852 Brown Univ., Providence, RI 02912, 401-863-2393

Hood, Rosemary, *BRITISH BOOK NEWS,* 65 Davies St., London W1Y 2AA, England, 01-499-8011

Hook, Brian, *CHINA QUARTERLY,* School of Oriental & African Studies, Malet St., London WC1E 7HP, England

Hooper, Shaun (see also McNally, W.J., III; Malin, Kathy), McNally & Loftin, West, 5390 Overpass Road, Santa Barbara, CA 93111, 805-964-7079; 964-5117

Hoopes, David S., Editor-in-Chief (see also Pusch, Margaret D.), Intercultural Press, Inc., PO Box 768, Yarmouth, ME 04096, 207-846-5168

Hoover, Carol F., Editor, Ariadne Press, 4817 Tallahassee Avenue, Rockville, MD 20853, 301-949-2514

Hoover, Paul (see also Chernoff, Maxine), *OINK!*, 1446 W Jarvis #3-D, Chicago, IL 60626

Hoover, Russell (see also Sukenick, Ronald; Russell, Charles; Ratner, Rochelle; Tytell, John), *THE AMERICAN BOOK REVIEW*, PO Box 188, Cooper Station, New York, NY 10003, 212-621-9289

Hope, James, Presto Books, PO Box 818, Shoreham, NY 11786

Horner, Britt (see also Ochester, Ed), Spring Church Book Company, PO Box 127, Spring Church, PA 15686

Hornick, Lita, Kulchur Foundation, 888 Park Ave., New York, NY 10021, 988-5193

Horotwitz, Mikhail, Contributing Editor (see also Golden, Michael; Elias, Viki; Harrison, Jim; Mungo, Raymond; Bukowski, Charles; Placidus, Max; Codrescu, Andrei; Ligi; Kramer, Glenn; Mitchell, Donna; Riedel, Robert), *SMOKE SIGNALS*, 1516 Beverly Road, Brooklyn, NY 11226

Horovitz, Michael, *NEW DEPARTURES*, Piedmont, Bisley, Stroud, Glos., England, England

Horowitz, Evelyn (see also Malinowitz, Michael; du Passage, Mary), *THE BAD HENRY REVIEW*, Box 45, Van Brunt Station, Brooklyn, NY 11215

Horowitz, Evelyn (see also Malinowitz, Michael; du Passage, Mary), 44 Press, Inc., Box 45, Van Brant Station, Brooklyn, NY 11215

Horton, Claude W., Sr., The White Cross Press, Route 1, Box 592, Granger, TX 76530, 512-859-2814

Horwitz, Adele D. (see also Griffin, Joan S.), Presidio Press, 31 Pamaron Way, Novato, CA 94947, 415-883-1373

Hosken, Fran P., Editor & Publisher, *WIN NEWS*, 187 Grant Street, Lexington, MA 02173, 617-862-9431

Hosler, Laddie, Editor and Publisher (see also Fudge, Gloria), *THE WISHING WELL*, Box 117, Novato, CA 94948

Hospers, John, Editor (see also Sugden, Sherwood), The Hegeler Institute, Box 600, La Salle, IL 61301, 815-223-1231

Hospers, John, Editor (see also Sugden, Sherwood J.B.), *THE MONIST: An International Quarterly Journal of General Philosophical Inquiry.*, Box 600, La Salle, IL 61301, 815-223-1231

Hostetler, Dale E., West Family Publishers, PO Box 1912, Beaverton, OR 97075, 503-641-0113

Hostrop, Richard W., ETC Publications, PO Drawer ETC, Palm Spring, CA 92263, 619-325-5352

Houedard, Dom Silvester (see also Furnival, John), Openings Press, Rooksmoor House, Woodchester, Glos, England

Hough, Lindy (see also Grossinger, Richard), *IO (named after moon of Jupiter)*, 2320 Blake St., Berkeley, CA 94704, 415-540-7934

Hough, Lindy (see also Grossinger, Richard), North Atlantic Books, 2320 Blake St., Berkeley, CA 94704, 415-540-7934

Housman, Katherine (see also Nicolson, Linda), Belle-Lettres Books, PO Box 20405, Oakland, CA 94620, 655-9783

Howard, Cheryl (see also Van Dyke, Annette), Woman Works Press, 622 Oakdale, Saint Paul, MN 55107, 612-291-8684

Howard, J. Kirk, Dundurn Press Ltd, PO Box 245 Station F, Toronto, Ontario M4Y 2L5, Canada, 416-368-9390

Howard, John, The Haven Corporation, 802 Madison Avenue, Evanston, IL 60202, 312-869-3434

82

Howard, Lee, Selective Publishers, Inc., Box 1140, Clearwater, FL 33517

Howard, Quentin R., *WIND LITERARY JOURNAL*, RFD Rt. 1 Box 809K, Pikeville, KY 41501, 606-631-1129

Howard, Richard, Poetry Editor (see also Boatwright, James), *SHENANDOAH*, PO Box 722, Lexington, VA 24450, 703-463-9111 ext 283

Howe, Florence, Publisher (see also Baird, Jo), The Feminist Press, Box 334, Old Westbury, NY 11568

Howe, Florence, Editor (see also Heineman, Barbara), *WOMEN'S STUDIES QUARTERLY*, Box 334, Old Westbury, NY 11568, 516-997-7660

Howell, Christopher, Poetry Editor (see also Stansberry, Domenic), Lynx House Press, PO Box 800, Amherst, MA 01004, 503-777-3102

Hower, Mary (see also Spangle, Douglas; Steger, Donna), *MOOSE MAGAZINE*, 3611 Southeast 15th, Portland, OR 97202, 503-232-3508

Hryciak, Marshall (see also Southward, Keith; Coney, Denise), Inkstone Press, PO Box 67, Station H, Toronto, Ontario M4C 5H7, Canada

Hryciuk, Marshall (see also Southward, Keith; Coney, Denise), *INKSTONE*, PO Box 67, Station H, Toronto, Ontario M4C 5H7, Canada, 656-0356

Huang, J. (see also Thoenen, B.; Jacobson, J.; Cohen, M.; McKale, A.), *THE DROOD REVIEW OF MYSTERY*, Box 8872, Boston, MA 02114

Hubbs, Clayton A., Editor & Publisher, *TRANSITIONS: The Resource Guide To Budget, Travel, Work, And Study Abroad*, 18 Hulst Rd., Amherst, MA 01002, 413-256-0373

Huehes, John (see also Elliott, Andrew), *NORTH*, 10 Stranmillis Park, Belfast BT9 5AU, Northern Ireland, 0232-662271

Huff, Casey (see also Kuhlken, Ken; Renfro, Elizabeth), Flume Press, 644 Citrus Avenue, Chico, CA 95926, 916-342-1583

Huffman, Katherine Gekker, The Huffman Press, 805 N. Royal Street, Alexandria, VA 22314, 703-683-1695

Huggon, Jas, Kropotkin's Lighthouse Publications, Box KLP, Housmans Bookshop, 5 Caledonian Road, London N19DX, England

Hughes, Eric, *COLLABORATION*, Matagiri Sri Aurobindo Center, Inc., Mt. Tremper, NY 12457, 914-679-8322

Hughes, Helen E., *THE CREATIVE WOMAN*, Governors State University, University Park, IL 60466, 312-534-5000, Ext. 2524

Hughes, John E. (see also Balsamo, Ron; Lee, Jean C.; Reed, W.A.; Reed, Vicki; Thompson, Catherine; Dennis, Deborah), *FARMER'S MARKET*, PO Box 1272, Galesburg, IL 61402

Hughes, Michael, Graphics (see also Michelson, Linda Brown; Bartlett, Elizabeth), *CROSSCURRENTS, A QUARTERLY*, 2200 Glastonbury Road, West Lake Village, CA 91361

Huizinga (see also Albert; Becker), New Society Publishers, 4722 Baltimore Avenue, Philadelphia, PA 19143, 215-726-6543

Humes, Harry, Editor, *YARROW, A JOURNAL OF POETRY*, English Dept., Lytle Hall, Kutztown State College, Kutztown, PA 19530, 683-4353

Humphry, Derek (see also Wickett, Ann), *HEMLOCK QUARTERLY*, PO Box 66218, Los Angeles, CA 90066, 213-391-1871

Humphry, Derek (see also Wickett, Ann), Hemlock Society, PO Box 66218, Los Angeles, CA 90066, 213-391-1971

Hundere, M.S., Myriad Moods, 313 Joliet, San Antonio, TX 78209, 3512-342-1652

Hundley Jr., Norris, *PACIFIC HISTORICAL REVIEW*, Department of History, University of California, Los Angeles, CA 90024

Hunker, Tracy, *TESTUBE NEWS/TESTUBE CASSETTEZINE (AUDIO VERSION)*, Testube, PO Box 89, Bascom, OH 44809, 419-937-2732

Hunt, Annice E., Editor, *CALLI'S TALES*, Box 1224, Palmetto, FL 33561, 813-722-2202

Hunt, Edmund (see also Ingram-Jope, Lynn), *OUTCROP*, 16 Kestrel Drive, Worle, Weston Supermare, Avon, England, 0934-415852

Hunt, Edmund (see also Ingram-Jope, Lynn), Outcrop Publications, 16 Kestrel Drive, Worle, Weston Supermare, Avon, England, 0934-415852

Hunt, Larry, Poetry Editor (see also Dominguez, Leonard J.; Cummings, Kathleen J.), *NIT&WIT, Chicago's Arts Magazine*, PO Box 14685, Chicago, IL 60614, 312-248-1183

Hunting, Constance, Puckerbrush Press, 76 Main St., Orono, ME 04473, 207-866-4868

Hunting, Constance, *THE PUCKERBRUSH REVIEW*, 76 Main St., Orono, ME 04473

Huntress, Diana (see also Trujillo, Paul), *RIO GRANDE WRITERS NEWSLETTER*, PO Box 40126, Albuquerque, NM 87106, 505-242-1050

Hurley, Rev. James, S.D.B., Editorial Director, Don Bosco Publications / Division of Don Bosco Mulitmedia, 475 North Avenue, Box T, New Rochelle, NY 10802, 914-576-0122

Hurley, Tom (see also Harman, Willis; O'Regan, Brendan; McNeill, Barbara), *INSTITUTE OF NOETIC SCIENCES NEWSLETTER*, Inst. Noetic Sciences, 475 Gate Five Road, Suite 300, Sausalito, CA 94965, 415-331-5650

Hurst, Bernice, Director (see also Hurst, Ray), The Elvendon Press, 33 Elvendon Road, Goring-on-Thames, Reading, Berkshire RG8 0DP, England, (0491) 873227

Hurst, Ray, Director (see also Hurst, Bernice), *The Elvendon Press*, 33 Elvendon Road, Goring-on-Thames, Reading, Berkshire RG8 0DP, England, (0491) 873227

Hussey, Valerie, Director, Kids Can Press, 585½ Bloor Street W, Toronto, Ontario M6G 1K5, Canada

Hutchison, Joseph, Poetry Editor (see also Nigg, Joe; Rea, David; Miller, Patty; Reilly, Gary; Schroeder, Gary), *PENDRAGON Journal of the Creative Arts*, 2640 E. 12th Avenue, Box 715, Denver, CO 80206, 303-444-4100

Hutchison-Cleaves, Geoffrey, Editor (see also Clarges, Robert), Papyrus Publishers, PO Box 466, Yonkers, NY 10704, 914-664-0840

Hutton, Linda, Mystery Time, PO Box 2377, Coeur d'Alene, ID 83814, 208-667-7511

Hutton, Linda, Editor, *MYSTERY TIME ANTHOLOGY*, PO Box 2377, Coeur d'Alene, ID 83814

Hutton, Linda, *RHYME TIME POETRY NEWSLETTER*, PO Box 2377, Coeur d'Alene, ID 83814, 208-667-7511

Hyde, Sue, News Editor (see also Morris, David; Patton, Cindy), *GAY COMMUNITY NEWS*, 167 Tremont Street 5th Floor, Boston, MA 02111, 617-426-4469

Hyman, Suzanne K., Managing Ed. (see also Poirier, Richard; Edwards, Thomas R.), *RARITAN: A Quarterly Review*, 165 College Avenue, New Brunswick, NJ 08903, 201-932-7852

Hymer, Bemett (see also Ronck, Ronn), Mutual Publishing of Honolulu, 2055 N. King, Honolulu, HI 96819

I

Ianniello, Pat (see also Ianniello, Tom; Blake, Mona), *THE CHORD*, Musician's Contact Service, PO Box 40708, Rochester, NY 14604, 716-244-3188

Ianniello, Tom (see also Ianniello, Pat; Blake, Mona), *THE CHORD*, Musician's Contact Service, PO Box 40708, Rochester, NY 14604, 716-244-3188

Igue, Robert B., North Country Books, Inc., 18 Irving Place, Utica, NY 13501, 315-733-7915

Inglis, Mary (see also Gaston, Robyn; Platts, David Earl), *ONE EARTH*, Findhorn Foundation, The Park, Forres, Morayshire 1V36 0TZ, Scotland, 030-93-2582

Ingram-Jope, Lynn (see also Hunt, Edmund), *OUTCROP*, 16 Kestrel Drive, Worle, Weston Supermare, Avon, England, 0934-415852

Ingram-Jope, Lynn (see also Hunt, Edmund), Outcrop Publications, 16 Kestrel Drive, Worle, Weston Supermare, Avon, England, 0934-415852

Inkster, Elke (see also Inkster, Tim), The Porcupine's Quill, Inc., 68 Main Street, Erin, Ontario N0B 1T0, Canada, 519-833-9158

Inkster, Tim (see also Inkster, Elke), *The Porcupine's Quill, Inc.*, 68 Main Street, Erin, Ontario N0B 1T0, Canada, 519-833-9158

Inness-Brown, Elizabeth, Associate Editor (see also Barthelme, Frederick; Herzinger, Kim A.), *MISSISSIPPI REVIEW*, Box 5144, Southern Station, Hattiesburg, MS 39406, 601-266-4321

Innis, Donald Q., Co-Editor (see also Innis, Wendy), *INDRA'S NET*, 78 Center Street, Geneseo, NY 14454

Innis, Wendy, Co-Editor (see also Innis, Donald Q.), *INDRA'S NET*, 78 Center Street, Geneseo, NY 14454

Ioan, Elwyn (see also Gruffudd, Robat), *LOL*, Lolfa, Y, Talybont, Dyfed, Wales SY24 5ER, United Kingdom, 0970 86 304

Iodice, Ruth G. (see also Kinnick, B. Jo; Witt, Harold), *BLUE UNICORN*, 22 Avon Road, Kensington, CA 94707, 415-526-8439

Ippolito, A. V., L D A Publishers, 42-36 209 Street, Bayside, NY 11361, 212-224-0485

Irving, Eric, Editor, The Doodly-Squat Press, Box 480740, Los Angeles, CA 90048, 213-856-4867

Irving, Eric, Editor, *THE HOT SPRINGS GAZETTE*, Box 480740, Los Angeles, CA 90066, 213-856-4867

Irwin, Miriam Owen, Mosaic Press, 358 Oliver Road, Dept. 45, Cincinnati, OH 45215, 513-761-5977

Isaacs, Ida (see also Isaacs, Tony), Indian House, Box 472, Taos, NM 87571, 505-776-2953

Isaacs, Tony (see also Isaacs, Ida), *Indian House*, Box 472, Taos, NM 87571, 505-776-2953

Islewright, Lee, Quorum Editions, 10 North Mill, Cranbury, NJ 08512

Ives, Kenneth, *SOCIOLOGICAL PRACTICE*, 401 E 32nd, #1002, Chicago, IL 60616, 312-225-9181

Ives, Kenneth H., *CASE ANALYSIS*, 401 E 32nd, #1002, Chicago, IL 60616, 312-225-9181

Ives, Kenneth H., Progresiv Publishr, 401 E. 32nd #1002, Chicago, IL 60616, 312-225-9181

Ives, Rich, *THE MONTANA REVIEW*, PO Box 2248, Missoula, MT 59806, 406-543-5307

Ives, Rich, Owl Creek Press, PO Box 2248, Missoula, MT 59806, 406-543-5307

J

Jabbari, Ahmad, Mazda Publishers, PO Box 136, Lexington, KY 40501, 614-766-2552

Jack, Alex, Kanthaka Press, PO Box 696, Brookline Village, MA 02147, 617-734-8146

Jackel, Harry, Editor (see also Reynolds, Louise T.; Reynolds, Louise E.; Bolton, Stanwood; Madrigal, Sylvia), *THE NEW RENAISSANCE, An International Magazine of Ideas & Opinions, Emphasizing Literature & The Arts*, 9 Heath Road, Arlington, MA 02174

Jackman, Patricia, Randatamp Press, Box 33, Dobbs Ferry, NY 10522, 914-693-9247

Jackson, Esther, Editor (see also Bond, Jean Carey; O'Dell, J. H.; Kaiser, Ernest; Baird, Keith E.; Hairston, Loyle), *FREEDOMWAYS - A Quarterly Review of the Freedom Movement*, Freedomways Associates, Inc., 799 Broadway Suite 542, New York, NY 10003

Jackson, Guida, Managing Editor (see also Laufer, William; Wegner, Frances), Houston Writers Guild, Drawer 42331, Houston, TX 77042, 713-669-9312

Jackson, Guida, Managing Editor (see also Laufer, William; Wegner, Francis), *TOUCHSTONE*, Drawer 42331, Houston, TX 77042, 713-669-9312

Jackson, Larry S., Heidelberg Graphics, 1116D Wendy Way, Chico, CA 95926, 916-342-6582

Jackson, Larry S., Editor and Publisher (see also Hemenway, Phillip), *PHANTASM*, 1116D Wendy Way, Chico, CA 95926, 916-342-6582

Jackson, Richard (see also Panori, Michael), *THE POETRY MISCELLANY*, English Dept. Univ of Tennessee, Chattanooga, TN 37402, 615-755-4213; 624-7279

Jackson, Thomas H., Editor (see also Barringer, Margot), *POESIS: A JOURNAL OF CRITICISM*, Department of English, Bryn Mawr College, Bryn Mawr, PA 19010, 215-645-5306

Jacob, John, Cat's Pajamas Press, 527 Lyman, Oak Park, IL 60304

Jacob, John (see also Jacob, Martha), *MOJO NAVIGATOR(E)*, 527 Lyman, Oak Park, IL 60304

Jacob, Martha, Fiction (see also Jacob, John), *MOJO NAVIGATOR(E)*, 527 Lyman, Oak Park, IL 60304

Jacobs, Laurence, Editor (see also Moselle, Gary), Craftsman Book Company, 6058 Corte Del Cedro, Carlsbad, CA 92008, 619-438-7828

Jacobs, Maria, Publisher, Editor (see also Billings, Robert), *POETRY TORONTO*, 217 Northwood Drive, Willowdale, Ontario M2M 2K5, Canada

Jacobsen, Bruce (see also Riggs, Rollin), RJ Publications, Inc., 4651 Yale Station, New Haven, CT 06520, 203-624-5485

Jacobson, Bonnie (see also Wallace, Robert; Seidler, C. M.), Bits Press, Deptartment of English, Case Western Reserve Univ., Cleveland, OH 44106, 216-795-2810

Jacobson, J. (see also Huang, J.; Thoenen, B.; Cohen, M.; McKale, A.), *THE DROOD REVIEW OF MYSTERY*, Box 8872, Boston, MA 02114

Jacobson, Robert, Editor-in-Chief (see also Reuling, Karl F.), *BALLET NEWS*, 1865 Broadway, New York, NY 10023, 582-3285

Jacoby, Julie, Southwest Research and Information Center, PO Box 4524, Albuquerque, NM 87106, 505-262-1862

Jacoby, Julie, Editor, *THE WORKBOOK*, PO Box 4524, Albuquerque, NM 87106, 505-262-1862

Jade, Savoy Rose, *DAY TONIGHT/NIGHT TODAY*, Day Tonight/Night Today, PO Box 353, Hull, MA 02045

Jaeger, Sharon Ann, Intertext, 2633 East 17th Avenue, Anchorage, AK 99508

Jaeger, Sharon Ann (see also Hammer, Louis), Sachem Press, PO Box 9, Old Chatham, NY 12136, 518-794-8077

Jaffe, Dan, Editor-in-Chief (see also KcKinley, Mary Ann), BkMk Press, University of Missouri-Kansas, 5100 Rockhill Road, Kansas City, MO 64110, 276-1305

Jaffe, Harold (see also McCaffery), *FICTION INTERNATIONAL*, San Diego State University, San Diego, CA 92182, 265-5443, 265-6220

Jaffe, Larry, Director of Publications, *PARACHUTIST*, 1440 Duke Street, Alexandria, VA 22314, 703-836-3495

Jamello, Nancy Portugal (see also Walatka, Pam Portugal; Stephens, Helen; Main, Jody; Davis, Annette), Wild Horses Publishing Company, 12310 Concepcion Road, Los Altos Hills, CA 94022, 415-941-3396

86

James, Clifford (see also Bevington, Stan; Young, David; Davey, Frank; Nichol, bp; Ondaatje, Michael; McCartney, Linda; Sheard, Sarah; Reid, Dennis), Coach House Press, 95 Rivercrest Road, Toronto, Ontario M6S 4H7, Canada, 416-767-6317

James, F., Editor, Jules Verne Circle, 125 Markyate Road, Dagenham, Essex RM82LB, England

James, F., Editor, *JULES VERNE VOYAGER*, 125 Markyate Road, Dagenham, Essex RM82LB, England

James, John, Mandorla Publications, PO Box 214, Wyong, N.S.W. 2259, Australia, 043-531266

James, Nancy E., Dawn Valley Press, Box 58, New Wilmington, PA 16142

James, Nancy E., *JUST REMINISCING: A Magazine of Memories*, Box 58, New Wilmington, PA 16142

James, Nancy E. (see also Rowland, Keith D.), *SUNRUST MAGAZINE*, Box 58, New Wilmington, PA 16142

James Nelson, Assistant Editor (see also Teacher, Lawrence; Tam Mossman), Running Press, 125 South Twenty-Second Street, Philadelphia, PA 19103, 215-567-5080

James, Susan (see also Emuss, John; George, Margaret; Pain, Margaret), Guildford Poets Press, 9 White Rose Lane, Woking, Surrey, GU22 73A, England

James, Susan (see also Clancy, John), *INSIGHT NORTHWEST*, 9123-25th NE, Seattle, WA 98115, 206-523-2101

James, Susan (see also Emuss, John; George, Margaret; Pain, Margaret), *WEYFARERS*, 9 Whiterose Lane, Woking, Surrey, England

Jamison, Bill, Milagro Press, PO Box 1804, Santa Fe, NM 87501, 505-982-2041

Janda, Judy (see also Georgakas, Dan; Bokhara, Elias), Smyrna Press, Box 1803 GPO, Brooklyn, NY 11202

Janisse, Thomas, Peninhand Press, 142 Sutter Creek Canyon, Volcano, CA 95689

Janisse, Thomas, Editor & Publisher (see also Warren, Lee; Luallin, Cherryl), *THE VOLCANO REVIEW*, 142 Sutter Creek Canyon, Volcano, CA 95689

Janney, Frank (see also Geist, Anthony; Pope, Randolph), Ediciones del Norte, Box A130, Hanover, NH 03755, 603-795-2433

Janz, Milli, ACCCA Press, 19 Foothills Drive, Pompton Plains, NJ 07444, 201-835-2661

Japikse, Carl, Ariel Press, 3391 Edenbrook Court, Columbus, OH 43220, 614-876-0211

Jappinen, Rae (see also Ryan, Tim), SourceNet, PO Box 6767, Santa Barbara, CA 93160, 805-685-3314

Jappinen, Rae (see also Ryan, Tim), *WHOLE AGAIN RESOURCE GUIDE*, PO Box 6767, Santa Barbara, CA 93160, 805-685-3314

Jaquith, Cindy, Editor (see also Jenness, Doug), *THE MILITANT*, 14 Charles Lane, New York, NY 10014, 212-243-6392

Jarman, A.O.H., *LLEN CYMRU*, 6 Gwennyth St., Cathays, Cardiff CF2 4YD, Wales, 0222-31919

Jarman, Mark (see also McDowell, Robert), *THE REAPER*, 8600 University Blvd, Evansville, IN 47712, 812-425-2840

Jarrett, Emmett, Contributing Editor (see also Hershon, Robert; Lourie, Dick; Pawlak, Mark; Schreiber, Ron; Levertov, Denise), *HANGING LOOSE*, 231 Wyckoff St, Brooklyn, NY 11217

Jarvis, Charles E. (see also Jarvis, Paul), Ithaca Press, PO Box 853, Lowell, MA 01853

Jarvis, Paul (see also Jarvis, Charles E.), *Ithaca Press*, PO Box 853, Lowell, MA 01853

Jauss, David, Fiction Editor (see also Murphy, Russell; Wojahn, David; Vannatta, Dennis), *CRAZYHORSE*, Dept of English, Unviersity of Arkansas at Little Rock, Little Rock, AR 72204, 501-569-3160

Jay, Peter, Editor (see also Sterland, Julia), Anvil Press Poetry, 69 King George St., London SE10 8PX, England, 01-858-2946

Jaycox, Elbert R., The Bee Specialist, 5775 Jornada Road North, Las Cruces, NM 88001

Jebb, Robert D., Teal Press, PO Box 4346, Portsmouth, NH 03801, 431-2319

Jeffery, Mildred (see also Baehr, Anne-Ruth; Hair, Jennie; Walker, Lois V.; Yaryura-Tobias, Anibal), Pleasure Dome Press (Long Island Poetry Collective Inc.), Box 773, Huntington, NY 11743, 516-691-2376

Jeffrey, Mildred, Editor (see also Baehr, Anne-Ruth; Hair, Jennie; Walker, Lois V.; Yaryura-Tobias, Anibal; Lucas, Barbara), *XANADU*, Box 773, Huntington, NY 11743, (516) 691-2376

Jenkins, Joyce, Publisher & Editor (see also Abbott, Steve; Silberg, Richard), *POETRY FLASH*, PO Box 4172, Berkeley, CA 94704, 415-548-6871

Jenkins, Meredith (see also Donnelly, Margarita; Malone, Ruth; Wendt, Ingrid; Wilner, Eleanor; Thompson, Joyce; Caday, Jan; Mclean, Cheryl; Gordon, Rebecca; Domitrovich, Lisa), *CALYX: A Journal of Art and Literature by Women*, PO Box B, Corvallis, OR 97339, 503-753-9384

Jenness, Doug, *INTERCONTINENTAL PRESS/INPRECOR*, 410 West Street, New York, NY 10014

Jenness, Doug, Editor (see also Jaquith, Cindy), *THE MILITANT*, 14 Charles Lane, New York, NY 10014, 212-243-6392

Jennings, Tom, Black Oak Press, PO Box 4663, University Place Station, Lincoln, NE 68504

Jenoff, Marvyne, Fiction (see also Lever, Bernice; Hamilton, Helen; Allison, Gay), *WAVES*, 79 Denham Drive, Thornhill, Ont. L4J 1P2, Canada, 416-889-6703

Jeppson, Buckley, Editorial Director, Peregrine Smith Books, PO Box 667, Layton, UT 84041, 801-376-9800

Jerome, Judson, Contributing Editor ('Poetry') (see also Fulton, Len; Ferber, Ellen; Urioste, Pat; Clifton, Merritt), *THE SMALL PRESS REVIEW*, P.O. Box 100, Paradise, CA 95969, 916-877-6110

Jirgens, Karl E., *RAMPIKE*, 95 Rivercrest Road, Toronto, Ontario M6S 4H7, Canada, 416-767-6713

Jobst, Debby, Assistant Editor (see also Kwain, Constance; Meagher, Rosann), *OYEZ REVIEW*, Roosevelt University, 430 S. Michigan Avenue, Chicago, IL 60614, 312-341-2017

Johanna, Betty (see also Adams, Jan; Gordon, Rebecca; Meyerding, Jane), *LESBIAN CONTRADIC-TION-A Journal of Irreverent Feminism*, 584 Castro Street, Suite 263, San Francisco, CA 94114

John, Roland (see also Martin, B.A.), Hippopotamus Press, 26 Cedar Road, Sutton, Surrey SM25DG, England, 01-643-1970

Johns, Bud, Synergetic Press, 3965 Sacramento St., San Francisco, CA 94118, 415-EV7-8180

Johnsen, Gretchen, Poetry Editor (see also Peabody, Richard Myers, Jr.), *GARGOYLE*, PO Box 3567, Washington, DC 20007, 202-333-1544

Johnson, Bennett J., President (see also Gilbert, Herman C.), Path Press, Inc., 53 West Jackson Blvd Suite 1040, Chicago, IL 60604, 312-663-0167

Johnson, Bonnie, Co-Editor & Business Manager (see also Brill, Kastle; Willoughby, Robin; Zuckerman, Ryki), *EARTH'S DAUGHTERS*, Box 41, c/o Bonnie Johnson, Central Park Stn., NY 14215, 716-837-7778

Johnson, Bryan R., Editor (see also Mattson, Francis, O.), *BOOK ARTS REVIEW*, 15 Bleecker St, New York, NY 10012

Johnson, Carol, Managing Editor (see also Calhoun, Richard; Hill, Robert), *SOUTH CAROLINA REVIEW*, English Dept, Clemson Univ, Clemson, SC 29631, 803-656-3229

Johnson, Christine L. (see also Straayer, Arny Christine; Soule, S. Janet; Connelly, Dolores), Metis Press, Inc., PO Box 25187, Chicago, IL 60625

Johnson, Curt, *DECEMBER MAGAZINE*, 3093 Dato, Highland Park, IL 60035, 312-973-7360

Johnson, Curt, December Press, 3093 Dato, Highland Park, IL 60035, 312-973-7360

Johnson, Curt, Contributing Editor (see also Kruchkow, Diane; Savitt, Lynne; Fox, Hugh; Melnicove, Mark), *STONY HILLS: News & Review of the Small Press*, Weeks Mills, New Sharon, ME 04955, 207-778-3436

Johnson, Debra Jo, Editor (see also Miller, Melissa), *THE HARVEST SUN*, 315 E. Dittlinger, Mew Braunfels, TX 78130

Johnson, Ellwood, Editor, *CONCERNING POETRY*, English Department, Western Wash. University, Bellingham, WA 98225

Johnson, Fred, The Dragonsbreath Press, 10905 Bay Shore Drive, Sister Bay, WI 54234, 414-854-2742

Johnson, G. Wesley, *THE PUBLIC HISTORIAN*, University of California Press, Berkeley, CA 94720, 415-642-7485

Johnson, Glenn, Engineering Press, Inc., PO Box 1, San Jose, CA 95103

Johnson, Harold Leland, Hearthstone Press, 708 Inglewood Drive, Broderick, CA 95605, 916-372-0250

Johnson, Jay E., Editor-in-Chief (see also Marron, Carol A.), Carnival Press, Inc., PO Box 19087, Minneapolis, MN 55419, 612-823-7216

Johnson, Ronna, Fiction Editor (see also Steinzor, Seth; Mabe, Eirard; Elder, John), *DARK HORSE*, Box 9, Somerville, MA 02143

Johnson, Ronna, Fiction (see also Hogan, Ed; Gubernat, Susan; Sagan, Miriam; Zeitlin, Leora), Zephyr Press, 13 Robinson Street, Somerville, MA 02145

Johnson, Tom, Two-Eighteen Press, PO Box 218 Village Station, New York City, NY 10014, 212-255-1723

Johnson, W. Max, Operations Manager (see also Casey, W. Wilson), CaseCo Publications, 1138 Edisto Drive, Spartanburg, SC 29302, 803-585-3298

Johnston, Gary (see also Grant, C.D.), Blind Beggar Press, Box 437, Bronx, NY 10467

Johnston, John Wayne, Editor, *THE INTERNATIONAL UNIVERSITY POETRY QUARTERLY*, 1301 S. Noland Rd., Independence, MO 64055

Johnston, John Wayne, Editor, The International University Press, 1301 S. Noland Rd., Independence, MO 64055

Johnston, Patricia Irwin, Perspectives Press, 905 West Wildwood Ave., Fort Wayne, IN 46807

Jones, Edward (see also Parker, Laurence), *PSYCHOLOGY AND SOCIAL THEORY*, East Hill Branch, Box 2740, Ithaca, NY 14850, 607-277-0509

Jones, Jean R., *Jelm Mountain Press/West*, 129 Santa Barbara Street, Modesto, CA 95354

Jones, Jean R., Editor & Owner, Jelm Mountain Publications, 209 Park, Laramie, WY 82070, 307-742-8053

Jones, Jennifer (see also Miller, Robert; Banning, Robert), Word Power, Inc., PO Box 17034, Seattle, WA 98107, 206-782-1437

Jones, Judie (see also Urfer, Pamela), Creative Arts Development, 144 Viking Court, Soquel, CA 95073, 408-475-2396

Jones, Keith, Asst. Editor (see also Anderson, Kathy Elaine; Hemphill, Essex C.; Williams, Cynthia L.), *NETHULA JOURNAL OF CONTEMPORARY LITERATURE*, 930 F Street, Suite 610, Washington, DC 20004

Jones, Lawrence T., III, *CONFEDERATE CALENDAR WORKS*, PO Box 2048, Austin, TX 78768

Jones, Lola E., Founder & Editor (see also Reckley, Ralph), *OUTREACH: A CREATIVE WRITER'S JOURNAL*, Morgan State University, Baltimore, MD 21239, 301-444-4189

Jones, Margaret K., Griffin Books, Inc., 50 Penn Place - Suite 380, Oklahoma City, OK 73118, 405-842-0398

Jones, Richard (see also Daniels, Kate), *POETRY EAST*, Star Rt. 1 Box 50, Earlysville, VA 22936, 804-973-5299

Jones, Stephen, Contributing Editor (see also Porter, Andrew; D'Ammassa, Don; Anderson, Kay; DiFate, Vincent; Pohl, Frederik; Silverberg, Robert; Fletcher, Jo; Carmody, Larry), *SCIENCE FICTION CHRONICLE*, PO Box 4175, New York, NY 10163, 212-643-9011

Jones, Whitney (see also Alta), Shameless Hussy Press, Box 3092, Berkeley, CA 94703

Jordan, John (see also McCarthy, Tom), *POETRY IRELAND REVIEW*, 106 Tritonville Road, Dublin 4, Republic of Ireland, 685210

Jorgensen, Arne, *OIKOS: A JOURNAL OF ECOLOGY AND COMMUNITY*, 130 Valley Road, Montclair, NJ 07042

Jorgensen, Erik, Axiom Press Publishers, PO Box 1668, Burlingame, CA 94011, 415-441-1211

Jorgensen, Rich, *THE STONE*, c/o Greenpeace, 1112-B Ocean, Santa Cruz, CA 95060, 408-429-9988

Joron, Andrew, *VELOCITIES*, 1509 Le Roy Ave., Berkeley, CA 94708

Joseph, David, Editor (see also Tarlen, Carol), Red Wheelbarrow Press, 298 9th Avenue, San Francisco, CA 94118, 415-387-3412

Joseph, David, Editor (see also Tarlen, Carol), *WORKING CLASSICS*, 298 9th Avenue, San Francisco, CA 94118, 415-387-3412

Joseph, Janet (see also Pfender, Elizabeth), Clear Beginnings-Women's Writing Workshops, 12970 Westchester Trail, Chesterland, OH 44026, 206-729-1659

Joseph, Jennifer, manic d press, 1853 Stockton, San Francisco, CA 94133, 415-788-6459

Joseph, Kerman (see also Kern, Holoman), *NINETEENTH-CENTURY MUSIC*, University of California Press, Berkeley, CA 94720, 415-642-7485

Josephine, Helen B., Associate Editor (see also Starr, Carol), Women Library Workers, 2027 Parker Street, Berkeley, CA 94704, 415-540-5322

Joy, Julie, Art Director (see also Campbell, John T.; Cole, Eddie-Lou), *WORLD OF POETRY*, 2431 Stockton Blvd., Sacramento, CA 95817, 916-731-8463

Joyner, Glenn P., Ginseng Press, Rt 2, Box 1105, Franklin, NC 28734, 704-369-9735

Juba, Robert Davis "Dr. Juba" (see also Lewis, Al; Chache, Miss Kalamu), *JOYFUL NOISE INTERNATIONAL*, 109 Minna St., Suite 153, San Francisco, CA 94105, 415-931-1009

Judge, Frank, Poetry, Managing Editor (see also FitzGerald, Gregory), *EXIT*, 50 Inglewood Dr, Rochester, NY 14619

Judson, John, Editor, Juniper Press, 1310 Shorewood Dr, La Crosse, WI 54601

Judson, John, *NORTHEAST/JUNIPER BOOKS*, 1310 Shorewood Dr., LaCrosse, WI 54601

Juergensen, Hans, Associate Editor (see also Ceconi, Isabel; Juergensen, Ilse; Collins, Pat), *GRYPHON*, Dept. of Humanities-LE3 370, The University of South Florida, Tampa, FL 33620

Juergensen, Ilse, Associate Editor (see also Juergensen, Hans; Ceconi, Isabel; Collins, Pat), *GRYPHON*, Dept. of Humanities-LE3 370, The University of South Florida, Tampa, FL 33620

Julty, Sam, Neild/Kuvet Publishing Company, Box 9184, Berkeley, CA 94709, 415-527-9645

Jutkowitz, Betty C., Director of Publications (see also Jutkowitz, Edward A.), Institute for the Study of Human Issues (ISHI), 3401 Market Street, Suite 252, Philadelphia, PA 19104, 215-387-9002

Jutkowitz, Edward A., Marketing Director (see also Jutkowitz, Betty C.), *Institute for the Study of Human Issues (ISHI)*, 3401 Market Street, Suite 252, Philadelphia, PA 19104, 215-387-9002

K

Kachmar, Jessie, Snow Press, 9300 Home Court, Des Plaines, IL 60016, 312-299-7605

Kadlec, Robert F., Vice-President (see also Powell, Mary A.; Weigle, Marta), Ancient City Press, PO Box 5401, Santa Fe, NM 87502, 505-982-8195

Kaesmayr, Benno, Maro Verlag, Riedinger Gewerbepark, Riedingerstr. 24/6f, Augsburg, West Germany, 0821-41 60 33

Kahn, Dr. Sy M. (see also Gray, Don), Sydon, Inc., c/o Drama Dept, University of the Pacific, Stockton, CA 95211

Kain, Sue, Editor (see also Walker, Lois V.; Hair, Jennie; Steinle, Rita Juul; Penha, James), *NEWSLETTER*, PO Box 773, Huntington, NY 11743

Kaiser, Ernest, Associate Editor (see also Jackson, Esther; Bond, Jean Carey; O'Dell, J. H.; Baird, Keith E.; Hairston, Loyle), *FREEDOMWAYS - A Quarterly Review of the Freedom Movement*, Freedomways Associates, Inc., 799 Broadway Suite 542, New York, NY 10003

Kalechofsky, Robert (see also Kalechofsky, Roberta), Micah Publications, 255 Humphrey St, Marblehead, MA 01945, 617-631-7601

Kalechofsky, Roberta (see also Kalechofsky, Robert), *Micah Publications*, 255 Humphrey St, Marblehead, MA 01945, 617-631-7601

Kaliss, Gail Darrow, *WEST END MAGAZINE*, c/o Kaliss, 31 Montague Place, Montclair, NJ 07042

Kalmbach, Ann (see also Kellner, Tatana), Women's Studio Workshop Print Center, PO Box V, Rosendale, NY 12472, 914-658-9133

Kamei, Marlene, Editor and Publisher, Plumbers Ink Books, PO Box 233, Cerrillos, NM 87010, 505-983-8962

Kamin, Franz, Contributing Editor (see also Quasha, George; Quasha, Susan; Martin, Michele; Coffey, Michael; Stein Charles; Nedds, Trish; Kelly, Robert; Auster, Paul; McClelland, Bruce), Station Hill Press, Station Hill Road, Barrytown, NY 12507, 914-758-5840

Kaminski, Mereda, Cove View Press, PO Box 810, Arcata, CA 95521

Kamiya, Margaretta, Editor (see also Klaber, Karen), *THE BERKELEY MONTHLY*, 910 Parker Street, Berkeley, CA 94710, 415-848-7900

Kamoroff, Bernard, Bell Springs Publishing, PO Box 640, Laytonville, CA 95454, 707-984-6746

Kanellos, Nicolas, Publisher, Arte Publico Press, University of Houston, Houston, TX 77004, 713-749-4768

Kannenstine, Louis, Editorial Director, Countryman Press, Woodstock, VT 05091, 802-457-1049

Kapitan, Lynn (see also Daniel, Eddee), *THIRD COAST ARCHIVES*, PO Box 11204, Shorewood, WI 53211, 414-964-0173

Kaplan, Edward (see also Gordon, Bonnie), *SAPIENS*, PO Box 209, Millburn, NJ 07041

Kaplan, Edward (see also Gordon, Bonnie), Sapiens Press, 3704 Hyde Park Avenue, Cincinnati, OH 45209

Kaplan, Jullie, *STAR LINE*, 8350 Poole Avenue, Sun Valley, CA 91352, 818-768-4970

Kaplan, Tobey (see also Dibz, A.), Ground Under Press, 2913 Shattuck Avenue, Berkeley, CA 94705

Karahan, Patricia, The Horse and Bird Press, PO Box 67C89, Los Angeles, CA 90067, 213-823-4364

Karman, Rita, Karmic Revenge Laundry Shop Press, Box 14, Guttenberg, NJ 07093

Kastan, Denise, Hoddypoll Press, 3841-B 24th Street, San Francisco, CA 94114

Kasu, Ephraim K. (see also Wanjie, Anne Catherine; Waiyaki, D. Nyoike; Njoroge, Fred N.), East African Publishing House, PO Box 30571, Nairobi, Kenya, Kenya, 557417, 557788

Kater, Louise N., Visa Books, PO Box 186, Glen Iris, Victoria 3146, Australia, 03-256-456

Katz, F.R., Co-Editor (see also Warsaw, Janine), *STORY QUARTERLY*, PO Box 1416, Northbrook, IL 60062, 312-272-9418

Katz, Menke, Editor-in-Chief, *BITTERROOT*, PO Box 453, Spring Glen, NY 12483

Kaufman, Amy R., *STORIES*, 14 Beacon St., Suite 614, Boston, MA 02108, 617-742-3345

Kaufman, Jodi, Palate Press, 10100 Santa Monica Boulevard, Los Angeles, CA 90067, 213-277-d9171

Kaufmann, William, William Kaufmann, Inc., 95 First Street, Los Altos, CA 94022, 415-948-5810

Kavacik, Karen, Art & Graphics Editor (see also Bourne, Daniel), *ARTFUL DODGE*, PO Box 1473, Bloomington, IN 47402, 812-332-0310

Kay, John (see also Mailman, Leo; Locklin, Gerald; Zepeda, Ray; Barker, David; Snider, Clifton; Salinas, Judy), *MAELSTROM REVIEW*, 8 Farm Hill Road, Cape Elizabeth, ME 04107

Kay, Phillip (see also Carthew, Sally), The Firebird Press, PO Box 10, Kingswood, N.S.W. 2750, Australia, 047 360344

Kay, Phillip (see also Carthew, Sally), *THE NEPEAN REVIEW*, PO Box 10, Kingswood, N.S.W. 2750, Australia, 047 360344

KcKinley, Mary Ann, Assistant Editor (see also Jaffe, Dan), BkMk Press, University of Missouri-Kansas, 5100 Rockhill Road, Kansas City, MO 64110, 276-1305

Keating, Martha, Fiction Editor (see also De Foe, Mark; Gamble, Mort; McAleavey, David; Pierce, Constance), *THE LAUREL REVIEW*, West Virginia Wesleyan College, Buckhannon, WV 26201, 304-473-8006

Keenan, Gerald, Managing Ed. (see also Pruett, F.A.), Pruett Publishing Company, 2928 Pearl, Boulder, CO 80301, 303-449-4919

Kefing, Omowali (see also Yeshitela, Omali), *THE BURNING SPEAR*, PO Box 27205, Oakland, CA 94602, 415-569-9620

Kefing, Omowali (see also Yeshitela, Omali), Burning Spear Publications, PO Box 27205, Oakland, CA 94602, 415-569-9620

Keith, Donald M. (see also Keith, Louis G.), The Center For Study of Multiple Birth, 333 East Superior Street, Suite 463-5, Chicago, IL 60611, 312-266-9093

Keith, Louis G. (see also Keith, Donald M.), *The Center For Study of Multiple Birth*, 333 East Superior Street, Suite 463-5, Chicago, IL 60611, 312-266-9093

Kelch, Richard (see also Reinhart, Rod), Operation D.O.M.E. Press, 625 Field #108, Detroit, MI 48214, 313-331-5682

Keller, Gary D., General Editor (see also Van Hooft, Karen S.), Bilingual Press, Office of the Graduate School, SUNY-Binghamton, Binghamton, NY 13901, 607-724-9495

Keller, Gary D., Editor (see also Van Hooft, Karen S.), *BILINGUAL REVIEW/Revista Bilingue*, Office of the Graduate School, SUNY-Binghamton, Binghamton, NY 13901, 313-487-0042

Kelley, Kate (see also Shobe, John), Divesports Publishing, PO Box 1397, Austin, TX 78767, 512-443-5883

Kellman, Lisa (see also Costello, Debbie), Black Oyster Press, PO Box 8550, Chicago, IL 60680, 312-743-5744

Kellner, Tatana (see also Kalmbach, Ann), Women's Studio Workshop Print Center, PO Box V, Rosendale, NY 12472, 914-658-9133

Kellogg, Peggy (see also Richard, Michel Paul; Moss, Leonard; Soffer, Walter), *THOUGHTS FOR ALL SEASONS: The Magazine of Epigrams*, State University College At Geneseo, Geneseo, NY 14454, 716-245-5336

Kelly, David J. (see also Shell, Jim), Peloria Publications, PO Box 50263, Raleigh, NC 27607, 919-828-7576

Kelly, John, *COUNTERSPY,* Box 647, Ben Franklin Station, Washington, DC 20044, 202-328-0178

Kelly, Kevin, *WALKING JOURNAL,* Orenda Media, PO Box 454, Athens, GA 30603, 404-546-1353

Kelly, Patrick, Chief Editor (see also Bradley, Jacqueline T.; Weissmann, G. Warren; Brunswick, S.J.; Mallory, Eugenia P.), *BLUE HORSE,* P.O. Box 6061, Augusta, GA 30906, 404-798-5628

Kelly, Patrick, Chief Editor (see also Bradley, Jacqueline), Blue Horse Publications, PO Box 6061, Augusta, GA 30906, (404) 798-5628

Kelly, Robert, Contributing Editor (see also Quasha, George; Quasha, Susan; Martin, Michele; Coffey, Michael; Stein Charles; Nedds, Trish; Auster, Paul; Kamin, Franz; McClelland, Bruce), Station Hill Press, Station Hill Road, Barrytown, NY 12507, 914-758-5840

Kemp, P.J., Editor, *FOURTH DIMENSION,* Box 129, Richford, VT 05476

Kempton, Karl, *KALDRON,* PO Box 541, Halcyon, CA 93420, 805-489-2770

Kendrick, Terry A., Compiler, *DIRECTORY OF NORTHERN ART GALLERIES & STUDIOS,* Mid Northumberland Arts Group, Ashington, Northumberland, England, 0670-814444

Kenin, Millea, Editor (see also Murcury, Miron), *EMPIRE: For the SF Writer,* 1025-55th Street, Oakland, CA 94608, 415-655-3024

Kenin, Millea, *OTHERGATES,* 1025 55th Street, Oakland, CA 94608, 415-655-3024

Kenin, Millea, Unique Graphics, 1025 55th Street, Oakland, CA 94608, 415-655-3024

Kennedy, Alan, Editor (see also Crowley, J.), *THE DALHOUSIE REVIEW,* Dalhousie Univ. Helen L. Gorman, Bus. Mgr., Sir James Dunn Bldg. Suite 314, Halifax, Nova Scotia B3H 3J5, Canada

Kennedy, Jon, *BAY AREA WRITERS NEWSLETTER,* 3156 Williamsburg Drive #1, San Jose, CA 95117

Kennedy, Jon, LIFE Style Publications, 3156 Williamsburg Drive #1, San Jose, CA 95117, 415-497-0574

Kennedy, Jon, *WRITER'S CONNECTION,* 10601 DeAnza Blvd. #301, Cupertino, CA 95014, 408-973-0227

Kennedy, Joyce Lain, Sun Features Inc., PO Box 368-P, Cardiff, CA 92007, 619-753-3489

Kennedy, Linda, VP-Publications Director (see also Everitt, Charles; Lynch, Kevin; Bandos, Kate), The Globe Pequot Press, Old Chester Road, Chester, CT 06412, 203-526-9571

Kennedy, Sylvia, Asst. Editor (see also Liu, Robert K.; Benesh, Carolyn L.E.), *ORNAMENT, A Quarterly of Jewelry and Personal Adornment,* PO Box 35029, Los Angeles, CA 90035, 213-652-9914

Kennedy, William S., *REFLECT,* 3306 Argonne Avenue, Norfolk, VA 23509, 804-857-1097

Kenny, Maurice (see also Gosciak, J.G.), *CONTACT/11: A Bimonthly Poetry Review Magazine,* PO Box 451, Bowling Green Station, New York, NY 10004, 212-425-5979 or 212-522-3227

Kenny, Maurice (see also Gosciak, J.G.), Contact II: Publications, PO Box 451, Bowling Green Station, New York, NY 10004, 212-522-3227

Kenny, Maurice, Strawberry Press, PO Box 451, Bowling Green Station, New York, NY 10004, 212-522-3227

Kent, Carol, Managing Editor (see also Kent, David L.), Erespin Press, 929 E 50 Street, Austin, TX 78751

Kent, David L., Copy Editor (see also Kent, Carol), *Erespin Press,* 929 E 50 Street, Austin, TX 78751

Kent, Rolly, The Maguey Press/Friends Of Tucson Public Library, Box 3395, Tucson, AZ 85722, 602-791-4391

Keolker, James, *THE OPERA COMPANION,* #40 Museum Way, San Francisco, CA 94114, 415-626-2741

Keppeler, Kurt, *COLORADO-NORTH REVIEW,* University Center, University of Northern Colorado, Greeley, CO 80639, 303-351-4347

Keppeler, Kurt, Student Publications Board, University Center, University of Northern Colorado, Greeley, CO 80639

Kercheval, Jesse Lee, Fiction Editor (see also Lott, Rick), *SUN DOG*, 406 Williams Bldg., English Dept., F.S.U., Tallahassee, FL 32306, 644-1248

Kerman, Judith, Mayapple Press, PO Box 3185, Kent, OH 44240, 216-678-2775

Kern, Coralee Smith, *MIND YOUR OWN BUSINESS AT HOME*, Box 14850, Chicago, IL 60614, 312-472-8116

Kern, Ellyn R., Cottontail Publications, PO Box 44761, Indianapolis, IN 46244, 317-638-2355; 359-7765

Kern, Holoman (see also Joseph, Kerman), *NINETEENTH-CENTURY MUSIC*, University of California Press, Berkeley, CA 94720, 415-642-7485

Kerr, Walter H. (see also Tuthill, Stacy; Zadravec, Katharine; Swope, Mary; Silva, Jayne), Scop Publications, Inc., Box 376, College Park, MD 20740, 301-345-8747

Kesend, Michael, Michael Kesend, Publishing, Ltd., PO Box 1184, Gracie Station, New York, NY 10028, 212-249-5150

Kesey, Ken (see also my; Leary, Timothy; Marrs, Lee; Loren, Richard; Babbs, Ken), *SPIT IN THE OCEAN*, 85829 Ridgeway Rd, Pleasant Hill, OR 97455, 503-747-5796

Kessler, Stephen, *ALCATRAZ*, 354 Hoover Road, Santa Cruz, CA 95065

Kessler, Stephen, Alcatraz Editions, 354 Hoover Road, Santa Cruz, CA 95065

Kettner, Kathleen McGann (see also Kettner, Michael E.), *CATALYST, AN ANNUAL COLLECTION OF EROTICA*, 5625 University Way N.E., Seattle, WA 98105, 206-523-4480

Kettner, Kathleen McGann (see also Kettner, Michael), McKettner Publishing, 5625 University Way N.E., Seattle, WA 98105, 206-634-1005

Kettner, Michael (see also Kettner, Kathleen McGann), *McKettner Publishing*, 5625 University Way N.E., Seattle, WA 98105, 206-634-1005

Kettner, Michael E. (see also Kettner, Kathleen McGann), *CATALYST, AN ANNUAL COLLECTION OF EROTICA*, 5625 University Way N.E., Seattle, WA 98105, 206-523-4480

Keyes, Claire, Advisory Editor, *SOUNDINGS/EAST*, English Dept., Salem State College, Salem, MA 01970, 745-0556

Keyishian, Harry, Co-Editor (see also Cummins, Walter; Green, Martin), *THE LITERARY REVIEW*, Fairleigh Dickinson University, 285 Madison Avenue, Madison, NJ 07940, 201 377-4050

Keyishian, M., Managing Editor (see also Zander, W.; Decavalles, A.; Cumming, W.), *JOURNAL OF NEW JERSEY POETS*, Fairleigh Dickinson Univ., English Dept., 285 Madison Avenue, Madison, NJ 07940, 01-377-4700

Khalsa, Gurubanda, Singh, Arcline, Box 1550, Pomona, CA 91769, 415-644-3229

Kiefer, Paul (see also Martin, Stephen-Paul; Royal, Richard; Ensler, Eve; Millis, Christopher; Sullivan, Mary Jane; Sanders, Catherine Marie), *CENTRAL PARK*, P.O. Box 1446, New York, NY 10023

Kiernan, Robert F., Associate Editor (see also Tollers, Vincent L.; O'Donnell, Mary Ann), *LITERARY RESEARCH NEWSLETTER* , Department of English and World Literature, Manhattan College, Bronx, NY 10471, 212-920-0121

Kilgore (see also Holsapple; Empfield), *CONTRABAND MAGAZINE*, PO Box 4073, Station A, Portland, ME 04101

Kilgore (see also Holsapple; Empfield), Contraband Press, PO Box 4073, Sta A, Portland, ME 04101

Kilodney, Crad, Charnel House, c/o Crad Kilodney, PO Box 281, Station S, Toronto, Ontario M5M 4L7, Canada, 416-482-1341

Kilroy, James (see also Davie, Donald; Touster, Eva), *CUMBERLAND POETRY REVIEW*, Poetics, Inc., PO Box 120128 Acklen Station, Nashville, TN 37212, 615-373-8948

94

Kimmett, Larry (see also Regis, Peggy), Periscope Press, PO Box 6926, Santa Barbara, CA 93160, 805-964-1749

Kindred, Wendy (see also Burns, Roland; Cooke, Roger), *THE BLACK FLY REVIEW*, University of Maine at Fort Kent, Fort Kent, ME 04743, 207-834-3162

King, Dennis, Associate Editor (see also Anbian, Robert; Spilker, John; Hellerman, Steve; Kosoua, Anna; Erfurdt, Jamie), *OBOE: A Journal of Literature & Fine Art*, 495 Ellis Street, Box 1156, San Francisco, CA 94102

King, Kathi, *VEGETARIAN LIFESTYLE INTERNATIONAL NEWSLETTER*, 1500-1176 West Georgia Street, Vancouver, B.C., V6E 4A2, Canada, 687-4300

King, Kathryn E., *COLUMBIA ROAD REVIEW: A Review Magazine of Southern Presses*, PO Box 19332, Washington, DC 20036, 202-332-7079

King, Kathryn E., Editor and Publisher, King Publications, P O Box 19332, Washington, DC 20036, 202-332-7079

King, Keith, Associate Editor (see also Aronson, Arnold; Margolis, Tina; Garren, Lois; Wells, Ann; Wolff, Fred M.; Rollins, Brook), *THEATRE DESIGN AND TECHNOLOGY*, 330 W. 42nd Street, New York, NY 10036, 212-563-5551

King, Rey, *BEYOND SCIENCE FICTION*, 4144 S. 41st Street, Richmond, CA 94804, 415-658-0233

King, Rey, Editor (see also Campbell, Kalynn), Cosmic Circus Productions, 414 So 41st Street, Richmond, CA 94804, 415-529-0716

King, Robert S., Editor, Ali Baba Press, Route 10, Box 353-C2, Gainesville, GA 30501

King, Robert S., Editor (see also Kistner, Diane), *LOCAL STORMS: A Review of Georgia Poetry*, Route 10, Box 353-C2, Gainesville, GA 30501

King, Robert S., Editor (see also Kistner, Diane), *LODESTAR*, Route 10, Box 353-C2, Gainesville, GA 30501

King, Royston (see also Ford, Eric; Cooper-Brown, Howard; Clare, Robert), High Orchard Press, 125 Markyate Road, Dagenham, Essex, England RM8 2LB, England

King, Royston, Technical Editor (see also Ford, Eric), *WELLSIANA, The World Of H.G. Wells*, High Orchard, 125 Markyate Rd, Dagenham, Essex RM8 2LB, England

King, Susan E., Paradise Press, PO Box 5306, Santa Monica, CA 90405, 213-473-4972

King, Una, Sunwest Publishing, PO Box 462, Bodega Bay, CA 94923, 707-875-3373

Kinnick, B. Jo (see also Iodice, Ruth G.; Witt, Harold), *BLUE UNICORN*, 22 Avon Road, Kensington, CA 94707, 415-526-8439

Kinzie, Mary, Poetry Editor (see also Nikolic, Djordje; Mills, Donna), Elpenor Books, Box 3152, Merchandise Mart Plaza, Chicago, IL 60654, 312-935-1343

Kippel, Leslie D., Publisher (see also Brown, Toni), *RELIX*, PO Box 94, Brooklyn, NY 11229, 212-645-0818

Kirby, Michael, Editor (see also Dolan, Jill), *THE DRAMA REVIEW*, MIT Press For New York University, 300 South Bldg. 51 W. 4th Street, New York, NY 10003, 212-598-2597

Kirchhofer, Mary V., Potentials Development, Inc., 775 Main Street, Suite 321, Buffalo, NY 14203, 716-842-2658

Kirk, Norman Andrew, Editor, West of Boston, PO Box 2, Cochituate Station, Wayland, MA 01778

Kirk, Pearl, *PATHWAYS*, Box 345, Middleton, ID 83644

Kirk, Pearl L., *INKY TRAILS and TIME TO PAUSE*, Inky Trails Publications, P.O.Box 345, Middleton, ID 83644

Kirk, Pearl L., Inky Trails Publications, PO Box 345, Middleton, ID 83644

Kirkpatrick, Douglas, Baker Publishing, 9348 Monogram Avenue, Sepulveda, CA 91343

Kirshenbaum, Sandra, Editor and Publisher (see also Bigelow, Charles; Taylor, W. Thomas), *FINE PRINT: A Review for the Arts of the Book*, P O Box 3394, San Francisco, CA 94119, 415-776-1530

Kisley, Lorraine, Publisher & Editor (see also Sheehy, John; Zaleski, Philip), *PARABOLA MAGA-ZINE*, 150 Fifth Avenue, New York, NY 10011, 212-924-0004

Kistner, Diane, Associate Editor (see also King, Robert S.), *LOCAL STORMS: A Review of Georgia Poetry*, Route 10, Box 353-C2, Gainesville, GA 30501

Kistner, Diane, Editor (see also King, Robert S.), *LODESTAR*, Route 10, Box 353-C2, Gainesville, GA 30501

Kitchen, Denis, Kitchen Sink Press, No. 2 Swamp Road, Princeton, WI 54968, 414-295-6922

Kitchen, Denis, *SNARF*, No. 2 Swamp Road, Princeton, WI 54968, 414-295-6922

Kitchen, Judith (see also Rubin, Stan Sanvel; Bennett, Bruce; Allardt, Linda), State Street Press, PO Box 252, Pittsford, NY 14534, 716-586-0154

Kitrilakis, Thalia (see also Duane, Kit; Rosenwasser, Rena; Lisanevich, Xenia; Loeb, Emily), Kelsey St. Press, PO Box 9235, Berkeley, CA 94709, AM: 415-845-2260; PM: 415-548-3826

Kitroeff, A. (see also Chouliaras, Y.; Pappas, P.; Roubatis, Y.), *JOURNAL OF THE HELLENIC DIASPORA*, 337 West 36th Street, New York, NY 10018, 212-279-9586

Kittredge, John, Associate Editor (see also Wendel, Wayne C.; Wells, Nancy), *NAUTICA, THE MAGAZINE OF THE SEA FOR YOUNG PEOPLE*, Spinnaker Press, Inc., Pickering Wharf, Salem, MA 01970, 617-745-6905

Kjellberg, Judith, Editor, *WOMEN AND ENVIRONMENTS*, c/o Center for Urban and Community Studies, 455 Spadina Avenue, Toronto, Ontario M5S 2G8, Canada, 416-978-4478

Klaber, Karen, Publisher (see also Kamiya, Margaretta), *THE BERKELEY MONTHLY*, 910 Parker Street, Berkeley, CA 94710, 415-848-7900

Klein, Gillian, Editor, *MULTICULTURAL TEACHING FOR PRACTITIONERS IN SCHOOLS AND COMMUNITY*, Keele University, Department of Education, Keele, Staffordshire ST5 5BG, England

Klein, William F., Editor (see also Church, Philip D.; Crump, Galbraith M.; Daniel, Robert W.), *THE KENYON REVIEW*, Kenyon College, Gambier, OH 43022, 614-427-3339

Kleinhans, Chuck (see also Hess, John; Lesage, Julia), *JUMP CUT, A Review of Contemporary Cinema*, P.O. Box 865, Berkeley, CA 94701, 415-658-4482

Kleinheksel, Karol, Grey Whale Press, 4820 S.E. Boise, Portland, OR 97206

Klienheksel, Karol, *BLOW*, 4820 S.E. Boise, Portland, OR 97206, 503-774-6304

Klotz, Saadi, Sufi Islamia/Prophecy Publications, 65 Norwich Street, San Francisco, CA 94110, 415-285-0562

Klotzer, Charles L., Editor & Publisher, Focus/Midwest Publishing Co., Inc., 8606 Olive Blvd., St Louis, MO 63132

Klotzer, Charles L., Editor-Publisher, *ST. LOUIS JOURNALISM REVIEW*, 928A N. McKnight, St. Louis, MO 63132, 314-991-1699

Knier, Timothy, Editor (see also Brilliant, Marilyn A.; Schultz, Cathy; Sitz, Carlton), Pine Mountain Press, Inc., Box 19746, West Allis, WI 53219, 414-778-1120

Kniffel, Leonard, *POETRY RESOURCE CENTER OF MICHIGAN (PRC) NEWSLETTER & CALEN-DAR*, 743 Beaubien, Detroit, MI 48226, 964-0888

Kniffel, Leonard J., Fallen Angel Press, 17606 Muirland, Detroit, MI 48221, 313-864-0982

Knight, Arthur Winfield (see also Knight, Kit), *THE UNSPEAKABLE VISIONS OF THE INDIVIDU-AL*, PO Box 439, California, PA 15419, 412-938-8956

Knight, Bill, *PRAIRIE SUN*, 2028 'P' Street NW, Washington, DC 20036

Knight, Kit (see also Knight, Arthur Winfield), *THE UNSPEAKABLE VISIONS OF THE INDIVIDU-AL*, PO Box 439, California, PA 15419, 412-938-8956

Knipe, Tony, Editor (see also Brown, Stuart), Ceolfrith Press, Sunderland, Tyne & Wear SR27DF, England, 0783-41214

Knowles, Ardeana Hamlin, Contrib. Editor (see also Rimm, Virginia M.; Perrin, Arnold; Grierson, Ruth; Briggs, Henry; Boisvert, Donald J.; McIntyre, Joan; Brown, Ronald G.; Beck, Raymond M.), *NEW ENGLAND SAMPLER*, RFD #1 Box 2280, Brooks, ME 04921, 207-525-3575

Knuth, Priscilla, Executive Editor (see also Vaughan, Thomas), *OREGON HISTORICAL QUARTER-LY*, 1230 S.W. Park Ave., Portland, OR 97205, 503-222-1741

Ko, Loretta (see also Dorsett, Robert), *THE ATAVIST*, Box 5643, Berkeley, CA 94705

Koehler, Michael (see also Moentmann, Uwe), S Press Tapes, Talsperren Strasse 21, D-5600 Wuppertal 21, West Germany

Koelsch, William A., Union Park Press, PO Box 2737, Boston, MA 02208

Koenig, Karl R., Chatham Publishing Company, PO Box 283, Burlingame, CA 94010, 415-348-0331

Koenigsberg, Allen, *ANTIQUE PHONOGRAPH MONTHLY*, 502 East 17th St., Brooklyn, NY 11226, 212-941-6835

Koenigsberg, Allen, APM Press, 502 East 17th St., Brooklyn, NY 11226, 212-941-6835

Kolm, Ron, Low-Tech Press, 30-73 47th Street, Long Island City, NY 11103, 212-721-0946

Koontz, Tom (see also Coghill, Sheila; Lowe, Kyrla; Tammaro, Thom), *BARNWOOD*, RR 2, Box 11C, Daleville, IN 47334

Koontz, Tom (see also Tammaro, Thom; Coghill, Sheila), The Barnwood Press, RR 2, Box 11C, Daleville, IN 47334, 317-378-0921

Kooser, Ted, Windflower Press, PO Box 82213, Lincoln, NE 68501

Kopelman, Sajjada (see also Kopelman, Sikander; de la Torre Bueno, Anka), Sufi Order Publications/Omega Press, PO Box 574, Lebanon Spring, NY 12114, 518-794-8181

Kopelman, Sikander (see also Kopelman, Sajjada; de la Torre Bueno, Anka), *Sufi Order Publications/Omega Press*, PO Box 574, Lebanon Spring, NY 12114, 518-794-8181

Koppenhaver, April M. (see also Frompovich, Catherine J.; Diana Witt), C J Frompovich Publications, RD 1, Chestnut Road, Coopersburg, PA 18036, 215-346-8461

Koran, Dennis (see also Guss, David), Panjandrum Books, 11321 Iowa Ave., Ste.1, Los Angeles, CA 90025, 213-477-8771

Koran, Dennis, Ed-in-Chief (see also Guss, David), *PANJANDRUM POETRY JOURNAL*, 11321 Iowa Ave. Ste.1, Los Angeles, CA 90025, 213-477-8771

Kornblum, Allan, *DENTAL FLOSS MAGAZINE*, P.O. Box 546, 626 E. Main, West Branch, IA 52358, 319-643-2604

Kornblum, Allan (see also Kornblum, Cinda), Toothpaste Press, PO Box 546, 626 E. Main, West Branch, IA 52358, 319-643-2604

Kornblum, Cinda (see also Kornblum, Allan), *Toothpaste Press*, PO Box 546, 626 E. Main, West Branch, IA 52358, 319-643-2604

Kosoua, Anna, Associate Editor (see also Anbian, Robert; Spilker, John; King, Dennis; Hellerman, Steve; Erfurdt, Jamie), *OBOE: A Journal of Literature & Fine Art*, 495 Ellis Street, Box 1156, San Francisco, CA 94102

Kostakis, Peter (see also Friedman, Richard; Pearlstein, Darlene), The Yellow Press, 2394 Blue Island Ave, Chicago, IL 60608

Kostelanetz, Richard, The Future Press, PO Box 73 Canal Street, New York, NY 10013

Kostelanetz, Richard (see also Scobie, Stephen; Frank, Sheldon; Zelevansky, Paul; Higgins, Dick; Essary, Loris; Young, Karl), *PRECISELY*, PO Box 73, Canal Street, New York, NY 10013

Kostick, Marilyn G., Editor-in-Chief, Dorison House Publishers, Inc., 824 Park Square Bldg, Boston, MA 02116, 617-426-1715

Kowaluk, L. (see also Roussopoulos, D.; Young, B.; Caloren, F.), *OUR GENERATION*, 3981 boul St Laurent, Montreal, Quebec H2W 1Y5, Canada

Krakowiak, Mary, Editor, *ENVIRONMENTAL PERIODICALS BIBLIOGRAPHY,* 2074 Alameda Padre Serra, Santa Barbara, CA 93103, 805-965-5010

Krakowiak, Mary, Editor (see also Garrison, Thomas S.; Williams, Susan), International Academy at Santa Barbara, 2074 Alameda Padre Serra, Santa Barbara, CA 93103, 805-965-5010

Kramer, Aaron (see also Everitt, Helen; Vondrasek, Bets; Andrew, Helen), *WEST HILLS REVIEW: A WALT WHITMAN JOURNAL,* Walt Whitman Birthplace Assn., 246 Walt Whitman Road, Huntington Station, NY 11746, (516) 427-5240

Kramer, Glenn, Associate Editor (see also Golden, Michael; Elias, Viki; Harrison, Jim; Mungo, Raymond; Bukowski, Charles; Placidus, Max; Codrescu, Andrei; Horotwitz, Mikhail; Ligi; Mitchell, Donna; Riedel, Robert), *SMOKE SIGNALS,* 1516 Beverly Road, Brooklyn, NY 11226

Krannich, Caryl Rae, Impact Publications (of Virginia)-A Division of Development Concepts Incorporated, 5311 Richardson Drive, Fairfax, VA 22032, 703-361-7300

Kranz, Henry, The Erie Street Press, 642 S Clarence Avenue, Oak Park, IL 60304, 312-848-5716

Kranz, Henry, *LUCKY STAR,* 642 S Clarence Avenue, Oak Park, IL 60304, 312-848-5716

Kratoville, Betty Lou, *ACADEMIC THERAPY,* 20 Commercial Boulevard, Novato, CA 94947, 415-883-3314

Kratoville, Betty Lou, Academic Therapy Publications, 20 Commercial Boulevard, Novato, CA 94947, 415-883-3314

Kratz, Dennis (see also Schulte, Rainer; Tobias, Ronald), *TRANSLATION REVIEW,* Univ. of Texas-Dallas, Box 688, Richardson, TX 75080, 214-690-2093

Kraus, Oswald, L., Brick Row Publishing Co. Ltd., Private Bag, Takapuna, Auckland 9, New Zealand, 444-5920

Krelove, Lillian, Asst. Ed. (see also Burns, Richard), *COME-ALL-YE,* P.O. Box 494, Hatboro, PA 19040, 215-675-6762

Krelove, Lillian (see also Burns, Richard K.), Legacy Books (formerly Folklore Associates), PO Box 494, Hatboro, PA 19040, 215-675-6762

Kremer, John, Ad-Lib Publications, PO Box 1102, Fairfield, IA 52556, 515-472-6617

Kriegel, Phyllis, Managing Editor, *NEW DIRECTIONS FOR WOMEN,* 108 West Palisade Avenue, Englewood, NJ 07631, 201-568-0226

Kroll, William, Editor, *FAMILY THERAPY,* 391 Willets Road, Roslyn Heights, L.I., NY 11577, (516) 484-4950

Kroll, William, President, Libra Publishers, Inc., 391 Willets Road, Roslyn Heights, L.I., NY 11577, (516) 484-4950

Kronen, H. B., *DANCE SCOPE,* 570 7 Ave. 20 Fl, New York, NY 10018, 212-691-4564

Kronenwetter, David, On Da Bayou Press & Publishing, PO Box 52467, New Orleans, LA 70152, 504-943-7041

Kronenwetter, David, *SOUTHERN AGITATOR,* PO Box 52467, New Orleans, LA 70152, 504-943-7041

Kruchkow, Diane, *SMALL PRESS NEWS,* Weeks Mills, New Sharon, ME 04955

Kruchkow, Diane, Editor (see also Johnson, Curt; Savitt, Lynne; Fox, Hugh; Melnicove, Mark), *STONY HILLS: News & Review of the Small Press,* Weeks Mills, New Sharon, ME 04955, 207-778-3436

Kruchkow, Diane, *ZAHIR,* Weeks Mills, New Sharon, ME 04955

Krueger, Caryl W., Belleridge Press, Box 970, Rancho Santa Fe, CA 92067, 619-756-3756

Kucak, Tanya, *RAIN: JOURNAL OF APPROPRIATE TECHNOLOGY,* 2270 NW Irving Street, Portland, OR 97210, 503-227-5110

Kucak, Tanya, The Rain Umbrella, 2270 NW Irving St, Portland, OR 97210, 503-227-5110

Kufeld, Adam, Editor, Solidarity Publications, PO Box 40874, San Francisco, CA 94140, 415-626-6626

98

Kuhlken, Ken (see also Huff, Casey; Renfro, Elizabeth), Flume Press, 644 Citrus Avenue, Chico, CA 95926, 916-342-1583

Kuhlken, Ken (see also Brashers, Charles), Helix House, 9231 Molly Woods Avenue, La Mesa, CA 92041, 619-460-4107

Kuhne, Barbara, Press Gang Publishers, 603 Powell Street, Vancouver, B.C. V6A 1H2, Canada, 253-2537

Kulp, Denise (see also Leonard, Vickie; Douglas, Carol Anne; Lootens, Tricia; Henry, Alice; Fugh-Berman, Adrianne; Moira, Fran; Dejanikus, Tacie; Sorrel, Lorraine), *OFF OUR BACKS*, 1841 Columbia Road NW Rm 212, Room 212, Washington, DC 20009, 202-234-8072

Kunreuther, Frances, *WOMEN'S WORKS IN REVIEW*, Dept. WR, 201 West 92nd Street, New York, NY 10025

Kunz, Christian, *FUTURE STUDIES CENTRE NEWSLETTER*, The Birmingham Settlement, 318 Summer Lane, Newtown, Birmingham B19 3RL, England, 021-359-3562

Kupferberg, Tuli, *PAPER NEWS*, 160 6th Avenue, New York, NY 10013, 212-925-3823

Kupferberg, Tuli, Vanity Press, 160 6th Avenue, New York, NY 10013, 212-925-3823

Kurzweil, Edith, Executive Editor (see also Phillips, William), *PARTISAN REVIEW*, 121 Bay State Road 3/F, Boston, MA 02215, 617-353-4260

Kwain, Constance, Editor (see also Jobst, Debby; Meagher, Rosann), *OYEZ REVIEW*, Roosevelt University, 430 S. Michigan Avenue, Chicago, IL 60614, 312-341-2017

Kwan, S. (see also Tajima, Renee; Lee, C.N.; Chow, P.; Chin, R.; Chu, B.; Francia, L.; Wu, S.; Lew, Walter; Hahn, Tomie), *BRIDGE: ASIAN AMERICAN PERSPECTIVES*, Asian Cine-Vision, Inc., 32 E Broadway, New York, NY 10002, 212-925-8685

L

La Brie, Henry G., III, Director, Mercer House Press, P.O. Box 681, Kennebunkport, ME 04046, 207-282-7116

La Russo, Carol (see also Allen, Marcus), Whatever Publishing, Inc./Rising Sun Records, 61 Camino Alto, Suite 100, PO Box 137, Mill Valley, CA 94941, 415-388-2100

Laba, Mark, Coma Goats Press, 729A Queen Street East, Toronto, Ontario M4M 1H1, Canada

Laba, Mark, *IN TENTS*, 729A Queen Street East, Toronto, Ontario M4M 1H1, Canada

Laba, Mark, Guest Editor (see also Curry, J.W.; Lefler, Peggy), *INDUSTRIAL SABOTAGE*, 729A Queen Street East, Toronto, Ontario M4M 1H1, Canada, 416-463-5867

Laba, Mark, Guest Editor (see also Curry, J.W.; Bennett, John M.), *1Cent*, 729a Queen Street East, Toronto, Ontario M4M 1H1, Canada

Laba, Mark (see also Curry, J.W.), Spider Plots in Rat-Holes, 729A Queen Street East, Toronto, Ontario M4M 1H1, Canada, 416-463-5867

Lagerquist, Dave, *CLOAD MAGAZINE*, PO Box 1448, Santa Barbara, CA 93102, 805-962-6271

LaGory, Michael, *LITERARY ARTS HAWAII*, PO Box 11213, Moiliili Station, Honolulu, HI 96828

Laing, Christine, Executive Editor (see also Bolotin, Norm), Creative Options, Box 601, Edmonds, WA 98020, 206-789-5808

Laird, W. David, Editor, *BOOKS OF THE SOUTHWEST*, Univ. of Az Library, A349 Main Library, U. of AZ, Tucson, AZ 85721

Lake, Paul, Poetry (see also Hall, B.C), *NEBO: A LITERARY JOURNAL*, Department of English, Arkansas Tech University, Russellville, AR 72801, 501-968-0256

Lally, Patrick, *THIRD EYE*, 189 Kelvin Drive, Buffalo, NY 14223, 716 832-1639

Lambe, Ron, *RFD,* Route 1, Box 127-E, Bakersville, NC 28705

Lamkin, Selma H., Nikmal Publishing, 698 River St., Mattapan, MA 02126, 617-361-2101

Lammi, Walter J., Editor (see also Chickering, A. Lawrence; Glynn, Patrick), Institute for Contemporary Studies, 785 Market Street, Suite 750, San Francisco, CA 94103, 415-543-6213

Lammi, Walter J., Editor (see also Chickering, A. Lawrence; Glynn, Patrick), *JOURNAL OF CONTEMPORARY STUDIES,* 785 Market Street, Suite 750, San Francisco, CA 94103, 415-543-6213

Lamperti, Claudia, New Victoria Publishers, 7 Bank St., Lebanon, NH 03766, 603-448-2264

Lance, Jeanne (see also Holland, Peter; Yurechko, John), *GALLERY WORKS,* 1465 Hammersley Avenue, Bronx, NY 10469, 212-379-1519

Landers, Daniel M., *JOURNAL OF SPORT PSYCHOLOGY,* Box 5076, Champaign, IL 61820, 217-351-5076

Lang, Doug, Poetry Editor (see also Swift, Mary; Rosenzweig, Phyllis; Wittenberg, Clarissa; Fleming, Lee), *WASHINGTON REVIEW,* P O Box 50132, Washington, DC 20004, 202-638-0515

Lang, Lillian (see also Schain, Stephen; Volz, Bill; Clark, Duane), *VERNAL,* 522 E. Third Avenue, Durango, CO 81301, 303-259-0221

Lang, Tom (see also Apglyn, Nic), *IDO-VIVO,* International Language (IDO) Society of Gt. Britain, 135 Stryd Keppoch, Caerdydd, Wales, 0222-497414

Lang, Tom (see also Apglyn, Nic), International Language (IDO) Society of Great Britain, 135 Stryd Keppoch, Caerdydd, Wales, 0222-497414

Langdon, Larry, Larry Langdon Publications, 34735 Perkins Creek Road, Cottage Grove, OR 97424

Lange, Gerald, The Bieler Press, PO Box 65856, St Paul, MN 55165, 612-292-9936

Langeuin, Michael Peter (see also Snyder, Jerry), *MAGICAL BLEND,* PO Box 11303, San Francisco, CA 94101

Langevil, Michael (see also Snyder, Jerry), Magical Blend, PO Box 11303, San Francisco, CA 94101

Langlais, Jacques, Associate Editor (see also Stark, Mary), *INTERCULTURE (Formerly THE MONCHANIN JOURNAL),* Centre Interculturel Monchanin, 4917 St-Urbain, Montreal, Quebec H2T 2W1, Canada, 514-288-7229

Langton, Roger W. (see also Fericano, Paul F.; Fericano, Katherine), Poor Souls Press/Scaramouche Books, PO Box 236, Millbrae, CA 94030

Lanigan, Thomas, Humana Press, PO Box 2148, Clifton, NJ 07015, 201-773-4389

Lanoux, Claude (see also Harris, Tina), Fablewaves Press, PO Box 7874, Van Nuys, CA 91409, 213-322-0236

Lansky, Vicki (see also Whelan, Sandra), *PRACTICAL PARENTING,* 18326B Minnetonka Blvd, Deephaven, MN 55391, 612-475-1505

Lant, Jeffrey, President, Jeffrey Lant Associates, Inc., 50 Follen Street, Suite 507, Cambridge, MA 02138, 617-547-6372

Lant, Jeffrey, President, JLA Publications, A Division Of Jeffrey Lant Associates, Inc., 50 Follen Street, Suite 507, Cambridge, MA 02138, 617-547-6372

Lape, Walter (see also Rikhoff, Jean; Weaver, Francis; Quirk, John; Porter, Regina), Loft Press, 93 Grant Avenue, Glens Falls, NY 12801

Lapolla, Paul (see also Gosney, Michael; Tobias, Michael), Avant Books, 3719 Sixth Avenue, San Diego, CA 92103, 619-295-0473

Laquer, Ann T., *INDIAN TRUTH,* 1505 Race St., Philadelphia, PA 19102, 215-563-8349

Lareau, George A., Afterimage Book Publishers, 1202 Commonwealth #406, Allston, MA 02134

Larsen, Ken, *ARC,* PO Box 1547, Mendocino, CA 95460, 707-937-5818

Larsen, Ken, Rural Arts Services, PO Box 765, Mendocino, CA 95460, 707-937-5818

Larson, Randall D., *CINEFAN,* PO Box 70868, Sunnyvale, CA 94086

Larson, Randall D., *CINEMASCORE—THE FILM MUSIC JOURNAL*, PO Box 70868, Sunnyvale, CA 94086

Larson, Randall D., Editor and Publisher, Fandom Unlimited Enterprises, PO Box 70868, Sunnyvale, CA 94086

Larson, Randall D., *REBORN*, PO Box 70868, Sunnyvale, CA 94022

Larson, Randall D., *THRESHOLD OF FANTASY*, PO Box 70868, Sunnyvale, CA 94086, 408-379-2446

LaRusso, Joseph, Managing Editor (see also Gibbons, Reginald; Penlongo, Bob; Hahn, Susan), *TRIQUARTERLY*, 1735 Benson Avenue, Northwestern Univ., Evanston, IL 60201, 312-492-3490

Lastname, Bradley, *BILE*, 932 W. Oakdale, Chicago, IL 60614, 312-929-3387

Lastname, Bradley, No Tickee/No Washee Enterprises Ltd, 932 W. Oakdale, Chicago, IL 60614, 312-929-3387

Lateiner, Bonnie, Vortex Editions, PO Box 42698, San Francisco, CA 94101

Latimer, Dan R. (see also Wright, Thomas L.), *SOUTHERN HUMANITIES REVIEW*, 9088 Haley Center, Auburn Univ., Auburn, AL 36830, 205-826-4606

Latta, John (see also Henkel, Chris), *CHIAROSCURO*, 108 North Plain Street, Ithaca, NY 14850, 607-272-1233

Latta, John (see also Henkel, Chris), Clearly Obscure Press, 108 North Plain Street, Ithaca, NY 14850

Latta, John (see also Hathaway, Baxter; Henkel, Christopher), Ithaca House, 108 North Plain Street, Ithaca, NY 14850, 607-272-1233

Lauber, Peg Carlson, Rhiannon Press, 1105 Bradley, Eau Claire, WI 54701, 715-835-0598

Laufer, William, Publisher (see also Jackson, Guida; Wegner, Frances), Houston Writers Guild, Drawer 42331, Houston, TX 77042, 713-669-9312

Laufer, William, Publisher (see also Wegner, Francis; Jackson, Guida), *TOUCHSTONE*, Drawer 42331, Houston, TX 77042, 713-669-9312

Laughlin, R. Owen, Lynn Corporation, Inc., 2484 Sharkey Road - 101, Clearwater, FL 33575, 813-797-0404

Laughter, Fred, Mismanaging Editor (see also Brennan, Barbara), Moonlight Publications, PO Drawer 2850, La Jolla, CA 92038

Laurans, Penelope, Associate Editor (see also Erikson, Kai T.; Wipprecht, Wendy), *THE YALE REVIEW*, 1902A Yale Station, New Haven, CT 06520

Lauritsen, John, Pagan Press, 26 St. Mark's Place, New York, NY 10003, 212-674-3321

Laverriere, Lorraine Moreau, Astra Publications, 24 Edgewood Terrace, Methuen, MA 01844, 617-686-5381

Laverriere, Lorraine Moreau, *REBIRTH OF ARTEMIS*, 24 Edgewood Terrace, Methuen, MA 01844, 617-686-5381

Laverrriere, Lorraine Moreau, *NEW VOICES*, 24 Edgewood Terrace, Methuen, MA 01844, 617-686-5381

Lawrence, Candida, Editor, *COYDOG REVIEW*, 203 Halton Lane, Watsonville, CA 95076, 408-688-2794

Lawrence, E.S. (see also de Faymonville, Denise; Sheroan, Dorsey F.), Wheat Forders, Box 6317, Washington, DC 20015, 202-362-1588

Lawson, Dr. Todd, Editor-in-Chief (see also Comen, Dr. Diane; Marsic, John; Rader, Steve; Monte, Oscar; Nishi, Mio; Ginsberg, Allen; Samolis, Dr. Sam; Graham, Joan; Ferlinghetti, Lawrence; Ramirez, Julio; Haynes, Dr. Robert; Snyder, Gary; Morris, Dr. Richard), *ALPS MONTHLY*, PO Box 99394, San Francisco, CA 94109, 415-771-3431

Lawson, Suzy, Amity Publications, 78688 Sears Road, Cottage Grove, OR 97424, 503-942-7501

Lawson, Todd S.J., Editor, Director (see also Comen, Diane; Marsic, John; Samolis, William; Comen, Diane; Graham, Joan; Rader, Steve), Peace & Pieces Press, Box 99394, San Francisco, CA 94109, 415-771-3431

Lea, Sydney, Editor (see also Scheley, James), Kenyon Hill Publications, PO Box 170, Hanover, NH 03755, 603-795-4027

Lea, Sydney, Editor (see also Schley, James), *NEW ENGLAND REVIEW and BREAD LOAF QUARTERLY (NER/BLQ)*, Box 170, Hanover, NH 03755, 603-795-4027

Leach, Susan L. (see also Tenpas, Kathleen M.), *ARACHNE*, Arachne, Inc., 162 Sturges Street, Jamestown, NY 14701, 716-488-0417

Leaper, Eric, *CURRENTS*, National Organization for River Sports, Box 6847, Colorado Springs, CO 80934, 303-473-2466

Lear, Robert, Contributing Editor (see also Osaki, Mark), *ROLLING THUNDER*, PO Box 9024, Berkeley, CA 94709

Learman, Rev. Roshi L.B.H. Kinzan, *THE JOURNAL OF SHASTA ABBEY*, PO Box 199, Mt. Shasta, CA 96067, 916-926-4208

Learnard, Stephen F., The Awareness Techniques Center, 15 Queens Lane, Box 338, Stow, MA 01775, 617-562-2154

Leary, Timothy (see also Kesey, Ken; my; Marrs, Lee; Loren, Richard; Babbs, Ken), *SPIT IN THE OCEAN*, 85829 Ridgeway Rd, Pleasant Hill, OR 97455, 503-747-5796

Leavell, Wm. A., *THE WASHINGTON REPORT*, Editors Release Service, PO Box 10309, St. Petersburg, FL 33733, 813-866-1598

Leaver, Anne, Director, Dolphin-Moon Press, PO Box 22262, Baltimore, MD 21203

LeBlond, William, Editor (see also Smith, Larry L.), Chronicle Books, 870 Market Street Suite 915, San Francisco, CA 94102, 415-777-7240

Lecard, Marc, Chance Additions, 395 Capp Street #11, San Francisco, CA 94110, 415-#11-826-6736

Leddy, Chris, Associate Editor (see also Gove, Jim; Mitchell, Charles), *MINOTAUR*, P.O. Box 4094, Burlingame, CA 94010

Lee, Anthony A., Editor (see also Caton, Margaret), Kalimat Press, 10889 Wilshire Blvd #700, Los Angeles, CA 90024, 213-208-8059

Lee, Barbara, Assistant Editor (see also Eshelman, Wm. R.), Scarecrow Press, P O Box 656, Metuchen, NJ 08840, 201-548-8600

Lee, C.N., Art Director (see also Tajima, Renee; Chow, P.; Chin, R.; Chu, B.; Francia, L.; Wu, S.; Lew, Walter; Hahn, Tomie; Kwan, S.), *BRIDGE: ASIAN AMERICAN PERSPECTIVES*, Asian Cine-Vision, Inc., 32 E Broadway, New York, NY 10002, 212-925-8685

Lee, Eric, Editor, Fist & Rose Publishers, Inc., PO Box 2126, Afula, Israel

Lee, Eric, Editor, *THE NEW INTERNATIONAL REVIEW*, PO Box 2126, Afula, Israel

Lee, Jean C. (see also Balsamo, Ron; Hughes, John E.; Reed, W.A.; Reed, Vicki; Thompson, Catherine; Dennis, Deborah), *FARMER'S MARKET*, PO Box 1272, Galesburg, IL 61402

Lee, Ralph E., Pro/Press Publishing Co., 5698 Hollyleaf Lane, San Jose, CA 95118, 408-266-1440

Lee, Susannah, Managing Editor (see also Henry, DeWitt; O'Malley, Peter; Peseroff, Joyce), *PLOUGHSHARES*, Box 529, Cambridge, MA 02139

Lees, John (see also Mortimer, Peter; Swan, Pete), Iron Press, 5 Marden Terrace, Cullercoats, North Shields Tyne & Near NE30 4PD, England

Leffler, Merrill (see also Lehrman, Neil), Dryad Press, PO Box 29161, Presidio, San Francisco, CA 94129

Lefler, Peggy, Guest Editor (see also Curry, J.W.; Laba, Mark), *INDUSTRIAL SABOTAGE*, 729A Queen Street East, Toronto, Ontario M4M 1H1, Canada, 416-463-5867

102

Lehman, David, Editor (see also Green, Stefanie; Black, Joel; Hartley, Glen T.), Nobodaddy Press, 159 Ludlowville Road, Lansing, NY 14882

Lehman, David (see also Green, Stefanie; Black, Joel; Hartley, Glen T.), *POETRY IN MOTION*, 159 Ludlowville Road, Lansing, NY 14882

Lehr, David, *THE ALTERNATIVE MAGAZINE*, Alternative Publications, Inc., PO Box 463, Zionsville, IN 46077, 317-251-1754

Lehrman, Neil (see also Leffler, Merrill), Dryad Press, PO Box 29161, Presidio, San Francisco, CA 94129

Leibowitz, Herbert, *PARNASSUS: POETRY IN REVIEW*, 205 West 89th Street, New York, NY 10024, 212-787-3569

Leighton, Betty (see also Wilson, Emily), The Jackpine Press, 1878 Meadowbrook Drive, Winston-Salem, NC 27104, 919-725-8828

Leighton, Elliott, *CONTACT*, PO Box 9248, Berkeley, CA 94709, 415-644-0696

Leimroth, Carol (see also Carney, Matthew), Caislan Press, Box 28371, San Jose, CA 95159, 408-723-8514

Leman, H. J., Cinema Publishing Company, 1612 NW Alta Vista Drive, Corvallis, OR 97330

LeMelle, Tilden J. (see also Hawley, Edward A.; Shepherd, George W., Jr.), *AFRICA TODAY*, c/o G.S.I.S, Univ of Denver, Denver, CO 80208

Lengyel, Cornel, Dragon's Teeth Press, 7700 Wentworth Springs Road, El Dorado Nat. Forest, Georgetown, CA 95634

Lenhart, Gary (see also Masters, Gregory; Scholnick, Michael), *MAG CITY*, 437 East 12 St. No. 26, New York, NY 10009

Lennard, Susan, Editoral Assistant (see also Osborne, Anne; Martindale, Sheila; Hancock, Geoff; Thom, Heather; Gibson, Brenda), *CANADIAN AUTHOR & BOOKMAN*, 25 Ryerson Aveune, 131 Bloor Street W, Toronto, Ontario M5t 2P3, Canada, 416-364-4203

Lennon, Nancy (see also Dellutri, Mary; Goldman, Richard), *RAMBUNCTIOUS REVIEW*, Rambunctious Press, Inc., 1221 West Pratt, Chicago, IL 60626

Lenson, David, Panache Books, PO Box 77, Sunderland, MA 01375, 413-665-7521

Lent, Max (see also Lent, Tina), The Garlic Press, 24 Wellington Avenue, Rochester, NY 14611, 716-328-5126

Lent, Tina (see also Lent, Max), *The Garlic Press*, 24 Wellington Avenue, Rochester, NY 14611, 716-328-5126

Leonard, Vickie (see also Douglas, Carol Anne; Lootens, Tricia; Henry, Alice; Fugh-Berman, Adrianne; Moira, Fran; Dejanikus, Tacie; Kulp, Denise; Sorrel, Lorraine), *OFF OUR BACKS*, 1841 Columbia Road NW Rm 212, Room 212, Washington, DC 20009, 202-234-8072

Lepler, H., Explorations Press, PO Box 907, Greenfield, MA 01302

Lesage, Julia (see also Hess, John; Kleinhans, Chuck), *JUMP CUT, A Review of Contemporary Cinema*, P.O. Box 865, Berkeley, CA 94701, 415-658-4482

Lesser, Wendy, Editor (see also Bowles, Paul; Berger, John; Hass, Robert; Vidal, Gore; Wasserman, Steve), *THE THREEPENNY REVIEW*, PO Box 9131, Berkeley, CA 94709, 415-849-4545

Lester, Paul, Protean Publications, 34 Summerfield Crescent, Flat 4, Edgbaston, Birmingham B16, England

Letcher, Tina, Editor (see also Suryanarayan, Indu; Tyler, Larry; Woodson, Jon), *NORTHEAST JOURNAL*, PO Box 217, Kingston, RI 02881

Letsinger, Sue (see also Brown, David; Halsted, Deb), Left Bank Books, 92 Pike Street, Seattle, WA 98101

Leukovins, Deborah, Art Editor (see also Wadden, Paul; Williams, Susan; DeGrazia, Emilio; Lund, Orval J.), *GREAT RIVER REVIEW*, 211 W 7th, Winona, MN 55987

Lev, Donald (see also Dame, Enid), *HOME PLANET NEWS*, P.O. Box 415 Stuyvesant Station, New York, NY 10009, 212-769-2854

Lev, Donald (see also Dame, Enid), Home Planet Publications, PO Box 415 Stuyvesant Station, New York, NY 10009, 212-769-2854

Lever, Bernice, Editor-Publisher (see also Hamilton, Helen; Allison, Gay; Jenoff, Marvyne), *WAVES*, 79 Denham Drive, Thornhill, Ont. L4J 1P2, Canada, 416-889-6703

Leverant, Robert (see also Bratman, David), Images Press, PO Box 756, Sebastopol, CA 95472, 707-823-4351

Levertov, Denise, Contributing Editor (see also Hershon, Robert; Lourie, Dick; Pawlak, Mark; Schreiber, Ron; Jarrett, Emmett), *HANGING LOOSE*, 231 Wyckoff St, Brooklyn, NY 11217

Levidow, Les (see also Young, Bob), Free Association Books (FAB), 26 Freegrove Road, London N7 9RQ, United Kingdom, 01-609-5646

Levin, Paul, *CONSTRUCTION COMPUTER APPLICATIONS NEWSLETTER*, 1105-F Spring Street, Silver Spring, MD 20910

Levin, Paul, Construction Industry Press, 1105-F Spring Street, Silver Spring, MD 20910

Levine, Dr. Barry B., *CARIBBEAN REVIEW*, Florida International University, Tamiami Trail, Florida International Univ., Miami, FL 33199, 305-554-2246

Levine, Mark L., Scarf Press, 58 E 83rd Street, New York, NY 10028, 212-744-3901

Levine, Samuel P., Samuel P. Levine, PO Box 174, Canoga Park, CA 91305, 818-343-0550

Levinson, Joan (see also Efros, Susan), Waterfall Press, 2122 Junction Avenue, El Cerrito, CA 94530, 415-232-5539

Levitt, Annabel, Publisher, Vehicle Editions Inc., 496 La Guardia Place #226, New York, NY 10012

Levy, Barry, Poetry Editor (see also Weinberger, Jerome), *GRINNING IDIOT: A MAGAZINE OF THE ARTS*, Grinning Idiot Press, PO Box 1577 General Post Office, Brooklyn, NY 11202

Levy, Barry, Poetry Editor (see also Weinberger, Jerome), Grinning Idiot Press, PO Box 1577, General Post Office, Brooklyn, NY 11202

Levy, Bronwen, Assistant Editor (see also Ferrier, Carole; Critchley, Cecily), *HECATE*, P.O. Box 99, St. Lucia, Queensland 4067, Australia

Levy, Herman (see also Partee, Phillip), Sprout Publications Inc, PO Box 4064, Sarasota, FL 33578, 813-349-6535

Lew, Walter (see also Tajima, Renee; Lee, C.N.; Chow, P.; Chin, R.; Chu, B.; Francia, L.; Wu, S.; Hahn, Tomie; Kwan, S.), *BRIDGE: ASIAN AMERICAN PERSPECTIVES*, Asian Cine-Vision, Inc., 32 E Broadway, New York, NY 10002, 212-925-8685

Lewandowski, Steve (see also Maloney, Dennis), *WHITE PINE JOURNAL*, 73 Putnam Street, Buffalo, NY 14213, 716-825-8671

Lewandowski, Steve (see also Maloney, Dennis), White Pine Press, 73 Putnam Street, Buffalo, NY 14213

Lewis, Al (see also Juba, Robert Davis "Dr. Juba"; Chache, Miss Kalamu), *JOYFUL NOISE INTERNATIONAL*, 109 Minna St., Suite 153, San Francisco, CA 94105, 415-931-1009

Lewis, Brian A., C.K. Smoley & Son, Inc., PO Box 274, Grand Haven, MI 49417, 616-842-9449

Lewis, Dale (see also Camp, Bill), Sunbeam Books, 23630 Old Owen Road, Monroe, WA 98272, 206-794-5919

Lewis, Harry (see also Breger, Brian; Wachtel, Chuck), *# MAGAZINE*, 339 W. 4th Street #2R, New York, NY 10014

Lewis, Monte (see also Rattan, Cleatus; Hammes, Ken), *CROSS TIMBERS REVIEW*, Cisco Junior College, Cisco, TX 76437, 817-442-2567

Lewis, R. (see also Toulson, S.), Keepsake Press, 26 Sydney Road, Richmond, Surrey, England, 01 940 9364

Leyland, Alice, *T-J TODAY*, PO Box 533, Watsonville, CA 95077, 408-728-3948

Leyland, Winston, Gay Sunshine Press, Inc., P.O. Box 40397, San Francisco, CA 94140, 415-824-3184

Leyner, Mark, Co-Director (see also Glynn, Thomas; White, Curtis), Fiction Collective, Inc., Brooklyn College, Dept. of English, Brooklyn, NY 11210, 212-780-5547

Libro, A.C., Editor, *ASPHODEL*, 613 Howard Avenue, Pitman, NJ 08071

Libro, A.C., Editor, Blackbird Press, 613 Howard Avenue, Pitman, NJ 08071

Liddy, John, *THE STONY THURSDAY BOOK*, 128 Sycamore Ave, Rath Bhan, Limerick, Republic of Ireland

Lieb, Patricia (see also Schott, Carol), Lieb/Schott Publications, PO Box 229, Bourbonnais, IL 60914

Lieb, Patricia (see also Schott, Carol), *PTERANODON*, PO Box 229, Bourbonnais, IL 60914

Ligi, Contributing Editor (see also Golden, Michael; Elias, Viki; Harrison, Jim; Mungo, Raymond; Bukowski, Charles; Placidus, Max; Codrescu, Andrei; Horotwitz, Mikhail; Kramer, Glenn; Mitchell, Donna; Riedel, Robert), *SMOKE SIGNALS*, 1516 Beverly Road, Brooklyn, NY 11226

Ligotti, Thomas, Contributing Editor (see also Wiloch, Thomas), *GRIMOIRE*, c/o Thomas Wiloch, 8181 Wayne Road Apt H2084, Westland, MI 48185

Lind, Alan R. (see also Benedict, Roy G.; Hansen, Zenon R.), Transport History Press, PO Box 201, Park Forest, IL 60466, 312-799-1785

Lind, Lars (see also Brewer, Merry), Poet Papers, P.O. Box 528, Topanga, CA 90290

Lindberg, Stanley W., Editor (see also Corey, Stephen), *THE GEORGIA REVIEW*, Univ. of Georgia, Athens, GA 30602, 404-542-3481

Lindeburg, Michael R., Professional Publications, Inc., PO Box 199, San Carlos, CA 94070, 415-593-9119

Linden, Eddie S., *AQUARIUS*, Flat 3, 114 Sutherland Avenue, London W9, England

Linder, Eric (see also Marion, Paul), Yellow Umbrella Press, 501 Main St., Chatham, MA 02633, 617-945-0144

Lindquist, Barbara (see also Arnold, Jeanne), Mother Courage Press, 1533 Illinois Street, Racine, WI 53405, 414-634-1047

Lindsay, Fay Diers, Executive Editor (see also Lindsay, Kenneth), AIGA Publications, PO Box 148, Laie, HI 96762, 808-293-5277

Lindsay, Kenneth, Technical Editor (see also Lindsay, Fay Diers), *AIGA Publications*, PO Box 148, Laie, HI 96762, 808-293-5277

Lindsey, Elbert, Jr., *STARWIND*, The Starwind Press, PO Box 98, Ripley, OH 45167, 513-392-4549

Lines, Marianna (see also Button, John; Gaston, Robin), The Findhorn Press, The Park, Forres, Morayshire 1V360TZ, Scotland, 030-93-2582

Ling, David, Editorial Director (see also McEwan, Graham), Heinemann Publisher's (NZ) Ltd, Box 36064, Auckland, New Zealand, 489154

Ling, Gilbert N. (see also Negemonk, William), *PHYSIOLOGICAL CHEMISTRY & PHYSICS*, Route 2, Box 28A, Wake Forest, NC 27587, 919-556-2940

Lingo, T.D., Director, Dormant Brain Research and Development Laboratory, PO Box 10, Black Hawk, CO 80422

Lipman, Burton E., Bell Publishing, 15 Surrey Lane, East Brunswick, NJ 08816, 201-257-7793

Lippert, Ronald S., *NEW METHODS JOURNAL (VETERINARY)*, PO Box 22605, San Francisco, CA 94122, 415-664-3469

Lisanevich, Xenia (see also Duane, Kit; Rosenwasser, Rena; Loeb, Emily; Kitrilakis, Thalia), Kelsey St. Press, PO Box 9235, Berkeley, CA 94709, AM: 415-845-2260; PM: 415-548-3826

Liszka, James Jakob, Philosophy Editor (see also Sexton, Thomas; Spatz, Ronald), *THE ALASKA QUARTERLY REVIEW*, Department of English/U of A, Anchorage, 3221 Providence, Anchorage, AK 99508, 907-786-1731

Little, Jeffrey B., Publisher, Liberty Publishing Company, Inc., 50 Scott Adam Road, Cockeysville, MD 21030, 301-667-6680

Liu, Robert K., Editor (see also Benesh, Carolyn L.E.; Kennedy, Sylvia), *ORNAMENT, A Quarterly of Jewelry and Personal Adornment*, PO Box 35029, Los Angeles, CA 90035, 213-652-9914

Livens, R. G. (see also Evans, D. Ellis; Smith, J. Beverley), *BULLETIN OF THE BOARD OF CELTIC STUDIES*, Univ. of Wales Press, 6 Gwennyth Street, Cathays, Cardiff CF2 4YD, Wales

Ljungkull, Christine, Design Editor (see also Boyer, Susan), *THE TOWNSHIPS SUN*, Box 28, Lennoxville, Quebec, Canada

Lloyd, D H (see also Hellen, Shelley), Applezaba Press, PO Box 4134, Long Beach, CA 90804, 213-591-0015

Lloyd, Robert (see also Hoffman, D. S.), Durak, RD 1 Box 20C, Rock Stream, NY 14878

Locke, Duane, *ABATIS*, Ut Review Press, University of Tampa, Tampa, FL 33606

Lockhart, Franklyn B. (see also Lockhart, Russell A.), The Lockhart Press, Box 1207, Port Townsend, WA 98368, 206-385-6412

Lockhart, Russell A. (see also Lockhart, Franklyn B.), *The Lockhart Press*, Box 1207, Port Townsend, WA 98368, 206-385-6412

Locklin, Gerald, Associate Editor (see also Mailman, Leo; Zepeda, Ray; Barker, David; Snider, Clifton; Salinas, Judy; Kay, John), *MAELSTROM REVIEW*, 8 Farm Hill Road, Cape Elizabeth, ME 04107

Lockwood, Guy, White Mountain Publishing Company, 13801 N. Cave Creek Rd, Phoenix, AZ 85022, 971-2720

Loeb, Catherine (see also Searing, Susan), *FEMINIST COLLECTIONS: WOMEN'S STUDIES LIBRARY RESOURCES IN WISCONSIN*, 112A Memorial Library, 728 State Street, Madison, WI 53706, 608-263-5754

Loeb, Catherine (see also Searing, Susan), *FEMINIST PERIODICALS: A CURRENT LISTING OF CONTENTS*, 112A Memorial Library, 728 State Street, Madison, WI 53706, 608-263-5754

Loeb, Catherine (see also Searing, Susan), *NEW BOOKS ON WOMEN & FEMINISM*, 112A Memorial Library, 728 State Street, Madison, WI 53706, 608-263-5754

Loeb, Catherine (see also Searing, Susan), Women's Studies Librarian-at-Large, 112A Memorial Library, 728 State Street, Madison, WI 53706

Loeb, Emily (see also Duane, Kit; Rosenwasser, Rena; Lisanevich, Xenia; Kitrilakis, Thalia), Kelsey St. Press, PO Box 9235, Berkeley, CA 94709, AM: 415-845-2260; PM: 415-548-3826

Loeb, Tim, Thorndike Press, PO Box 157, Thorndike, ME 04986, 207-948-2962

Loeffler, Carl, Contemporary Arts Press, PO Box 3123, Rincon Annex, San Francisco, CA 94119, 415-431-7524

Loeffler, Carl E., *ART COM*, PO Box 3123, Rincon Annex, San Francisco, CA 94119, 415-431-7672/431-7524

Loeffler, Mark (see also Essary, Loris), *INTERSTATE*, PO Box 7068, U.T. Sta., Austin, TX 78713

Loeffler, Mark (see also Essary, Loris), Noumenon Press, PO Box 7068, University Station, Austin, TX 78713

Logan, Karen, National Literary Guild, 210 North Pass Avenue #204, Burbank, CA 91505, 213-845-2687

Logsdon, Loren, Fiction (see also Robinson, Forrest; Mann, John), *MISSISSIPPI VALLEY REVIEW*, Dept. of English, Western Ill. University, Macomb, IL 61455, 309-298-1514

Lohmann, Charles, Airplane Press, 400 S. Laurel Street, Richmond, VA 23220

Lohmann, Charles M., Editor, *THE NEW SOUTHERN LITERARY MESSENGER*, 400 S. Laurel Street, Richmond, VA 23220, 804-780-1244

Loiry, William S., Executive Editor, Loiry Publishing House, 635 South Orange Avenue Suite 6, Sarasota, FL 33577, 813-365-1959

LoNano, Mari, Associated Writing Programs, AWP c/o Old Dominion University, Norfolk, VA 23508

Lond, Harley W., *INTERMEDIA*, PO Box 27670, Los Angeles, CA 90027

Lone Dog, Lcota (see also Smith, Barbara; Rhodes, Gina; Oliveira, Ana), Kitchen Table: Women of Color Press, Box 2753, New York, NY 10185, 212-308-5389

Loomis, Mildred J., Editor Emeritus (see also Rarihokwats), *FOUR ARROWS*, PO Box 3177, York, PA 17402, 717-993-6664

Lootens, Tricia (see also Leonard, Vickie; Douglas, Carol Anne; Henry, Alice; Fugh-Berman, Adrianne; Moira, Fran; Dejanikus, Tacie; Kulp, Denise; Sorrel, Lorraine), *OFF OUR BACKS*, 1841 Columbia Road NW Rm 212, Room 212, Washington, DC 20009, 202-234-8072

Lopilato, Peter, *THE RYDER*, 104½ E. Kirkwood, Bloomington, IN 47401, 339-2001

Loren, Richard (see also Kesey, Ken; my; Leary, Timothy; Marrs, Lee; Babbs, Ken), *SPIT IN THE OCEAN*, 85829 Ridgeway Rd, Pleasant Hill, OR 97455, 503-747-5796

Lorrah, Jean (see also Wickstrom, Lois), Empire Books, 10612 Altman Street, Tampa, FL 33612

Lorrah, Jean (see also Wickstrom, Lois), *PANDORA, An Original Anthology of Role-expanding Science Fiction and Fantsy*, PO Box 625, Murray, KY 42071

Lorrance, Arleen (see also Pike, Diane Kennedy), LP Publications, (The Love Project), PO Box 7601, San Diego, CA 92107, 619-225-0133

Lorrance, Arleen (see also Pike, Diane K.), *THE SEEKER MAGAZINE*, PO Box 7601, San Diego, CA 92107, 619-225-0133

Lotgrave, Janet (see also Beckman, Lanny; Maurer, Ralph), New Star Books Ltd., 2504 York Avenue, Vancouver, B.C. V6K 1E3, Canada, 604-738-9429

Lott, Clarinda Harriss, Editor-in-Chief, The New Poets Series, Inc., 541 Piccadilly Rd., Baltimore, MD 21204, 301-321-2868

Lott, Rick, Poetry Editor (see also Kercheval, Jesse Lee), *SUN DOG*, 406 Williams Bldg., English Dept., F.S.U., Tallahassee, FL 32306, 644-1248

Louder, Fred (see also Sarah, Robyn; Hannan, Jack), *FOUR BY FOUR: A SELECTION OF POETS*, 4647, rue Hutchison, Montreal, Quebec H2V 4A2, Canada, 514-274-1902

Louder, Fred (see also Sarah, Robyn), *Villeneuve Publications*, 4647, rue Hutchison, Montreal, Quebec H2V 4A2, Canada, 514-274-1902

Lourie, Dick (see also Hershon, Robert; Pawlak, Mark; Schreiber, Ron; Levertov, Denise; Jarrett, Emmett), *HANGING LOOSE* , 231 Wyckoff St, Brooklyn, NY 11217

Lovelock, Yann, Assistant Editor (see also Toczek, Nick), *THE LITTLE WORD MACHINE*, 5 Beech Terrace, Undercliffe, Bradford, West Yorkshire, BD3 0PY, England

Lovgren, George K., Editor, Karl Bern Publishers, 9939 Riviera Drive, Sun City, AZ 85351

Lowe, Kyrla (see also Coghill, Sheila; Koontz, Tom; Tammaro, Thom), *BARNWOOD*, RR 2, Box 11C, Daleville, IN 47334

Lowe, Lorilee (see also Bass, Lorena), Coriander Press, PO Box 337, Ashland, OR 97520, 503-488-1016

Lowery, Robert G., Editor-Publisher (see also Murphy, Maureen), *IRISH LITERARY SUPPLE-MENT*, 114 Paula Boulevard, Selden, NY 11784, 516-698-8243

Lowy, David C., President, Janitor, Sergeant-at-Arms, Lowy Publishing, 5047 Wigton, Houston, TX 77096, 713-723-3209

Loyd, Bonnie, Managing Editor (see also Boyd, Blair), *LANDSCAPE*, PO Box 7107, Berkeley, CA 94707, 415-549-3233

Luain, Cathal O, *CARN (a link between the Celtic nations)*, 9 Br Cnoc Sion, Ath Cliath 9, Republic of Ireland, Dublin 373957

Luallin, Cherryl, Associate Editor (see also Janisse, Thomas; Warren, Lee), *THE VOLCANO REVIEW*, 142 Sutter Creek Canyon, Volcano, CA 95689

Luboff, Ken, John Muir Publications, Inc., PO Box 613, Santa Fe, NM 87501, 505-982-4078

Lucas, Barbara, Associate Editor (see also Baehr, Anne-Ruth; Hair, Jennie; Jeffrey, Mildred; Walker, Lois V.; Yaryura-Tobias, Anibal), *XANADU*, Box 773, Huntington, NY 11743, (516) 691-2376

Lucas, John (see also Rodway, Allan; Parfitt, George), Byron Press, The English Dept., Univ. Park, Nottingham, England

Lucia, Joseph, *CREEPING BENT*, 433 W. Market Street, Bethlehem, PA 18018, 215-691-3548

Luckman, John, Editor (see also Schwartz, Howard), GBC Press, Gambler's Book Club, 630 S. 11th St., Box 4115, Las Vegas, NV 89127, 702-382-7555

Luden, Charles, Astro Black Books, P O Box 46, Sioux Falls, SD 57101, 605-338-0277

Luke, Hugh, Editor (see also Raz, Hilda), *PRAIRIE SCHOONER*, 201 Andrews Hall, Univ. of Nebraska, Lincoln, NE 68588

Lum, Darrell (see also Chock, Eric), *BAMBOO RIDGE, THE HAWAII WRITERS' QUARTERLY*, 990 Hahaione Street, Honolulu, HI 96825, 808-395-7098

Lum, Darrell (see also Chock, Eric), Bamboo Ridge Press, 990 Hahaione Street, Honolulu, HI 96825, 808-395-7098

Lumpkin, Kirk, Managing Editor & Sound Direction (see also Gravelle, Barbara; Bertolet, Bebe), *ZYGA MAGAZINE ASSEMBLAGE*, PO Box 7452, Oakland, CA 94601, 415-261-6837

Lumpkin, Kirk, Managing Editor, Sound Direction, & Publisher (see also Gravelle, Barbara; Bertolet, Bebe), Zyga Multimedia Research, PO Box 7452, Oakland, CA 94601, 415-261-6837

Lund, Orval J., Fiction Editor (see also Wadden, Paul; Williams, Susan; DeGrazia, Emilio; Leukovins, Deborah), *GREAT RIVER REVIEW*, 211 W 7th, Winona, MN 55987

Lund, Peder C., President and Publisher (see also Thomas, Virginia), Paladin Enterprises, Inc., PO Box 1307, Boulder, CO 80306, 303-443-7250

Lundberg, David W., Voice of Liberty Publications, 3 Borger Place, Pearl River, NY 10965, (914) 735-8140

Lunde, David, Editor (see also Henris, Marilyn), The Basilisk Press, P.O. Box 71, Fredonia, NY 14063, 716-934-4199

Luneau, Lynn, Associate Editor (see also Cruickshank, Douglas; McGowan, Cese), Mho & Mho Works, Box 33135, San Diego, CA 92103, 619-488-4991

Lunn, Jean, Poetry Editor (see also Dunning, Barbara Renkens), *SANDSCRIPT*, Box 333, Cummaquid, MA 02637, 617-362-6078

Lurkis, Alexander, President, Icare Press Inc., 193-12 Nero Avenue, Jamaica, NY 11423, 212-465-2843

Luschei, Glenna, Publisher (see also Berry-Horton, Glenna), *CAFE SOLO*, 7975 San Marcos, Atascadero, CA 93422, 805-466-0947

Lush, Richard M. (see also Greenwald, Roger), Anjou, PO Box 322 Station P, Toronto Ontario, Canada, 416-368-9739

Lush, Richard M, Associate Editor (see also Greenwald, Roger), *WRIT*, Two Sussex Avenue, Toronto, Canada, 416-978-4871

Lutz, Dick, Dimi Press, 3820 Oak Hollow Lane, SE, Salem, OR 97302, 503-364-7698

Luxton, Stephen (see also Allen, Robert; Draper, Jan; Dow, Hugh), *THE MOOSEHEAD REVIEW*, Box 169, Ayer's Cliff, Quebec, Canada, 819-842-2835, 838-4801

Lybrand, Bert, Spectrum Books, Box 20822, Portland, OR 97220

Lybrand, Lisa (see also Worden, Mark; Butkus, Greg), *POETRY TODAY*, Box 20822, Portland, OR 97220, 213-334-4732

Lyle, John, *TRANSFORMACTION*, Harpford, Sidmouth, Devon EX10 0NH, England

Lynch, Joan Cornell, Associate Editor (see also Lynch, Michael), *PARIS/ATLANTIC INTERNATIONAL MAGAZINE OF POETRY*, 31 Avenue Bosquet, Paris, 75007, France, 555-91-73

Lynch, Kevin, Production Director (see also Everitt, Charles; Kennedy, Linda; Bandos, Kate), The Globe Pequot Press, Old Chester Road, Chester, CT 06412, 203-526-9571

Lynch, Michael, Editor (see also Lynch, Joan Cornell), *PARIS/ATLANTIC INTERNATIONAL MAGAZINE OF POETRY*, 31 Avenue Bosquet, Paris, 75007, France, 555-91-73

Lynskey, Edward C., *CROP DUST*, Route 2, Box 389-1, Bealeton, VA 22712, 703-439-2140

Lynskey, Edward C., Crop Dust Press, Route 2, Box 389-1, Bealeton, VA 22712, 703-439-2140

Lyon, Elisabeth (see also Bergstrom, Janet; Penley, Constance), *CAMERA OBSCURA: A Journal of Feminism and Film Theory*, PO Box 25899, Los Angeles, CA 90025

Lyon, Ted, *CHASQUI*, Dept of Spanish, Brigham Young University, Provo, UT 84602

Lyon, Thomas J., *WESTERN AMERICAN LITERATURE*, UMC 32, Utah State Univ., Logan, UT 84322

Lyons, Joan, (Cordinator, USW Press), Visual Studies Workshop Press, 31 Prince Street, Rochester, NY 14607, 716-442-8676

Lyons, Nathan, Editor, *AFTERIMAGE*, 31 Prince Street, Rochester, NY 14607, 716-442-8676

M

Maas, Paula Dianne (see also Stach, Alex), *Western Sun Publications*, PO Box 1470, 290 S First Avenue, Yuma, AZ 85364, 602-782-4646

Mabe, Eirard, Art Editor (see also Steinzor, Seth; Johnson, Ronna; Elder, John), *DARK HORSE*, Box 9, Somerville, MA 02143

Mac, Vicki, Coordinating Editor (see also Phebe(Karen Beiser)), *DINAH, a lesbian-feminist publication*, Lesbian Activist Bureau, P.O. Box 1485, Cincinnati, OH 45201

McAleavey, David, Poetry Editor (see also De Foe, Mark; Keating, Martha; Gamble, Mort; Pierce, Constance), *THE LAUREL REVIEW*, West Virginia Wesleyan College, Buckhannon, WV 26201, 304-473-8006

McAlister, Kim (see also Rowell, Carol), *FEMINIST BULLETIN*, PO Box 350, San Diego, CA 92101, 714-233-8984

McAllister, Bruce (see also Fox, William L.), West Coast Poetry Review Press, 1335 Dartmouth Dr, Reno, NV 89509, 702-322-4467

McAllister, Lesley, *IDENTITY*, 336 Queen Street East, Toronto, Ontario M5A 1S8, Canada, 416-366-2347

McAllister, Paul W. (see also Finley, Sara; Thorne, J.), Three Tree Press, PO Box 10044, Lansing, MI 48901

McAnally, Mary, Cardinal Press, Inc., 76 N Yorktown, Tulsa, OK 74110, 918-583-3651

Macarow, Leo, Greenview Publications, Box 7051, Chicago, IL 60630, 312-282-5289

McBee, Denis (see also van Valkenburg, Rick; Henderson, Jock), *BEATNIKS FROM SPACE*, Box 8043, Ann Arbor, MI 48107, 313-668-6867

McBee, Denis (see also van Valkenburg, Rick; Henderson, Jock), The Neither/Nor Press, Box 8043, Ann Arbor, MI 48107, 313-668-6867

McBride, John (see also Vangelisti, Paul), *INVISIBLE CITY*, PO Box 2853, San Francisco, CA 94126

McBride, John (see also Vangelisti, Paul), Red Hill Press, San Francisco + Los Angeles, PO Box 2853, San Francisco, CA 94126

McBride, Mekeel, Contributing Editor (see also Murphy, George; Carver, Raymond; Gallagher, Tess; Galvin, Brendan; Matthews, William; Mueller, Lisel), *TENDRIL*, Box 512, Green Harbor, MA 02041, 617-834-4137

McCaffery (see also Jaffe, Harold), *FICTION INTERNATIONAL*, San Diego State University, San Diego, CA 92182, 265-5443, 265-6220

McCaffrey, Phillip, The Charles Street Press, P.O. Box 4692, Baltimore, MD 21212

McCall, Karen E. (see also Schultz, Alixa), *GATHERING POST*, PO Box 3, St. Peter, MN 56082, 507-931-6391

McCall, Karen E. (see also Olson, David; Sherman, Jack), *THEATERWORK MAGAZINE*, 120 South Broad, Mankato, MN 56001, 507-345-7885

McCallum, Tracy (see also MacNaughton, Anne; Douthit, Peter), Minor Heron Press, PO Box 2615, Taos, NM 87571, 505-758-0081

McCann, Michael, *ART HAZARDS NEWSLETTER*, 5 Beekman Street, New York, NY 10038, 212-227-6220

McCarthy, M.L. (see also Wincote, Basil), Red Candle Press, 19 South Hill Park, London NW3 2ST, England

McCarthy, Tom (see also Jordan, John), *POETRY IRELAND REVIEW*, 106 Tritonville Road, Dublin 4, Republic of Ireland, 685210

McCartney, Linda (see also Bevington, Stan; Young, David; Davey, Frank; James, Clifford; Nichol, bp; Ondaatje, Michael; Sheard, Sarah; Reid, Dennis), Coach House Press, 95 Rivercrest Road, Toronto, Ontario M6S 4H7, Canada, 416-767-6317

McCarville, Mike, *BYLINE*, 7901 NE 10th S204, Midwest City, OK 73110, 405-733-1129

McClelland, Bruce, Contributing Editor (see also Quasha, George; Quasha, Susan; Martin, Michele; Coffey, Michael; Stein Charles; Nedds, Trish; Kelly, Robert; Auster, Paul; Kamin, Franz), Station Hill Press, Station Hill Road, Barrytown, NY 12507, 914-758-5840

McCormick, Pat, Art (see also Neeld, Judith; Truscott, Robert Blake), *STONE COUNTRY*, PO Box 132, Menemsha, MA 02552, 617-693-5832

McCormick, Pat, Art Editor (see also Neeld, Judith), Stone Country Press, PO Box 132, Menemsha, MA 02552, 617-693-5832

McCoy, Barbara, Haiku Editor (see also Craig, David; Christian, Paula; White, Gail), *PIEDMONT LITERARY REVIEW*, P.O.Box 3656, Danville, VA 24541, 804-793-0956

McCrady, Ellen, *ABBEY NEWSLETTER: Bookbinding & Conservation*, c/o School of Library Service, 516 Butler Library Columbia University, New York, NY 10027, 212-280-4014

McCreary, Susan A., Strawberry Patchworks, 517 Northview Drive, Fayetteville, NC 28303, 919-484-4976

McCune, Kate, *AWP NEWSLETTER*, AWP c/o Old Dominion University, Norfolk, VA 23508

McCunn, Donald, Editor, Design Enterprises of San Francisco, PO Box 14695, San Francisco, CA 94114

McCurry, Jim, Libra Press, PO Box 341, Wataga, IL 61488

McDevitt, T.J., M.D., Little Red Hen, Inc., PO Box 4260, Pocatello, ID 83201, 208-233-3755

MacDonald, Angus, Editor & Publisher (see also MacDonald, Barry Myles; Rickenbacher, William F.), *ST. CROIX REVIEW*, Box 244, Stillwater, MN 55082, 612-439-7190

MacDonald, Barry Myles, Editor (see also MacDonald, Angus; Rickenbacher, William F.), *ST. CROIX REVIEW*, Box 244, Stillwater, MN 55082, 612-439-7190

Macdonald, Ian, Gleniffer Press, 11 Low Road, Castlehead, Paisley PA2 6AQ, Scotland, 041-889-9579

MacDonald, Lachlan P., Padre Productions, PO Box 1275, San Luis Obispo, CA 93406, 805-543-5404

MacDonald, Lachlan P., Editor, *PUBLISHING IN THE OUTPUT MODE,* P.O.Box 1275, San Luis Obispo, CA 93406, (805) 543-5404

McDonald, Susan, Associate Editor (see also Mitchell, Steven L.), Northland Press, PO Box N, Flagstaff, AZ 86002, 602-774-5251

McDonald, Susan (see also Wiener, Phyllis; Ochtrup, Monica), *WARM JOURNAL,* 414 First Avenue North, Minneapolis, MN 55401, 612-332-5672

McDonald, Susan (see also Wiener, Phyllis; Ochtrup, Monica), Women's Art Registry of Minnesota, 414 First Avenue North, Minneapolis, MN 55401, 612-332-5672

McDougall, Betsy, Managing Editor (see also Spiegelman, Willard), *SOUTHWEST REVIEW,* Southern Methodist Univ., Dallas, TX 75275, 214-692-2263

McDowell, Mike, Editor-Publisher, *BLITZ,* PO Box 48124, Los Angeles, CA 90048

McDowell, Paul, Highway Book Shop, 4338-199A Street, Langley, B.C. V3A 4V7, Canada

McDowell, Robert (see also Jarman, Mark), *THE REAPER,* 8600 University Blvd, Evansville, IN 47712, 812-425-2840

Mace, Scott, *BUG TAR,* Box 1534, San Jose, CA 95109

Mcelhearn, Kirk (see also Goldberg, Jay), *BOGUS REVIEW,* 120 West 97th Street #10A, New York, NY 10025, 222-1731

Mcelhearn, Kirk (see also Goldberg, Jay), Bogusbooks, 120 West 97th Street #10A, New York, NY 10025

McElligot, Pat (see also Pride, Anne; Balogh, Paulette), *MOTHEROOT JOURNAL,* 214 Dewey Street, Pittsburgh, PA 15218, 412-731-4453

McElligott, Pat (see also Pride, Anne; Balogh, Paulette), Motheroot Publications, 214 Dewey Street, Pittsburgh, PA 15218

McEwan, Graham, Educational Director (see also Ling, David), Heinemann Publisher's (NZ) Ltd, Box 36064, Auckland, New Zealand, 489154

McFadden, S. Michele (see also Wilson, Roberta), Career Publishing, Inc., PO Box 5486, Orange, CA 92667, 714-771-5155/In CA 1-800-821-0543/Outside CA 1-800-854-4014

McFale, Patricia, Publisher & Editor, Galvanic, 127 East 73rd Street, New York, NY 10021

McFale, Patricia, Publisher & Editor (see also Gyongy, Adrienne), *SCANDINAVIAN REVIEW,* 127 East 73rd Street, New York, NY 10021, 212-879-9779

McFarland, Ron, Editor (see also Snyder, Margaret; Buxton, Karen; Foriyes, Tina), *SNAPDRAGON,* English Department, University of Idaho, Moscow, ID 83843, 208-885-6156

McGarey, Gladys (see also McGarey, William), Gabriel Press, 35 E. Vernon Avenue, Phoenix, AZ 85004, 602-955-0551

McGarey, William (see also McGarey, Gladys), *Gabriel Press,* 35 E. Vernon Avenue, Phoenix, AZ 85004, 602-955-0551

McGee, Deborah Jaffe (see also McGee, Hal), *12 SECONDS OF LAUGHTER,* 821 N Pennsylvania Street #22, Indianapolis, IN 46204, 317-297-1222

McGee, Hal (see also McGee, Deborah Jaffe), *12 SECONDS OF LAUGHTER,* 821 N Pennsylvania Street #22, Indianapolis, IN 46204, 317-297-1222

McGilligan, Pat (see also Edelson, Morris; Bondy, Melissa; Fellner, Mike; Edelson, Olga), Quixote Press, 1812 Marshall, Houston, TX 77098

McGivern, Gary (see also Culp, Marguerite), *CLEARWATER NAVIGATOR,* 112 Market Street, Poughkeepsie, NY 12601, 914-454-7673

McGlynn, Brian (see also DiPresso, Stephen J.), *RAPSCALLION'S DREAM*, PO Box 183, Bronx, NY 10470, (212) 549-2374

McGonigle, Thomas, *ADRIFT*, 239 East 5th Street #4D, New York, NY 10003

McGovern, Edythe M., Mar Vista Publishing Company, 11917 Westminster Place, Los Angeles, CA 90066, 213-391-1721

McGovern, Jack (see also Giovannini, Carolyn), The Rubicon Press, 5638 Riverdsle Road S, Salem, OR 97302

McGovern, Robert, Co-Editor (see also Snyder, Richard), The Ashland Poetry Press, Ashland College, Ashland, OH 44805, 419-289-4096

McGovern, Wendla, Managing Editor, *LIFESTYLE*, 2194 Palou Avenue, San Francisco, CA 94124, 415-824-2900

McGowan, Cese, Assistant Editor (see also Cruickshank, Douglas; Luneau, Lynn), Mho & Mho Works, Box 33135, San Diego, CA 92103, 619-488-4991

McGowan, James, Editor (see also Sutherland, Robert D.; Scrimgeour, James R.; White, Curtis), *THE PIKESTAFF FORUM*, PO Box 127, Normal, IL 61761, 309-452-4831

McGowan, James, Editor (see also Sutherland, Robert D.; Scrimgeour, James R.; White, Curtis), The Pikestaff Press, PO Box 127, Normal, IL 61761, 309-452-4831

McGraw, Erin, Associate Editor (see also Hilberry, Jane), *INDIANA REVIEW*, 316 North Jordan Avenue, Indiana University, Bloomington, IN 47405, 812-335-3439

McGraw, Woody, Trinity House, Inc., 5311 Montfort Lane, Crestwood, KY 40014, 502-241-1492

McGuill, Mike (see also Rayher, Ed; Conoley, Gillian; Stansberry, Domenic; Ruhl, Steven), *TIGHTROPE*, 72 Colonial Village, Amherst, MA 01002

McGuire, Jerry L. (see also Miklitsch, Robert), *MODERN POETRY STUDIES*, 207 Delaware Avenue, Buffalo, NY 14202, 716-847-2555

Macias, Reynaldo (see also Gomez-Quinones, Juan; McKenna, Teresa; Romero, Annelisa), *AZTLAN: International Journal of Chicano Studies Research*, University of California-Los Angeles, 405 Hilgard Avenue, Los Angeles, CA 90025, 213-825-2642

Macias, Reynaldo F. (see also Gomez-Quinones, Juan; McKenna, Teresa; Romero, Annelisa), Chicano Studies Research Center Publications, University of California-Los Angeles, 405 Hilgard Avenue, Los Angeles, CA 90024, 213-825-2642

Maciejewksi, Jeffrey (see also Smith, Steven G.), *TREND MAGAZINE*, PO Box 15563, Milwaukee, WI 53215, 414-647-1944

McIntosh, A.S., Survivors' Manual Books, PO Box 263, Division of Independent Learning Assoc., Rockville Centre, NY 11571

McIntosh, Grant, Publisher (see also Morgan, David), *STRIPS*, PO Box 2896, Auckland, New Zealand

MacIntosh, Keitha K., Sunken Forum Press, Dewittville, Quebec J0S1C0, Canada, 514-264-2866

McIntyre, Joan, Book Reviews Editor (see also Rimm, Virginia M.; Perrin, Arnold; Grierson, Ruth; Briggs, Henry; Boisvert, Donald J.; Knowles, Ardeana Hamlin; Brown, Ronald G.; Beck, Raymond M.), *NEW ENGLAND SAMPLER*, RFD #1 Box 2280, Brooks, ME 04921, 207-525-3575

McKale, A. (see also Huang, J.; Thoenen, B.; Jacobson, J.; Cohen, M.), *THE DROOD REVIEW OF MYSTERY*, Box 8872, Boston, MA 02114

McKay, Don (see also Dragland, Stan), Brick Books, Box 219, Ilderton, Ontario N0M 2AO, Canada, 519-666-0283

McKay, Jean (see also Dragland, Stan), *BRICK: A Journal Of Reviews*, Box 219, Ilderton, Ontario N0M 2AO, Canada, (519) 666-0283

McKellip, Doris, Unicorn Rising, Route 2, Box 360, Sheridan, OR 97378, 503-843-3902

112

McKenna, Teresa (see also Gomez-Quinones, Juan; Macias, Reynaldo; Romero, Annelisa), *AZTLAN: International Journal of Chicano Studies Research*, University of California-Los Angeles, 405 Hilgard Avenue, Los Angeles, CA 90025, 213-825-2642

McKenna, Teresa (see also Gomez-Quinones, Juan; Macias, Reynaldo F.; Romero, Annelisa), Chicano Studies Research Center Publications, University of California-Los Angeles, 405 Hilgard Avenue, Los Angeles, CA 90024, 213-825-2642

McKenzie, Gilbert S., Astrosonics Research Institute, 11037½ Freeman Ave., Lennox, CA 90304, 213-673-4679

McKernan, John, *THE LITTLE REVIEW*, Marshall University, Box 205, Huntington, WV 25701

McKinley, Mae Pohle, Publisher (see also Pohe, Robert W., Jr.), *THE BOOK-MART*, PO Drawer 72, Lake Wales, FL 33853

McKinney, Ruth, Editor-in-Chief (see also Fisher, Eunice M.), *THE ROCKFORD REVIEW*, PO Box 858, Rockford, IL 61105, 815-962-1353

Mclean, Cheryl (see also Donnelly, Margarita; Malone, Ruth; Wendt, Ingrid; Wilner, Eleanor; Thompson, Joyce; Caday, Jan; Gordon, Rebecca; Domitrovich, Lisa; Jenkins, Meredith), *CALYX: A Journal of Art and Literature by Women*, PO Box B, Corvallis, OR 97339, 503-753-9384

McLeester, Dick, Food For Thought Publications, PO Box 331, Amherst, MA 01004, 413-253-5432

MacLennan, Kathy, Roush Books, Box 4203, Valley Village, North Hollywood, CA 91607, 213-762-3740

McLeod, Kathy, Fiction Editor (see also Clark, Susan; Marple, Vivian), *THE RADDLE MOON*, Creative Writing Department, Univ. of Victoria, Box 1700, B.C., Victoria, B.C. V8W 2Y2, Canada, 604-721-7306

Macleod, Norman, Founding Editor (see also Stephenson, Shelby), *PEMBROKE MAGAZINE*, PO Box 60, PSU, Pembroke, NC 28372, 919-521-4214 ext 246

McMahill, Cheiron (see also Yates, Barbara; Watana, Mieko), *NEW YARN*, Fujicho 6-5-20, Hoyashi, Tokyo 202, Japan, 0424-67-3809

McMahon, Peggy O'Mara, *MOTHERING*, PO Box 2208, Albuquerque, NM 87103, 505-867-3110

McManis, Jack, *PIVOT*, Pivot Associates, 538 Burrowes Building, University Park, PA 16802

MacManus, Yvonne (see also Prather, Jo Anne), Timely Books, PO Box 267, New Milford, CT 06776, 203-744-4719

McMillan, Peter, *ILLUMINATIONS*, The Rathasker Press, 1712 Henderson Street, Columbia, SC 29201, 803-256-3727

McMillan, Sally Hill, The East Woods Press, 429 East Boulevard, Charlotte, NC 28203, 704-334-0897

McNally, Mrs. J.H., *TOWPATHS*, 1341 West 112th Street, Cleveland, OH 44102, 216-226-7890

McNally, W.J., III (see also Hooper, Shaun; Malin, Kathy), McNally & Loftin, West, 5390 Overpass Road, Santa Barbara, CA 93111, 805-964-7079; 964-5117

McNamara, Bob, Editor (see also Culligan, Bridget), L'Epervier Press, 762 Hayes #15, Seattle, WA 98109

McNamara, Eugene (see also Stevens, Peter), Sesame Press, c/o English Dept Univ of Windosr, Windsor, Ontario N9B3P4, Canada

McNamara, Eugene, *UNIVERSITY OF WINDSOR REVIEW*, c/o University of Windsor, Windsor, Ontario N9B3P4, Canada

McNamara, Kevin (see also Gullikson, Sandy), *CLEARWATER JOURNAL*, 1115 V Avenue, La Grande, OR 97850, 503-963-8212

MacNaughton, Anne (see also Douthit, Peter; McCallum, Tracy), Minor Heron Press, PO Box 2615, Taos, NM 87571, 505-758-0081

MacNeil, Maura, Editor, *HUBRIS*, PO Box 1543, Concord, NH 03301

McNeill, Barbara (see also Harman, Willis; O'Regan, Brendan; Hurley, Tom), *INSTITUTE OF NOETIC SCIENCES NEWSLETTER*, Inst. Noetic Sciences, 475 Gate Five Road, Suite 300, Sausalito, CA 94965, 415-331-5650

McPhee, Linda (see also Strempek, Stephen; Anastas, Charles), *HARBOR REVIEW*, c/o English Department, UMass/Boston, Boston, MA 02125

McPherson, Bruce R., McPherson & Company Publishers, PO Box 638, New Paltz, NY 12561, 914-255-7084

McQueen, Robert I., Editor (see also Frisch, Peter), *THE ADVOCATE*, 1730 S. Amphlett, Suite 225, San Mateo, CA 94402, 415-573-7100

McQuilkin, Frank (see also Sill, Geoffrey M.), *THE MICKLE STREET REVIEW*, 46 Centre Street, Haddonfield, NJ 08033, (609) 795-7887

MacShane, Frank, Director (see also Payne, Robert; Smith, William Jay; Cook, Diane G.H.), *TRANSLATION*, 307A Mathematics, Columbia University, New York, NY 10027, 212-280-2305

MacShane, Frank (see also Cook, Diane G.H.; Payne, Robert; Smith, William Jay; Galvin, Dallas), Translation, 307A Mathematics, Columbia University, New York, NY 10027, 280-2305

McWaters, Barry (see also Clark, Stephen), Evolutionary Press, Santa Barbara Office, PO Box 40391, Santa Barbara, CA 93103, 415-221-9222

McWaters, Barry, *GAIA*, 2418 Clement Street, San Francisco, CA 94121, 415-221-9222

Madhubuti, Haki R., Third World Press, 7524 So. Cottage Grove Ave., Chicago, IL 60619, (312) 651-0700

Madrigal Ecay, Roberto (see also Ballagas, Manuel F.), *TERMINO*, PO Box 8905, Cincinnati, OH 45208, 513-232-1548

Madrigal, Sylvia, Assistant Editor (see also Reynolds, Louise T.; Jackel, Harry; Reynolds, Louise E.; Bolton, Stanwood), *THE NEW RENAISSANCE, An International Magazine of Ideas & Opinions, Emphasizing Literature & The Arts*, 9 Heath Road, Arlington, MA 02174

Madsen (see also Engh; Eriksen; Seglen; Ostenstad), Futurum Forlag, Hjelmsgt. 3, 0355 Oslo 3, Norway, (02) 69 12 84

Madsen (see also Engh; Eriksen; Selgen; Ostenstad), *GATEAVISA*, Hjelmsgt 3, 0355 Oslo 3, Norway, (02) 69 12 84

Madson, Jerry, *TRULY FINE PRESS, A Review*, PO Box 891, Bemidji, MN 56601

Madson, Jerry, Truly Fine Press, PO Box 891, Bemidji, MN 56601

Magary, Alan (see also Cole, Tom), Lexikos, 1012 14th Street, San Francisco, CA 94114, 415-861-4916

Magliocco, Peter, *ART: MAG*, 18570 Sherman Way, C-1, Reseda, CA 91335, 213-345-4794

Magnin, Joseph T. (see also Gorham, Daniel J.), Axios Newletter, Inc., 800 South Euclid Avenue, Fullerton, CA 92634

Magnuson, Gordon, Associate Editor (see also Harkey, Joseph; Hite, Rick; Orr, Anderson), *INLET*, Virginia Wesleyan College, Norfolk, VA 23455

Mahapatra, Jayanta, *CHANDRABHAGA*, Tinkonia Bagicha, Cuttack 753 001, Orissa, India, 20-566

Mahler, Carol, Co-editor (see also Miller, A. McA.), *NEW COLLAGE MAGAZINE*, 5700 North Trail, Sarasota, FL 33580, 813-355-7671, Ex 203

Mahler, Carol, Co-Editor (see also Miller, A. McA), New Collage Press, 5700 North Trail, Sarasota, FL 33580, 813-355-7671, Ex 203

Mailman, Leo, Editor & Publisher, Maelstrom Press, 8 Farm Hill Road, Cape Elizabeth, ME 04107

Mailman, Leo (see also Locklin, Gerald; Zepeda, Ray; Barker, David; Snider, Clifton; Salinas, Judy; Kay, John), *MAELSTROM REVIEW*, 8 Farm Hill Road, Cape Elizabeth, ME 04107

114

Main, Jody (see also Walatka, Pam Portugal; Stephens, Helen; Jamello, Nancy Portugal; Davis, Annette), Wild Horses Publishing Company, 12310 Concepcion Road, Los Altos Hills, CA 94022, 415-941-3396

Makowsky, Andrew, Assistant Editor (see also Stettner, Irving), *STROKER*, 129 2nd Ave. No. 3, New York, NY 10003

Makuck, Peter, *TAR RIVER POETRY*, Department of English, East Carolina University, Greenville, NC 27834

Malaschak, Dolores (see also Douglas, Prentice), *LINCOLN LOG (POETRY JOURNAL)*, Route 2, Box 126-C, Raymond, IL 62560

Malik, Keshav, Indian Academy of Letters, 35 Feroze Shah Road, New Delhi 110001, India, 388667

Malik, Keshav (see also Bhavan, Rabindra), *INDIAN Literature*, 35 Feroze Shah Road, New Delhi 110001, India, 388667

Malin, Kathy (see also McNally, W.J., III; Hooper, Shaun), McNally & Loftin, West, 5390 Overpass Road, Santa Barbara, CA 93111, 805-964-7079; 964-5117

Malinowitz, Michael (see also Horowitz, Evelyn; du Passage, Mary), *THE BAD HENRY REVIEW*, Box 45, Van Brunt Station, Brooklyn, NY 11215

Malinowitz, Michael (see also Horowitz, Evelyn; du Passage, Mary), 44 Press, Inc., Box 45, Van Brant Station, Brooklyn, NY 11215

Mallis, Jackie, Editorial Director, Multi Media Arts, PO Box 14486, Austin, TX 78761, 512-837-5503

Mallory, Eugenia P., Graphics Editor (see also Bradley, Jacqueline T.; Kelly, Patrick; Weissmann, G. Warren; Brunswick, S.J.), *BLUE HORSE*, P.O. Box 6061, Augusta, GA 30906, 404-798-5628

Malmquist, Niels, Nordic Books, PO Box 1941, Philadelphia, PA 19105, 215-574-4258

Malone, Marvin, Editor (see also Stranger, Ernest), *THE WORMWOOD REVIEW*, PO Box 8840, Stockton, CA 95208, 209-466-8231

Malone, Marvin, Editor (see also Stranger, Ernest), The Wormwood Review Press, P O Box 8840, Stockton, CA 95208, 209-466-8231

Malone, Robert L., Ark and Arbor Press, Box 901, Little Compton, RI 02837, 401-635-2053

Malone, Ruth (see also Donnelly, Margarita; Wendt, Ingrid; Wilner, Eleanor; Thompson, Joyce; Caday, Jan; Mclean, Cheryl; Gordon, Rebecca; Domitrovich, Lisa; Jenkins, Meredith), *CALYX: A Journal of Art and Literature by Women*, PO Box B, Corvallis, OR 97339, 503-753-9384

Maloney, Dennis (see also Lewandowski, Steve), *WHITE PINE JOURNAL*, 73 Putnam Street, Buffalo, NY 14213, 716-825-8671

Maloney, Dennis (see also Lewandowski, Steve), White Pine Press, 73 Putnam Street, Buffalo, NY 14213

Maloney, Roy T., Dropzone Press, PO Box 882222, San Francisco, CA 94188, 415-776-7164

Maltbie, Cynthia (see also Mays, Bruce), Diversity Press, 2738 N. Racine, Chicago, IL 60614, 312-472-5662

Maltz, Patricia M. (see also Gritta, Patricia E.), Peregrine Associates, PO Box 22292, Ft. Lauderdale, FL 33316, 987-2423

Manago, James V., Editor, *JOURNAL OF CHRISTIAN CRITICISM*, 114-41 Queens Blvd., #195, Forest Hills, NY 11375, 805-1682

Mandel, Charlotte, Editor, Saturday Press, Inc., PO Box 884, Upper Montclair, NJ 07043, 201-256-1731

Mandel, Gerry (see also Rubel, William), *STONE SOUP, The Magazine By Children*, Box 83, Santa Cruz, CA 95063, 408-426-5557

Mandel, William A., Editor & Publisher, Crystal Press, Ltd., PO Box 215, Crystal Bay, NV 89402, 702-831-3846

Mandelblat, Reuben (see also Mandell, Richard; Mandell, Alan; Rasch, William), Hermes House Press, Inc., 127 W 15th Street, Apt 3F, New York, NY 10011, 212-691-9773/415-655-8571

Mandell, Alan (see also Mandell, Richard; Mandelblat, Reuben; Rasch, William), *Hermes House Press, Inc.*, 127 W 15th Street, Apt 3F, New York, NY 10011, 212-691-9773/415-655-8571

Mandell, Alan (see also Rasch, William; Mandell, Richard), *KAIROS, A Journal of Contemporary Thought and Criticism*, 127 W 15th Street, Apt 3F, New York, NY 10011, 212-691-9773

Mandell, Richard (see also Mandelblat, Reuben; Mandell, Alan; Rasch, William), Hermes House Press, Inc., 127 W 15th Street, Apt 3F, New York, NY 10011, 212-691-9773/415-655-8571

Mandell, Richard (see also Mandell, Alan; Rasch, William), *KAIROS, A Journal of Contemporary Thought and Criticism*, 127 W 15th Street, Apt 3F, New York, NY 10011, 212-691-9773

Manesse, Daniel, Editor, *PHILOSOPHY AND THE ARTS*, PO Box 431, Jerome Avenue Station, Bronx, NY 10468

Manesse, Daniel, Editor, Philosophy and the Arts Press, PO Box 431, Jerome Avenue Station, Bronx, NY 10468

Mangan, Patricia (see also Dailey, Joel), Acre Press, 1804 E Main Street, Endicott, NY 13760

Mann, Ernest, Editor-Publisher, *LITTLE FREE PRESS*, Box 8201, Minneapolis, MN 55408

Mann, Jim, Jim Mann & Associates, 9 Mount Vernon Drive, Gales Ferry, CT 06335, 203-464-2511

Mann, Jim, *MEDIA MANAGEMENT MONOGRAPHS*, 9 Mount Vernon Drive, Gales Ferry, CT 06335, 203-464-2511

Mann, John, Poetry (see also Robinson, Forrest; Logsdon, Loren), *MISSISSIPPI VALLEY REVIEW*, Dept. of English, Western Ill. University, Macomb, IL 61455, 309-298-1514

Mansell, Chris, *COMPASS*, PO Box 51, Burwood, NSW 2134, Australia, (02) 560 8729

Mansell, Chris, Editor, Compass Poetry & Prose, PO Box 51, Burwood, NSW 2134, Australia, (02) 560 8729

Manthe, George L. (see also Glean, Katherine B.), Cube Publications Inc, 1 Buena Vista Road, Port Jefferson, NY 11777, 516-331-4990

Maravelas, Paul, The Press of Paul Maravelas, Box 637, Watertown, MN 55388

Marcan, Peter, Peter Marcan Publications, 31 Rowliff Road, High Wycombe, Bucks, United Kingdom

Marcinko, Bill-Dale, *AFTA—The Alternative Magazine*, Afta Press, Inc., 153 George Street, Second Floor, New Brunswick, NJ 08901, 201-828-5467

Marcus, Stanley, Somesuch Press, PO Box 188, Dallas, TX 75221, 214-748-1842

Marder, Louis, *THE SHAKESPEARE NEWSLETTER*, 1217 Ashland Ave., Chicago Circle, Evanston, IL 60202, 312-475-7550

Marecki, Joan (see also Arrathoon, Dr. Leigh A.), Solaris Press, Inc., PO Box 1009, Rochester, MI 48063, 313-656-0667

Margolin, Malcolm, Heyday Books, Box 9145, Berkeley, CA 94709, 415-549-3564

Margolis, Tina, Advertising Director (see also Aronson, Arnold; Garren, Lois; King, Keith; Wells, Ann; Wolff, Fred M.; Rollins, Brook), *THEATRE DESIGN AND TECHNOLOGY*, 330 W. 42nd Street, New York, NY 10036, 212-563-5551

Mariah, Paul (see also Tagett, Richard), Manroot Books, Box 982, So San Francisco, CA 94080

Mariani, Phil (see also Wallis, Brian), *WEDGE*, 141 Perry Street, New York, NY 10014, 212-243-6296

Marier, Don, Director (see also Stoiaken, Larry), *ALTERNATIVE SOURCES of ENERGY MAGAZINE*, 107 S. Central Avenue, Milaca, MN 56353, 612-983-6892

Marilyn, Sandra (see also Eldrege, Joss), *TRADESWOMEN MAGAZINE*, Tradeswomen Inc., PO Box 40664, San Francisco, CA 94140, 415-989-1566

Marion, Paul (see also Linder, Eric), Yellow Umbrella Press, 501 Main St., Chatham, MA 02633, 617-945-0144

Mark, Linda, Managing Editor (see also Rader, Hannelore), *REFERENCE SERVICES REVIEW*, PO Box 1808, Ann Arbor, MI 48106, 313-434-5530

Mark, Linda, Managing Editor (see also Hepfer, Will; Mueller, Carolyn), *SERIALS REVIEW*, PO Box 1808, Ann Arbor, MI 48106, 313-434-5530

Markert, Lawrence (see also Codrescu, Andrei), *EXQUISITE CORPSE*, PO Box 20889, Baltimore, MD 21209, 301-578-0146

Markland, Murray F., *UNIVERSITY JOURNAL*, Graduate School, CSU, Chico, Chico, CA 95926, 916-895-5700

Markowski, Michael A., Ultralight Publications, Inc., PO Box 234, Hummelstown, PA 17036, 717-566-0468 (office); 800-441-7527 (orders only or messages)

Marks, Tracy, Sagittarius Rising, PO Box 252, Arlington, MA 02174, 617-646-2692

Marlatt, Daphne (see also Marshall, John), *ISLAND*, Box 256, Lantzville B C, Canada, 604-390-3508

Marlatt, Daphne (see also Marshall, John), Island, Box 256, Lantzville BC, Canada, 604-390-3508

Marles, Bill, *LITERARY MARKETS*, 4340 Coldfall Road, Richmond, B.C. V7C 1P8, Canada, 604-277-4829

Marovich, David M. (see also Waskowsky, Nicolaus), *PRACTICES OF THE WIND*, PO Box 214, Kalamazoo, MI 49005, 616-344-1602

Marple, Vivian, Poetry Editor (see also Clark, Susan; McLeod, Kathy), *THE RADDLE MOON*, Creative Writing Department, Univ. of Victoria, Box 1700, B.C., Victoria, B.C. V8W 2Y2, Canada, 604-721-7306

Marron, Carol A., Editor (see also Johnson, Jay E.), Carnival Press, Inc., PO Box 19087, Minneapolis, MN 55419, 612-823-7216

Marrs, Lee (see also Kesey, Ken; my; Leary, Timothy; Loren, Richard; Babbs, Ken), *SPIT IN THE OCEAN*, 85829 Ridgeway Rd, Pleasant Hill, OR 97455, 503-747-5796

Marsh, William Parker (see also Bamford, Christopher), *THE LINDISFARNE LETTER*, R.D. #2, West Stockbridge, MA 01266, 413-232-4377

Marsh, William Parker (see also Bamford, Christopher), The Lindisfarne Press, RD #2, West Stockbridge, MA 01266, 413-232-4377

Marshall, Ann, Editor, *SIGNPOST*, 16812 36th Avenue W, Lynwood, WA 98037, 206-743-3947

Marshall, John (see also Marlatt, Daphne), *ISLAND*, Box 256, Lantzville B C, Canada, 604-390-3508

Marshall, John (see also Marlatt, Daphne), Island, Box 256, Lantzville BC, Canada, 604-390-3508

Marshall, Louise, President, Northwest Trails Association, 16812 36th Avenue W, Lynwood, WA 98036, 206-743-3947

Marshall, Lucie (see also Tarbell, Jim; Tarbell, Judith), *RIDGE REVIEW*, Box 90, Mendocino, CA 95460, 707-937-4275

Marshall, Ron, Publisher, *PHOTOFLASH: Models & Photographers Newsletter*, PO Box 7946, Colorado Springs, CO 80933

Marshall, Sol H., Creative Book Company, 8210 Varna Ave., Van Nuys, CA 91402, 213-988-2334

Marsic, John, Associate Editor (see also Lawson, Dr. Todd; Comen, Dr. Diane; Rader, Steve; Monte, Oscar; Nishi, Mio; Ginsberg, Allen; Samolis, Dr. Sam; Graham, Joan; Ferlinghetti, Lawrence; Ramirez, Julio; Haynes, Dr. Robert; Snyder, Gary; Morris, Dr. Richard), *ALPS MONTHLY*, PO Box 99394, San Francisco, CA 94109, 415-771-3431

Marsic, John, Assistant and Contributing Editor (see also Comen, Diane; Lawson, Todd S.J.; Samolis, William; Comen, Diane; Graham, Joan; Rader, Steve), Peace & Pieces Press, Box 99394, San Francisco, CA 94109, 415-771-3431

Marston, Betsy, Editor (see also Marston, Ed), *HIGH COUNTRY NEWS,* PO Box V, Paonia, CO 81428, 303-527-4898

Marston, Ed, Publisher (see also Marston, Betsy), *HIGH COUNTRY NEWS,* PO Box V, Paonia, CO 81428, 303-527-4898

Marston, Will, The Oleander Press, 17 Stansgate Ave., Cambridge CB2 2QZ, England

Martello, Leo Louis, Hero Press, 153 West 80th Street, Suite 1B, New York City, NY 10024

Martello, Leo Louis, *WITCHCRAFT DIGEST MAGAZINE (THE WICA NEWSLETTER),* 153 West 80th Street, Suite 1B, New York, NY 10024

Martens Ph.D., Rainer (see also Simon Ph.D., Julie), Human Kinetics Pub. Inc., Box 5076, Champaign, IL 61820, 217-351-5076

Martens, Robert, Star Rover House, 1914 Foothill Blvd., Oakland, CA 94606, 415-532-8408

Martensen, Jean, Cobbers, Box 261, Williamsburg, VA 23185, 804-220-2828

Marti, Eric, Assistant Editor (see also Poole, Robert, Jr.; Gordon, Paul), *FRONTLINES,* Box 40105, Santa Barbara, CA 93103, 805-963-5993

Martin, Andrea, Managing Editor (see also Burch, Charlton), *LIGHTWORKS MAGAZINE,* PO Box 1202, Birmingham, MI 48012, 313-642-7207

Martin, B.A., Business Manager (see also John, Roland), Hippopotamus Press, 26 Cedar Road, Sutton, Surrey SM25DG, England, 01-643-1970

Martin, Karen, Managing Editor (see also Springer, Eleanor K.), *BUSINESS VIEW OF SOUTHWEST FLORIDA,* Collier County Magazines Inc., PO Box 1546, Naples, FL 33939, 813-263-7525

Martin, Leslie, Editor (see also Baron, Magda), *AMERICAN DANCE GUILD NEWSLETTER,* 570 7 Ave. 20 Floor, New York, NY 10018, 212-944-0557

Martin, Michele, Associate Editor (see also Quasha, George; Quasha, Susan; Coffey, Michael), Open Book Publications, A Division of Station Hill Press, Station Hill Road, Barrytown, NY 12507

Martin, Michele, Managing Editor (see also Quasha, George; Quasha, Susan; Coffey, Michael; Stein Charles; Nedds, Trish; Kelly, Robert; Auster, Paul; Kamin, Franz; McClelland, Bruce), Station Hill Press, Station Hill Road, Barrytown, NY 12507, 914-758-5840

Martin, Pam, Editor (see also Walsh, Susan), *THE NORTH WIND,* Box 65583, Vancouver 12, B. C. V5N 5K5, Canada

Martin, Robert, Editor-in-Chief (see also Nicholson, Ann Winston), AUBURN-WOLFE PUBLISH-ING CO, 584 Castro #351, San Francisco, CA 94114, 916-583-0708

Martin, Stephen-Paul (see also Royal, Richard; Ensler, Eve; Millis, Christopher; Kiefer, Paul; Sullivan, Mary Jane; Sanders, Catherine Marie), *CENTRAL PARK,* P.O. Box 1446, New York, NY 10023

Martindale, Sheila, Poetry Editor (see also Osborne, Anne; Hancock, Geoff; Thom, Heather; Gibson, Brenda; Lennard, Susan), *CANADIAN AUTHOR & BOOKMAN,* 25 Ryerson Aveune, 131 Bloor Street W, Toronto, Ontario M5t 2P3, Canada, 416-364-4203

Martinez, Elizabeth Sutherland, Senior Editor, Synthesis Publications, 2703 Folsom Street, San Francisco, CA 94110, 415-550-1284

Martinson, Sue Ann, Editor, *SING HEAVENLY MUSE! WOMEN'S POETRY AND PROSE,* PO Box 14059, Minneapolis, MN 55414, 612-822-8713; 612-823-6934

Martone, Michael, *POET & CRITIC,* English Dept., ISU, 203 Ross Hall, Ames, IA 50011, 515-294-2180

Marunas, P. Raymond, Art Editor (see also Ferguson, David; Garber, Thomas; Padol, Brian; Gateff, Amy H.; Smith, Charlotte; Goldman, Bill), *BOX 749,* Box 749, Old Chelsea Station, New York, NY 10011, 212-98-0519

Mason, Jim, Co-Editor (see also Moss, Doug; Moretti, Laura; Mola, Noreen), *AGENDA: Newsmagazine of the Animal Rights Network,* Box 5234, Westport, CT 06881, 203-226-8826

Massie, Allan, *NEW EDINBURGH REVIEW,* 1 Buccleuch Place, Edinburgh EH8, Scotland, 031-667-5718

Masters, Gregory (see also Scholnick, Michael; Lenhart, Gary), *MAG CITY,* 437 East 12 St. No. 26, New York, NY 10009

Masters, Heidi, *LITERARY ART PRESS NEWSLETTER,* 5210-16th Street N.E., Seattle, WA 98105, 206-524-4385

Masters, Heidi (see also Stablein, Marilyn), Wash 'n Press, 5210-16th Street N.E., Seattle, WA 98105, 206-524-4385

Mathews, Richard (see also Russ, Barbara), *KONGLOMERATI,* PO Box 5001, Gulfport, FL 33737, 813-323-0386

Mathews, Richard (see also Russ, Barbara), Konglomerati Press, PO Box 5001, Gulfport, FL 33737, 813-323-0386

Mathias, Steven (see also Nagorka, Henry J.; Nagorka, Rev. Diane S.), ESPress, Inc., Box 8606, Washington, DC 20011, 202-723-4578

Mathias, Steven (see also Nagorka, Henry J.; Nagorka, Rev. Diane S.), *THE PSYCHIC OBSERVER,* Box 8606, Washington, DC 20011, 202-723-4578

Matta, John (see also Palmer, Jill; Nikides, George), *SCRIVENER,* McGill University, 853 Sherbrooke Street W., Montreal, P.Q. H3A 2T6, Canada

Matthews, Allan F., *THE DEVELOPING COUNTRY COURIER,* PO Box 239, McLean, VA 22101, 703-356-7561

Matthews, David (see also C., G.C.; Oliveros, Chuck), Dead Angel Press, 1206 Lyndale Drive SE, Atlanta, GA 30316, 404-624-1524

Matthews, David (see also Oliveros, Chuck; C., G.C.), *DEAD ANGEL,* 1206 Lyndale Drive SE, Atlanta, GA 30316

Matthews, Kenneth, Aaron Publishers, Inc., PO Box 2572, Sarasota, FL 33578, 813-371-0249

Matthews, William, Contributing Editor (see also Murphy, George; Carver, Raymond; Gallagher, Tess; Galvin, Brendan; McBride, Mekeel; Mueller, Lisel), *TENDRIL,* Box 512, Green Harbor, MA 02041, 617-834-4137

Mattson, Francis, O., Calendar Editor (see also Johnson, Bryan R.), *BOOK ARTS REVIEW,* 15 Bleecker St, New York, NY 10012

Maurer, Ralph (see also Beckman, Lanny; Lotgrave, Janet), New Star Books Ltd., 2504 York Avenue, Vancouver, B.C. V6K 1E3, Canada, 604-738-9429

May, Chris, *BLACK MUSIC & JAZZ REVIEW (BM),* Napheld Ltd., 153 Praed Street, London W2, England, 01-402 5996

May, Dorothy G., Meadowlark Press, PO Box 8172, Prairie Village, KS 66208

Mayer, Bernadette (see also Warsh, Lewis), *UNITED ARTISTS,* 172 E. 4th Street, 9-B, New York, NY 10009

Mayer, Bernadette (see also Warsh, Lewis), United Artists, 172 E. 4th Street, 9-B, New York, NY 10009

Mayerski, Alfred, Gem Guides Book Co., 3677 San Gabriel Pkwy., Pico Rivera, CA 90660, 213-692-5492

Mayfield, Carl, Editor (see also Baker, Morrow), *THE MARGARINE MAYPOLE ORANGOUTANG EXPRESS,* 3209 Wellesley, NE 1, Albuquerque, NM 87107

Maynard, Jim, Quicksilver Productions, P.O.Box 340, Ashland, OR 97520, (503) 482-5343

Mayne, S. (see also Aster, H.; Walsh, M.; Potichnyj, P.), Mosaic Press/Valley Editions, PO Box 1032, Oakville, Ontario L6J 5E9, Canada

Mayor, D.F., *REVEALER CASSETTES,* 2 Hall Cottages, Kimpton Hall Farm, Kimpton (Near Hitchin) Herts, England, (01) 961-2538

Mays, Blaine C., Editor-in-Chief, *NEW THOUGHT*, International New Thought Alliance, 7314 E Stetson Drive, Scottsdale, AZ 85251, 602-945-0744

Mays, Bruce (see also Maltbie, Cynthia), Diversity Press, 2738 N. Racine, Chicago, IL 60614, 312-472-5662

Mayseung, Jew, *TORONTO CLARION*, 73 Bathurst Street, Toronto, Ontario M5V 2P6, Canada, 363-4404

Mazandarani, Aliya B.H. (see also Gallaghan, Haj Hayder), *NURADEEN*, PO Box 730, Blanco, TX 78606, 512-698-3239

Mazandarani, Batul H. (see also Anees, M.; Bilgrami, M.; Gallaghan, Haj Haydar), Zahra Publications, PO Box 730, Blanco, TX 78606, 512-698-3239

Mead, Howard, Editor (see also Schwanz Pogorsch, Susan), Tamarack Press, P.O.Box 5650, Madison, WI 53705, 608-231-2444

Mead, Howard, Editor (see also Schwanz Pigorsch, Susan), *WISCONSIN TRAILS*, PO Box 5650, Madison, WI 53705, 608-231-2444

Mead, Jean, Misty Mountain Press, 2231 Fairview Avenue, Casper, WY 82609, 307-266-6743

Meade, Laura, Editor (see also Meade, Richard), Story Press, Box 10040, Chicago, IL 60610

Meade, Richard, Editor (see also Meade, Laura), *Story Press*, Box 10040, Chicago, IL 60610

Meagher, Rosann, Assistant Editor (see also Kwain, Constance; Jobst, Debby), *OYEZ REVIEW*, Roosevelt University, 430 S. Michigan Avenue, Chicago, IL 60614, 312-341-2017

Medcalf Jr., Robert Randolph, *APOGEE/LYRICAL WAYS*, Box 7635, Baltimore, MD 21207

Medcalf, Robert Randolph, Jr., Quixsilver Press, Box 7635, Baltimore, MD 21207

Medina, Robert C., Bilingue Publications, PO Drawer H, Las Cruces, NM 88004, 505-526-1557

Mehra, Ravi, General Hall, Inc., 23-45 Corporal Kennedy Street, Bayside, NY 11360, 212-423-9397

Meier, Joyce (see also Schulte, Rainer), *SANDS*, 17302 Club Hill Drive, Dallas, TX 75248

Meier, Klaus, *JOURNAL OF THE PHILOSOPHY OF SPORT*, Box 5076, Champaign, IL 61820, 217-351-5076

Meiselma, Stephanie, Assistant Editor (see also Slezak, Ellen), Pluribus Press, Inc. (A division of Teach'em, Inc.), 160 E. Illinois Street, Chicago, IL 60611, 312-467-0424

Mekas, Jonas (see also Sitney, P. Adams; Melton, Hollis), *FILM CULTURE*, G. P. O. Box 1499, New York, NY 10001

Mekas, Jonas (see also Sitney, P. Adams; Melton, Hollis), Film Culture Non-Profit, Inc., GPO Box 1499, New York, NY 10001

Mele, Jim (see also Norris, Ken), Cross Country Press, Ltd., PO Box 492, Ridgefield, CT 06877, 203-431-8225

Mele, Jim (see also Norris, Ken), *CROSSCOUNTRY*, PO Box 492, Ridgefield, CT 06877, 203-431-8225

Melius, Ken, Tensleep Publications, PO Box 925, Aberdeen, SD 57401, 605-226-0488

Melnicove, Mark, The Dog Ear Press, PO Box 143, S. Harpswell, ME 04079, 207-833-6314

Melnicove, Mark, *DOG EAR RAG*, PO Box 143, S. Harpswell, ME 04079, 207-833-6314

Melnicove, Mark, Contributing Editor (see also Kruchkow, Diane; Johnson, Curt; Savitt, Lynne; Fox, Hugh), *STONY HILLS: News & Review of the Small Press*, Weeks Mills, New Sharon, ME 04955, 207-778-3436

Melnyczuk, Askold, Founding and Advisory Editor (see also Dunn, Sharon; Dukes, Norman), *THE AGNI REVIEW*, PO Box 229, Cambridge, MA 02238, 617-491-1079

Melton, Hollis (see also Mekas, Jonas; Sitney, P. Adams), *FILM CULTURE*, G. P. O. Box 1499, New York, NY 10001

120

Melton, Hollis (see also Mekas, Jonas; Sitney, P. Adams), Film Culture Non-Profit, Inc., GPO Box 1499, New York, NY 10001

Memmott, Roger Ladd, *EUREKA REVIEW*, 16 Samuelson Road, Weston, CT 06883

Memmott, Roger Ladd, Orion Press, 16 Samuelson Road, Weston, CT 06883

Mendel, Roberta, The Pin Prick Press, 2664 S Green RD, Shaker Heights, OH 44122, 216-932-2173

Merians, Valerie (see also Duer, David), Dog Hair Press, PO Box 372, West Branch, IA 52358, 319-643-7324

Mernit, Susan (see also Ratner, Rochelle), *HAND BOOK*, 314 E 78 Street #1, New York, NY 10021

Merrill, Lisa, Director of Publications (see also Brewer, Daryln), Poets & Writers, Inc., 201 West 54th Street, New York, NY 10019, 212-757-1766

Merrill, Susan, Managing Editor (see also Schechter, Ruth Lisa; Thomas, Dan B.; Bluestein, Dan T.; Crisci, Pat J.; Stettan, Leonard), *CROTON REVIEW*, P.O. Box 277, Croton on Hudson, NY 10520, 914-271-3144

Merwin, Miles, Associate Editor (see also Williams, Gregory), International Tree Crops Institute, Route 1, Black Lick Road, Gravel Switch, KY 40328, 606-332-7606

Merwin, Miles L., Assoc. Editor (see also Williams, Greg), *AGROFORESTRY REVIEW*, Route One, Gravel Switch, KY 40328, 606-332-7606

Mesmer, Sharon (see also Deanovich, Connie; Pintonelli, Debbie), *B-CITY*, B-City Press, 1555 W. Pratt Boulevard, Chicago, IL 60626, 312-743-4806

Messerli, Douglas (see also Fox, Howard N.), Sun & Moon Press, 4330 Hartwick Road, #418, College Park, MD 20740, 301-864-6921

Messina, Kathlyn, *Hampton Court Publishers*, PO Box 655, Lake Mahopac, NY 10541, 914-628-6155

Metras, Gary, Adastra Press, 101 Strong Street, Easthampton, MA 01027, 413-527-3324

Meyer, Linda D., The Chas. Franklin Press, 18409 90th Avenue W, Edmonds, WA 98020, 206-774-6979

Meyerding, Jane (see also Adams, Jan; Gordon, Rebecca; Johanna, Betty), *LESBIAN CONTRADIC-TION-A Journal of Irreverent Feminism*, 584 Castro Street, Suite 263, San Francisco, CA 94114

Meyers, Alison (see also Ziesing, Michael), Lysander Spoon Society, PO Box 806, Willimantic, CT 06226, 203-423-5836

Meyers, George (see also Wilson, Merrill), Chockstone Press, 526 Franklin Street, Denver, CO 80218, 303-377-1970

Meyerson, Jeffrey, *THE POISONED PEN*, 50 First Place, Brooklyn, NY 11231, 212-596-7739

Michael, Ann (see also Small, Robert; Steptoe, Lamont B.; Gabriele, Mary), *HEAT*, 1220 S. 12th Street, 3rd Floor, Philadelphia, PA 19147, 215-271-6569 or 382-6644

Michael, Ann E. (see also Dunn, David), LiMbo bar&grill Books, 7446 Overhill Road, Melrose Park, PA 19126

Michaels, Joanne (see also Ober, Stuart), Beekman Publishers, Inc., Po Box 888, Woodstock, NY 12498, 914-679-2300

Michaels, Neal, *BOOK BUSINESS MART*, 16254 Wedgewood, Fort Worth, TX 76133, 817-293-7030

Michaels, Neal (see also Bates, Owen), *BOOK NEWS & BOOK BUSINESS MART*, Box 16254, Fort Worth, TX 76133, 817-293-7030

Michaels, Neal (see also Bates, Owen), Premier Publishers, Inc., Box 16254, Fort Worth, TX 76133, 817-293-7030

Michaels, Neal, Premier Wholesale Book News, 16254 Wedgewood, Fort Worth, TX 76133

Michael-Titus, C. (see also Michael-Titus, N.M.), Panopticum Press London, 44, Howard Road, Upminster, England, (04022) 22100

Michael-Titus, C., *THE REMINDER*, 44, Howard Road, Upminster, RM14 2UF, England, (04022) 22100

Michael-Titus, N.M. (see also Michael-Titus, C.), Panopticum Press London, 44, Howard Road, Upminster, England, (04022) 22100

Michalson, Greg, Managing Editor (see also Morgan, Speer), *THE MISSOURI REVIEW*, Dept. of English, 231 Arts & Science, University of Missouri-Columbia, Columbia, MO 65211

Michelson, Linda Brown, Editor-in-Chief (see also Hughes, Michael; Bartlett, Elizabeth), *CROSS-CURRENTS, A QUARTERLY*, 2200 Glastonbury Road, West Lake Village, CA 91361

Mihopoulos, Effie, *MATI*, 5548 N. Sawyer, Chicago, IL 60625

Mihopoulos, Effie, Ommation Press, 5548 North Sawyer, Chicago, IL 60625

Mihopoulos, Effie, Editor, *SALOME: A LITERARY DANCE MAGAZINE*, 5548 N. Sawyer, Chicago, IL 60625, 312-539-5745

Mikesell, Suzanne, Editor (see also Winch, Bradley L.), Jalmar Press, Division of B.L. Winch & Associates, 45 Hitching Post Drive, Building 2, Rolling Hills Estates, CA 90274, 213-547-1240

Mikesell, Suzanne, Senior Editor, B. L. Winch & Associates, 45 Hitching Post Dr. Bldg 2, Rolling Hills Estate, CA 90274

Miki, Roy, *LINE: A Journal of the Contemporary Literature Collection*, The Library, Simon Fraser University, Burnaby, B.C. V5A 1S6, Canada

Miklitsch, Robert (see also McGuire, Jerry L.), *MODERN POETRY STUDIES*, 207 Delaware Avenue, Buffalo, NY 14202, 716-847-2555

Mikolowski, Ann (see also Mikolowski, Ken), *THE ALTERNATIVE PRESS*, 3090 Copeland Rd, Grindstone City, MI 48467

Mikolowski, Ken (see also Mikolowski, Ann), *THE ALTERNATIVE PRESS*, 3090 Copeland Rd, Grindstone City, MI 48467

Miles, Elaine (see also Miles, Robert), R. & E. Miles, PO Box 1916, San Pedro, CA 90733, 213-833-8856

Miles, Robert (see also Miles, Elaine), *R. & E. Miles*, PO Box 1916, San Pedro, CA 90733, 213-833-8856

Miller, A. McA., General Editor (see also Mahler, Carol), *NEW COLLAGE MAGAZINE*, 5700 North Trail, Sarasota, FL 33580, 813-355-7671, Ex 203

Miller, A. McA, General Editor (see also Mahler, Carol), New Collage Press, 5700 North Trail, Sarasota, FL 33580, 813-355-7671, Ex 203

Miller, Adam David (see also Nakano, Mei), Mina Press, PO Box 854, Sebastopol, CA 95472, 707-829-0854

Miller, Anita (see also Miller, Jordan), Academy Chicago Limited, 425 North Michigan 5th Floor, Chicago, IL 60611, 312-644-1723

Miller, Chuck, Underwood/Miller & Brandywyne Books, 651 Chestnut Street, Columbia, PA 17512, 717-684-7335

Miller, David (see also Miller, Meg), *GRASS ROOTS*, Box 900, Shepparton, Victoria 3630, Australia

Miller, David (see also Miller, Meg), Night Owl Publishers, PO Box 900, Shepparton 3630, Australia

Miller, Dean, Exanimo Press, PO Box 18, 23250 Highway 12, Segundo, CO 81070

Miller, Donald Britton, Vitality Associates, P.O. Box 2154, Saratoga, CA 95070, 408-867-1241

Miller, Faren, Assistant Editor (see also Brown, Charles N.; Holmen, Rachel), *LOCUS: The Newspaper of the Science Fiction Field*, Box 13305, Oakland, CA 94661, 415-339-9196

Miller, Jack, Editor, Anvil Press, Po Box 37, Millville, MN 55957, 507-798-2366

Miller, Jack, Editor (see also Redmond, Pauline; Schaefer, Paul), *NORTH COUNTRY ANVIL*, PO Box 37, Millville, MN 55957, 507-798-2366

122

Miller, J.E., *THE ORCADIAN*, The Firm of W. R. Mackintosh, THE ORCADIAN Office, PO Box 18, Kirkwall, Orkney, Scotland

Miller, Jeff, *NEW UNIONIST*, 621 West Lake Street, Rm 210, Minneapolis, MN 55408, 612-823-2593

Miller, Jeffrey, Cadmus Editions, PO Box 687, Tiburon, CA 94920

Miller, Jerome K., President, Copyright Information Services, Box 2419, Station A, Champaign, IL 61820, 217-356-7590

Miller, Jordan (see also Miller, Anita), Academy Chicago Limited, 425 North Michigan 5th Floor, Chicago, IL 60611, 312-644-1723

Miller, Karl, *LONDON REVIEW OF BOOKS*, 6A Bedford Square, London WC1B 3RA, England, 01-631-0884

Miller, Kitty, Editor and Publisher (see also Rindock, Kathy Miller), Log Cabin Publishers, PO Box 1536, Allentown, PA 18105, 215-434-2448

Miller, Marge, Vice President (see also Planz, Allen; Everett, Graham), Backstreet Editions, Inc., c/o Box 555, Port Jefferson, NY 11777

Miller, Marilee, Kindred Joy Publications, 554 W. 4th, Coquille, OR 97423, 503-396-4154

Miller, Meg (see also Miller, David), *GRASS ROOTS*, Box 900, Shepparton, Victoria 3630, Australia

Miller, Meg (see also Miller, David), Night Owl Publishers, PO Box 900, Shepparton 3630, Australia

Miller, Melissa, Editor (see also Johnson, Debra Jo), *THE HARVEST SUN*, 315 E. Dittlinger, Mew Braunfels, TX 78130

Miller, Nolan, Fiction Ed. (see also Fogarty, Robert; St. John, David; Holyoke, Tom), *THE ANTIOCH REVIEW*, PO Box 148, Yellow Springs, OH 45387, 513-767-7386

Miller, Patty, Art Editor (see also Hutchison, Joseph; Nigg, Joe; Rea, David; Reilly, Gary; Schroeder, Gary), *PENDRAGON Journal of the Creative Arts*, 2640 E. 12th Avenue, Box 715, Denver, CO 80206, 303-444-4100

Miller, Robert, Noble House Publishing, 256 South Robertson, Beverly Hills, CA 90211

Miller, Robert (see also Banning, Robert; Jones, Jennifer), Word Power, Inc., PO Box 17034, Seattle, WA 98107, 206-782-1437

Miller, Shirley, Editor (see also Welles, Lynn), Mexico West Travel Club, Inc., 2424 Newport Blvd. #91, Costa Mesa, CA 92627, (714) 536-8081

Miller, Steve, Co-Editor (see also Botnick, Ken), The Red Ozier Press, PO Box 101, Old Chelsea Station, New York, NY 10113, 212-620-3154

Miller, Thomas, Lancaster, Miller, & Schnobrich Publishers, PO Box 3056, PO Box 3056, Berkeley, CA 94703, 415-652-6004

Miller, Yvette E., *LATIN AMERICAN LITERARY REVIEW*, Dept. of Hispanic Language & Lit., 1309 Cathedral of Learning, U. of Pitts., Pittsburgh, PA 15260, 412-624-6222

Miller, Yvette E., Latin American Literary Review Press, PO Box 8385, Pittsburgh, PA 15218, 412-624-0870

Millett, John, Managing Editor (see also Perry, Grace), *POETRY AUSTRALIA*, Market Place, Berrima, N.S.W. 2577, Australia

Millis, Christopher (see also Martin, Stephen-Paul; Royal, Richard; Ensler, Eve; Kiefer, Paul; Sullivan, Mary Jane; Sanders, Catherine Marie), *CENTRAL PARK*, P.O. Box 1446, New York, NY 10023

Mills, Charlotte, Northwest Matrix Bookmakers, 385 East 11th #3, Eugene, OR 97401, 503-343-7449

Mills, Donna, Editor (see also Nikolic, Djordje; Kinzie, Mary), Elpenor Books, Box 3152, Merchandise Mart Plaza, Chicago, IL 60654, 312-935-1343

Mills, Joseph A., Jotarian Productions, 3976 Warner Avenue #A-4, Landover Hills, MD 20784, 301-322-2480

Mills, Stephanie, Editor, *CALIFORNIA TOMORROW,* 512 Second Street - 4th Floor, San Francisco, CA 94107, 415-543-5000

Mills, Susie, *BULLDOG PRESS,* PO Box 1344, Denton, TX 76201, 817-382-2319

Millsaps, Daniel, *WASHINGTON INTERNATIONAL ARTS LETTER,* Box 15240, Washington, DC 20003, 202-328-1900

Milroy, Vivian, *SELF AND SOCIETY,* F.C. Barnwell Press, 62 Southwark Bridge Road, London, England

Milton, John R., *SOUTH DAKOTA REVIEW,* Box 111, University Exchange, Vermillion, SD 57069, 605-677-5229

Min, D. (see also Taryor, Nya Kwiawon), Strugglers' Community Press, 2003 West 67th Place, Chicago, IL 60636, 312-776-6400

Miner, Tom (see also Goossens, Elisabeth), *PINCHPENNY,* 4851 Q Street, Sacramento, CA 95819, 916-451-3042

Mirchandani, Ravi (see also Cooney, Rian), *THE CAMBRIDGE POETRY MAGAZINE,* 602 King's College, Cambridge CB2 1ST, England

Miriam, Selma (see also Beaver, Betsey; Furie, Noel), Sanguinaria Publishing, 85 Ferris Street, Bridgeport, CT 06605, 203-576-9168

Mirsky, Mark, *FICTION,* c/o Dept. of English, City College, 138th Street & Convent Ave., New York, NY 10031

Mish, Jo, Serpent & Eagle Press, 1 Dietz Street, Oneonta, NY 13820, 607-432-5604

Mitchell, Barbara, Drama (see also Cooper, Peter S.; Bean, Joyce Miller; Steger, Linda; Fielding, Cynthia), *MIDWAY REVIEW,* 3400 West 11th Street, Suite 134, Chicago, IL 60655, 312-233-6002

Mitchell, Char, Assistant Editor (see also Brady, Steven R.), *CACHE REVIEW,* 4805 E. 29th Street, Tucson, AZ 85711, 602-748-0600

Mitchell, Charles, Associate Editor (see also Gove, Jim; Leddy, Chris), *MINOTAUR,* P.O. Box 4094, Burlingame, CA 94010

Mitchell, Donna, Associate Editor (see also Golden, Michael; Elias, Viki; Harrison, Jim; Mungo, Raymond; Bukowski, Charles; Placidus, Max; Codrescu, Andrei; Horotwitz, Mikhail; Ligi; Kramer, Glenn; Riedel, Robert), *SMOKE SIGNALS,* 1516 Beverly Road, Brooklyn, NY 11226

Mitchell, Larry, Calamus Books, Box 689, Cooper Station, New York, NY 10003

Mitchell, Steven L., Editor (see also McDonald, Susan), Northland Press, PO Box N, Flagstaff, AZ 86002, 602-774-5251

Moeller, Nancy L., *PORTLAND REVIEW,* PO Box 751, Portland, OR 97207, 229-4468

Moentmann, Uwe (see also Koehler, Michael), S Press Tapes, Talsperren Strasse 21, D-5600 Wuppertal 21, West Germany

Moeser, David, Editor, Cincinnati Chess Federation, PO Box 30072, Cincinnati, OH 45230, 513-232-3204

Moeser, David, Editor, *J'ADOUBE!, THE CINCINNATI CHESS MAGAZINE,* PO Box 30072, Cincinnati, OH 45230, 513-232-3204

Moffeit, Tony (see also Scherzer, Joel), Pueblo Poetry Project, Room 31, Union Depot, Pueblo, CO 81003

Moira, Fran (see also Leonard, Vickie; Douglas, Carol Anne; Lootens, Tricia; Henry, Alice; Fugh-Berman, Adrianne; Dejanikus, Tacie; Kulp, Denise; Sorrel, Lorraine), *OFF OUR BACKS,* 1841 Columbia Road NW Rm 212, Room 212, Washington, DC 20009, 202-234-8072

Mola, Noreen, Co-Editor (see also Moss, Doug; Mason, Jim; Moretti, Laura), *AGENDA: Newsmagazine of the Animal Rights Network,* Box 5234, Westport, CT 06881, 203-226-8826

124

Mole, John (see also Scupham, Peter), The Mandeville Press, 2 Taylor's Hill, Hitchin, Hertfordshire SG49AD, England

Moleah, Alfred T., Disa Press, Inc., PO Box 9284, Wilmington, DE 19809

Moliken, Mary, Gypsy Press, 1627 New Jersey Avenue #3, New Castle, DE 19720, 215-627-2821

Molmen, Marcia E. M., The Athena Press, 602 South 4th Street, Grand Forks, ND 58201, 701-775-9156

Momsen, Bill, Nautical Brass, PO Box 744DB, Montrose, CA 91020, 818-248-2616

Momsen, Bill, *NAUTICAL BRASS, ETC.*, PO Box 744DB, Montrose, CA 91020, 818-248-2616

Monaco, James, New York Zoetrope, 80 East 11th Street, Suite 516, New York, NY 10003, 420-0590

Monahan, Gordon (see also Pearson, Tina), *MUSICWORKS*, 30 St. Patrick Street, Toronto, Ontario, Canada, 416-593-7088

Monks, Clifford, *TOWARDS*, 3442 Grant Park Drive, Carmichael, CA 95608, 213-349-2780

Monroe, Elvira, Wide World Publishing/TETRA, PO Box 476, San Carlos, CA 94070, 415-593-2839

Montague, Don (see also Rosa, Linda), *SOUTH AMERICAN EXPLORER*, 2239 E. Colfax, Denver, CO 80206, 320-0388

Monte, Oscar, Associate Editor-at-Large (see also Lawson, Dr. Todd; Comen, Dr. Diane; Marsic, John; Rader, Steve; Nishi, Mio; Ginsberg, Allen; Samolis, Dr. Sam; Graham, Joan; Ferlinghetti, Lawrence; Ramirez, Julio; Haynes, Dr. Robert; Snyder, Gary; Morris, Dr. Richard), *ALPS MONTHLY*, PO Box 99394, San Francisco, CA 94109, 415-771-3431

Montgomery, John M., Editor and Publisher, Fels and Firn Press, 944 Sir Francis Drake Blvd #7, Kentfield, CA 94904, 415-457-4361

Monti, David A., Co-Author, Editor& Officer; Vice-President (see also Ganci, Michael T.; Ganci, Joseph A.), Avanti Assocciates, Publishers Inc., 9 Marrietta Lane, Mercerville, NJ 08619

Moody, Eric N., Editor (see also Mortensen, Lee), Great Basin Press, Box 11162, Reno, NV 89510, (702) 826-7729

Moody, Rodger, Editor, *SILVERFISH REVIEW*, PO Box 3541, Box 565, Apt 11, Eugene, OR 97403, 503-687-9625

Moomaw, G. Dunbar, Publisher, Mu Publications, Box 612, Dahlgren, VA 22448

Mooradian, K. A. (see also Mooradian, V. A.), Gilgamesh Press Ltd., 1059 W Ardmore Avenue, Chicago, IL 60660, 312-334-0327

Mooradian, V. A. (see also Mooradian, K. A.), *Gilgamesh Press Ltd.*, 1059 W Ardmore Avenue, Chicago, IL 60660, 312-334-0327

Moore, Charles, Richboro Press, Box 1, Richboro, PA 18954, 215-355-6084

Moore, Jack Henry (see also Haynes, Jim), '*THE CASSETTE GAZETTE*', Atelier A2, 83 rue de la Tombe-Issoire, Paris 75014, France, 327-1767

Moore, John Rees, *THE HOLLINS CRITIC*, P.O. Box 9538, Hollins College, VA 24020

Moore, J.W., Sunrise Press, 2004 Grant Street, Evanston, IL 60201, 312-475-3651

Moore, Mary Jane, Editor-in-Chief (see also Brown, Jae), *A LETTER AMONG FRIENDS*, PO Box 1198, Groton, CT 06340, 203-536-3494

Moorhead, Andrea, *OSIRIS*, Box 297, Deerfield, MA 01342

Moot, Andrew, Editor (see also Dutch, Peter), *PACIFIC BRIDGE*, PO Box 6328, San Francisco, CA 94101, 415-863-3622

Morain, Lloyd L., Editor (see also Harnack, William J.), *THE HUMANIST*, 7 Harwood Drive, Amherst, NY 14226, 716-839-5080

Morales, Goldie L. (see also Schuler, Ruth Wildes; Schuler, Jeanne Leigh), *PROPHETIC VOICES*, 94 Santa Maria Drive, Novato, CA 94947

Moran, John C., Founder Editor (see also Herron, Don; Eng, Steve), The F. Marion Crawford Memorial Society, Saracinesca House, 3610 Meadowbrook Avenue, Nashville, TN 37205

Moran, John C., Founder, Editor (see also Herron, Don; Eng, Steve), *THE ROMANTIST*, Saracinesca House, 3610 Meadowbrook Avenue, Nashville, TN 37205, 615-228-5939

Moran, Margaret, *NEW TIMES*, 1000 21st Street, Rock Island, IL 61201, 309-786-6944

Moran, Marilyn, *CabArt*, CabPress, 403½ Montgomery, Ann Arbor, MI 48103, 313-769-3685

Moran, Patrick R. (see also Burrows, Arthur A.; Clark, Raymond C.), ProLingua Associates, 15 Elm Street, Brattleboro, VT 05301, 802-257-7779

Morant, Mack B. (see also Nichols, Mosezelle), R & M Publishing Company, Inc, PO Box 1276, Holly Hill, SC 29059, 803-534-6894, 531-2053

Mordenski, Jan, *MOVING OUT: Feminist Literary & Arts Journal*, PO Box 21249, Detroit, MI 48221, 313-833-1403

Moreno, Catherine, Hartmus Press, 23 Lomita Drive, Mill Valley, CA 94941

Moretti, Laura, Co-Editor (see also Moss, Doug; Mason, Jim; Mola, Noreen), *AGENDA: Newsmagazine of the Animal Rights Network*, Box 5234, Westport, CT 06881, 203-226-8826

Morgan, David (see also McIntosh, Grant), *STRIPS*, PO Box 2896, Auckland, New Zealand

Morgan, Frederick, Co-editor (see also Deitz, Paula), *THE HUDSON REVIEW*, 684 Park Avenue, New York, NY 10021, 212-650-0020

Morgan, Jane, Director, *COMMUNITY SERVICE NEWSLETTER*, Box 243, Yellow Springs, OH 45387, 513-767-2161

Morgan, Kenneth O. (see also Griffiths, Ralph A.), *WELSH HISTORY REVIEW*, 6 Gwenyth Street, Cathays, Cardiff CF2 4YD, Wales, Cardiff 31919

Morgan, Melanie (see also Chesson, Lela), Falls of the Tar Publications, PO Box 4194, Rocky Mount, NC 27801

Morgan, Richard (see also Silkin, Jon; Tracy, Lorna; Blackburn, Michael), *STAND*, 179 Wingrove Road, Newcastle-on-Tyne NE49DA, England

Morgan, Speer, Editor (see also Michalson, Greg), *THE MISSOURI REVIEW*, Dept. of English, 231 Arts & Science, University of Missouri-Columbia, Columbia, MO 65211

Morgan, Sue A., *MODERN IMAGES*, Box 912, Mattoon, IL 61938

Morice, Dave, The Happy Press, Box 585, Iowa City, IA 52244, 319-338-0084

Morrill, Tom, *ABORNING*, Route 16, Box 9047, Tallahassee, FL 32304, 904-576-1206

Morris, David, Features Editor (see also Patton, Cindy; Hyde, Sue), *GAY COMMUNITY NEWS*, 167 Tremont Street 5th Floor, Boston, MA 02111, 617-426-4469

Morris, Dr. Richard, Small Press Coordinator (see also Lawson, Dr. Todd; Comen, Dr. Diane; Marsic, John; Rader, Steve; Monte, Oscar; Nishi, Mio; Ginsberg, Allen; Samolis, Dr. Sam; Graham, Joan; Ferlinghetti, Lawrence; Ramirez, Julio; Haynes, Dr. Robert; Snyder, Gary), *ALPS MONTHLY*, PO Box 99394, San Francisco, CA 94109, 415-771-3431

Morris, Linda, Managing Editor (see also Allen, William), *THE OHIO JOURNAL*, OSU Dept. of English, 164 W. 17th Avenue, Columbus, OH 43210, 614-422-2242

Morris, Richard, *COSMEP NEWSLETTER*, PO Box 703, San Francisco, CA 94101, 415-922-9490

Morrison, C.L., *FORMAT*, 405 S. 7th Street, St. Charles, IL 60174, 312-584-0187

Morrison, C.L., Seven Oaks Press, 405 S. 7th Street, St. Charles, IL 60174, 312-584-0187

Morrison, John, Poetry Editor (see also Blythe, Will; Carroll, Ron), *THE BLACK WARRIOR REVIEW*, P.O. Box 2936, University, AL 35486, 205-348-4518

Morrone, John, P E N American Center, 47 5th Ave, New York, NY 10003

Morrow, Bradford, Editor, *CONJUNCTIONS*, 33 W. 9th Street, New York, NY 10011

Morrow, Bradford, Senior Editor, Conjunctions, Inc., 33 W. 9th Street, New York, NY 10011

Morrow, Sandra, Managing Editor (see also Peters, Lana), Newsletter Makers, 1540 Pleasant Lane, Lafayette, CA 94549, 415-930-8584

Morrow, Sandra, Managing Editor (see also Peters, Lana), *POETIC IMAGES*, 1540 Pleasant Lane, Lafayette, CA 94549, 415-930-8584

Mortensen, Lee, Editor (see also Moody, Eric N.), Great Basin Press, Box 11162, Reno, NV 89510, (702) 826-7729

Mortimer, Peter, Editor (see also Swan, Pete), *IRON*, 5 Marden Terrace, Cullercoats, North Shields, Tyne & Wear NE30 4PD, England, 0632-531901

Mortimer, Peter, Art Editor, Editor (see also Swan, Pete; Lees, John), Iron Press, 5 Marden Terrace, Cullercoats, North Shields Tyne & Near NE30 4PD, England

Morton, Brian N. (see also Morton, Jacqueline), The Olivia and Hill Press, Inc., PO Box 7396, Ann Arbor, MI 48107, 313-663-0235

Morton, Jacqueline (see also Morton, Brian N.), *The Olivia and Hill Press, Inc.*, PO Box 7396, Ann Arbor, MI 48107, 313-663-0235

Morton, W. C., Chase Avenue Press, 107 East Spring Street, Apt 9, Oxford, OH 45056, 513-523-1682

Moseley, Amelia, Feldspar, PO Box 2375, Stanford, CA 94305, 415-323-7907

Moseley, Ray, Raymond's Quiet Press, 6336 Leslie N E, Albuquerque, NM 87109, 505-821-3627

Moselle, Gary, Publisher (see also Jacobs, Laurence), Craftsman Book Company, 6058 Corte Del Cedro, Carlsbad, CA 92008, 619-438-7828

Moser, N., *ILLUMINATIONS*, 2110 9th Street, Apt B, Berkeley, CA 94710, 415-849-2102

Moser, N., Chief Editor (see also Fingland, Randy), Illuminations Press, 2110 9th Street, Apt B, Berkeley, CA 94710, 415-849-2102

Moser, Robin S., Editorial Asst. (see also Skeens, Gary S.), *GREEN FEATHER*, PO Box 2633, Lakewood, OH 44107

Moser, Robin S., Assoc. Editor (see also Skeens, Gary S.), Quality Publications, Inc., PO Box 2633, Lakewood, OH 44107

Moser, Robin S., Assoc. Editor (see also Skeens, Gary S.), S-W Enterprises, PO Box 2633, Lakewood, OH 44107

Moses, Claire, Managing Editor, *FEMINIST STUDIES*, c/o Women's Studies Program, Univ of MD, College Park, MD 20742, 301-454-2363

Moses, Patricia, Aarben Presentations, PO Box 24627, Minneapolis, MN 55424

Moses, W.R. (see also Schneider, Harold W.; Nyberg, Ben; Rees, John), *KANSAS QUARTERLY*, Denison Hall, Kansas St. Univ., Manhattan, KS 66506, 913-532-6716

Mosher, Robin, Associate Editor (see also Clift, G.W.; Carrell, Ann; Roper, J.V.; Salah-Din, Hakim), *LITERARY MAGAZINE REVIEW*, English Department, Kansas State University, Manhattan, KS 66506, 913-532-6719

Mosier, John, *NEW ORLEANS REVIEW*, Loyola University, New Orleans, LA 70118, 504-865-2295

Moss, Doug, Co-Editor (see also Mason, Jim; Moretti, Laura; Mola, Noreen), *AGENDA: Newsmagazine of the Animal Rights Network*, Box 5234, Westport, CT 06881, 203-226-8826

Moss, Leonard (see also Richard, Michel Paul; Kellogg, Peggy; Soffer, Walter), *THOUGHTS FOR ALL SEASONS: The Magazine of Epigrams*, State University College At Geneseo, Geneseo, NY 14454, 716-245-5336

Moss, Mark (see also Eilenberg, Jeff; Gorka, John), *SING OUT! The Folk Song Magazine*, PO Box 1071, Easton, PA 18042, 215-253-8105

Moss, Stanley, The Sheep Meadow Press/Flying Point Books, c/o Persea Books, 225 Lafayette St., New York, NY 10012, 212-431-5270

Motion, Andrew, *POETRY REVIEW*, 21 Earls Court Square, London SW5, England, 01-373-7861

Motta, Marcelo, Editor. Supervisor General, O.T.O., *THE EQUINOX - THE ORIFLAMME*, PO Box 90144, Nashville, TN 37209

Motta, Marcelo, Supervisor General, O.T.O., Society Ordo Templi Orientis International, Box 90144, Nashville, TN 37209

Mottet, Arthur L., Jr. (see also Elbert, N.E.; Fox, C.L.), Pacific Scientific Press, Inc., 3506 Pennsylvania, Longview, WA 98632, 206-425-8592

Mountaingrove, Jean (see also Mountaingrove, Ruth), New Woman Press, 2000 Mountain Trail S.V., Wolf Creek, OR 97497

Mountaingrove, Jean (see also Mountaingrove, Ruth), *WOMANSPIRIT*, 2000 King Mt. Trail, Wolf Creek, OR 97497

Mountaingrove, Ruth (see also Mountaingrove, Jean), New Woman Press, 2000 Mountain Trail S.V., Wolf Creek, OR 97497

Mountaingrove, Ruth (see also Mountaingrove, Jean), *WOMANSPIRIT*, 2000 King Mt. Trail, Wolf Creek, OR 97497

Moyer, Greg, *NUTRITION ACTION*, 1501 16th Street N.W., Washington, DC 20036, 202-332-9110

Moyse, Arthur (see also Witte, Jan), *ZERO ONE*, 39 Minford Gardens, West Kensington, London W14 0AP, England

Mudd, C.P., Poetry Editor (see also Burns, William; Empereur, Jake, S.J.), *MODERN LITURGY*, Box 444, Saratoga, CA 95071, 408-252-4195

Mudfoot, Judyl, *INKLINGS*, 209 West De la Guerra, Santa Barbara, CA 93101, (805) 962-9996

Mudfoot, Judyl (see also Newborn, Sasha), Mudborn Press, 209 West De la Guerra, Santa Barbara, CA 93101, 805-962-9996

Mueller, Carolyn, Co-Editor (see also Mark, Linda; Hepfer, Will), *SERIALS REVIEW*, PO Box 1808, Ann Arbor, MI 48106, 313-434-5530

Mueller, L. W., Harlo Press, 50 Victor, Detroit, MI 48203

Mueller, Lisel, Contributing Editor (see also Murphy, George; Carver, Raymond; Gallagher, Tess; Galvin, Brendan; Matthews, William; McBride, Mekeel), *TENDRIL*, Box 512, Green Harbor, MA 02041, 617-834-4137

Mueller, Milton (see also Grossberg, Michael), *FREE PRESS NETWORK*, PO Box 1743, Apple Valley, CA 92307, 619-242-4899, 415-834-6880

Mulhallen, Karen, *DESCANT*, P.O. Box 314 Station P, Toronto, Ontario M5S 2S8, Canada

Mumford, Clive, *SCILLONIAN MAGAZINE*, c/o T. Mumford, St. Mary's, Isles of Scilly, Cornwall, England

Munday, Georgette (see also Hol, Jim), *THE AGENT*, New Agency, 46 Denbigh Street, London SW1, England

Mungo, Raymond, Contributing Editor (see also Golden, Michael; Elias, Viki; Harrison, Jim; Bukowski, Charles; Placidus, Max; Codrescu, Andrei; Horotwitz, Mikhail; Ligi; Kramer, Glenn; Mitchell, Donna; Riedel, Robert), *SMOKE SIGNALS*, 1516 Beverly Road, Brooklyn, NY 11226

Munini, Diane J., Developmental Arts, PO Box 389, Arlington, MA 02174, 617-729-5221

Murcko, Terry, Poetry (see also Villani, Jim; Sayre, Rose; George Peffer), Pig Iron Press, P.O. Box 237, Youngstown, OH 44501

Murcury, Miron, Art Director (see also Kenin, Millea), *EMPIRE: For the SF Writer*, 1025-55th Street, Oakland, CA 94608, 415-655-3024

Murphy, George, Editor-in-Chief (see also Carver, Raymond; Gallagher, Tess; Galvin, Brendan; Matthews, William; McBride, Mekeel; Mueller, Lisel), *TENDRIL*, Box 512, Green Harbor, MA 02041, 617-834-4137

Murphy, George E., Jr., Director, Wampeter Press, Box 512, Green Harbor, MA 02041, 617-834-4137

Murphy, James J., *RHETORICA: A Journal of the History of Rhetoric,* Department of Rhetoric, University of California, Davis, CA 95616

Murphy, Maureen, Features Editor (see also Lowery, Robert G.), *IRISH LITERARY SUPPLEMENT,* 114 Paula Boulevard, Selden, NY 11784, 516-698-8243

Murphy, Robert A. (see also Adams Suzanne), Higginson Books, Derby Square, Salem, MA 01970, 617-744-0470

Murphy, Russell, Managing Editor (see also Jauss, David; Wojahn, David; Vannatta, Dennis), *CRAZYHORSE,* Dept of English, Unviersity of Arkansas at Little Rock, Little Rock, AR 72204, 501-569-3160

Murray, Steven T., Editor (see also Doran, Susan), Fjord Press, PO Box 615, Corte Madera, CA 94925, 415-924-9566/549-1910

Muses, Dr. Charles (see also Beeman, Rockne), Sceptre Publishing, 1442A Walnut Street, Suite 61, Berkeley, CA 94709, 415-525-1481

my (see also Kesey, Ken; Leary, Timothy; Marrs, Lee; Loren, Richard; Babbs, Ken), *SPIT IN THE OCEAN,* 85829 Ridgeway Rd, Pleasant Hill, OR 97455, 503-747-5796

Myers, Carol A., *BOOK TALK,* 8632 Horacio Pl NE, Albuquerque, NM 87111, 505-299-8940

Myers, George, Editor-in-Chief, *MENU,* PO Box 36027, Grosse Pointe Farms, MI 48236

Myers, George, Jr., *CUMBERLAND JOURNAL,* 8 Oakwood Circle, Camp Hill, PA 17011

Myers Jr., George, Consultant Editor (see also Bianco, David), The Lunchroom Press, PO Box 36027, Grosse Pointe Farms, MI 48236

Myles, Colette (see also Myles, Glenn), Artman's Press, 1511 McGee Avenue, Berkeley, CA 94703, 415-527-2710

Myles, Glenn (see also Myles, Colette), *Artman's Press,* 1511 McGee Avenue, Berkeley, CA 94703, 415-527-2710

Myss, Caroline M., Editor, Stillpoint Publishing, Box 640, Walpole, NH 03608, 603-756-3508

Mytinger, Melissa, Christopher's Books, 390 62nd Street, Oakland, CA 94618, 415-428-1120

N

Naatz, Robert (see also Dell, Barbara), Precipice Press, 106 Pinion Lane, Manitou Springs, CO 80829

Nading, Lee (see also Addleman, Rex; Simmons, Jim), *VERIDIAN,* PO Box 2324, Bloomington, IN 47402

Nagorka, Henry J. (see also Mathias, Steven; Nagorka, Rev. Diane S.), ESPress, Inc., Box 8606, Washington, DC 20011, 202-723-4578

Nagorka, Henry J. (see also Mathias, Steven; Nagorka, Rev. Diane S.), *THE PSYCHIC OBSERVER,* Box 8606, Washington, DC 20011, 202-723-4578

Nagorka, Rev. Diane S., Assistant Editor (see also Nagorka, Henry J.; Mathias, Steven), ESPress, Inc., Box 8606, Washington, DC 20011, 202-723-4578

Nagorka, Rev. Diane S., Assistant Editor (see also Nagorka, Henry J.; Mathias, Steven), *THE PSYCHIC OBSERVER,* Box 8606, Washington, DC 20011, 202-723-4578

Nakagawa, Atsuo, *POETRY NIPPON,* 11-2, 5-chome, Nagaike-cho, Showa-ku, Nagoya 466, Japan

Nakagawa, Atsuo, The Poetry Nippon Press, 11-2, 5-Chome, Nagaike-cho, Showa-ku, Nagoya 466, Japan, 052-833-5724

Nakano, Mei (see also Miller, Adam David), Mina Press, PO Box 854, Sebastopol, CA 95472, 707-829-0854

Nall, Barbara, Patrick Walsh Press, 2017 S. Ventura, Tempe, AZ 85282, 602-894-1230

Names, Larry D. (see also Eagan, Peggy), Larantor Press, Box 253, 211 Main Street, Neshkoro, WI 54960, 414-293-4377

Nantier, Terry, NBM Publishing Company, PO Box 281, Peck Slip Station, New York, NY 10272, 202-788-6498

Napier, Ronald, The Avondale Press, P.O. Box 451, Willowdale, Ontario M2N5T1, Canada, (416) 640-2946

Narby, Mary A., *THE HORSE, THE FORCE—MAGAZINE OF MOUNTED LAW ENFORCEMENT,* LBN Publishing Company, 42 Avondale Park, Rochester, NY 14620, 716-473-5161

Nash, Grinley, The Blackhole School of Poethnics, Box 555, Port Jefferson, NY 11777

Nash, Helen, Editor (see also Bush, G. F.), *LETTERS MAGAZINE,* MAINE WRITERS WORK-SHOP, RFD 1, Box 905, Stonington, ME 04681

Nash, Helen, Editor (see also Bush, G. F.), Mainespring Press, MAINE WRITERS WORKSHOP, Box 905, R. F. D., Stonington, ME 04681

Nash, Valery (see also Ayyildiz, Judy; Ferguson, Maurice; Bullins, Amanda; Sheffler, Natalie; Steinke, Paul; Weinstein, Ann), *ARTEMIS,* PO Box 945, Roanoke, VA 24005, 703-981-9318

Naslund, Alan, Publisher (see also Neumayer, Richard L.), River City Review Press, Inc., PO Box 34275, Louisville, KY 40232

Naslund, Sena Jeter, Faculty Editor (see also Well, Mary), *THE LOUISVILLE REVIEW,* Univ. of Louisville, English Dept., 315 Bingham Humanities, Louisville, KY 40292, 502-588-5921

Natambu, Kofi, *SOLID GROUND: A NEW WORLD JOURNAL,* Go-For-What-You-Know, Inc., 4929 Scotten, Detroit, MI 48210, 313-874-0594

Nathan, Ronald G., Ph.D (see also Charleworth, Edward A., Ph.D.), Biobehavioral Publishers and Distributors, Inc., 10603 Grant, Suite #204, PO Box 1102, Houston, TX 77251, 713-890-8575

Natov, Roni (see also DeLuca, Geraldine), *THE LION AND THE UNICORN: A Critical Journal of Children's Literature,* Dept of English, Brooklyn College, Brooklyn, NY 11210, 780-5195

Nauman-Haight, Sheila, Editor & Publisher (see also Rognlie, Tammy), *HEALTH LITERATURE REVIEW,* PO Box 8029, St. Paul, MN 55113, 612-731-1816

Nauman-Haight, Sheila, Editor & Publisher (see also Rognlie, Tammy), True-To-Form Press, PO Box 8029, St. Paul, MN 55113, 612-731-1816

Navaretta, Cynthia, Editor, Midmarch Associates, 3304 Grand Central Sta, New York City, NY 10163, 212-666-6990

Navaretta, Cynthia, Exec. Editor (see also Hausen, Rena), *WOMEN ARTISTS NEWS,* Box 3304, Grand Central, New York City, NY 10163, 212-666-6990

Nealon, Jean, *PHOEBUS MAGAZINE,* PO Box 3085, Phoebus Station, Hampton, VA 23663

Necakov, Lillian, *ELVIS CAR,* PO Box 789 Stn. F, Toronto, Ontario M4Y 2N7, Canada

Necakov, Lillian, Surrealist Poets' Gardening Association, PO Box 789, Stn. F, Toronto, Ontario M4Y 2N7, Canada

Nedds, Trish, Contributing Book Artist (see also Quasha, George; Quasha, Susan; Martin, Michele; Coffey, Michael; Stein Charles; Kelly, Robert; Auster, Paul; Kamin, Franz; McClelland, Bruce), Station Hill Press, Station Hill Road, Barrytown, NY 12507, 914-758-5840

Neeld, Judith, Editor and Publisher (see also McCormick, Pat; Truscott, Robert Blake), *STONE COUNTRY,* PO Box 132, Menemsha, MA 02552, 617-693-5832

Neeld, Judith, Editor and Publisher (see also McCormick, Pat), Stone Country Press, PO Box 132, Menemsha, MA 02552, 617-693-5832

Negemonk, William (see also Ling, Gilbert N.), *PHYSIOLOGICAL CHEMISTRY & PHYSICS,* Route 2, Box 28A, Wake Forest, NC 27587, 919-556-2940

Neill, Peter (see also Press, Michelle), Leete's Island Books, Box 1131, New Haven, CT 06505, 203-481-2536

Neill, William, Gaelic Editor (see also Green, J.C.R.), Club Leabhar, PO Box 1, Portree, Isle of Skye, Scotland

Neill, William, Editor, *TIANABHIAG*, PO Box 1, Portree, Isle of Skye, Scotland

Nelson, B.J., Ram Publishing Co., PO Box 38649, Dallas, TX 75238, 214-278-8439

Nelson, Bonnie E., Editor & Publisher, Lintel, Box 8609, Roanoke, VA 24014, 703-982-2265

Nelson, Tony, Managing Editor (see also Cummins, Rich), *SONORA REVIEW*, Dept of English, University of Arizona, Tucson, AZ 85721, (602) 626-1387

Nemeth, Doris, Editor (see also Bearden, Wanda), The Poet, 2314 West Sixth Street, Mishawaka, IN 46544, 219-255-8606

Nestor, Jack (see also Trowbridge, C.H.), *THE HOBOKEN TERMINAL*, The Hoboken Terminal, PO Box 841, Hoboken, NJ 07030, 201-798-1696

Nestor, Sarah, Book Editor (see also Shattuck-Rosenfelt, Jane), Museum of New Mexico Press, PO Box 2087, Santa Fe, NM 87503, 505-827-6454

Neumayer, Richard L., Editor (see also Naslund, Alan), River City Review Press, Inc., PO Box 34275, Louisville, KY 40232

New, W.H., *CANADIAN LITERATURE*, University of British Columbia, 2021 West Mall, Vancouver, B.C. V6T 1W5, Canada, 604-228-2780

Newborn, Sasha, Bandanna Books, 209 West De la Guerra, Santa Barbara, CA 93101, 805-962-9996

Newborn, Sasha (see also Mudfoot, Judyl), Mudborn Press, 209 West De la Guerra, Santa Barbara, CA 93101, 805-962-9996

Newcomb, Justine Webb (see also Webb, David Maryland), Webb-Newcomb Company, Inc., 308 N.E. Vance Street, Wilson, NC 27893, 919-291-7231; 919-735-5865

Newhouse, Sally, Co-Editor (see also Holley, Barbara), *EARTHWISE NEWSLETTER*, PO Box 680-536, Miami, FL 33168, 305-688-8558

Newman, Felice (see also Delacoste, Frederique), Cleis Press, PO Box 8933, Pittsburgh, PA 15221

Newman, George, Blossom Valley Press, PO Box 4044, Blossom Valley Station, Mountain View, CA 94040, 415-941-7525

Newman, William S., *THE DEKALB LITERARY ARTS JOURNAL*, 555 N. Indian Creek Dr, Clarkston, GA 30021

Newton, J., Editor (see also Nuse, B.; Zavitz, C.; Rooney, F.; Andersen, M.; Wine, J.; Prentice, A.; Scane, J.; Caplan, Paula; Van Kirk, Sylvia), *RESOURCES FOR FEMINIST RESEARCH/DOCUMEN-TATION SUR LA RECHERCHE FEMINISTE*, Ont Inst for Stud in Educ, Centre for Women's Studies in Education, 252 Bloor Street W., Toronto, Ontario M5S 1V6, Canada, 416-923-6641

Nichol, bp (see also Bevington, Stan; Young, David; Davey, Frank; James, Clifford; Ondaatje, Michael; McCartney, Linda; Sheard, Sarah; Reid, Dennis), Coach House Press, 95 Rivercrest Road, Toronto, Ontario M6S 4H7, Canada, 416-767-6317

Nichols, Mosezelle (see also Morant, Mack B.), R & M Publishing Company, Inc, PO Box 1276, Holly Hill, SC 29059, 803-534-6894, 531-2053

Nicholson, Ann Winston (see also Martin, Robert), AUBURN-WOLFE PUBLISHING CO, 584 Castro #351, San Francisco, CA 94114, 916-583-0708

Nicolson, Linda (see also Housman, Katherine), Belle-Lettres Books, PO Box 20405, Oakland, CA 94620, 655-9783

Niers, Gert, Executive Editor (see also Steinitz, Hans), *AUFBAU*, 2121 Broadway, New York, NY 10023, 212-873-7400

Nigg, Joe, Press Editor (see also Hutchison, Joseph; Rea, David; Miller, Patty; Reilly, Gary; Schroeder, Gary), *PENDRAGON Journal of the Creative Arts*, 2640 E. 12th Avenue, Box 715, Denver, CO 80206, 303-444-4100

Nikides, George (see also Palmer, Jill; Matta, John), *SCRIVENER*, McGill University, 853 Sherbrooke Street W., Montreal, P.Q. H3A 2T6, Canada

Nikolic, Djordje, Publisher (see also Mills, Donna; Kinzie, Mary), Elpenor Books, Box 3152, Merchandise Mart Plaza, Chicago, IL 60654, 312-935-1343

Nilsen, Mary, *IOWA WOMAN*, PO Box 680, Iowa City, IA 52244

Nimimosha, Co-Editor (see also Sun Bear; Wabun), Bear Tribe Publishing, PO Box 9167, Spokane, WA 99209, 509-258-7755

Nimimosha (see also Wabun; Sun Bear), *MANY SMOKES EARTH AWARENESS MAGAZINE*, PO Box 9167, Spokane, WA 99209, 509-258-7755

Nimmo, Kurt, *PLANET DETROIT*, 8214 St. Marys, Detroit, MI 48228, 313-582-6362

Nimmo, Kurt, Planet Detroit Chapbook Series, 8214 St. Marys, Detroit, MI 48228, 313-582-6362

Ninkovich, Tom, National Reunion Association, PO Box 295, Nevada City, CA 95959, 916-265-6644

Nirmala, Kammana (see also Dorsett, Thomas), *KAVITHA*, 4408 Wickford Road, Baltimore, MD 21210, 301-467-4316

Nishi, Mio, Assistant Editor-at-Large (see also Lawson, Dr. Todd; Comen, Dr. Diane; Marsic, John; Rader, Steve; Monte, Oscar; Ginsberg, Allen; Samolis, Dr. Sam; Graham, Joan; Ferlinghetti, Lawrence; Ramirez, Julio; Haynes, Dr. Robert; Snyder, Gary; Morris, Dr. Richard), *ALPS MONTHLY*, PO Box 99394, San Francisco, CA 94109, 415-771-3431

Nisley, Rebecca (see also Buck, Harry), *ANIMA*, 1053 Wilson Avenue, Chambersburg, PA 17201, 717-263-8303

Niven, Dr. Alastair (see also Calder, Dr. Angus), *THE JOURNAL OF COMMONWEALTH LITERATURE*, Africa Centre, 38 King Street, London, England, 01-836-1973

Njoroge, Fred N. (see also Wanjie, Anne Catherine; Waiyaki, D. Nyoike; Kasu, Ephraim K.), East African Publishing House, PO Box 30571, Nairobi, Kenya, Kenya, 557417, 557788

Norby, Mary, Assistant Editor (see also Behm, Richard), *SONG*, 808 Illinois, Stevens Pt, WI 54481, 715-344-6836

Norman, Gina, Assistant Editor (see also Peabody, Melissa), *U.S. INFORMATION MOSCOW*, 2300 Leghorn St., Mountain View, CA 94043, 415-493-1885

Norris, Addis Lynne, The Olive Press Publications, PO Box 99, Los Olivos, CA 93441

Norris, Ken (see also Mele, Jim), Cross Country Press, Ltd., PO Box 492, Ridgefield, CT 06877, 203-431-8225

Norris, Ken (see also Mele, Jim), *CROSSCOUNTRY*, PO Box 492, Ridgefield, CT 06877, 203-431-8225

Northway, Martin, Highlander Press, PO Box 183, Nashville, IN 47448

Norton, Phil, Editor & publisher, BikePress U.S.A./BikePress Canada, PO Box 326, Mars, PA 16046, 412-625-1180

Novak, Don (see also Novak, Louella), Joshua Publishing Company, 8033 Sunset Blvd., Suite 306, Los Angeles, CA 90046, 213-650-8127

Novak, Don (see also Novak, Louella), *SCRIPTWRITERS MARKET*, 8033 Sunset Blvd., Suite 306, Los Angeles, CA 90046, 213-650-8127

Novak, Louella (see also Novak, Don), Joshua Publishing Company, 8033 Sunset Blvd., Suite 306, Los Angeles, CA 90046, 213-650-8127

Novak, Louella (see also Novak, Don), *SCRIPTWRITERS MARKET*, 8033 Sunset Blvd., Suite 306, Los Angeles, CA 90046, 213-650-8127

Novak, Robert, *THE WINDLESS ORCHARD,* Indiana Univ Eng Dept, Ft. Wayne, IN 46805

Novey, Jeffrey H. (see also Zerkin, E. Leif), Haight-Ashbury Publications, 409 Clayton Street, San Francisco, CA 94117, 415-626-2810

Novey, Jeffrey H. (see also Zerkin, E. Leif), *JOURNAL OF PSYCHOACTIVE DRUGS,* 409 Clayton Street, San Francisco, CA 94117, 415-626-2810

Nowicki, Ron, *SAN FRANCISCO REVIEW OF BOOKS,* PO Box 33-0090, San Francisco, CA 94133, 415-777-2923

Noyce, John L., *LIBRARIANS FOR SOCIAL CHANGE,* PO Box 450, Brighton, Sussex BN1 8GR, England

Noyce, John L., John L Noyce, Publisher, P.O. Box 450, Brighton, Sussex BN1 8GR, England

Noyce, John L., *POPULAR CULTURE IN BRITAIN,* P.O. Box 450, Brighton BN18GR, England

Nunn, Walter, Rose Publishing Co., 301 Louisiana Street, Little Rock, AR 72201, 501-372-1666

Nuse, B., Editor (see also Newton, J.; Zavitz, C.; Rooney, F.; Andersen, M.; Wine, J.; Prentice, A.; Scane, J.; Caplan, Paula; Van Kirk, Sylvia), *RESOURCES FOR FEMINIST RESEARCH/DOCUMEN-TATION SUR LA RECHERCHE FEMINISTE,* Ont Inst for Stud in Educ, Centre for Women's Studies in Education, 252 Bloor Street W., Toronto, Ontario M5S 1V6, Canada, 416-923-6641

Nuttall, Suse, Administrative Circulation (see also Stainsby, Charles), *LIBERAL NEWS,* 1 Whitehall Place, London SW1A2HE, England, 01 839 1533

Nutton, V. (see also Bynum, W.F.), *MEDICAL HISTORY,* 183 Euston Road, London NW1 2BP, England

Nyberg, Ben (see also Schneider, Harold W.; Moses, W.R.; Rees, John), *KANSAS QUARTERLY,* Denison Hall, Kansas St. Univ., Manhattan, KS 66506, 913-532-6716

Nye, Naomi Shihub, Poetry Editor (see also Yates, David C.; O'Keefe, John), *CEDAR ROCK,* 1121 Madeline, New Braunfels, TX 78130, 512-625-6002

Nyerges, Christopher (see also Deyans, Vernon), *BURWOOD JOURNAL,* Box 42152, Los Angeles, CA 90042, 213-255-9502

Nyerges, Christopher (see also Devons, Vernon), Survival News Service, Box 42152, Los Angeles, CA 90042, 213-255-9502

O

Oakes, Elizabeth (see also Steele, Frank; Steele, Peggy), *PLAINSONG,* Box U245, Western Kentucky University, Bowling Green, KY 42101, 502-745-3043

OakGrove, Artemis, Editor, Lace Publications, PO Box 10037, Denver, CO 80210, 303-221-4405

Oaks Smith, David, *OUIJA MADNESS,* PO Box 42212, San Francisco, CA 94142, 415-747-0486

Oaks Smith, David, Ouija Madness Press, PO Box 42212, San Francisco, CA 94142, 415-747-0486

Oandasan, William, *A, a journal of contemporary literature,* Box 42A510, York Station, CA 90042, 213-390-4517

Oandasan, William, A Publications, Box 42A510, York Station, CA 90042, 213-390-4517

Oandasan, Willian, *AMERICAN INDIAN CULTURE AND RESEARCH JOURNAL,* 3220 Campbell Hall UCLA, Los Angeles, CA 90024, 213-825-4777

Oates, Joyce Carol, Associate Editor (see also Smith, Raymond J.), *THE ONTARIO REVIEW,* 9 Honey Brook Drive, Princeton, NJ 08540

Oates, Joyce Carol, Assoc. Editor (see also Smith, Raymond J.), The Ontario Review Press, 9 Honey Brook Drive, Princeton, NJ 08540

Ober, Stuart (see also Michaels, Joanne), Beekman Publishers, Inc., Po Box 888, Woodstock, NY 12498, 914-679-2300

Ober, Stuart A., *O.I.L. OIL INCOME LETTER*, PO Box 888, Mill Hill Road, Woodstock, NY 12498, 914-679-2300 or 2301

O'Brien, Aline (see also Rasmussen, Chrys; Costello, Catherine), Continuing Saga Press, PO Box 194, San Anselmo, CA 94960, 415-454-4411

O'Brien, John, *THE REVIEW OF CONTEMPORARY FICTION*, 1817 79th Avenue, Elmwood Park, IL 60635

O'Brien, William (see also Steinke, Russell; DiFranco, Anthony), *LONG POND REVIEW*, English Dept, Suffolk Community College, Selden Long Island, NY 11784

O'Callaghan, Robert J., Editor-in-Chief (see also Carrington, Stephen M.), Pine Tree Publishing, PO Box 93, Phippsburg, ME 04562, 207-389-2428

Ochester, Ed (see also Horner, Britt), Spring Church Book Company, PO Box 127, Spring Church, PA 15686

Ochtrup, Monica, Poetry Editor (see also McDonald, Susan; Wiener, Phyllis), *WARM JOURNAL*, 414 First Avenue North, Minneapolis, MN 55401, 612-332-5672

Ochtrup, Monica, Poetry Editor (see also McDonald, Susan; Wiener, Phyllis), Women's Art Registry of Minnesota, 414 First Avenue North, Minneapolis, MN 55401, 612-332-5672

Ockerse, Thomas, Tom Ockerse Editions, 37 Woodbury Street, Providence, RI 02906, 401-331-0783

O'Connell, Bonnie P. (see also O'Connell, G.A.), The Penumbra Press, Box 12, Lisbon, IA 52253, 319-455-2182

O'Connell, G.A. (see also O'Connell, Bonnie P.), *The Penumbra Press*, Box 12, Lisbon, IA 52253, 319-455-2182

O'Connell, Richard, *POETRY NEWSLETTER*, Dept. of English, Temple University, Philadelphia, PA 19122

O'Daly, Bill, *WILLOW SPRINGS*, Pub, PO Box 1063, Eastern Washington University, Cheney, WA 99004, 359-7061

O'Dell, J. H., Associate Editor (see also Jackson, Esther; Bond, Jean Carey; Kaiser, Ernest; Baird, Keith E.; Hairston, Loyle), *FREEDOMWAYS - A Quarterly Review of the Freedom Movement*, Freedomways Associates, Inc., 799 Broadway Suite 542, New York, NY 10003

O'Donnell, Mary Ann, Associate Editor (see also Tollers, Vincent L.; Kiernan, Robert F.), *LITERARY RESEARCH NEWSLETTER*, Department of English and World Literature, Manhattan College, Bronx, NY 10471, 212-920-0121

Oei, Perry (see also Sullivan, Patrick S.), *CEILIDH: AN INFORMAL GATHERING FOR STORY & SONG*, 986 Marquette Lane, Foster City, CA 94404, 415-341-6228

Oei, Perry (see also Sullivan, Patrick S.), Ceilidh, Inc., 986 Marquette Lane, Foster City, CA 94404, 415-341-6228

O'Gara, Geoffrey, Trotevale, Inc., PO Box 58, Lander, WY 82520, 307-332-7044

O'Hara, William F., International Sport Fishing Publications, PO Box 873, Captiva Island, FL 33924

Ohe, Yun J., Editor, Old Dominion Press, PO Box 10423, Alexandria, VA 22310, 703-922-8741

Ohlsen, Linda, Editor (see also Eades, Joan; Eades, Dan), *BLOODROOT*, PO Box 891, Grand Forks, ND 58206, 701-775-6079

Ohlsen, Linda, Editor (see also Eades, Dan; Eades, Joan), Bloodroot, Inc., PO Box 891, Grand Forks, ND 58206, 70l-775-6079

O'Keefe, John, Fiction Editor (see also Yates, David C.; Nye, Naomi Shihub), *CEDAR ROCK*, 1121 Madeline, New Braunfels, TX 78130, 512-625-6002

Olivares, Julian (see also Saldivar, Jose), *REVISTA CHICANO-RIQUENA*, University of Houston, Houston, TX 77004, 219-749-4768

Oliveira, Ana (see also Smith, Barbara; Lone Dog, Lcota; Rhodes, Gina), Kitchen Table: Women of Color Press, Box 2753, New York, NY 10185, 212-308-5389

Oliveros, Chuck (see also Matthews, David; C., G.C.), Dead Angel Press, 1206 Lyndale Drive SE, Atlanta, GA 30316, 404-624-1524

Oliveros, Chuck (see also C., G.C.; Matthews, David), *DEAD ANGEL*, 1206 Lyndale Drive SE, Atlanta, GA 30316

Olleson, Edward (see also Fortune, Nigel), *MUSIC AND LETTERS*, Oxford Journals, Walton Street, Oxford 0X2 6DP, England

Olmstead, Robert, Executive Director, Conservatory of American Letters, PO Box 123, So. Thomaston, ME 04858

Olmsted, Elaine (see also Olmsted, Robert; Danbury, Richard S., III), Dan River Press, PO Box 88, Thomaston, ME 04861

Olmsted, Robert (see also Olmsted, Elaine; Danbury, Richard S., III), *Dan River Press*, PO Box 88, Thomaston, ME 04861

Olmsted, Robert W., Publisher, Northwoods Press, PO Box 88, South Thomaston, ME 04861, 207-354-6550

Olsen, Don, Ox Head Press, 414 N 6th St, Marshall, MN 56258

Olsen, Humphrey A., Nonfiction Prose Editor, & Business Manager (see also Seaburg, Alan), *SNOWY EGRET*, 205 S. Ninth St., Williamsburg, KY 40769, 606-549-0850

Olson, C.L., *FRUITION*, PO box 872-db, Santa Cruz, CA 95061, 408-429-3020

Olson, David (see also McCall, Karen E.; Sherman, Jack), *THEATERWORK MAGAZINE*, 120 South Broad, Mankato, MN 56001, 507-345-7885

Olwell, Carol, Publisher, Antelope Island Press, Box 220, St. George, UT 84770, 801-673-6093

O'Malley, Peter (see also Henry, DeWitt; Lee, Susannah; Peseroff, Joyce), *PLOUGHSHARES*, Box 529, Cambridge, MA 02139

Ondaatje, Michael (see also Bevington, Stan; Young, David; Davey, Frank; James, Clifford; Nichol, bp; McCartney, Linda; Sheard, Sarah; Reid, Dennis), Coach House Press, 95 Rivercrest Road, Toronto, Ontario M6S 4H7, Canada, 416-767-6317

O'Neal, Amy (see also O'Neal, Jim), *LIVING BLUES*, 2615 N. Wilton, Chicago, IL 60614, 312-281-3385

O'Neal, Jim (see also O'Neal, Amy), *LIVING BLUES*, 2615 N. Wilton, Chicago, IL 60614, 312-281-3385

O'Neill, Michael (see also Reeves, Gareth), *POETRY DURHAM*, Dept. of English, Univ. of Durham, Elvet Riverside, New Elvet, Durham DH1 3JT, England, 0385-64466 ext. 440

Onley, James (see also Simpson, Lewis P.), *THE SOUTHERN REVIEW*, 43 Allen Hall, Louisiana State University, Baton Rouge, LA 70803, 504-388-5108

Opperman, Harry, Fiction Editor (see also Colquitt, Betsy Feagan), *DESCANT*, English Department, TCU, Fort Worth, TX 76129

Opperman, Harry, Fiction Editor (see also Colquitt, Betsy Feagan), Texas Christian University Press, English Department, TCU, Fort Worth, TX 76129

O'Regan, Brendan (see also Harman, Willis; McNeill, Barbara; Hurley, Tom), *INSTITUTE OF NOETIC SCIENCES NEWSLETTER*, Inst. Noetic Sciences, 475 Gate Five Road, Suite 300, Sausalito, CA 94965, 415-331-5650

Orfield, H.M. (Barney), Publisher (see also Orfield, Olivia), prism press, 11706 Longleaf Lane, Houston, TX 77024, 713-782-5189

Orfield, Olivia, Editor (see also Orfield, H.M. (Barney)), *prism press*, 11706 Longleaf Lane, Houston, TX 77024, 713-782-5189

O'Roarke, Seamus (see also Green, Theo), *INKBLOT*, 439-49th Street #11, Oakland, CA 94609, 415-652-7127

O'Rourke, Paddy (see also Forrie, Allan; Sorestad, Glen; Sorestad, Sonia), Thistledown Press Ltd., 668 East Place, Saskatoon, Saskatchewan S7J2Z5, Canada, 374-1730

O'Rourke, Seamus (see also Green, Theo), Inkblot Press, 439-49th Street #11, Oakland, CA 94609, 415-652-7127

Orowan, Florella (see also Andersen, Len J.; Cornish, Sam), *FICTION, LITERATURE & THE ARTS REVIEW*, Arcade, 318 Harvard Street, Brookline, MA 02146, 617-232-2674

Orr, Anderson, Associate Editor (see also Harkey, Joseph; Hite, Rick; Magnuson, Gordon), *INLET*, Virginia Wesleyan College, Norfolk, VA 23455

Ortenberg, Neil (see also Webster, Lee), *ACM (ANOTHER CHICAGO MAGAZINE)*, c/o Neil Ortenberg, PO Box 780, New York, NY 10025, 312-524-1289

Ortenberg, Neil (see also Webster, Lee), Thunder's Mouth Press, c/o Neil Ortenberg, PO Box 780, New York, NY 10025, 212-595-2025

Ortiz, Roxanne Dunbar (see also Cottier, Chockie), *INDIGENOUS WORLD/EL MUNDO INDIGE-NA*, 275 Grand View Avenue #103, San Francisco, CA 94114, 415-647-1966

Ortner-Zimmerman, Toni, *CONNECTIONS MAGAZINE*, Bell Hollow Road, Putnam Valley, NY 10579

Osaki, Mark, Editor (see also Lear, Robert), *ROLLING THUNDER*, PO Box 9024, Berkeley, CA 94709

Osborne, Anne, Editor (see also Martindale, Sheila; Hancock, Geoff; Thom, Heather; Gibson, Brenda; Lennard, Susan), *CANADIAN AUTHOR & BOOKMAN*, 25 Ryerson Aveune, 131 Bloor Street W, Toronto, Ontario M5t 2P3, Canada, 416-364-4203

Osborne, Karen (see also Hettich, Michael; Ahern, Colleen), Moonsquilt Press, 16401 NE 4th Avenue, North Miami Beach, FL 33162, 305-947-9534

Osborne, Mitchel L., Picayune Press, 326 Picayune Place #200, New Orleans, LA 70130, 504-522-1871

O'Shaughnessy, Virginia, Managing Editor (see also Poe, Michael), Spuyten Duyvil, 520 Cathedreal Parkway, #5-C, New York, NY 10025, 212-666-3648

O'Shaunnessay, William, Dir. of Publ. (see also Cummings, Albert), Golden West Historical Publications, PO Box 1906, Ventura, CA 93002

Osley, Carol Ann, S.O.C.O. Publications, Box 733, Herkimer, NY 13350

Osmanski, Edna Ann, Business Manager (see also Bayes, Ron; Roper, John H.; Diogo, Judith A.), Saint Andrews Press, St Andrews College, Laurinburg, NC 28352, 919-276-3652

Ostenstad (see also Engh; Eriksen; Madsen; Seglen), Futurum Forlag, Hjelmsgt. 3, 0355 Oslo 3, Norway, (02) 69 12 84

Ostenstad (see also Engh; Eriksen; Madsen; Selgen), *GATEAVISA*, Hjelmsgt 3, 0355 Oslo 3, Norway, (02) 69 12 84

Ott, Carol J., Publisher & Editor-in-Chief, *N. Y. HABITAT*, 928 Broadway, Suite 405, New York, NY 10010, 212-505-2030

Ott, Gil, Editor, *PAPER AIR*, 825 Morris Road, Blue Bell, PA 19422

Ott, Gil, Editor & Publisher, Singing Horse Books, 825 Morris Road, Blue Bell, PA 19422

Otter, Nancy Clarke (see also Allison, Dorothy; Bulkin, Elly; Clarke, Cheryl; Waddy, Adrianne), *CONDITIONS*, PO Box 56, Van Brunt Sta., Brooklyn, NY 11215, 212-788-8654

Otto, A. Stuart, Dominion Press, P O Box 37, San Marcos, CA 92069, 619-746-9430

Otto, A. Stuart, Editor, *THEOLOGIA 21*, PO Box 37, San Marcos, CA 92069, 619-746-9430

Overson, Beth E., Writer's Group Bulletin Board Editor (see also Woodhams, Stephen; Gabbard, D.C.; Gabbard, Dwight C.; Caquelin, Anthony; Salmon-Heynemen, Jana; Goodwin, Tema; Shames,

136

Terry; Rajfur, Ted), *FICTION MONTHLY*, Malvolio Press, 545 Haight Street, Suite 67, San Francisco, CA 94117, 415-621-1646

Owen, Maureen, Telephone Books, 109 Dunk Rock Rd., Guilford, CT 06437, 203-453-4415

P

Pacernick, Dorothea (see also Pacernick, Gary), *IMAGES*, English Dept, Wright State Univ., Dayton, OH 45435

Pacernick, Gary (see also Pacernick, Dorothea), *IMAGES*, English Dept, Wright State Univ., Dayton, OH 45435

Pacey, Michael, Editor-in-Chief (see also Seniuk, Lasha), *PRISM INTERNATIONAL*, E459-1866 Main Mall, University of British Columbia, Vancouver BC, Canada, 604-228-2514

Pacholczyk, J.M., *THE ETHNODISC JOURNAL OF RECORDED SOUND*, Box 35549, Tucson, AZ 85740, 602-297-4797

Padgett, Ron (see also Simon, Joan; Waldman, Anne), Full Court Press, Inc., 138-140 Watts St., New York, NY 10013

Padgett, Ron, Teachers & Writers Collaborative, 5 Union Square West, New York, NY 10003, 212-691-6590

Padgett, Ron, *TEACHERS & WRITERS MAGAZINE*, 5 Union Square West, New York, NY 10003, 212-691-6590

Padol, Brian (see also Ferguson, David; Marunas, P. Raymond; Garber, Thomas; Gateff, Amy H.; Smith, Charlotte; Goldman, Bill), *BOX 749*, Box 749, Old Chelsea Station, New York, NY 10011, 212-98-0519

Paehlke, Robert (see also Torgerson, Donalas), *ALTERNATIVES: Perspectives in Society and Environment*, Trent University, c/o Traill College, Peterborough, On K9J7B8, Canada

Paffrath, Chris, J P Publications, 2952 Grinnel, Davis, CA 95616, 916-758-9727

Page, Don, *HUMANIST IN CANADA*, Canadian Humanist Publications, 2007, Postal Station D, Ottawa, Ontario K1P 5W3, Canada, 613-283-7210

Page, Linda (see also Wigginton, Eliot), Foxfire Press, Box B, Rabun Gap, GA 30568, 404-746-5828

Page, William, Faculty Editor, *MEMPHIS STATE REVIEW*, Department of English, Memphis State University, Memphis, TN 38152, 901-454-2668

Paher, Stanley W., Nevada Publications, 4135 Badger Circle, Reno, NV 89509, 702-747-0800

Pain, Margaret (see also Emuss, John; George, Margaret; James, Susan), Guildford Poets Press, 9 White Rose Lane, Woking, Surrey, GU22 73A, England

Pain, Margaret (see also Emuss, John; George, Margaret; James, Susan), *WEYFARERS*, 9 Whiterose Lane, Woking, Surrey, England

Paine, T., Editor (see also Pinsonneault, Claude; Galt, John), *COMMON SENSE*, PO Box 650051, Miami, FL 33165, 305-937-6080

Paladino, Thomas, Editor (see also Stanson, Diane; Cutty, Robert B.), *THE THIRD WIND*, PO Box 8277, Boston, MA 02114

Paley, Morton D. (see also Eaves, Morris), *BLAKE, AN ILLUSTRATED QUARTERLY*, Dept. of English, Univ. of New Mexico, Albuquerque, NM 87131, 505-277-3103

Palmer, Jill (see also Matta, John; Nikides, George), *SCRIVENER*, McGill University, 853 Sherbrooke Street W., Montreal, P.Q. H3A 2T6, Canada

Palmer, Michele, Rocking Horse Press, 32 Ellise Road, Storrs, CT 06268, 203-429-1474

Panich, Holly, Ohio University Press/Swallow Press, Ohio University Press, Scott Quadrangle, Athens, OH 45701, 614-594-5505

Panori, Michael (see also Jackson, Richard), *THE POETRY MISCELLANY*, English Dept. Univ of Tennessee, Chattanooga, TN 37402, 615-755-4213; 624-7279

Paolucci, Anne (see also Paolucci, Henry; Grande, Frank D.), Griffon House Publications, PO Box 81, Whitestone, NY 11357

Paolucci, Henry (see also Paolucci, Anne; Grande, Frank D.), *Griffon House Publications*, PO Box 81, Whitestone, NY 11357

Papalia, Donna M. (see also Roes, Nicholas A.), *TEACHER UPDATE*, Box 205, Saddle River, NJ 07458, 201-327-8486

Papalia, Donna M. (see also Roes, Nicholas A.), Teacher Update, Inc., Box 205, Saddle River, NJ 07458, 201-327-8486

Papethanasiou, Leandros, Publisher, President, Pella Publishing Co, 337 West 36th Street, New York, NY 10018, 212-279-9586

Papineau, Lou, Editor (see also Davis, Ty), *THE NEWPAPER*, Box 2393, Providence, RI 02906, 401-273-NEWP

Pappas, Evangeline, Associate Editor (see also Flynn, Richard; Walthall, Hugh; Weber, Lilian; Weber, Ron), S.O.S. Books, 1821 Kalorama Road NW, Washington, DC 20009, 703-524-4460

Pappas, P. (see also Chouliaras, Y.; Kitroeff, A.; Roubatis, Y.), *JOURNAL OF THE HELLENIC DIASPORA*, 337 West 36th Street, New York, NY 10018, 212-279-9586

Paradis, Adrian A., Phoenix Publishing, Canaan Street, Canaan, NH 03741, 603-523-9901-2

Parchman, J.I., Associate Editor (see also Vaughan, M.K.), Mallema Press, Box 22485, Houston, TX 77227, 713-850-0481

Parfitt, George (see also Lucas, John; Rodway, Allan), Byron Press, The English Dept., Univ. Park, Nottingham, England

Parisi, Joseph, Acting Editor, *POETRY*, Box 4348, Chicago, IL 60680, 312-996-7803

Park, C.I., *THE COINT REPORTS (*Communication and Information Technology)*, PO Box 165, Morton Grove, IL 60053

Parker, Arri (see also Satow, Donna), *THE WOMAN'S NEWSPAPER OF PRINCETON*, PO Box 1303, Princeton, NJ 08542, 609-466-9330

Parker, Jim, Editor, *D.I.N. NEWSERVICE*, PO Box 5115, Phoenix, AZ 85010, 602-257-0797

Parker, Jim, Editor (see also Christina, Dye), D.I.N. Publications, PO Box 5115, Phoenix, AZ 85010, 602-257-0797

Parker, Laurence (see also Jones, Edward), *PSYCHOLOGY AND SOCIAL THEORY*, East Hill Branch, Box 2740, Ithaca, NY 14850, 607-277-0509

Parkhurst, Liz, Editor (see also Parkhurst, Ted), August House Inc., Publishers, PO Box 3223, Little Rock, AR 72203, 501-663-7300

Parkhurst, Ted, Director (see also Parkhurst, Liz), *August House Inc., Publishers*, PO Box 3223, Little Rock, AR 72203, 501-663-7300

Parlatore, Anselm, *BLUEFISH*, PO Box 1601, Southampton, NY 11968, 516-283-8811

Parman, Frank (see also Henderson, Arn), Point Riders Press, PO Box 2731, Norman, OK 73070

Parman, Frank, Editor (see also Griffin, Larry D.), *TERRITORY OF OKLAHOMA: Literature & the Arts*, PO Box 5036, Norman, OK 73070, 405-521-0046

Parman, John, Co-Editor (see also Snowden, Elizabeth), *DESIGN BOOK REVIEW*, 1414 Spring Way, Berkeley, CA 94708, 415-848-2001; 486-1956

Parrish, A.S., Director, Westwind Press, Route 1, Box 208, Farmington, WV 26571, 304-287-7160

Parrish, J Richard, President, Book Publishers of Texas, 1609 Southpoint, Tyler, TX 75701, 214-595-4222

Parry, Anne Spencer (see also Pizer, Marjorie), Pinchgut Press, 6 Oaks Avenue, Cremorne, Sydney, N.S.W. 2090, Australia, 90-5548

Parson, Ann, Managing Editor (see also Bromell, Nicholas), Boston Critic, Inc., 991 Massachusetts Avenue, No. 4, Cambridge, MA 02138

Parson, Ann, Managing Editor (see also Bromell, Nicholas), *BOSTON REVIEW*, 991 Massachusetts Avenue, No.4, Cambridge, MA 02138, 617-492-5478

Parson, Tom, Now It's Up To You Publications, 157 S Logan, Denver, CO 80209, 303-777-8951

Parsons, James, *THE CREATIVE WEST*, Box 1589, Taos, NM 87571

Parsons, James (see also Bareiss, Philip), Gallery West, Inc., Box 1589, Taos, NM 87571, 758-9637

Partee, Phillip (see also Levy, Herman), Sprout Publications Inc, PO Box 4064, Sarasota, FL 33578, 813-349-6535

Paskin, Sylvia (see also Godbert, Geoffrey; Ramsay, Jay), *THE THIRD EYE*, 3 South Villas, Camden Square, London NW1, England

Patrick, Dee, Chantry Press, PO Box 144, Midland Park, NJ 07432, 201-423-2921

Patten, Karl (see also Taylor, Robert), *WEST BRANCH*, Department of English, Bucknell University, Lewisburg, PA 17837, 717-524-4591

Patterson, Ian (see also Vas Dias, Robert; Buck, Paul), Spectacular Diseases, 83(b) London Road, Peterborough, Cambs, England

Patton, Cindy, Managing Editor (see also Morris, David; Hyde, Sue), *GAY COMMUNITY NEWS*, 167 Tremont Street 5th Floor, Boston, MA 02111, 617-426-4469

Paul, Bil, Alchemist/Light Publishing, PO Box 881444, San Francisco, CA 94188, 415-345-7021

Pavloff, Gerald, Managing Editor, *SOURCES/THE MAGAZINE ABOUT PEOPLE AT WORK*, PO Box 8089, Atlanta, GA 30306, 404-875-0975

Pavlos, Mike, Poet Gallery Press, 224 West 29th Street, New York, NY 10001

Pawlak, Mark (see also Hershon, Robert; Lourie, Dick; Schreiber, Ron; Levertov, Denise; Jarrett, Emmett), *HANGING LOOSE*, 231 Wyckoff St, Brooklyn, NY 11217

Pawlowski, Lois, Assistant Editor (see also Tapley, Lance), *COPING*, Box 2439, Augusta, ME 04330, 207-622-1179

Paxton, Larry R., *OHIO CHESS BULLETIN*, 212 Victor Avenue #12, Dayton, OH 45405, 513-277-7025

Payack, Millie Lorenzo, Managing Editor (see also Payack, Paul J.J.), Chthon Press/Nonesuch Publications/Spindle City Editions, 77 Mark Vincent Drive, Westford, MA 01886

Payack, Paul J.J., Editor (see also Payack, Millie Lorenzo), *Chthon Press/Nonesuch Publications/Spindle City Editions*, 77 Mark Vincent Drive, Westford, MA 01886

Payack, Peter, Founding Editor (see also Pease, Roland), The Imaginary Press, Box 1321, Cambridge, MA 02238

Payack, Peter, Founding Editor (see also Pease, Roland), *PHONE-A-POEM*, PO Box 1321, Cambridge, MA 02238, 617-492-1144

Payne, Alex, Alex Payne Publishing, 2515 Rainbow Glen Road, Fallbrook, CA 92028, 714-728-7353

Payne, Robert (see also Smith, William Jay; MacShane, Frank; Cook, Diane G.H.), *TRANSLATION*, 307A Mathematics, Columbia University, New York, NY 10027, 212-280-2305

Payne, Robert (see also Cook, Diane G.H.; MacShane, Frank; Smith, William Jay; Galvin, Dallas), Translation, 307A Mathematics, Columbia University, New York, NY 10027, 280-2305

Peabody, Melissa, Editor (see also Norman, Gina), *U.S. INFORMATION MOSCOW*, 2300 Leghorn St., Mountain View, CA 94043, 415-493-1885

Peabody, Richard Myers, Jr., Editor & Publisher (see also Johnsen, Gretchen), *GARGOYLE*, PO Box 3567, Washington, DC 20007, 202-333-1544

Peabody, Richard Myers, Jr., Editor, Paycock Press, PO Box 3567, Washington, DC 20007, 202-333-1544

Pearce, Zachary, The Pterodactyl Press, PO Box 205, Cumberland, IA 50843, 712-774-2244

Pearlstein, Darlene (see also Friedman, Richard; Kostakis, Peter), The Yellow Press, 2394 Blue Island Ave, Chicago, IL 60608

Pearson, Tina (see also Monahan, Gordon), *MUSICWORKS*, 30 St. Patrick Street, Toronto, Ontario, Canada, 416-593-7088

Pease, Roland, Associate Editor (see also Payack, Peter), The Imaginary Press, Box 1321, Cambridge, MA 02238

Pease, Roland, Associate Editor (see also Payack, Peter), *PHONE-A-POEM*, PO Box 1321, Cambridge, MA 02238, 617-492-1144

Peattie, Noel, Konocti Books, Route 1, Box 216, Winters, CA 95694

Peattie, Noel, *SIPAPU*, Route 1, Box 216, Winters, CA 95694, 916-662-3364; 916-752-1032

Peck, Tom, Editor (see also Youngson, Jeanne), *THE COUNT DRACULA FAN CLUB NEWSLET-TER-JOURNAL*, Penthouse North, 29 Washington Square W., New York, NY 10011, 212-533-5018

Peck, Tom, Editor (see also Youngson, Jeanne), Dracula Press, Penthouse North, 29 Washington Square West, New York, NY 10011, 212-533-5018

Peckenpaugh, Angela, Sackbut Press, 2513 E Webster Place, Milwaukee, WI 53211

Pedersen, Marquerite, Editor, Sovereign Press, 326 Harris Rd, Rochester, WA 98579

Pedrick, Jean (see also Veenendaal, Cornelia; Aisenberg, Nadya), Rowan Tree Press, 124 Chestnut Street, Boston, MA 02108, 617-523-7627

Peebles, J. Winston, General Editor (see also Staton, Marjorie E.), Winston-Derek Publishers, Inc., Pennywell Drive, PO Box 90883, Nashville, TN 37209, 615-329-1319

Peebles, Marvin L., MLP Enterprises, 236 E. Durham Street, Philadelphia, PA 19119

Peebles, Marvin L., J.D., *CBO MANAGEMENT REPORT*, 236 E. Durham Street, Philadelphia, PA 19119

Peffer, George, Editor(poetry) (see also Villani, Jim; Sayre, Rose; Remick, Jace), *PIG IRON*, P.O. Box 237, Youngstown, OH 44501, 216-744-2258

Pellicano, Cheryl, Editor (see also Baldwin, Howard), *LOS GATOS MAGAZINE*, 251 East 7th Street, Long Beach, CA 90813, 408-866-1888

Penha, James, Contributing Editor (see also Kain, Sue; Walker, Lois V.; Hair, Jennie; Steinle, Rita Juul), *NEWSLETTER*, PO Box 773, Huntington, NY 11743

Penley, Constance (see also Bergstrom, Janet; Lyon, Elisabeth), *CAMERA OBSCURA: A Journal of Feminism and Film Theory*, PO Box 25899, Los Angeles, CA 90025

Penlongo, Bob, Executive Editor (see also Gibbons, Reginald; LaRusso, Joseph; Hahn, Susan), *TRIQUARTERLY*, 1735 Benson Avenue, Northwestern Univ., Evanston, IL 60201, 312-492-3490

Penzler, Otto, Executive Editor (see also Seidman, Michael), The Mysterious Press, 129 West 56th Street, New York, NY 10019, 212-765-0923

Perkins, Barbara, Managing Editor (see also Perkins, George), *JOURNAL OF NARRATIVE TECHNIQUE*, English Dept, Eastern Michigan University, Ypsilanti, MI 48197, 313-487-0151

Perkins, E., Co-ordinating Editor (see also Frost, Cheryl), English Language Literature Association, English Department, James Cook University of North Quebec, Townsville 4811, Australia

Perkins, E., Co-ordinating Editor (see also Frost, Cheryl), *LINQ*, English Dept., James Cook University of North Queensland, Townsville 4811, Australia

Perkins, George, General Editor (see also Perkins, Barbara), *JOURNAL OF NARRATIVE TECH-NIQUE*, English Dept, Eastern Michigan University, Ypsilanti, MI 48197, 313-487-0151

Perlman, James, Holy Cow! Press, PO Box 618, Minneapolis, MN 55440

Perlman, Jim, Assistant Editor (see also White, William; Folsom, Ed), *WALT WHITMAN QUARTER-LY REVIEW*, 308 EPB The University of Iowa, Iowa City, IA 52240, 319-353-3698; 353-5650

Perlman, Sue, *ISSUES*, PO Box 11250, San Francisco, CA 94101, 415-864-2600

Perras, Wayne (see also Scavone, Dave; Skinner, Elizabeth), *THE HIGH ROCK REVIEW*, PO Box 614, Saratoga Springs, NY 12866, 518-584-4080

Perrett, Thomas I., Photography Research Institute Carson Endowment, 21237 S. Moneta Avenue, Carson, CA 90745

Perri, Michael W, Editor (see also Zed, Xenia Z.), *ART PAPERS*, 972 Peachtree Street NE, Atlanta, GA 30309, 404-885-1273

Perrin, Arnold, Poetry Editor (see also Rimm, Virginia M.; Grierson, Ruth; Briggs, Henry; Boisvert, Donald J.; McIntyre, Joan; Knowles, Ardeana Hamlin; Brown, Ronald G.; Beck, Raymond M.), *NEW ENGLAND SAMPLER*, RFD #1 Box 2280, Brooks, ME 04921, 207-525-3575

Perrin, Arnold, Wings Press, R2, Box 730, Belfast, ME 04915, 207-338-2005

Perry, Grace, Editor (see also Millett, John), *POETRY AUSTRALIA*, Market Place, Berrima, N.S.W. 2577, Australia

Perry, Grace, Editor, South Head Press, Market Place, Berrima, N.S.W. 2577, Australia

Person, Tom, Editor, *LAUGHING BEAR*, PO Box 36159, Bear Valley Station, Denver, CO 80236, 303-989-5614

Person, Tom, Editor, Laughing Bear Press, PO Box 36159, Bear Valley Station, Denver, CO 80236, 408-578-7558

Persun, Terry L. (see also Schwartz, Irwin; Strauss, Robert), *MYTHOS*, Box 6236, Wilmington, DE 19804

Peseroff, Joyce, Director (see also Henry, DeWitt; O'Malley, Peter; Lee, Susannah), *PLOUGHS-HARES*, Box 529, Cambridge, MA 02139

Peters, Lana, Art Editor (see also Morrow, Sandra), Newsletter Makers, 1540 Pleasant Lane, Lafayette, CA 94549, 415-930-8584

Peters, Lana, Art Editor (see also Morrow, Sandra), *POETIC IMAGES*, 1540 Pleasant Lane, Lafayette, CA 94549, 415-930-8584

Peters, Nancy J. (see also Ferlinghetti, Lawrence; Sharrard, Robert), City Lights Books, 261 Columbus Ave., San Francisco, CA 94133, 415-362-8193

Peters, Nancy J. (see also Ferlinghetti, Lawrence; Sharrard, Robert), *CITY LIGHTS JOURNAL*, 261 Columbus Avenue, San Francisco, CA 94133, 415-362-8193

Peterson, Jim, Editor, *THE DEVIL'S MILLHOPPER*, Route 3, Box 29, Elgin, SC 29049, 803-777-2760

Peterson, Mary Ellis, Balance Beam Press, Inc., 12711 Stoneridge Road, Dayton, MN 55327, 612-427-3168

Peterson, Perry L. (see also Hayes, Ann M.), *WOODROSE*, PO Box 2537, Madison, WI 53701

Peterson, Perry L. (see also Hayes, Ann M.), Woodrose Editions, PO Box 2537, Madison, WI 53701, 608-256-6155

Peterson, Robert, *KAYAK*, 325 Ocean View, Santa Cruz, CA 95062

Peterson, Robert, Kayak Press, 325 Ocean View, Santa Cruz, CA 95062

Petralia, Joseph F., Sierra Trading Post, PO Box 2497, San Francisco, CA 94126, 415-421-1040

Petrillo, Jim (see also Davids, Betsy), Rebis Press, P.O. Box 2233, Berkeley, CA 94702, 415-527-3845

Petrosky, Anthony (see also Petrosky, Patricia), Slow Loris Press, 923 Highview Street, Pittsburgh, PA 15206

Petrosky, Patricia (see also Petrosky, Anthony), *Slow Loris Press*, 923 Highview Street, Pittsburgh, PA 15206

Petrosky, Patricia, *SLOW LORIS READER*, 923 Highview St, Pittsburgh, PA 15206

Petruzzi, Anthony, Offshore Press, 294 Mt. Auburn St., Watertown, MA 02172

Pfefferle, W.T. (see also Pietrzyk, Leslie), *FOLIO*, MFA Program, Dept. of Literature, American University, Washington, DC 20016, 202-244-0525

Pfeil, Fred (see also Rice-Sayre, Laura; Sprinker, Michael), *THE MINNESOTA REVIEW*, Dept. of English, Oregon State University, Corvallis, OR 97331

Pfender, Elizabeth (see also Joseph, Janet), Clear Beginnings-Women's Writing Workshops, 12970 Westchester Trail, Chesterland, OH 44026, 206-729-1659

Phebe(Karen Beiser), Coordinating Editor (see also Mac, Vicki), *DINAH, a lesbian-feminist publication*, Lesbian Activist Bureau, P.O. Box 1485, Cincinnati, OH 45201

Philby, Ruth, Early Stages Press/Contemporary Literature Series, PO Box 31463, San Francisco, CA 94131, 415-282-2526

Philips, Graham, Submissions Editor (see also Cameron, Kenneth P.), Alchemy Books, 681 Market, Suite 755, San Francisco, CA 94105, 415-777-9509

Phillips, Ben (see also Phillips, Julie), The Folks Upstairs Press, 426 College Street, Toronto, Ontario M5T 1T3, Canada

Phillips, Glyn O., *Y GWYDDONYDD*, 6 Gwennyth St., Cathays, Cardiff LCF2 4YD, Wales, Cardiff 31919

Phillips, Jim, Phillips Publications, Inc., PO box 168, Williamstown, NJ 08094, 609-567-0695

Phillips, Julie (see also Phillips, Ben), The Folks Upstairs Press, 426 College Street, Toronto, Ontario M5T 1T3, Canada

Phillips, Maxine, Man. Editor (see also Harrington, Michael; Ehrenreich, Barbara), *DEMOCRATIC LEFT*, 853 Broadway, Suite 801, New York, NY 10003, 212-260-3270

Phillips, Meredith, Perseverance Press, PO Box 384, Menlo Park, CA 94026, 415-323-5572

Phillips, Tina W., Editor, *ANGELTREAD*, PO Box 2199, University Station, Murray, KY 42071

Phillips, William, Editor (see also Kurzweil, Edith), *PARTISAN REVIEW*, 121 Bay State Road 3/F, Boston, MA 02215, 617-353-4260

Piccone, Paul, *TELOS*, PO Box 3111, St Louis, MO 63130, 314-361-8472

Piccone, Paul, Telos Press, PO Box 3111, St Louis, MO 63130, 314-361-8472

Pichaske, David, The Ellis Press, PO Box 1443, Peoria, IL 61655, 309-676-7611, x394

Pickelsimer, Lisa, Editor (see also Blythe, Randall), *NEW BEGINNINGS MAGAZINE*, Route #2, Box 27-D, Pisgah Forest, NC 28768, 704-883-3973

Pickerill, Julie, CRCS Publications, PO Box 20850, Reno, NV 89515

Pierce, Constance, Poetry Editor (see also De Foe, Mark; Keating, Martha; Gamble, Mort; McAleavey, David), *THE LAUREL REVIEW*, West Virginia Wesleyan College, Buckhannon, WV 26201, 304-473-8006

Pietrzyk, Leslie (see also Pfefferle, W.T.), *FOLIO*, MFA Program, Dept. of Literature, American University, Washington, DC 20016, 202-244-0525

Pike, Diane K. (see also Lorrance, Arleen), *THE SEEKER MAGAZINE*, PO Box 7601, San Diego, CA 92107, 619-225-0133

Pike, Diane Kennedy (see also Lorrance, Arleen), LP Publications, (The Love Project), PO Box 7601, San Diego, CA 92107, 619-225-0133

Pilarski, Jan (see also Holzman, David; Bossong, Ken), Citizen's Energy Project, 1110 6th Street, NW, Washington, DC 20001

Pink, Holly (see also Campbell, John), *CROWDANCING*, Route 1, Box 189A, Winters, CA 95694, 916-795-4323

Pinkvoss, Joan (see also Wieser, Barb), Aunt Lute Book Company, Publishers of Women's Work, Box 2723, Iowa City, IA 52240, 338-7022

142

Pinsonneault, Claude, Managing Editor (see also Galt, John; Paine, T.), *COMMON SENSE*, PO Box 650051, Miami, FL 33165, 305-937-6080

Pinto, Michael, *THE STAR BLAZERS FANDOM REPORT*, PO Box 1047, Bellmore, NY 11710, 516-623-2833

Pintonelli, Debbie (see also Deanovich, Connie; Mesmer, Sharon), *B-CITY*, B-City Press, 1555 W. Pratt Boulevard, Chicago, IL 60626, 312-743-4806

Piper, Paul (see also Borneman, Bill), *WORLD WAR IV*, 1733 South 5th W., Missoula, MT 59801, 442-0656

Pippin, Ann, Communication Creativity, PO Box 213, Saguache, CO 81149, 303-655-2504

Pisani, George R., Managing Editor, *ASC NEWSLETTER*, Museum of Natural History, University of Kansas, Lawrence, KS 66045, 913-864-4867/4301

Pisano, Vivian M., Managing Editor (see also Cabello-Argandona, Roberto; Claire Splan), *LECTOR*, PO Box 4273, Berkeley, CA 94704, 415-893-8702

Pittore, Carlo, *ME MAGAZINE*, PO Box 1132, Peter Stuyvesant Station, New York, NY 10009, 212-673-2705

Pittore, Carlo, Pittore Euforico, PO Box 1132, Stuyvesant Station, New York, NY 10009

Pizer, Marjorie (see also Parry, Anne Spencer), Pinchgut Press, 6 Oaks Avenue, Cremorne, Sydney, N.S.W. 2090, Australia, 90-5548

Placidus, Max, Contributing Editor (see also Golden, Michael; Elias, Viki; Harrison, Jim; Mungo, Raymond; Bukowski, Charles; Codrescu, Andrei; Horotwitz, Mikhail; Ligi; Kramer, Glenn; Mitchell, Donna; Riedel, Robert), *SMOKE SIGNALS*, 1516 Beverly Road, Brooklyn, NY 11226

Plante, Tom, *BERKELEY WORKS*, 2206 Martin Luther King Way Apt C, Berkeley, CA 94704, 415-849-3979

Plante, Tom (see also Harrod, Elizabeth; Emerson, Ann), Owlseye Publications, 23650 Stratton Court, Hayward, CA 94541, 415-537-6858

Plante, Tom (see also Harrod, Elizabeth; Emerson, Ann), *POETALK QUARTERLY*, 23650 Stratton Court, Hayward, CA 94541, 415-537-6858

Plantos, Ted, Editor, *CROSS-CANADA WRITERS' QUARTERLY*, Cross-Canada Writers, Inc., Box 277, Station F, Toronto, Ontario M4Y 2L7, Canada, 416-690-0917

Planz, Allen, President (see also Miller, Marge; Everett, Graham), Backstreet Editions, Inc., c/o Box 555, Port Jefferson, NY 11777

Plath, James, Editor & Publisher (see also Emery, Mary Ann; Blum, John; Williams, Elizabeth), *CLOCKWATCH REVIEW*, 737 Penbrook Way, Hartland, WI 53029, 414-367-8315

Plath, James, Editor & Publisher, Driftwood Publications, 737 Penbrook Way, Hartland, WI 53029

Platt, Tony (see also Takagi, Paul), *CRIME AND SOCIAL JUSTICE*, 2701 Folsom Street, San Francisco, CA 94110, 415-550-1703

Platt, Tony, Crime and Social Justice Associates, Inc., 2701 Folsom Street, San Francisco, CA 94110, 415-550-1703

Platts, David Earl (see also Inglis, Mary; Gaston, Robyn), *ONE EARTH*, Findhorn Foundation, The Park, Forres, Morayshire 1V36 0TZ, Scotland, 030-93-2582

Playle, Ron, R & D Services, PO Box 644, Des Moines, IA 50303, 515-288-8391

Pletta, Robert E., Acheron Press, Bear Creek at the Kettle, Friendsville, MD 21531, 301-746-5885

Plimpton, George A., Editor, *PARIS REVIEW*, 45-39 171 Place, Flushing, NY 11358, 539-7085

Plutchak, T. Scott, Editor, *WISCONSIN REVIEW*, Box 276, Dempsey Hall, University Wisconsin-Oshkosh, Oshkosh, WI 54901, 715-424-2267

Poe, Michael, Publisher (see also O'Shaughnessy, Virginia), Spuyten Duyvil, 520 Cathedreal Parkway, #5-C, New York, NY 10025, 212-666-3648

Pohe, Robert W., Jr., Editor (see also McKinley, Mae Pohle), *THE BOOK-MART*, PO Drawer 72, Lake Wales, FL 33853

Pohl, Frederik, Contributing Editor (see also Porter, Andrew; D'Ammassa, Don; Anderson, Kay; DiFate, Vincent; Silverberg, Robert; Jones, Stephen; Fletcher, Jo; Carmody, Larry), *SCIENCE FICTION CHRONICLE*, PO Box 4175, New York, NY 10163, 212-643-9011

Pohrt, Karl (see also Robbins, David), Bear Claw Press, 13 East Wheelock #1E, Hanover, NH 03755, 313-668-6634

Poirier, Richard, Editor-in-Chief (see also Edwards, Thomas R.; Hyman, Suzanne K.), *RARITAN: A Quarterly Review*, 165 College Avenue, New Brunswick, NJ 08903, 201-932-7852

Politis, John, Editor, Cupola Productions, 966 N. Randolph Street, Philadelphia, PA 19123

Polk, James, Editorial Director (see also Wall, Ann), House of Anansi Press Limited/Publishing Co., 35 Britain St., Toronto M5A1R7, Canada, 416-363-5444

Polk, Noel, Advisory Editor (see also Prenshaw, Peggy W.; Tharpe, Jac L.; Richardson, Thomas J.; Saunders, Cheryl), *SOUTHERN QUARTERLY: A Journal of the Arts in the South*, Box 5078, Southern Stn., USM, Hattiesburg, MS 39406, 601-266-4370

Polkinhorn, Christa (see also Cook, Ralph; Polkinhorn, Harry; Cook, Deborah), Atticus Press, PO Box 34044, San Diego, CA 92103, 619-299-3088

Polkinhorn, Harry (see also Cook, Ralph; Cook, Deborah; Polkinhorn, Christa), *Atticus Press*, PO Box 34044, San Diego, CA 92103, 619-299-3088

Polkinhorn, Harry (see also Cook, Ralph), *ATTICUS REVIEW*, PO Box 34044, San Diego, CA 92103, 619-299-3088

Pollack, Jeremy A., *CHICAGO SHEET*, Box 3667, Oak Park, IL 60303, 312-383-0277

Polley, Simon (see also Rippington, Geoff; Bailey, Chris; Sutherland, Allen; Swinden, Dave), British Science Fiction Assoc. Ltd., 269 Wykeham Road, Reading RG6 1PL, England, 0734-666142

Polley, Simon, *MATRIX*, 269 Wykeham Road, Reading RG6 1PL, England

Pond, Lily, *YELLOW SILK: Journal Of Erotic Arts*, PO Box 6374, Albany, CA 94706, 415-841-6500

Poole, Gary (see also Donato, Vince), *THE LAUGH FACTORY*, Fell Great Publishing Co., 1370 Windsor Road, Teaneck, NJ 07666, 201-833-0068

Poole, Robert, Jr., Editor (see also Gordon, Paul; Marti, Eric), *FRONTLINES*, Box 40105, Santa Barbara, CA 93103, 805-963-5993

Poore, Nancy Victoria (see also Cohen, Jocelyn Helaine), Helaine Victoria Press,Inc., 4080 Dynasty Lane, Martinsville, IN 46151, 317-537-2868

Poore, Patricia, *THE OLD-HOUSE JOURNAL*, 69A Seventh Avenue, Brooklyn, NY 11217, 212-636-4514

Pope, Chris (see also Heseltine, Nigel), *RENEWABLE ENERGY NEWS*, Box 4869, Station E, Ottawa, Ontario K1S 5J1, Canada, 613-238-5591

Pope, Nancy C., *THE LOST ROAD EXPLORER DIGEST*, PO Box 1936, Anderson, IN 46014

Pope, Randolph (see also Janney, Frank; Geist, Anthony), Ediciones del Norte, Box A130, Hanover, NH 03755, 603-795-2433

Poplaski, Peter, *STEVE CANYON MAGAZINE*, No. 2 Swamp Road, Princeton, WI 54968, 414-295-6922

Porges, Timothy, Associate Editor (see also Spector, Buzz), *WHITE WALLS: A Magazine of Writings by Artists*, PO Box 8204, Chicago, IL 60680

Porter, Andrew, Editor & Publisher, Algol Press, PO Box 4175, New York, NY 10163, 212-643-9011

Porter, Andrew, Editor, Publisher (see also D'Ammassa, Don; Anderson, Kay; DiFate, Vincent; Pohl, Frederik; Silverberg, Robert; Jones, Stephen; Fletcher, Jo; Carmody, Larry), *SCIENCE FICTION CHRONICLE*, PO Box 4175, New York, NY 10163, 212-643-9011

Porter, Bern, Bern Porter Books, 22 Salmond Road, Belfast, ME 04915, 207-338-3763

Porter, Regina (see also Rikhoff, Jean; Lape, Walter; Weaver, Francis; Quirk, John), Loft Press, 93 Grant Avenue, Glens Falls, NY 12801

Posey, Jeff, Editor, *DUCK SOUP*, 5001 N. MacArthur Blvd., Irving, TX 75062, 214-659-5270

Posner, Neil (see also Delson, Donn), Bradson Press, 120 Longfellow Street, Thousand Oaks, CA 91360, 805-496-8212

Post, Robert, Blue Mountain Press, Route 3, Box 316-A, South Haven, MI 49090, 349-3924

Potichnyj, P. (see also Mayne, S.; Aster, H.; Walsh, M.), Mosaic Press/Valley Editions, PO Box 1032, Oakville, Ontario L6J 5E9, Canada

Potra, George G., *ROMANIAN REVIEW*, Piata Scinteii 1, Bucharest, Romania, 173836

Poulin, A, Jr., BOA Editions, Ltd., 92 Park Avenue, Brockport, NY 14420, 716-637-3844

Powell, Jim, *INPRINT*, 429 East Vermont Street, Indianapolis, IN 46202, 317-253-3733

Powell, Jim, Editor, Writers' Center Press, 429 East Vermont Street, Indianapolis, IN 46202, 317-253-3733

Powell, Mary A., General Manager (see also Kadlec, Robert F.; Weigle, Marta), Ancient City Press, PO Box 5401, Santa Fe, NM 87502, 505-982-8195

Powell, Patricia, Editor, *WISCONSIN ACADEMY REVIEW*, 1922 University Ave., Madison, WI 53705, 608-263-1692

Powell, Richard J., Publisher, *TEMPO*, 610 Mulberry Steet, Scranton, PA 18510, 717-961-3355

Poynter, Dan, Publisher, Para Publishing, PO Box 4232-Q, Santa Barbara, CA 93103, 805-968-7277

Poynter, Rhonda C., Editor, *FIRE*, L&L Press, PO Box 811, Rochester, MN 55903

Prather, Jo Anne (see also MacManus, Yvonne), Timely Books, PO Box 267, New Milford, CT 06776, 203-744-4719

Precious, P.J., The Curlew Press, Hare Cott, Kettlesing, Harrogate, Yorkshire, England, Harrogate 770686

Precious, P.J., *POETRY QUARTERLY (previously CURLEW)*, Harecott, Kettlesing, Harrogate, Yorkshire, England, Harrogate 770686

Prenshaw, Peggy W., Editor (see also Polk, Noel; Tharpe, Jac L.; Richardson, Thomas J.; Saunders, Cheryl), *SOUTHERN QUARTERLY: A Journal of the Arts in the South*, Box 5078, Southern Stn., USM, Hattiesburg, MS 39406, 601-266-4370

Prentice, A., Editor (see also Nuse, B.; Newton, J.; Zavitz, C.; Rooney, F.; Andersen, M.; Wine, J.; Scane, J.; Caplan, Paula; Van Kirk, Sylvia), *RESOURCES FOR FEMINIST RESEARCH/DOCUMENTATION SUR LA RECHERCHE FEMINISTE*, Ont Inst for Stud in Educ, Centre for Women's Studies in Education, 252 Bloor Street W., Toronto, Ontario M5S 1V6, Canada, 416-923-6641

Press, Michelle (see also Neill, Peter), Leete's Island Books, Box 1131, New Haven, CT 06505, 203-481-2536

Presti, Santo M., Editor, Bristol Publishing Company, PO Box 22, Fairport, NY 14450, 716-248-5064; 223-3366

Price, Janis Bryant, Quartus Books, PO Box 26683, Austin, TX 78755, 512-345-3823

Pride, Anne (see also Balogh, Paulette; McElligot, Pat), *MOTHEROOT JOURNAL*, 214 Dewey Street, Pittsburgh, PA 15218, 412-731-4453

Pride, Anne (see also Balogh, Paulette; McElligott, Pat), Motheroot Publications, 214 Dewey Street, Pittsburgh, PA 15218

Priesnitz, Wendy, Village Books, 195 Markville Road, Unionville, Ont. L3R4V8, Canada

Prince, Scott, Charlton House Publishing, PO Box 2474, Newport Beach, CA 92663, 714-760-8528

Prior, Pedyr, Celtic League, 9 Br Cnoc Sion,, Ath Cliath 9, Republic of Ireland, Dublin 373957

Prising, Robin (see also Coakley, William Leo), Helikon Press, 120 West 71st Street, New York City, NY 10023

Pritchard, Ruth, Editorial Director, Cougar Books, PO Box 22246, Sacramento, CA 95822, 916-428-3271

Procario, Saverio (see also Gullickson, James R.), Sleepy Hollow Press, 150 White Plains Road, Tarrytown, NY 10591, 914-631-8200

Prochak, Michael (see also Graham, Chael), & (Ampersand) Press, Michael S. Prochak, 141 Barrack Street, Colchester, Essex, United Kingdom

Prochak, Michael S., Co-Editor (see also Graham, Chael), *STARDANCER*, 141 Barracks Street, Colchester, Essex, England

Proffer, Carl R. (see also Proffer, Ellendea), *RUSSIAN LITERATURE TRIQUARTERLY*, 2901 Heatherway, Ann Arbor, MI 48104, 313-971-2367

Proffer, Ellendea (see also Proffer, Carl R.), *RUSSIAN LITERATURE TRIQUARTERLY*, 2901 Heatherway, Ann Arbor, MI 48104, 313-971-2367

Prohlo, Irwin M. (see also Caldwell, E.T.), Heavy Evidence Productions, 1315½ 7th Street, Menomonie, WI 54751

Prohlo, Irwin M. (see also Caldwell, E.T.), *HEAVY EVIDENCE*, 1315½ 7th Street, Milwaukee, WI 54751

Prophet, Colleen, Organizing Editor (see also Shaw, Darla K.; Erickson, Dave), *COE RE-VIEW:Annual Anthology of Experimental Literature*, 1220 First Avenue N.E., Coe College, Cedar Rapids, IA 52402, 319-399-8660

Pruett, F.A., President (see also Keenan, Gerald), Pruett Publishing Company, 2928 Pearl, Boulder, CO 80301, 303-449-4919

Pryor, William (see also Finch, Vivienne), *TANGENT*, 58 Blakes Lane, New Malden, Surrey, England KT3 6NX, England

Pryor, William (see also Finch, Vivienne), Tangent Books, 58 Blakes Lane, New Malden, Surrey, England KT3 6NX, England, 01-942-0979

Pultz, Jane, Publisher, Press Pacifica, PO Box 47, Kailua, HI 96734, 808-261-6594

Pursyn, Nowan, The Intercollective, PO Box 5446, Berkeley, CA 94705, 415-929-0671

Pursyn, Nowan, *The Networker Collective*, 1531 Fulton Street, San Francisco, CA 94117, 415-929-0671

Pusch, Margaret D. (see also Hoopes, David S.), Intercultural Press, Inc., PO Box 768, Yarmouth, ME 04096, 207-846-5168

Pyros, Andrea (see also Pyros, John), *DRAMATIKA*, 429 Hope Street, Tarpon Springs, FL 33589

Pyros, Andrea (see also Pyros, John), Dramatika Press, 429 Hope Street, Tarpon Springs, FL 33589

Pyros, John (see also Pyros, Andrea), *DRAMATIKA*, 429 Hope Street, Tarpon Springs, FL 33589

Pyros, John (see also Pyros, Andrea), Dramatika Press, 429 Hope Street, Tarpon Springs, FL 33589

Q

Quasha, George, Publisher, Editor (see also Quasha, Susan; Coffey, Michael; Martin, Michele), Open Book Publications, A Division of Station Hill Press, Station Hill Road, Barrytown, NY 12507

Quasha, George, Publisher & Director (see also Quasha, Susan; Martin, Michele; Coffey, Michael; Stein Charles; Nedds, Trish; Kelly, Robert; Auster, Paul; Kamin, Franz; McClelland, Bruce), Station Hill Press, Station Hill Road, Barrytown, NY 12507, 914-758-5840

Quasha, Susan, Co-Publisher, Designer (see also Quasha, George; Coffey, Michael; Martin, Michele), Open Book Publications, A Division of Station Hill Press, Station Hill Road, Barrytown, NY 12507

Quasha, Susan, Associate Publisher & Co-Director (see also Quasha, George; Martin, Michele; Coffey, Michael; Stein Charles; Nedds, Trish; Kelly, Robert; Auster, Paul; Kamin, Franz; McClelland, Bruce), Station Hill Press, Station Hill Road, Barrytown, NY 12507, 914-758-5840

Quatrone, Lorraine A. (see also Quatrone, Richard P.), *PASSAIC REVIEW*, Forstmann Library, 195 Gregory Avenue, Passaic, NJ 07055, 201-460-1774

Quatrone, Richard P. (see also Quatrone, Lorraine A.), *PASSAIC REVIEW*, Forstmann Library, 195 Gregory Avenue, Passaic, NJ 07055, 201-460-1774

Quinn, A., Runa Press, Monkstown, Co Dublin, Eire, Republic of Ireland

Quirk, John (see also Rikhoff, Jean; Lape, Walter; Weaver, Francis; Porter, Regina), Loft Press, 93 Grant Avenue, Glens Falls, NY 12801

R

Raborg, Frederick A., Editor, *AMELIA*, 329 "E" Street, Bakersfield, CA 93304, 805-323-4064

Rabson, Diane, Editor, *WAYWARD WIND*, PO Box 7427, Boulder, CO 80306

Racz, Jeanette G., Business Manager, Racz Publishing Co., PO Box 287, Oxnard, CA 93032, 805-642-1186

Rader, Hannelore, Editor (see also Mark, Linda), *REFERENCE SERVICES REVIEW*, PO Box 1808, Ann Arbor, MI 48106, 313-434-5530

Rader, Mary-Jane Grandinetti, Co-Editor (see also Rader, R.W. Grandinetti), *MUSE-PIE: A Journal of Poetry*, 73 Pennington Avenue, Passaic, NJ 07055, 201-777-3588

Rader, R.W. Grandinetti, Editor (see also Rader, Mary-Jane Grandinetti), *MUSE-PIE: A Journal of Poetry*, 73 Pennington Avenue, Passaic, NJ 07055, 201-777-3588

Rader, Steve, Editor-at-Large (see also Lawson, Dr. Todd; Comen, Dr. Diane; Marsic, John; Monte, Oscar; Nishi, Mio; Ginsberg, Allen; Samolis, Dr. Sam; Graham, Joan; Ferlinghetti, Lawrence; Ramirez, Julio; Haynes, Dr. Robert; Snyder, Gary; Morris, Dr. Richard), *ALPS MONTHLY*, PO Box 99394, San Francisco, CA 94109, 415-771-3431

Rader, Steve, Contributing Editor (see also Comen, Diane; Lawson, Todd S.J.; Marsic, John; Samolis, William; Comen, Diane; Graham, Joan), Peace & Pieces Press, Box 99394, San Francisco, CA 94109, 415-771-3431

Radican, E.J., J Rad Publications, PO Box 214741, Sacramento, CA 95821, 916-486-3857

Radin, Jessica (see also Stein, Charlotte M.; Rubenstein, Nancy), Double M Press, 16455 Tuba Street, Sepulveda, CA 91343, 213-360-3166

Rafalsky, Stephen Mark, *THE LIGHTNING HERALD: UN JOURNAL DE POETES TERRIBLES*, PO Box 371, Woodstock, NY 12498

Rafferty, Larry, hit & run Press, 61 Moraga Way #3, Orinda, CA 94563, 707-964-0843

Ragnar, F. Lie, Bactrianus Enterprises, Solliveien 37, 1370 Asker, Norway

Ragner, F. Lie, *HOWL'T*, Solliveien 37, 1370 Asker, Norway

Rainey, Albert, *PROPHET NEWSLINE*, 1015 N. El Centro Avenue, Los Angeles, CA 90038, 213-463-7876

Rainwater, Richard, *Mister Production Enterprise*, 11822 Rosecrans Blvd, Norwalk, CA 90650, 213-863-2179

Rainwater, Sylvan (see also Waygren, Leslie), Lez Press, PO Box 4387, Portland, OR 97208, 503-287-1838

Raiziss, Sonia, Editor (see also de Palchi, Alfredo; Swann, Brian; Foerster, Richard), *CHELSEA*, Box 5880, Grand Central Station, New York, NY 10163

Rajfur, Ted, Art Director (see also Woodhams, Stephen; Gabbard, D.C.; Gabbard, Dwight C.; Overson, Beth E.; Caquelin, Anthony; Salmon-Heynemen, Jana; Goodwin, Tema; Shames, Terry), *FICTION MONTHLY*, Malvolio Press, 545 Haight Street, Suite 67, San Francisco, CA 94117, 415-621-1646

Ramey, Frederick, Editor (see also Holte, Susan), Arden Press, 1127 Pennsylvania, Denver, CO 80203, 303-837-8913

Ramirez, Alphonse F., Editor, General Manager, Treasurer (see also Ramirez, Eleanor Gude), *"RAM, - THE LETTER BOX" Poetry Magazine (All Moral)*, Alphonse F. Ramirez & Eleanor Gude, 430 4th Street, Brooklyn, NY 11215, 212-SO8-5415

Ramirez, Bruno (see also D'Alfonso, Antonio; Tassinar, Lamberto; Caccia, Fulvio), *VICE VERSA*, P.O. Box 633, Sta N.D.G., Montreal, Quebec H4A 3R1, Canada

Ramirez, Eleanor Gude, Editor-in-Chief (see also Ramirez, Alphonse F.), *"RAM, - THE LETTER BOX" Poetry Magazine (All Moral)*, Alphonse F. Ramirez & Eleanor Gude, 430 4th Street, Brooklyn, NY 11215, 212-SO8-5415

Ramirez, Julio, T.V. Literature Manager (see also Lawson, Dr. Todd; Comen, Dr. Diane; Marsic, John; Rader, Steve; Monte, Oscar; Nishi, Mio; Ginsberg, Allen; Samolis, Dr. Sam; Graham, Joan; Ferlinghetti, Lawrence; Haynes, Dr. Robert; Snyder, Gary; Morris, Dr. Richard), *ALPS MONTHLY*, PO Box 99394, San Francisco, CA 94109, 415-771-3431

Ramsay, Jay (see also Godbert, Geoffrey; Paskin, Sylvia), *THE THIRD EYE*, 3 South Villas, Camden Square, London NW1, England

Ramsey, John, Brainchild Books, PO Box 837, Paia, Maui, HI 96779, 527-9102

Rand, Elizabeth, Editor & Publisher, Rand Editions/Tofua Press, Po Box 2610, Leucadia, CA 92024, 619-753-2500

Randall, James, Pym-Randall Press, 73 Cohasset Street, Roslindale, MA 02131, 617-323-1133

Ranker, Camille, Editor (see also Avery, Amanda), Mendocino Graphics, PO Box 1580, Mendocino, CA 95460, 707-964-3831

Ranker, Camille, *MENDOCINO REVIEW*, PO Box 888, Mendocino, CA 95460, 707-964-3831

Raphael, Dan (see also Whited, David), *NRG*, 6735 S E 78th, Portland, OR 97206

Raphael, Dan (see also Fish, Mara), Skydog Press, 6735 S E 78th, Portland, OR 97206

Rapoport, Janis, *ETHOS*, 316 Dupont Street, Toronto, Ontario M5R 1V9, Canada, 416-926-8157

Rarihokwats (see also Loomis, Mildred J.), *FOUR ARROWS*, PO Box 3177, York, PA 17402, 717-993-6664

Rasch, William (see also Mandell, Richard; Mandelblat, Reuben; Mandell, Alan), Hermes House Press, Inc., 127 W 15th Street, Apt 3F, New York, NY 10011, 212-691-9773/415-655-8571

Rasch, William (see also Mandell, Alan; Mandell, Richard), *KAIROS, A Journal of Contemporary Thought and Criticism*, 127 W 15th Street, Apt 3F, New York, NY 10011, 212-691-9773

Rasmussen, Chrys (see also O'Brien, Aline; Costello, Catherine), Continuing Saga Press, PO Box 194, San Anselmo, CA 94960, 415-454-4411

Rateaver, Bargyla (see also Rateaver, Gylver), The Rateavers, 9049 Covina Street, San Diego, CA 92126, 619-566-8994

Rateaver, Gylver (see also Rateaver, Bargyla), *The Rateavers*, 9049 Covina Street, San Diego, CA 92126, 619-566-8994

Rath, E. (see also Gaard, F.; Baird, A.), *ARTPOLICE*, 133 E. 25th Street, Minneapolis, MN 55404, 612-825-3673

Ratner, Megan (see also Halpern, Daniel), *ANTAEUS*, 18 West 30th Street, New York, NY 10001, 212-685-8240

Ratner, Megan (see also Halpern, Daniel), The Ecco Press, 18 West 30th Street, New York City, NY 10001, 212-685-8240

Ratner, Rochelle (see also Sukenick, Ronald; Russell, Charles; Tytell, John; Hoover, Russell), *THE AMERICAN BOOK REVIEW*, PO Box 188, Cooper Station, New York, NY 10003, 212-621-9289

Ratner, Rochelle (see also Mernit, Susan), *HAND BOOK*, 314 E 78 Street #1, New York, NY 10021

Rattan, Cleatus (see also Lewis, Monte; Hammes, Ken), *CROSS TIMBERS REVIEW*, Cisco Junior College, Cisco, TX 76437, 817-442-2567

Rauner, Judy, Marlborough Publications, PO Box 16406, San Diego, CA 92116, 619-280-8310

Ravens, Debi, Art & Graphic Editor (see also Summers, Anthony J.; Finnegan, James J.), Cornerstone Press, PO Box 28048, St. Louis, MO 63119, 314-752-3703

Ravens, Debi, Art & Graphic Editor (see also Summers, Anthony J.; Finnegan, James J.), *IMAGE MAGAZINE*, P.O. Box 28048, St. Louis, MO 63119, 314-752-3703

Ray, David, *NEW LETTERS*, University of Missouri, Kansas City, MO 64110, 816-276-1168

Ray, MaryEllen, Co-Editor (see also Edwards, Ellen), Rising Publishing, PO Box 72478, Los Angeles, CA 90002, 213-746-7483

Rayher, Ed, Editor-in-Chief (see also McGuill, Mike; Conoley, Gillian; Stansberry, Domenic; Ruhl, Steven), *TIGHTROPE*, 72 Colonial Village, Amherst, MA 01002

Rayher, Ed Tyrant, Swamp Press, 72 Colonial Village, Amherst, MA 01002

Raymond, J. H., Pegasus Books/Press, PO Box 1350, Yashon, WA 98070, 206-567-5224/206-463-5755

Raymond, Kathy, *MUSE'S BREW POETRY REVIEW*, PO Box 9561, Forestville, CT 06010, 203-589-5039

Raymond, Kathy, Muse's Brew Publications, PO Box 9561, Forestville, CT 06010, 203-589-5039

Raymond, Stephen (see also Szebedinszky, Janos), and books, 702 South Michigan, Suite 836, South Bend, IN 46618

Raynes, Livia (see also Frisch, Annette), Odin Press, PO Box 536, New York, NY 10021, 212-744-2538

Rayson, Dr. Ann Louise, The Bess Press, PO Box 22388, Honolulu, HI 96822, 808-734-7159

Raz, Hilda, Poetry Editor (see also Luke, Hugh), *PRAIRIE SCHOONER*, 201 Andrews Hall, Univ. of Nebraska, Lincoln, NE 68588

Rea, Barbara (see also Rea, Tom), Dooryard Press, Box 221, Story, WY 82842, 307-683-2937

Rea, David, Prose Editor (see also Hutchison, Joseph; Nigg, Joe; Miller, Patty; Reilly, Gary; Schroeder, Gary), *PENDRAGON Journal of the Creative Arts*, 2640 E. 12th Avenue, Box 715, Denver, CO 80206, 303-444-4100

Rea, Tom (see also Rea, Barbara), Dooryard Press, Box 221, Story, WY 82842, 307-683-2937

Read, Patricia, Director Publications, The Foundation Center, 888 Seventh Avenue, New York, NY 10106, 212-975-1120

Reaves, Elizabeth, The Fisher Institute, 6350 LBJ Freeway, Suite 183E, Dallas, TX 75240, 214-233-1041

Reckenbeil, Robert, Publisher, Meridional Publications, Route 2, Box 28A, Wake Forest, NC 27587, 919-556-2940

Reckley, Ralph, Co-Editor (see also Jones, Lola E.), *OUTREACH: A CREATIVE WRITER'S JOURNAL*, Morgan State University, Baltimore, MD 21239, 301-444-4189

Redin, Barbara, Editor-In-Chief, Bookworm Publishing Company, PO Box 1792, Russellville, AR 72801

Redmond, Pauline, Associate Editor (see also Miller, Jack; Schaefer, Paul), *NORTH COUNTRY ANVIL*, PO Box 37, Millville, MN 55957, 507-798-2366

Reed, Catherine (see also Strang, Steven), *THE PALE FIRE REVIEW*, 162 Academy Avenue, Providence, RI 02908

Reed, Donn, Brook Farm Books, Glassville, New Brunswick, E0J 1L0, Canada

Reed, Ishmael (see also Young, Al), *QUILT,* 1446 Sixth Street #D, Berkeley, CA 94710, 415-527-1586

Reed, Ishmael (see also Cannon, Steve), I. Reed Books, 1446 Sixth Street #D, Berkeley, CA 94710, 415-527-1586

Reed, M., Editor, Gibson-Hiller Co., PO Box 22 1254 Canfield Avenue, Dayton, OH 45406, 513-277-2427

Reed, Paul, Editor, Submissions (see also Wood, Philip; Wan, Jackie; Young, George), Ten Speed Press, PO Box 7123, Berkeley, CA 94707, 415-845-8414

Reed, Paul Richard (see also Exander, Max), *Folsom House* , PO Box 14793, San Francisco, CA 94114

Reed, Vicki (see also Balsamo, Ron; Hughes, John E.; Lee, Jean C.; Reed, W.A.; Thompson, Catherine; Dennis, Deborah), *FARMER'S MARKET,* PO Box 1272, Galesburg, IL 61402

Reed, W.A. (see also Balsamo, Ron; Hughes, John E.; Lee, Jean C.; Reed, Vicki; Thompson, Catherine; Dennis, Deborah), *FARMER'S MARKET,* PO Box 1272, Galesburg, IL 61402

Rees, John (see also Schneider, Harold W.; Nyberg, Ben; Moses, W.R.), *KANSAS QUARTERLY,* Denison Hall, Kansas St. Univ., Manhattan, KS 66506, 913-532-6716

Reese, Harry E. (see also Reese, Sandra Liddell), Turkey Press, 6746 Sueno Road, Isla Vista, CA 93117, 685-3603

Reese, Sandra Liddell (see also Reese, Harry E.), *Turkey Press,* 6746 Sueno Road, Isla Vista, CA 93117, 685-3603

Reeve, Franklin, *THE POETRY REVIEW,* 15 Gramercy Park, New York, NY 10003, 212-254-9628

Reeve, Franklin, Editor, *THE POETRY SOCIETY OF AMERICA BULLETIN,* 15 Gramercy Park, New York, NY 10003, 254-9628

Reeves, Gareth (see also O'Neill, Michael), *POETRY DURHAM,* Dept. of English, Univ. of Durham, Elvet Riverside, New Elvet, Durham DH1 3JT, England, 0385-64466 ext. 440

Reginald, Robert, Publisher (see also Burgess, Mary), The Borgo Press, Box 2845, San Bernardino, CA 92406, (714) 884-5813

Regis, Peggy (see also Kimmett, Larry), Periscope Press, PO Box 6926, Santa Barbara, CA 93160, 805-964-1749

Rehwaldt, Anny, The Fairisher Press, PO Box 9090, Rapid City, SD 57709, 605-342-6223

Reid, Clifton O. (see also Reid, Desmond A.), Theo. Gaus, Ltd., PO Box 1168, Brooklyn, NY 11202, 212-625-4651

Reid, Dennis (see also Bevington, Stan; Young, David; Davey, Frank; James, Clifford; Nichol, bp; Ondaatje, Michael; McCartney, Linda; Sheard, Sarah), Coach House Press, 95 Rivercrest Road, Toronto, Ontario M6S 4H7, Canada, 416-767-6317

Reid, Desmond A. (see also Reid, Clifton O.), Theo. Gaus, Ltd., PO Box 1168, Brooklyn, NY 11202, 212-625-4651

Reid, Gayla (see also Wachtel, Eleanor), Growing Room Collective, Box 46160, Station G, Vancouver BC V6R 4G5, Canada, 604-733-3889

Reid, Gayla (see also Wachtel, Eleanor; Freeman, Victoria; Schendlinger, Mary; Wexler, Jeannie), *ROOM OF ONE'S OWN,* PO Box 46160, Station G, Vancouver, British Columbia V6R 4G5, Canada, 604-733-3889

Reilly, Gary, Prose Editor (see also Hutchison, Joseph; Nigg, Joe; Rea, David; Miller, Patty; Schroeder, Gary), *PENDRAGON Journal of the Creative Arts,* 2640 E. 12th Avenue, Box 715, Denver, CO 80206, 303-444-4100

Reilly, Jon, Druid Books, Ephraim, WI 54211

Reimers, Ronald, Publisher, Palimpsest Books, PO Box 280, Santa Monica, CA 90406

Reimers, Ronald, Co-Editor (see also Cohen, Sande), *THE PALIMPSEST REVIEW*, PO Box 1280, Santa Monica, CA 90406

Reimers, Ronald (see also Gorton, Gregg), *PRAXIS: A Journal of Cultural Criticism*, PO Box 1280, Santa Monica, CA 90406

Reinhart, Rod (see also Kelch, Richard), Operation D.O.M.E. Press, 625 Field #108, Detroit, MI 48214, 313-331-5682

Reisman, Ellen, North Coast Publishing, Box 1119, Shaker Heights, OH 44120, 216-491-8699

Reitz, Del, Editor and Publisher, *NEWSLETTER INAGO*, Inago Press, PO Box 7541, Tucson, AZ 85725, 602-294-7031

Remick, Jace, Contributing Editor (see also Villani, Jim; Sayre, Rose; Peffer, George), *PIG IRON*, P.O. Box 237, Youngstown, OH 44501, 216-744-2258

Rendleman, Danny, Editor, JETT Press, English Department, 326 CROB Univ. of Michigan-Flint, Flint, MI 48503, 313-762-3285

Rendleman, Danny, Editor, *JOURNAL OF ENGLISH TEACHING TECHNIQUES*, English Department, 326 CROB Univ. of Michigan-Flint, Flint, MI 48503, 313-762-3285

Renfro, Elizabeth (see also Huff, Casey; Kuhlken, Ken), Flume Press, 644 Citrus Avenue, Chico, CA 95926, 916-342-1583

Renner, Dick A. (see also Rippy, Frances Mayhew), *BALL STATE UNIVERSITY FORUM*, Ball State Univ., Muncie, IN 47306

Renner, Ginger, Asst. Editor (see also Waage, Frederick O.), *SECOND GROWTH: Appalachian Nature and Culture*, P.O. Box 24, 292, East Tennessee State Univ., Johnson City, TN 37619, 615-929-7466

Rennie, Michael, *WORD LOOM*, Box 20, 242 Montrose, Winnipeg, Manitoba, Canada

Renwick, Morag, Rennan Publications, Quennel Road, Nanaimo, B.C. V9R 5X9, Canada, 245-2824

Reppen, Joseph, *REVIEW OF PSYCHOANALYTIC BOOKS*, 211 East 70th Street, New York, NY 10021

Requard, Margo, Business Manager, *NEW AMERICA*, c/o Dept. of American Studies, University of New Mexico, Albuquerque, NM 87131, 505-277-6347

Reuling, Karl F., Managing Editor (see also Jacobson, Robert), *BALLET NEWS*, 1865 Broadway, New York, NY 10023, 582-3285

Rexner, Romulus, Editor-in-Chief (see also Anders, Irene), *COSMOPOLITAN CONTACT*, P. O. Box 1566, Fontana, CA 92335

Reyes, Carlos (see also Steinman, Lisa), *HUBBUB*, 2754 S.E. 27th Avenue, Portland, OR 97202, 503-775-0370

Reyes, Carlos, Trask House Books, Inc., 2754 S.E. 27th Ave., Portland, OR 97202, 503-235-1898

Reynolds, Julie (see also Darlington, Sandy), Arrowhead Press, 3005 Fulton, Berkeley, CA 94705, 415-540-7010

Reynolds, Louise E., Manager (see also Reynolds, Louise T.; Jackel, Harry; Bolton, Stanwood; Madrigal, Sylvia), *THE NEW RENAISSANCE, An International Magazine of Ideas & Opinions, Emphasizing Literature & The Arts*, 9 Heath Road, Arlington, MA 02174

Reynolds, Louise T., Editor (see also Jackel, Harry; Reynolds, Louise E.; Bolton, Stanwood; Madrigal, Sylvia), *THE NEW RENAISSANCE, An International Magazine of Ideas & Opinions, Emphasizing Literature & The Arts*, 9 Heath Road, Arlington, MA 02174

Rhoads, Linda Smith, Assoc. Editor (see also Fowler, William M.), *THE NEW ENGLAND QUARTERLY*, 243 Meserve Hall, Northeastern University, Boston, MA 02115, 617-437-2734

Rhoads, Linda Smith, Assoc. Editor (see also Fowler, William M., Jr.), The New England Quarterly, Inc., 243 Meserve Hall, Northeastern University, Boston, MA 02115, 617-437-2734

Rhodes, Gina (see also Smith, Barbara; Lone Dog, Lcota; Oliveira, Ana), Kitchen Table: Women of Color Press, Box 2753, New York, NY 10185, 212-308-5389

Rice, Felicia, Moving Parts Press, 419 A Maple Street, Santa Cruz, CA 95060, 408-427-2271

Rice, Jim, *THE SPORTS DESK*, Box 1303, Iowa City, IA 52244

Rice Jr., Jon F., The Committee, Box 1082, Evanston, IL 60204, 312-288-4935

Rice-Sayre, Laura (see also Pfeil, Fred; Sprinker, Michael), *THE MINNESOTA REVIEW*, Dept. of English, Oregon State University, Corvallis, OR 97331

Richard, Michel Paul (see also Kellogg, Peggy; Moss, Leonard; Soffer, Walter), *THOUGHTS FOR ALL SEASONS: The Magazine of Epigrams*, State University College At Geneseo, Geneseo, NY 14454, 716-245-5336

Richardson Jr, Robert D., Book Review Editor (see also Gould, Eric), *DENVER QUARTERLY*, University of Denver, Denver, CO 80208, 303-753-2869

Richardson, Thomas J., Advisory Editor (see also Prenshaw, Peggy W.; Polk, Noel; Tharpe, Jac L.; Saunders, Cheryl), *SOUTHERN QUARTERLY: A Journal of the Arts in the South*, Box 5078, Southern Stn., USM, Hattiesburg, MS 39406, 601-266-4370

Richie, E. Daniel (see also Claire, F.B.; Wasserman, Rosanne; Rovner, Arkady), The Groundwater Press, 40 Clinton Street #1A, New York, NY 10002, 212-228-5750

Richter, Karl (see also Amodeo, Ron), *ALLEGHENY REVIEW*, Box 32, Allegheny College, Meadville, PA 16335, 814-724-6553; 724-4343

Rickenbacher, William F., Editor (see also MacDonald, Angus; MacDonald, Barry Myles), *ST. CROIX REVIEW*, Box 244, Stillwater, MN 55082, 612-439-7190

Riedel, Robert, Associate Editor (see also Golden, Michael; Elias, Viki; Harrison, Jim; Mungo, Raymond; Bukowski, Charles; Placidus, Max; Codrescu, Andrei; Horotwitz, Mikhail; Ligi; Kramer, Glenn; Mitchell, Donna), *SMOKE SIGNALS*, 1516 Beverly Road, Brooklyn, NY 11226

Riessman, Frank, Editor (see also Gartner, Audrey), *SOCIAL POLICY*, Room 1212, 33 W 42nd St, New York, NY 10036, 212-840-7619

Rifkin, Andrew (see also Rifkin, Frank Ray), *NUTRITION HEALTH REVIEW*, 143 Madison, New York, NY 10016

Rifkin, Frank Ray (see also Rifkin, Andrew), *NUTRITION HEALTH REVIEW*, 143 Madison, New York, NY 10016

Riggs, Rollin (see also Jacobsen, Bruce), RJ Publications, Inc., 4651 Yale Station, New Haven, CT 06520, 203-624-5485

Rikhoff, Jean (see also Lape, Walter; Weaver, Francis; Quirk, John; Porter, Regina), Loft Press, 93 Grant Avenue, Glens Falls, NY 12801

Riley, Jan (see also Glazier, Loss), *ORO MADRE*, 4429 Gibraltar Drive, Fremont, CA 94536, 415-797-9096

Riley, Jan (see also Glazier, Loss), Ruddy Duck Press, 4429 Gibraltar Drive, Fremont, CA 94536, 415-797-9096

Rimm, Virginia M., Editor (see also Perrin, Arnold; Grierson, Ruth; Briggs, Henry; Boisvert, Donald J.; McIntyre, Joan; Knowles, Ardeana Hamlin; Brown, Ronald G.; Beck, Raymond M.), *NEW ENGLAND SAMPLER*, RFD #1 Box 2280, Brooks, ME 04921, 207-525-3575

Rindock, Kathy Miller, Assistant Editor (see also Miller, Kitty), Log Cabin Publishers, PO Box 1536, Allentown, PA 18105, 215-434-2448

Ringold, Francine, *NIMROD*, Arts and Humanities Council of Tulsa, 2210 So. Main, Tulsa, OK 74114

Rinker, Harry L., Warman Publishing Co., Inc., PO Box 26742, Elkins Park, PA 19117

Riordan, Michael, Cheshire Books, 514 Bryant Street, Palo Alto, CA 94301, 415-321-2449

Rios, Herminio, Editor-in-Chief, Editorial Justa Publications, Inc., P. O. Box 2131-C, Berkeley, CA 94702, 415 848-3628

Rippington, Geoff (see also Polley, Simon; Bailey, Chris; Sutherland, Allen; Swinden, Dave), British Science Fiction Assoc. Ltd., 269 Wykeham Road, Reading RG6 1PL, England, 0734-666142

Rippington, Geoff, *VECTOR*, 269 Wykeham Road, Reading RG6 1PL, England, 0734-666142

Rippy, Frances Mayhew (see also Renner, Dick A.), *BALL STATE UNIVERSITY FORUM*, Ball State Univ., Muncie, IN 47306

Risoli, Vincent, Mogul Book and FilmWorks, PO Box 2773, Pittsburgh, PA 15230, 412-653-6577

Risseeuw, John L., The Cabbagehead Press, 1272 E. Loma Vista Drive, Tempe, AZ 85282

Ritter, Jeff (see also Grinberg, Gordon), *BROADSIDE*, Broadside Ltd., PO Box 1464, New York, NY 10023

Ritter, M. R., Back Row Press, 1803 Venus Ave., St. Paul, MN 55112, 612-633-1685

Rizzon, Barbara, Editor (see also Rizzon, Bruce), Gearhead Press, 835 9th NW, Grand Rapids, MI 49504, 459-7861 or 459-4577

Rizzon, Bruce, Editor (see also Rizzon, Barbara), *Gearhead Press*, 835 9th NW, Grand Rapids, MI 49504, 459-7861 or 459-4577

Roach, Harry, *MILITARY IMAGES MAGAZINE*, 918 Liberty Street, Allentown, PA 18102

Roark, Randy, *FRICTION*, Laocoon Press, 2130 Arapahoe, Boulder, CO 80302, 303-443-7514

Robbie Rubinstein (see also Scherzer, Joel), Quick Books, PO Box 222, Pueblo, CO 81002

Robbins, David (see also Pohrt, Karl), Bear Claw Press, 13 East Wheelock #1E, Hanover, NH 03755, 313-668-6634

Roberge, Victor, Metamorphous Press, PO Box 1712, Lake Oswego, OR 97034, 503-635-6709

Roberts, Helen, Bragdon Books, 1322 Bragdon, Pueblo, CO 81004, 303-542-2231

Roberts, Nancy, Managing Editor (see also Garlington, Jack; Shapard, Robert), *WESTERN HUMANITIES REVIEW*, University of Utah, Salt Lake City, UT 84112, 801-581-7438

Roberts, T.A., *EFRYDIAU ATHRONYDDOL*, 6 Gwennyth St., Cathays, Cardiff CF2 4YD, Wales, Cardiff 31919

Robertson, Carolyn (see also Robertson, James), The Yolla Bolly Press, PO Box 156, Covelo, CA 95428, 707-983-6130

Robertson, Foster (see also Foreman, Paul), Thorp Springs Press, 803 Red River, Austin, TX 78701

Robertson, James (see also Robertson, Carolyn), The Yolla Bolly Press, PO Box 156, Covelo, CA 95428, 707-983-6130

Robertson, Kirk, Duck Down Press, PO Box 1047, Fallon, NV 89406, 702-423-6643

Robertson, Kirk, *SCREE*, PO Box 1047, Fallon, NV 89406, 702-423-6643

Robinson, Chris, Editor (see also Bellis, Lewis), *RECON*, P.O. Box 14602, Philadelphia, PA 19134

Robinson, Chris, Editor (see also Bellis, Lewis), Recon Publications, PO Box 14602, Philadelphia, PA 19134

Robinson, David (see also Schendlinger, Mary; Siegler, Karl), Talon Books Ltd., 201/1019 East Cordova Street, Vancouver, British Columbia V6A 1M8, Canada, 604-253-5261

Robinson, Forrest, Editor (see also Logsdon, Loren; Mann, John), *MISSISSIPPI VALLEY REVIEW*, Dept. of English, Western Ill. University, Macomb, IL 61455, 309-298-1514

Robinson, Ian (see also Vas Dias, Robert; Frazer, Tony), *NINTH DECADE*, 52 Cascade Avenue, London N10, United Kingdom, 01-444-8591

Robinson, Robert H., Sussex Prints, Inc., PO Box 469, Georgetown, DE 19947, 302-856-0026

Robson, Andy, *KRAX*, 63 Dixon Lane, Leeds, Yorkshire LS12 4RR, England

Robson, Deborah, Tree Toad Press, PO Box 263, Rockville Centre, NY 11571

Robson, Ernest (see also Robson, Marion), Primary Press, Box 105A, Parker Ford, PA 19457, 215-495-7529

Robson, Marion (see also Robson, Ernest), *Primary Press*, Box 105A, Parker Ford, PA 19457, 215-495-7529

Roccia, M, Surrey Press, 224 Surrey Road, Warminster, PA 18974, 215-675-4569

Rodecker, Shirley J. (see also Cloke, Richard; Smith, Lori C.), Cerulean Press (Subsidiary of Kent Publications), 18301 Halsted St., Northridge, CA 91325

Rodecker, Shirley J., Asst. Editor (see also Cloke, Richard; Smith, Lori C.), Kent Publications, Inc., 18301 Halsted Street, Northridge, CA 91325, 213-349-2080

Rodecker, Shirley J., Associate Editor (see also Cloke, Richard; Smith, Lori C.), *SAN FERNANDO POETRY JOURNAL*, 18301 Halstead Street, Northridge, CA 91325

Rodgers, James L., Executive Director, Valentine Publishing & Drama Co., PO Box 461, Rhinebeck, NY 12572, 914-876-3589

Rodieck, P. Anna, Open Hand Publishing Inc., 210 7th Street SE Suite A24, Washington, DC 20003, 206-624-5875

Rodriguez, Aleida (see also De Angelis, Jacqueline), Books of a Feather, PO Box 3095, Terminal Annex, Los Angeles, CA 90051

Rodriguez, Aleida (see also De Angelis, Jacqueline), *RARA AVIS*, P.O. Box 3095, Terminal Annex, Los Angeles, CA 90051

Rodriguez, Juan, *CARTA ABIERTA*, Center for Mexican American Studies, Texas Lutheran College, Seguin, TX 78155, 512-379-4161 X 331

Rodriquez, E., Art Editor (see also Haus, Henn), *LOCAL DRIZZLE*, farmOut, P.O.Box 388, Carnation, WA 98014, (206) 333-4980

Rodway, Allan (see also Lucas, John; Parfitt, George), Byron Press, The English Dept., Univ. Park, Nottingham, England

Roes, Nicholas A. (see also Papalia, Donna M.), *TEACHER UPDATE*, Box 205, Saddle River, NJ 07458, 201-327-8486

Roes, Nicholas A. (see also Papalia, Donna M.), Teacher Update, Inc., Box 205, Saddle River, NJ 07458, 201-327-8486

Rogak, Lisa, *CONSUMING PASSIONS NEWSLETTER*, PO Box 77, Norwood, NJ 07648

Rogers, Katherin A., Executive Editor (see also Bush, Erwin H.), *PHILOSOHICAL SPECULATIONS in Science Fiction & Fantasy*, 103 Middleton Place, Jeffersonville, PA 19403, 215-275-5396

Rogers, Steven B., Editor and Publisher (see also Goebel, Robert), Rainfeather Press, 3201 Taylor Street, Mt. Rainier, MD 20712

Rogers, Steven B., Editor and Publisher (see also Goebel, Robert), *ROADRUNNER-BIO: A Broadside Series*, 3201 Taylor Street, Mt. Rainier, MD 20712

Rognlie, Tammy, Managing Editor (see also Nauman-Haight, Sheila), *HEALTH LITERATURE REVIEW*, PO Box 8029, St. Paul, MN 55113, 612-731-1816

Rognlie, Tammy, Managing Editor (see also Nauman-Haight, Sheila), True-To-Form Press, PO Box 8029, St. Paul, MN 55113, 612-731-1816

Rogs, Larry, Gryphon House, Inc., PO Box 275, Mt. Ranier, MD 20712, 301-779-6200

Rohe, Fred, Editor (see also Feuerstein, Georg), The Dawn Horse Press, PO Box 3270, Clearlake, CA 95422, 707-994-8281

Rohe, Fred, Editor-in-Chief (see also Feuerstein, Georg), *THE LAUGHING MAN: On the Principles and Secrets of Religion, Spirituality and Human Culture*, PO Box 3270, Clearlake, CA 95422, 707-928-5469

Rohmer, Harriet (see also Cherin, Robin), Children's Book Press/Imprenta de Libros Infantiles, 1461 9th Ave., San Francisco, CA 94122, 415-664-8500

Rolfe, Bari, Personabooks, 434 66th Street, Oakland, CA 94609, 415-658-2482

Rollins, Brook, Associate Editor (see also Aronson, Arnold; Margolis, Tina; Garren, Lois; King, Keith; Wells, Ann; Wolff, Fred M.), *THEATRE DESIGN AND TECHNOLOGY*, 330 W. 42nd Street, New York, NY 10036, 212-563-5551

Rollins, Scott, Bridges, The Bridges Foundation, Ceintuurbaan 374-3, 1073 El Amsterdam, The Netherlands

Rollo, Vera F., Maryland Historical Press, 9205 Tuckerman St, Lanham, MD 20706, 301-577-2436 and 557-5308

Rolph, Ken, Editor, Hexagon Press, P.O. Box 269, Greenacre, N.S.W. 2190, Australia, 02-724-4444

Romano-V, Octavio I., *GRITO DEL SOL COLLECTION,* PO Box 9275, Berkeley, CA 94709, 415-655-8036

Romano-V, Octavio I., Tonatiuh - Quinto Sol International Inc., PO Box 9275, Berkeley, CA 94709, 415-655-8036

Romero, Annelisa, Managing Editor (see also Gomez-Quinones, Juan; McKenna, Teresa; Macias, Reynaldo), *AZTLAN: International Journal of Chicano Studies Research,* University of California-Los Angeles, 405 Hilgard Avenue, Los Angeles, CA 90025, 213-825-2642

Romero, Annelisa, Managing Editor (see also Gomez-Quinones, Juan; McKenna, Teresa; Macias, Reynaldo F.), Chicano Studies Research Center Publications, University of California-Los Angeles, 405 Hilgard Avenue, Los Angeles, CA 90024, 213-825-2642

Romey, Bill, Ash Lad Press, P.O. Box 396, Canton, NY 13617, 315-386-8820

Ronck, Ronn (see also Hymer, Bemett), Mutual Publishing of Honolulu, 2055 N. King, Honolulu, HI 96819

Rooke, Constance, Editor (see also Scobie, Stephen), *THE MALAHAT REVIEW,* PO Box 1700, Victoria, British Columbia V8W 2Y2, Canada

Rooney, Carol, *SOLAR FLASHES,* 512 Ross, Alamosa, CO 81101, 303-589-2233

Rooney, F., Editor (see also Nuse, B.; Newton, J.; Zavitz, C.; Andersen, M.; Wine, J.; Prentice, A.; Scane, J.; Caplan, Paula; Van Kirk, Sylvia), *RESOURCES FOR FEMINIST RESEARCH/DOCUMENTATION SUR LA RECHERCHE FEMINISTE,* Ont Inst for Stud in Educ, Centre for Women's Studies in Education, 252 Bloor Street W., Toronto, Ontario M5S 1V6, Canada, 416-923-6641

Roper, John H., Executive Editor (see also Bayes, Ron; Osmanski, Edna Ann; Diogo, Judith A.), Saint Andrews Press, St Andrews College, Laurinburg, NC 28352, 919-276-3652

Roper, John H., *SAINT ANDREWS REVIEW,* St. Andrews College, Laurinburg, NC 28352, 919-276-3652

Roper, J.V., Associate Editor (see also Clift, G.W.; Carrell, Ann; Mosher, Robin; Salah-Din, Hakim), *LITERARY MAGAZINE REVIEW,* English Department, Kansas State University, Manhattan, KS 66506, 913-532-6719

Rorke, Raymond, Design Editor (see also Beam, Joe; Bernstein, Carole; Caplan, Leslie; Simpson, Chris; Sorensen, Sally Jo), *PAINTED BRIDE QUARTERLY,* 230 Vine Street, Philadelphia, PA 19106, 215-925-9914

Rosa, Linda (see also Montague, Don), *SOUTH AMERICAN EXPLORER,* 2239 E. Colfax, Denver, CO 80206, 320-0388

Rosalea, *THURDS: FROM THE ART OF ROSALEA'S HOTEL,* PO Box 121, Harper, KS 67058

Rose, I. (see also Degnore, R.P.), I.R.D. Productions - Alien Prods, Box 366, Canal Street Station, New York, NY 10013, 212-420-9043

Rose, Kenneth (see also Schlegel, Lee-Lee), *DEROS,* 6009 Edgewood Lane, Alexandria, VA 22310, 703-971-2219

Rose, Kenneth (see also Schlegel, Lee-Lee), Miriam Press, Inc., 6009 Edgewood Lane, Alexandria, VA 22310, 703-971-2219

Rose, Leo E. (see also Scalapino, Robert A.), *ASIAN SURVEY,* University of California Press, Berkeley, CA 94720, 415-642-0978

Rosemont, Franklin, Black Swan Press, 1726 W Jarvis, Chicago, IL 60626

Rosen, Joan, *NEWSREAL,* Box 40323, Tucson, AZ 85717, 887-3982

Rosenberg, Ann, *THE CAPILANO REVIEW,* 2055 Purcell Way, North Vancouver, B.C. V7J3H5, Canada, 604-986-1911

Rosenberg, David, Kangaroo Press, 3 Whitehall Road, PO Box 75, Kenthurst, Sydney, NSW 2154, Australia, 02-654-1502

Rosenberg, L.M., Co-Editor (see also Higgins, Joanna; Gardner, John), *MSS (Manuscripts),* SUNY, Binghamton, NY 13901, 607-798-2000

Rosenblum, Martin J., Editor, Lionhead Publishing/Roar Recording, 2521 East Stratford Court, Shorewood, WI 53211, 414-332-7474

Rosenblum, Martin J., *ROAR: A Tapebook Series,* 2521 East Stratford Court, Shorewood, WI 53211, 414-332-7474

Rosenburg, Robert K., Linden Press Baltimore, 3601 Greenway, Baltimore, MD 21218, 301-338-1689

Rosenfeld, Dr. Sybil (see also Armstrong, W.A., Professor; Booth, Michael, Professor), *THEATRE NOTEBOOK,* 103 Ralph Court, Queensway, London W2 5HU, England

Rosenthal, Odeda, Starchand Press, Box 468, Wainscott, NY 11975

Rosenus, Alan, Urion Press, PO Box 10085, San Jose, CA 95157, 408-867-7695

Rosenwasser, Rena (see also Duane, Kit; Lisanevich, Xenia; Loeb, Emily; Kitrilakis, Thalia), Kelsey St. Press, PO Box 9235, Berkeley, CA 94709, AM: 415-845-2260; PM: 415-548-3826

Rosenzweig, Phyllis, Poetry Reviews Editor, Film Reviews (see also Swift, Mary; Lang, Doug; Wittenberg, Clarissa; Fleming, Lee), *WASHINGTON REVIEW,* P O Box 50132, Washington, DC 20004, 202-638-0515

Rosler, Martha, *POSTCARD ART/POSTCARD FICTION,* 53 Pearl Street, Brooklyn, NY 11201

Rosler, Martha, Rosler, Martha, 53 Pearl Street, Brooklyn, NY 11201

Roslund, Kathy, Editor, *FAMILY FESTIVALS,* PO Box 37, Saratoga, CA 95071

Ross, Charlie (see also Banta, Mary Lu), Smithereens Press, Box 1036, Bolinas, CA 94924, 415-868-0149

Ross, Charlie (see also Banta, Mary Lu), *SMITHEREENS SEASONAL SAMPLER,* Box 1036, Bolinas, CA 94924, 415-868-0149

Ross, Franz, Ross Books, Box 4340, Berkeley, CA 94704, (415) 841-2474

Ross, Stuart, *MONDO HUNKAMOOGA,* PO Box 789, Station F, Toronto, Ontario M4Y 2N7, Canada

Ross, Stuart, Proper Tales Press, PO Box 789, Station F, Toronto, Ontario M4Y 2N7, Canada

Rossi, Betty, Editor (see also Elliott, William; Sliney, Jean), *LOONFEATHER: Minnesota North Country Art,* Bemidji Community Arts Center, 426 Bemidji Avenue, Bemidji, MN 56601, 218-751-7570

Rossiter, Charles, *ESKER PRODUCTIONS,* 3820 East 39th Street N.W., Washington, DC 20016, 301-694-7274

Roth, Bonnie, *NOSTALGIA WORLD,* PO box 231, North Haven, CT 06473, 203-239-4891

Roth, Hal, *WIND CHIMES,* PO Box 601, Glen Burnie, MD 21061

Roth, Hal, Wind Chimes Press, PO Box 601, Glen Burnie, MD 21061

Rothfork, John (see also Bradley, Jerry), Saurian Press, Box A, New Mexico Tech., Socorro, NM 87801, 505-835-5445

Rothstein, Haskell (see also Rothstein, Margaret), Arbor Publications, PO Box 8185, Ann Arbor, MI 48107, 313-662-5786

Rothstein, Margaret (see also Rothstein, Haskell), *Arbor Publications,* PO Box 8185, Ann Arbor, MI 48107, 313-662-5786

Rothwell, Edward, Editor-in-Chief (see also Attebury, Jean), The Garlinghouse Company, 320 S.W. 33rd Street, PO Box 299, Topeka, KS 66601, 913-267-2490

Rottman, Gordon L., Brown Mouse Publishing Company, PO Box 20082, Houston, TX 77225, 713-699-1277

Roubatis, Y. (see also Chouliaras, Y.; Kitroeff, A.; Pappas, P.), *JOURNAL OF THE HELLENIC DIASPORA*, 337 West 36th Street, New York, NY 10018, 212-279-9586

Rouig, Lynn, Fiction Assistant (see also Freeman, Stephanie Anne; Damon, John Edward), *JEOPARDY*, Western Washington University, Humanities 350, WWU, Bellingham, WA 98225

Rousseau, Richard W., Ridge Row Press, 10 South Main Street, Montrose, PA 18801, 717-278-1141

Roussopoulos, D. (see also Kowaluk, L.; Young, B.; Caloren, F.), *OUR GENERATION*, 3981 boul St Laurent, Montreal, Quebec H2W 1Y5, Canada

Rovner, Arkady (see also Richie, E. Daniel; Claire, F.B.; Wasserman, Rosanne), The Groundwater Press, 40 Clinton Street #1A, New York, NY 10002, 212-228-5750

Rowan, John (see also Cobbing, Bob), Writers Forum, 262 Randolph Ave., London W9, England, 01-624-8565

Rowe, Charlene M. (see also Shane, Sheila), Rowe Publishing Corporation, 3906 N. 69th Street, Milwaukee, WI 53216, 414-438-0685

Rowell, Carol (see also McAlister, Kim), *FEMINIST BULLETIN*, PO Box 350, San Diego, CA 92101, 714-233-8984

Rowell, Charles H., Editor, *CALLALOO*, Department of English, University of Kentucky, Lexington, KY 40506, 606-257-6984, 257-3114, 257-2901

Rowland, Keith D. (see also James, Nancy E.), *SUNRUST MAGAZINE*, Box 58, New Wilmington, PA 16142

Roy, Terina Lee, Production (see also Ford, E.), Edwardian Studies Association, 125 Markyate Road, Dagenham Essex RM8 2LB, England

Royal, Richard (see also Martin, Stephen-Paul; Ensler, Eve; Millis, Christopher; Kiefer, Paul; Sullivan, Mary Jane; Sanders, Catherine Marie), *CENTRAL PARK*, P.O. Box 1446, New York, NY 10023

Rubel, William (see also Mandel, Gerry), *STONE SOUP, The Magazine By Children*, Box 83, Santa Cruz, CA 95063, 408-426-5557

Rubenstein, Lenny (see also Crowdus, Gary; Georgakas, Dan), *CINEASTE MAGAZINE*, 200 Park Avenue South, Room 1320, New York, NY 10003

Rubenstein, Nancy (see also Stein, Charlotte M.; Radin, Jessica), Double M Press, 16455 Tuba Street, Sepulveda, CA 91343, 213-360-3166

Rubin, Lorna (see also Freeman, Lenore), Triad Publishing Co. Inc., 1110 NN 8th Avenue Suite C, Gainesville, FL 32601, 904-373-5308

Rubin, Samuel K., *CLASSIC IMAGES*, PO Box 4079, Davenport, IA 52808

Rubin, Stan Sanvel (see also Kitchen, Judith; Bennett, Bruce; Allardt, Linda), State Street Press, PO Box 252, Pittsford, NY 14534, 716-586-0154

Rubinstein, Robbie (see also Scherzer, Joel), *LOOK QUICK*, PO Box 222, Pueblo, CO 81002

Rubio, Mary (see also Waterston, Elizabeth), *CANADIAN CHILDREN'S LITERATURE*, PO Box 335, Guelph Ontario, Canada

Rudinger, Joel, Publisher, Cambric Press, 312 Park Street, c/o Firelands College, Huron, OH 44839, 419-433-5660; 433-6266

Rudinger, Joel, *POETRY PROJECTS*, 312 Park Street, Firelands College, Huron, OH 44839, 419-433-5660; 433-6266

Rudolf, Anthony, The Menard Press, 8 The Oaks, Woodside Avenue, London N12 8AR, England

Ruffin, Paul, *THE TEXAS REVIEW*, English Department, Sam Houston State University, Huntsville, TX 77341

Ruggie, Cathie, The Hosanna Press, 5372 West Kimball Place, Oak Lawn, IL 60453, 312-423-6177

Ruggieri, Ford F. (see also Ruggieri, Helen), Allegany Mountain Press, 111 N. 10th St., Olean, NY 14760, 716-372-0935

Ruggieri, Ford F. (see also Ruggieri, Helen), *UROBOROS*, 111 N. 10th St., Olean, NY 14760, 716-372-0935

Ruggieri, Helen (see also Ruggieri, Ford F.), Allegany Mountain Press, 111 N. 10th St., Olean, NY 14760, 716-372-0935

Ruggieri, Helen (see also Ruggieri, Ford F.), *UROBOROS*, 111 N. 10th St., Olean, NY 14760, 716-372-0935

Ruhl, Steven (see also Rayher, Ed; McGuill, Mike; Conoley, Gillian; Stansberry, Domenic), *TIGHTROPE*, 72 Colonial Village, Amherst, MA 01002

Rumsey, Anne M., Poetry (see also Gennrich, Suzanne J.), *THE MADISON REVIEW*, Dept of English, H.C. White Hall, 600 N. Park Street, Madison, WI 53706, 263-3303

Rusch, Robert D., *CADENCE: THE AMERICAN REVIEW OF JAZZ & BLUES*, Cadence Building, Redwood, NY 13679, 315-287-2852

Russ, Barbara (see also Mathews, Richard), *KONGLOMERATI*, PO Box 5001, Gulfport, FL 33737, 813-323-0386

Russ, Barbara (see also Mathews, Richard), Konglomerati Press, PO Box 5001, Gulfport, FL 33737, 813-323-0386

Russ, Raymond, Editor, *THE JOURNAL OF MIND AND BEHAVIOR*, PO Box 522, Village Station, New York, NY 10014, 212-783-1471

Russell, Charles (see also Sukenick, Ronald; Ratner, Rochelle; Tytell, John; Hoover, Russell), *THE AMERICAN BOOK REVIEW*, PO Box 188, Cooper Station, New York, NY 10003, 212-621-9289

Ruthel, Rod, Managing Editor, *BIRD TALK MAGAZINE*, 5509 Santa Monica Blvd., Los Angeles, CA 90038, 209-736-0505

Rutter, Frances T., Tompson & Rutter, Inc., PO Box 297, Grantham, NH 03753, 603-863-4392

Ryan, David Stuart, Kozmik Press Centre, 134 Elsenham Street, London SW18 5NPL, United Kingdom, 874-8218

Ryan, Frank, Editor (see also Schulz, Paul J.), Muse-ed Company, 14141 Margate Street, Van Nuys, CA 91331, 213-789-3310

Ryan, Tim (see also Jappinen, Rae), SourceNet, PO Box 6767, Santa Barbara, CA 93160, 805-685-3314

Ryan, Tim (see also Jappinen, Rae), *WHOLE AGAIN RESOURCE GUIDE*, PO Box 6767, Santa Barbara, CA 93160, 805-685-3314

Ryan, William, Editor (see also Gellen, Karen; Farley, Gay), *GUARDIAN*, 33 W 17th St, New York, NY 10011, 212-691-0404

Ryan, William, Editor (see also Gellen, Karen; Farley, Gay), Institute for Independent Social Journalism, Inc., 33 W 17th St, New York, NY 10011, 212-691-0404

Ryde, Fred M., *THE INQUIRER*, 1-6 Essex Street, London WC2R 3HY, England

Ryder, Virginia P., Amigo Press, 620 Lombardy Lane, Laguna Beach, CA 92651, 714-494-2302

S

Safran, Rose, Tide Book Publishing Company, Box 268, Manchester, MA 01944, 617-872-6100

Safransky, Sy, *THE SUN, A MAGAZINE OF IDEAS*, 412 W. Rosemary Street, Chapel Hill, NC 27514, 942-5282

Sagan, Miriam, Poetry (see also Hogan, Ed; Gubernat, Susan; Johnson, Ronna; Zeitlin, Leora), Zephyr Press, 13 Robinson Street, Somerville, MA 02145

Sage, Howard, Sage Press, 720 Greenwich St, New York City, NY 10014

Sagstetter, Brad, Managing Editor, The Larksdale Press, 133 S Heights Blvd, Houston, TX 77007, 869-9092

Salah-Din, Hakim, Associate Editor (see also Clift, G.W.; Carrell, Ann; Roper, J.V.; Mosher, Robin), *LITERARY MAGAZINE REVIEW,* English Department, Kansas State University, Manhattan, KS 66506, 913-532-6719

Salander, Eric L., Delgren Books, 3833 N. Fairview #25, Tucson, AZ 85705

Salantrie, Frank, *THE ORIGINAL ART REPORT (TOAR),* P.O. Box 1641, Chicago, IL 60690

Saldivar, Jose (see also Olivares, Julian), *REVISTA CHICANO-RIQUENA,* University of Houston, Houston, TX 77004, 219-749-4768

Salinas, Judy (see also Mailman, Leo; Locklin, Gerald; Zepeda, Ray; Barker, David; Snider, Clifton; Kay, John), *MAELSTROM REVIEW,* 8 Farm Hill Road, Cape Elizabeth, ME 04107

Salmon-Heynemen, Jana, Calendar Editor (see also Woodhams, Stephen; Gabbard, D.C.; Gabbard, Dwight C.; Overson, Beth E.; Caquelin, Anthony; Goodwin, Tema; Shames, Terry; Rajfur, Ted), *FICTION MONTHLY,* Malvolio Press, 545 Haight Street, Suite 67, San Francisco, CA 94117, 415-621-1646

Samolis, Dr. Sam, Photographer (see also Lawson, Dr. Todd; Comen, Dr. Diane; Marsic, John; Rader, Steve; Monte, Oscar; Nishi, Mio; Ginsberg, Allen; Graham, Joan; Ferlinghetti, Lawrence; Ramirez, Julio; Haynes, Dr. Robert; Snyder, Gary; Morris, Dr. Richard), *ALPS MONTHLY,* PO Box 99394, San Francisco, CA 94109, 415-771-3431

Samolis, William, Secretary (see also Comen, Diane; Lawson, Todd S.J.; Marsic, John; Comen, Diane; Graham, Joan; Rader, Steve), Peace & Pieces Press, Box 99394, San Francisco, CA 94109, 415-771-3431

San Souci, Robert D., Downey Place Publishing House, Inc., PO Box 1352, El Cerrito, CA 94530, 415-529-1012

Sanders, Catherine Marie (see also Martin, Stephen-Paul; Royal, Richard; Ensler, Eve; Millis, Christopher; Kiefer, Paul; Sullivan, Mary Jane), *CENTRAL PARK,* P.O. Box 1446, New York, NY 10023

Sanders, D.M., The Rubric Press, Maon Beit Brodetaky, 36 Rechov Brodetaky, Ramat Aviv 69051 Tel Aviv, Israel

Sanders, Ken, Publisher (see also Brown, Marc; Firmage, Richard), Dream Garden Press, 1199 Iola Avenue, Salt Lake City, UT 84104, 801-355-2154

Sanders, Mark (see also Brummels, J.V.), Sandhills Press, 219 S 19th Street, Ord, NE 68862

Sanderson, George S., *THE ANTIGONISH REVIEW,* St Francis Xavier University, Antigonish, Nova Scotia B2G1CO, Canada

Sandow, Stuart A., President, Sterling-Miller, PO Box 2413, Staunton, VA 24401

Sandstrom, Roy, Managing Editor, Whitmore Publishing Company, 35 Cricket Terrace, Ardmore, PA 19003, 215-896-6116

Santos, Rosario, Managing Editor, Center For Inter-American Relations, 680 Park Avenue, New York, NY 10021

Santos, Rosario, *REVIEW. LATIN AMERICAN LITERATURE & ARTS,* Center For Inter-American Relations, 680 Park Avenue, New York, NY 10021

Sapiro, Leland (see also Boggs, Redd; Smith, Sheryl; Emerson, Mary), *RIVERSIDE QUARTERLY,* Box 863-388, Wildcat Station, Plano, TX 75086, 214-234-6795

Sarah, Robyn (see also Louder, Fred; Hannan, Jack), *FOUR BY FOUR: A SELECTION OF POETS,* 4647, rue Hutchison, Montreal, Quebec H2V 4A2, Canada, 514-274-1902

Sarah, Robyn (see also Louder, Fred), *Villeneuve Publications,* 4647, rue Hutchison, Montreal, Quebec H2V 4A2, Canada, 514-274-1902

Sargent, Bob, Treasurer (see also Alenier, Karren L.; Baldwin, Deirdra; Beall, Jim), The Word Works, Inc., PO Box 42164, Washington, DC 20015, (202) 554-3014

Sargent, Colin W., *GREATER PORTLAND MAGAZINE*, 142 Free Street, Portland, ME 04101, 207-772-2811

Sargent, L. (see also Herman, E.; Walsh, S.; Geiger, K.), South End Press, 302 Columbus Avenue, Boston, MA 02116, 617-266-0629

Sargent, Robert, Treasurer (see also Cochrane, Shirley; Wyman, Hastings), Washington Writers Publishing House, PO Box 50068, Washington, DC 20004, 202-546-1020

Saricyan-Jamieson, Ligia (see also Cleary, Michael; Schwartz, Magi), *THE SOUTH FLORIDA POETRY REVIEW*, PO Box 7072, Hollywood, FL 33081, 305-474-5285

Sato, Kazuo, Japan (see also Harr, Lorraine Ellis; Harr, Carl F.; Yagi, Kametaro), *DRAGONFLY: A Quarterly Of Haiku*, 4102 N.E. 130th Pl., Portland, OR 97230

Satow, Donna (see also Parker, Arri), *THE WOMAN'S NEWSPAPER OF PRINCETON*, PO Box 1303, Princeton, NJ 08542, 609-466-9330

Saunders, Cheryl, Managing Editor (see also Prenshaw, Peggy W.; Polk, Noel; Tharpe, Jac L.; Richardson, Thomas J.), *SOUTHERN QUARTERLY: A Journal of the Arts in the South*, Box 5078, Southern Stn., USM, Hattiesburg, MS 39406, 601-266-4370

Saunders, Leslie (see also Harrison, Jeanne; Folsom, Eric), *NEXT EXIT*, Box 143, Tamworth, Ontario K0K 3G0, Canada, 613-379-2339

Savage, Alice (see also Cannon, Melissa), *CAT'S EYE*, 1005 Clearview Drive, Nashville, TN 37205

Saville, Ken, The Transientpress, Box 4662, Albuquerque, NM 87196, (505) 242-6600

Savion, Thom (see also Cotolo, F.M.; Tabor, B. Lyle; Stevroid, Lionel; Clendaniel, Nancy), *FAT TUESDAY*, 853 N Citrus, Los Angeles, CA 90038

Savitt, Lynne, Contributing Editor (see also Kruchkow, Diane; Johnson, Curt; Fox, Hugh; Melnicove, Mark), *STONY HILLS: News & Review of the Small Press*, Weeks Mills, New Sharon, ME 04955, 207-778-3436

Savory, Teo, Editor, Unicorn Press, P.O. Box 3307, Greensboro, NC 27402

Say, Daniel, *ENTROPY NEGATIVE*, Box 65583, Vancouver 12, B.C. V5N 5K5, Canada

Say, Daniel, *GUARD THE NORTH*, Box 65583, Vancouver 12, B. C. V5N 5K5, Canada

Sayre, Rose, Associate Editor (see also Villani, Jim; Peffer, George; Remick, Jace), *PIG IRON*, P.O. Box 237, Youngstown, OH 44501, 216-744-2258

Sayre, Rose, Associate Editor (see also Villani, Jim; Murcko, Terry; George Peffer), Pig Iron Press, P.O. Box 237, Youngstown, OH 44501

Scalapino, Robert A. (see also Rose, Leo E.), *ASIAN SURVEY*, University of California Press, Berkeley, CA 94720, 415-642-0978

Scammacca, Nat (see also Cane, Crescenzio), *COOP. ANTIGRUPPO SICILIANO*, Villa Schammacha-nat, Via Argenteria Km 4, Trapani, Sicily, Italy, 0923-38681

Scammacca, Nat (see also Certa, Rolando), *IMPEGNO 80*, Villa Schammachanat, Via Argentaria Km 4, Trapani, Sicily, Italy

Scammacca, Nat (see also Certa, Rolando), Sicilian Antigruppo/Cross-Cultural Communications, Villa Schammchanat, via Argenteria Km 4, Trapani, Sicily, Italy, 0923-38681

Scane, J., Editor (see also Nuse, B.; Newton, J.; Zavitz, C.; Rooney, F.; Andersen, M.; Wine, J.; Prentice, A.; Caplan, Paula; Van Kirk, Sylvia), *RESOURCES FOR FEMINIST RESEARCH/DOCUMENTATION SUR LA RECHERCHE FEMINISTE*, Ont Inst for Stud in Educ, Centre for Women's Studies in Education, 252 Bloor Street W., Toronto, Ontario M5S 1V6, Canada, 416-923-6641

Scates, Maxine, Poetry Editor (see also Witte, John; Casey, Deb), *NORTHWEST REVIEW*, 369 P.L.C., University of Oregon, Eugene, OR 97403, 503-686-3957

Scavone, Dave (see also Perras, Wayne; Skinner, Elizabeth), *THE HIGH ROCK REVIEW*, PO Box 614, Saratoga Springs, NY 12866, 518-584-4080

Schaefer, Jay, Editor (see also Ellison, Heidi), *FICTION NETWORK MAGAZINE*, PO Box 5651, San Francisco, CA 94101, 415-552-3223

Schaefer, Jim, Publisher (see also Schaefer, Karen), *RIPPLES*, 1426 Las Vegas, Ann Arbor, MI 48103

Schaefer, Karen, Editor (see also Schaefer, Jim), *RIPPLES*, 1426 Las Vegas, Ann Arbor, MI 48103

Schaefer, Karen, Editor, Shining Waters Press, 1426 Las Vegas, Ann Arbor, MI 48103

Schaefer, Paul, Associate Editor (see also Miller, Jack; Redmond, Pauline), *NORTH COUNTRY ANVIL*, PO Box 37, Millville, MN 55957, 507-798-2366

Schafer, Joachim, Nexus Verlag, Fichardstr. 38, Frankfurt/M. 6000, West Germany, 0611-59-99-70

Schain, Stephen (see also Volz, Bill; Clark, Duane; Lang, Lillian), *VERNAL*, 522 E. Third Avenue, Durango, CO 81301, 303-259-0221

Schapiro, Nancy, *WEBSTER REVIEW*, Webster University, Webster Groves, MO 63119, 314-432-2657

Schapp, William, Director, Sheridan Square Publications, Inc., PO Box 677, New York, NY 10013, 212-254-1061

Schappes, Morris U., *JEWISH CURRENTS*, 22 E 17th Street, Suite 601, New York, NY 10003, 212-WA4-5740

Scharf, Lauren Barnett, *LONE STAR: A MAGAZINE OF HUMOR* , PO Box 29000 Suite #103, San Antonio, TX 78229

Scharf, Lauren Barnett, *LONE STAR COMEDY MONTHLY*, PO Box 42821, Suite 204, Houston, TX 77042

Scharf, Lauren Barnett, Lone Star: Publications of Humor, PO Box 29000 Suite #103, San Antonio, TX 78229

Scharper, Philip J., Editor-in-Chief (see also Eagleson, John; Higgins, Elizabeth), Orbis Books, Attention: Robert N. Quigley, Maryknoll, NY 10545, 914-941-7590

Schechter, Joel, Editor, *THEATER*, 222 York Street, New Haven, CT 06520, 203-436-1417

Schechter, Ruth Lisa, Editor (see also Thomas, Dan B.; Bluestein, Dan T.; Crisci, Pat J.; Merrill, Susan; Stettan, Leonard), *CROTON REVIEW*, P.O. Box 277, Croton on Hudson, NY 10520, 914-271-3144

Scheibli, Silvia, *THE CYPRESS REVIEW*, Box 673, Half Moon Bay, CA 94019, 726-4911

Scheibli, Silvia, Cypress Review Press, Box 673, Half Moon Bay, CA 94019, 726-4911

Scheley, James, Managing Editor (see also Lea, Sydney), Kenyon Hill Publications, PO Box 170, Hanover, NH 03755, 603-795-4027

Schell, Nixa, Fiction Editor (see also Gilbert, Elliot; Swanson, Robert), *THE CALIFORNIA QUARTERLY*, 100 Sproul Hall, Univ of Calif, Davis, CA 95616

Schendlinger, Mary (see also Reid, Gayla; Wachtel, Eleanor; Freeman, Victoria; Wexler, Jeannie), *ROOM OF ONE'S OWN*, PO Box 46160, Station G, Vancouver, British Columbia V6R 4G5, Canada, 604-733-3889

Schendlinger, Mary (see also Robinson, David; Siegler, Karl), Talon Books Ltd, 201/1019 East Cordova Street, Vancouver, British Columbia V6A 1M8, Canada, 604-253-5261

Scherzer, Joel (see also Rubinstein, Robbie), *LOOK QUICK*, PO Box 222, Pueblo, CO 81002

Scherzer, Joel (see also Moffeit, Tony), Pueblo Poetry Project, Room 31, Union Depot, Pueblo, CO 81003

Scherzer, Joel (see also Robbie Rubinstein), Quick Books, PO Box 222, Pueblo, CO 81002

Schick, James B., Editor (see also Heffernan, Michael; Daniel, Bruce), *THE MIDWEST QUARTER-LY*, Pittsburg State University, Pittsburg, KS 66762, 316-231-7000

161

Schiffman, Glenn (see also Elman, Barbara), *WORD PROCESSING NEWS*, 211 East Olive #210, Burbank, CA 91502, 818-845-7809

Schiller, Karen, Managing Editor (see also Weinstock, A.), *PLEXUS: The West Coast Women's Press*, 545 Athol Avenue, Oakland, CA 94606, 415-451-2585

Schimmel, Bruce, Publisher (see also Hill, Chris), *PHILADELPHIA CITY PAPER*, 6381 Germantown Avenue, Philadelphia, PA 19144, 215-848-3885

Schimmel, Nancy, Sisters' Choice Press, 1450-6th Street, Berkeley, CA 94710, 415-524-5804

Schizzano, Adrienne, Spectrum Productions, 979 Casiano Rd., Los Angeles, CA 90049

Schlegel, Lee-Lee (see also Rose, Kenneth), *DEROS*, 6009 Edgewood Lane, Alexandria, VA 22310, 703-971-2219

Schlegel, Lee-Lee (see also Rose, Kenneth), Miriam Press, Inc., 6009 Edgewood Lane, Alexandria, VA 22310, 703-971-2219

Schlegel, Lee-Lee, *UP AGAINST THE WALL, MOTHER...*, 6009 Edgewood Lane, Alexandria, VA 22310, 703-971-2219

Schleich, David John, *QUARRY MAGAZINE*, Box 1061, Kingston, Ontario K7L 4Y5, Canada, 613-549-0379

Schleich, David John, Quarry Press, Box 1061, Kingston, Ontario K7L 4Y5, Canada

Schley, James, Editor (see also Lea, Sydney), *NEW ENGLAND REVIEW and BREAD LOAF QUARTERLY (NER/BLQ)*, Box 170, Hanover, NH 03755, 603-795-4027

Schmidt, Dorey, Gen. Ed. (see also de la Fuente, Patricia), *RIVERSEDGE*, PO Box 3185, Edinburg, TX 78539, 512-381-3429

Schmidt, Dorey, Gen. Ed. (see also de la Fuente, Patricia), Riversedge Press, PO Box 3185, Edinburg, TX 78539

Schmidt, Michael, Carcanet Press, 208-212 Corn Exchange Buildings, Manchester, England M4 3BQ, England, (061) 834-8730

Schmidt, Michael, *PN REVIEW*, 208-212 Corn Exchange, Manchester M4 3BQ, England

Schneider, Duane, Croissant & Company, P.O. Box 282, Athens, OH 45701, 614-593-3008

Schneider, Harold W. (see also Nyberg, Ben; Moses, W.R.; Rees, John), *KANSAS QUARTERLY*, Denison Hall, Kansas St. Univ., Manhattan, KS 66506, 913-532-6716

Schneider, Ralph, *CARP NEWSLETTER QUARTERLY*, PO Box 236, Eleva, WI 54738, 715-287-4224

Schneider, Ralph, Pleasant Valley Press, PO Box 236, Eleva, WI 54738, 715-287-4224

Schneider, Rex (see also Buchman, Chris), Blue Mouse Studio, Box 312, Union, MI 49130

Schneider, Susan W., Executive Editor (see also Cantor, Aviva; Freedman, Reena Sigman), *LILITH*, 250 W 57th, Suite 1328, New York, NY 10019, (212) 757-0818

Schneidre, P., Illuminati, 8812 West Pico Blvd. Suite #203, Los Angeles, CA 90035, 213-273-8372

Schneidre, P., *ORPHEUS*, c/o Illuminati, 8812 West Pico Blvd. #203, Los Angeles, CA 90035

Schoenberg, Al (see also Dahl, Bard), *PANGLOSS PAPERS*, Box 18917, Los Angeles, CA 90018, 213-663-1950

Schoenberg, Al (see also Dahl, Bard), Pangloss Press, Box 18917, Los Angeles, CA 90018, 213-663-1950

Schofield, Paul, Editor, *POETRY NEWSLETTER*, Dept. DB-1984, Box 2279, Santa Cruz, CA 95063, 408-429-1122

Scholes, Randall W., Art Director (see also Buchwald, Emilie), *MILKWEED CHRONICLE*, Box 24303, Minneapolis, MN 55424, 612-332-3192

Scholl, S.J., Ana-Doug Publishing, 424 W. Commonwealth, Fullerton, CA 92632, 714-871-4060

Scholnick, Michael (see also Masters, Gregory; Lenhart, Gary), *MAG CITY*, 437 East 12 St. No. 26, New York, NY 10009

Schori, Ward, The Press of Ward Schori, 2716 Noyes Street, Evanston, IL 60201, 312-475-3241

Schorre, Val (see also Cooper, W. Norman), Truth Center, A Universal Fellowship, 6940 Oporto Drive, Los Angeles, CA 90068, 213-876-6295

Schott, Carol (see also Lieb, Patricia), Lieb/Schott Publications, PO Box 229, Bourbonnais, IL 60914

Schott, Carol (see also Lieb, Patricia), *PTERANODON*, PO Box 229, Bourbonnais, IL 60914

Schramm, Henning (see also Sulberg, Walter), IKO-Verlag Fur Interkultu Relle Kommunikation, PO Box 90 90 65, 6000 Frankfurt 90, West Germany

Schreiber, Ron (see also Hershon, Robert; Lourie, Dick; Pawlak, Mark; Levertov, Denise; Jarrett, Emmett), *HANGING LOOSE*, 231 Wyckoff St, Brooklyn, NY 11217

Schriber, Charlotte J., Editor, M-R-K Publishing, Rural Route #6, Petaluma, CA 94952, 707-763-0056

Schroeder, Gary, Poetry Editor (see also Hutchison, Joseph; Nigg, Joe; Rea, David; Miller, Patty; Reilly, Gary), *PENDRAGON Journal of the Creative Arts*, 2640 E. 12th Avenue, Box 715, Denver, CO 80206, 303-444-4100

Schroer, Steve (see also Heminger, Steve), *CHICAGO REVIEW*, University of Chicago, Faculty Exchange, Box C, Chicago, IL 60637, 312-753-3571

Schubert, Cynthia, Senior Editor (see also Galasso, Al; Choate, Lon), American Bookdealers Exchange, PO Box 2525, La Mesa, CA 92041, 619-462-3297

Schubert, Cynthia, Senior Editor (see also Galasso, Al; Choate, Lon), *BOOK DEALERS WORLD*, PO Box 2525, La Mesa, CA 92041, 619-462-3297

Schubert, Susan J., Charles River Press, PO Box 8277, Boston, MA 02114

Schuck, Marjorie, Publisher & Editor, Valkyrie Publishing House, 8245 26th Avenue N, St. Petersburg, FL 33710, 813-345-8864

Schuler, Burton S., The La Luz Press, Inc., 2401 W. 15th Street, Panama City, FL 32401

Schuler, Jeanne Leigh (see also Schuler, Ruth Wildes; Morales, Goldie L.), *PROPHETIC VOICES*, 94 Santa Maria Drive, Novato, CA 94947

Schuler, Ruth Wildes (see also Morales, Goldie L.; Schuler, Jeanne Leigh), *PROPHETIC VOICES*, 94 Santa Maria Drive, Novato, CA 94947

Schulte, Rainer, *MUNDUS ARTIUM: A Journal of International Literature & the Arts*, University of Texas at Dallas, Box 830688, Richardson, TX 75083

Schulte, Rainer, Translations (see also Meier, Joyce), *SANDS*, 17302 Club Hill Drive, Dallas, TX 75248

Schulte, Rainer (see also Kratz, Dennis; Tobias, Ronald), *TRANSLATION REVIEW*, Univ. of Texas-Dallas, Box 688, Richardson, TX 75080, 214-690-2093

Schultz, Alixa, Poetry (see also McCall, Karen E.), *GATHERING POST*, PO Box 3, St. Peter, MN 56082, 507-931-6391

Schultz, Cathy, Senior Editor, Med-Psych. Pub. (see also Brilliant, Marilyn A.; Knier, Timothy; Sitz, Carlton), Pine Mountain Press, Inc., Box 19746, West Allis, WI 53219, 414-778-1120

Schultz, Owen C., Postroad Press, Inc., PO Box 1212, Roanoke, VA 24006, 703-342-9797

Schulz, Paul J., Author (see also Ryan, Frank), Muse-ed Company, 14141 Margate Street, Van Nuys, CA 91331, 213-789-3310

Schwanz Pigorsch, Susan, Managing Editor (see also Mead, Howard), *WISCONSIN TRAILS*, PO Box 5650, Madison, WI 53705, 608-231-2444

Schwanz Pogorsch, Susan, Assistant Managing Editor (see also Mead, Howard), Tamarack Press, P.O.Box 5650, Madison, WI 53705, 608-231-2444

Schwartz, Howard, Editor, *CASINO & SPORTS*, 630 S. 11th St., Box 4115, Las Vegas, NV 89127, 702-382-7555

Schwartz, Howard, Editor (see also Luckman, John), GBC Press, Gambler's Book Club, 630 S. 11th St., Box 4115, Las Vegas, NV 89127, 702-382-7555

Schwartz, Howard, Editor, *SYSTEMS & METHODS*, 630 So. 11th St., Box 4115, Las Vegas, NV 89127, 702-382-7555

Schwartz, Irwin (see also Strauss, Robert; Persun, Terry L.), *MYTHOS*, Box 6236, Wilmington, DE 19804

Schwartz, Magi (see also Cleary, Michael; Saricyan-Jamieson, Ligia), *THE SOUTH FLORIDA POETRY REVIEW*, PO Box 7072, Hollywood, FL 33081, 305-474-5285

Scilken, Marvin H., Editor (see also Scilken, Mary P.), *THE U*N*A*B*A*S*H*E*D LIBRARIAN, THE "HOW I RUN MY LIBRARY GOOD" LETTER*, G.P.O. Box 2631, New York, NY 10116

Scilken, Mary P., Assoc. Editor (see also Scilken, Marvin H.), *THE U*N*A*B*A*S*H*E*D LIBRARIAN, THE "HOW I RUN MY LIBRARY GOOD" LETTER*, G.P.O. Box 2631, New York, NY 10116

Scithers, George H., Owlswick Press, Box 8243, Philadelphia, PA 19101, 215-EV2-5415

Scobie, Stephen, Associate Editor (see also Rooke, Constance), *THE MALAHAT REVIEW*, PO Box 1700, Victoria, British Columbia V8W 2Y2, Canada

Scobie, Stephen (see also Kostelanetz, Richard; Frank, Sheldon; Zelevansky, Paul; Higgins, Dick; Essary, Loris; Young, Karl), *PRECISELY*, PO Box 73, Canal Street, New York, NY 10013

Scott, A., *CANADIAN PUBLIC POLICY- Analyse de Politiques*, Room 039, MacKinnon Bldg., University of Guelph, Guelph, Ontario N1G 2W1, Canada, 519-824-4120 ext. 3330

Scott, Stanely J., Editor, *NORTHERN LIGHTS STUDIES IN CREATIVITY*, University of Maine at Presque Isle, Presque Isle, ME 04769, 207-764-0311

Scott, Virginia, Editor, Sunbury Press, 22 Catherine Street, Basement Workshop, New York, NY 10038

Scrimgeour, James R., Editor (see also Sutherland, Robert D.; McGowan, James; White, Curtis), *THE PIKESTAFF FORUM*, PO Box 127, Normal, IL 61761, 309-452-4831

Scrimgeour, James R., Editor (see also Sutherland, Robert D.; McGowan, James; White, Curtis), The Pikestaff Press, PO Box 127, Normal, IL 61761, 309-452-4831

Scrimgeour, James R., Editor (see also Sutherland, Robert D.), *THE PIKESTAFF REVIEW*, PO Box 127, Normal, IL 61761, 309-452-4831

Scupham, Peter (see also Mole, John), The Mandeville Press, 2 Taylor's Hill, Hitchin, Hertfordshire SG49AD, England

Seaburg, Alan, Poetry & Fiction Editor (see also Olsen, Humphrey A.), *SNOWY EGRET*, 205 S. Ninth St., Williamsburg, KY 40769, 606-549-0850

Searing, Susan (see also Loeb, Catherine), *FEMINIST COLLECTIONS: WOMEN'S STUDIES LIBRARY RESOURCES IN WISCONSIN*, 112A Memorial Library, 728 State Street, Madison, WI 53706, 608-263-5754

Searing, Susan (see also Loeb, Catherine), *FEMINIST PERIODICALS: A CURRENT LISTING OF CONTENTS*, 112A Memorial Library, 728 State Street, Madison, WI 53706, 608-263-5754

Searing, Susan (see also Loeb, Catherine), *NEW BOOKS ON WOMEN & FEMINISM*, 112A Memorial Library, 728 State Street, Madison, WI 53706, 608-263-5754

Searing, Susan (see also Loeb, Catherine), Women's Studies Librarian-at-Large, 112A Memorial Library, 728 State Street, Madison, WI 53706

Searle, Karen, Publisher & Editor (see also Baizerman, Suzanne), Arana Press Inc., PO Box 14-23849, St. Paul, MN 55114, 303-449-1170

Searle, Karen (see also Baizerman, Suzanne), Dos Tejedoras Fiber Arts Publications, 3036 N. Snelling, St. Paul, MN 55113

Searle, Karen, Publisher & Editor (see also Baizerman, Suzanne), *THE WEAVER'S JOURNAL*, PO Box 14-238, St. Paul, MN 55114

Seastone, Leonard, Tideline Press, P.O. Box 786, Tannersville, NY 12485, 518-589-6344

Segerstrom, Jane, Triad Press, PO Box 42006 1-D, Houston, TX 77242, 713-465-1463

Seglen (see also Engh; Eriksen; Madsen; Ostenstad), Futurum Forlag, Hjelmsgt. 3, 0355 Oslo 3, Norway, (02) 69 12 84

Seidler, C. M. (see also Wallace, Robert; Jacobson, Bonnie), Bits Press, Deptartment of English, Case Western Reserve Univ., Cleveland, OH 44106, 216-795-2810

Seidman, Michael, Editor-In-Chief, *THE ARMCHAIR DETECTIVE*, 129 West 56th Street, New York, NY 10019, 212-765-0900

Seidman, Michael, Editor-in-Chief (see also Penzler, Otto), The Mysterious Press, 129 West 56th Street, New York, NY 10019, 212-765-0923

Seijo, N., Palmyra Publications, Inc., PO Box 450004, Shenandoah Station, Miami, FL 33145, 858-6830

Sein, Nels, Coelacanth Publications, 55 Bluecoat, Irvine, CA 92714, 714-544-0914

Sein, Steve, Managing Editor (see also Agetstein, Stephen), *VIDEO 80 MAGAZINE*, 1250-17th Street, San Francisco, CA 94107, 415-863-8434

Seldin, Donna, *SOURCE NOTES IN THE HISTORY OF ART*, 10 Columbus Circle, Suite 1230, New York, NY 10019

Selgen (see also Engh; Eriksen; Madsen; Ostenstad), *GATEAVISA*, Hjelmsgt 3, 0355 Oslo 3, Norway, (02) 69 12 84

Selkin, Carl, Associate Editor (see also Shectman, Robin), *THE ALTADENA REVIEW*, P.O. Box 212, Altadena, CA 91001

Selkin, Carl, Associate Editor (see also Shectman, Robin), The Altadena Review, Inc., PO Box 212, Altadena, CA 91001

Sellin, Eric, Editor, *CELFAN REVIEW*, Department of French and Italian, Temple University, Philadelphia, PA 19122

Selman, L. H., Paperweight Press, 761 Chestnut Street, Santa Cruz, CA 95060, 408-427-1177

Seltzer, Barbara Hartley (see also Seltzer, Richard; Seltzer, Robert Richard; Seltzer, Heather Katherine; Seltzer, Michael Richard), The B & R Samizdat Express, PO Box 161, West Roxbury, MA 02132, 617-469-2269

Seltzer, Heather Katherine (see also Seltzer, Barbara Hartley; Seltzer, Richard; Seltzer, Robert Richard; Seltzer, Michael Richard), *The B & R Samizdat Express*, PO Box 161, West Roxbury, MA 02132, 617-469-2269

Seltzer, Michael Richard (see also Seltzer, Barbara Hartley; Seltzer, Richard; Seltzer, Robert Richard; Seltzer, Heather Katherine), *The B & R Samizdat Express*, PO Box 161, West Roxbury, MA 02132, 617-469-2269

Seltzer, Richard (see also Seltzer, Barbara Hartley; Seltzer, Robert Richard; Seltzer, Heather Katherine; Seltzer, Michael Richard), *The B & R Samizdat Express*, PO Box 161, West Roxbury, MA 02132, 617-469-2269

Seltzer, Robert Richard (see also Seltzer, Barbara Hartley; Seltzer, Richard; Seltzer, Heather Katherine; Seltzer, Michael Richard), *The B & R Samizdat Express*, PO Box 161, West Roxbury, MA 02132, 617-469-2269

Senay, Donna, President, Rainbow Publishing Co., PO Box 397, Chesterland, OH 44026, 216-256-8519

Seniuk, Lasha, Managing Editor (see also Pacey, Michael), *PRISM INTERNATIONAL*, E459-1866 Main Mall, University of British Columbia, Vancouver BC, Canada, 604-228-2514

Sennett, John (see also Bullen, Donald), *MAGIC CHANGES*, 553 W Oakdale #317, Chicago, IL 60657, 312-327-5606

Sergeant, Howard, *OUTPOSTS POETRY QUARTERLY,* 72 Burwood Road, Walton-On-Thames, Surrey KT12 4AL, England

Sergeant, Howard, Outposts Publications, 72 Burwood Rd, Walton-on-Thames, Surrey KT12 4AL, England, Walton-on-Thames 240712

Severin, C. Sherman (see also Bell, Rebecca S.), CSS Publications, PO Box 23, Iowa Falls, IA 50126, 515-648-2716; 243-6407

Severin, Dorothy Sherman, Professor, *BULLETIN OF HISPANIC STUDIES,* School Of Hispanic Studies, The University, PO Box 147, Liverpool L69 3BX, England, 051 709 6022 extn. 3055

Severin, Dorothy Sherman, Professor, Liverpool University Press, School of Hispanic Studies, The Univ., PO Box 147, Liverpool L69 3BX, England, 051 709 6022 extn. 3055

Sexson, Lynda, Co-Editor (see also Sexson, Michael), *CORONA,* Dept. of Hist. & Phil., Montana State University, Bozeman, MT 59717, 406-994-5200

Sexson, Michael, Co-Editor (see also Sexson, Lynda), *CORONA,* Dept. of Hist. & Phil., Montana State University, Bozeman, MT 59717, 406-994-5200

Sexton, Thomas, Poetry Editor (see also Spatz, Ronald; Liszka, James Jakob), *THE ALASKA QUARTERLY REVIEW,* Department of English/U of A, Anchorage, 3221 Providence, Anchorage, AK 99508, 907-786-1731

Seymour, James D., *SPEAHRhead: BULLETIN OF THE SOCIETY FOR THE PROTECTION OF EAST ASIANS' HUMAN RIGHTS,* PO Box 1212, Cathedral Station, New York, NY 10025

Shadle, Carolyn, *FOR PARENTS,* Interpersonal Communication Services, Inc., 7052 West Lane, Eden, NY 14057, 716-649-3493

Shah, Kirit N., Kirit N. Shah, 980 Moraga Avenue, Piedmont, CA 94611, 415-658-6970

Shambaugh, Joan Dibble, Acorn, 185 Merriam Street, Weston, MA 02193, 617-893-8661

Shambaugh, Joan Dibble, Editor, *TREES,* 185 Merriam Street, Weston, MA 02193, 617-893-8661

Shames, Terry, Assistant Editor (see also Woodhams, Stephen; Gabbard, D.C.; Gabbard, Dwight C.; Overson, Beth E.; Caquelin, Anthony; Salmon-Heynemen, Jana; Goodwin, Tema; Rajfur, Ted), *FICTION MONTHLY,* Malvolio Press, 545 Haight Street, Suite 67, San Francisco, CA 94117, 415-621-1646

Shane, Sheila (see also Rowe, Charlene M.), Rowe Publishing Corporation, 3906 N. 69th Street, Milwaukee, WI 53216, 414-438-0685

Shankel-Lecrenski, Miklyn, Co-Editor (see also Florence, Jerry), *HARDSCRABBLE,* Blue Sheep Press, 10th & Ingersoll, Coos Bay, OR 97420, 267-3104 ext. 244

Shanken, Phyliss, Philmer Enterprises, #4 Hunter's Run, Spring House, PA 19477, 215-643-2976

Shannon, Foster H. (see also Hewett, James), Green Leaf Press, PO Box 6880, Alhambra, CA 91802, 818-281-6809

Shannon, H.T., *ANAPRESS,* 114 Albert Road, South Melbourne, Melbourne, Victoria 3205, Australia, 697-0100

Shannon, Mike (see also Harrison, W. J.), *SPITBALL,* 1721 Scott Street, Covington, KY 41011, 606-261-3024

Shapard, Robert, Managing Editor (see also Garlington, Jack; Roberts, Nancy), *WESTERN HUMANITIES REVIEW,* University of Utah, Salt Lake City, UT 84112, 801-581-7438

Shar, Bob, Fiction Editor (see also Gibson, Becky Gould), *THE CRESCENT REVIEW,* PO Box 15065, Winston-Salem, NC 27103, 919-768-5943

Sharif, Jonaid, *THE SOUTHWESTERN REVIEW,* PO Box 44691, Lafayette, LA 70504, 318-231-6908

Sharp, Jonathan, Chandler & Sharp Publishers, Inc., 11A Commercial Blvd., Novato, CA 94947, 415-883-2353

Sharpe, D. W., Applied Probability Trust, Department of Probability and Statistics, The University, Sheffield S3 7RH, England, England

Sharpe, D.W., *MATHEMATICAL SPECTRUM,* Dept of Probability and Statistics, The University, Sheffield S3 7RH, England

Sharrard, Robert (see also Ferlinghetti, Lawrence; Peters, Nancy J.), City Lights Books, 261 Columbus Ave., San Francisco, CA 94133, 415-362-8193

Sharrard, Robert (see also Ferlinghetti, Lawrence; Peters, Nancy J.), *CITY LIGHTS JOURNAL,* 261 Columbus Avenue, San Francisco, CA 94133, 415-362-8193

Shattuck-Rosenfelt, Jane, Editor (see also Nestor, Sarah), Museum of New Mexico Press, PO Box 2087, Santa Fe, NM 87503, 505-827-6454

Shattuck-Rosenfelt, Jane, Editor, *EL PALACIO,* PO Box 2087, Santa Fe, NM 87503, 505-827-6454

Shaw, Darla K., Poetry Editor (see also Prophet, Colleen; Erickson, Dave), *COE REVIEW:Annual Anthology of Experimental Literature,* 1220 First Avenue N.E., Coe College, Cedar Rapids, IA 52402, 319-399-8660

Sheahen, Al, Editor, Gain Publications, PO Box 2204, Van Nuys, CA 91404, 818-785-1895

Sheahen, Al, Editor, *NATIONAL MASTERS NEWS,* PO Box 2372, Van Nuys, CA 91404, 818-785-1895

Sheard, Sarah (see also Bevington, Stan; Young, David; Davey, Frank; James, Clifford; Nichol, bp; Ondaatje, Michael; McCartney, Linda; Reid, Dennis), Coach House Press, 95 Rivercrest Road, Toronto, Ontario M6S 4H7, Canada, 416-767-6317

Shectman, Robin, Editor (see also Selkin, Carl), *THE ALTADENA REVIEW,* P.O. Box 212, Altadena, CA 91001

Shectman, Robin, Editor (see also Selkin, Carl), The Altadena Review, Inc., PO Box 212, Altadena, CA 91001

Sheehy, John, Associate Publisher (see also Kisley, Lorraine; Zaleski, Philip), *PARABOLA MAGA-ZINE,* 150 Fifth Avenue, New York, NY 10011, 212-924-0004

Sheffler, Natalie (see also Ayyildiz, Judy; Ferguson, Maurice; Bullins, Amanda; Nash, Valery; Steinke, Paul; Weinstein, Ann), *ARTEMIS,* PO Box 945, Roanoke, VA 24005, 703-981-9318

Shell, Jim (see also Kelly, David J.), Peloria Publications, PO Box 50263, Raleigh, NC 27607, 919-828-7576

Shelton, Donald (see also Cooper, Michael), GloryPatri Publishers, 2891 Richmond Road Suite 202, Lexington, KY 40509, 606-269-3391

Shep, R.L., Editor (see also Bach, Pieter), *THE TEXTILE BOOKLIST,* Box C-20, Lopez Island, WA 98261, 206-468-2021

Shepard, Judith (see also Shepard, Martin), The Permanent Press, RD 2, Noyac Road, Sag Harbor, NY 11963, 516-725-1101

Shepard, Judith (see also Shepard, Martin), The Second Chance Press, Rd 2, Noyac Road, Sag Harbor, NY 11963, 516-725-1101

Shepard, Martin (see also Shepard, Judith), The Permanent Press, RD 2, Noyac Road, Sag Harbor, NY 11963, 516-725-1101

Shepard, Martin (see also Shepard, Judith), The Second Chance Press, Rd 2, Noyac Road, Sag Harbor, NY 11963, 516-725-1101

Shephard, D., Woods Hole Press, PO Box 44, Woods Hole, MA 02543, 617-548-9600

Shepherd, George W., Jr. (see also Hawley, Edward A.; LeMelle, Tilden J.), *AFRICA TODAY,* c/o G.S.I.S, Univ of Denver, Denver, CO 80208

Shepherd, James M., President, Shepherd Publishers, 100 Sheriffs Place, Williamsburg, VA 23185, 804-229-0661

Sheppard, Ann (see also Weisman, Dale; Taylor, R.D.), Curbstone Publishing Co.- Austin/New York, PO Box 7445, Austin, TX 78712

Sheppard, Judith (see also Sheppard, Roger), Trigon Press, 117 Kent House Road, Beckenham, Kent BR3 1JJ, England, 01-778-0534

167

Sheppard, Roger (see also Sheppard, Judith), *Trigon Press*, 117 Kent House Road, Beckenham, Kent BR3 1JJ, England, 01-778-0534

Sherer, Joan M., *THE YELLOW BUTTERFLY*, The Yellow Butterfly Press, 835 West Carolina Street, Lebanon, OR 97355, 503-451-3011

Sherman, Jack (see also McCall, Karen E.; Olson, David), *THEATERWORK MAGAZINE*, 120 South Broad, Mankato, MN 56001, 507-345-7885

Sherman, James R., Pathway Books, 700 Parkview Terrace, Golden Valley, MN 55416, 612-377-1521

Sheroan, Dorsey F. (see also Lawrence, E.S.; de Faymonville, Denise), Wheat Forders, Box 6317, Washington, DC 20015, 202-362-1588

Sherraden, Jim, *FRONT STREET TROLLEY*, 2125 Acklen Avenue, Nashville, TN 37212

Sherraden, Jim, Trolley, Inc, 2125 Acklen Ave., Nashville, TN 37212

Sherwin, Dr. Byron L., Cabala Press, 2421 W. Pratt, Suite 810, Chicago, IL 60645, 312-761-0682

Shideler, James, *AGRICULTURAL HISTORY*, University of California Press, Berkeley, CA 94720, 415-642-7485

Shields, Mike, Publisher, *ORBIS*, 199 The Long Shoot, Nuneaton, Warwickshire CV11 6JQ, England, 0203-327440

Shields, Steven L., *RESTORATION*, PO Box 547, Bountiful, UT 84010, 801-298-4058

Shields, Steven L., Restoration Research, PO Box 547, Bountiful, UT 84010, 801-298-4058

Shinn, Duane, Keyboard Workshop, PO Box 192, Medford, OR 97501, 664-2317

Shinn, Sharon, Contributing Editor (see also Bieberle, Gordon F.; Ullman, Rosanne; Davis, Allison), *PUBLISHING TRADE*, 1495 Oakwood, Des Plaines, IL 60016, 312-298-8291

Shobe, John (see also Kelley, Kate), Divesports Publishing, PO Box 1397, Austin, TX 78767, 512-443-5883

Shoemaker, Jack (see also Shoemaker, Vicki), Sand Dollar, PO Box 7400, Landscape Station, Berkeley, CA 94707

Shoemaker, Vicki (see also Shoemaker, Jack), *Sand Dollar*, PO Box 7400, Landscape Station, Berkeley, CA 94707

Shouldice, Larry (see also Allard, Diane), *ELLIPSE*, Univ. de Sherbrooke, Box 10 Faculte des Arts, Sherbrooke, Quebec J1K2R1, Canada, 819-565-4576

Shows, Charles, Windsong Books International, Box 867, Huntington Beach, CA 92648

Shurtleff, William, The Soyfoods Center, PO Box 234, Lafayette, CA 94549, 415-283-2991

Shute, Allan, *MOUNTAIN STANDARD TIME*, 10144-89 Street, Edmonton, Alberta T5H 1P7, Canada

Shute, Allan, Tree Frog Press Limited, 10144-89 St., Edmonton, Alberta T5H 1P7, Canada, 403-429-1947

Sibley, Brian, *THE MERVYN PEAKE REVIEW*, 46 Belmont Lane, Chisleturst, Kent BR7 6BJ, England

Sicoli, Dan (see also Borgatti, Robert; Farallo, Livio), *SLIPSTREAM*, Slipstream Publications, Box 2071, New Market Station, Niagara Falls, NY 14301, 716-282-2616

Sieckmann, Jochen, Edition am Mehringdamm, PO Box 148, Rensselaer Falls, NY 13680, 315-344-2351

Siegel, Steven W., *TOLEDOT: The Journal of Jewish Genealogy*, 155 East 93rd Street, Suite 3C, New York, NY 10128, 212-427-5395

Siegler, Karl (see also Schendlinger, Mary; Robinson, David), Talon Books Ltd, 201/1019 East Cordova Street, Vancouver, British Columbia V6A 1M8, Canada, 604-253-5261

Silberg, Richard, Associate Editor (see also Jenkins, Joyce; Abbott, Steve), *POETRY FLASH*, PO Box 4172, Berkeley, CA 94704, 415-548-6871

Silkin, Jon (see also Glover, Jon; Wainwright, Jeffrey), Northern House, 179 Wingrove Road, Newcastle upon Tyne NE49DA, England

Silkin, Jon (see also Tracy, Lorna; Blackburn, Michael; Morgan, Richard), *STAND*, 179 Wingrove Road, Newcastle-on-Tyne NE49DA, England

Sill, Geoffrey M. (see also McQuilkin, Frank), *THE MICKLE STREET REVIEW*, 46 Centre Street, Haddonfield, NJ 08033, (609) 795-7887

Silva, Jayne (see also Tuthill, Stacy; Kerr, Walter H.; Zadravec, Katharine; Swope, Mary), Scop Publications, Inc., Box 376, College Park, MD 20740, 301-345-8747

Silver, Gary, Director, *MID-PENINSULA NEWS AND NOTES*, Mid-Peninsula Library Cooperative, 424 Stephenson Avenue, Iron Mountain, MI 49801, 906-774-3005

Silver, Gary, Director, Ralph W. Secord Press, Mid-Peninsula Library Cooperative, 424 Stephenson Avenue, Iron Mountain, MI 49801, 906-774-3005

Silverberg, Robert, Contributing Editor (see also Porter, Andrew; D'Ammassa, Don; Anderson, Kay; DiFate, Vincent; Pohl, Frederik; Jones, Stephen; Fletcher, Jo; Carmody, Larry), *SCIENCE FICTION CHRONICLE*, PO Box 4175, New York, NY 10163, 212-643-9011

Simmons, Jim (see also Addleman, Rex; Nading, Lee), *VERIDIAN*, PO Box 2324, Bloomington, IN 47402

Simms, Clif, Editor (see also Simms, Lynn L.), *WIDE OPEN: MAGAZINE OF POETRY*, Wide Open Press, 1150-A Caddington Center, Suite 108, Santa Rosa, CA 95401, 707-545-3821

Simms, Lynn L., Co-Editor (see also Simms, Clif), *WIDE OPEN: MAGAZINE OF POETRY*, Wide Open Press, 1150-A Caddington Center, Suite 108, Santa Rosa, CA 95401, 707-545-3821

Simms, Norman (see also Carlton, Charles), *MIORITA*, Dept of F.L.L.L., Univ of Rochester, Dewey Hall 482, Rochester, NY 14627

Simms, Norman, Outrigger Publishers, PO Box 13-049, Hamilton, New Zealand

Simms, Norman, *PACIFIC QUARTERLY MOANA*, PO Box 13-049, Hamilton, New Zealand

Simon, B., Rossi, PO Box 2001, Beverly Hills, CA 90213, 213-556-0337

Simon, Joan (see also Padgett, Ron; Waldman, Anne), Full Court Press, Inc., 138-140 Watts St., New York, NY 10013

Simon Ph.D., Julie, Marketing Director (see also Martens Ph.D., Rainer), Human Kinetics Pub. Inc., Box 5076, Champaign, IL 61820, 217-351-5076

Simpson, Chris (see also Beam, Joe; Bernstein, Carole; Caplan, Leslie; Rorke, Raymond; Sorensen, Sally Jo), *PAINTED BRIDE QUARTERLY*, 230 Vine Street, Philadelphia, PA 19106, 215-925-9914

Simpson, Lewis P. (see also Onley, James), *THE SOUTHERN REVIEW*, 43 Allen Hall, Louisiana State University, Baton Rouge, LA 70803, 504-388-5108

Simpson, Lucy Picco, *TABS: AIDS FOR ENDING SEXISM IN SCHOOL*, 744 Carroll Street #621, Brooklyn, NY 11215, 212-788-3478

Singer, Patricia (see also Frink, Sharon; Frakes, Carol), Seaworthy Press, 4200 Wisconsin Avenue NW, Suite 106-143, Washington, DC 20016, 1983

Singer, Philip, General Editor (see also Titus, Professor Elizabeth), Trado-Medic Books, 102 Normal Ave.(Symphony Circle), Buffalo, NY 14213, 716-885-3686

Singham, Nancy, Managing Editor, Vanguard Books, P.O. Box 3566, Chicago, IL 60654, 312-342-3425

Singleton, Ralph S. (see also Vietor, Joan E.), Lone Eagle Publishing, Inc., 9903 Santa Monica Blvd., Suite #204, Beverly Hills, CA 90212, 213-274-4766

Sitney, P. Adams (see also Mekas, Jonas; Melton, Hollis), *FILM CULTURE*, G. P. O. Box 1499, New York, NY 10001

Sitney, P. Adams (see also Mekas, Jonas; Melton, Hollis), Film Culture Non-Profit, Inc., GPO Box 1499, New York, NY 10001

Sitz, Carlton, Senior Editor (see also Brilliant, Marilyn A.; Knier, Timothy; Schultz, Cathy), Pine Mountain Press, Inc., Box 19746, West Allis, WI 53219, 414-778-1120

Skeens, Gary S., Editor (see also Moser, Robin S.), *GREEN FEATHER*, PO Box 2633, Lakewood, OH 44107

Skeens, Gary S., Exec. Editor (see also Moser, Robin S.), Quality Publications, Inc., PO Box 2633, Lakewood, OH 44107

Skeens, Gary S., Executive Editor (see also Moser, Robin S.), S-W Enterprises, PO Box 2633, Lakewood, OH 44107

Skelley, Jack, Fred & Barney Press, 1140½ Nowita Place, Venice, CA 90291, 213-392-2886

Skildum, Paige, Editor, *THE PHOTOLETTER*, Photosearch International, Department 56, Osceola, WI 54020, (715) 248-3800

Skildum, Paige, Editor, Photosearch International, Department 56, Osceola, WI 54020

Skiles, Jackie, *WOMEN IN THE ARTS BULLETIN/NEWSLETTER*, 325 Spring St, Room 200, New York, NY 10013, 212-691-0988

Skiles, Jackie, Editor, Women In The Arts Foundation, Inc., 325 Spring St, New York, NY 10013

Skinner, Elizabeth (see also Perras, Wayne; Scavone, Dave), *THE HIGH ROCK REVIEW*, PO Box 614, Saratoga Springs, NY 12866, 518-584-4080

Skinner, Knute, Editor (see also Hodson, Stanley), *THE BELLINGHAM REVIEW*, 412 N State Street, Bellingham, WA 98225, 206-734-9781

Skinner, Knute, Editor (see also Hodson, Stanley), Signpost Press Inc., 412 N State Street, Bellingham, WA 98225

Sklar, Morty, *THE SPIRIT THAT MOVES US*, PO Box 1585, Iowa City, IA 52244, 319-338-5569

Sklar, Morty, Ed-Publ., The Spirit That Moves Us, Inc., PO Box 1585, Iowa City, IA 52244, 319-338-5569

Skloot, Floyd, Assoc. Editor (see also Slate, Ron), *THE CHOWDER REVIEW*, 648 Canton Ave, Milton, MA 02186

Skrabanek, D. W. (see also Souby, Anne R.), S & S Press, PO Box 5931, Austin, TX 78763

Sky-Peck, Kathryn, Samuel Weiser, Inc., PO Box 612, York Beach, ME 03910, 207-363-4393

Slade, Joseph W., *THE MARKHAM REVIEW*, Horrmann Library, Wagner College, Staten Island, NY 10301

Slate, Ron, Editor, Chowder Chapbooks, 648 Canton Ave, Milton, MA 02186

Slate, Ron, Editor (see also Skloot, Floyd), *THE CHOWDER REVIEW*, 648 Canton Ave, Milton, MA 02186

Slezak, Ellen, Associate Editor (see also Meiselma, Stephanie), Pluribus Press, Inc. (A division of Teach'em, Inc.), 160 E. Illinois Street, Chicago, IL 60611, 312-467-0424

Sliney, Jean, Art Editor (see also Elliott, William; Rossi, Betty), *LOONFEATHER: Minnesota North Country Art*, Bemidji Community Arts Center, 426 Bemidji Avenue, Bemidji, MN 56601, 218-751-7570

Sloan, William, *FILM LIBRARY QUARTERLY*, c/o Museum of Modern Art, 11 West 53rd Street, New York, NY 10019

Slohm, Natalie, Natalie Slohm Associates, Inc., Box 273, Cambridge, NY 12816, 518-677-3040

Smalheiser, Marvin, Editor, *TAI CHI*, PO Box 26156, Los Angeles, CA 90026, 213-665-7773

Smalheiser, Marvin, Wayfarer Publications, PO Box 26156, Los Angeles, CA 90026

Small, Robert (see also Michael, Ann; Steptoe, Lamont B.; Gabriele, Mary), *HEAT*, 1220 S. 12th Street, 3rd Floor, Philadelphia, PA 19147, 215-271-6569 or 382-6644

170

Smart, Ian I. (see also Cyrus, Stanley A.), *AFRO-HISPANIC REVIEW*, 3306 Ross Place, NW, Washington, DC 20008, 202-966-7783

Smetzer, Mike, *NAKED MAN*, c/o English Department, Bowling Green State University, Bowling Green, OH 43403

Smetzer, Mike, Editor, Naked Man Press, c/o English Department, Bowling Green State Univesity, Bowling Green, OH 43403

Smith, Barbara (see also Lone Dog, Lcota; Rhodes, Gina; Oliveira, Ana), Kitchen Table: Women of Color Press, Box 2753, New York, NY 10185, 212-308-5389

Smith, Bill, *CODA: The Jazz Magazine*, Box 87 Stn. J., Toronto, Ont. M4J4X8, Canada, 416-593-7230

Smith, Bruce (see also Balakian, Peter), *GRAHAM HOUSE REVIEW*, Box 5000, Colgate University, Hamilton, NY 13346

Smith, Charlotte (see also Ferguson, David; Marunas, P. Raymond; Garber, Thomas; Padol, Brian; Gateff, Amy H.; Goldman, Bill), *BOX 749*, Box 749, Old Chelsea Station, New York, NY 10011, 212-98-0519

Smith, Chuck (see also Duran, Erin), Word for Today, PO Box 8000, Costa Mesa, CA 92628, 714-979-0706

Smith, Clark C., *THE SHORT-TIMER'S JOURNAL: SOLDIERING IN VIETNAM*, PO Box 9462, N. Berkeley Station, CA 94709

Smith, Clark C., Winter Soldier Archive, PO Box 9462, N. Berkeley Station, CA 94709, 415-527-0616

Smith, Donald, Gamma Books, 400 Nelson Road, Ithaca, NY 14850, 607-237-8801

Smith, Esther K. (see also Faust, Dikko), Purgatory Pie Press, 238 Mott 4B, New York, NY 10072, 212-925-3462

Smith, Genny, Genny Smith Books, 1304 Pitman Avenue, Palo Alto, CA 94301, 415-321-7247

Smith, Harry (see also Bernard, Sidney; Tolnay, Tom), *PULPSMITH*, 5 Beekman Street, New York, NY 10038

Smith, J. Beverley (see also Evans, D. Ellis; Livens, R. G.), *BULLETIN OF THE BOARD OF CELTIC STUDIES*, Univ. of Wales Press, 6 Gwennyth Street, Cathays, Cardiff CF2 4YD, Wales

Smith, James Clois, Jr., The Sunstone Press, PO Box 2321, Santa Fe, NM 87501, 505-988-4418

Smith, Karen J., The Informed Performer, PO Box 793, Ansonia Station, New York, NY 10011, 212-362-6377

Smith, Larry L., Editorial Director (see also LeBlond, William), Chronicle Books, 870 Market Street Suite 915, San Francisco, CA 94102, 415-777-7240

Smith, Lori C. (see also Cloke, Richard; Rodecker, Shirley J.), Cerulean Press (Subsidiary of Kent Publiations), 18301 Halsted St., Northridge, CA 91325

Smith, Lori C., Editor-in-Chief (see also Cloke, Richard; Rodecker, Shirley J.), Kent Publications, Inc., 18301 Halsted Street, Northridge, CA 91325, 213-349-2080

Smith, Lori C., Associate Editor (see also Cloke, Richard; Rodecker, Shirley J.), *SAN FERNANDO POETRY JOURNAL*, 18301 Halstead Street, Northridge, CA 91325

Smith, Mary Bround, *MINNESOTA LITERATURE NEWSLETTER*, 1 Nord Circle, St. Paul, MN 55110, 612-483-3904

Smith, Mary Carol, Editor, *THE A.L.S. FORUM & NEWSLETTER*, PO Box 21271, Eugene, OR 97402, 503-345-3043

Smith, Mary Carol, Editor and Publisher, Titania Publications, PO Box 21271, Eugene, OR 97402, 503-345-3043

Smith, Michael, Editor (see also Grady, Wayne), *BOOKS IN CANADA: A National Review Of Books*, 366 Adelaide St East, Toronto, Ontario M5A 3X9, Canada, 416-363-5426

Smith, Patrick, Pancake Press, 163 Galewood Circle, San Francisco, CA 94131, 415-648-3573

Smith, Paul, *START,* Burslem Leisure Centre, Market Place, Burslem, Stoke-on-Trent, ST6 3DS, England, 0782-813363

Smith, Quinn, *POETRY DETROIT,* 4709 Second, Apt 4, Detroit, MI 48201, 313-832-2537

Smith, Raymond J., Editor (see also Oates, Joyce Carol), *THE ONTARIO REVIEW,* 9 Honey Brook Drive, Princeton, NJ 08540

Smith, Raymond J., Editor (see also Oates, Joyce Carol), The Ontario Review Press, 9 Honey Brook Drive, Princeton, NJ 08540

Smith, Robert Ellis, *PRIVACY JOURNAL,* PO Box 15300, Washington, DC 20003, 202-547-2865

Smith, Ron (see also Guppy, Stephen; Bailey, Rhonda), Oolichan Books, P.O. Box 10, Lantzville, British Columbia V0R2H0, Canada, 604-390-4839

Smith, Sheryl, Poetry (see also Sapiro, Leland; Boggs, Redd; Emerson, Mary), *RIVERSIDE QUARTERLY,* Box 863-388, Wildcat Station, Plano, TX 75086, 214-234-6795

Smith, Steven G. (see also Maciejewksi, Jeffrey), *TREND MAGAZINE,* PO Box 15563, Milwaukee, WI 53215, 414-647-1944

Smith, Virgil, Catcher Press, 215 West Elm, Kent, OH 44240, 216-673-1880

Smith, William Jay (see also Payne, Robert; MacShane, Frank; Cook, Diane G.H.), *TRANSLATION,* 307A Mathematics, Columbia University, New York, NY 10027, 212-280-2305

Smith, William Jay (see also Cook, Diane G.H.; MacShane, Frank; Payne, Robert; Galvin, Dallas), Translation, 307A Mathematics, Columbia University, New York, NY 10027, 280-2305

Smothermon, Ron, Context Publications, 20 Lomita Avenue, San Francisco, CA 94122, (415) 664-4477

Smyth, Donna, Co-Editor (see also Clark, Susan; Conrad, Margaret), *ATLANTIS: A Women's Studies Journal/Journal D'Etudes Sur La Femme,* Mount Saint Vincent University, Halifax Nova Scotia B3M 2J6, Canada

Smyth, Robert B., Yellow Moon Press, 1725 Commonwealth Ave. #5, Brighton, MA 02135, 617-782-3183

Snider, Clifton (see also Mailman, Leo; Locklin, Gerald; Zepeda, Ray; Barker, David; Salinas, Judy; Kay, John), *MAELSTROM REVIEW,* 8 Farm Hill Road, Cape Elizabeth, ME 04107

Snowden, Elizabeth, Co-Editor (see also Parman, John), *DESIGN BOOK REVIEW,* 1414 Spring Way, Berkeley, CA 94708, 415-848-2001; 486-1956

Snowden, Roger, Bingo Bugle, Inc, PO Box 322, Gig Harbor, WA 98335, 206-265-6241

Snyder, Arnold (see also Finlay, Alison), *BLACKJACK FORUM,* 2000 Center St. #1067, Berkeley, CA 94704, 415-540-5209

Snyder, Arnold (see also Finlay, Alison), R.G.E., 2000 Center St. #1067, Berkeley, CA 94704

Snyder, Gary, Poet-at-Large (see also Lawson, Dr. Todd; Comen, Dr. Diane; Marsic, John; Rader, Steve; Monte, Oscar; Nishi, Mio; Ginsberg, Allen; Samolis, Dr. Sam; Graham, Joan; Ferlinghetti, Lawrence; Ramirez, Julio; Haynes, Dr. Robert; Morris, Dr. Richard), *ALPS MONTHLY,* PO Box 99394, San Francisco, CA 94109, 415-771-3431

Snyder, Jerry (see also Langeuin, Michael Peter), *MAGICAL BLEND,* PO Box 11303, San Francisco, CA 94101

Snyder, Jerry (see also Langevil, Michael), Magical Blend, PO Box 11303, San Francisco, CA 94101

Snyder, Margaret, Editor (see also McFarland, Ron; Buxton, Karen; Foriyes, Tina), *SNAPDRAGON,* English Department, University of Idaho, Moscow, ID 83843, 208-885-6156

Snyder, Richard, Co-Editor (see also McGovern, Robert), The Ashland Poetry Press, Ashland College, Ashland, OH 44805, 419-289-4096

Socolofsky, Homer, Book Review Editor (see also Higham, Robin; Clark, Patricia), *JOURNAL OF THE WEST,* 1531 Yuma, Manhattan, KS 66502, 913-532-6733; 539-3668

Soffer, Walter (see also Richard, Michel Paul; Kellogg, Peggy; Moss, Leonard), *THOUGHTS FOR ALL SEASONS: The Magazine of Epigrams*, State University College At Geneseo, Geneseo, NY 14454, 716-245-5336

Soled, Alex J., Chancery Publishers, Inc., 401 Washington Avenue, Baltimore, MD 21204, 301-821-5143

Solensten, Lori, Sunstone Publications, PO Box 788, Cooperstown, NY 13326, 607-547-8207

Somerville, Jane, *GAMBIT*, PO Box 1122, Marietta, OH 45750

Soos, *A POET*, 2745 Monterey Road #76, San Jose, CA 95111

Soos, *OCCASIONAL REVIEW*, 2745 Monterey Road #76, San Jose, CA 95111, 408-578-3546

Soos, Realities, 2745 Monterey Road #76, San Jose, CA 95111

Sorensen, Sally Jo, Managing Editor (see also Beam, Joe; Bernstein, Carole; Caplan, Leslie; Rorke, Raymond; Simpson, Chris), *PAINTED BRIDE QUARTERLY*, 230 Vine Street, Philadelphia, PA 19106, 215-925-9914

Sorenson, Elizabeth (see also Weaver, David), Great Circle Productions, 43A Upland Road, W. Somerville, MA 02144, 617-776-7072

Sorestad, Glen (see also Forrie, Allan; Sorestad, Sonia; O'Rourke, Paddy), Thistledown Press Ltd., 668 East Place, Saskatoon, Saskatchewan S7J2Z5, Canada, 374-1730

Sorestad, Sonia (see also Forrie, Allan; Sorestad, Glen; O'Rourke, Paddy), *Thistledown Press Ltd.*, 668 East Place, Saskatoon, Saskatchewan S7J2Z5, Canada, 374-1730

Sorfleet, John R., Managing Ed., *JOURNAL OF CANADIAN FICTION*, 2050 Mackay Street, Montreal, Quebec H3G 2J1, Canada

Sorrel, Lorraine (see also Leonard, Vickie; Douglas, Carol Anne; Lootens, Tricia; Henry, Alice; Fugh-Berman, Adrianne; Moira, Fran; Dejanikus, Tacie; Kulp, Denise), *OFF OUR BACKS*, 1841 Columbia Road NW Rm 212, Room 212, Washington, DC 20009, 202-234-8072

Sossaman, Stephen, New Traditions Publications, Allen Coit Road, Norwich Hill, Huntington, MA 01050

Sotsisowah, Editor, *AKWESASNE NOTES*, Mohawk Nation, Rooseveltown, NY 13683, 518-358-9531

Souby, Anne R. (see also Skrabanek, D. W.), S & S Press, PO Box 5931, Austin, TX 78763

Souder, Mark, *SIGN OF THE TIMES-A CHRONICLE OF DECADENCE IN THE ATOMIC AGE*, PO Box 6464, Portland, OR 97228, 503-238-8965

Soule, S. Janet (see also Straayer, Arny Christine; Johnson, Christine L.; Connelly, Dolores), Metis Press, Inc., PO Box 25187, Chicago, IL 60625

Southward, Keith (see also Hryciuk, Marshall; Coney, Denise), *INKSTONE*, PO Box 67, Station H, Toronto, Ontario M4C 5H7, Canada, 656-0356

Southward, Keith (see also Hryciak, Marshall; Coney, Denise), Inkstone Press, PO Box 67, Station H, Toronto, Ontario M4C 5H7, Canada

Sowell, Carol (see also Buh, Lisa), Barrington Press, 5933 Armaga Springs Road, Suite A, Palos Verdes, CA 90274, 213-544-2597

Spadaccini, Vic, Editor, Blue Sky Marketing, Incorporated, 2006 Arkwright Street, Saint Paul, MN 55117, 612-774-2920

Spangle, Douglas (see also Hower, Mary; Steger, Donna), *MOOSE MAGAZINE*, 3611 Southeast 15th, Portland, OR 97202, 503-232-3508

Spangler, David M. (see also Doremus, Paul N.), *LORIAN JOURNAL*, PO Box 147, Middleton, WI 53562, 608-833-0455

Spangler, David M. (see also Doremus, Paul N.), Lorian Press, PO Box 147, Middleton, WI 53562, 608-833-0455

Spatz, Ronald, Fiction Editor (see also Sexton, Thomas; Liszka, James Jakob), *THE ALASKA QUARTERLY REVIEW*, Department of English/U of A, Anchorage, 3221 Providence, Anchorage, AK 99508, 907-786-1731

Spector, Buzz, Editor (see also Porges, Timothy), *WHITE WALLS: A Magazine of Writings by Artists*, PO Box 8204, Chicago, IL 60680

Spector, Norma, Editor, *WREE-VIEW OF WOMEN*, 130 E 16th Street, New York, NY 10003

Speer, Allen, *HEMLOCKS AND BALSAMS*, Box 128, Lees-McRae College, Banner Elk, NC 28604, 704-898-4284

Spencer, Mickey (see also Taylor, Polly), *BROOMSTICK: A PERIODICAL BY, FOR, AND ABOUT WOMEN OVER FORTY*, 3543 18th Street, San Francisco, CA 94110, 415-552-7460

Spender, Philip, Asst. Editor (see also Theiner, George), *INDEX ON CENSORSHIP*, 39c Highbury Place, London N5 1QP, England, 01-359-0161

Sperling, Ehud C., President & Publisher (see also Sperling, Lisa), Inner Traditions/Destiny Books, 377 Park Ave. South, New York, NY 10016, 212-889-8350

Sperling, Lisa, Senior Editor (see also Sperling, Ehud C.), *Inner Traditions/Destiny Books*, 377 Park Ave. South, New York, NY 10016, 212-889-8350

Sperling, Roberta, *RUBBERSTAMPMADNESS*, PO Box 168, Newfield, NY 14867, 607-564-7673

Speth, Lee (see also Goodknight, Glen H.), *MYTHLORE*, PO Box 4671, Whittier, CA 90607

Spicer, David, *OUTLAW*, 323 Hodges Street, Memphis, TN 38111

Spicer, David, Editor (see also Tickle, Phyllis), *RACCOON*, 1407 Union Avenue, Suite 401, Memphis, TN 38104, (901) 357-5441

Spicer, David, Raccoon Editor (see also Tickle, Phyllis; Eason, Roger R.), St. Luke's Press, Suite 401, 1407 Union Avenue, Memphis, TN 38104, 901-357-5441

Spiegel, Richard, Co-Editor (see also Fisher, Barbara), Ten Penny Players, Inc., 799 Greenwich Street, New York, NY 10014, 212-929-3169

Spiegel, Richard, Co-Editor (see also Fisher, Barbara), *WATERWAYS: Poetry in the Main Stream*, 799 Greenwich St., New York, NY 10014

Spiegelman, Willard, Editor (see also McDougall, Betsy), *SOUTHWEST REVIEW*, Southern Methodist Univ., Dallas, TX 75275, 214-692-2263

Spielmann, Katherine, Editor (see also Stirling, Patty), *PUNCTURE*, 1674 Filbert #3, San Francisco, CA 94123, 415-771-5127

Spiess, Robert, *MODERN HAIKU*, PO Box 1752, Madison, WI 53701, 608-255-2660

Spilker, John, Associate Editor (see also Anbian, Robert; King, Dennis; Hellerman, Steve; Kosoua, Anna; Erfurdt, Jamie), *OBOE: A Journal of Literature & Fine Art*, 495 Ellis Street, Box 1156, San Francisco, CA 94102

Spingarn, Lawrence P., Perivale Press, 13830 Erwin Street, Van Nuys, CA 91401, 213-785-4671

Spiro, Penelope (see also Hawkes, John E.), *FEDORA*, PO Box 577, Siletz, OR 97380, 503-444-2757

Sprague, J.M., *CLARITY*, 3 Greenway, Berkhamsted, Herts HP4 3JD, England

Springer, Eleanor K., Publisher (see also Martin, Karen), *BUSINESS VIEW OF SOUTHWEST FLORIDA*, Collier County Magazines Inc., PO Box 1546, Naples, FL 33939, 813-263-7525

Springer, Garrett (see also Weldon, Paul), Indian Publications, 1869 2nd Avenue, New York, NY 10029

Springer, Jane, Managing Editor, Women's Educational Press, 16 Baldwin Street, Toronto, Ontario, Canada, 416-598-0082

Springer, Jane, Women's Press, 16 Baldwin Street, Toronto, Ontario M5T 1L2, Canada

Sprinker, Michael (see also Pfeil, Fred; Rice-Sayre, Laura), *THE MINNESOTA REVIEW*, Dept. of English, Oregon State University, Corvallis, OR 97331

Spurgeon, Dickie, Pantagraph, Southern Illinois University, Edwardsville, IL 62026

Spurgeon, Dickie, *SOU'WESTER*, Southern Illinois University, Edwardsville, IL 62026

Squires, Dana Leigh, Art Director (see also Foster, John), Lost Music Network, PO Box 2391, Olympia, WA 98507, 206-352-9735

Squires, Dana Leigh, Art Director (see also Foster, John), *OP: Independent Music*, PO Box 2391, Olympia, WA 98507, 206-866-7955, 352-9735

Sroda, George, George Sroda, Publisher, Amherst Jct., WI 54407, 715-824-3868

St. Cyr, Napoleon, *THE SMALL POND MAGAZINE OF LITERATURE*, PO Box 664, Stratford, CT 06497, 203-378-4066

St. John, David, Poetry Ed. (see also Fogarty, Robert; Holyoke, Tom; Miller, Nolan), *THE ANTIOCH REVIEW*, PO Box 148, Yellow Springs, OH 45387, 513-767-7386

Stablein, Marilyn (see also Masters, Heidi), Wash 'n Press, 5210-16th Street N.E., Seattle, WA 98105, 206-524-4385

Stach, Alex (see also Maas, Paula Dianne), *Western Sun Publications*, PO Box 1470, 290 S First Avenue, Yuma, AZ 85364, 602-782-4646

Stafford, Laura, Director, *GUEST EDITOR*, 179 Duane Street, New York, NY 10013, 212-925-6315

Stainsby, Charles, Editor (see also Nuttall, Suse), *LIBERAL NEWS*, 1 Whitehall Place, London SW1A2HE, England, 01 839 1533

Staley, Thomas F., Editor, Academic Publications, Univ of Tulsa, 600 S. College, Tulsa, OK 74104

Staley, Thomas F., *JAMES JOYCE QUARTERLY*, University of Tulsa, 600 S. College, Tulsa, OK 74104

Stanford, Don (see also Stanford, Judith), *JAM TO-DAY*, PO Box 249, Northfield, VT 05663

Stanford, Judith (see also Stanford, Don), *JAM TO-DAY*, PO Box 249, Northfield, VT 05663

Stanley, E.G. (see also Fleeman, J.D.; Hewitt, D.), *NOTES & QUERIES: for Readers & Writers, Collectors & Librarians*, Oxford Journals, Walton Street, Oxford 0X2 6DP, England

Stansberry, Domenic, Fiction Editor (see also Howell, Christopher), Lynx House Press, PO Box 800, Amherst, MA 01004, 503-777-3102

Stansberry, Domenic (see also Rayher, Ed; McGuill, Mike; Conoley, Gillian; Ruhl, Steven), *TIGHTROPE*, 72 Colonial Village, Amherst, MA 01002

Stanson, Diane, Associate Editor (see also Paladino, Thomas; Cutty, Robert B.), *THE THIRD WIND*, PO Box 8277, Boston, MA 02114

Stark, Mary, Associate Editor (see also Langlais, Jacques), *INTERCULTURE (Formerly THE MONCHANIN JOURNAL)*, Centre Interculturel Monchanin, 4917 St-Urbain, Montreal, Quebec H2T 2W1, Canada, 514-288-7229

Starnes, Jo Anne (see also Hershey, Jon), *THE OLD RED KIMONO*, Humanities, Floyd College, PO Box 1864, Rome, GA 30161, 404-295-6312

Starr, Carol, Editor, *WLW JOURNAL: News/Views/Reviews for Women and Libraries*, 2027 Parker Street, Berkeley, CA 94704

Starr, Carol, Editor (see also Josephine, Helen B.), Women Library Workers, 2027 Parker Street, Berkeley, CA 94704, 415-540-5322

Stathatos, John, Oxus Press, 16 Haslemere Rd., London N.8., England

Staton, Marjorie E., Juvenile (see also Peebles, J. Winston), Winston-Derek Publishers, Inc., Pennywell Drive, PO Box 90883, Nashville, TN 37209, 615-329-1319

Stec, Helen M., Success Publications, 2257 Elphinstone Street, Regina, Sask. S4T 3N9, Canada

Steele, Frank (see also Steele, Peggy; Oakes, Elizabeth), *PLAINSONG*, Box U245, Western Kentucky University, Bowling Green, KY 42101, 502-745-3043

Steele, Peggy (see also Steele, Frank; Oakes, Elizabeth), *PLAINSONG*, Box U245, Western Kentucky University, Bowling Green, KY 42101, 502-745-3043

Steffey, Ron Squire, B.O.O.S.T. Publishing Co. (Teen Esteem Publishing Co.), PO Box 7357, Portsmouth, VA 23707, 703-886-6172

Steger, Donna (see also Hower, Mary; Spangle, Douglas), *MOOSE MAGAZINE*, 3611 Southeast 15th, Portland, OR 97202, 503-232-3508

Steger, Linda, Articles (see also Cooper, Peter S.; Bean, Joyce Miller; Mitchell, Barbara; Fielding, Cynthia), *MIDWAY REVIEW*, 3400 West 11th Street, Suite 134, Chicago, IL 60655, 312-233-6002

Stein Charles, Contributing Editor (see also Quasha, George; Quasha, Susan; Martin, Michele; Coffey, Michael; Nedds, Trish; Kelly, Robert; Auster, Paul; Kamin, Franz; McClelland, Bruce), Station Hill Press, Station Hill Road, Barrytown, NY 12507, 914-758-5840

Stein, Charlotte M. (see also Rubenstein, Nancy; Radin, Jessica), Double M Press, 16455 Tuba Street, Sepulveda, CA 91343, 213-360-3166

Stein, Howard, Editor, *THE JOURNAL OF PSYCHOANALYTIC ANTHROPOLOGY*, 2315 Broadway, New York, NY 10024, 212-873-3760

Steinberg, David, Red Alder Books, Box 2992, Santa Cruz, CA 95063, 408-426-7082

Steinberg, Jon, *HEALTH/PAC BULLETIN*, 17 Murray Street, New York, NY 10007

Steiner, Peter, Summerthought Ltd., PO Box 1420, Banff, Alberta T0L0C0, Canada, 762-3919

Steinitz, Hans, Editor (see also Niers, Gert), *AUFBAU*, 2121 Broadway, New York, NY 10023, 212-873-7400

Steinke, Paul, Poetry & Fiction Editors (see also Ayyildiz, Judy; Ferguson, Maurice; Bullins, Amanda; Nash, Valery; Sheffler, Natalie; Weinstein, Ann), *ARTEMIS*, PO Box 945, Roanoke, VA 24005, 703-981-9318

Steinke, Russell (see also O'Brien, William; DiFranco, Anthony), *LONG POND REVIEW*, English Dept, Suffolk Community College, Selden Long Island, NY 11784

Steinle, Rita Juul, Contributing Editor (see also Kain, Sue; Walker, Lois V.; Hair, Jennie; Penha, James), *NEWSLETTER*, PO Box 773, Huntington, NY 11743

Steinman, Lisa (see also Reyes, Carlos), *HUBBUB*, 2754 S.E. 27th Avenue, Portland, OR 97202, 503-775-0370

Steinzor, Seth, Editor (see also Johnson, Ronna; Mabe, Eirard; Elder, John), *DARK HORSE*, Box 9, Somerville, MA 02143

Stephens, Christopher P., Ultramarine Publishing Co., Inc., PO Box 303, Hastings-on-Hudson, NY 10706, 914-478-2522

Stephens, Helen (see also Walatka, Pam Portugal; Main, Jody; Jamello, Nancy Portugal; Davis, Annette), Wild Horses Publishing Company, 12310 Concepcion Road, Los Altos Hills, CA 94022, 415-941-3396

Stephens, Jack, Editor-in-Chief (see also Wendell, Julia), The Galileo Press, Box 16129, Baltimore, MD 21218, 301-771-4544

Stephens, Jack, Editor (see also Wendell, Julia), *TELESCOPE*, Box 16129, Baltimore, MD 21218, 301-771-4544

Stephens, Meic (see also Finch, Peter), Oriel, 53 Charles St., Cardiff, Wales CF14ED, Great Britain, 0222-395548

Stephenson, Shelby, Editor (see also Macleod, Norman), *PEMBROKE MAGAZINE*, PO Box 60, PSU, Pembroke, NC 28372, 919-521-4214 ext 246

Steptoe, Lamont B. (see also Michael, Ann; Small, Robert; Gabriele, Mary), *HEAT*, 1220 S. 12th Street, 3rd Floor, Philadelphia, PA 19147, 215-271-6569 or 382-6644

Sterland, Julia, Editorial Assistant (see also Jay, Peter), Anvil Press Poetry, 69 King George St., London SE10 8PX, England, 01-858-2946

176

Sterling, Sharon (see also Godfrey, W.D.; Godfrey, Ellen; Truscott, Gerry; Allen, Kelly), Press Porcepic Limited, 235-560 Johnson St., Victoria, B.C. V8W 3C6, Canada, 604-381-5502

Stetler, Russell, Ramparts Press, Box 50128, Palo Alto, CA 94303, 415-325-7861

Stetser, Carol, Padma Press, PO Box 56, Oatman, AZ 86433

Stetser, Virginia M., Laridae Press, 3012 Wesley Avenue, Ocean City, NJ 08226, 609-399-3222

Stettan, Leonard, Art Editor, Design (see also Schechter, Ruth Lisa; Thomas, Dan B.; Bluestein, Dan T.; Crisci, Pat J.; Merrill, Susan), *CROTON REVIEW*, P.O. Box 277, Croton on Hudson, NY 10520, 914-271-3144

Stettner, Irving, Editor (see also Makowsky, Andrew), *STROKER*, 129 2nd Ave. No. 3, New York, NY 10003

Stetzel, Warren, Raven Rocks Press, 54118 Crum Road, Beallsville, OH 43716, 614-926-1705

Stevens, Paul Drew, Editor, Sharp & Dunnigan, PO Box 660, Forest Ranch, CA 95942, 916-891-5908

Stevens, Peter (see also McNamara, Eugene), Sesame Press, c/o English Dept Univ of Windosr, Windsor, Ontario N9B3P4, Canada

Stevens-Cox, G., *THOMAS HARDY YEARBOOK*, Mt Durand, St Peter Port, Guernsey CI, England

Stevens-Cox, Gregory (see also Stevens-Cox, James), Toucan, Mt. Durand, St Peter Port, Guernsey, England

Stevens-Cox, James (see also Stevens-Cox, Gregory), *Toucan*, Mt. Durand, St Peter Port, Guernsey, England

Stevenson, Jack, *THE LIVING COLOR*, 417 Euclid Ave, Elmira, NY 14905

Stevenson, Ralph L., Editor, Publisher, The Sirius League, PO Box 40507, Albuquerque, NM 87196, 505-262-0720

Stevroid, Lionel (see also Cotolo, F.M.; Tabor, B. Lyle; Savion, Thom; Clendaniel, Nancy), *FAT TUESDAY*, 853 N Citrus, Los Angeles, CA 90038

Stewart, Fern (see also De Mente, Boye), Phoenix Books/Publishers, P.O.Box 32008, Phoenix, AZ 85064, 602-952-0163

Stickney, John, Editor, League Books, PO Box 98101, Cleveland, OH 44101, 216-348-4544

Stickney, John, Editor, *POETS' LEAGUE of GREATER CLEVELAND NEWSLETTER*, PO Box 91801, Cleveland, OH 44101

Stiefel, Janice, The Second Hand, PO Box 204, Plymouth, WI 53073, 414-893-5226

Stilwell, Steve, *THE MYSTERY FANCIER*, 3004 E. 25th Street, Minneapolis, MN 55406, 612-729-9200

Stirling, Dale A., Editor & Publisher, *POETRY NORTH REVIEW*, 3809 Barbara Drive, Anchorage, AK 99503, 907-248-1294

Stirling, Patty, Articles Editor (see also Spielmann, Katherine), *PUNCTURE*, 1674 Filbert #3, San Francisco, CA 94123, 415-771-5127

Stocking, David M. (see also Stocking, Marion K.), *BELOIT POETRY JOURNAL*, Box 154, RFD 2, Ellinsworth, ME 04605, 207-667-5598

Stocking, David M. (see also Stocking, Marion K.), The Latona Press, RFD 2, Box 154, Ellsworth, ME 04605

Stocking, Marion K. (see also Stocking, David M.), *BELOIT POETRY JOURNAL*, Box 154, RFD 2, Ellinsworth, ME 04605, 207-667-5598

Stocking, Marion K. (see also Stocking, David M.), The Latona Press, RFD 2, Box 154, Ellsworth, ME 04605

Stoiaken, Larry, Editor-Chief (see also Marier, Don), *ALTERNATIVE SOURCES of ENERGY MAGAZINE*, 107 S. Central Avenue, Milaca, MN 56353, 612-983-6892

Stone, Bradley, El Camino Publishers, 4010 Calle Real Suite 4, Santa Barbara, CA 93110, 805-687-2959; 682-9340

Stone, Jenifer, Nova, Inc., PO Box 948, Rockefeller Center Station, New York, NY 10185

Stone, Ken, *THIRTEEN*, Box 392, Portlandville, NY 13834, 607-286-7500

Stone, Nancy, The New South Company, PO Box 24918, Los Angeles, CA 90024, 213-489-5700/299-7666

Storey, M. John, Publisher (see also Griffith, Roger), Garden Way Publishing Company, Schoolhouse Road, Pownal, VT 05261, 802-823-5108

Stork, Joe, *MERIP REPORTS*, PO Box 43445, Columbia Heights Station, Washington, DC 20010, 202-667-1188

Stoumen, Tatiana, Editor, *NETWORK*, Box 810, Gracie Station, New York, NY 10028, 212-737-7536

Straayer, Arny Christine (see also Johnson, Christine L.; Soule, S. Janet; Connelly, Dolores), Metis Press, Inc., PO Box 25187, Chicago, IL 60625

Strahan, Bradley R., Black Buzzard Press, 4705 South 8th Road, Arlington, VA 22204

Strahan, Bradley R., Publisher, Poetry Editor (see also Sullivan, Shirley G.; Black, Harold; Gill, Ursula), *VISIONS*, 4705 South 8th Road, Arlington, VA 22204, 703-521-0142

Strand, Eric (see also Strand, Mary), Maric Publishing, 203 North Fifth, Delavan, WI 53115, 414-728-3382

Strand, Mary (see also Strand, Eric), *Maric Publishing*, 203 North Fifth, Delavan, WI 53115, 414-728-3382

Strang, Steven (see also Reed, Catherine), *THE PALE FIRE REVIEW*, 162 Academy Avenue, Providence, RI 02908

Strange, Florence, Manzanita Press, PO Box 4027, San Rafael, CA 94903, 415-479-9636

Stranger, Ernest, Art Ed. (see also Malone, Marvin), *THE WORMWOOD REVIEW*, PO Box 8840, Stockton, CA 95208, 209-466-8231

Stranger, Ernest, Art Editor (see also Malone, Marvin), The Wormwood Review Press, P O Box 8840, Stockton, CA 95208, 209-466-8231

Strauss, David Levi, Editor, *ACTS*, 324 Bartlett Street #9, San Francisco, CA 94110, 415-647-2961

Strauss, Robert (see also Schwartz, Irwin; Persun, Terry L.), *MYTHOS*, Box 6236, Wilmington, DE 19804

Strauss, Susan, Editor (see also Cooley, Peter), *THE TULANE LITERARY MAGAZINE*, University Center, New Orleans, LA 70118

Strawn, John T., Strawn Studios Inc., 208 Fifth Street, West Des Moines, IA 50265, 515-224-4760

Strempek, Stephen (see also McPhee, Linda; Anastas, Charles), *HARBOR REVIEW*, c/o English Department, UMass/Boston, Boston, MA 02125

Stricker, N.L. ('Sam'), The Biting Idge Press, 410 Central Ave., #6, Sandusky, OH 44870

Strizek, Norman (see also Willkzie, Philip; Emond, Paul; Young, Tom; Baysans, Greg), *JAMES WHITE REVIEW; a gay men's literary quarterly*, PO Box 3356, Traffic Station, Minneapolis, MN 55403, 612-291-2913; 871-2248

Strobel, Ray G., Printed Matter Publishing Company Inc, 1151 W. Webster, Chicago, IL 60614, 312-870-8742

Stroblas, Laurie, Editor (see also Fox, Jane), *CAROUSEL*, 4800 Sangamore Road, Bethesdn, MD 20816, 301-229-0930

Stroh, Luella, Assistant Editor (see also Zimmer, David), Good Vibes, PO Box 32413, Fridley, MN 55432, 612-571-9274

Strong, Bethany, Parable Press, 136 Gray Street, Amherst, MA 01002, 413-253-5634

Stroud, Drew, Saru, Kawauchi Urban Heights 203, Kawauchi Sanjunin-machi 5-85, Sendai-shi, Miyagi-ken 980, Japan

Struna, Nancy, *QUEST*, Box 5076, Champaign, IL 61820, 217-351-5076

Stuart, Friend, Editor, *MASTER THOUGHTS*, PO Box 37, San Marcos, CA 92069, 619-746-9430

Stuart, Kiel, Assistant Editor (see also Wendell, Leilah), *UNDINAL SONGS*, Undinal Songs Press, PO Box 70, Oakdale, NY 11769, 516-589-8715

Stubblefield, Al, Writer's Service, Inc., PO Box 152, Miami Springs, FL 33166, 305-887-2398

Stuhlman, Daniel D., BYLS Press, 6247 N. Francisco Avenue, Chicago, IL 60659, 312-262-8959

Stumm, Jim, *LIVING FREE*, Box 29, Hiler Branch, Buffalo, NY 14223

Style, Al, Pacific Gallery Publishers, PO Box 19494, Portland, OR 97219

Succop, Greg, Publisher, Editor (see also Doria, Charles), *ASSEMBLING*, Box 1967, Brooklyn, NY 11202

Succop, Greg (see also Doria, Charles), Assembling Press, PO Box 1967, Brooklyn, NY 11202

Sugden, Sherwood, Managing Editor (see also Hospers, John), The Hegeler Institute, Box 600, La Salle, IL 61301, 815-223-1231

Sugden, Sherwood, Sherwood Sugden & Company, Publishers, 1117 Eighth Street, La Salle, IL 61301, 815-223-1231

Sugden, Sherwood J.B., Managing Editor (see also Hospers, John), *THE MONIST: An International Quarterly Journal of General Philosophical Inquiry.*, Box 600, La Salle, IL 61301, 815-223-1231

Sukenick, Ronald, Publisher (see also Russell, Charles; Ratner, Rochelle; Tytell, John; Hoover, Russell), *THE AMERICAN BOOK REVIEW*, PO Box 188, Cooper Station, New York, NY 10003, 212-621-9289

Sulberg, Walter (see also Schramm, Henning), IKO-Verlag Fur Interkultu Relle Kommunikation, PO Box 90 90 65, 6000 Frankfurt 90, West Germany

Sullivan, Jamie (see also Vorda, Allan; DeSalvo, Jules), *THE FABULIST REVIEW*, PO Box 770851, Houston, TX 77215, 713-978-6191

Sullivan, Mary Jane (see also Martin, Stephen-Paul; Royal, Richard; Ensler, Eve; Millis, Christopher; Kiefer, Paul; Sanders, Catherine Marie), *CENTRAL PARK*, P.O. Box 1446, New York, NY 10023

Sullivan, Patrick S. (see also Oei, Perry), *CEILIDH: AN INFORMAL GATHERING FOR STORY & SONG*, 986 Marquette Lane, Foster City, CA 94404, 415-341-6228

Sullivan, Patrick S. (see also Oei, Perry), Ceilidh, Inc., 986 Marquette Lane, Foster City, CA 94404, 415-341-6228

Sullivan, Shirley G., Associate Editor (see also Strahan, Bradley R.; Black, Harold; Gill, Ursula), *VISIONS*, 4705 South 8th Road, Arlington, VA 22204, 703-521-0142

Sullivan, Wm. J., *CELEBRATION*, 2707 Lawina Road, Baltimore, MD 21216, 301-542-8785

Summers, Anthony J. (see also Finnegan, James J.; Ravens, Debi), Cornerstone Press, PO Box 28048, St. Louis, MO 63119, 314-752-3703

Summers, Anthony J. (see also Finnegan, James J.; Ravens, Debi), *IMAGE MAGAZINE*, P.O. Box 28048, St. Louis, MO 63119, 314-752-3703

Sun Bear, Co-Editor (see also Wabun; Nimimosha), Bear Tribe Publishing, PO Box 9167, Spokane, WA 99209, 509-258-7755

Sun Bear (see also Wabun; Nimimosha), *MANY SMOKES EARTH AWARENESS MAGAZINE*, PO Box 9167, Spokane, WA 99209, 509-258-7755

Super, Gary Lee (see also Goodman, Michael), Nexus Press, 608 Ralph McGill Boulevard N.E., Atlanta, GA 30312, (404) 577-3579

Sura, Thurman, Senior Editor (see also DeRay, Norton), Seed Center, PO Box 658, Garberville, CA 95440, 707-986-7575

Suryanarayan, Indu, Editor (see also Letcher, Tina; Tyler, Larry; Woodson, Jon), *NORTHEAST JOURNAL*, PO Box 217, Kingston, RI 02881

Sussler, Betsy, Bomb, PO Box 178, Prince Station, New York City, NY 10012, 212-431-3943

Sussler, Betsy, *BOMB MAGAZINE*, PO Box 178, Prince Station, New York City, NY 10012, 212-431-3943

Sussman, Art (see also Frazier, Louie), Garcia River Press, PO Box 527, Pt. Arena, CA 95468, 707-882-9956

Sutherland, Allen (see also Rippington, Geoff; Polley, Simon; Bailey, Chris; Swinden, Dave), British Science Fiction Assoc. Ltd., 269 Wykeham Road, Reading RG6 1PL, England, 0734-666142

Sutherland, Allen (see also Bailey, Chris; Swinden, Dave), *FOCUS*, 269 Wykeham Road, Reading RG6 1PL, England

Sutherland, Robert D., Editor (see also Scrimgeour, James R.; McGowan, James; White, Curtis), *THE PIKESTAFF FORUM*, PO Box 127, Normal, IL 61761, 309-452-4831

Sutherland, Robert D., Editor (see also Scrimgeour, James R.; McGowan, James; White, Curtis), The Pikestaff Press, PO Box 127, Normal, IL 61761, 309-452-4831

Sutherland, Robert D., Editor (see also Scrimgeour, James R.), *THE PIKESTAFF REVIEW*, PO Box 127, Normal, IL 61761, 309-452-4831

Swan, Pete, Art Editor (see also Mortimer, Peter), *IRON*, 5 Marden Terrace, Cullercoats, North Shields, Tyne & Wear NE30 4PD, England, 0632-531901

Swan, Pete, Reviews Editor (see also Mortimer, Peter; Lees, John), Iron Press, 5 Marden Terrace, Cullercoats, North Shields Tyne & Near NE30 4PD, England

Swanberg, Ingrid, Editor (see also Woessner, Warren; Hilton, David), *ABRAXAS*, 2518 Gregory St., Madison, WI 53711, 608-238-0175

Swanberg, Ingrid, Editor, Ghost Pony Press, 2518 Gregory Street, Madison, WI 53711, 608-238-0175

Swann, Brian, Associate Editor (see also Raiziss, Sonia; de Palchi, Alfredo; Foerster, Richard), *CHELSEA*, Box 5880, Grand Central Station, New York, NY 10163

Swann-Rogak, Lisa, Revelations Press, Inc., PO Box 77, Norwood, NJ 07648

Swansea, Charleen, Red Clay Books, 1710 I'On Avenue, Sullivans Island, SC 29482, 803-883-9262

Swanson, Murray A., Medic Publishing Co., PO Box 89, Redmond, WA 98052, 881-2883

Swanson, Robert, Poetry Editor (see also Gilbert, Elliot; Schell, Nixa), *THE CALIFORNIA QUARTERLY*, 100 Sproul Hall, Univ of Calif, Davis, CA 95616

Swartz, F. Randolph, Footnotes, Box 328, Philadelphia, PA 19105

Swenson, Tree (see also Hamill, Sam), Copper Canyon Press/Copperhead, P.O. Box 271, Port Townsend, WA 98368

Swiderski, Richard M., Tree Shrew Press, 285 Adams Street, Holliston, MA 01746

Swift, Mary, Managing Editor (see also Lang, Doug; Rosenzweig, Phyllis; Wittenberg, Clarissa; Fleming, Lee), *WASHINGTON REVIEW*, P O Box 50132, Washington, DC 20004, 202-638-0515

Swinden, Dave (see also Rippington, Geoff; Polley, Simon; Bailey, Chris; Sutherland, Allen), British Science Fiction Assoc. Ltd., 269 Wykeham Road, Reading RG6 1PL, England, 0734-666142

Swinden, Dave (see also Bailey, Chris; Sutherland, Allen), *FOCUS*, 269 Wykeham Road, Reading RG6 1PL, England

Swisher, Doug, Technical Editor (see also Welch, Jennifer Groce; Welch, Rick), *PUDDING MAGAZINE*, 2384 Hardesty Dr. So., Columbus, OH 43204, 614-279-4188

Swisher, Doug, Technical Editor (see also Welch, Jennifer Groce; Welch, Rick), Pudding Publications, 2384 Hardesty Drive, South, Columbus, OH 43204, 614-279-4188

Swope, Mary (see also Tuthill, Stacy; Kerr, Walter H.; Zadravec, Katharine; Silva, Jayne), Scop Publications, Inc., Box 376, College Park, MD 20740, 301-345-8747

Sykes, Michael, *FLOATING ISLAND,* Floating Island Publications, P.O. Box 516, Point Reyes Station, CA 94956

Sykes, Michael, Floating Island Publications, PO Box 516, Pt Reyes Sta, CA 94956

Szabo, Marilyn (see also Berg, Neal; Udinotti, Angese), *CHIMERA,* 4215 N. Marshall Way, Scottsdale, AZ 85251, 602-275-7924

Szebedinszky, Janos, Editor (see also Raymond, Stephen), and books, 702 South Michigan, Suite 836, South Bend, IN 46618

T

Tabor, B. Lyle (see also Cotolo, F.M.; Savion, Thom; Stevroid, Lionel; Clendaniel, Nancy), *FAT TUESDAY,* 853 N Citrus, Los Angeles, CA 90038

Tagett, Richard (see also Mariah, Paul), Manroot Books, Box 982, So San Francisco, CA 94080

Taggart, David P., Director of Communications Services, The Media Institue, 3017 M Street NW, Washington, DC 20007, 202-298-7512

Tajima, Renee, Managing Editor (see also Lee, C.N.; Chow, P.; Chin, R.; Chu, B.; Francia, L.; Wu, S.; Lew, Walter; Hahn, Tomie; Kwan, S.), *BRIDGE: ASIAN AMERICAN PERSPECTIVES,* Asian Cine-Vision, Inc., 32 E Broadway, New York, NY 10002, 212-925-8685

Takagi, Paul (see also Platt, Tony), *CRIME AND SOCIAL JUSTICE,* 2701 Folsom Street, San Francisco, CA 94110, 415-550-1703

Tall, Deborah, *SENECA REVIEW,* Hobart & William Smith Colleges, Geneva, NY 14456, 315-789-5500 ext. 437

Talley, Ruth, Director of Publications, International Childbirth Education Association, Inc., PO Box 20048, Minneapolis, MN 55420

Tam Mossman, Editor (see also Teacher, Lawrence; James Nelson), Running Press, 125 South Twenty-Second Street, Philadelphia, PA 19103, 215-567-5080

Tamar, Rima, Publisher's contact (see also Tulku, Tarthang), Dharma Publishing, 2425 Hillside Avenue, Berkeley, CA 94704

Tammaro, Thom (see also Coghill, Sheila; Koontz, Tom; Lowe, Kyrla), *BARNWOOD,* RR 2, Box 11C, Daleville, IN 47334

Tammaro, Thom (see also Koontz, Tom; Coghill, Sheila), The Barnwood Press, RR 2, Box 11C, Daleville, IN 47334, 317-378-0921

Tanis, Norman E., Editor, Santa Susana Press, University Libraries, CSUN, 18111 Nordhoff Street, Northridge, CA 91330, 213-885-2271

Tapley, Lance, Editor (see also Pawlowski, Lois), *COPING,* Box 2439, Augusta, ME 04330, 207-622-1179

Tapley, Lance, Publisher, Heron Books, 86 Winthrop Street, PO Box 2439, Augusta, ME 04330, 207-622-1179

Tapp, Roland W. (see also Baird, J. Arthur), The Iona Press, Box C-3181, Wooster, OH 44691, 216-262-2300 ext. 470

Tarachow, Michael, Pentagram, Box 379, Markesan, WI 53946, 414-398-2161

Tarakan, Sheldon L. (see also Curtin, Nancy), *E. A. R. for Children,* 40 Holly Lane, Roslyn Heights, NY 11577, 516-621-2445

Tarbell, Jim, An Apple Press, Box 90, Mendocino, CA 95460, 707-937-4275

Tarbell, Jim, *BIG RIVER NEWS,* Box 169, Mendocino, CA 95460, 707-937-4020

Tarbell, Jim, Big River Publishing Company, Box 169, Mendocino, CA 95460, 707-937-4020

Tarbell, Jim (see also Tarbell, Judith; Marshall, Lucie), *RIDGE REVIEW*, Box 90, Mendocino, CA 95460, 707-937-4275

Tarbell, Judith (see also Tarbell, Jim; Marshall, Lucie), *RIDGE REVIEW*, Box 90, Mendocino, CA 95460, 707-937-4275

Tarlen, Carol, Associate Editor (see also Belfiglio, Genevieve), *REAL FICTION*, 298-9th Avenue, San Francisco, CA 94118

Tarlen, Carol, Assistant Editor (see also Joseph, David), Red Wheelbarrow Press, 298 9th Avenue, San Francisco, CA 94118, 415-387-3412

Tarlen, Carol, Assistant Editor (see also Joseph, David), *WORKING CLASSICS*, 298 9th Avenue, San Francisco, CA 94118, 415-387-3412

Tarver, David P., *AQUATICS*, 2416 McWest Street, Tallahassee, FL 32303, 904-562-1870

Taryor, Nya Kwiawon (see also Min, D.), Strugglers' Community Press, 2003 West 67th Place, Chicago, IL 60636, 312-776-6400

Taskans, Andris, *PRAIRIE FIRE*, 374 Donald Street, 3rd Floor, Winnipeg MB R3B 2J2, Canada, 204-942-6134

Tassinar, Lamberto (see also D'Alfonso, Antonio; Caccia, Fulvio; Ramirez, Bruno), *VICE VERSA*, P.O. Box 633, Sta N.D.G., Montreal, Quebec H4A 3R1, Canada

Tate, Cassandra, J & B Publishers, Box 2866, Taos, NM 87571

Tate, Eugene D., Editor, *CANADIAN JOURNAL OF COMMUNICATION*, St. Thomas More College, 1437 College Drive, Saskatoon, Saskatchewan, Canada, 306-343-4561

Tatelbaum, Brenda L., Brush Hill Press, PO Box 96, Boston, MA 02137, 617-333-0612

Tatelbaum, Brenda L., *EIDOS: EROTICA FOR WOMEN*, PO Box 96, Boston, MA 02137, 617-333-0512

Tavernier-Courbin, Jacqueline, *THALIA: Studies in Literary Humor*, Dept of English, Univ of Ottawa, Ottawa KN1 6N5, Canada, 613-231-2311

Taylor, Alexander (see also Doyle, Judy), Curbstone Press, 321 Jackson Street, Willimantic, CT 06226, 423-9190

Taylor, Constance, Fathom Publishing Co., Box 821, Cordova, AK 99574, 907-424-3116

Taylor, Duane, Editor (see also Galvin, Zanne T.), *ILLINOIS WRITERS REVIEW*, PO Box 562, Macomb, IL 61455, 217-357-2225

Taylor, Jack (see also Walker, Tom), Boyd & Fraser Publishing Company, 3627 Sacramento St., San Francisco, CA 94118, 415-346-0686

Taylor, James D., ParkSide Press Publishing Co., 17221 E. 17th Street, Santa Ana, CA 92701, 714-541-5160

Taylor, Joe, *SWALLOW'S TALE MAGAZINE*, PO Box 4328, Tallahassee, FL 32315, 386-8069

Taylor, Michael, Fiction Editor (see also Conway, Don; Gibbs, Robert; Trethewey, Eric; Hawkes, Robert; Butlin, Ron; Thompson, Kent; Davey, Bill; Boyles, Ann; Bauer, William), *THE FIDDLE-HEAD*, The Observatory, Univ. New Brunswick, PO Box 4400, Fredericton, NB E3B 5A3, Canada, 506-454-3591

Taylor, Polly (see also Spencer, Mickey), *BROOMSTICK: A PERIODICAL BY, FOR, AND ABOUT WOMEN OVER FORTY*, 3543 18th Street, San Francisco, CA 94110, 415-552-7460

Taylor, R.D. (see also Sheppard, Ann; Weisman, Dale), Curbstone Publishing Co.- Austin/New York, PO Box 7445, Austin, TX 78712

Taylor, Robert (see also Patten, Karl), *WEST BRANCH*, Department of English, Bucknell University, Lewisburg, PA 17837, 717-524-4591

Taylor, Robert T. (see also Taylor, William R.), Editorial Review, 1009 Placer Street, Butte, MT 59701, 406-782-2546

Taylor, W. Thomas, Associate Editor (see also Kirshenbaum, Sandra; Bigelow, Charles), *FINE PRINT: A Review for the Arts of the Book*, P O Box 3394, San Francisco, CA 94119, 415-776-1530

Taylor, William R. (see also Taylor, Robert T.), Editorial Review, 1009 Placer Street, Butte, MT 59701, 406-782-2546

te Neues, Hendrik, Managing Partner (see also Ashley, Robin), te Neues Publishing Company, 15 East 76th Street, New York, NY 10021, 212-288-0265

Teacher, Lawrence, Editoral Director (see also Tam Mossman; James Nelson), Running Press, 125 South Twenty-Second Street, Philadelphia, PA 19103, 215-567-5080

Teague, Toney (see also Bradley, Beth; Thompson, Sandra S.), *ANGELSTONE*, 316 Woodland Drive, Birmingham, AL 35209, 205-870-7281

Teague, Toney (see also Bradley, Beth; Thompson, Sandra S.), Angelstone Press, 316 Woodland Drive, Birmingham, AL 35209, 205-870-7281

Tembeck, Shoshana, Managing Editor (see also Utne, Eric), *THE UTNE READER*, LENS Publishing Co., 4306 Upton Avenue South, Minneapolis, MN 55410, 612-929-2670

Tennyson, Doris M., Director Publications and Print Production (see also Darling, Denise L.), Hanley-Wood, Inc., 15th and M Streets N W, Washington, DC 20005, 202-822-0394

Tennyson, G.B. (see also Wortham, Thomas), *NINETEENTH-CENTURY FICTION*, University of California Press, Berkeley, CA 94720, 415-642-7485

Tenpas, Kathleen M. (see also Leach, Susan L.), *ARACHNE*, Arachne, Inc., 162 Sturges Street, Jamestown, NY 14701, 716-488-0417

Terrell, C.F. (see also Hatlen, Burton), National Poetry Foundation, 305 EM Building, University of Maine, Orono, ME 04469, 207-581-3814

Terrell, C.F. (see also Hatlen, Burton), *PAIDEUMA*, 305 EM Building, University of Maine, Orono, ME 04469, 207-581-3814

Terrell, C.F. (see also Hatlen, Burton), *SAGETRIEB*, 305 EM Building, University of Maine, Orono, ME 04469, 207-581-3814

Terrill, Thomas S., Editor-in-Chief, *COUNTERFORCE: (A QUARTERLY COMMENTARY RE: STANDARD ENGLISH)*, 522 Gloria Drive, Baton Rouge, LA 70819, 505-892-8635

Terrill, Thomas S., Dolly Varden Publications, 522 Gloria Drive, Baton Rouge, LA 70819, 504-275-8148

Tetreault, Wilfred F. (see also Clements, Robert W.), American Business Consultants, Inc., 1540 Nuthatch Lane, Sunnyvale, CA 94087, 408-732-8931/738-3011

Tharpe, Jac L., Advisory Editor (see also Prenshaw, Peggy W.; Polk, Noel; Richardson, Thomas J.; Saunders, Cheryl), *SOUTHERN QUARTERLY: A Journal of the Arts in the South*, Box 5078, Southern Stn., USM, Hattiesburg, MS 39406, 601-266-4370

Theiner, George, Editor (see also Spender, Philip), *INDEX ON CENSORSHIP*, 39c Highbury Place, London N5 1QP, England, 01-359-0161

Thoenen, B. (see also Huang, J.; Jacobson, J.; Cohen, M.; McKale, A.), *THE DROOD REVIEW OF MYSTERY*, Box 8872, Boston, MA 02114

Thom, Heather, Book Reviews Editor (see also Osborne, Anne; Martindale, Sheila; Hancock, Geoff; Gibson, Brenda; Lennard, Susan), *CANADIAN AUTHOR & BOOKMAN*, 25 Ryerson Aveune, 131 Bloor Street W, Toronto, Ontario M5t 2P3, Canada, 416-364-4203

Thomas, Dan B., Editor (see also Schechter, Ruth Lisa; Bluestein, Dan T.; Crisci, Pat J.; Merrill, Susan; Stettan, Leonard), *CROTON REVIEW*, P.O. Box 277, Croton on Hudson, NY 10520, 914-271-3144

Thomas, Diane, Hunter Publishing, Co., P.O. Box 9533, Phoenix, AZ 85068, 602-944-1022

Thomas, F. Richard, *CENTERING: A Magazine of Poetry*, ATL EBH, Michigan State University, E. Lansing, MI 48824

Thomas, F. Richard, Years Press, Dept. of ATL, EBH, Michigan State Univ, E. Lansing, MI 48824, 517-332-5983

Thomas, Hazel F., Consultant (see also Wicker, Nina A.; Thomas, Kate Kelly), *MANNA*, Route 8, Box 368, Sanford, NC 27330

Thomas, Irv, *BLACK BART*, PO Box 48, Canyon, CA 94516

Thomas, Kate Kelly, Consultant (see also Wicker, Nina A.; Thomas, Hazel F.), *MANNA*, Route 8, Box 368, Sanford, NC 27330

Thomas, Lew, Not-For-Sale-Press, 420 F 4th Street, c/o Harold Jones, Tucson, AZ 85705, 415-647-4290

Thomas, Sherry, Spinsters, Ink, 803 De Haro Street, San Francisco, CA 94107, 415-647-9360

Thomas, Virginia, Senior Editor (see also Lund, Peder C.), Paladin Enterprises, Inc., PO Box 1307, Boulder, CO 80306, 303-443-7250

Thompson, Catherine (see also Balsamo, Ron; Hughes, John E.; Lee, Jean C.; Reed, W.A.; Reed, Vicki; Dennis, Deborah), *FARMER'S MARKET*, PO Box 1272, Galesburg, IL 61402

Thompson, Jacqueline, Editorial Services Co., 96 State Street, Brooklyn, NY 11201, 212-625-2485

Thompson, Joyce (see also Donnelly, Margarita; Malone, Ruth; Wendt, Ingrid; Wilner, Eleanor; Caday, Jan; Mclean, Cheryl; Gordon, Rebecca; Domitrovich, Lisa; Jenkins, Meredith), *CALYX: A Journal of Art and Literature by Women*, PO Box B, Corvallis, OR 97339, 503-753-9384

Thompson, Kent, Fiction Editor (see also Conway, Don; Gibbs, Robert; Trethewey, Eric; Hawkes, Robert; Butlin, Ron; Taylor, Michael; Davey, Bill; Boyles, Ann; Bauer, William), *THE FIDDLEHEAD*, The Observatory, Univ. New Brunswick, PO Box 4400, Fredericton, NB E3B 5A3, Canada, 506-454-3591

Thompson, Pat (see also Youra, Dan), Still Publishing, PO Box 353, Port Ludlow, WA 98365, 206-437-9172

Thompson, Sandra S. (see also Bradley, Beth; Teague, Toney), *ANGELSTONE*, 316 Woodland Drive, Birmingham, AL 35209, 205-870-7281

Thompson, Sandra S. (see also Bradley, Beth; Teague, Toney), Angelstone Press, 316 Woodland Drive, Birmingham, AL 35209, 205-870-7281

Thomson, Derick S., *GAIRM*, 29 Waterloo Street, Glasgow, Scotland

Thomson, Derick S., Gairm Publications, 29 Waterloo Street, Glasgow, Scotland

Thomson, R.D.B., *CANADIAN SLAVONIC PAPERS*, Dept. of Slavic Languages & Literatures, University of Toronto, Toronto, Ontario M5S 1A1, Canada

Thomson, T.L. (see also Fitting, Frances), San Diego Publishing Company, PO Box 9222, San Diego, CA 92109, 619-698-5105

Thorne, J. (see also Finley, Sara; McAllister, Paul W.), Three Tree Press, PO Box 10044, Lansing, MI 48901

Thornton, Elizabeth (see also Dietz, Chris; Gregory, Michael), The Bisbee Press Collective, Drawer HA, Bisbee, AZ 85617

Thorpe, Lynne, Parkhurst Press, PO Box 143, Laguna Beach, CA 92652, 714-494-3092

Thorsgood, Antoinette (see also B'orlaug, Ruby), Ide House, Inc., 4631 Harvey Drive, Mesquite, TX 75149, 214-681-2552

Thrasivoulos, Jacquelyn, Coordinating Editor, Reference Series, Porter Sargent Publishers, Inc., 11 Beacon St., Boston, MA 02108, 617-523-1670

Tickle, Phyllis, Managing Editor (see also Spicer, David), *RACCOON*, 1407 Union Avenue, Suite 401, Memphis, TN 38104, (901) 357-5441

Tickle, Phyllis, Senior Editor (see also Spicer, David; Eason, Roger R.), St. Luke's Press, Suite 401, 1407 Union Avenue, Memphis, TN 38104, 901-357-5441

Tierney, Frank (see also Clever, Glenn), Borealis Press Limited, 9 Ashburn Drive, Nepean Ontario, Canada, 613-224-6837

Tierney, Frank M. (see also Clever, W. Glenn), *JOURNAL OF CANADIAN POETRY*, 9 Ashburn Drive, Nepean Ontario, Canada, (613) 224-6837

Tindal, Amalia, *READER'S CHOICE*, 205 Station S, Toronto, Ontario M5M 4L7, Canada, 416-783-7028

Tinsley, Lyn D., *ILLINOIS LIBERTARIAN*, 822 Thacker Street, Des Plaines, IL 60016, 312-297-8219

Tipton, David (see also Borman, Kevin), Rivelin Press, 24 Aireville Road, Bradford, England, 0274-498135

Titus, Mary, *CAROLINA QUARTERLY*, Greenlaw Hall 066-A, Univ of N. Carolina, Chapel Hill, NC 27514, 919-962-0244

Titus, Professor Elizabeth, Associate Editor (see also Singer, Philip), Trado-Medic Books, 102 Normal Ave.(Symphony Circle), Buffalo, NY 14213, 716-885-3686

Tobias, Michael (see also Gosney, Michael; Lapolla, Paul), Avant Books, 3719 Sixth Avenue, San Diego, CA 92103, 619-295-0473

Tobias, Ronald (see also Schulte, Rainer; Kratz, Dennis), *TRANSLATION REVIEW*, Univ. of Texas-Dallas, Box 688, Richardson, TX 75080, 214-690-2093

Toczek, Nick, Editor (see also Lovelock, Yann), *THE LITTLE WORD MACHINE*, 5 Beech Terrace, Undercliffe, Bradford, West Yorkshire, BD3 0PY, England

Tollers, Vincent L., Editor (see also O'Donnell, Mary Ann; Kiernan, Robert F.), *LITERARY RESEARCH NEWSLETTER*, Department of English and World Literature, Manhattan College, Bronx, NY 10471, 212-920-0121

Tolnay, Tom (see also Smith, Harry; Bernard, Sidney), *PULPSMITH*, 5 Beekman Street, New York, NY 10038

Tomlinson, T. B., Managing Editor (see also Goldberg, S. L.), *THE CRITICAL REVIEW*, History of Ideas Unit, Australian National University, G.P.O. Box 4, Canberra, A.C.T. 2601, Australia

Topham, J., Editor, American Poetry Press, PO Box 2013, Upper Darby, PA 19082, 215-352-5438

Torczyner, Leslie, Editor (see also Durst, James), *SONGSMITH JOURNAL*, PO Box 608036, Chicago, IL 60626, 312-274-0054

Torgerson, Donolas (see also Paehlke, Robert), *ALTERNATIVES: Perspectives in Society and Environment*, Trent University, c/o Traill College, Peterborough, On K9J7B8, Canada

Toro, Louis, Editor, *FARMING UNCLE*, Box 91, Liberty, NY 12754

Toulson, S. (see also Lewis, R.), Keepsake Press, 26 Sydney Road, Richmond, Surrey, England, 01 940 9364

Touster, Eva (see also Davie, Donald; Kilroy, James), *CUMBERLAND POETRY REVIEW*, Poetics, Inc., PO Box 120128 Acklen Station, Nashville, TN 37212, 615-373-8948

Towner, George, *THE ECPHORIZER*, San Francisco Regional Mensa, 814 Gail Avenue, Sunnyvale, CA 94086, 408-738-0430

Townley, John C., Editor, *CONCERTINA AND SQUEEZEBOX MAGAZINE*, PO Box 68, Gloucester Point, VA 23062, 804-642-2305

Townley, John C., Ocran Industries, Route 1, Box 718, White Stone, VA 23578, 804-435-6494

Townley, John M., Jamison Station Press, 7115 Pembroke Drive, Reno, NV 89502, 702-359-2178

Townsend, Guy M., Brownstone Books, 1711 Clifty Drive, Madison, IN 47250, 812-273-6908

Tracy, Jack W., Gaslight Publications, 112 East Second, Bloomington, IN 47401, 812-332-5169

Tracy, Lorna (see also Silkin, Jon; Blackburn, Michael; Morgan, Richard), *STAND*, 179 Wingrove Road, Newcastle-on-Tyne NE49DA, England

Trawick, Leonard (see also Turner, Alberta), Cleveland State Univ. Poetry Center, Dept English, Cleveland State Univ, Cleveland, OH 44115, 216-687-3986

Trechak, John, *AMBASSADOR REPORT*, PO Box 4068, Pasadena, CA 91106

Tremblay, Bill, Poetry (see also Ude, Wayne; Crow, Mary), *COLORADO STATE REVIEW*, 322 Eddy, English Department, Colorado State University, Fort Collins, CO 80523, 303-491-6428

Trembly, Dean, Erin Hills Publishers, 1390 Fairway Dr, San Luis Obispo, CA 93401, (805) 543-3050

Trethewey, Eric, Poetry Editor (see also Conway, Don; Gibbs, Robert; Hawkes, Robert; Butlin, Ron; Taylor, Michael; Thompson, Kent; Davey, Bill; Boyles, Ann; Bauer, William), *THE FIDDLEHEAD*, The Observatory, Univ. New Brunswick, PO Box 4400, Fredericton, NB E3B 5A3, Canada, 506-454-3591

Trimble, Bjo (see also Trimble, John), *TO THE STARS*, 3963 Wilshire Blvd. #142, Los Angeles, CA 90010

Trimble, John (see also Trimble, Bjo), *TO THE STARS*, 3963 Wilshire Blvd. #142, Los Angeles, CA 90010

Trotta, Anna, J & A Enterprises, 5522 West Acoma Road, Glendale, AZ 85306

Trotta, Anna, *"STARR"*, 5522 West Acoma Road, Glendale, AZ 85306, 602-978-4740

Trowbridge, C.H. (see also Nestor, Jack), *THE HOBOKEN TERMINAL*, The Hoboken Terminal, PO Box 841, Hoboken, NJ 07030, 201-798-1696

Troy, Betty (see also Troy, Con), Trojan Books, 1330 Cleveland Avenue, Wyomissing, PA 19610, 215-372-8041

Troy, Con, Publisher (see also Troy, Betty), *Trojan Books*, 1330 Cleveland Avenue, Wyomissing, PA 19610, 215-372-8041

Truesdale, C. W., New Rivers Press, Inc., 1602 Selby Avenue, St. Paul, MN 55104, 612-645-6324

Truffer, Michael, *SKYDIVING*, Po Box 189, Deltona, FL 32728

Trujillo, Paul (see also Huntress, Diana), *RIO GRANDE WRITERS NEWSLETTER*, PO Box 40126, Albuquerque, NM 87106, 505-242-1050

Truscott, Gerry (see also Godfrey, W.D.; Godfrey, Ellen; Sterling, Sharon; Allen, Kelly), Press Porcepic Limited, 235-560 Johnson St., Victoria, B.C. V8W 3C6, Canada, 604-381-5502

Truscott, Robert Blake, Reviews (see also Neeld, Judith; McCormick, Pat), *STONE COUNTRY*, PO Box 132, Menemsha, MA 02552, 617-693-5832

Trusky, T. (see also Burmaster, O.; Boyer, D.), Ahsahta, Boise State University, Department of English, Boise, ID 83725, 208-385-1190 or 1999

Tucker, George Elliott, *THE INDEPENDENT JOURNAL OF PHILOSOPHY*, 38, rue St-Louis-in-l'Ile, F-75004 Paris, France

Tucker, George Elliott, The Independent Philosophy Press, 38, rue St-Louis-in-l'Ile, F-75004 Paris, France

Tucker, Martin, *CONFRONTATION*, English Dept., Long Island University, C.W. Post, Greenvale, NY 11548

Tuel, Ted (see also Conway, Connie), *MISSOURI VALLEY SOCIALIST*, PO Box 31321, Omaha, NE 68131, 402-553-2314

Tulku, Tarthang, President (see also Tamar, Rima), Dharma Publishing, 2425 Hillside Avenue, Berkeley, CA 94704

Turner, Alberta (see also Trawick, Leonard), Cleveland State Univ. Poetry Center, Dept English, Cleveland State Univ, Cleveland, OH 44115, 216-687-3986

Turner, Irene (see also Wellman, Don; Franzen, Cole), *O.ARS*, Box 179, Cambridge, MA 02238, 617-641-1027

Tuthill, Stacy (see also Kerr, Walter H.; Zadravec, Katharine; Swope, Mary; Silva, Jayne), Scop Publications, Inc., Box 376, College Park, MD 20740, 301-345-8747

Tuynman, Carol E., Editor-In-Chief, *EAR MAGAZINE*, 325 Spring Street, #208, New York City, NY 10013, 212-807-7944

Tvedten, Brother Benet, O.S.B., *BLUE CLOUD QUARTERLY*, Blue Cloud Abbey, Box 98, Marvin, SD 57251, 605-432-5528

Twine, Jeff, Synerjy, Box 4790, Grand Central Station, New York, NY 10017, 212-865-9595

Twine, Jeff, *SYNERJY: A Directory of Energy Alternatives*, Box 4790, Grand Central Station, New York, NY 10017, 212-865-9595

Tyler, Larry, Associate Editor (see also Letcher, Tina; Suryanarayan, Indu; Woodson, Jon), *NORTHEAST JOURNAL*, PO Box 217, Kingston, RI 02881

Tytell, John (see also Sukenick, Ronald; Russell, Charles; Ratner, Rochelle; Hoover, Russell), *THE AMERICAN BOOK REVIEW*, PO Box 188, Cooper Station, New York, NY 10003, 212-621-9289

U

Ude, Wayne, Fiction (see also Tremblay, Bill; Crow, Mary), *COLORADO STATE REVIEW*, 322 Eddy, English Department, Colorado State University, Fort Collins, CO 80523, 303-491-6428

Udinotti, Angese (see also Szabo, Marilyn; Berg, Neal), *CHIMERA*, 4215 N. Marshall Way, Scottsdale, AZ 85251, 602-275-7924

Ulery, L. K., Psychic Books, 440 Avalon Place, Oxnard, CA 93033, 805-488-8670

Ulisse, Peter, Co-Editor (see also Young, Virginia Brady; Harding, May), *CONNECTICUT RIVER REVIEW: A Journal of Poetry*, 184 Centerbrook Road, Hamden, CT 06518, 203-281-0235

Ullman, Rosanne, Managing Editor (see also Bieberle, Gordon F.; Davis, Allison; Shinn, Sharon), *PUBLISHING TRADE*, 1495 Oakwood, Des Plaines, IL 60016, 312-298-8291

Ulrich, Betty (see also Bailey, Marilyn; Hall, John), *THE INKLING JOURNAL*, PO Box 128, Alexandria, MN 56308, 612-762-2020

Ulrich, Betty (see also Bailey, Marilyn; Hall, John), Inkling Publications, Inc., PO Box 128, Alexandria, MN 56308, 612-762-2020

Upasaka Chou Li-ren, Chinese Editor (see also Bhikshuni Heng Ch'ih; Bhikshuni Heng Ch'ing; Bhikshuni Heng Tao), *VAJRA BODHI SEA*, 1731 15th St, Gold Mountain Monastery, San Francisco, CA 94103, 861-9672

Uphoff, Joseph A., Jr., Director, *Arjuna Library Press* , 1025 Garner Street, Box 18, Colorado Springs, CO 80905

Uphoff Jr., Joseph A., Director, *JOURNAL OF REGIONAL CRITICISM*, 1025 Garner Street, Box 18, Colorado Springs, CO 80905

Urban, Tom (see also Doty, Ruth; Valentine, Jody), *BLUE BUILDINGS*, 1215 25th Street #F, Des Moines, IA 50311, 515-277-2709

Urfer, Pamela (see also Jones, Judie), Creative Arts Development, 144 Viking Court, Soquel, CA 95073, 408-475-2396

Urick, Kevin, The White Ewe Press, Box 996, Adelphi, MD 20783, 301-439-1470

Urie, Sherry, Sherry Urie, RFD #3, Box 63, Barton, VT 05822, 802-525-4482

Urioste, Pat, Contributing Editor ('Feedback') (see also Fulton, Len; Ferber, Ellen; Clifton, Merritt; Jerome, Judson), *THE SMALL PRESS REVIEW*, P.O. Box 100, Paradise, CA 95969, 916-877-6110

Urushibara, Hideko, Asst. Administrator (see also Ainlay Jr., Thomas; Zuckerman, Matthew), Tokyo English Literature Society (TELS), TELS 'Tomeoki', Koishikawa Post Office, Bunkyo-ku, Tokyo 112, Japan, 03-312-0481

Usher, Peter D., *THE ASTRONOMY QUARTERLY*, Box 35549, Tucson, AZ 85740, 602-297-4797

Utne, Eric, Publisher, Editor (see also Tembeck, Shoshana), *THE UTNE READER*, LENS Publishing Co., 4306 Upton Avenue South, Minneapolis, MN 55410, 612-929-2670

V

Vajda, David C., *PTOLEMY/BROWNS MILLS REVIEW*, Box 908, Browns Mills, NJ 08015, 609-893-7594

Vale, V., *RE/SEARCH*, 20 Romolo, Suite B, San Francisco, CA 94133, 415-362-1465

Vale, V., Re/Search Publications, 20 Romolo, Suite B, San Francisco, CA 94133, 415-362-1465

Valenti, Dan, Cellarway Press, PO Box 1845, Pittsfield, MA 01201

Valenti, Dan, *LITERATIONS*, PO Box 2204, Pittsfield, MA 01202

Valentine, Jody (see also Doty, Ruth; Urban, Tom), *BLUE BUILDINGS*, 1215 25th Street #F, Des Moines, IA 50311, 515-277-2709

Van Atta, Marian (see also Wilcox, Kathleen), Geraventure Corp., PO Box 2131, Melbourne, FL 32902, 305-723-5554

Van Atta, Marian (see also Wilcox, Kathleen), *LIVING OFF THE LAND, Subtropic Newsletter*, PO Box 2131, Melbourne, FL 32902, 305-723-5554

Van Dyke, Annette (see also Howard, Cheryl), Woman Works Press, 622 Oakdale, Saint Paul, MN 55107, 612-291-8684

Van Hooft, Karen S., Managing Editor (see also Keller, Gary D.), Bilingual Press, Office of the Graduate School, SUNY-Binghamton, Binghamton, NY 13901, 607-724-9495

Van Hooft, Karen S., Managing Editor (see also Keller, Gary D.), *BILINGUAL REVIEW/Revista Bilingue*, Office of the Graduate School, SUNY-Binghamton, Binghamton, NY 13901, 313-487-0042

Van Kirk, Sylvia, Editor (see also Nuse, B.; Newton, J.; Zavitz, C.; Rooney, F.; Andersen, M.; Wine, J.; Prentice, A.; Scane, J.; Caplan, Paula), *RESOURCES FOR FEMINIST RESEARCH/DOCUMENTA-TION SUR LA RECHERCHE FEMINISTE*, Ont Inst for Stud in Educ, Centre for Women's Studies in Education, 252 Bloor Street W., Toronto, Ontario M5S 1V6, Canada, 416-923-6641

Van Troyer, Gene (see also Frazier, Robert), Science Fiction Poetry Assoc., 8350 Poole Avenue, Sun Valley, CA 91352, 818-768-4970

van Valkenburg, Rick (see also McBee, Denis; Henderson, Jock), *BEATNIKS FROM SPACE*, Box 8043, Ann Arbor, MI 48107, 313-668-6867

van Valkenburg, Rick (see also McBee, Denis; Henderson, Jock), The Neither/Nor Press, Box 8043, Ann Arbor, MI 48107, 313-668-6867

Vander Werff, Engbert, The Van Press, PO Box 6053, London ON N5V 2Y3, Canada, 519-453-4529

Vandermeulen, Carl, The Middleburg Press, Box 166, Orange City, IA 51041, 712-737-4198

Vangelisti, Paul (see also McBride, John), *INVISIBLE CITY*, PO Box 2853, San Francisco, CA 94126

Vangelisti, Paul (see also McBride, John), Red Hill Press, San Francisco + Los Angeles, PO Box 2853, San Francisco, CA 94126

Vannatta, Dennis, Review and Criticism Editor (see also Murphy, Russell; Jauss, David; Wojahn, David), *CRAZYHORSE*, Dept of English, Unviersity of Arkansas at Little Rock, Little Rock, AR 72204, 501-569-3160

Vas Dias, Robert (see also Frazer, Tony; Robinson, Ian), *NINTH DECADE*, 52 Cascade Avenue, London N10, United Kingdom, 01-444-8591

Vas Dias, Robert, Permanent Press, 52 Cascade Avenue, London N10, United Kingdom

Vas Dias, Robert (see also Buck, Paul; Patterson, Ian), Spectacular Diseases, 83(b) London Road, Peterborough, Cambs, England

188

Vaughan, M.K., Chief Editor (see also Parchman, J.I.), Mallema Press, Box 22485, Houston, TX 77227, 713-850-0481

Vaughan, Thomas, Editor-In-Chief (see also Knuth, Priscilla), *OREGON HISTORICAL QUARTERLY,* 1230 S.W. Park Ave., Portland, OR 97205, 503-222-1741

Veenendaal, Cornelia (see also Pedrick, Jean; Aisenberg, Nadya), Rowan Tree Press, 124 Chestnut Street, Boston, MA 02108, 617-523-7627

Venn, Lisa, Devida Publication, 9115 Reisterstown Road, Owings Mills, MD 21117, 301-363-2093

Verlag, K. G. Saur, Hans Zell Publishers, PO Box 56, Oxford OX1 3EL, England, 0865-512934

Vernuccio Jr., Frank V., Editor-in-Chief, *THE SPACE PRESS,* Vernuccio Publications, 645 West End Avenue, New York, NY 10025, 212-724-5919

Viano, Emilio C., *VICTIMOLOGY AN INTERNATIONAL JOURNAL,* P O Box 39045, Washington, DC 20016, 703-528-8872

Vidal, Gore, Consulting Editor (see also Lesser, Wendy; Bowles, Paul; Berger, John; Hass, Robert; Wasserman, Steve), *THE THREEPENNY REVIEW,* PO Box 9131, Berkeley, CA 94709, 415-849-4545

Vietor, Joan E. (see also Singleton, Ralph S.), Lone Eagle Publishing, Inc., 9903 Santa Monica Blvd., Suite #204, Beverly Hills, CA 90212, 213-274-4766

Vilips, Kathryn L. (see also Holley, Barbara; Carter, Kaye Edwards), *EARTHWISE LITERARY CALENDAR,* PO Box 680-536, Miami, FL 33168

Villa, Jose Garcia (see also Cowen, John), *BRAVO,* 1081 Trafalgar Street, Teaneck, NJ 07666, 201-836-5922

Villa, Jose Garcia, King and Cowen (New York), 1081 Trafalgar Street (John Cowen), Teaneck, NJ 07666, 201-836-5922

Villani, Jim, Editor (see also Sayre, Rose; Peffer, George; Remick, Jace), *PIG IRON,* P.O. Box 237, Youngstown, OH 44501, 216-744-2258

Villani, Jim, Editor (see also Sayre, Rose; Murcko, Terry; George Peffer), Pig Iron Press, P.O. Box 237, Youngstown, OH 44501

Villegas, Robert, Jr., Lion Enterprises, 8608 Old Dominion Court, Indianapolis, IN 46231, 219-369-9498

Vincent, Bob, Main Track Publications, 12435 Ventura Court, Studio City, CA 91604, 213-506-0151

Vincent, Stephen, Momo's Press, 45 Sheridan, San Francisco, CA 94103, 415-863-3009

Vinciguerra, Theresa, The Poet Tree, Inc, 2791 24th St. #8, Sacramento, CA 95818, 616-739-1885

Vinciguerra, Theresa, *QUERCUS,* 2791 24th Street, Suite #8, Sacramento, CA. 95818, 916-739-1885

Vines, Jay, *ULULATUS,* 3006 South 40th St., Fort Smith, AR 72903

Vineyard, Paula L., Editor, Work At Home Press, PO Box 5520, Ocala, FL 32678, 904-237-6095

Vining, Donald, The Pepys Press, 1270 Fifth Avenue, New York, NY 10029, 212-348-6847

Virato, Swami, *NEW FRONTIER,* 129 N 13th Street, Philadelphia, PA 19107, 215-235-0312

Virato, Swami, New Frontier Education Society, 129 N 13th Street, Philadelphia, PA 19107, 215-235-0312

Vitucci, Donna D., Poetry Editor (see also Gonzalez, Lupe A.; Feinberg, Karen), La Reina Press, PO Box 8182, Cincinnati, OH 45208

Vlli Diemer, *CONNEXIONS,* 427 Bloor Street, West, Toronto, Ontario M5S 1X7, Canada, 960-3903

Voelpel, Jack, Senior Editor, Beekman Hill Press, 342 East 51st Street, 3A, New York, NY 10022, 212-755-0218

Vogelsang, Arthur (see also Bonanno, David; Berg, Stephen), *AMERICAN POETRY REVIEW*, 1616 Walnut St., Room 405, Philadelphia, PA 19103, 215-732-6770

Voldeseth, Beverly, *RAG MAG*, Box 12, Goodhue, MN 55027

Volz, Bill (see also Schain, Stephen; Clark, Duane; Lang, Lillian), *VERNAL*, 522 E. Third Avenue, Durango, CO 81301, 303-259-0221

von Koschembahr, Daniel Talbot, The Square-Rigger Press, 106 Westgate Drive, Lexington, KY 40504, 606-253-3862

von Rosenberg, Helena, Editorial Assistant (see also Borrelli, Peter), *THE AMICUS JOURNAL*, 122 E 42nd Street, New York, NY 10168, 949-0049

Vondrasek, Bets (see also Kramer, Aaron; Everitt, Helen; Andrew, Helen), *WEST HILLS REVIEW: A WALT WHITMAN JOURNAL*, Walt Whitman Birthplace Assn., 246 Walt Whitman Road, Huntington Station, NY 11746, (516) 427-5240

Vorda, Allan (see also DeSalvo, Jules; Sullivan, Jamie), *THE FABULIST REVIEW*, PO Box 770851, Houston, TX 77215, 713-978-6191

Vorhies, Aleen, Production & Design (see also Campbell, Kimo), Pueo Press, PO Box 2066, San Rafael, CA 94912, 415-456-6480

W

Waage, Frederick O. (see also Renner, Ginger), *SECOND GROWTH: Appalachian Nature and Culture*, P.O. Box 24, 292, East Tennessee State Univ., Johnson City, TN 37619, 615-929-7466

Wabun, Co-Editor (see also Sun Bear; Nimimosha), Bear Tribe Publishing, PO Box 9167, Spokane, WA 99209, 509-258-7755

Wabun (see also Sun Bear; Nimimosha), *MANY SMOKES EARTH AWARENESS MAGAZINE*, PO Box 9167, Spokane, WA 99209, 509-258-7755

Wachtel, Chuck (see also Breger, Brian; Lewis, Harry), *# MAGAZINE*, 339 W. 4th Street #2R, New York, NY 10014

Wachtel, Eleanor (see also Reid, Gayla), Growing Room Collective, Box 46160, Station G, Vancouver BC V6R 4G5, Canada, 604-733-3889

Wachtel, Eleanor (see also Reid, Gayla; Freeman, Victoria; Schendlinger, Mary; Wexler, Jeannie), *ROOM OF ONE'S OWN*, PO Box 46160, Station G, Vancouver, British Columbia V6R 4G5, Canada, 604-733-3889

Wadden, Paul, Poetry Editor (see also Williams, Susan; DeGrazia, Emilio; Lund, Orval J.; Leukovins, Deborah), *GREAT RIVER REVIEW*, 211 W 7th, Winona, MN 55987

Waddy, Adrianne (see also Allison, Dorothy; Bulkin, Elly; Clarke, Cheryl; Otter, Nancy Clarke), *CONDITIONS*, PO Box 56, Van Brunt Sta., Brooklyn, NY 11215, 212-788-8654

Wade, David (see also Dimitrios, Bro.), *FROZEN WAFFLES*, Writers-Action, PO Box 1941, Bloomington, IN 47402, 812-334-0381

Wade, David (see also Dimitrios, Bro.), Frozen Waffles Press & Tapes, Writers-Action, Inc., PO Box 1941, Bloomington, IN 47402, 812-334-0381

Wade, David (see also Dimitrios, Brother), Pitjon Press/BackPack Media, Writers-Action, Inc., PO Box 1941, Bloomington, IN 47402, 812-334-0381

Wade, Seth, *PAN AMERICAN REVIEW*, 1101 Tori Lane, Edinburg, TX 78539, 512-383-7893

Wade, T.E., Jr., Gazelle Publications, 5580 Stanley Drive, Auburn, CA 95603, 916-878-1223

Wadland, John H., *JOURNAL of CANADIAN STUDIES/Revue d'etudes canadiennes*, Trent Univ., Peterborough, Ont. K9J 7B8, Canada

Wadland, John H., Trent University, Trent University, Peterborough ON K9J 7B8, Canada

Wadsworth, Charles (see also Wadsworth, Jean), The Tidal Press, Box X, Cranberry Isles, ME 04625, 207-244-3090

Wadsworth, Jean (see also Wadsworth, Charles), *The Tidal Press*, Box X, Cranberry Isles, ME 04625, 207-244-3090

Wagar, Samuel, Obscure Anarchist Press, 861A Danforth Avenue, Toronto, Ontario M4J 1L8, Canada

Wagenheim, Kal, Co-Editor (see also Wagenheim, Olga Jimenez), Waterfront Press, 52 Maple Avenue, Maplewood, NJ 07040

Wagenheim, Olga Jimenez (see also Wagenheim, Kal), *Waterfront Press*, 52 Maple Avenue, Maplewood, NJ 07040

Wagner, Linda, *THE CENTENNIAL REVIEW*, 110 Morrill Hall, Mich. State Univ., E. Lansing, MI 48824, 517-355-1905

Wagner, Pete (see also Anger, Lance), *MINNE HA! HA!*, PO Box 14009, Minneapolis, MN 55414, 612-378-9156

Wagner, Pete, Designer (see also Anger, Lance), Minne Ha! Ha!, PO Box 14009, Minneapolis, MN 55414

Wagner, Ruth M, Woodcock Press, PO Box 4744, Santa Rosa, CA 95402, 415-533-4399

Wagoner, David, *POETRY NORTHWEST*, 4045 Brooklyn NE, Ja-15, Univ. Of Washington, Seattle, WA 98105

Wainer, Dorothy, Author! Author! Publishing Co., 210 E 58th Street, New York, NY 10022

Wainhouse, Austryn, Director, The Marlboro Press, Box 157, Marlboro, VT 05344, 802-257-0781

Wainwright, Ann, *POETIC LICENCE*, Flat 8, 84 High Street, Norton, Cleveland, England, 0642-534778

Wainwright, Ann, Poetic Licence Collective, Flat 8, 84 Hight Street, Norton, Cleveland, England, 0642-534778

Wainwright, Ann, *STATION IDENTIFICATION*, Flat 8, High Street, Norton, Cleveland, England, 0642-534778

Wainwright, Don, The Unitrade Press, PO Box 172, Station A, Toronto, Ontario M5W 1B2, Canada, 416-787-5658

Wainwright, Jeffrey (see also Silkin, Jon; Glover, Jon), Northern House, 179 Wingrove Road, Newcastle upon Tyne NE49DA, England

Waite, Arthur, *FREELANCE WRITING*, 5/9 Bexley Square, Salford, Manchester M3 6DB, England, 061-832-5079

Waiyaki, D. Nyoike (see also Wanjie, Anne Catherine; Kasu, Ephraim K.; Njoroge, Fred N.), East African Publishing House, PO Box 30571, Nairobi, Kenya, Kenya, 557417, 557788

Wakin, Edward, Ph.D., *IMAGROUP*, 475 North Avenue Box T, New Rochelle, NY 10802, 914-576-0122

Walatka, Pam Portugal (see also Stephens, Helen; Main, Jody; Jamello, Nancy Portugal; Davis, Annette), Wild Horses Publishing Company, 12310 Concepcion Road, Los Altos Hills, CA 94022, 415-941-3396

Waldauer, Karen, Publisher, The Middle Atlantic Press, Box 263, Wallingford, PA 19086, 215-565-2445

Waldman, Anne (see also Padgett, Ron; Simon, Joan), Full Court Press, Inc., 138-140 Watts St., New York, NY 10013

Waldrop, Keith (see also Waldrop, Rosmarie), Burning Deck Press, 71 Elmgrove Ave., Providence, RI 02906

Waldrop, Rosmarie (see also Waldrop, Keith), *Burning Deck Press*, 71 Elmgrove Ave., Providence, RI 02906

Walker, Anne S., Executive Director + Editor, *THE TRIBUNE*, 777 United Nations Plaza, 12th floor, New York, NY 10017, 212-687-8633

Walker, Jinx, Peripatos Press, PO Box 550, Wainscott, NY 11975, 516-324-6396

Walker, Lois V., Contributing Editor (see also Kain, Sue; Hair, Jennie; Steinle, Rita Juul; Penha, James), *NEWSLETTER*, PO Box 773, Huntington, NY 11743

Walker, Lois V. (see also Baehr, Anne-Ruth; Hair, Jennie; Jeffery, Mildred; Yaryura-Tobias, Anibal), Pleasure Dome Press (Long Island Poetry Collective Inc.), Box 773, Huntington, NY 11743, 516-691-2376

Walker, Lois V., Editor (see also Baehr, Anne-Ruth; Hair, Jennie; Jeffrey, Mildred; Yaryura-Tobias, Anibal; Lucas, Barbara), *XANADU*, Box 773, Huntington, NY 11743, (516) 691-2376

Walker, Rod, Pandemonium Press, 1273 Crest Drive, Encinitas, CA 92024

Walker, Rod, *PELLENNORATH*, 1273 Crest Drive, Encinitas, CA 92024

Walker, Ron, Assistant Editor (see also Walker, Sue), *NEGATIVE CAPABILITY*, 6116 Timberly Road N., Mobile, AL 36609, 205-661-9114

Walker, Ron, Assistant Editor (see also Walker, Sue), Negative Capability Press, 6116 Timberly Road N., Mobile, AL 36609, 205-661-9114

Walker, Scott, The Graywolf Press, P.O. Box 142, Port Townsend, WA 98368, 206-385-1160

Walker, Sue, Editor (see also Walker, Ron), *NEGATIVE CAPABILITY*, 6116 Timberly Road N., Mobile, AL 36609, 205-661-9114

Walker, Sue, Chief Editor (see also Walker, Ron), Negative Capability Press, 6116 Timberly Road N., Mobile, AL 36609, 205-661-9114

Walker, Tom (see also Taylor, Jack), Boyd & Fraser Publishing Company, 3627 Sacramento St., San Francisco, CA 94118, 415-346-0686

Walker, Wilbert L., Heritage Press, PO Box 18625, Baltimore, MD 21216, 301-383-9330

Walker, William D., Editor, Publisher (see also Griggs, Lonnie R.; Green, Perry John), *JOINT ENDEAVOR*, PO Box 32, Huntsville, TX 77340

Wall, Ann, Publisher (see also Polk, James), House of Anansi Press Limited/Publishing Co., 35 Britain St., Toronto M5A1R7, Canada, 416-363-5444

Wall, Elizabeth S., Bayshore Books, Box 848, Nokomis, FL 33555, 813-485-2564

Wallace, Deborah A., Senior Editor, Psychological Press, PO Box 45435, Seattle, WA 98105, 206-323-5753

Wallace, Robert (see also Seidler, C. M.; Jacobson, Bonnie), Bits Press, Deptartment of English, Case Western Reserve Univ., Cleveland, OH 44106, 216-795-2810

Wallia, C.J. Singh, *THE BAY REVIEW*, California Publishing Institute, 2601 College Avenue, Berkeley, CA 94704, 848-8200

Wallis, Brian (see also Mariani, Phil), *WEDGE*, 141 Perry Street, New York, NY 10014, 212-243-6296

Walsh, John J., Publisher, Black Swan Books Ltd., PO Box 327, Redding Ridge, CT 06876, 203-938-9548

Walsh, Joy (see also Dardess, George), Moody Street Irregulars, Inc., PO Box 157, Clarence Center, NY 14032, (716) 741-3393

Walsh, Joy (see also Dardess, George), *MOODY STREET IRREGULARS: A Jack Kerouac Magazine*, PO Box 157, Clarence Center, NY 14032, 716-741-3393

Walsh, Joy, Textile Bridge Press, PO Box 157, Clarence Center, NY 14032

Walsh, M. (see also Mayne, S.; Aster, H.; Potichnyj, P.), Mosaic Press/Valley Editions, PO Box 1032, Oakville, Ontario L6J 5E9, Canada

Walsh, S. (see also Sargent, L.; Herman, E.; Geiger, K.), South End Press, 302 Columbus Avenue, Boston, MA 02116, 617-266-0629

Walsh, Susan, Co-Editor (see also Martin, Pam), *THE NORTH WIND*, Box 65583, Vancouver 12, B. C. V5N 5K5, Canada

Walters, James L., Assoc. Editor (see also Bradt, George), Bradt Enterprises, 93 Harvey Street, Cambridge, MA 02140

Walthall, Hugh, General Editor & Publisher (see also Flynn, Richard; Pappas, Evangeline; Weber, Lilian; Weber, Ron), S.O.S. Books, 1821 Kalorama Road NW, Washington, DC 20009, 703-524-4460

Walton, Michael, Melrose, 14 Clinton Rise, Beer, E. Devon EX12 3DZ, England, 0297-20619

Wamaling, Mark, *THE ALTERNATIVE ART PAPER*, 8123-19th Place, Adelphi, MD 20783, 301-434-4559

Wamaling, Mark, Newark Press, 8123-19th Place, Adelphi, MD 20783, 301-434-4559

Wan, Jackie, Editor (see also Wood, Philip; Young, George; Reed, Paul), Ten Speed Press, PO Box 7123, Berkeley, CA 94707, 415-845-8414

Wanjie, Anne Catherine (see also Waiyaki, D. Nyoike; Kasu, Ephraim K.; Njoroge, Fred N.), East African Publishing House, PO Box 30571, Nairobi, Kenya, Kenya, 557417, 557788

Ward, Dan S. (see also Hamilton, Michael), *The Publishing Ward, Inc.*, PO Box 9077, Fort Collins, CO 80525, 303-226-5107

Ward, Dave, *SMOKE*, 22 Roseheath Drive, Halewood, Liverpool L26 9UH, England

Ward, Dave, Windows Project, 22 Roseheath Drive, Halewood, Liverpool L26 9UH, England

Ward, Hiley H., Ph.D., *MEDIA HISTORY DIGEST*, 575 Lexington Avenue, New York, NY 10022, 212-752-7050

Ward, Tony, Arc Publications, 17 Pudsey Road, Corn Holme, Todmorden, Lancs, England, 070681-3622

Ware, Norman, Editor (see also Herdeck, Donald), Three Continents Press, Inc., 1346 Connecticut Ave NW, Suite 224, Washington, DC 20036, 202-457-0288

Warne, Gary, *THE ANSWER MAN NEWSLETTER*, PO Box 11263, San Francisco, CA 94101, 415-863-8114

Warner, Elizabeth (see also Brown, Harvey), Frontier Press, P O Box 5023, Santa Rosa, CA 95402, 707-544-5174

Warner, Ralph (see also Elias, Stephen), Nolo Press, 950 Parker Street, Berkeley, CA 94710, 415-549-1976

Warner, Sharon Oard, Assistant Editor (see also Christensen, Erleen), *COTTONWOOD (formerly COTTONWOOD REVIEW)*, Box J, Kansas Union, Univ. of Kansas, Lawrence, KS 66045

Warnick, Marilyn (see also Worden, Catherine), Quartet Books Inc., 360 Park Avenue South, New York, NY 10010, 212-684-2233

Warnken, Kelly, *THE JOURNAL OF FEE-BASED INFORMATION SERVICES*, c/o Information Alternative, PO Box 5571, Chicago, IL 60680, 914-679-2549

Warren, Lee, Fiction Editor (see also Janisse, Thomas; Luallin, Cherryl), *THE VOLCANO REVIEW*, 142 Sutter Creek Canyon, Volcano, CA 95689

Warsaw, Janine, Co-Editor (see also Katz, F.R.), *STORY QUARTERLY*, PO Box 1416, Northbrook, IL 60062, 312-272-9418

Warsh, Lewis (see also Mayer, Bernadette), *UNITED ARTISTS*, 172 E. 4th Street, 9-B, New York, NY 10009

Warsh, Lewis (see also Mayer, Bernadette), United Artists, 172 E. 4th Street, 9-B, New York, NY 10009

Was, Elizabeth (see also And, Miekal), *SPEK*, 1341 Williamson, Madison, WI 53703

Was, Elizabeth (see also And, Miekal; Boyer, Chuck), Xerox Sutra Editions, 1341 Williamson #B, Madison, WI 53703

Waskowsky, Nicolaus, Practices of the Wind, c/o David M. Marovich, Box 214, Kalamazoo, MI 49005, 616-345-1602

Waskowsky, Nicolaus (see also Marovich, David M.), *PRACTICES OF THE WIND*, PO Box 214, Kalamazoo, MI 49005, 616-344-1602

Wasserman, Rosanne (see also Richie, E. Daniel; Claire, F.B.; Rovner, Arkady), The Groundwater Press, 40 Clinton Street #1A, New York, NY 10002, 212-228-5750

Wasserman, Steve, Consulting Editor (see also Lesser, Wendy; Bowles, Paul; Berger, John; Hass, Robert; Vidal, Gore), *THE THREEPENNY REVIEW*, PO Box 9131, Berkeley, CA 94709, 415-849-4545

Watana, Mieko (see also Yates, Barbara; McMahill, Cheiron), *NEW YARN*, Fujicho 6-5-20, Hoyashi, Tokyo 202, Japan, 0424-67-3809

Waters, Chocolate, Director, Eggplant Press, 343 E. 9th Street #4, New York, NY 10003, 303 841-1442

Waters, W. George, *PACIFIC HORTICULTURE*, Box 485, Berkeley, CA 94701, 415-524-1914

Waterston, Elizabeth (see also Rubio, Mary), *CANADIAN CHILDREN'S LITERATURE*, PO Box 335, Guelph Ontario, Canada

Watkins, Melvin, Managing Ed. (see also Fordham, Monroe; Williams, Lillian S.), *AFRO-AMERICANS in NEW YORK LIFE & HISTORY*, PO Box 1663, Buffalo, NY 14216

Watkins, Ralph E., Prairie Publishing Company, Box 24 Station C, Winnipeg R3M 3S7, Canada, 204-885-6496

Watson, Lewis (see also Watson, Sharon), Stonehouse Publications, Timber Butte Road, Box 390, Sweet, ID 83670

Watson, Richard A., Editor, Cave Books, 756 Harvard Avenue, Saint Louis, MO 63130, 314-862-7646

Watson, Sharon (see also Watson, Lewis), Stonehouse Publications, Timber Butte Road, Box 390, Sweet, ID 83670

Watten, Barrett (see also Hejinian, Lyn), *POETICS JOURNAL*, 2639 Russell Street, Berkeley, CA 94705, 415-535-1952

Watten, Barrett, *THIS*, 2020 9th Avenue, Oakland, CA 94606

Watten, Barrett, This Press, c/o Small Press Distribution, Inc., 1784 Shattuck Avenue, Berkeley, CA 94709

Waygren, Leslie (see also Rainwater, Sylvan), Lez Press, PO Box 4387, Portland, OR 97208, 503-287-1838

Weaver, David (see also Sorenson, Elizabeth), Great Circle Productions, 43A Upland Road, W. Somerville, MA 02144, 617-776-7072

Weaver, Francis (see also Rikhoff, Jean; Lape, Walter; Quirk, John; Porter, Regina), Loft Press, 93 Grant Avenue, Glens Falls, NY 12801

Weaver, Michael S., Editor (see also Brown, Melvin E.), *BLIND ALLEYS*, PO Box 13224, Baltimore, MD 21203, 301-235-3857

Weaver, Michael S. (see also Brown, Melvin E.), Seventh Son Press, PO Box 13224, Baltimore, MD 21203, 301-235-3857

Webb, Colin David, Editor, Kawabata Press, Knill Cross House, Higher Anderton Road, Millbrook, Nr Torpoint, Cornwall, England

Webb, Colin David, Editor, *SEPIA*, Knill Cross House, Higher Anderton Road, Millbrook, Nr Torpoint, Cornwall, England

Webb, David Maryland (see also Newcomb, Justine Webb), Webb-Newcomb Company, Inc., 308 N.E. Vance Street, Wilson, NC 27893, 919-291-7231; 919-735-5865

Webb, G.H., O.B.E., *THE KIPLING JOURNAL*, 18 Northumberland Ave., London WC2N 5BJ, England, 01-930-6733

Weber, Lilian, Associate Editor (see also Flynn, Richard; Walthall, Hugh; Pappas, Evangeline; Weber, Ron), S.O.S. Books, 1821 Kalorama Road NW, Washington, DC 20009, 703-524-4460

Weber, Ron, Associate Editor (see also Flynn, Richard; Walthall, Hugh; Pappas, Evangeline; Weber, Lilian), *S.O.S. Books*, 1821 Kalorama Road NW, Washington, DC 20009, 703-524-4460

Webster, Lee (see also Ortenberg, Neil), *ACM (ANOTHER CHICAGO MAGAZINE)*, c/o Neil Ortenberg, PO Box 780, New York, NY 10025, 312-524-1289

Webster, Lee (see also Ortenberg, Neil), Thunder's Mouth Press, c/o Neil Ortenberg, PO Box 780, New York, NY 10025, 212-595-2025

Weeds, Betty (see also Demeter, Lise), Hungarica Publishing House, Fraser Valley Region, PO Box 86788, North Vancouver, B.C. V7L 4L3, Canada, 604-986-3539

Wegner, Frances, Fiction Editor (see also Laufer, William; Jackson, Guida), Houston Writers Guild, Drawer 42331, Houston, TX 77042, 713-669-9312

Wegner, Francis, Editor (see also Laufer, William; Jackson, Guida), *TOUCHSTONE*, Drawer 42331, Houston, TX 77042, 713-669-9312

Weichel, Ken, *ANDROGYNE*, 930 Shields, San Francisco, CA 94132, 586-2697

Weichel, Ken, Androgyne Books, 930 Shields, San Francisco, CA 94132, 586-2697

Weidner, James H., Foris Publications USA, Box C-50, Cinnaminson, NJ 08077, 609-829-6830

Weigle, Marta, President and Editor (see also Kadlec, Robert F.; Powell, Mary A.), Ancient City Press, PO Box 5401, Santa Fe, NM 87502, 505-982-8195

Weil, Lise, Co-Editor (see also Dellenbaugh, Anne G.), *TRIVIA, A JOURNAL OF IDEAS*, Box 606, North Amherst, MA 01059, 413-367-2254

Weinberger, Jerome, Fiction Editor (see also Levy, Barry), *GRINNING IDIOT: A MAGAZINE OF THE ARTS*, Grinning Idiot Press, PO Box 1577 General Post Office, Brooklyn, NY 11202

Weinberger, Jerome, Fiction Editor (see also Levy, Barry), Grinning Idiot Press, PO Box 1577, General Post Office, Brooklyn, NY 11202

Weingarten, Henry, Editor-in-Chief (see also Brockway, Laurie Sue), ASI Publishers, Inc., 63 West 38th Street, New York, NY 10018, 212-679-0645

Weinstein, Ann, Art Editor (see also Ayyildiz, Judy; Ferguson, Maurice; Bullins, Amanda; Nash, Valery; Sheffler, Natalie; Steinke, Paul), *ARTEMIS*, PO Box 945, Roanoke, VA 24005, 703-981-9318

Weinstein, Joel, *MISSISSIPPI MUD*, 1336 SE Marion Street, Portland, OR 97202, 503-236-9962

Weinstein, Joel (see also Darroch, Lynn), Mud Press, 1336 S.E. Marion Street, Portland, OR 97202

Weinstein, Michael, Polygonal Publishing House, 210 Broad Street, Washington, NJ 07882, 201-689-3894

Weinstein, Ms. G.M., President, Amen Publishing Co., Box 3612, Arcadia, CA 91006, 355-9336

Weinstock, A., Reviews (see also Schiller, Karen), *PLEXUS: The West Coast Women's Press*, 545 Athol Avenue, Oakland, CA 94606, 415-451-2585

Weintraub, Stanley, Pennsylvania State University Press, S-234 Burrowes Building, University Park, PA 16802

Weintraub, Stanley, *SHAW. THE ANNUAL OF BERNARD SHAW STUDIES*, S-234 Burrowes Building, University Park, PA 16802, 814-865-4242

Weir, Stanley, Editor, Singlejack Books, Miles & Weir, Ltd., PO Box 1906, San Pedro, CA 90733, 213-548-5964

Weisman, Dale (see also Sheppard, Ann; Taylor, R.D.), Curbstone Publishing Co.- Austin/New York, PO Box 7445, Austin, TX 78712

Weiss, Renee (see also Weiss, Theodore), *QRL POETRY SERIES*, 26 Haslet Ave, Princeton, NJ 08540, 921-6976

Weiss, Theodore (see also Weiss, Renee), *QRL POETRY SERIES*, 26 Haslet Ave, Princeton, NJ 08540, 921-6976

Weissman, Walter, President, Foundation for the Community of Artists, 280 Broadway, Suite 412, New York, NY 10007, 212-227-3770

Weissmann, G. Warren, Editor At Large (see also Bradley, Jacqueline T.; Kelly, Patrick; Brunswick, S.J.; Mallory, Eugenia P.), *BLUE HORSE*, P.O. Box 6061, Augusta, GA 30906, 404-798-5628

Weixlmann, Joseph, *BLACK AMERICAN LITERATURE FORUM*, Indiana State University, Parsons Hall 237, Terre Haute, IN 47809, 812-232-6311, Ext. 2760

Welch, Jennifer Groce, Editor (see also Swisher, Doug; Welch, Rick), *PUDDING MAGAZINE*, 2384 Hardesty Dr. So., Columbus, OH 43204, 614-279-4188

Welch, Jennifer Groce, Editor (see also Swisher, Doug; Welch, Rick), Pudding Publications, 2384 Hardesty Drive, South, Columbus, OH 43204, 614-279-4188

Welch, John, Dawnwood Press, Two Park Avenue, Suite 2650, New York, NY 10016, 212-532-7160

Welch, John, The Many Press, 15 Norcott Road, London N16 7BJ, England, 01-806-5723

Welch, John, *THE MANY REVIEW*, 15 Norcott Road, London N16 7BJ, England, 01-806-5723

Welch, John B., Walter H. Baker Company (Baker's Plays), 100 Chauncy St., Boston, MA 02111, 617-482-1280

Welch, Nancy, Apple Tree Lane, 801 La Honda Road, Woodside, CA 94062, 415-851-3800

Welch, Rick, Managing Editor (see also Welch, Jennifer Groce; Swisher, Doug), *PUDDING MAGAZINE*, 2384 Hardesty Dr. So., Columbus, OH 43204, 614-279-4188

Welch, Rick, Managing Editor (see also Welch, Jennifer Groce; Swisher, Doug), Pudding Publications, 2384 Hardesty Drive, South, Columbus, OH 43204, 614-279-4188

Weldon, Paul (see also Springer, Garrett), Indian Publications, 1869 2nd Avenue, New York, NY 10029

Welker, Robert L., Editor, Huntsville Literary Association, c/o English Department, University of Alabama, Huntsville, AL 35899

Welker, Robert L., *POEM*, c/o English Department, University of Alabama, Huntsville, AL 35899

Well, Mary, Editor (see also Naslund, Sena Jeter), *THE LOUISVILLE REVIEW*, Univ. of Louisville, English Dept., 315 Bingham Humanities, Louisville, KY 40292, 502-588-5921

Welles, Lynn, Assistant Editor (see also Miller, Shirley), Mexico West Travel Club, Inc., 2424 Newport Blvd. #91, Costa Mesa, CA 92627, (714) 536-8081

Wellman, Don (see also Franzen, Cole; Turner, Irene), *O.ARS*, Box 179, Cambridge, MA 02238, 617-641-1027

Wells, Ann, Associate Editor (see also Aronson, Arnold; Margolis, Tina; Garren, Lois; King, Keith; Wolff, Fred M.; Rollins, Brook), *THEATRE DESIGN AND TECHNOLOGY*, 330 W. 42nd Street, New York, NY 10036, 212-563-5551

Wells, Dean, Editor (see also Wells, Lawrence), Yoknapatawpha Press, Box 248, Oxford, MS 38655, 601-234-0909

Wells, Lawrence, Director (see also Wells, Dean), *Yoknapatawpha Press*, Box 248, Oxford, MS 38655, 601-234-0909

Wells, Nancy, Managing Editor (see also Wendel, Wayne C.; Kittredge, John), *NAUTICA, THE MAGAZINE OF THE SEA FOR YOUNG PEOPLE*, Spinnaker Press, Inc., Pickering Wharf, Salem, MA 01970, 617-745-6905

Wendel, Wayne C., Editor-In-Chief (see also Wells, Nancy; Kittredge, John), *NAUTICA, THE MAGAZINE OF THE SEA FOR YOUNG PEOPLE*, Spinnaker Press, Inc., Pickering Wharf, Salem, MA 01970, 617-745-6905

Wendell, Julia, Editor-in-Chief (see also Stephens, Jack), The Galileo Press, Box 16129, Baltimore, MD 21218, 301-771-4544

Wendell, Julia, Editor (see also Stephens, Jack), *TELESCOPE*, Box 16129, Baltimore, MD 21218, 301-771-4544

Wendell, Leilah, Managing Editor, Publisher (see also Stuart, Kiel), *UNDINAL SONGS*, Undinal Songs Press, PO Box 70, Oakdale, NY 11769, 516-589-8715

Wendt, Ingrid (see also Donnelly, Margarita; Malone, Ruth; Wilner, Eleanor; Thompson, Joyce; Caday, Jan; Mclean, Cheryl; Gordon, Rebecca; Domitrovich, Lisa; Jenkins, Meredith), *CALYX: A Journal of Art and Literature by Women*, PO Box B, Corvallis, OR 97339, 503-753-9384

Wenig, M. Judith (see also Freundlich, Paul; Collins, Chris; Hirsch, Audrey), *COMMUNITIES*, Box 426, Louisa, VA 23093, 703-894-5126

Wenig, M. Judith (see also Freundlich, Paul; Collins, Chris; Hirsch, Audrey), *Communities Publishing Cooperative*, Box 426, Louisa, VA 23093, 703-894-5126

Werderman, Richard L., Publisher, Wolf House Books, PO Box 6657, Grand Rapids, MI 49506, 616-245-8812

Wergeland, Steve, Wordland, Department ID-19, 947 W Bishop Suite A, Santa Ana, CA 92703, 714-953-2900

Werner, Hans-Peter, Editor, *PRELUDE TO FANTASY*, Route 3, Box 193, Richland Center, WI 53581

Wescott, Juanita, Abbetira Publications, PO Box 17600, Tucson, AZ 85731, 714-885-8557

Wesolowski, Paul G. (see also Dixon, Peter; Gorman, Neal E.), *THE FREEDONIA GAZETTE*, Darien B-28 at Village II, New Hope, PA 18938, 215-862-9734

West, Celeste, Editor, Booklegger Press, 555 29th St, San Francisco, CA 94131

West, Charlee, *THE HER STREET JOURNAL*, Drake Office Center, 363 W. Drake, Fort Collins, CO 80526, 303-223-9372

West, Linda (see also Brockway, R.; Brockway, Katie; Blanar, Mike; Hanly, Ken; Blaikie, John; Gentleman, Dorothy Corbett), Pierian Press, 5, Brandon University, Brandon, Manitoba, Canada, 727-2577

West, Linda (see also Brockway, R.; Brockway, Katie; Blanar, Mike; Hanly, Ken; Blaikie, John; Gentleman, Dorothy Corbett), *PIERIAN SPRING*, 5, Brandon University, Brandon, Manitoba, Canada, 727-2577

Westburg, Gregory G., Design & Production Editor (see also Westburg, John; Westburg, Mildred; Westburg, Martial), *NORTH AMERICAN MENTOR MAGAZINE*, 1745 Madison Street, Fennimore, WI 53809

Westburg, Gregory G., Design & Production Editor (see also Westburg, John E.; Westburg, Mildred; Westburg, Martial R.), Westburg Associates, Publishers, 1745 Madison Street, Fennimore, WI 53809, 608-822-6237

Westburg, John, General Editor (see also Westburg, Mildred; Westburg, Gregory G.; Westburg, Martial), *NORTH AMERICAN MENTOR MAGAZINE*, 1745 Madison Street, Fennimore, WI 53809

Westburg, John E., Gen'l. Ed. (see also Westburg, Mildred; Westburg, Gregory G.; Westburg, Martial R.), Westburg Associates, Publishers, 1745 Madison Street, Fennimore, WI 53809, 608-822-6237

Westburg, Martial, Art Consultant (see also Westburg, John; Westburg, Mildred; Westburg, Gregory G.), *NORTH AMERICAN MENTOR MAGAZINE*, 1745 Madison Street, Fennimore, WI 53809

Westburg, Martial R., Art Consultant (see also Westburg, John E.; Westburg, Mildred; Westburg, Gregory G.), Westburg Associates, Publishers, 1745 Madison Street, Fennimore, WI 53809, 608-822-6237

Westburg, Mildred, General Editor (see also Westburg, John; Westburg, Gregory G.; Westburg, Martial), *NORTH AMERICAN MENTOR MAGAZINE*, 1745 Madison Street, Fennimore, WI 53809

Westburg, Mildred, Gen'l. Ed (see also Westburg, John E.; Westburg, Gregory G.; Westburg, Martial R.), Westburg Associates, Publishers, 1745 Madison Street, Fennimore, WI 53809, 608-822-6237

Westcott, Michelle Anne (see also Westcott, W.F.), Blue Heron Press, PO Box 1326, Alliston, Ontario L0M 1A0, Canada, 705-435-9914

Westcott, W.F. (see also Westcott, Michelle Anne), *Blue Heron Press*, PO Box 1326, Alliston, Ontario L0M 1A0, Canada, 705-435-9914

Westerfield, M. J., Publisher, Ashford Press, PO Box 513, Willimantic, CT 06226

Westerfield, M. J., Publisher, *WESTERFIELD'S REVIEW*, PO Box 513, Willimantic, CT 06226

Wetherby, Phyllis, Know, Inc., P.O. Box 86031, Pittsburgh, PA 15221

Wexler, Jeannie (see also Reid, Gayla; Wachtel, Eleanor; Freeman, Victoria; Schendlinger, Mary), *ROOM OF ONE'S OWN*, PO Box 46160, Station G, Vancouver, British Columbia V6R 4G5, Canada, 604-733-3889

Whalen, Tom, *LOWLANDS REVIEW*, 6048 Perrier, New Orleans, LA 70118

Wharton, John, The Global Press, 2239 E. Colfax Avenue #202, Denver, CO 80206, 303-393-7647

Whealy, Kent, *SEED SAVERS EXCHANGE*, 203 Rural Avenue, Decorah, IA 52101, 319-382-3949

Wheeler, Tony (see also Hart, Jim), Lonely Planet Publications, P.O. Box 88, South Yarra, Victoria 3141, Australia, 03 429-5100

Wheelwright, Henry C., Stone Wall Press, Inc, 1241 30th Street NW, Washington, DC 20007, 202-333-1860

Wheelwright, Thea, President, The Kennebec River Press, Inc., R.R. 1, Box 164, Woolwich, ME 04579, 207-442-7632

Wheelwright, Thea, TBW Books, R.R.1, Box 164, Day's Ferry Road, Woolwich, ME 04579, 207-442-7632

Whelan, Sandra (see also Lansky, Vicki), *PRACTICAL PARENTING*, 18326B Minnetonka Blvd, Deephaven, MN 55391, 612-475-1505

Whitaker, B., *MINORITY RIGHTS GROUP REPORTS*, MRG, 36 Craven St., London WC2N5NG, England, 01-930-6659

White, Bruce W., Expedition Press, 301 Douglas Apt. #3, Kalamazoo, MI 49007

White, Curtis, Co-Director (see also Glynn, Thomas; Leyner, Mark), Fiction Collective, Inc., Brooklyn College, Dept. of English, Brooklyn, NY 11210, 212-780-5547

White, Curtis, Editor (see also Sutherland, Robert D.; Scrimgeour, James R.; McGowan, James), *THE PIKESTAFF FORUM*, PO Box 127, Normal, IL 61761, 309-452-4831

White, Curtis, Editor (see also Sutherland, Robert D.; Scrimgeour, James R.; McGowan, James), The Pikestaff Press, PO Box 127, Normal, IL 61761, 309-452-4831

White, Gail, Poetry Editor (see also Craig, David; Christian, Paula; McCoy, Barbara), *PIEDMONT LITERARY REVIEW*, P.O.Box 3656, Danville, VA 24541, 804-793-0956

White, J. Claire, Editor, *THE CONNECTICUT POETRY REVIEW*, PO Box 3783, Amity Station, New Haven, CT 06525

White, Patricia, Director (see also Crudup, Sonya), Bond Publishing Company, 226 Massachusetts Avenue NE, Suite 21, Washington, DC 20002, 202-547-3140

White, Richard, Chief Editor (see also Hall, Timothy), White Tower Inc. Press, PO Box 42216, Los Angeles, CA 90042, 213-254-1326

White, Robert, Editor, *THE DUCK BOOK DIGEST*, Robert White Inc., Box 1928, Cocoa, FL 32923, 305-636-4823

White, Shirley (see also Fowler, Gus), Amistad Brands, Inc., 22 Division Ave., N.E., Washington, DC 20019, 301-593-7276

White, William, Co-Editor (see also Folsom, Ed; Perlman, Jim), *WALT WHITMAN QUARTERLY REVIEW*, 308 EPB The University of Iowa, Iowa City, IA 52240, 319-353-3698; 353-5650

Whited, David (see also Raphael, Dan), *NRG*, 6735 S E 78th, Portland, OR 97206

Whiten, Clifton, Publisher and Editor, *POETRY CANADA REVIEW*, PO Box 1280, Station A, Toronto, Ontario M5W 1G7, Canada, 416-927-8001

Whitmore, Keith A., I. S. C. Press, PO Box 779, Fortuna, CA 95540, 707-768-3284

Whitton, Tom (see also Whitton, Wendy), Second Back Row Press, P.O. Box 43, Leura NSW 2781, Australia

Whitton, Wendy (see also Whitton, Tom), *Second Back Row Press*, P.O. Box 43, Leura NSW 2781, Australia

Whyte, Dr. Malcolm Arthur, Alco Press, 554 West 156th Street, New York, NY 10032, 212-862-7193

Whyte, Raewyn, *DANCE NEWS*, NZ Dance Federation, Box 5138, Wellington 1, New Zealand, 89-4639

Wicker, Nina A., Editor (see also Thomas, Hazel F.; Thomas, Kate Kelly), *MANNA*, Route 8, Box 368, Sanford, NC 27330

Wickett, Ann (see also Humphry, Derek), *HEMLOCK QUARTERLY*, PO Box 66218, Los Angeles, CA 90066, 213-391-1871

Wickett, Ann (see also Humphry, Derek), Hemlock Society, PO Box 66218, Los Angeles, CA 90066, 213-391-1971

Wickstrom, Lois (see also Lorrah, Jean), Empire Books, 10612 Altman Street, Tampa, FL 33612

Wickstrom, Lois (see also Lorrah, Jean), *PANDORA, An Original Anthology of Role-expanding Science Fiction and Fantsy*, PO Box 625, Murray, KY 42071

Widdowson, J.D.A., *LORE AND LANGUAGE*, The Centre for English Cultural Tradition and Language, The University, Sheffield S10 2TN, England, Sheffield 78555 ext 6295

Wiebe, Dallas, *CINCINNATI POETRY REVIEW*, Dept of English (069), University of Cincinnati, Cincinnati, OH 45221, 513-475-4484

Wiener, Phyllis (see also McDonald, Susan; Ochtrup, Monica), *WARM JOURNAL*, 414 First Avenue North, Minneapolis, MN 55401, 612-332-5672

Wiener, Phyllis (see also McDonald, Susan; Ochtrup, Monica), Women's Art Registry of Minnesota, 414 First Avenue North, Minneapolis, MN 55401, 612-332-5672

Wienert, Christopher, Editor, White Dot Press, 2607 Manhattan Avenue, Baltimore, MD 21215, 301-542-2846

Wieser, Barb (see also Pinkvoss, Joan), Aunt Lute Book Company, Publishers of Women's Work, Box 2723, Iowa City, IA 52240, 338-7022

Wiggins, Reynold, *DR. DOBB'S JOURNAL*, 1263 El Camino, P. O. Box E, Menlo Park, CA 94025, 415-323-3111

Wiggins, Reynold, Editor-in-Chief, Books + Periodicals, People's Computer Co., 1263 El Camino Real, PO Box E, Menlo Park, CA 94025, 415-323-3111

Wiggins, Sarah Woolfolk, Editor, *ALABAMA REVIEW*, PO Box CS, University of Alabama, University, AL 35486

Wigginton, Eliot, Supervisor, *FOXFIRE*, Box B, Rabun Gap, GA 30568, 404-746-5318

Wigginton, Eliot (see also Page, Linda), Foxfire Press, Box B, Rabun Gap, GA 30568, 404-746-5828

Wiig, Howard C., Clean Energy Press, 3593-a Alani Dr, Honolulu, HI 96822, 808-988-4155

Wilber, Ken, Editor-in-Chief (see also Gaffney, Rachel), *ReVISION JOURNAL*, PO Box 316, Cambridge, MA 02238, 617-354-5827

Wilcox, Jackson, *SILVER WINGS*, PO Box 5201, Mission Hills, CA 91345, 818-893-2889

Wilcox, Kathleen (see also Van Atta, Marian), Geraventure Corp., PO Box 2131, Melbourne, FL 32902, 305-723-5554

Wilcox, Kathleen (see also Van Atta, Marian), *LIVING OFF THE LAND, Subtropic Newsletter*, PO Box 2131, Melbourne, FL 32902, 305-723-5554

Wilcox, Laird M., Editorial Research Service, P.O.Box 1832, Kansas City, MO 64141, 913-342-6768

Wilcox, Patricia, Iris Press, Inc., 27 Chestnut St., Binghamton, NY 13905, 607-722-6739

Wilder, John, *THE VERY BEGINNING*, Dept. L-2, PO Box 2191, Iowa City, IA 52244, 319-353-8883

Wilder, John, Writers House Press, Dept. L-2, PO Box 2191, Iowa City, IA 52244, 319-353-8883

Wilder, John R., Editor & Publisher, *BEGINNING: THE MAGAZINE FOR THE WRITER IN THE COMMUNITY*, Dept. L-2, PO Box 2191, Iowa City, IA 52244, 319-353-8883

Wilensky, L., *PEDESTRIAN RESEARCH*, PO Box 624, Forest Hills, NY 11375

Wilentz, Joan (see also Wilentz, Ted), Corinth Books Inc., 4008 East West Highway, Chevy Chase, MD 20815, 301-652-1016

Wilentz, Ted (see also Wilentz, Joan), *Corinth Books Inc.*, 4008 East West Highway, Chevy Chase, MD 20815, 301-652-1016

Wilhelm, Roger P., Editor (see also Allton, George), *THRESHOLD MAGAZINE*, Wilhelm Publishing, Inc., PO Box 922, Columbia, MO 65205, 314-442-6134

Wilkins, Frederick C., *THE EUGENE O'NEILL NEWSLETTER*, Department of English, Suffolk University, Boston, MA 02114, 617-723-4700 ext. 272

Williams, Cynthia L., Art Editor (see also Anderson, Kathy Elaine; Jones, Keith; Hemphill, Essex C.), *NETHULA JOURNAL OF CONTEMPORARY LITERATURE*, 930 F Street, Suite 610, Washington, DC 20004

Williams, Deborah H. (see also Williams, Gil), Bellevue Press, 60 Schubert St., Binghamton, NY 13905, 607-729-0819

Williams, Elizabeth, Asst. Editor (see also Plath, James; Emery, Mary Ann; Blum, John), *CLOCKWATCH REVIEW*, 737 Penbrook Way, Hartland, WI 53029, 414-367-8315

Williams, Fred, *TYPE & PRESS*, 24667 Heather Court, Hayward, CA 94545

Williams, Gil (see also Williams, Deborah H.), Bellevue Press, 60 Schubert St., Binghamton, NY 13905, 607-729-0819

Williams, Gordon, *TRIVIUM*, Dept. Of English, St. David's University College, Lampeter, Dyfed SA48 7ED, Great Britain, 0570-422351 ext 253

Williams, Greg, Editor (see also Merwin, Miles L.), *AGROFORESTRY REVIEW*, Route One, Gravel Switch, KY 40328, 606-332-7606

Williams, Gregory, Editor (see also Merwin, Miles), International Tree Crops Institute, Route 1, Black Lick Road, Gravel Switch, KY 40328, 606-332-7606

Williams, Helen (see also Abercrombie, V.T.), Brown Rabbit Press, Box 19111, Houston, TX 77024, 713-622-1844/465-1168

Williams, J.E. Caerwyn, *STUDIA CELTICA*, University of Wales Press, 6 Gwennyth St., Cathays, Cardiff CF2 4YD, Wales, Cardiff 31919

Williams, Lillian S., Assoc. Ed. (see also Fordham, Monroe; Watkins, Melvin), *AFRO-AMERICANS in NEW YORK LIFE & HISTORY*, PO Box 1663, Buffalo, NY 14216

Williams, Linda, *SLICK PRESS*, 125 Dyna Drive #206, Houston, TX 77060

Williams, M.K., President, Ahnene Publications, Box 456, Maxville Ontario K0C 1T0, Canada

Williams, M.K., President, *POETRY 'N PROSE*, Box 456, Maxville, Ontario K0C 1T0, Canada

Williams, Paul, Editor, Entwhistle Books, Box 611, Glen Ellen, CA 95442

Williams, Phillip, The P. Gaines Co., Publishers, PO Box 2253, Oak Park, IL 60303, 312-524-1073

Williams, Reese, Tanam Press, 40 White Street, New York, NY 10013

Williams, S.E., *CONTRIBUTORS BULLETIN*, 5/9 Bexley Square, Salford, Manchester, England M3 6DB, England, 061-832 5079

Williams, Susan, Editor, *ENERGY REVIEW*, 2074 Alameda Padre Serra, Santa Barbara, CA 93103, 805-965-5010

Williams, Susan, Book Review Editor (see also Wadden, Paul; DeGrazia, Emilio; Lund, Orval J.; Leukovins, Deborah), *GREAT RIVER REVIEW*, 211 W 7th, Winona, MN 55987

Williams, Susan, Editor (see also Garrison, Thomas S.; Krakowiak, Mary), International Academy at Santa Barbara, 2074 Alameda Padre Serra, Santa Barbara, CA 93103, 805-965-5010

Williamson, Robin, Editor, Pig's Whisker Music, PO Box 27522, Los Angeles, CA 90027, 213-665-3613

Willkzie, Philip (see also Emond, Paul; Young, Tom; Baysans, Greg; Strizek, Norman), *JAMES WHITE REVIEW; a gay men's literary quarterly*, PO Box 3356, Traffic Station, Minneapolis, MN 55403, 612-291-2913; 871-2248

Willoughby, Robin, Co-Editor (see also Brill, Kastle; Johnson, Bonnie; Zuckerman, Ryki), *EARTH'S DAUGHTERS*, Box 41, c/o Bonnie Johnson, Central Park Stn., NY 14215, 716-837-7778

Willson, A. Leslie, Editor, *DIMENSION*, Box 26673, Austin, TX 78755, 512-345-0622

Willson, Robert, Tejas Art Press, 207 Terrell Road, San Antonio, TX 78209, 512-826-7803

Wilner, Eleanor (see also Donnelly, Margarita; Malone, Ruth; Wendt, Ingrid; Thompson, Joyce; Caday, Jan; Mclean, Cheryl; Gordon, Rebecca; Domitrovich, Lisa; Jenkins, Meredith), *CALYX: A Journal of Art and Literature by Women*, PO Box B, Corvallis, OR 97339, 503-753-9384

Wiloch, Thomas, Editor (see also Ligotti, Thomas), *GRIMOIRE*, c/o Thomas Wiloch, 8181 Wayne Road Apt H2084, Westland, MI 48185

Wilson, Barbara (see also da Silva, Rachel; Conlon, Faith), The Seal Press, Box 13, Seattle, WA 98111, 624-5262

Wilson, David A., Lorien House, PO Box 1112, Black Mountain, NC 28711, 704-669-6211

Wilson, Del, Senior Editor (see also Crombie, Daniel, Jr.), Crossroads Communications, PO Box 7, Carpentersville, IL 60110

Wilson, Don D., Editor, Singular Speech Press, 507 Dowd Avenue, Canton, CT 06019, 203-693-6059

Wilson, Emily (see aiso Leighton, Betty), The Jackpine Press, 1878 Meadowbrook Drive, Winston-Salem, NC 27104, 919-725-8828

Wilson, Marian M., Simon & Pierre Publishing Co. Ltd., Box 280, Adelaide St. P.O., Toronto, Ontario M5C2J4, Canada, 416-363-6767

Wilson, Merrill (see also Meyers, George), Chockstone Press, 526 Franklin Street, Denver, CO 80218, 303-377-1970

Wilson, Robert S., Wilson Brothers Publications, PO Box 712, Yakima, WA 98907, 509-457-8275

Wilson, Roberta (see also McFadden, S. Michele), Career Publishing, Inc., PO Box 5486, Orange, CA 92667, 714-771-5155/In CA 1-800-821-0543/Outside CA 1-800-854-4014

Wilson, Robley, Jr., *THE NORTH AMERICAN REVIEW*, Univ. Of Northern Iowa, Cedar Falls, IA 50614, 319-266-8487/273-2681

Wilson, Sharon, Managing Editor (see also Friedmann, Peggy), *KALLIOPE, A Journal of Women's Art*, 3939 Roosevelt Blvd, Florida Junior College at Jacksonville, Jacksonville, FL 32205, 904-387-8211 or 904-387-8272

Winans, A.D., *SECOND COMING*, PO Box 31249, San Francisco, CA 94131, 415-647-3679

Winans, A.D., Second Coming Press, PO Box 31249, San Francisco, CA 94131, 415-647-3679

Winch, Bradley L., President (see also Mikesell, Suzanne), Jalmar Press, Division of B.L. Winch & Associates, 45 Hitching Post Drive, Building 2, Rolling Hills Estates, CA 90274, 213-547-1240

Wincote, Basil, *CANDELABRUM POETRY MAGAZINE*, 19 South Hill Park, London NW3 2ST, England

Wincote, Basil (see also McCarthy, M.L.), Red Candle Press, 19 South Hill Park, London NW3 2ST, England

Wine, J., Editor (see also Nuse, B.; Newton, J.; Zavitz, C.; Rooney, F.; Andersen, M.; Prentice, A.; Scane, J.; Caplan, Paula; Van Kirk, Sylvia), *RESOURCES FOR FEMINIST RESEARCH/DOCUMEN-TATION SUR LA RECHERCHE FEMINISTE*, Ont Inst for Stud in Educ, Centre for Women's Studies in Education, 252 Bloor Street W., Toronto, Ontario M5S 1V6, Canada, 416-923-6641

Winke, Jeffrey, Distant Thunder Press, 1007 Sunnyvale Lane Apt #E, Madison, WI 53713

Winner, W. P., Aviation Book Company, 1640 Victory Blvd., Glendale, CA 91201, 213-240-1711

Wipprecht, Wendy, Assistant Editor (see also Erikson, Kai T.; Laurans, Penelope), *THE YALE REVIEW*, 1902A Yale Station, New Haven, CT 06520

Witt, Harold (see also Iodice, Ruth G.; Kinnick, B. Jo), *BLUE UNICORN*, 22 Avon Road, Kensington, CA 94707, 415-526-8439

Witt, Roselyn (see also Field, Filip), *AGAPE*, 6940 Oporto Drive, Los Angeles, CA 90068, 213-876-6295

Witte, Jan (see also Moyse, Arthur), *ZERO ONE*, 39 Minford Gardens, West Kensington, London W14 0AP, England

Witte, John, Editor (see also Casey, Deb; Scates, Maxine), *NORTHWEST REVIEW*, 369 P.L.C., University of Oregon, Eugene, OR 97403, 503-686-3957

Wittenberg, Clarissa, Art Editor (see also Swift, Mary; Lang, Doug; Rosenzweig, Phyllis; Fleming, Lee), *WASHINGTON REVIEW*, P O Box 50132, Washington, DC 20004, 202-638-0515

Wodetzki, Tom, Times Change Press, c/o Publishers Services, Box 3914, San Rafael, CA 94901, 415-883-3530

Woessner, Warren, Senior Editor (see also Swanberg, Ingrid; Hilton, David), *ABRAXAS*, 2518 Gregory St., Madison, WI 53711, 608-238-0175

Wojahn, David, Poetry Editor (see also Murphy, Russell; Jauss, David; Vannatta, Dennis), *CRAZYHORSE*, Dept of English, Unviersity of Arkansas at Little Rock, Little Rock, AR 72204, 501-569-3160

Wojahn, David, Contributing Editor (see also Bowden, Michael), San Pedro Press, 212 Clawson Street, Bisbee, AZ 85603

Wojahn, David, Contributing Editor (see also Bowden, Michael), *WHETSTONE*, 212 Clawson Street, Bisbee, AZ 85603

Wolf, Samuel, Swand Publications, 120 N. Longcross Road, Linthicum Heights, MD 21090, 301-859-3725

Wolfe, Michael, Tombouctou Books, Box 265, Bolinas, CA 94924, 415-868-1082

Wolfe, William G., President, The Riverside Press, PO Box 133, Riverside, CT 06878, 203-637-3084

Wolff, Fred M., Associate Editor (see also Aronson, Arnold; Margolis, Tina; Garren, Lois; King, Keith; Wells, Ann; Rollins, Brook), *THEATRE DESIGN AND TECHNOLOGY*, 330 W. 42nd Street, New York, NY 10036, 212-563-5551

Wolfshohl, Clarence, Timberline Press, Box 327, Fulton, MO 65251, 314-642-5035

Woo, John, Basement Workshop, Inc., 102 Third Avenue #2, New York, NY 10003, 212-254-4938

Wood, Deloris (see also Wood Jr., Dr. Thomas W.), *LOST GENERATION JOURNAL*, Department of Journalism, Temple University, Philadelphia, PA 19122, (314) 729-5669: (501) 568-6241

Wood Jr., Dr. Thomas W. (see also Wood, Deloris), *LOST GENERATION JOURNAL*, Department of Journalism, Temple University, Philadelphia, PA 19122, (314) 729-5669: (501) 568-6241

Wood, Marilyn (see also Hayes, Marshall), *BOOK FORUM*, Hudson River Press, 38 East 76 Street, New York, NY 10021, 212-861-8328

Wood, Philip, Publisher (see also Wan, Jackie; Young, George; Reed, Paul), Ten Speed Press, PO Box 7123, Berkeley, CA 94707, 415-845-8414

Wood, Wilbur, *AERO SUN-TIMES,* 324 Fuller #C-4, Helena, MT 59601, 406-443-7272

Woodhams, Stephen, Editor (see also Gabbard, D.C.; Gabbard, Dwight C.; Overson, Beth E.; Caquelin, Anthony; Salmon-Heynemen, Jana; Goodwin, Tema; Shames, Terry; Rajfur, Ted), *FICTION MONTHLY,* Malvolio Press, 545 Haight Street, Suite 67, San Francisco, CA 94117, 415-621-1646

Woodman, Allen (see also Hamby, Barbara), *APALACHEE QUARTERLY,* DDB Press, PO Box 20106, Tallahassee, FL 32316

Woodman, Allen, *WORD BEAT,* PO Box 10509, Tallahassee, FL 32302

Woodman, Allen, Word Beat Press, PO Box 10509, Tallahassee, FL 32302

Woods, Edward, *INS & OUTS,* PO Box 3759, Amsterdam, Holland, 276868

Woods, Edward, Ins & Outs Press, PO Box 3759, Amsterdam, Holland, 276868

Woodson, Jon, Associate Editor (see also Letcher, Tina; Suryanarayan, Indu; Tyler, Larry), *NORTHEAST JOURNAL,* PO Box 217, Kingston, RI 02881

Woolf, Robert, Technical Editor, Quartz Publications, 16 Hilltop Road, RD 5, Freehold, NJ 07728, 201-462-7182

Woolley, Pat, Wild & Woolley, PO Box 41, Glebe NSW 2037, Australia, 02-692-0166

Worden, Catherine (see also Warnick, Marilyn), Quartet Books Inc., 360 Park Avenue South, New York, NY 10010, 212-684-2233

Worden, Mark (see also Lybrand, Lisa; Butkus, Greg), *POETRY TODAY,* Box 20822, Portland, OR 97220, 213-334-4732

Works, Jan (see also Works, Pat), RWunderground Parachuting Publications, 1656 Beechwood Avenue, Fullerton, CA 92635, 714-990-0369

Works, Pat (see also Works, Jan), *RWunderground Parachuting Publications,* 1656 Beechwood Avenue, Fullerton, CA 92635, 714-990-0369

Worman, A. Lee (see also Elder, Karl), *SEEMS,* c/o Lakeland College, Box 359, Sheboygan, WI 53082

Wortham, Jim, Marathon International Publishing Company, Deptartment SPR, PO Box 33008, Louisville, KY 40232

Wortham, Thomas (see also Tennyson, G.B.), *NINETEENTH-CENTURY FICTION,* University of California Press, Berkeley, CA 94720, 415-642-7485

Wray, Elizabeth (see also Austin, Alan; Zu-Bolton, Ahmos; Becker, Anne), *BLACK BOX MAGAZINE,* PO Box 50145, Washington, DC 20004, 202-347-4823

Wray, Elizabeth, Co-Producer (see also Becker, Anne; Austin, Alan), Watershed Tapes, PO Box 50145, Washington, DC 20004

Wray, Jeanne Adams, Managing Editor (see also Hackett, Neil J.), *CIMARRON REVIEW,* Oklahoma State University Press, Oklahoma State University, Stillwater, OK 74074, (405) 624-6573

Wright, A.J., Doctor Jazz Press, 2208 Chapel Hill Road, Birmingham, AL 35216, 205-822-5564

Wright, C. D., Editor (see also Gander, Forrest), Lost Roads Publishers, PO Box 5848, Weybosset Hill Station, Providence, RI 02903, 401-941-4188

Wright, Jeff, Hard Press, 340 East Eleventh Street, New York, NY 10003

Wright, Thomas L. (see also Latimer, Dan R.), *SOUTHERN HUMANITIES REVIEW,* 9088 Haley Center, Auburn Univ., Auburn, AL 36830, 205-826-4606

Wrigley, Robert, Editor (see also Hepworth, James), Confluence Press, Inc., Spalding Hall, Lewis-Clark State College, Lewiston, ID 83501

Wrigley, Robert, Editor (see also Hepworth, James), *THE SLACKWATER REVIEW,* Spalding Hall, Lewis-Clark Campus, Lewiston, ID 83501, 208-746-2341

Wu, S. (see also Tajima, Renee; Lee, C.N.; Chow, P.; Chin, R.; Chu, B.; Francia, L.; Lew, Walter; Hahn, Tomie; Kwan, S.), *BRIDGE: ASIAN AMERICAN PERSPECTIVES*, Asian Cine-Vision, Inc., 32 E Broadway, New York, NY 10002, 212-925-8685

Wujciak, Dick (see also Baron, Matt; Zuk, Sue), Cornell Design Publishers, PO Box 278, E. Hanover, NJ 07936

Wyatt, Cosmo (see also Wyatt, Marjorie), *PROGRESSIVE PLATTER*, Journal Publishing, PO Box 638, Boston, MA 02215, 617-267-4255/247-1144

Wyatt, Margaret, Editor, *THE ARTFUL REPORTER*, 12 Harter Street, 4th Floor, Manchester, England

Wyatt, Marjorie (see also Wyatt, Cosmo), *PROGRESSIVE PLATTER*, Journal Publishing, PO Box 638, Boston, MA 02215, 617-267-4255/247-1144

Wyly, R.D., *SCHOLIA SATYRICA*, English Department, University of South Florida, Tampa, FL 33620, 974-2421

Wyman, Hastings, President (see also Cochrane, Shirley; Sargent, Robert), Washington Writers Publishing House, PO Box 50068, Washington, DC 20004, 202-546-1020

Wysocki, Sharon, *THE WIRE*, 7320 Colonial, Dearborn Heights, MI 48127, 517-394-3736

X

Xelina (see also Alurista), *MAIZE: Notebooks of Xicano Art and Literature*, The Colorado College, Box 10, Colorado Springs, CO 80903, 303-636-3249, 473-2233 ext. 624

Xelina (see also Alurista), Maize Press, The Colorado College, Box 10, Colorado Springs, CO 80903, 303-636-3249; 473-2233, ext. 624

Xianyi, Yang, Chinese Literature, Baiwanzhang St., Beijing, People's Republic of China

Xianyi, Yang, *CHINESE LITERATURE*, Baiwanzhang St., Beijing, People's Republic of China

Y

Yaffe, Richard, Editor (see also Cantor, Aviva), *ISRAEL HORIZONS*, 150 Fifth Avenue, Room 1002, New York, NY 10011, 212-255-8760

Yagi, Kametaro, Japan (see also Harr, Lorraine Ellis; Harr, Carl F.; Sato, Kazuo), *DRAGONFLY: A Quarterly Of Haiku*, 4102 N.E. 130th Pl., Portland, OR 97230

Yaryura-Tobias, Anibal (see also Baehr, Anne-Ruth; Hair, Jennie; Jeffery, Mildred; Walker, Lois V.), Pleasure Dome Press (Long Island Poetry Collective Inc.), Box 773, Huntington, NY 11743, 516-691-2376

Yaryura-Tobias, Anibal, Editor (see also Baehr, Anne-Ruth; Hair, Jennie; Jeffrey, Mildred; Walker, Lois V.; Lucas, Barbara), *XANADU*, Box 773, Huntington, NY 11743, (516) 691-2376

Yates, Barbara (see also McMahill, Cheiron; Watana, Mieko), *NEW YARN*, Fujicho 6-5-20, Hoyashi, Tokyo 202, Japan, 0424-67-3809

Yates, David C., Editor & Publisher (see also O'Keefe, John; Nye, Naomi Shihub), *CEDAR ROCK*, 1121 Madeline, New Braunfels, TX 78130, 512-625-6002

Yates, David C., Publisher, Cedar Rock Press, 1121 Madeline, New Braunfels, TX 78130

Yeatman, Ted P., Nonfiction Editor (see also Eng, Steve), Depot Press, PO Box 60072, Nashville, TN 37206, 226-1890

Yefimov, Igor (see also Yefimov, Marina), Hermitage (Ermitazh), 2269 Shadowood Drive, Ann Arbor, MI 48104, 313-971-2968

Yefimov, Marina (see also Yefimov, Igor), *Hermitage (Ermitazh)*, 2269 Shadowood Drive, Ann Arbor, MI 48104, 313-971-2968

Yeshitela, Omali (see also Kefing, Omowali), *THE BURNING SPEAR*, PO Box 27205, Oakland, CA 94602, 415-569-9620

Yeshitela, Omali (see also Kefing, Omowali), Burning Spear Publications, PO Box 27205, Oakland, CA 94602, 415-569-9620

Yoder, Bart, *ELECTRUM*, 1435 Louise Street, Santa Ana, CA 92706, 714-543-5800

Yoder, Bart, Medina Press, 1435 Louise Street, Santa Ana, CA 92706, 714-543-5800

Yoder, Carolyn, Editor, *COBBLESTONE: The History Magazine for Young People*, 20 Grove Street, Peterborough, NH 03458, 603-924-7209

York, Lamar, *THE CHATTAHOOCHEE REVIEW*, 2101 Womack Road, Dunwoody, GA 30338, 393-3300

Yots, Michael, Editor, *THE PANHANDLER*, University of West Florida, English Dept., Pensacola, FL 32514, 904-474-2923

Young, Al (see also Reed, Ishmael), *QUILT*, 1446 Sixth Street #D, Berkeley, CA 94710, 415-527-1586

Young, B. (see also Roussopoulos, D.; Kowaluk, L.; Caloren, F.), *OUR GENERATION*, 3981 boul St Laurent, Montreal, Quebec H2W 1Y5, Canada

Young, Bob (see also Levidow, Les), Free Association Books (FAB), 26 Freegrove Road, London N7 9RQ, United Kingdom, 01-609-5646

Young, David (see also Bevington, Stan; Davey, Frank; James, Clifford; Nichol, bp; Ondaatje, Michael; McCartney, Linda; Sheard, Sarah; Reid, Dennis), Coach House Press, 95 Rivercrest Road, Toronto, Ontario M6S 4H7, Canada, 416-767-6317

Young, David (see also Friebert, Stuart), *FIELD*, Rice Hall, Oberlin College, Oberlin, OH 44074

Young, Gary, Greenhouse Review Press, 3965 Bonny Doon Road, Santa Cruz, CA 95060, 408-426-4355

Young, Geoffrey, The Figures, RD 3 Box 179, Great Barrington, MA 01230, 413-528-0458

Young, George, Editorial Director (see also Wood, Philip; Wan, Jackie; Reed, Paul), Ten Speed Press, PO Box 7123, Berkeley, CA 94707, 415-845-8414

Young, Grahaeme Barrasford, Bran's Head At The Hunting Raven Press, 45 Milk Street, Frome, Somerset, England

Young, Grahaeme Barrasford, *LABRYS*, 45, Milk Street, Frome, Somerset, England

Young, James Dean, *CRITIQUE: Studies in Modern Fiction*, Dept. of English, Georgia Tech, Atlanta, GA 30332

Young, Joyce LaFray, *CUISINE TAMPA BAY*, 3210 9th Street N., St. Petersburg, FL 33734

Young, Joyce LaFray, La Fray Young Publishing Company, 3210 9th Street N, St. Petersburg, FL 33734

Young, Karl, Publisher, Membrane Press, PO Box 11601-Shorewood, Milwaukee, WI 53211

Young, Karl (see also Kostelanetz, Richard; Scobie, Stephen; Frank, Sheldon; Zelevansky, Paul; Higgins, Dick; Essary, Loris), *PRECISELY*, PO Box 73, Canal Street, New York, NY 10013

Young, Karl, *STATIONS*, PO Box 11601 Shorewood, Milwaukee, WI 53211

Young, Lincoln B., Fine Arts Press, PO Box 3491, Knoxville, TN 37927, 615-637-9243

Young, Natrelle, *VANDERBILT REVIEW*, 911 W. Vanderbilt, Stephenville, TX 76401, 817-968-4267

Young, Natrelle, Vanderbilt Street Press, 911 W. Vanderbilt, Stephenville, TX 76401, 817-968-4267

Young, Noel, Capra Press, P.O. Box 2068, Santa Barbara, CA 93120, 805-966-4590

Young, Tom (see also Willkzie, Philip; Emond, Paul; Baysans, Greg; Strizek, Norman), *JAMES WHITE REVIEW; a gay men's literary quarterly*, PO Box 3356, Traffic Station, Minneapolis, MN 55403, 612-291-2913; 871-2248

Young, Virginia Brady, Senior Editor (see also Harding, May; Ulisse, Peter), *CONNECTICUT RIVER REVIEW: A Journal of Poetry*, 184 Centerbrook Road, Hamden, CT 06518, 203-281-0235

Youngson, Jeanne, Publisher (see also Peck, Tom), *THE COUNT DRACULA FAN CLUB NEWSLETTER-JOURNAL*, Penthouse North, 29 Washington Square W., New York, NY 10011, 212-533-5018

Youngson, Jeanne, Publisher (see also Peck, Tom), Dracula Press, Penthouse North, 29 Washington Square West, New York, NY 10011, 212-533-5018

Youra, Dan (see also Thompson, Pat), Still Publishing, PO Box 353, Port Ludlow, WA 98365, 206-437-9172

Yurechko, John (see also Holland, Peter; Lance, Jeanne), *GALLERY WORKS*, 1465 Hammersley Avenue, Bronx, NY 10469, 212-379-1519

Z

Zaage, Herman, Art Director (see also Goodson, Arthur; Zekowski, Arlene; Berne, Stanley), Berne, PO Box 5645, Coronado Station, Santa Fe, NM 87502, 505-356-4082

Zadravec, Katharine (see also Tuthill, Stacy; Kerr, Walter H.; Swope, Mary; Silva, Jayne), Scop Publications, Inc., Box 376, College Park, MD 20740, 301-345-8747

Zaleski, Philip, Executive Editor (see also Kisley, Lorraine; Sheehy, John), *PARABOLA MAGAZINE*, 150 Fifth Avenue, New York, NY 10011, 212-924-0004

Zander, W. (see also Keyishian, M.; Decavalles, A.; Cumming, W.), *JOURNAL OF NEW JERSEY POETS*, Fairleigh Dickinson Univ., English Dept., 285 Madison Avenue, Madison, NJ 07940, 01-377-4700

Zavitz, C., Editor (see also Nuse, B.; Newton, J.; Rooney, F.; Andersen, M.; Wine, J.; Prentice, A.; Scane, J.; Caplan, Paula; Van Kirk, Sylvia), *RESOURCES FOR FEMINIST RESEARCH/DOCUMENTATION SUR LA RECHERCHE FEMINISTE*, Ont Inst for Stud in Educ, Centre for Women's Studies in Education, 252 Bloor Street W., Toronto, Ontario M5S 1V6, Canada, 416-923-6641

Zavrian, Suzanne, SZ/Press, PO Box 20075, Cathedral Finance Station, New York, NY 10025, 212-749-5906

Zed, Xenia Z., Editor (see also Perri, Michael W), *ART PAPERS*, 972 Peachtree Street NE, Atlanta, GA 30309, 404-885-1273

Zeitlin, Leora (see also Hogan, Ed; Gubernat, Susan; Johnson, Ronna; Sagan, Miriam), Zephyr Press, 13 Robinson Street, Somerville, MA 02145

Zekowski, Arlene (see also Goodson, Arthur; Berne, Stanley; Zaage, Herman), Berne, PO Box 5645, Coronado Station, Santa Fe, NM 87502, 505-356-4082

Zelevansky, Lynn (see also Zelevansky, Paul), Zartscorp, Inc. Books, 333 West End Avenue, New York, NY 10023, 724-5071

Zelevansky, Paul (see also Kostelanetz, Richard; Scobie, Stephen; Frank, Sheldon; Higgins, Dick; Essary, Loris; Young, Karl), *PRECISELY*, PO Box 73, Canal Street, New York, NY 10013

Zelevansky, Paul (see also Zelevansky, Lynn), Zartscorp, Inc. Books, 333 West End Avenue, New York, NY 10023, 724-5071

Zell, Hans M., *THE AFRICAN BOOK PUBLISHING RECORD*, PO Box 56, Oxford OX13EL, England, 0865-512934

Zenofon, Fonda, *MATILDA LITERARY & ARTS MAGAZINE*, 7 Mountfield Street, Brunswick, Melbourne, Victoria, Australia, (03) 386 5604

Zenofon, Fonda, Matilda Publications, 7 Mountfield Street, Brunswick, Melbourne, Victoria, Australia, 03-386-5604

Zepeda, Ray (see also Mailman, Leo; Locklin, Gerald; Barker, David; Snider, Clifton; Salinas, Judy; Kay, John), *MAELSTROM REVIEW*, 8 Farm Hill Road, Cape Elizabeth, ME 04107

Zerkin, E. Leif (see also Novey, Jeffrey H.), Haight-Ashbury Publications, 409 Clayton Street, San Francisco, CA 94117, 415-626-2810

Zerkin, E. Leif (see also Novey, Jeffrey H.), *JOURNAL OF PSYCHOACTIVE DRUGS*, 409 Clayton Street, San Francisco, CA 94117, 415-626-2810

Ziegler, Alan (see also Zirlin, Larry; Greenberg, Harry), Release Press, 411 Clinton Street, Apt 8, Brooklyn, NY 11231

Zieroth, Dale, *EVENT*, Kwantlen College, PO Box 9030, Surrey, B.C. V3T 5H8, Canada

Ziesing, Michael (see also Meyers, Alison), Lysander Spoon Society, PO Box 806, Willimantic, CT 06226, 203-423-5836

Zigal, Thomas, Editor, *THE PAWN REVIEW*, 2903 Windsor Road, Austin, TX 78703

Zimbelman, Karen, Director of Publications, North American Students of Cooperation, Box 7715, Ann Arbor, MI 48107, 313-663-0889

Zimmer, David, Editor (see also Stroh, Luella), Good Vibes, PO Box 32413, Fridley, MN 55432, 612-571-9274

Zimmerman, William E., Chief Editor & Publisher, Guarionex Press Ltd., 201 West 77th Street, New York, NY 10024, 212-724-5259

Zirker, Lorette, Editor and Publisher, Iroquois House, Publishers, Box 211, Mountain Park, NM 88325, 505-682-2751

Zirker, Lorette, Editor and Publisher, *TRIBUTARIES*, Box 211, Mountain Park, NM 88325

Zirlin, Larry (see also Greenberg, Harry; Ziegler, Alan), Release Press, 411 Clinton Street, Apt 8, Brooklyn, NY 11231

Zobel, Jan, Editor, People's Yellow Pages Press, PO Box 31291, San Francisco, CA 94131

Zu-Bolton, Ahmos (see also Austin, Alan; Wray, Elizabeth; Becker, Anne), *BLACK BOX MAGAZINE*, PO Box 50145, Washington, DC 20004, 202-347-4823

Zuckerman, Matthew, *PRINTED MATTER (Japan)*, TELS "Tomeoki", Koishikawa Post Office, Bunkyo-ku, Tokyo 112, Japan

Zuckerman, Matthew, Editor (see also Ainlay Jr., Thomas; Urushibara, Hideko), Tokyo English Literature Society (TELS), TELS 'Tomeoki', Koishikawa Post Office, Bunkyo-ku, Tokyo 112, Japan, 03-312-0481

Zuckerman, Philip W., Apple-wood Books, Box 2870, Cambridge, MA 02139, 617-923-9337

Zuckerman, Ryki, Co-Editor (see also Brill, Kastle; Johnson, Bonnie; Willoughby, Robin), *EARTH'S DAUGHTERS*, Box 41, c/o Bonnie Johnson, Central Park Stn., NY 14215, 716-837-7778

Zuk, Sue (see also Baron, Matt; Wujciak, Dick), Cornell Design Publishers, PO Box 278, E. Hanover, NJ 07936

Zweig, Connie, Managing Editor (see also Ferguson, Marilyn), *BRAIN/MIND BULLETIN*, P O Box 42211, Los Angeles, CA 90042, 213-223-2500

Zweig, Connie, Managing Editor (see also Ferguson, Marilyn), Interface Press, PO Box 42211, Los Angeles, CA 90042, 213-223-2500

Zweig, Connie, Managing Editor (see also Ferguson, Marilyn), *LEADING EDGE*, PO Box 42211, Los Angeles, CA 90042, 213-223-2500
e also Hogan, Ed; Gubernat, Susan; Johnson, Ronna; Sagan, Miriam), Zephyr Press, 13 Robinson Street, Somerville, MA 02145

Zekowski, Arlene (see also Goodson, Arthur; Berne, Stanley; Zaage, Herman), Berne, PO Box 5645, Coronado Station, Santa Fe, NM 87502, 505-356-4082

Zelevansky, Lynn (see also Zelevansky, Paul), Zartscorp, Inc. Books, 333 West End Avenue, New York, NY 10023, 724-5071

Zelevansky, Paul (see also Kostelanetz, Richard; Scobie, Stephen; Frank, Sheldon; Higgins, Dick; Essary, Loris; Young, Karl), *PRECISELY*, PO Box 73, Canal Street, New York, NY 10013

Zelevansky, Paul (see also Zelevansky, Lynn), Zartscorp, Inc. Books, 333 West End Avenue, New York, NY 10023, 724-5071

Zell, Hans M., *THE AFRICAN BOOK PUBLISHING RECORD*, PO Box 56, Oxford 0X13EL, England, 0865-512934

Zenofon, Fonda, *MATILDA LITERARY & ARTS MAGAZINE*, 7 Mountfield Street, Brunswick, Melbourn